by

New York Times Bestseller
PEPPER WINTERS

Published: Pepper Winters 2016: pepperwinters@gmail.com
Cover Design: by Kellie Dennis http://www.bookcoverbydesign.co.uk/
Editing by: Jenny Sims: http://www.editing4indies.com

OTHER WORK BY PEPPER WINTERS

Pepper Winters is a New York Times, Wall Street Journal, and USA Today International Bestseller.

Her Dark Romance books include:
Monsters in the Dark Trilogy
Tears of Tess (Monsters in the Dark #1)
Quintessentially Q (Monsters in the Dark #2)
Twisted Together (Monsters in the Dark #3)

Indebted Series
Debt Inheritance (Indebted #1)
First Debt (Indebted Series #2)
Second Debt (Indebted Series #3)
Third Debt (Indebted Series #4)
Fourth Debt (Indebted Series #5)
Final Debt (Indebted Series #6)
Indebted Epilogue (Indebted Series #7)

Her Grey Romance books include:
Destroyed
Ruin & Rule (Pure Corruption MC #1)
Sin & Suffer (Pure Corruption MC #2)

Her Upcoming Releases include:
2016: **Je Suis a Toi (Monsters in the Dark Novella)**
2016: **Super Secret Series**
2016: **Indebted Beginnings (Indebted Series Prequel)**

Her Audio Books include:
Monsters in the Dark Series (releasing early 2016)
Indebted Series (releasing early 2016)
Ruin & Rule / Sin & Suffer (Out now)
Destroyed / Unseen Messages (releasing early 2016)

To be the first to know of upcoming releases, please join Pepper's Newsletter (she promises never to spam or annoy you.)

Pepper's Newsletter

Or follow her on her website
Pepper Winters

UNSEEN MESSAGES

a survival romance novel

by

New York Times Bestseller
PEPPER WINTERS

Note from Author

The following novel is a blend of truth and fable. The messages truly happened; the outcome & subsequent fate did not.

This story was inspired by my flight home in 2015. Each thing that happened, happened to me. Each issue and fear was my own experience, right down to the clothes Estelle wears, to what she shoves in her pocket.
That's complete truth.
What happened afterward...
I'll let the characters tell you their tale.

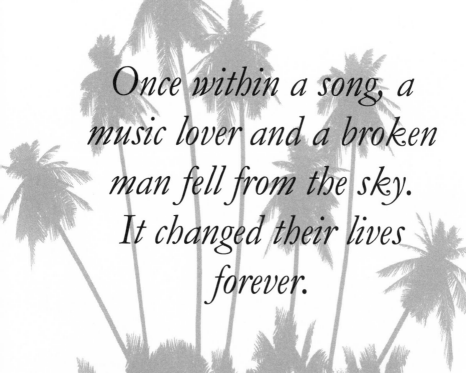

Once within a song, a music lover and a broken man fell from the sky. It changed their lives forever.

Prologue

ESTELLE

. . . . . .

I'm a song wrapped in paper; a sonnet scribbled by a singer.
Every composition takes a part of me until I'm nothing more than crotchets and
quavers. My story began ~~on paper~~ on sheet music. A fresh page of bars and
ledgers, governed by a sturdy treble clef. But my life ~~ended~~ changed. And the
things of importance faded from superfluous to survival.
~~*I'm a writer. I'm a singer.*~~
Not anymore, I'm a survivor.
Taken from the notepad of E.E.

. . .

LIFE OFFERS EVERYONE messages.

Either unnoticeable or obvious, it's up to us to pay attention.

I didn't pay attention.

Instinct tried to take notice; the world tried to prevent my downfall.

I didn't listen.

I'll forever wonder what would've happened if I *had* paid attention to those messages. Would I have survived? Would I have fallen in love? Would I have been happy?

Then again, perhaps just as the messages exist, fate exists, too.

And no matter what life path we choose, fate always has the final say.

I didn't listen, but it doesn't mean I didn't live.

I lived and breathed and cried and laughed and *existed* in a totally different tale than the one I'd envisioned.

Away from my home.

Away from my family.

Away from everything comfortable and familiar.

But I wasn't alone…

I was with him.

A stranger turned lover. An enemy turned friend.
I was with him.
And he became my entire universe.

Chapter One

••

E S T E L L E

••••••

No one can truly soothe your fears, your tears, your rolodex of emotions. No one
can truly make it right, fix the wrong, or make your dreams come true. Only you.
Only you, only you, only you.
You're the anchor in rough seas, the roof in churning storms. ~~You're the survivor~~
~~in adversity~~.
You are trust. You are home.
Only you, only you, only you.
Lyrics: 'Only You' Taken from the notepad of E.E.

•••

THE FIRST MESSAGE warning my life would end came ten
minutes after the taxi dropped me off at the airport.

I didn't know it would be my last car ride. My last grumble over
a fare. My last foray on a road, in a city, in a society surrounded by
people and chaos and noise.

My last taste of *normalcy*.

Not that my life had been normal the past two years.

Ever since my 'supposedly' best friend secretly uploaded an
original song of mine, I'd gone from a simple retail assistant to an
internet sensation.

The whirlwind career change was both a good and bad thing.

Good because I could now afford the things I'd never dared
dream of, brought security to my family (not that I had a family
anymore), and formed a nest egg for retirement. And bad because
such wonder came at great cost and I feared I didn't have enough in
which to pay it.

After two months on the road—on a self-funded and mostly
organised by 'supposedly best friend' singing tour, I was a masticated
piece of chewing gum with no flavour left to give.

Not that I wasn't grateful. I was. So, so, *so* grateful. Meeting
fans, singing until my throat bled, signing postcards and hastily
printed posters—it had been surreal.

I couldn't get my head around how quickly my world switched from helping rich housewives spend their husband's money on unneeded fashion to blinking in spotlights and performing secrets (pieces of my heart and soul bound in lyrics) that people seemed to connect to. They connected enough to want me to sing for them. *Me.* An utter nobody suddenly traded the safety of non-recognition for high-risk fame.

I could handle sharing myself and my songs. I could handle chipping away at my secrets and giving them to others to glue their patch-worked souls. What I couldn't handle were the endless airports and suitcases. The constant noise and chatter and calamity of living on tour.

I never wanted to stay in another hotel again. I craved space and silence with the passion of a million wishes.

Madeline didn't understand how hard being in the limelight was for me. Even working in retail (while I decided what to do with my life now I was alone) had been a struggle: the constant dealing with people, the endless questions, the draining nature of mingling. Add loud music, screaming fans, and countless demands for social events, encores, and media obligations, I was wrung dry. I was worse than chewing gum. I was the grime left over from a well-trodden shoe.

I'm shoeless.

My fingers itched to write the line down. The beginning of a new sonnet wisped into creation. I deliberated over dropping my suitcase and grabbing my notepad. But it was a single sentence. I'd remember it.

Hopefully.

Besides, I had something much more important to think about.

It's over now.

My lips turned from sad frown to happy anticipation.

I wasn't unappreciative for the rapid notoriety and vocal success I'd been given. But I couldn't change who I was at heart.

I was a homebody.

A girl who kept to herself, preferred to curl up with her flat-faced Persian than attend a party, and had a hard time making small talk with strangers, which meant singledom wasn't a choice but a by-product of being an introvert. Add a recent funeral for the three most important people in my life and…well, the outside world was as enjoyed as much as bug spray was to a butterfly.

Crossing the threshold into the airport terminal, I forcibly removed all thoughts of drudgery and schedules and relaxed for the first time in seventy-two days.

This was it.

This had been my only requirement which Madeline (said best friend and slave driver) didn't understand. No matter we'd been friends for almost two decades, she still didn't 'get me.' She didn't understand my pathological need to be alone after months of belonging to other people.

I'd agreed to eight singing venues; I'd bowed to her every whim of newspaper interviews, blogger podcasts, and high-society power dinners. But I'd stood firm on two things.

Number one: I refused to share a hotel room with her. I loved her but after monopolising my time eighteen hours a day, I needed an empty space. It was my recharge station after others drained me dry.

Number two: I wanted to travel back on my own.

Alone.

Just me.

For seventy-two days, she'd tried to convince me to amend my itinerary and celebrate with her in Bora Bora. In her mind, the money pouring in from endorsements and a newly signed record deal meant we should live large. In my mind, I should save every penny, because, as fast as luck had shined on me, it could eclipse me just as quickly.

Look at how swiftly death had visited when supposed perfection reigned.

I hadn't budged—no matter how hard she moaned—and here I was.

A single person in a whitewash of crowds and mayhem.

Slamming to a stop, I narrowly avoided a bulldozer conveniently dressed as a man. He charged past, sweaty and swearing, obviously late for his flight.

Not me.

I had plenty of time to meander through security, grab a coffee, read my book, and then slip quietly onto the plane to unwind on my journey home.

I sighed in bliss.

Feeling much happier, I dragged my suitcase to the Fiji Airways check-in desk. They'd been the best value in ticket prices when I'd booked from Sydney three months ago. The aircraft had been clean and staff attentive. And the fact that the service had been half-full made me happy. Fingers crossed they'd be quiet on the way back, too.

There wasn't a line, which made my day even brighter.

"Hello, Miss?" The elderly gentleman waved me toward the first class check-in, even though I wasn't first class. "I can check you in over here if you'd like."

I'm going home.

I smiled as genuine joy and relaxation fluttered. Carting my heavy suitcase to his counter, I fumbled in my handbag for my documentation. "Thank you."

He grinned, tapping a pen on the keyboard. "Don't mention it. Happens I don't like being bored and you're the first one to check in. I'm assuming you're on the service flying to Nadi?"

I managed to yank my passport and ticket from my overstuffed handbag without turfing out every other item and handed it over. "That's right."

The man eyed my paperwork. "Going onward to Sydney from there?"

"Yes."

His blue eyes warmed. "Been there myself. Great place."

"Yes, it is."

Small talk...once again, I sucked at it.

I'd adored every minute of meeting my agent and recording manager in New York—doing my best to chat about important things. And now, knowing I was only two plane rides away from my own bed made my willingness to engage with strangers more bearable.

"I'm dying to get back to the Northern Beaches. That's where I'm from."

The guy beamed, treating me like his new best friend. "It's a special existence having the ocean so close. I live in Venice Beach and there's something about waking up and seeing an empty horizon that helps balance city life." Pointing at the scales, he said, "If you can put your luggage there, I'll get you sorted."

I placed my weighty suitcase—full of gifts from aspiring songwriters and appreciative listeners—onto the scales. At the same time, I subtly shoved my carry-on behind the counter where he wouldn't see. Most of the heavier stuff was in there.

Glancing at the scales, his eyes crinkled. "Glad to see you're under the maximum weight."

"Me too." I laughed softly.

That had been another argument with Madi. She couldn't understand why, after the success of the tour, I hadn't upgraded my economy class ticket for business. She'd shaken her head as if I were a freak for not spending my new wealth. But I couldn't. It didn't seem real. If I was honest, it didn't feel like I'd earned it.

I'd made it doing something I loved. Weren't you supposed to scrimp and slave in a job you hated to save up as much as I'd made in the past year?

Either way, I wouldn't waste a penny. Economy class was good enough for me—just like it had been for the past twenty-five years of my life.

Tapping on his keyboard, Mark, according to his nametag, said, "Your bag will go all the way through to Sydney, so you don't have to worry about it in Fiji."

"Great. That's good to know."

He focused on his computer screen. His smile slowly morphed into confusion. "Eh, are you sure you have the right day?"

"Yes." Nerves quivered in my belly. "I'm one of those people who has to check a bazillion times. I even woke up three times last night to make sure I read the time as a.m. and not p.m. I'm very sure."

He looked up. "You don't have a reservation, I'm afraid."

"What?"

He pointed at the screen I couldn't see. "It says here your ticket was cancelled."

"No." I squashed down the panic. *So close. I'm so close to home.* This couldn't happen. I wouldn't *let* it happen. "That can't be true." Fossicking in my handbag for my cell-phone, I trembled as I tried to find the email of my itinerary. "I have proof. I'll find what my travel agent sent through."

Damn Madeline. If she'd somehow done this, she was in *huge* trouble.

I was idiotic to blame a friend I would never see again.

I should've listened.

This was the first message.

Mark returned to checking the screen while I scrolled through my emails. Stupid Gmail had archived the file and I couldn't find it.

"Did you have a delay coming here? Did you miss your flight?"

"Ah, yes!" Relief flooded. "My connecting flight was late. I missed the leg to New York and had to wait twenty-four hours before the next service." I moved closer to the desk, trying to refrain from seeming desperate. "But that was the airline's fault, not mine. They assured me the rest of my ticket was unaffected."

"That's fine." Mark pursed his lips. "And that's true, normally. I just can't find a ticket number." Chewing the inside of his cheek, he mumbled, "Don't worry. Give me five minutes and I'll build you a new booking then reissue your ticket."

I sighed, wanting to puddle to the floor and magically teleport myself home. I didn't have the strength to go through the highs and lows of travel. I was done. Empty.

My shoulders rolled. "Okay."

There was nothing I could do.

I stood there and waited as Mark fixed Message Number One.

I should've paid attention.

I should've walked right out the doors and hailed the nearest cab back to downtown Hollywood.

But I didn't.

....

"I'm sorry, ma'am."

A male's hand shot out, preventing me from moving forward.

I blanched, slamming to a halt. "Excuse me?"

Now, what have I done?

His eyes narrowed in reproof. "The body scanner picked up metal objects on your person. You'll be required to undergo a pat-down in a private room with a female officer. Do you consent?"

All around me, other passengers shoved and bumped, grabbing items from the X-ray belt and rushing to their chosen destinations.

I envied them.

"But...I don't have anything to declare."

The dark-haired officer cocked his head at the screen showing a few large splodges on a stick figure that I assumed was me. "The scanner has highlighted a few areas of concern."

A furl of unease nudged its way into being.

First, the missing booking and now, security.

Can't I just get on the plane without talking to anyone else?

I'd hoped once Mark handed over my reissued boarding pass and wished me a pleasant flight that my problems were over.

Desperate to just be left alone, I lifted up my pink jumper, revealing a black tank with glittering diamantes on the chest. "I should've thought before dressing in this to travel. I think those set it off."

The officer cleared his throat, doing his best not to look at my boobs. "That may be the case, but there are multiple points to check."

I glanced at the image. More black spots on my ankles and wrists.

"Ah, it's my jewellery and the zips in my jeans." Shoving back my sleeves, I revealed three bracelets on each wrist. All gold on my left and all silver on my right. Then pointed at the zippers in my skinny jeans at my ankles. "See?"

"I'm sorry. We'll still need to do a pat down."

"Are you sure—"

"Are you refusing to undergo the requirement to travel?" The agent crossed his arms, his biceps straining against the dark material of his uniform.

There was nothing I could do.

"No." My voice turned weary. "I consent."

A female officer came forward, waving me to follow her. "Come with me. We'll get you sorted."

Message Number Two went unheeded.

······························

NOT PERMITTED TO TRAVEL.

"Oh, my God. *Now,* what?"

The unease grew to unrest, prickling my spine.

"Come on." I stabbed the screen, removing and inserting my passport a few times into the do-it-yourself e-reader. Where were the good old days of customer service and officers who personally asked if you had explosives in your carry-on? Why had machines replaced a friendly face?

I didn't want to have to deal with robots, all lined up in military precision, unable to empathize or wish me a pleasant journey—extending my misery that much more.

NOT PERMITTED TO TRAVEL. PLEASE REMOVE PASSPORT AND SEE OFFICER.

I growled under my breath. "Fine."

Stealing my passport and deleting the half-finished clearance, I looked around for a saviour to help.

No one.

Brilliant.

Not one single person to help guide me through this frustrating dilemma.

Slinging my handbag further up my arm, I hugged my jacket and wheeled my heavy carry-on to the glass booths guarding the gate lounge.

Other disgruntled people rolled their eyes, obviously victims of the same masquerade of machines.

The line took a few moments.

I wasted each minute by willing it away when I should've been holding each tightly, refusing to let time move forward.

Finally, a dark-skinned youngish man waved me over.

Trooping toward him, I smiled and handed over my ticket, clearance card, and passport. "The machine won't accept me."

He scowled. "It's because only US and Canadian citizens are allowed to use the e-gates."

I pointed at the sign above the hated machines. "It says anyone with an e-reader passport."

He huffed as if I'd read it wrong. "It's not for Australians."

His attitude pissed me off, but I fought my rising annoyance. "Great. Well, I'm glad I'm in your care."

He didn't reply.

Frowning, he passed my passport through his computer and did whatever he needed to do. "I require your fingerprints for identification."

I placed my first four fingers on the sticky scanner and held them until he told me to flip to my thumb. Rubbing the tacky residue, I resisted the urge to pull out my hand sanitizer and disinfect whatever germs had just contaminated me.

The officer looked up, his forehead furrowing. "Um, that's odd."

The unease grew again, a bubble glistening with fear, puffing fresh breath with every issue. "What's odd?"

"Your fingerprints correspond to a different name in the system." He glowered as if I were a super spy or wanted villain.

My heart raced. "Look, I am who I say I am—Estelle Evermore."

"Place your fingers on the scanner again."

Cringing at the thought of touching the unsanitary device, I did as he asked.

A few seconds later and more keyboard tapping, the computer chimed happily.

My shoulders slouched in relief.

The officer handed back my documents. Suspicion didn't leave his gaze as he looked me up and down. "Have a pleasant day."

Hasn't been very pleasant so far.

I didn't reply.

Wait...

The nerves dancing on my spine switched from waltz to hip-hop, picking up in strength and number.

There was something wrong with this...surely?

Don't people say things happen in threes?

Well, three things had just tried to prevent me from getting on the plane.

The thought of home battled against the fear of idiotic superstitions. I couldn't stand another night in a foreign bed. I wanted my apartment. I wanted to shoo away the house sitter and cuddle my cat, Shovel-Face (named for his flat little nose and saucerish eyes), while catching up on the latest TV shows.

No. There's nothing wrong.

I was just tired and overly sensitive.

Ignoring my paranoia and ridiculous excuses, I made my way through duty-free and found my gate.

I'm here.

Sitting in an uncomfortable chair, I turned on my e-book and prepared to relax.

I'm going home.

This entire mess would be forgotten.

How stupid of me to ignore yet another message.

....

The fourth and final message trying to prevent my imminent demise happened an hour later.

"Flight FJ811 to Nadi is now boarding all remaining passengers."

I'd patiently waited for most people to board. I didn't do well standing in the air-bridge, squashed like hamsters in a toilet roll, waiting to enter an overcrowded airplane. I preferred to get on last, regardless if I didn't get convenient overhead storage.

Ever since I'd said goodbye to Madeline, I'd been tired. But it was nothing compared to the sudden lethargy as I handed over my boarding pass.

The air-bridge beckoned, and beyond that, the airplane that would take me home.

Home.

Yes, please.

"Afternoon." The lady took my pass, inserting it into the reader.

Instantly a siren sounded; red codes popped up on the screen.

Oh, my God. Now *what?*

"Is everything okay?" My tiredness evaporated, drowned out by escalating unease.

I'm not meant to get on this plane.

The lady frowned. "It says you're not permitted to board. There's an issue with your visa."

My heart stopped beating.

Why is this happening?

Anxiousness lodged in my throat. I wanted to grab my carry-on and back away from the boarding gate. I wanted to listen. To finally give into premonition and paranoia and stay in America until fate stopped playing roulette with my life.

"Look, I don't know what's going on but I've changed my mind—"

"Wait." The woman silenced the blinking lights and alarm. "You don't need a visa. You're flying to Australia and have an

Australian passport. Stupid machine. You're returning to your own country."

I swallowed hard. "It's okay. If you could just offload my luggage—"

She waved away my concerns. "Don't be absurd, dear. Just a glitch. We'll get it sorted in a sec."

"What seems to be the problem?" A supervisor came over, wiping his hands importantly on black slacks.

The blonde haired woman shrugged. "I'm not sure. The machine has gone crazy."

I'm not meant to get on the plane.

Do. Not. Get. On. That. Plane.

Goosebumps darted down my arms, my eyes dancing between the two agents. "I'm okay to wait. If it says I don't have a visa, I'll stay here until it's sorted out." My feet itched to bolt. My eyes landed on the plane, the air-bridge linking to its fuselage like an artery to a heart. "If someone could help with my belongings, I'll happily wait for the next service."

"No, don't be silly." The supervisor pulled wire-rimmed glasses from his pocket and took over from the blonde agent. "It's just a malfunction. That's all." His fingers flew over the keyboard, inputting code and hitting commands.

The same message popped up. *DO NOT BOARD. NO VISA.*

"If you could stand to the side, ma'am." The supervisor waved to the glass windows away from foot traffic. "Once the final stragglers are on board, I'll be sure to fix it."

I didn't move. I *couldn't* move.

My heart flew, pounding against rib after rib. My body turned into stone.

Stop being ridiculous, Stel.

Overtiredness had finally caught up with me and I was reading into things. There was no earthly reason why I shouldn't get on the plane.

I'd always loved flying. In fact, when I left school, I'd been an air-hostess for two years before I realised dealing with humans in a claustrophobic tube wasn't the best condition for my personality.

However, the travel had been incredible. The aeronautical calling breathed in my blood. I knew how airports ran. I knew the codes. I knew the lingo. I knew what pilots and air-hostesses got up to on overnight flights away.

What I didn't know was why—when I'd spent the past seven weeks flying every other day with no problems—every issue appeared all at once.

Another warning went off. I wrenched my head up.

The supervisor glanced at a new crowd. "Ah, Mr and Mrs Evermore. Are you related to Ms. Estelle Evermore by any chance?"

A family I'd never seen before with two children looked at me. Their plaid jumpers and matching backpacks would've been comical if they didn't share my last name. What were the odds? Were we related and I never knew?

Mr. Evermore shook his head. "Not that I'm aware."

We made eye contact. Mr. Evermore was the postcard-perfect American with a bushy beard, floppy hair, and kind eyes. His wife smiled, hugging the child closest to her. The boy couldn't have been older than thirteen, but he took after his father. The youngest, a rosy-cheeked girl, yawned, holding the arm of a stuffed kitten.

Shovel-Face.

An image of my ugly but gorgeously affectionate cat hit me hard.

A lick of terror erupted down my spine.

I couldn't explain it. I had no words to describe it.

But I'd never been so afraid of something I couldn't see, hear, or touch.

I had the strangest sensation that I'd never see my favourite companion again.

Don't be so stupid, Stel!

The supervisor cleared his throat, shattering my fear, returning to my problematic booking. "No worries. It's just a bit strange that there's more than one Evermore party on this flight and you're not related."

Yet another strange message.

Another unknown issue.

I don't want to get on the plane.

I didn't speak as the Evermores laughed, took their passes, and drifted down the air-bridge.

Another gust of fear darted down my back.

Get it together.

They didn't seem anxious. They had children to protect. Instincts behaving themselves. Nothing was going to happen.

Pinching my wrist, I grounded myself firmly in reality and shoved away scepticism of flying.

Looking up, my gaze fell on a man with sexy dark hair and the most insanely bright blue eyes I'd ever seen.

He jogged toward the counter, handing over his boarding pass in a rush of crumpled clothing and messily packed messenger bag.

The blonde agent blinked, eyeing his clean-shaven jaw, his height, and well-formed biceps. He wore hard work like an aftershave while the provocative black rims of his glasses firmly placed him as intellectually mysterious.

My songwriter's brain went into overdrive, penning him a song of outdoorsy carpenter or wildlife patroller. Sunshine existed in his gaze, wildness wept from his flawless skin. I'd never seen a man so tamed by scruffy jeans, grey t-shirt, and glasses but somehow still look so recklessly undomesticated.

His boarding pass went through without complaint.

His eyes met mine.

He paused, lips twitching into a small smile. A bolt of interested attraction sparked from me to him. My mouth responded against my will, parting beneath his attention.

Who is he?

Sunlight reflected off his glasses, blinding me for a moment.

"Have a nice flight, Mr. Oak." The blonde agent returned his pass.

The connection between us vanished as he pinched it from her fingers and hoisted the bag strap up his shoulder. "Cheers."

An accent. English, by the sounds of it. Before I could conjure more tales of fancy, he disappeared down the air-bridge.

A moment later, the supervisor clapped his hands. "Hurrah. All done." Giving me a new boarding pass, he grinned. "All sorted, Ms. Evermore. You're free to board. Sorry for the delay."

Taking the documentation, I put one foot in front of the other.

I ignored every warning bell in my blood.

I followed the Evermore family, the enticing Mr. Oak, and willingly gave my life to fate.

I put my previous fear down to overwork and stress.

I convinced myself I was reading into things, that disasters happened to other people; that life didn't send messages to those about to die.

I didn't listen.

I ignored the signs.

I got on the plane.

Chapter Two

....

GALLOWAY

......

I HATED FLYING.

The only reason I agreed to fly halfway across the bloody world was to complete my apprenticeship under one of the best builders in the style of architecture I wanted to specialise in.

For the past six months, I'd lived on his estate. I'd listened to my mentor by night. I'd worked beside him by day. He taught me how little I knew and how much I needed to learn if I wanted to excel in the profession I'd chosen (not to mention reminding me how close I was to throwing it all away).

To work with wood, to build and create with a natural resource—first, you had to understand how it worked. My teacher had come from a long line of craftsmen from furniture makers to sky-scraper designers.

The fact he had Inuit blood and could trace his family tree back to the natives on his mother's side was a plus for learning, not just about how to hammer a nail or finesse a dovetail joint, but how to nurture the trees we used. How to take a wooden plank and turn it into a home.

I'd learned more living with his wife and two sons, absorbing every lesson, than I ever did at university (or at my more recent abode). Then again, that education had been of a different nature.

You promised you wouldn't think about it.

For the hundredth time, I gritted my teeth and pushed away thoughts that only pissed me off and hurt. Clenching my fists, I followed the herd down the air-bridge and onto the plane.

I was sad to leave.

But eager to put a stamp on my new career. My new life. A life I was eternally thankful for after everything I'd done to screw it up.

I didn't deserve it, but my father had agreed to help fund me. Acting as guarantor for the business loan I'd applied for: Opulent Oak Construction. Not to mention, he'd been fundamental for me securing the work permit for entry into the USA. Without him…well, my second chance wouldn't have mattered.

He'd given me my world back. He trusted I wouldn't let him down.

I had no intention of doing that. *Ever again.*

He'd granted endless support and fatherly devotion, even after everything I'd done. However, he had a condition—completely adamant with no concessions.

So, I did the only thing I could.

I gave in.

I agreed to fly to Fiji (the one place I'd always wanted to visit as a kid) and live a little before burying myself in my new company in England. He wanted me to sample freedom before I shackled myself to a long-term commitment.

He wanted me to have *fun.*

Ha!

After everything that'd happened, he thought I knew what that word meant.

I have no bloody clue.

How could he expect me to be an average twenty-seven-year old bloke after the history I'd already clocked up? Even now, he still looked at me like the golden son…not the black stain I'd become. I didn't deserve fun. Not after what I'd done; *especially* at a time he needed me the most.

Fun.

I *hated* the word.

And even if I *did* remember how to indulge, I wouldn't waste my time on girls and booze because I had a driving need to create something from nothing after I'd destroyed everything. I had a lot of sins to make up for, and if my father wouldn't let me start atoning at home, well, I would have to find another way.

I'm a bastard, pure and simple.

I hated that I'd lied when conceding to his terms. I'd looked him in the eye and agreed to go to Fiji under the proviso of sunbaking, drinking, and having a one-night stand or ten. However, instead of reserving a bed in a gross backpackers with other self-centred idiots, I volunteered my skills to a local firm who built homes for under privileged locals.

I needed to find redemption before I drove myself insane with sickening memories and overflowing self-hatred.

Only thing was, the company expected me to start work first thing tomorrow. Otherwise, they'd give the contract to another applicant. No tardiness. No excuses. Be there or miss out.

I won't miss out.

Trudging onto the plane, my mind skipped to the last time I'd seen my father. Over six months had passed since our last embrace. He'd slapped my back and whispered in my ear. *"Learn, study, and behave. But once your training is up, fly to Fiji, get lost in warm seas, and remember how to live. Then come home refreshed and I'll do whatever you want to make your business a success."*

He'd even pulled the cheap shot guaranteed to make me crumple like a little kid. He'd argued that if Mum were still alive, she would've said that work didn't equal a life, even if it was a passion. There were other important things and having unplanned experiences was one of them.

Asshole.

Poor, grieving asshole.

Me, too. We were both grieving assholes, missing the one person who gave our souls purpose only to ruin us when she died.

What happened wasn't her fault.

My nostrils flared, pushing her out of my mind.

I pulled the crumpled boarding pass from my back pocket, trying to find my seat.

Goddammit.

Fifty-nine D. Right down the back of the plane.

The thought of having to squish around people pissed me off. But the sooner I was seated, the sooner I could pull out my headphones and lose myself in a movie.

Waiting for a family to shove their luggage into the overhead compartment, I hoisted my bag onto my shoulder and pulled out my phone. I'd promised my father I'd text him before we took off. Ever since losing Mum, he'd been neurotic at the thought of losing me.

Tapping a generic *'I love you and talk to you soon'* message, I pressed send.

Huh, that's strange.

I tapped the screen, waiting for confirmation that it'd sent. However, the sending icon just swirled around and around, never connecting.

The family finally slid into their row, granting me the freedom to carry on down the aisle.

Giving up on the message, I shoved the phone back into my jeans and hurried to my seat. An air-hostess stood blocking it. She backed away when I raised an eyebrow.

"You're lucky last, huh?" Her red hair caught the glare of false illumination.

"Yup. That's me. Always lucky."

Luck had nothing to do with it. I was the opposite of luck. I was misfortune.

The air-hostess disappeared to help another with their seating.

I stowed my luggage, slammed into my chair, and looked out the window.

The memory of my mother's struggle and what happened afterward clenched my heart as passengers settled and the cabin prepared for flight.

A flash of blonde caught my eye as I scanned my fellow travellers. The flight wasn't full, providing a good view across to the other side of the plane.

That girl again.

Her carry-on, as she wedged it above her head, looked fit to explode like a shrapnel grenade.

She was pretty—*very* pretty.

There was something about her. Something intrinsic— something that singled her out and made me notice.

Long blonde hair, translucent skin…large hazel eyes.

She deserved to be investigated and appraised. I was interested.

When our gazes met at the boarding gate, I'd felt the first hint of normalcy in over five years. I *liked* that she'd affected me, but I also wouldn't let it happen again.

Women like her were dangerous, especially for men like me.

The girl had barely sat down and fastened her seat belt before the fuselage creaked as the captain pushed off from the gate and the terminal grew smaller as we lined up to defy gravity.

Tearing my eyes away from her, I stared out the window at the blurry world and the last glimpse of Los Angeles.

After waiting our turn, the engines screamed and we shot down the runway, hurtling from stationery to rocket.

My ears popped as we traded concrete for open air.

The eleven-hour flight had commenced.

"Welcome on board this service to Nadi." The captain's drone dripped from the overhead speakers. "The current temperature at our destination is a humid twenty-seven degrees centigrade with a chance of rain closer to arrival. The flight today will take approximately ten hours and forty-five minutes. We encourage you to sit back, relax, and allow us to fly you to your destination in style."

Style has nothing to do with it.

Reclining in my shitty economy class seat, I peered through the row and eyed the blonde. My glasses fogged a little, obscuring her until she glowed with a halo. I didn't mean to glance her way. I should forget all about her.

But I couldn't shake my interest.

Her side profile, as she bent over a tatty notebook, was as beautiful as front on. She was stunning, if not a little strange—the perfect paragon of sharp and shy.

I want to talk to her.

My legs bunched to stand. I swallowed with disbelief. *What the hell?*

The aircraft skipped with minor turbulence, wrenching the girl's head up.

An air-hostess nudged my elbow as she darted up the aisle, dragging the trolley with scents of food. That solved my dilemma. I couldn't go talk to her because I had to remain seated for the service and I wouldn't go talk to her because I had no intention of spreading the bad luck I brought onto others.

I was better off alone.

It was the way it had to be.

End of bloody story.

Pressing the button to recline my chair, I gripped the hand-rails and closed my eyes. For the next eleven hours, I would forget about her, then disembark and never see her again.

I didn't know it but the opposite was true.

Getting on that plane inexplicably tied our fates together.

....

The ending credits scrolled over my screen.

Stretching, I switched off the movie, removed my glasses, and rubbed my eyes. I didn't know exactly how much time had passed, but I'd eaten (extremely crappy airplane food), I'd watched two movies (nothing to gush about) and I'd stolen a few more looks at Unknown Girl across the plane (okay, more than just a few).

I hadn't forgotten my pledge to forget about her, but the tiredness of a long journey, coupled with the dark gloom of the cabin, didn't put me in the best of moods. The darkness reminded me too much of the place I'd lived in before escaping to America. The loud hum of engines irritated me to the point of violence.

I didn't want anything to do with the girl across the aisle.

So why do you keep looking at her?

I was happier on my own. Being on my own meant I didn't have to answer to anyone, share my past, or worry about their reaction to who I truly was.

Dad had told me time and time again that one day my need for space would be trumped by the perfect woman.

He didn't have a damn clue.

I didn't want to find love. I wasn't *worthy* of finding love.

I'd seen what Mum's death did to him. He'd become hollow. A father with no spark. A man with no happiness.

I could handle being on my own.

Why would I ruin that by weakening myself and handing over my heart to a woman who could crush me?

I stole another look at Unknown Girl. She'd scooped her hair into a ponytail and slicked pink lipstick on her very kissable mouth.

Tearing my eyes away, I yanked on my headphones.

Goddammit, what was it about her that interested me?

Who is she?

Pity fate couldn't talk. If it could, I would've heard the reply:

She's your beginning.

Your end.

Your salvation.

Chapter Three

....

ESTELLE

••••••

~~There is such a thing as loneliness~~. *Loneliness is the stalker you've been running from, the parent you've been hiding from, the disappointment you've been escaping from.*
It's a sticky entity crouching in your heart, filling your soul with echoes, carving out your hope with ten thousand spades of hollowness.
Empty, so, so empty.
~~Empty as silence. Empty as an argument.~~
Lyrics: 'So Empty' Taken from the notepad of E.E.

...

TEN HOURS INTO the flight.

See? I worried for nothing.

Dinner had been delivered and cleaned away. I'd watched three movies, and the near-empty cabin was fast asleep—minus a few annoying kids a few rows away and a squalling baby in her mother's arms by the toilets.

Only forty-five minutes to go, then I would be one flight closer to home.

Heavenly home.

I can't wait.

My transfer in Fiji was a quick two-hour turnaround and the flight onward would only take a few more hours before I could sleep in my own bed, wear fresh clothes than the ones in my suitcase, and decompress for a few days with takeout and pyjamas.

Luckily, the flight wasn't full, which meant I had a window, middle, and aisle to myself. Unfortunately, I was also the last row of the cabin.

The traipsing passengers and constant flushes of the facilities meant I couldn't sleep or relax. Elbows and knees constantly hit mine as weary travellers marched the tiny space, doing their best to keep their circulation flowing and muscles from seizing.

Rubbing my eyes, I pulled up the airplane journey on my in-seat screen. The small aircraft flying over the flattened atlas showed we were somewhere over the Pacific Ocean. Far below me existed atolls and paradisiacal archipelagos.

Fiji wasn't too much further. I'd made it this far, including the last nine hours without another nerve-wracking incident. The turbulence at the beginning of the flight freaked me out, but it had been smooth since.

I could make it home before succumbing to sleep deprivation.

A kid with grubby hands brushed my forearm as he charged back to his parents, leaving the bathroom door hanging open.

I groaned under my breath, reaching behind me to secure it.

Never again.

I would never sit at the back of the airplane.

You should've upgraded to business class.

Plopping my headphones over my ears, I rolled my eyes. Just because business class would've offered more comfort, I refused to start being that person. The one who expected better service just because they'd had a windfall. The asshole who felt more deserving than others just because money had changed their financial situation.

No, I wouldn't be that person.

Changing the atlas for the latest movie channels, I laughed at myself for being so nervous. I'd spent the entire flight wound up and petrified of the simplest noise.

I'd burned through enough calories to sustain me for a week. I was wired on adrenaline and desperate to put as much space between me and flying as possible.

But there'd been nothing to worry about, after all.

There was no such thing as messages or premonition.

I was living proof.

My fingers itched for my notepad to add more lyrics to my half-cooked idea. There was a song lurking in my unwarranted fear. It could become a metaphor for other terrifying things in life.

That was where my true passion lay. Not in performing or seeing my name on billboards or screamed by strangers. My passion was fresh paper, sharpened pencil, and the joy of taking innocent words and stringing them into a necklace of rhythm.

My foot tapped a non-existent beat, gathering depth the more I composed.

My stress levels faded. I stopped flicking through the movie selection to focus inward, letting the melody cast me away from the plane, sink me deep into my art, and allow me to conjure music all while sitting in a tiny seat thousands of feet above the earth.

Love doesn't live in first glances.
Life doesn't dwell in second chances.
Our path exists in unseen messages.
~~Power to transform from unknown wreckages~~.

No, that last line wouldn't work.

I pursed my lips, mulling over words that could replace it.

For a few wondrous seconds, I lived in my calling and allowed a new song to form.

But then…a reminder.

A hint that I hadn't been stupid to listen. I'd been stupid to *ignore.*

Another message.

The plane rocked with a buffet of air, sloshing the half-finished water on my tray table.

The lyrics in my head screeched to a halt.

I froze…waiting.

A minute t..i..c..k..e..d past.

All was well.

Another minute as I stared at the bright screen enticing me to click on a romantic comedy.

Then…my screen went blank.

The plane suddenly hopscotched across clouds.

The sparse cabin cracked as the hopscotch turned into a rodeo.

Passengers woke up. Headphones were wrenched off. Slumber turned to screams.

My fingers clutched the arm-rests; my lap drenched in water as the plastic cup toppled over.

However, as quickly as the turbulence hit, it was over.

My heart raced and strangers made eye contact, searching for answers.

The seat belt sign pinged; the captain came over the intercom. "Ladies and gentlemen, we apologise for the slight discomfort. We'd hoped to avoid the storm but it's inevitable if we wish to land in Fiji. We're descending and confident we can avoid the majority of turbulence. Please keep your seat belts fastened and refrain from using the facilities at this time. We'll have you on the ground at 6:45 p.m. local time."

His words were soothing.

His voice was not.

He's afraid.

I'd been in the industry. I knew the inner lingo.

I hoped I was wrong, but nerves fledged into fully spread wings, careening around my ribcage like a startled crow.

My eyes remained glued to the seat belt sign. If it flickered again, the pilot wanted the head stewardess to call him.

Don't flicker.

Don't flicker.

Bing Bong.

It flickered.

The purser hightailed it up the aisle, her hands gripping the headrests for balance, disappearing past the dividing curtain.

Whatever existed outside the metal walls of the aircraft was enough for fear to pollute the cabin.

I couldn't ignore it anymore.

The messages.

The signs.

I should've listened.

I didn't care if it was stupid. I didn't care if paranoia rotted my brain. I couldn't switch off the instinct howling inside.

Something's wrong.

My previous training on how to survive a ditching came back. I'd done the drills on how to escape wrecked fuselage. I'd completed exams on how best to protect passengers. What I hadn't done was experience a true crash.

We're over the ocean. I'm in the tail of the plane.

Contrary to what people said, the safest possible place in a ditching was over the wing. Yes, the fuel tanks were below, but if the pilot was good, the plane would skim like a skipping stone before diving and flipping. The nose would snap, the tail would break, and water would gush—

Stop it!

Needing to do something, *anything*, I shoved up my tray table and reached between my legs for my handbag. Yanking it onto my lap, my hands trembled.

If something happened, I wouldn't be allowed to take anything. The only thing we could take would be what was on our person.

Don't be ridiculous. Nothing's going to happen.

My life sped up as another bout of turbulence shook the plane—disagreeing with my positivity.

Pessimism launched into full alert.

Something is going to happen.

My heart lodged in my throat as I tore open my bag and took

stock of what I had. The puffer jacket I wore had deep pockets. Without hesitation, I stuffed my passport, money, and credit cards into the inner chest pocket, zipping tight. Rushing, I made sure my phone was turned off and the solar powered charger was in my left pocket.

Another jolt and the plane twisted with an unnatural groan.

Working faster, I tucked my compact mirror, carry-on sized toothpaste and toothbrush, jewellery that I wouldn't check in my suitcase, three hair-ties, a pen, and an unopened poncho I'd bought from a convenience store when a thunderstorm hit unexpectedly last week in Texas.

Everything I could fit disappeared into deep pockets and secured with a zip.

Once my jacket bulged with possessions, I caressed my song notebook where every tune and melody I'd ever created, every lyric and musical tale I ever thought of rested. This notebook was as precious as gold to me. Worth more than my newly signed record deal. Better than any accolade or list appearance. Without my jotted ideas, my magic would go. I would lose the symphonic world I'd become so fond of.

But the book wouldn't fit in my bursting pockets.

Another crush of air tossed us around like a ping-pong ball. I dropped the notepad into my handbag, letting it plummet to my feet.

I listened.

Are you happy?

The sky said no.

The wind prepared to pay.

And fate shattered any hope of ever going home.

Chapter Four

....

GALLOWAY

......

"THANK CHRIST."

The grateful curse fell from my lips as airplane tyres bounced onto the Fijian runway. My fingers ached from clutching the armrests and my heart had permanently rehomed itself in my throat.

I wasn't a pussy—most things didn't scare me—how could it when I'd lived what I'd lived? But when it came to that kind of event (the kind that so eloquently reminded us we were *nothing* in the scheme of things), then yeah, I had a healthy dose of terror.

The entire descent, my mind had exploded with worst-case scenarios of agonising pain and horrific death. Of slamming into the earth, erupting into fire, burning to char with the scent of flesh in my nostrils.

The atmosphere of the flight had switched completely the moment the first judder bar turned into a bloody loop de loop. It wasn't ordinary turbulence—this had been mean, furious—a demon dog toying with its prey.

While passengers had remained locked in their useless seats, air-hostesses quickly secured the cabin and buckled in. The wind howled louder outside, continuing to tumble us through the clouds.

I'd looked across the cabin to Unknown Girl and wished I'd been a better person, a braver bloody man. I should've said hello, given fate time to show why we had a connection.

But I hadn't, and that opportunity had been snatched away as the wings of the plane shuddered and bowed.

The closer we plummeted to earth, the more adrenaline drenched my bloodstream—especially when the TV screens hissed with white noise and a few overhead lockers popped open, raining baggage from above.

Human screams punctured the mechanical screams of engines. Our velocity increased as the same substance we flew through made its life mission to tear us apart and leave the scattered pieces in the Pacific Ocean. The blackness outside hid our destination, but streaks of angry raindrops slurped their way along the window—tasting us…preparing to kill us.

I'd expected the captain to yell, *"Brace, brace, brace."* I'd prepared myself for a crash and the highly unwanted repercussion of death.

But he never did.

And as close as death had come…we'd survived.

After forty-five minutes of fear and spine-jarring bucking, the captain had managed to save us from turning into road kill. We were intact—minus a few bumps and bruises from pelting luggage. We were no longer at the mercy of storms but secured firmly on the earth thanks to gravity's hold.

An eerie quiet filled the plane as we taxied to a gate. No one spoke or clapped at the safe landing or even laughed with nervousness. It was as if the harrowing ordeal had stolen any holiday cheer, showing us how killable we were when nature wanted us.

The plane rocked as we turned toward the terminal. The waiting air-bridge danced in the storm, drenched with rain and occasional flashes of lightning.

I waited while the plane slowed and the usual rustling of passengers announced we would soon be free. The instant we docked, people launched themselves from their seats, scrambling for luggage and family members.

"Welcome to Nadi, ladies and gentlemen." The captain's voice cut through the raucous. "I appreciate your patience and want to thank you for remaining calm. We have just been informed by air traffic control that the storm is currently making its way north and will soon be over for those transporting to hotels and homes. However, for those travelling on outgoing services—either international connections or island links—your services have been postponed until further notice."

An annoyed moan crested as people glared at the speakers, blaming the captain for their derailed plans.

Bloody idiots.

Were their attention spans so short they forget what we just lived through?

Shit, what about my flight?

I had to get to Kadavu—the island where I'd be building homes for locals for three months—before tonight. Otherwise, I'd have no job or place to live.

Waiting until the aisle cleared from annoying passengers, I grabbed my messenger bag and slipped from my row. My eyes flickered to the left, looking for Unknown Girl.

She wasn't there.

She'd bolted.

Not that I could blame her. She'd been nervous as hell most of the flight, let alone the mayhem and turbulence at the end. I wasn't an anxious flyer, but even I had expected to be shark bait rather than disembarking on two legs.

Well, good riddance.

She'd gone.

I was safe—just like I wanted.

Keeping my head down, I followed the crowd down the air-bridge and into the heaving terminal. Apparently, another flight had just arrived suffering the same warm welcome we had. Voices escalated with tales of drama and danger as people made their way to immigration.

Nothing like a shared tragedy to turn strangers into best friends.

Hooking my bag higher on my shoulder, I brushed past gossipers and beelined for the departure board. The captain had said the storm was moving away. With a little luck, the sea-plane I was meant to catch in an hour to Kadavu would still depart.

It wasn't that I was eager to get back in the air where my life expectancy became a debate but because I'd made a promise. I'd committed to something I believed in.

It'd been so long since I'd put myself out there—*wanted* to put myself out there—that I wouldn't let a little rain and wind stop me. Not now, when I was so close to finding redemption for the shitty human I'd become.

I have no choice.

I'm going.

Tonight.

Scowling at the departure board, I repositioned my glasses and brushed a hand over my face as nothing but red lettering and flashing DELAYED announced no one was getting anywhere fast.

All around me the havoc of families and screeching children amplified in decibels, sending seething frustration through my blood.

I couldn't stay here. I couldn't let my one opportunity to rewrite the wrongs I've done slip away.

The storm will blow over by the time you clear customs.

Holding onto that thought, I navigated the airport and dutifully lined up for my turn at immigration. My back ached from the landing-rodeo, but the line didn't take too long. Handing over my passport and already organised work permit, I was ushered through with no issues.

Marching toward the baggage claim, my dinged-up, overstuffed backpack slid down the chute directly in front of me. Hoisting the weight onto my back, I rearranged my messenger bag and scanned the terminal.

Thanks to my tall height, I skimmed the heads of most people to the services offered beyond. Exits beckoned newly freed passengers to enter their tropical destination and shuttle operators sold vouchers to drive them to hotels.

I didn't want to head out there without finding out about my flight or securing another alternative.

Spotting the airline who my new employer had arranged to fly me to the island, I stalked toward the booth, dodging flustered holidaymakers.

There was a small line, but I grudgingly stayed patient. Shuffling farther up the queue, I tossed my backpack onto the floor to rescue my spine.

Finally, it was my turn.

A Fijian woman with thick black hair and wide smile motioned me forward. "May I help you?"

"I hope so." Kicking my backpack to lean against the counter, I placed my arms on the top and smiled. Dad always said I had a nice smile—straight teeth and honest intentions. I agreed with the straight teeth but not so much about the honest intentions. I'd been bloody lucky to get the work visa.

Someone like me didn't normally find such hospitable welcomes.

Smiling wider, I hoped I could work some charm and get what I wanted. "I'm starting work tomorrow on Kadavu. I'm booked on your service to fly there tonight."

"Okay, wonderful." She grabbed a paper with six names on it. "And you are?"

I stabbed the sheet with my index. "Galloway Oak." Conveniently located at the top of the list. "That's me."

Her black eyes met mine. "Thank you for flying with us, but I do have some unfortunate news, I'm afraid."

Shit.

My heart sank, along with an unwanted dose of anger. "If it's about the storm—the pilot on my inbound flight said it's blowing over."

She nodded, her gaze warm and gentle. "That's true. Fiji has many storms, all which blow over very fast. But I'm sorry, Mr. Oak, the rain has delayed our schedule. We won't be flying tonight."

My gut clenched. "But I have a commitment."

Shaking her head, she drew a tick beside my name. "You've been booked on our first available service tomorrow."

It might still work.

If I get there before six a.m.

Swallowing my frustration, I asked, "What time is that?"

She beamed, her hair catching the overhead lights. "A very suitable hour of midday. You can relax at a local hotel and come back after a delicious breakfast. No early starts."

I dragged a hand over my face, suddenly feeling the effects of jetlag. "That won't work. I have to start work at eight."

"I'm sorry." She curled the corner of the page. "That's just not possible. It's our first available—"

"What about another airline? Is anyone else flying?"

She pointed at the madness behind me. "No one is leaving tonight, Mr. Oak. The international airlines will resume in an hour when the storm is over, but the local planes will not. We are all working hard to ferry you to respective hotels then have you on your way tomorrow."

I groaned.

I couldn't wait.

If I did, I'd have no accommodation because the deal was my labour for bed and food. I didn't have any money to stay in fancy hotels.

"Surely, there must be something you can do?"

Her friendliness faded. "Mr. Oak. The storm is—"

"If the weather calms enough for other planes to depart, surely it's safe to fly tonight?"

She grabbed a pen, scratching out my name on the manifest and scrawling a hotel name beside it. "Our airline has decided not to take that chance." Passing over an envelope, she said, "Here is your voucher for dinner and breakfast along with a shuttle to take you to your hotel." Her smile returned, a little more forced than before. "Have a pleasant night, Mr. Oak. See you in the morning."

Before I could argue, she snapped her fingers, looking over my shoulder. "Next."

A man rudely bumped me, squeezing his considerable bulk between me and the desk, effectively shoving me away.

Bloody—

I bit my tongue.

I'd always had an issue with my temper. It'd gotten me into far too much strife. I'd made a personal promise the day I left England that I would rein it in. Working with timber and innocuous items helped calm me when others pissed me off (yet another reason why I loved my vocation).

I might've been able to control my outward reaction, but inside, all I wanted to do was shove the asshole's head multiple times against the desk.

Don't have time for that.

Kadavu was a short flight away. The storm was fading. I would find a way to get there tonight.

I grabbed my bag from the floor and stalked away to find a solution to my nightmare.

Chapter Five

······································

ESTELLE

······

I've made mistakes, so many mistakes. I shut out those who told me to abandon lyrics. I avoided those who didn't understand g-sharps and b-flats. I ignored those who didn't realise my pronunciation came in the form of octaves and arpeggiated chords.
I'm a mistake. I'm my own person.
I made wrong choices. I made the only choices I could.
I died. I lived.
I didn't listen. I listened.
Taken from the notepad of E.E.
...

HOLY MOTHER OF God.

Hadn't I lived through enough drama on this trip? First, all the issues with security and boarding, and then, an attempted crash landing.

I couldn't stop shaking.

I'd vomited in the stupid bag the air-hostesses provided for inflight sickness. I'd hugged my jacket full of belongings as if by some miracle I would survive with a pocket mirror and travel-sized toothpaste. And I hated how the fear of dying had shown me just how much of my life I'd wasted. How I'd pinned happiness on a future I couldn't predict. How I let fear rule my decisions rather than doing what I quoted in my songs.

You're alive.

Be grateful.

I was grateful.

Beyond grateful.

But despite my thankfulness, I couldn't stop trembling at how close to death I'd come.

It was a minor storm. You weren't anywhere near death.

I moved through immigration in a strange mind-space, unable to untangle the last hour of turbulence, terror, and finally, landing intact. I didn't understand how strangely accepting I'd been in those final moments where I'd truly, deeply looked at who I was and was forced to stare at the one conclusion I'd been running from.

I found myself *lacking*.

It was odd to drift through the airport, still looking and sounding and moving like myself when something so irreversible had changed.

I thought I was dead.

You're overdramatizing the situation.

Regardless, the thought of saying goodbye had forced my eyes wide open. I'd been slammed into my deepest, darkest secrets, and I didn't like what I'd come face-to-face with.

In those horrifying moments of mortality, I introduced the ideal me to the real me.

And I didn't like it.

I'm afraid.

Not just of failure and dying but of success and *living*.

Madeline had given me a dream career after a decade of meaningless labour. She'd given me something priceless after the death of my family. And all I could do was moan about crowds and cower in corners when people wanted to befriend and congratulate.

Who did that?

Who willingly choose a life of loneliness because she was too afraid to risk sharing herself with others?

Who am I?

I didn't know.

Not anymore.

The girl I'd been when I boarded in America had died as truly as if we *had* crash-landed. I no longer wanted to be that Estelle. I wanted to be something more. Something better. Someone I could be proud of. If another life-or-death moment came along and made me score-card my life, I wanted to be happy not afflicted.

I wanted no regrets, and right now…I had millions of them.

Grabbing my suitcase as it appeared on the carousel (so much for having it go through to Sydney), I clutched my hotel and shuttle voucher and made my way outside. My suitcase creaked behind me. I needed a new one. The wheels on it had well and truly given up— I might as well cart it on sheer plastic for how useful they were.

The minute I get home, I'm going to reinvent myself.

Home.

The thought of sleeping in yet another hotel brought frustrated tears to my eyes. I'd begged at the check-in counter for a reprieve. I was happy to wait in the terminal for a possible departure. I was content to be patient. But the crew had been adamant that despite the fact the storm was passing, and other airlines would depart later tonight, they wouldn't risk flying.

That was their final decision, and I had no way of getting home (unless I wanted to swim).

I need to sleep. I want this day to be over.

I hated the whiny voice inside, complaining of inconvenience and delays. Only moments ago, I'd admitted I didn't like my desire to hide away and run from human contact.

Perhaps this was what the messages had been trying to say—not to avoid calamity but to walk right into it, so I could realise what was missing before it was too late.

Maybe the messages weren't about dying but awakening.

Is that what this is?

A wake-up call?

Something to show me how much I needed to immerse myself in a life that I was squandering away, letting every experience and priceless moment pass by in a blur of non-requited joy?

If it was…what should I do about it? Be more spontaneous? Be brave, try new things, and accept deviations to my regimented plan?

"Are you with the Evermore party?" A wiry man in a turquoise shirt with a frangipani sewn on the breast pocket smiled as I stopped at Collection Point C. I'd been told to wait there and I'd be taken to my hotel.

A hotel full of noisy people. Of stress. Of sleeplessness.

I shuddered.

Stop that.

Reinvention…remember?

You might meet a handsome stranger in the hotel restaurant and have the time of your life before flying home as planned tomorrow.

I scoffed.

As if.

"Miss…is your name Ms. Evermore?"

I frowned. "I'm Estelle Evermore, but I'm travelling on my own."

The guy's forehead furrowed. "Oh? You're not with Duncan, Amelia, Conner, and Pippa Evermore?"

"What? No…" I looked past the guide and froze. By the frangipani-decorated van stood the family who'd boarded while I'd been stuck at the gate in Los Angeles.

The wife smiled, waving a little. "Hello again."

I swallowed. "Uh, hi."

The driver tapped his clipboard. "So you know each other? You family or not?"

"We've met but aren't related." The husband with his bushy beard grinned. "We're strangers but more than happy to travel in the same van." He strode toward me, hand outstretched. "I'm Duncan. Nice to meet you…"

My manners kicked in. "Estelle. Pleasure to meet you…for the second time."

"Likewise, Estelle. That was rather random back in the States, huh? Never met another Evermore before. Perhaps we *are* related and just don't know it." He winked as his large hand wrapped around mine, squeezing warmly. "Oh well, any girl as pretty as you is welcome to join our family." Turning to face his loved ones, he pointed at each in turn. "My wife Amelia, and our rug-rats, Conner and Pippa." He rolled his eyes at his brood. "Say hi, kids."

The little girl hugged her tatty-stuffed kitten. "Hi."

The teenage boy didn't look up from his gaming device, his fingers flying over the controls.

I waved lamely. "Hi, guys."

"Don't mind them. Just tired and need sleep." Duncan took a step back. "So, what brings you to Fiji?"

Before I could answer, footsteps sounded behind me followed by an intake of breath. *"You."*

My heart skipped as I whirled around. My gaze locked onto the vibrant blue eyes framed so deliciously in black glasses.

The man from Los Angeles.

"You."

He smirked. "I already said that."

"What are you doing here?" Nerves scattered over my skin, adding to the residual trembling from turbulence.

"I think the same reason why you're here."

The driver butted in. "Are you Mr. Oak?"

The man tore his eyes from mine. "I am." Hoisting his backpack higher onto his shoulder, he swiped a hand through his thick dark hair. The locks immediately flopped back over his forehead as if they'd claimed that part of his face and refused to behave. His skin was the perfect alabaster of a true Englishman while his height and broadness of well-used muscles hinted he might be more farm boy than aristocrat.

A mental movie unravelled in my head of him toiling away beneath the hot sun (shirtless, of course) with his glasses sliding down his sweaty nose.

I'd never thought of glasses as a sex statement (more of an inconvenience) but on him…holy crap.

His attention fell back to me. He cocked his head, running his tongue along his bottom lip. "I wondered where you disappeared to."

"Pardon?" I hated the way his gravelly voice slipped beneath my clothes as if he'd already seen me naked. I loathed the way his accent made me want to revoke my many rules and beg to listen to who he was and share my tale in exchange. I *never* wanted to talk about myself…so why him? What made him so different?

"On the plane. You bolted when we landed."

My heart stopped. "Wait. You could see me on board?" Embarrassment flushed my skin. He'd seen me throwing up? He'd witnessed a neurotic idiot shove as many belongings as she could into pockets of a jacket that'd become far too stifling in the muggy heat, all because she'd had a hare-brained idea of surviving after plummeting thousands of feet into a stormy ocean?

Wonderful.

Flipping brilliant.

"I saw you. I was even tempted to come and talk to you." His eyes slipped over my nose, cheeks, and lips, taking far more liberties than a stranger should. His damn glasses glittered in the lights, drawing all my focus to the one part of him I wanted to escape.

Wait…

Tempted to talk to me but didn't…. *Guess he did see me in all my crazy glory.*

My voice cracked with nerves. "And why didn't you?"

Why would you ask that?

I didn't want to know what'd turned him off. I'd made a pact to reinvent myself when I returned home. Whoever he'd seen on the plane no longer existed.

Then why do you care if you're no longer that person?

Shut up!

God, I was annoying myself.

His eyebrows quirked in an entirely roguish way. "Why didn't I what?" The connection between us grew heavier by the second.

Seriously?

He'd baited me, and, like a stupid fish, I couldn't ignore the hook. "Come talk to me?"

Suddenly, the smouldering awareness snipped free with one caustic laugh from him. "Oh. Let's just say, I have my reasons."

My cheek smarted as if he'd slapped me physically rather than just figuratively. I didn't know how to take that.

Should I be impressed that he noticed me and not care why he hadn't approached, or jilted that I'd interested him but not enough to enlist conversation?

Egotistical jerk.

Duncan laughed under his breath, returning to his wife.

Mr. Oak noticed we had an audience and the brief glimpse into the man who chased what he wanted (but for some reason didn't chase me) shut down, leaving a polite stranger in his wake.

He waved at the Evermore family. "Galloway." His eyes once again landed on mine. Leaning forward, he held out his hand. "Anyway, we've talked now, so no harm done. Like I just said…I'm Galloway."

Automatically, social graces made me loop my fingers with his.

Big mistake.

Colossal mistake.

The second we touched, the embarrassment flushing my skin turned to sexual mist, mingling with sweat from the humid tropics and rolling in a dirty droplet down my spine.

His touch felt like a hundred fireflies—bright, flickering, and completely alive against my flesh.

His mouth parted.

His fingers tightened around mine.

And the driver coughed loudly, hacking a spit-ball by my feet.

Eww!

I leapt to the side, wrenching my hand from Galloway's, leaving me confused and not entirely sad that the touch had been severed.

What the hell was that?

And why did I have equal measures of fascination and abhorrence for this cocky English man who complimented me and insulted me all in one breath?

"Ready to go?" The driver marched to the van door and tossed his clipboard inside. Coming toward me, he stole my suitcase and yanked it toward the trailer attached to the back. "We're all here. Let's go. Perfect time to get you to your hotel before the rain starts again."

The shock of having my suitcase stolen deleted all thoughts of Galloway and the unwelcome power he'd had. I was a professional songwriter and singer. I wasn't a dumb mute rendered idiotic by a handsome man.

Slipping my heavy jacket from my shoulders, I wiped beaded sweat from my forehead. "Wait…are you sure there isn't another flight leaving tonight? I'd rather stay at the airport, just in case—"

"She's right," Galloway muttered. His five o' clock shadow bristled in the low illumination. "I need to leave tonight. Not in the morning. I don't care what they say; I'm travelling to Kadavu."

The driver cocked his head. "Kadavu?"

Galloway crossed his arms. "I start work first thing. If I don't get there on time, I'll lose my contract." He took a step toward the driver. "Surely, you must know of someone willing to fly." Pointing at the storm-slashed but now calm sky, he added, "There's hardly any wind and it's not raining anymore. The storm's gone—just like they said. It's safe to travel."

Duncan Evermore came forward. "Don't mean to interrupt, but we're trying to get to Matava Resort. If you want, we can join forces and see if we can hire a boat or something?" He looked over his shoulder at his family. "I'd much prefer to get to our hotel and start our vacation now, rather than waste time in the morning with packing and checking in for another flight."

The driver tutted under his breath. "Boat would take too long and no one would go in the dark."

Galloway ignored him, focusing on Duncan's potential solution. "I'm with you. I'm happy to split the cost if it means getting to where we want tonight."

"Not possible." The driver shook his head. "No one will travel tonight."

Amelia (Duncan's wife) caught my eye. We smiled, shrugging. *Men.*

Even though they'd been told multiple times they couldn't travel, it didn't stop their pig-headedness at trying.

Galloway opened his messenger bag and pulled out an envelope with a wad of currency. "We'll pay." Wafting it in front of the driver, he taunted. "You help us arrange what we need, and you'll get a bonus."

Unable to take his eyes off the money, the driver rubbed his chin. "Kadavu and Matava?"

Galloway and Duncan nodded together. "That's right. But it has to be tonight, and it has to be for all of us."

All of us not including me, of course.

My heart raced as I was ignored completely. The only person paying attention to me was the little girl hugging her stuffed kitten.

Somehow, we were all strangers, but I'd become the odd one out.

Again.

Normally, I preferred it that way. I deliberately pulled back, letting others bond so I could remain quiet and on the outskirts where I liked it.

But this time, I felt left out—as if an adventure was forming and I hadn't been given an invitation.

Is this another message?

Another hint that life happened all around me and unless I was brave enough to jump in, I would miss yet another opportunity.

My heart raced.

Perhaps my reinvention needed to happen here…not when I got home to Australia.

The driver dug a cell-phone from his back pocket. "Wait a minute." Pacing away, he held the phone to his ear and conversed with someone on the other end.

Duncan shook Galloway's hand. "Looks like we might be in luck, my boy."

Galloway crumpled the cash-filled envelope, shoving it deep into his bag. "Hope so. I have no choice. I'm not accepting no for an answer." His eyes found their way back to me.

Not succumbing to his power again, I deliberately looked away, feigning interest in a billboard for a diving site complete with jewelled fish and reef sharks. The advertisement held the true colours of Fiji—bright pinks and blues and yellows. It was nothing like the dismal evening where black was the colour palate and the whiff of warm asphalt and rotting rubbish overshadowed holiday welcome.

Finally, the driver returned. "Matava Resort is on the island of Kadavu, yes?" Tapping his phone against his thigh, a glint formed in his gaze. "Very exclusive resort. Expensive."

Duncan stiffened, understanding the undertone. "If it's about cost, name it. I'm sure we can come to an arrangement."

Galloway didn't move. He held himself rigid but beneath I sensed an anxious need to move forward rather than stay stationary. Whatever his destination or reason, he wouldn't back down or accept defeat.

I envied him.

I was jealous that he had such passion for bending the rules and getting what he wanted.

"I'm with Duncan," Galloway said. "Find a way to get us there tonight and money can be discussed."

The driver slouched against his van, oblivious to the chaos of other passengers being ferried to their destinations. "I might have a friend."

Duncan slapped him on the shoulder. "Great. What's the

damage?"

"Damage?" The driver immediately looked at his vehicle as if we'd vandalized it while he was on the phone. "What damage?"

Galloway chuckled. "He means how much?"

The driver smiled. "Five hundred US per person."

"No way. Five hundred for all of us." Pointing at his family and Galloway, Duncan clipped, "Five hundred for five people."

Wait.

What was I supposed to do? Travel meekly to a hotel I didn't want to go to, check into a room I had no interest in, and sleep in a bed I already despised?

No.

They had their plans while I rotted in indecision. I had no backbone to my life. I was done being a passenger as tides took me this way and that. I wanted some direction for once.

I wanted to *live.*

I wouldn't ignore the messages any longer.

If I couldn't get home, I would go somewhere second best. I would celebrate like Madi said I should. I would enjoy a holiday, new experiences, and something spontaneous—all because I could.

"Um, Mr. Evermore?"

Duncan paused, smiling kindly. "Yes?"

I ignored Galloway watching me. "This resort you mentioned. Is it quiet?"

Amelia answered on his behalf, tucking copper hair behind her ear. "It's an eco-lodge. Thatched bures with solar power and no carbon footprint. It's for those who crave solitude and silence."

Holy crap, that sounds amazing.

Idyllic.

Custom made for me.

I could relax around the pool (if there was a pool), write, daydream, and plan a future where I wasn't afraid of living.

My heart skipped but this time with hope. "Do you think they'd have vacancy?"

Duncan scratched his chin. "I only made the reservation last week and they said they were at half occupancy. If I were you, I'd be willing to take the risk."

Thoughts of peace and tranquillity enticed me more and more. I could take a week off and recuperate from my tour, before returning home where the internet would hound me, my work would crush me, and obligations awaited.

Why did I want to rush back if I could have a week just for me?

I'd always been a structured person. I didn't take gambles or make spur-of-the-moment decisions, but what if this was *exactly* what I needed?

And they're going without me.

What would I regret more? Letting them find a way to paradise and holing up in some awful hotel, or taking a risk, going with them, and finding the best experience of my life?

I smiled at the driver. "We'll pay six hundred for six people."

Galloway raised an eyebrow. "You're coming, too? But I thought you said—"

"I don't care. I've changed my mind."

"You can do that? Just *change* your mind?"

My smile hardened. "I can do whatever I want."

"But don't you have to—" He scowled. "I dunno. Work or something?"

His body language switched from eager to standoffish. Why did he have a problem with me hitching a ride? It wasn't as if I was asking him to marry me. We'd never see each other again after this.

"What the hell is your deal?"

Galloway flinched. "What do you mean? I don't have a deal."

"You don't want me to travel with you."

"I never said that."

"You did."

"Whatever. Hear what you want to hear. I was merely concerned for your welfare."

I planted hands on my hips. "My welfare. What do you care about my welfare? You don't even know me."

"That's right. He doesn't." Duncan stepped between us, acting as referee. "Six people. No problem at all." Patting me on the shoulder, he grinned. "Pleasure to have you along for the ride, Estelle."

"Estelle?" Galloway's voice stole my name, turning it from a simple address to an angry caress. "That's your name?"

"Don't tell me you have a problem with that, too?"

His face tightened. "I don't have any problem with you. No problems. None."

"Then stop being one for me." The snapped command hovered between us, neither dispersing nor fading.

His eyes turned to steely flint as the friendliness and whatever bond we'd had evaporated.

Jerk.

He'd had the opportunity to talk to me on the plane and didn't. He'd deemed me unworthy of his time, insulted me more times than anyone, and we'd only just met.

The moment we got to where we were going, I'd put him out of my mind and never waste another second on him.

Unless it's to write a nasty song where he meets an unfortunate end.

"Okay, six people for six hundred. Done." The driver pushed off from his slouch and wrenched open the sliding door of his van. "Get in."

The Evermore children climbed in first, followed by Amelia and Duncan. Galloway planted himself in front of me, pausing to talk to the driver. "Where exactly are you taking us?"

The driver said, "I have a cousin who flies produce and supplies to outlying islands. He can help."

"He can get us there tonight?"

The man nodded. "Tonight. No problem."

"Great." With a cold smile, Galloway clambered inside the van.

Hugging my jacket with my pockets filled with random survival gear, I squeezed in after him, taking the spare seat beside Pippa. The little girl smiled, stroking the foot of her kitten. We shared a look as the driver slammed the door, cocooning us in the tight space.

My mind skipped ahead to the idea of waking up tomorrow on a quiet beach, eating fresh fruit, and penning lyrics in the sunshine. Pure excitement fell like silky petals.

I was pissed off at Galloway and more tired than I'd ever been after two months on the road, but for the first time...I was uncomplicatedly happy.

I'm proud of myself.

I'd finally listened to the messages to live deeper, louder, brighter.

I'd finally paid attention and decided not to squander my life away with mediocrity.

Pity, I completely misread the signs.

They weren't there to be adventurous. To live in the moment. To be reckless and stupid and alive.

They were there as a barricade against the exact same flaws I'd just embraced.

Ironically, I'd done the exact opposite of what I should.

By trying to live, I killed myself.

Chapter Six

GALLOWAY

I COULDN'T STOP looking at her.

My gaze somehow found their way to her no matter how much she pissed me off.

What the hell is she doing here?

She wasn't like me.

She didn't have an obligation to uphold.

She had a plane reservation leaving in the morning and every reason to stay in the crappy hotel supplied by the airline and leave the moment she could. So why the hell had she thrown that away to come with us?

Stupid girl.

Stupid, beautiful, sexy-as-hell girl.

Why couldn't she vanish and let me live my damn life?

You don't know anything about her.

I didn't want to. I'd only had a few conversations with her, and already, I guessed she was a high-maintenance shrew with the personality of a pencil.

My fists curled as the van bumped over badly paved roads, heading through villages shrouded in darkness.

I couldn't stop staring.

Why the hell can't I stop staring?

I was glad I hadn't talked to her on the plane. I wished I didn't have to talk to her at all. Not only had she ruined the perception I had of a sweet woman who would've let me walk all over her and not held my balls in her hands, but now, I also had the unwanted situation of sharing transportation with her.

And what was worse…she would be on my island.

Kadavu.

She would check into the resort where the Evermores were staying and infect my piece of paradise. She would be close enough to visit, apologise to, let down my walls, turn off my temper, and truly see what the hell had happened between us when we touched.

She didn't look my way—not once.

I cleaned my glasses; just to be sure I'd catch any glimpse of her sneaking a look.

But nothing.

Her eyes locked on the passing Fijian countryside, her fingers tapping a nonsensical beat on her puffer jacket in her lap. She'd removed her pink jumper and the delicate lines of her naked shoulders and the hint of bra straps beneath her black tank top pissed me off even more.

How dare she have this effect on me? It wasn't permitted. Not when I was so close to doing something right for a change. Not when I wanted nothing to do with complications and relationships that I didn't deserve.

The little girl sitting beside her tugged her jacket, poking at the bulging pockets.

Estelle (what sort of sexy, delicious name was that anyway?) giggled, leaning closer to chat with the kid.

The fearful tension she'd worn on the plane had faded, revealing another layer to the woman I didn't want to know.

Now, she looked almost…excited. Free. Younger and wiser all at the same time.

What made her change her mind?

Where had she been going before throwing her plans to fate and deciding to hook up with a bunch of strangers to fly to an island in the middle of nowhere?

Who *did* that?

Who lived so freely?

My lips drifted to her mouth.

What would she taste like if I kissed her? Would she let me or would she kick me in the balls instead?

I don't want to bloody kiss her, goddammit.

I groaned, rubbing my temples, trying to get myself under control.

I wanted to open the door and shove her outside mid-drive. I wanted her far, far away from me before I could give into the itch inside. Because if I gave into the itch, I was screwed. She would be, too.

I don't have time for this.

Duncan and his family remained quiet as fat raindrops

intermittently splashed the van's roof. Palm trees swayed in the dark, lit with an occasional streetlight, turning them into eerie skeletons the deeper into the bush we drove.

The journey didn't take long. After all, Viti Levu wasn't a big island. However, the rain had drenched the trees and banana plantations. The storm might have passed, but precipitation and humidity meant the tropics were never truly dry.

My teeth jarred as we turned right over a pothole and down a long driveway, arriving beside an airstrip where the carcasses of propeller aircraft and a few sad looking helicopters rested in the night.

Estelle glanced out the window as we pulled to a stop outside a thatched bungalow. The driver climbed out and opened our door.

We all tumbled out in a mix of curses.

Suitcases and carry-ons were hauled from the van's trailer and carted as quickly as possible into the decrepit office with dull lights swinging from the ceiling. The humidity did its best to drench us, turning weary passengers into a sodden pile of jetlagged clothing.

Dropping our bags in the foyer beside a counter with an ancient printer and fax machine, our sad little group surveyed the not-too-inviting office.

The driver pointed at the floor in the universal sign of 'stay here' and disappeared down a corridor to where I assumed was the main traffic control.

Estelle looked at me fleetingly as she investigated sepia photographs on the wall depicting planes and helicopters flying over pretty islands.

The tiny glance harpooned my attention, reeling me in despite my wishes. Opening lines and snippy arguments filled my head. If I had to put up with the weird connection between us, she ought to be as uncomfortable as I was.

Before I could think up a callous, witty remark, Estelle turned her back on me and traced a large map of Fiji with its widespread islands pasted crookedly on the wall. The Evermore family drifted off, murmuring and soothing the kids that soon they'd be in paradise and able to sleep.

I stood there like a bloody idiot.

Needing to do something, I ran a hand over my hair to dispel raindrops and prowled after the driver. At the end of the corridor, I entered the office where he'd disappeared.

Two men conversed in Hindi, letting me know they were Indian-Fijian descent. Their hands punctured their sentences as I skirted the perimeter, scanning the rudimentary graphs and diagrams of flight paths and other aeronautical paraphernalia.

Our driver pointed outside to the wet night, nodding as if it was a perfect evening to fly. The other man shook his head, waggling his wristwatch in his friend's face, scrunching his nose with disagreement.

Goddammit, he had to take us.

If it weren't important, I'd happily stay the night in some shitty backpackers. But it *was* important. I had to be there. I wouldn't fail again.

Shoving my hands into my jean pockets, I approached them. "Look, we're happy to pay. How long is the flight? An hour or so? That means you make some good coin and get home all within a couple of hours." Forcing a smile, I pulled the wad of cash from my back pocket (it was all I had left). "Need to know we're good for it? We'll pay you up-front. How about that?"

The remaining US currency was convenient. I'd pay for all of us, and they could pay me back on the flight.

The driver cleared his throat, gesturing to his friend and the money in my hand.

I smiled. "See, a good gig."

Frowning, the other man—who I assumed would be our pilot—came closer. Ignoring the money, he held out his hand waiting for me to shake. Transferring the bills to my left, I clasped his right, completing social niceties.

Letting our handheld introduction break, the man said, "I'm Akin. You are?"

"Galloway."

"Mr. Galloway, you do realise a storm is threatening Fiji. It's not safe—"

"The pilot on the flight here said the weather pattern was leaving."

Akin paced around me, making me feel like a naughty student listening to his professor. The guy wasn't old, but his face was lined with stress and hardship. "That might be, but these things create wind thermals and downdraughts. The cumulus nimbus of a thunderstorm can be deadly with turbulent air."

My heart fisted at the thought of having this last chance stolen. I wasn't an idiot. If a professional said it was risky…then what did I value more? My life or a job?

But I valued this second chance almost as much. It wasn't just a job. It was the opportunity to find happiness again.

My fingers clutched the money. Words filled my mouth to argue, but I wouldn't fight. I'd done my best. If it was too dangerous, then…fine. Yet another dream dashed. I'd have to change my flight to fly back to England tomorrow rather than in three months' time. I'd have to admit to my father that I lied to him. I'd have to accept that I wasn't worthy of what I wished for. *Goddammit.*

Our driver struck up conversation in Hindi again. I left them to it. I'd tried and failed.

Heading down the corridor, my eyes met Estelle's. The green and brown of swirling hazel warmed first with anticipation and then cooled with disappointment. She understood just by looking at me that we wouldn't be going anywhere—not tonight. I hoped she had better things to go back to than I did.

Duncan moved away from his wife and kids. "What's the update? When do we leave?"

I gripped the back of my neck, squeezing at the sudden headache building at the base of my spine. "We don't—"

"How many people?" Akin interrupted me, shooting me a look as he appeared in entrance to the corridor.

"Huh?"

Estelle answered for me. "Six, plus luggage."

Akin crossed his arms. "No. I have an R44 and maximum capacity is four people." He scowled at the children. "I've stripped the cabin of all unnecessary gear so I can transport more supplies for work. It's possible to squeeze in the kids but luggage can't go."

Amelia came forward. "But we need our bags. How are we supposed—"

"I'll bring them over tomorrow when I fly my regular route to bring produce to outlying hotels." Akin cocked his chin. "Those are my terms. Fly now and have a night with limited supplies or leave tomorrow with your belongings on a bigger service."

My heart leapt. I didn't care. I had most of my toiletries in my messenger bag and nothing of value in my luggage. "If we can take bare necessities, I'm in."

Estelle cleared her throat, hugging her jacket.

Why the hell was she still holding that thing? She must be sweltering beneath the puffy weight—even if she wasn't wearing it.

Glancing at her overstuffed suitcase, she sighed. "If I can bring my handbag, I'm okay with that, too. As long as my valuables like my laptop are safe to leave here overnight?"

"Very safe." Akin nodded. "I'll take great care of your belongings until I bring them to you." Fixing his gaze on the Evermore family, he asked, "What's it to be? I'll agree to take you to Kadavu with my helicopter. But we leave now and you follow my every instruction."

My eyes drifted to our shuttle driver. He stood behind Akin, leaning against the wall. What did he say to him to change his mind? Akin had been rather adamant about not flying in the storm.

"And you're sure it's safe?" I muttered. "After your unwillingness before?"

Akin glared in my direction. "Yes, I checked the weather and you're right. The storm is heading away. I'm comfortable enough to do a quick flight." His eyes flashed. "Believe me, if I didn't think it was safe, I wouldn't go. After all, it's not just your lives on the line, is it?"

Good point. "Fair enough."

"There is one thing I need to mention and then it's your choice." Akin waited for complete attention before continuing. "My R44 has a faulty ELT. It's your own risk."

"What's an ELT?" Duncan asked.

"Emergency Locator Beacon," Akin said. "I'm due to get it fixed, but my workload means I can't give up time for a maintenance overhaul." He spread his hands in surrender. "Your choice. I trust my machine and it's never failed me. But full disclosure."

Amelia tugged Duncan's sleeve. "I'm not so sure—"

"It's just like riding a rickety bus, Emmy." Duncan kissed his wife's cheek. "They never break down but they look God awful." Looking at Akin, he smiled. "I'm okay with that."

Akin glanced at me. "You?"

I looped my fingers around my bag's strap. "I guess."

"And you?" Akin pointed at Estelle.

She pursed her lips. I fully expected her to refuse. But once again she surprised me.

"Okay." Turning to grab her handbag from the stash of belongings, she rummaged in the white leather to make sure she had whatever she needed. Dropping to her haunches, she unzipped her suitcase and pulled out a silky nightgown (that made my mouth go dry), a black bikini, a t-shirt, shorts, and mini-skirt. Stuffing them all into her handbag, she stood. "All ready."

Fine.

If Ms. Preparedness had the forethought to think about waking tomorrow and not having things to wear, I would, too.

Ripping out a pair of khaki pants to work in, a pair of shorts to relax in, a couple of t-shirts, and board-shorts from my backpack, I stuffed them into my messenger bag. It bulged but it would do. My toothbrush and deodorant were already in there—travel compact size.

Without a word, Duncan followed suit. Grabbing his wife's large tote, he stuffed in a few belongings and children clothes followed by whatever else he needed into his own small backpack.

A few moments later, the rustling and sounds of zippers ceased and we turned to face Akin.

"Ready when you are."

Akin held out his hand.

Knowing what he wanted, I planted the money into his outstretched palm.

His fingers tightened over the bills before marching to the counter and inserting the money into a locked drawer.

"Let's go." Without a backward glance, he strode out the door.

Well, that was the fastest boarding sequence I've ever been through.

Duncan caught my eye as we all trudged after our pilot.

Lingering rain splashed onto our shoulders and mud squelched beneath our shoes as we exchanged bungalow for open sky.

The helicopter welcomed us into its belly.

After pre-flight checks and pilot given instructions, we left land for horizon for the second time and left Nadi behind.

Forever.

Chapter Seven

· ···

ESTELLE

······

Have you ever tried and failed, leapt and fell, believed and floundered? Defeat comes swift. Tragedy strikes fast. The world is dangerous, monstrous, unthinkable. But the unthinkable is where magic exists. Hidden between unthought thoughts and unspoken verses. ~~Mysterious behind unseen messages.~~ The unthinkable is where greatness exists.
~~*Be unthinkable. Be untameable. Be unstoppable.*~~
Lyrics: 'Unthinkable' Taken from the notepad of E.E.

···

THE *WHOP* OF rotor blades.

The swoop of gravity.

The soar of flying.

I'd never been in a helicopter before. Even when I was lucky enough to score a job as an air-hostess, I'd never swapped fixed wings for propellers above my head.

I'm in a helicopter.

I'm going to an unknown resort rather than home to my comfy bed.

What the hell am I doing?

My fingers tightened the harness around my middle for the billionth time. The crackle in my headset was foreign and unwelcome. But despite the sway and rock of the machine, and the fear that I'd overstepped some sort of code keeping my life in balance, I was alive.

I was aware of *everything.*

From the slipperiness of the bench seat beneath me, the whirl of engines, the warmth of strangers wedged beside me to the tingling sensation of unwanted attraction for a man who confused and frustrated me.

E..v..e..r..ything.

Every heartbeat, every swallow, every trepidation of what awaited.

Whereas before, I'd felt nothing. I'd willingly wrapped myself in sameness so I never felt out of place because...why was that? Because I was afraid of change or the consequences of moving on by myself?

My life had changed more than once in the last few years. My family had left me alone (through no fault of their own), Madeline had uploaded something intrinsically private and made it global property, and I'd shed all notion of who I was to do something stupidly spontaneous.

But the rush as we soared away from Viti Levu and disappeared into the inky sky of raindrops and ocean made me thankful that I'd had the courage to leap without evaluating first.

If I'd remained afraid, I'd most likely be sitting in a nondescript hotel room waiting for my flight tomorrow. Instead, I was flying with complete strangers, at the mercy of the occasional wind buffets and cloud-blanketed stars, living more in the moment than I ever had before.

This would be a splendid song.

Half-formed lyrics filled my head, threading around the racket of the helicopter.

Pippa, the daughter of Duncan Evermore, grinned my way. She perched on her mother's lap beside me. I sat in the middle while Duncan rested on my right with his son, Conner, on his knee. Galloway sat up front with the pilot. I was the lucky one holding everyone's luggage.

Even though I'd been transformed into a suitcase holder, it couldn't dampen my enjoyment. The view outside was just black—like the void of a nightmare or kiss of goodbye. An occasional sparkle of light from a boat below or island in the distance glittered as raindrops smeared over the windows.

Akin, the pilot, had made us all pull on inflatable life-jackets. I'd panicked for a moment, remembering the delays and random occurrences warning me not to board my commercial flight. But there'd been nothing since I'd decided to leap into the unknown. I had no fear. No reservations.

This felt right.

Akin's voice filled my head through the heavy headset. It cancelled out some of the rotor noise but not enough to hear him clearly. "Going to get a bit bumpy. Air mass up ahead."

My chest tightened. *Okay, perhaps I spoke too soon.* Fear unspooled as the first turbulent jiggle shook us.

The Evermores clutched their children.

I hugged my collection of handbags and backpacks.

Another jolt of air pressure and slam of rotor blades reminded me we weren't safely on the ground anymore. We were high in the sky, at the mercy of gravity and nasty weather.

Why did I do this again?

No one spoke as we flew farther out to sea.

My breathing turned shallow as the turbulence steadily became worse. I stopped breathing a couple of times as pockets of air opened beneath us, hurtling us down only for an updraft to propel us back up.

I'd never suffered airsickness (until my previous flight), but the brewing of illness returned, steadily growing the longer we flew. We became a snake in the sky, slithering left then right. We'd yaw sideways then correct. We'd bounce upward then stabilize.

Through it all, Galloway sat up front, muttering to the pilot on a frequency I couldn't hear. The tension in the two men's shoulders fed my anxiety. Galloway's chocolate hair looked almost as dark as Akin's black in the gloom.

Akin was a good pilot, remaining calm and focused. But he couldn't hide the discomfort or immense concentration it took to remain airborne in such storm-churned weather.

I closed my eyes.

Don't think about that.

Think about where you'll be in an hour or so.

It wouldn't be long before I could check into heaven, say goodbye to pig-headed Galloway, and be on my own once again. I'd rent a private room with no noise or city chaos. I'd have the best sleep of my life and then relax and compose new songs around the pool after a delicious breakfast of pastries and fresh fruit.

Sounds perfect.

After a week of recharging, I'd return home fully relaxed and able to work hard for my new agent and producer.

The stress trickled from my blood, even as another swirl of bumpy air jerked me against my seat belt.

"Bit rough, isn't it?" Duncan nudged his shoulder with mine.

Unwillingly, I let my illusion dissolve to look at him. "We'll be okay." I didn't know where my words of comfort came from—they had no foundation.

Amelia shifted Pippa on her knee, bumping me. "I never did like flying. Would much prefer a boat or something closer to the ground."

I smiled, forcing myself to be friendly even while squashed in a helicopter and drowning in people's bags. Galloway's messenger bag sat on top, right beneath my nose. The scent of his aftershave (or was it possible to smell that good with no manmade sprays?) intoxicated me with every inhale. A delectable-terrible mix of musk, cedar, and…was that *liquorice?*

It was one of the best scents in the world—much better than the oil-fumy helicopter.

Damn him for enticing my nose as well as my eyes.

Pippa reached out and grabbed my wrist. Her warm fingers clutched me as another burp of air buffeted us.

Without thinking, I brought my wrist to my lips and kissed her knuckles. "It's okay. Just the wind."

Amelia gave me a grateful smile.

Pippa hugged her stuffed kitten.

"What's your cat called?" I had to yell rather than whisper comfortingly with the crackling headset.

Pippa bit her lip, shaking her head shyly.

Amelia answered for her. "Puffin."

"Puffin? That's an interesting name for a kitten."

Amelia smoothed her daughter's matching copper hair. "Puss in Boots. But someone had trouble with the 'Puss in' part and it slowly morphed to Puffin."

"Ah." I ran my fingers over the well-loved cuddly toy. "It's a perfect name."

Pippa beamed.

Focusing on the little girl rather than the rocking helicopter, I said, "Want to know a secret?"

Pippa's eyes shot wide, the headset far too big for her tiny head. She nodded.

"I have a kitty, too. But it's real. I have a house sitter looking after him while I travel, but I can't wait to cuddle him like you are."

Pippa's mouth fell open.

Amelia laughed. "Isn't that cool, Pip? Perhaps, if you're good when we get home, we can see about getting one, too."

The undiluted joy on the girl's face almost brought me to tears.

For a while, we all sat in our individual thoughts. We flew quickly over islands and ocean. My daydream came back, and I allowed the trance of icy cocktails and sunbaking to steal me away from the *whop whop* of rotor blades.

I lost track of time.

Sleepiness found me, even with the air turning us into a tennis ball and hitting us with its battering blows. Conner's voice mingled with his father's as they tried to play 'I Spy' out the rain-drenched windows.

Pippa snuggled with Puffin, nuzzling into her mother's neck, and Galloway turned to check on us, his eyes shadowed by his glasses but still intense enough to conjure goosebumps.

I sat frozen beneath his inspection. His throat worked as he swallowed, never tearing his gaze from mine. I waited for him to turn around so I could breathe again.

But he didn't.

Slowly, his eyes dropped to my lips, warming and cooling at the same time.

What do you want from me?

Who are you?

Questions glowed on his face, mimicking mine. I'd never met someone I'd had such an instantaneous reaction (both good and bad) with. Half of me wanted to argue with him while the other half wanted to silently stare.

His hand moved to the microphone by his lips. His mouth parted to speak.

I didn't move or blink, waiting to see what he would do.

But then, it happened.

The bottom of the sky vanished.

We fell.

My stomach was left a few metres above, making me horribly hollow.

A microsecond later, we slammed into a wall of air, curtailing our fall and crunching our spines into the leathered bench.

"Oh, my God!" Amelia screamed.

Pippa's eyes welled up with tears.

What the hell was that?

"Hold on!" Akin bellowed in the headphones. "The storm was bigger than I thought and left behind disrupted air pockets. I'm going to have to go around and avoid what I can't see."

Galloway spun to face the front. His voice came over the frequency. "What flight range does this thing have?"

Good question.

Fear of running out of fuel and nosediving into the sea swamped me.

Akin never answered, focusing too hard on swooping us to the right and hurtling us higher into the sky.

I hugged my lap of luggage.

Please let us be okay.

Please.

Pippa cried on her mother's knee while Conner clutched his

father. Duncan gave me a worried smile that was anything but encouraging. My racing heart turned into a jackhammer, splitting my ribcage with panic.

There were no more sparkly lights outside. No sign of life or habitation. It was just us and blackness as we bounced and skipped wherever the wind wanted to take us.

This was a stupid, *stupid* idea.

We were all idiots to fly in such weather.

"Shit!" Akin's curse sliced through my ears, bringing a rush of prickly adrenaline.

A second later, the world ended.

It was quieter than I'd imagined. Less sharp with imminent death and more befuddled with confusion.

The engine screamed, trying to get us to a safe altitude. But we lost height instead. We didn't plunge like before but hovered—almost as if the moon cast a fishing line and hooked us, dangling us as bait for something big to snatch.

Our trajectory stalled.

We were weightless

soundless

motionless.

Then the inevitable happened.

I said inevitable because everything (every delay, every occurrence, every unseen message) had been warning me of this and I didn't listen.

I didn't listen!

Whatever creature the moon had been fishing for, took hold. We jerked then an explosion ricocheted through the cabin. The rotor blades suddenly flapped down so they were visible through the windows, bending like broken wings. The spectacle disappeared as quickly as it happened, snapping upward and tearing free from the mast.

They came free.

The blades keeping us airborne—the very things determining if we survived or died—snapped off.

They abandoned us.

No!

We turned from flying machine to plummeting grenade.

Falling,

falling,

falling.

Dying…

Through fear and disbelief one thought blared.

One number.
One date.
29th of August.
The day we left the world of the living and became lost.

Chapter Eight

GALLOWAY

I'D THOUGHT ABOUT death.

Who wouldn't when their mother died right in front of them? How could I not when I'd been the cause of someone else's?

I'd wondered if there was an existence after death. I'd sat in the dark and begged for no afterlife because if there was a heaven, then there was a hell, and I would rot there forever.

I hated myself for wishing away a heaven where my dead mother might've found peace purely because I worried for my immortal soul.

But I was a prick, a bastard, and now, the world had finally agreed to kill me. I wasn't worth its resources any longer.

I had to be exterminated.

There would be no reincarnation—not after what I'd done. I didn't want my fate, but I accepted it. I just hated that innocent people had to die beside me.

The helicopter went from saviour to dementor.

The air turned violent, spewing us from its domain.

The spinning blades keeping us afloat vanished.

I couldn't breathe.

We spun like a top, over and over and *over*.

My ears popped.

My head pounded.

My life unravelled heartbeat by heartbeat.

There was no way to stop it. Gravity wanted us. It would have us.

All of us. Not just me.

I forced my eyes open. The water-drenched windshield showed no answers but I knew. I *felt* it. I sensed the earth coming faster and faster to meet us. A killing welcome party of water or land, waves or trees.

I couldn't see.

I can't see!

My fingers dug into the worn leather of the seat, the life-jacket cocooned me, and the seat belt across my chest kept me pinned for the worst adventure of my life.

Screams echoed behind me as the helicopter ripped itself apart.

The handbags and belongings Estelle held tore from her grip, clattering around the cabin.

The kids wailed.

The pilot cursed.

And through it all, I chanted.

Please let them live.

Please let them live.

Don't make them pay, too.

But no answers came. Noise shattered everything.

That noise was all I would remember of the crash. Like a hurricane...no, a goddamn tornado—the god of wind had revenge on his mind.

My life was over before it even began.

I should've fought harder.

Started living sooner.

I should never have done what I did.

I should've, should've, *should've.*

And now, I can't.

Regret crushed me that I wouldn't grow old. Wouldn't have kids or a wife.

I thought I could ignore affection—that I didn't need it. Fuck yes, I needed it. I *desperately* needed it. And now, I'd never experience it.

Idiot.

Moron.

Loser.

I squeezed my eyes as the whining of engines stole my sanity.

My teeth clattered as the helicopter vibrated to a frequency guaranteed to destroy us. The earth came faster, faster, *faster...*we were airborne no longer.

We were no longer moving toward the world.

We were there.

We slammed into treetops, bouncing like a tombstone over trunks and twigs.

And the last thing I remembered—the final thought I had—

wasn't the answer to life's ultimate question or peace at accepting my gruesome end.

It was the crack and shudder of trees being annihilated, carving a path of destruction, welcoming us into its home, tearing us apart piece by piece.

My head bashed against the window.

My glasses shattered.

And then…nothing.

Chapter Nine

....

E S T E L L E

......

All things end. *All things don't end. Love doesn't end just because hate manifests. A tree doesn't end just because it's transformed into fire. Life doesn't end just because it ceases to be what you know. Life cannot simply unexist. So why does an ending seem like a beginning? So why are endings so damn hard to survive?*

Taken from the notepad of E.E.

...

ONCE WITHIN A song, a girl who was terrified of everything finally found a reason to be afraid of nothing.

All my life, I'd used words to invoke emotion and deliver a scene or circumstance. I'd borrowed the power of rhythm to reveal magnitude and depth of feeling.

But this.

There were no words for this.

No beat or riff could compare.

No simple explanation of what it felt like to be torn from reality and deposited into a nightmare.

All I knew was pain.

Pain.

We crashed.

Those two words were woefully unjust.

We turned into helicopter mincemeat.

We ceased to exist as whole creatures and became splinters instead.

I didn't see.

I didn't understand.

I couldn't register anything in the speed it took to go from alive to dead.

One moment, we were friends to the sky, and the next, an enemy to earth.

I couldn't explain how we'd gone from flying to being crumpled at the bottom of a palm tree.

I couldn't find the articulation to say how I'd survived.

All I could do was live in tragedy.

Every part of me hurt.

My chest bellowed from where my seat belt cut into my chest. My head pounded from snapping back and forth. And the terror at realising I was all alone...well, that was the worst part.

Horror crept over my injuries, hurting me right in my solar plexus.

I was the only one remaining in the helicopter.

To my left was empty. To my right was empty.

The Evermores were gone.

The pilot gone.

Galloway...*gone.*

My heart bled with fear, staining ribs that I was sure were broken.

Where is everybody?

My hands and feet tingled; the smell of gasoline made my vision swim.

You have to get out.

My fingers took control; my brain ignored confusion, making way for survival.

Another whiff of gasoline made my hands scramble faster. Every twist and breath killed my bleeding chest and ribs.

But I didn't care.

Get out. Get out!

The harness snapped open; I fell sideways.

I cried as I tumbled from the empty cabin, rolling from the wreckage. The helicopter had come to a halt, resting on its side. The rotor blades were gone, the straps and pulleys of the flying mechanism were a gruesome massacre. The stab of bracken and foliage struck my palms as I crawled away from the mangled transport.

Another gasp burned through my bruised chest. Another lungful of gasoline.

Tears formed like a swelling tsunami, but I wouldn't let them fall. I wouldn't. Not yet. Not until I comprehended the situation.

I was alive.

I didn't have time for tears.

I didn't know if the helicopter would catch fire.

I didn't know if an explosion was imminent.

All I knew was I had to get as far away as possible…just in case.

Crawling, I inched my way along the trail path of our unscheduled landing. The scar in the earth was the perfect runway for me to follow.

My other senses returned.

I was soaking.

Rain sluiced from above, blackening the sky, slicking dirt into mud and leaves into slippery devils.

I couldn't hear properly.

My ears rang with the final scream of the helicopter engine. The occasional boom of thunder in the distance grew louder the farther I crawled.

I tasted copper.

My face scrunched up as I investigated the cause of the metallic residue in my mouth. I'd bitten a chunk off the inside of my cheek upon impact.

I was in pain.

My injuries were localized—mainly throbbing in my chest—but they radiated out, stealing my energy far too fast.

I have to stop.

My crawling turned into a face plant on the sodden ground while the rain gathered strength and pummelled my back. The wet splatter against my uninflated life-jacket mocked me; wasn't this safety device supposed to protect rather than ridicule?

Sadness I'd never felt before crushed me deeper into the dirt, hitching a ride on my aching shoulder blades, riding me into depression.

What would happen now?

Where am I?

Would someone find me?

I couldn't think about the future. So I did the only thing I could.

I kept going.

Holding my side as pain spilled from my lips, I somehow managed to stumble to my feet. My chest compounded in agony and my suspicions about broken ribs were confirmed the longer I hobbled away from the crash.

As I moved, I took inventory.

My fingers worked. My arms and legs, too. I wasn't bleeding too badly apart from a cut on my forehead and a long slice down my chest from the harness.

I was lucky.

I'd survived.

I'm the only one.

My feet suddenly refused to keep moving. What if they were back there? In serious pain and needing help? I froze, listening for an explosion from the spilling fuel tanks.

But there was no catastrophic boom, only the heavy splatter of rain and occasional sheet of lightning above the palm trees.

I'd flown with six other people, yet they'd all disappeared.

Where are they?

My eyes widened, doing their best to see through the dark wetness. But I couldn't see. No hint of human shuffle or tease of companions.

I had to find them. I had to *help* them.

But I had to help myself, too.

If we'd landed on an inhabited island, I could alert the officials for ambulances and rescue.

Yes…

The idea formed and adrenaline flowed at the thought of falling into the arms of a doctor who could take away my pain and tell me it would all be okay. I would find a saviour, then I'd return to save the others.

One foot in front of the other.

Moving. Walking. Slogging through a forest where rain was the sky rather than the moon.

I'll find someone to help us.

The world was a populated place. Someone close by would know what to do.

All I could do was keep moving.

Until I couldn't anymore.

I was shattered pieces strung up with despair. The island was loneliness and terror. The sky my crying eyes. The drenched dirt my hopeless hope.

Time held no meaning as I finally reached the end of destruction from our crash. Before me rested pristine overgrown jungle, barricading my way with vines and densely grown weeds.

The loudest ricochet of thunder cymbaled across the earth.

I sucked in a panicked breath, wrenching my ribs with agony.

This can't be real.

Let it all be a dream.

Feeling helpless, useless, and woefully unprepared for whatever my future held, I fell to my knees and looked to the heavens. Rainwater mixed with the blood on my forehead, turning into pink cascades, washing away my life as I knew it.

Anyone...please...

The tears I'd swallowed returned, and this time, I couldn't stop them.

I cried.

I sobbed.

I begged.

Anyone...please...

Help us.

Chapter Ten

GALLOWAY

••••••

I WAS NUMB.

But it was a crap load better than being in pain.

I didn't remember anything past hitting the treetops and my head crunching against something hard. My brain shut down and the torrenting rain had woken me by trying to drown me as I rested unconscious on my back.

I'd somehow managed to cough myself awake, tear myself free from a strangling life-jacket, and scramble onto my elbows to assess what the hell had happened.

I didn't know how I ended up with half a ripped seat belt still attached to me while lying in the middle of a jungle. I didn't know how we'd gone from flying to *this*. But just because I couldn't understand it, didn't mean it hadn't happened.

Lightning forked overhead. Each flash illuminated the forest with white light.

Nothing was familiar.

No buildings, no people, no signs of humanity anywhere; only the unapologetic backdrop of trees and undergrowth.

Tearing my gaze from my surroundings, I took stock of my injuries. Everything was slightly hazy. My eyes overcompensated to drag clarity with corneas that required glasses for proper use.

My glasses.

They'd vanished. The dent on the bridge of my nose gave me a clue that something had slammed the frame into my face. No doubt the optical prescription would be shattered.

You can order more online.

Taking comfort that my vision could be rectified the moment I was rescued, I glanced at my body.

The moment I looked at my right leg, I knew I was screwed.

My heart sank.

I was hurt.

Badly.

My leg bellowed, centring in my lower shin, ankle, and foot. My jeans were intact, no blood staining the denim so my flesh wasn't broken, but I didn't need an X-ray to know a few bones were. The angle my ankle rested at sent a wash of sickness through me. The heat of my lower leg and odd swelling on my shoeless foot painted a horrendous injury.

Where are my flip-flops?

I prodded it with a finger and almost passed out from the backwash of agony.

Goddammit.

Breathing hard, I glanced away. I was afraid to study it any longer in case it grew worse. The rest of my body had fared okay. A few scrapes on my arms and torso from no doubt slamming into trees and a decent amount of blood pooled from a cut on my left thigh, peeking through torn jeans, gleaming black in the darkness.

Adrenaline pumped through my system, stealing the resonating pain in my ankle as my body went into shock. The natural instinct of my nervous system blocked me from feeling, but it couldn't camouflage the rapidly swelling and contorted shape of my lower leg.

How bad was it? How did you even fix something like that?

I needed an ambulance and fast.

My entire system turned wobbly and weak. My hands shook, my teeth chattered, and my vision wavered in and out from the bump on my head.

Shit.

Forcing myself to focus, I did my best to work out our flight path. Akin said he had to fly around the storm. How long had he diverted before he told us the severity of the problem? Were we close to Kadavu or miles off?

Where the hell are we?

My heart rate increased the longer I sat in the rain. It was eerie sitting in a spooky forest on my own with no pollution from human habitation or chatter from voices.

"Anyone there?"

The storm stole my voice with a wet snatch.

Fumbling with the broken remains of my seat belt, I gritted my teeth against my crippled ankle and shuffled backward, using my hands as anchors and dragging my legs in front of me.

There was no way I could stand. Not without support or some serious medical attention.

A palm tree welcomed my back, shielding me partially from the heavy rain. Squinting into the droplets, I cursed.

Turns out the weather hadn't moved away.

The wind whistled through the canopy, gusting through leaves with mini hurricanes.

What caused us to crash?

I wasn't clued up on helicopter mechanics, but I'd watched a documentary about skiers who died while flying up a popular mountain. The cause of the accident was turbulent air causing a thing called mast bump. It would correspond to what happened in our case: the blades flapping down and bouncing off like a damn traitor.

My ears strained for a reply to my call. No rustling indicated they'd heard me. No footsteps heralded help.

Nothing.

Just me in a Fiji wilderness with no sign of the helicopter, pilot, or passengers.

Estelle.

My heart raged. Where was she? Was she hurt? What about those poor kids? What the hell *happened* to everyone?

My fingers dug into the ground, fighting to get to my feet and find them. But the moment I added the tiniest amount of weight to my leg, I grunted in agony.

Sweat sprouted on my forehead, which had nothing to do with the outside temperature and everything to do with how badly I was hurt.

How did I fly from the cockpit? Why was I alone? And why the hell had Akin said it was safe to fly when he obviously had reservations. Yes, we were adamant about leaving. Yes, it was our fault for being stupidly reckless just because we were impatient. But he'd put his life on the line, too. And for what? A few measly bucks?

"Christ!" I pounded the muddy ground with a fist. No wildlife sprang away. No one appeared from the bushes.

I was alone. A broken man beneath an angry storm.

I was completely insignificant.

Time ticked onward, and still, no one came. My eyes strained, willing a recognisable face to morph from the shadows. Nothing moved apart from tree trunks swaying in the high winds and palm fronds snapping in the gusts.

My ears did their best to listen to noises other than angry

droplets but there was nothing.

Nothing

nothing

nothing.

Had they died on impact? What about the pilot? Were they all dead and decaying in different stages of agony?

Another flush of pain worked up my leg. I shifted to find a more comfortable position (not that there was one) and every inch of me howled. The thought of a hospital and competent doctors felt like an entire solar system away from the wreckage of my present.

What do I do?

Did I just sit there, drowning as the skies washed away the earth? Did I try to stand and find shelter? Seek the others? Do my best to survive?

So many questions and no answers.

My leg meant I was screwed unless I could figure out a way to secure the broken limb and somehow haul myself to my feet (or rather foot—the other was broken, too).

The cut on my thigh oozed but wasn't life threatening. While the storm raged, I couldn't do a damn thing. I'd only slip on the soggy ground and cause myself more pain.

So…even though I hated every wasted second, I did the only thing I could.

I slouched against the palm tree, cursed my brokenness, and willed the storm to leave so the sun could rise and this whole bloody nightmare could be over.

Chapter Eleven

· ·

ESTELLE

· · · · · ·

~~I am nothing but loneliness.~~ *I am nothing but hope. I am numb but full of intensity. I am alone but not lost. I belonged to society, but now, I'm ~~abandoned~~ free. Free or dead?*
All freedom can seem like death for those unprepared.
~~I am unprepared.~~ *I'll survive this.*
Taken from the notepad of E.E.

· · ·

THE BLUSH OF dawn came on the heels of the storm.

Slowly, the sky switched from dismal black to watery grey. The rain turned from deluge to drizzle, the wind stopped howling, and the earth breathed a sigh of relief as the clouds dispersed and left us to dry off.

I wriggled out from beneath the bush where I'd huddled. I hadn't been able to sleep (who could dripping wet and terrified), but I had been able to rest my broken ribs and figure out a plan (sort of. Not really).

I'd rested there, grieved there, until the depressive burden had eased. Until my eyes stopped weeping, my courage stopped failing, and my fear stopped choking.

I'm alive.

It was a gift. A triumph after a blurry blender of battery.

Goosebumps covered my bare arms, mottling white skin with bruises and minor cuts. I looked as if I'd painted myself in mud from crawling in the storm.

I would've given anything to have my puffer jacket. It wouldn't have kept me dry, but at least, the feathers and duck down would've kept me slightly warmer than bare skin.

Not to mention, the items I'd stowed in the pockets on a

paranoid whim that'd turned out to be far too premonitive. I'd stuffed nonsense things with my fear of crashing. And now, I'd crashed, and I had no idea where my jacket was.

Had I jinxed myself or had fate merely toyed with me, leading me to believe I could circumnavigate the future while I ended up walking straight into its trap?

Either way, I was alone and hurt. I had to get help and find a way back to society.

Every step killed my broken ribs. I kept my arms wrapped snug around myself, fighting against tiredness, shock, and hunger as I headed back the way I'd crawled. I'd decided, while curled up beneath my bush, that hacking through dense forest without returning for supplies or checking on the others was suicide.

Going back to the helicopter, now the risk of an explosion was less likely, made the most logical sense.

I breathed with relief as the cool breeze switched to muggy warmth the longer I walked. The forest steamed as it steadily grew warmer, turning fresh air into an oxygen-rich soup.

It'd been cold last night, but now, the increasing humidity sprang with full force.

Stopping, I called, "Hello? Can anyone hear me?"

I waited for a reply.

One minute.

Two.

Nothing.

Fighting the heavy weight of worry, I supported my throbbing ribs and trudged forward.

Where? I had no idea.

Why? I had nothing better to do.

I could remain under my bush and hope to God someone found me or I could be proactive and seek help on my own. Besides, there'd been seven of us when we crashed. I needed to know if seven of us survived.

My ballet flats scuffed fallen palm fronds. Thirst attacked me now I was moving in the heat, and I folded to my knees to lap a large puddle where rainwater had gathered on a glossy leaf.

You need to store some of it…before it's too late.

I rolled my eyes at my stupidity.

This wasn't that type of crash. We were in a high-traffic tourist destination. The chances of no one being on this island were slim. The chances of having to wait a few days for help even slimmer.

I bet the moment I cut through the forest I'll find a resort with staff, a doctor on call, and a room I can check into.

Even as I forced the rationale to take hold, I couldn't stop the whisper of common sense.

Water food shelter safety.

Water food shelter safety.

My mind took over, switching from hopeful naïvety to haphazard survival. I didn't know a thing about how to source fresh water once the rain evaporated. I didn't know how to check which plants were edible and which were poisonous. I didn't know how to hunt, track, build, fish...

Oh, God.

My heart rate exploded.

Millennia of evolution had been lost by living in cities, eating prepared meals, letting the cogs of society keep us insulated from truly living. I was ruined for whatever potential scenario I had to face. Money was the only weapon you needed in the pampered lap of the modern world.

Had I been stripped from that forever? How many days would I have to remain here before I was found and returned to the only life I knew?

Don't think that way.

But it was hard not to.

Questions poured into my mind of what-if, and when, and how, and why, and, and, *and...*

Stop it!

Halting in my tracks, I took a deep breath. I focused on the stretching of my lungs, the rain-sweetened sky, and the sharp agony of my ribs. The pleasant petrichor perfumed the air with post-shower fragrance.

Words.

They were my lifeboat in a sea of sensation. Words were my weapons, and it soothed me being able to assign such a pretty phrase like 'petrichor' to the dewy scent lingering around me.

I had my life, my dictionary of favourite letters. I had enough to be strong.

First things first.

I needed to understand this new world. I needed to explore and figure out just how bad things were before jumping to idiotic conclusions.

There was no saying we didn't land on an island where people lived. Just because there'd been no lights or signs of life last night didn't mean they didn't exist.

This isn't one of those islands where marooned travellers die, stranded and alone.

That wasn't possible. Not in this day and age. Not with technology and satellites and beacons.

My phone!

My footsteps switched into a quick jog before I groaned and slowed from my ribs. If I could find my jacket, I could call for help. My phone was waterproof. It would've survived the storm last night with no ill effects.

See? You're being ridiculous for nothing.

Food and shelter—ha! I would be off this island (if it even were an island) by lunchtime.

Striding forward with renewed purpose, I kept to the trails between tightly growing plants. I didn't know the names. I was clueless what undergrowth I brushed against and what shade covered me.

Time lost all meaning as I kept moving. The air temperature increased until my tank top hung wetly with sweat as much as rainwater. Splices of sunshine kissed the forest floor, stealing the raindrops, reminding me that soon…there would be no water.

Drink. Before there's nothing left.

I hated the instinctual reversion of my thoughts. Where had the sudden drive to store rainwater come from? Was I being overly pessimistic or cautiously smart?

In the end, it didn't matter because I was thirsty again and found a few more leaves with fresh puddles. Cupping the greenery, I managed to scoop them from the forest floor and create a funnel so I didn't lose the precious water, tipping mouthfuls down my throat.

Store it.

The thought came again, only more persistent. I would've willingly given in to my dominating mind but how? Store it in what? I hadn't come equipped with bottles, decanters, and crystal glasses. I didn't know how to weave a waterproof container from leaves.

I'm not a naturalist or botanist or survivalist.

I'm a lyricist and occasional singer.

Swiping away a pitiful tear, I moved onward. The longer I walked, the less dense the forest became. It took longer than I remembered to return to the crash and worry crept that I'd bypassed or taken a wrong turn.

The thinning undergrowth kept me going, however, encouraging me to follow the beckoning sunshine and soft crash of waves.

Waves.

A beach!

My walk became a painful jog. I burst from the trees and onto the soft sugar sand of a perfect bay.

Shielding my eyes from the sun's glare, I made my way to the water's edge and looked back. The lap of warm tide licked my ankles, filling my ballet shoes as my gaze landed on the storm-ravaged island.

All around me, the beach was littered with flotsam and jetsam of the tropics. A plastic bottle, smoothed and beaten flat by the waves, nestled in a vortex of seaweed.

The trees I'd just appeared from soared high but tentative, as if afraid the sky would slap them for being so prideful and riddle them with rain-bullets again.

Tropical colours sparkled, white sand glittered, and beauty existed in every inch of this wild, savage place.

Looking to my left, the beach disappeared around a bend, leading off to unknown territory. Looking to my right, the bay continued with sandy welcome until the same thing happened and the shoreline vanished. There was no inlet, no sandbank, no hint this island connected to a larger one or civilisation.

No sun-loungers or happy holidaymakers.

My heart did its best to reassure me. There was still more territory to explore, another coast to traipse, hope still lingering in the trees.

But for now, I had nothing left.

My worst fears suffocated me.

I'm alone.

On an island.

Turning to face the sea, my hope shattered and tears sprang to my eyes.

The island held no salvation but perhaps the ocean would.

A boat?

A plane?

My gaze bounced from whitecap to reef, searching.

But nothing.

Just pristine, perfect, periwinkle blue water.

Chapter Twelve

•••

GALLOWAY

••••••

DIZZINESS STOLE MY eyesight as I tried yet again to stand.
Come on. Get to your bloody feet!
I'd burned all the energy I had, ignored every minor cut and
scrape, and done my best to stand on a severely broken ankle and
leg.
I'd tried over and over again. I'd clung to the tree behind me.
I'd crawled sideways, back-ways, front-ways (all which damn-near
killed me) all in the name of getting off my ass.
But I couldn't do it.
I was still ground-locked, reclining against the palm tree, doing
my best not to focus on the resonating throb now that shock and
adrenaline had left my system.
One more try.
Gathering everything I had left, I planted my hands into the
mulch and pushed upward. My good leg bent, ready to hurl me
upright, but the minute my broken one shifted with pressure, I
collapsed with a shard of blistering agony.
"Goddammit!"
Balling my hands, I sucked in lungfuls of air. Frustration and
fear sat in equal measures on my thoughts. The storm had passed,
the sun had risen, and *still*, no one had come to investigate.
The fact that no one had appeared to rubberneck or call
authorities gave me all the answers I needed.
This wasn't an island with resorts and humans. This was an
island that could very quickly become my grave if I didn't get to my
feet.
All my life, I'd been so confident, acting immortal in my
younger years. I'd been arrogant with no thought to the

consequences. After what happened with my mum, I'd learned a hard lesson: I was nothing.

And this…

This simple task of climbing to my feet taught me another lesson. I was useless. Completely utterly *useless*.

I punched the ground, adding bruised knuckles to my list of injuries.

A crash in the bushes wrenched my head up.

"Hello?"

The thought of company (even if they turned out to be cannibals) was a damn sight better than being on my own.

"Hello? Can you hear me?"

The noise came again, followed by the most beautiful sound in the world.

Footsteps.

"I'm over here." I hauled myself into a less slouchy position. My legs splayed in front of me, dirt covered every inch from trying to move all night.

My heart raced as eyes met mine, appearing from the greenery. I held my breath as a hesitant boy stepped from the undergrowth.

A kid.

Conner Evermore.

Thank God more than one of us survived.

"Hey." I smiled, swiping at dirt sticking to my chin. "Remember me? I won't hurt you."

The kid shuffled closer, keeping his hands behind his back, protecting something.

Holding out my palm, I beckoned him forward. "It's okay. Come here."

One footstep. Two. Slowly, he traversed the sodden ground and stopped within a few metres. His gaze fell on my jeans, flinching when he understood what the swelling and odd position of my ankle meant.

He shifted from one foot to the other, clearly uncomfortable. He dropped his eyes. "You okay?"

I ignored the question. I wouldn't be such a selfish bastard to accept the concern of a kid. "Don't worry about that." Pointing at what he hid behind him, I said, "I'm more interested if *you're* okay."

Conner shrugged. "I'll live."

Spunky kid.

I hated that he'd lived through the crash and whatever would come next, but I liked that he was here. As much as I pushed people away, I didn't want to be alone. Not now. Not like this.

A twig snapped behind Conner. He spun in place. "I told you to wait—"

I smiled as another survivor appeared. Thank God, they'd both lived. They were children and didn't deserve to die so young.

Not moving, so I didn't spook the little girl, I spoke to Conner. "You found your sister. That's great."

Conner nodded as the copper-haired girl darted toward him, coming to stand within touching distance. She had a wicked bruise on her cheekbone and blood covered her top. She trembled as tears glittered in her orb-like eyes.

My own pain was forgotten as something inside me softened. I'd never been around kids before. I didn't know how to relate to them. But seeing anything in distress (either human or animal) turned me into some comic book superhero, fighting to the death to avenge and help.

That's what happened with Mum and look how that turned out.

I snorted, cutting off my thoughts before they led me back into darkness. I was the only adult and these two kids needed guidance. They deserved a grown-up to tell them comforting lies that everything would be okay.

I would be that liar.

I would protect them...somehow.

"Not the best landing, huh?" I smiled. "You okay...Pippa, right?"

The little girl nodded. I guessed she was about seven or eight-years-old. She was taller than other kids but skinny, and the mud smearing both her and her brother mixed with blood that I didn't know how to deal with.

"Where are we?" Conner stood protectively by his sister. He didn't let go of his right wrist, cupping it protectively. He also had a large bruise, but unlike Pippa's, his marred his neck in a purple splodge.

"Somewhere in the Fijian Islands."

Conner pursed his lips, unhappy with my unhelpful answer.

I couldn't blame him. If I were him, I'd be pissed, too.

I tried to do better. "Hopefully, we're on an island with a hotel or local village. They'll know what to do."

Instead of my lie being believable, the kids looked at each other with uncertainty.

What the hell happened to these two?

Where was the helicopter?

Where are their parents?

I swallowed the question. Something like that could come with disastrous answers.

However, Conner gave me no choice but to learn. "You're the only one we've found alive."

Christ.

Pippa swallowed a sob, drifting closer to me as if I could stop the truth. "They didn't move."

Conner went with his sister. "It's okay, Pip. It will be okay."

"How? She wouldn't wake up!" Pippa fell forward onto my lap. Her bony arms landed on my broken shin.

Holy bloody hell, that hurts.

It took every ounce of control not to toss her away. Instead, I gritted my teeth so hard they almost cracked and hugged the little girl. She needed comfort more than I did. No one ought to see their dead loved ones—especially so young.

The moment I touched her, my fingers came away with rusty crimson.

Shit, shit, shit.

Tugging at her shredded t-shirt, I peered at her back. Blood rivered over her shoulder, a large gash oozing and full of island filth.

My heart sank.

There was no way I could tend to her. No way I would be of any use to these kids…these…orphaned kids.

"You're hurt."

She nodded, her head burrowing into my lap.

Conner grabbed his little sister, tugging her from my arms. His demeanour was feral—treating me as the enemy while so much responsibility had just been dumped on his young shoulders. "She'll be okay. She's brave. Aren't you, Pip?"

Pippa sniffed, licking at tears rolling close to her lips. She didn't look away from me as she whispered, "Conner said I can have any to—toy I want of his as lo—long as I don't cry and do what he tells me."

Conner's boyish jaw clenched. "Anything you want, you get, sis."

Pippa smiled; it was pain-filled and tears still leaked, but it was an attempt to behave for her older brother.

I had to look away from the pure love between the siblings. Conner was barely in his teens, yet the steadfast bravery and wisdom aged him overnight.

We didn't speak for a few minutes, all coming to terms with what this meant.

Conner said I'm the only one he's come across alive. Does that mean…Estelle—

I cut myself off.

The thought of Conner's parents dying gutted me. The image of the woman I'd immediately connected with destroyed me.

Taking a deep breath, I did my best to keep my questions cryptic so as not to unsettle Pippa. "Conner...when you say I'm the only one..."

Conner understood straight away. Glancing into the foliage from where they'd come, he shuddered. "They're dead." Balling his hands, he forced himself to continue. "Mum and Dad are over there. And the pilot is by the helicopter."

"Mummy and Daddy?" Pippa perked up. "They might just be sleeping, Co." She tugged on his hand. "I want to go back. I want Mummy to stop the pain."

Conner squeezed his eyes before jerking his sister close and kissing her temple. She cried out as his arm stuck to her bleeding shoulder but didn't try to squirm away.

"Pip, Mummy can't help you. Remember what I said?"

Shit, he'd had the conversation alone?

This kid was something else.

Pippa frowned. "You said they were sleeping."

"What else did I tell you?"

She looked at the ground. "That it was a forever kind of sleep, and they wouldn't wake up."

Conner scowled, fighting his own grief in order to hide the trauma from his sister. "And do you remember why I said they wouldn't wake up? Remember what happened to Chi-Chi when she went to heaven?"

"The kitty went to sleep and remained very still. She didn't purr or swat at me with her paw. She just kept sleeping."

"Exactly." His jaw ticked with pain. "And that's what Mum and Dad are doing. They're forever sleeping and no matter how much you want them to, they won't wake up. Okay?"

Pippa froze, the realisation finally settling deep into her too-young-for-loss soul. "But—"

Conner swallowed his grief, doing his best to be brave. "But nothing, Pip. They're dead. Got it? They're not coming—"

Pippa wrenched from his hold. "I don't believe you!"

"You don't *have* to believe me! It's true."

The two siblings glared at each other.

"I want to go back!"

"We can't go back! They're dead, Pip."

"I don't *want* them to be dead." Pippa burst into fresh tears. "They *can't* be dead."

I cursed that I couldn't get to my feet and hug them. They were too young to deal with death, too innocent to deal with pain, and too damn precious to be stranded in a crash and left alone.

Screw this.

Gritting my teeth, I bent my good leg and pushed upward. The world tilted, pain greyed my vision, and the breaks in my bones toppled me back down again.

Goddammit!

Pippa pummelled Conner's chest as he tried to grab her. "I want to go home. I don't like this place."

"You think I don't want that, too?" He caught her flailing fists. "I want them to wake up just as much as you do!"

Gasping with agony, I growled, "Guys, quit it. You can't—"

"Oh, my God. You're alive."

The squabble ceased as we all wrenched our heads to the newcomer's voice.

My heart tripped over as the blonde, hazel-eyed apparition turned into a dirty but sexy-as-hell woman. Leggy and lovely, she represented everything I thought I'd lost and everything I'd been too afraid to want.

She was safety to me. Even while granting jeopardy in the worst way.

"Estelle?" My voice echoed shock and relief. "You survived."

She flicked me a smile but beelined toward the kids. Pippa stood frozen with tears cascading down her cheeks.

Estelle didn't say a word, merely stopped in front of them, dropped to her knees, and grabbed them in a hug.

Pippa dissolved, burying her face into the stranger's damp hair, sobbing with no restraint. It bloody hurt to see a child come so undone, but it was for the best. She needed to grieve; only then could she face what her new future held.

Conner stood rigidly, his arms dead straight and hands balled tight, unyielding in Estelle's arms. But slowly his pale bravery cracked and his tears flowed.

Bowing over Estelle, he let himself be hugged, allowing the weight of death to smother thanks to a random act of kindness.

I hated that I couldn't join in; that I couldn't offer what Estelle did so easily. All I could do was sit there, fighting against uselessness and grieve with them. If Conner was right and his parents and the pilot were dead, that meant our seven had become four and who knew what the future held.

I had no way of judging time, but slowly, Pippa's tears stopped and Conner moved away.

Kissing Pippa's cheek, Estelle stood upright, wincing a little as she held her chest.

She's hurt, too.

We were all damaged in some way.

Making eye contact with me, Estelle's gaze cut me to the core. She made me feel lacking; she made me feel brave. She made me feel like she needed me even while I needed her in return.

I didn't even know her, but she dragged so many emotions from me. Emotions I wanted nothing to do with because she made me weak and I had to be strong in this place. Strong for her and for them.

But how could I stop her power when all I wanted was for her to hug me the way she'd done with the kids?

Clearing my throat, I looked away.

Estelle came to stand over me. "Is it broken?" She pointed at my ankle.

I squinted; the sun silhouetted her through the trees. "I'm not a doctor, but I'm pretty sure a normal leg and foot isn't supposed to bend like that."

She scowled. "You don't have to be pissy about it. It was a simple question."

What?

I hadn't meant my answer to come across surly and rude. She unnerved me. It made me try too hard and sprout crap I didn't mean.

Dragging long hair over her shoulder, she muttered, "Can you stand at least?"

Keeping my eyes down, I did my best to answer without any hint of attitude. "No." I wouldn't give her any other reason to think I was an asshole.

"The pain is that bad? Or you just didn't try?"

Way to make me feel like even more of a loser than I am.

My teeth clenched. "Of course, I fucking tried."

She sucked in a gasp at my curse.

The children drifted closer, drying their eyes and focusing on me rather than their dead parents.

"On a scale of one to ten, how bad?" Estelle squatted beside me, resting her tiny hands on my quad.

I flinched. The heat of her fingers lacerated me through my jeans. Even with a crashed landing, immense pain, and night in a storm, my cock still twitched with longing.

I didn't know this woman, yet everything about her shackled a collar around my neck and made me want to beg for scraps of attention. Why did she have to be on my flight? Why did she have to sign up for a stupid helicopter taxi? Why couldn't she have stayed away?

"Are you going to answer me?" Her head tilted. Sunshine dappled her bare arms, highlighting cuts, scrapes, and mud but somehow making her even more beautiful. Twigs and leaves tangled her hair as if she'd slept in a tree, and her lips were wet and pink.

What the hell did she ask me?

I forced myself not to look at the glittering gemstones on her top, beckoning me to peer down her cleavage to the hint of bra beneath.

"Earth to Galloway."

My heart raced hearing my name on her lips.

She leaned closer, giving me a glimpse down her shirt and the full swell of her breasts. Desire shot between my legs before horror replaced it at the slice across her perfect skin. Blood splattered, rust-coloured, and no longer flowing but the large laceration showed just how hurt she was.

Shit.

"Who cares about me? What about you. How badly are *you* hurt?"

Her eyebrow rose as she followed my gaze. Slapping a hand over the gaping top, she sniffed. "That's none of your business. I asked about you."

I reached for her, wanting to rip the neckline and force her to admit that she wasn't okay. That it ought to be *me* taking care of *her* not the other way around. "Let me see—"

She swatted my hand. "No chance." Temper glowered on her face. "Answer the damn question and forget about me. On a scale of one—"

"One to ten?" Fine, if she didn't want me to care for her, she could just leave me the hell alone. "I'd say a fucking eleven."

Her forehead furrowed. "Don't swear."

Great, now I was aroused and annoyed and pissed off that I couldn't do a damn thing to help the people around me. They deserved attention far more than I did. I didn't do well being told off—no matter that she was right.

Breathing shallowly, her fingers suddenly splayed along the length of my leg, travelling from swollen shin, deformed ankle, to my mangled foot below.

Every muscle in my body clenched. I swallowed my agonising groan.

"I don't know what I'm doing, but I think you're right." She bit her lip. "I don't want to be a pessimist but I think a few metacarpals in your foot are broken, your ankle most definitely is, and perhaps your tibia, too."

She leaned closer, and I had no hope in hell of not staring at her parted mouth and thick eyelashes. The island faded. My leg faded. Everything faded but the chemistry dragging me deeper into her spell.

"I'm so sorry, Galloway."

Who are *you?*

She had no idea the effect she had on me (or if she did, she wanted nothing to do with it).

"It's swollen and hot and the deformity is worrying." Sitting on her haunches, she gave me a weary smile. "I guess all we can do is hope your body knows how to heal and do as much as we can to prevent a clean knit...until we're found, of course."

So basically...I'm screwed.

I didn't want to think about my disability. I didn't want to come to terms with what the injury would mean. All I wanted was a simple reminder of happier things and for whatever reason...she had the power to make me forget.

I couldn't stop staring at her. The make-up she'd been wearing last night had washed off in the storm and a rivulet of mascara smudged below her eye.

Without thinking, I ran my thumb along the soft skin of her cheekbone.

She turned frigid. "What on earth do you think you're doing?"

Now, what was her problem? I couldn't be nice? I couldn't tend to her while she tended to me?

I shrugged, doing my best to downplay what'd happened. "You had dirt on your face."

Conner snickered. "We're all covered in dirt. I don't think a speck on her face is gonna be a problem."

I glared at him. I liked the kid, but he'd better not form a habit of making me look like an idiot. I did that fine all on my own.

Estelle ran her hand where my thumb had touched her. Her eyes softened just a little. "Well...thank you. But Conner's right. I'm filthy. We all are."

I wanted to bring up the fact she was hurt again but didn't know how to do it without her slapping me or worse...leaving me with no way of chasing after her.

Pippa tugged Estelle's hair. "My Mummy never lets me get this messy. Can I have a shower so I don't get into trouble?"

All of us collectively tensed. Poor girl. The simple necessities of showering and eating with utensils had been stripped for the foreseeable future.

You don't know that for sure.

Estelle plastered a fake smile on her face. "I've got something even better than a shower."

Pippa brightened. "Oh?"

"How about a bath in the ocean? It's so blue and pretty and maybe a dolphin will come and swim with you."

Conner sucked in a ragged breath—not because Estelle soothed his baby sister but because of the word 'ocean.'

I latched onto it, too.

"You've been on the beach?" My voice was gruff and snappy.

Estelle narrowed her eyes. "I have."

My patience stretched too thin. "And..."

"And what?"

"And what did you see? Are we close to another island? Do you recognise where we are?"

She smoothed Pippa's hair with gentle fingers while her voice hardened. "How would I recognise it? I've never been to Fiji before."

Conner said, "Did you find help?"

Estelle's anger faded—it seemed only I deserved her wrath. "No, I'm afraid not."

I butted in again. "Where did you end up? After the crash, I mean?"

Annoyance glowed in her gaze. "I was in the helicopter. I was the only one."

I did my best to understand how I'd been thrown clear, along with the Evermores. Estelle had been in the middle of the cabin, protected on both sides. It would make sense that she would be the last to be flung free.

Conner took Pippa's hand, looking at Estelle. "We walked back to the helicopter last night. Did you see the pilot?"

Pippa shivered. "He's sleeping like Mummy and Daddy."

Estelle swallowed hard. "You mean he's—"

"Didn't make it. Yes," I snapped, worried about Pippa and how she'd react bringing it up again. Couldn't she see things like that ought to be discussed when juvenile ears weren't around to hear?

Estelle's nostrils flared. "Will you stop? Just stop. Okay?"

"Stop what?" I drowned in her angry eyes. They turned more green than hazel when she was mad.

"You *know* what."

I did know what, but I wasn't sure how to stop it. She brought out the worst in me.

I hoisted myself higher. "Look, help me up, then if you want to leave, you can. I won't bother you again." Holding out my hand, I did my best not to piss her off. "Please. Just help me stand and I'll be a lot less annoying. I promise."

She didn't warm to my peace offering. "For now, I think you should stay there. I've explored one side of the island. There's nothing but beach and sea for miles." Looking over her shoulder, she looked into the thicket in the opposite direction. "However, I haven't explored that way yet. Perhaps, there are people. I'll try and find help for your leg."

My heart leapt but the niggle of doubt was too big to ignore. "And if there's no one else on this island?"

"Then I guess we'd better make more of an effort to get along and remember how to survive better than what credit cards and home delivery has taught us." Striding away, she left without another word.

Damn woman.

Damn gorgeous, opinionated, strong-as-hell woman.

Conner and Pippa gawked after her. Pointing at his sister, Conner ordered. "Stay with Galloway. I'm going with her."

"But—" Pippa tried to grab her brother.

"No, Pip." Conner pushed her. I managed to snag her wrist as she stumbled closer to me.

I wanted him to go with Estelle. Someone needed to be with her and, hopefully, keep her safe.

"Keep me company. I'd love that." Winking at Conner, I added, "I've got her. Go ahead. Fingers crossed you find civilisation and this will all be over."

Conner jogged after Estelle, still protecting his wrist.

Pippa sniffed, sliding unwillingly into a cross-legged pose beside me. Her brown eyes met mine, almost identical to the copper-brown on her head. She'd been well-dressed and excited when we'd boarded the helicopter last night. Now, she looked wild and unkempt.

We both did.

Holding out my arm, I invited, "You must be tired. How about you get some rest and I'll keep an eye out?"

"But I wanna know when Conner comes back." Her voice argued, but her body accepted my offer, slotting beneath my arm. Her little head rested on my chest.

I tried not to think about the blood from her shoulder. She

needed to be tended to—disinfected and bandaged. But all of that would have to come later.

"I'll wake you the second he comes back. How about that?"

She bit her lip, pondering. Finally, she nodded. "Okay."

As the little girl fell asleep on my chest in the middle of unchartered waters, I fixated on the spot where Estelle and Conner had disappeared.

I wanted to know, too.

I wanted to know what they found.

I was just terrified of the answer.

Chapter Thirteen

....

ESTELLE

......

Breathe. That's all you have to do. Breathe. When life shines brightly. Breathe. When the world turns its back. Breathe. When nothing works out. Breathe. When luck favours kindly. Inhale with hope and exhale with distrust. Breathe.
~~*That's all you've got.*~~
After all...that's all you can ever do.
Lyrics: 'Breathe' Taken from the notepad of E.E.

...

"THAT'S IT, THEN."

My voice was calm and accepting while inside, I was a crying disaster. However, I couldn't break down. I couldn't scream with fear or beg fate for a second chance. Not with a child beside me. A child looking up to me to be strong and brave.

"I guess." Conner gasped in pain as we leapt over a fallen palm tree and padded down the beach to the shore. We'd explored the other side of the island. We'd found that there was nothing on this side, just like there was nothing on that.

We were stranded.

Alone.

Utterly marooned and unwanted.

Tears welled but I forced them down. The pain from my ribs kept me centred and the knowledge that things had to be taken care of (if we had any hope of existing past the next couple of days) weighed heavier and heavier on my mind.

Where do we begin?

How do we begin?

Conner groaned as his wrist bounced again. He'd nursed it every step we'd taken. It killed me to see him in pain and not help.

Yanking him to a stop, I asked, "You're hurt?"

Bravado existed in his gaze but he couldn't hide it. He looked away, gnawing on his bottom lip. "I'm all right."

"You can tell me."

He sighed, glancing at the sand beneath our feet. He still wore his sneakers—scuffed and highlighter green—while I wore my silver ballet flats. Blisters had formed on my instep and big toe, but I couldn't take them off—not yet. Not until I found my handbag and the pair of flip-flops I'd hurriedly packed before boarding the helicopter.

What I wouldn't give for my suitcase.

I had sunblock in there. A floppy hat. A first-aid kit.

Everything I didn't think I'd need for an overnight stay had suddenly turned into every precious requirement.

"Ouch." Conner flinched as I ran my fingers along his wrist.

The skin puffed with swelling, red with discomfort.

My stomach twisted. Not only was Galloway, myself, and Pippa hurt, but it looked like Conner was as well.

Damn, were we all in pieces?

I delivered the news as gently as I could. "You're going to be okay, but..."

"It's broken, isn't it?"

I glanced up, meeting his angry, fearful eyes. "I think so."

He huffed. "Figured."

"It doesn't mean it can't be set."

"How? Do you see a doctor and an X-ray machine around here?"

I smiled at his morbid humour. "Not exactly, but humans healed from breaks long before a doctor had the ability to make plaster casts."

Conner stiffened. "Whatever."

Sliding my fingers from his wrist, I took his hand. "May I?"

His eyes widened but he nodded.

Guiding him toward the border of where the forest met the beach, I sat down in the soft sand, taking him with me. Switching to face each other, I gently felt his wrist again—just as I'd done with Galloway's leg.

Unlike Galloway, my lungs didn't asphyxiate with overpowering desire. I didn't understand my snappy shyness or nonsensical attraction toward him. When he'd looked down my top and seen the cut from the seat belt, I'd wanted to slap him for thinking he had the right to protect me but also for the way his eyes burned with lust.

The opinionated Englishman rose full force in my thoughts.

Conner and I had been gone for over an hour, but the annoyance Galloway caused still simmered.

What was his deal? I was only trying to help, but he kept growling at me as if he couldn't stand to have me near.

He'd wanted me (unless I misread the way he watched me) but that had no place here.

We didn't have time for egos or desire. Not now. If this truly was an island and we were the only people on it, we had to stick together and find some way to survive side by side.

Conner didn't move as I felt along the bony angles of his wrist.

I had no idea what I was feeling for. Sharp edges? Misaligned ligaments? Even if I did, I wouldn't know if it was normal or wrong. Plus, if I *did* somehow know what was wrong, what on earth could I do about it?

I couldn't even offer generic painkillers, let alone assure him he'd heal intact with no ill effects. However, I knew from experience that fake confidence was better than panicked horror, especially where children were concerned.

Smiling brightly, I let him go. "I might be wrong. It could just be a nasty sprain. But let's be on the safe side and make you a splint. How does that sound?"

"A splint?"

Grabbing a straight-ish stick, I nodded. The bark had weathered into the silvery softness of driftwood. It wouldn't stab him and would hopefully keep his bone in line to heal. I didn't know how long it would take to knit together, but this was all I could offer.

What can I use as a bandage?

Twisting in the sand (killing my ribs in the process), I looked for a possibility. "Yes, you know? Like a cast but without the plaster."

Dammit, there was nothing to wrap his arm with. The only thing I could think of was my top. I wasn't precious with my clothes and didn't hesitate.

Dropping the stick, I grabbed my hem and ripped the soft cotton with my teeth. With a quick yank, a section came away. I repeated it so I had a few strips to use.

"You just ruined your top." Conner rolled his eyes. "I don't see a mall to buy another one."

Laughing as if he'd told the funniest joke, I grabbed his wrist again and placed the stick on his forearm. As a quick addition, I picked up a newly fallen leaf and wrapped it around his skin to protect him as much as possible from the stick. "Oh, well. I'm not exactly going for best dressed or a fancy party, am I?"

Conner grinned. "I guess not. However, I'd still vote for you as prettiest girl, even though you are completely filthy."

My hands froze. I could barely deal with Galloway and his snide comments and he was closer to my age for sexual innuendo arguments. Conner was too young. How did I deal with pubescent testosterone when it was just him and me and no referee?

I forced myself to meet his eyes. "How old are you, Conner?"

"Thirteen. Why?"

"And Pippa? How old is she?"

He frowned. "She's seven. Turns eight in a few months."

"I bet she seems really young to you."

He smirked. "Hell, yeah. A baby, really."

Please don't let this backfire.

I hated confrontation (a nasty symptom of being an introvert) but if we had any chance of surviving together, then boundaries had to be put in place immediately.

I straightened. "Well, the way you think of Pippa, with how young she is…that's how I think of you."

Conner sucked in a sharp breath.

I didn't say a word, merely waited for the backlash. Only…it didn't come. "Do you understand what I'm saying? I want to be your friend, Conner. But I'm too old for you…"

His face didn't hint his thoughts. His skin had already caught the sunshine. His brow and square nose had turned pink and his brown eyes glowed warmly. He was a great looking boy, and I had no doubt would break many female hearts…when he came of age. I just hoped I hadn't emasculated him by treating him like a child.

He burst out laughing. "Ah, I get it."

"You do?"

"You have the hots for Gal."

"Gal?"

"Galloway."

Embarrassment flushed my cheeks. "No. That's not it at *all.*"

He leaned closer, encroaching on my personal bubble, making me slightly uncomfortable. How could a boy unnerve me so much?

Because he's nailed it.

I acted as if Galloway pissed me off because I didn't want to face reality. I was attracted to him. When I'd touched him to check his broken ankle, all I thought about was skimming my hands higher and seeing what *wasn't* broken.

I'd never wanted to do that to anyone, let alone a complete stranger.

It was better for me to keep my distance, and if Conner kept his distance from me, believing I liked Galloway…well, where was the harm in that?

Besides, we were on a freaking island!

Alone.

We had more pressing things to worry about than romantic wishes and misunderstood arguments.

Clearing my throat, I picked up the stick again. "Hold that."

Still chuckling, Conner did as I asked as I wrapped the leaf tighter and positioned the stick along his wrist from his palm to middle forearm. Once in place, I used my makeshift bandage, wrapping the fabric strips around him and binding tight.

It wasn't pretty, but at least it would give him support and allow the bones – if they were broken—to knit correctly.

Galloway.

I'll have to do the same for him.

He could growl and grumble all he wanted, but his leg wouldn't heal without some sort of attention.

Conner sighed as soon as the knot was finished. "Thanks. That already feels better."

I stood up. "No worries." My eyes drifted from bright beach to gloomy jungle. We'd achieved more than just setting a damaged wrist. We'd formed the foundations of a friendship that I hoped would benefit both of us—no matter what happened.

My stomach rumbled and thirst nagged my dry throat. We'd wasted enough time exploring and hoping that help was just around the corner.

We had to face facts.

We had to be smarter and focus on items that would keep us alive rather than kill us faster. "Want to go back and get the others? I think it's time for some food, don't you?"

As if on cue, Conner's tummy mimicked mine, growling with emptiness. "Food would be good…but what?" He scanned the island that'd become our prison, protector, and home. "Just like I don't see a mall, I don't see a supermarket or fast food joint."

"Think you're so smart, huh?" I laughed, doing my best to keep my tone jovial. Pretending everything was fine helped keep my unravelling despair from taking over.

Earlier, when I'd come back from the other side of the island and found Galloway propped up and the two children fighting, for a single horrible moment I'd wished they hadn't survived. One awful, spiteful, selfish second, I wished such innocence hadn't survived so they wouldn't know the hardships of what was to come.

There was no luxury of purging myself with tears of self-pity. No way of screaming for help like a crazy person. I had to be the one others leaned on. I had to fight, not just for me, but for these precious children who deserved so much more than what they'd been given.

Brushing sand from my jeans, I strode back into the forest. "I know where some food might be. Let's go check the helicopter. You said you knew where it was?"

"I do. But the dead pilot is that way."

I fought my shudder. "I guess that can't be helped."

"I didn't tell Pippa this, but I hate seeing dead people as much as she does." His breathing stuttered. "I really miss them. It—it doesn't feel real."

What rational answer could I give to such an awful sentence? I drew a blank so didn't reply. "We won't go close to the pilot. We'll grab our bags and any other supplies we might need and leave."

Conner scrunched up his face, swiping at a rogue tear. The heartbreak of his parents' death never left his eyes. "Okay."

I waved him ahead. "Lead the way, Mr. Explorer. Let's go get lunch so we can tend to the other invalids."

....

Tears, fears, disbelief, every gauntlet of emotion lodged all at once in my throat as the helicopter (or what was left of it) appeared before us.

"This way." Conner led me forward, ducking under fallen trees and clambering awkwardly over others. Scars left on tree trunks and snapped limbs all added to the chequered disaster of our crash.

I couldn't speak as I moved around the carnage. Without torrential rain and darkness, the aftermath of the helicopter astounded me. I was shocked we'd survived, let alone remained so intact.

The poor machine resembled a morbid form of entrails.

The detached rotor blades had landed not far away, spearing into the ground like javelins. The sides of the chopper were wrenched open and dust turned the machine into a relic. It hadn't been too shiny and new to begin with, but now, it looked ancient. Tired and derelict and in no way ever majestic enough to take to the skies and soar.

I actually felt sympathy for the aircraft. We'd all suffered our own trauma, but this…it was destroyed.

Conner scrambled into the fuselage and disappeared.

"Hey, wait!"

I jogged and tripped, gasping thanks to broken ribs, wishing the blood on my chest would disappear so I didn't have to explain my injuries to Galloway.

Clunking and the occasional bang came from the cockpit as Conner did who knew what. Skirting the torn fuselage, I stood on part of the skid and hauled myself up to see.

Conner bent over, bracing himself against flattened boxes and dangling seat belts. He kept his strapped wrist against his chest, rummaging with his healthy one. His coppery hair flopped over his forehead as he searched faster, throwing junk and paraphernalia out of the way. "I can't find my father's backpack."

I was responsible for that. I'd been the one holding the luggage. I was the one who'd let them go. "Sorry, I lost them."

"I wasn't blaming you."

"I know. But if I'd been able to hold onto them—"

"They can't be far." He made his way toward me carefully, stepping on an old magazine and ducking beneath some wiring that'd unspooled. "If we find his backpack, we'll find food." He swallowed as memories of his dad took him.

I didn't speak as the air turned stagnant with grief.

I was as useless and soothing as a discarded tissue. How could I be brave when his misery reduced me to nothing more than helpless sentiment?

Sniffing, Conner forced his sadness away with the bravery of a man twice his age. "He always has a water bottle and muesli bars in there. He gets really jittery and hangry if he doesn't have food."

I flinched at the turn of phrase: *has* a water bottle. Not *had*. Doing my best to put a stopper in the pain in my heart, I was careful to stay on neutral topics. "Hangry?"

"Yeah, you know? Hungry-angry? Hangry."

"How is it that I'm in the middle of the Pacific and learning a new word?"

Conner smirked, wisely focusing on easier subjects. "'Cause you're shacked up with me."

I studied him, slightly in awe. "You're not like a normal thirteen-year-old."

"Mum always said that." His eyes dimmed. "Said I was an old soul."

"I think she was right." Prickles ran over my skin to talk of a woman I'd only just met but had sat next to and chatted. She'd been so nice—a great mother to have raised such decent children. *A good person who didn't deserve to die.*

Conner clambered toward me and used the skid to lower himself to the forest floor. "It's my fault they're dead."

He said it so quietly that I almost missed it.

Frissons of fear made me snap, "Don't *ever* say something like that. This isn't your fault. *At all.*"

He ignored me, jumping the final distance and pacing away.

I chased after him, tugging his elbow. "Conner, listen to me—"

He spun, his age-free face scrunched with tears. "I forced them to come. Dad had been so busy, and Pippa kept begging him to spend time with us, but he wouldn't. Mum asked me what I wanted for my birthday—delayed by months, by the way—and I said a trip to Fiji."

He grew angry, wrenching himself from my hold. "He said he couldn't go. That this time of year wasn't possible. I called him a pussy and told him he sucked as a father." His eyes tightened with regret. "I didn't mean it. But the next day, he cancelled his work trip and booked the hotel on Kadavu. He's a bank manager. Always stressed. I think Mum chose the resort hoping an island with no internet or phones would help him remember us. We all got excited. I was so happy. Even if I did hate what I'd said to him."

He hung his head, kicking at a fallen coconut. "I never told him I was sorry. I pretended like going away wasn't a big deal when it was the best present in the world."

My heart resembled a pickaxe, eroding me beat by beat.

I knew the feeling of wanting to retract words spoken in heated moments. I would take back many things said to my own parents and sister before they died a year ago. However, life didn't work like that. And regret and guilt only hurt the living with no power to bring back the dead.

I didn't touch him or try to hug away his pain. "He knew, Conner. He booked that trip because you were right and he loved you."

He wiped his running nose on his forearm. "It doesn't change what I said."

"No, it doesn't. But it was a reminder to him that work isn't important. That his family was. You did the right thing."

"How can you say that? That's the point. I *didn't* do the right thing." His grief rose again. "If I'd kept my mouth shut, he'd still be alive. My mum would still be alive. We'd be at home, together, and none of this would've happened."

I had no response to that. I wouldn't lie and say that wasn't true because chances were it would be. His parents would still be alive but who knew what might've happened in return. "You can't torture yourself with what-ifs. You and Pippa are alive. That's enough to be grateful—"

"Shut up. I don't want to talk about it anymore." He sliced his hand through the air. "Forget I said anything, okay?"

An awkward silence fell but I nodded. "All right."

Conner stormed back to the chopper and hauled himself inside. A few moments later, his voice sailed back. "Do you think we could use this?"

Hoisting myself into the cabin, I winced with pain from my ribs.

Conner held up a metal panel that'd come unscrewed. "Can we use it for like, I don't know, digging or something?"

I smiled. "I guess."

Passing me the piece of metal, Conner made his way into the cockpit. I stayed in the cabin but narrowed my eyes at the smashed front window thanks to a palm tree spearing through. Something red and sinister trailed down the jagged glass, leading to...

I slapped a hand over my mouth. "Oh, my God. Is that—"

Conner looked up. "Oh, yeah. The pilot's outside. I wouldn't look if I were you."

Legs bent unnaturally while foliage hid the rest of the pilot's mangled body.

A rush of nausea hit me. I'd never seen a dead body until I had to identify my family after the car wreck. I still had nightmares about their ice-cold skin and waxy faces. Some things you just couldn't unsee.

I looked away. Spidery horror crawled over my flesh. "Let's grab what we can and go. We'll come back later to collect more supplies."

The thought of returning to the crash site and dealing with a decomposing body after a few hours in the hot sunshine did not appeal. But depending on how long we were stranded, the helicopter would become a great asset.

"They'll rescue us, right?" Conner climbed toward me, a black rucksack in his hands labelled with the same registration number painted on the tail of the helicopter.

I didn't want to lie, but I also didn't want to be pessimistic. "I'm sure they will. Fiji is a popular tourist destination. There'll be countless boats and planes around here."

Conner shook his head. "I wouldn't be so sure. I researched when dad told us where we were going. A friend of mine mentioned he'd been to Bali and bragged about an awesome waterpark in Kuta. I wanted to know if Fiji had one." He smiled wryly. "It doesn't, by the way. All it has is over three hundred islands and only one hundred and ten are inhabited. I think it said there are over eighteen thousand, three hundred square kilometres that make up the archipelago of Fiji."

Frigid terror melted down my spine.

Eighteen thousand, three hundred square kilometres?

Three hundred islands and only a hundred with people on them?
Crap.

The hope I clung to popped like a helium balloon. The police
would search for us…*I mean why wouldn't they?* I was important.
Conner, Pippa, Galloway, we were *all* important in the citizenship of
earth.

But really…we weren't.

We were just four people in four billion. Just four people
thrown into four different compass directions while four people died
every second around the globe.

Why would they come for us?

Why should we expect them to?

Madeline will try. She'll look for me.

Would she?

She was expecting me home. She didn't know I'd been stupid
enough to hitch a ride without thinking. I was never spontaneous.
Why would they think to search for me in a helicopter disappearance?

My cat. The house sitter. My freshly signed record deal. What
would happen to all of that? Who would be there to issue the
paperwork when my life suddenly ended?

I laughed out loud as I remembered the final nail in our coffin.
The Emergency Locator Beacon wasn't working when we crashed.
Akin had warned us, and we all believed we were invincible to require
it. We'd willingly charted a helicopter when commercial airlines had
refused to fly because of the weather. We'd walked right into death
with so much blasé stupidity we didn't *deserve* to be found.

We'd done this.

Our past was over. Our lives before the crash…deleted.

This was our reality now, and we had no one else to blame but
each other.

Chapter Fourteen

....

GALLOWAY

......

THE ANSWER I didn't want blurted the moment Estelle and Conner arrived.

The starkness of our circumstances plastered all over their faces' as they morphed from the forest with their arms full of junk.

I met Estelle's gaze. I didn't want to believe it. My heart thudded with frustrated rage; I looked away just as quickly.

We're alone.

My shoulders rolled while increasing pain in my ankle drenched my skin with a mixture of sweat and nausea.

Pippa slept soundly on my chest. I hugged her closer, finding comfort in her warm body. I hoped the kid had good dreams...she'd need them to get through reality.

Taking a deep breath, I looked up again. Estelle moved with decision and purpose, but her hips still swung in an intrinsically feminine way.

Why did she have to infuriate and beguile me all at once?

I wanted her but she'd never reciprocate.

No one wanted a long-term commitment with a guy like me.

The moment I'd set eyes on her, I couldn't explain the sudden rush and confusing link tugging me to *know* her.

I'd never had that before.

With anyone.

And I didn't want it now when she was the only woman around and I had no way to give her what she deserved.

My temper rose again at the flush of her skin and obvious pain in her eyes from carrying such heavy items. *I* should be the one exploring and carting bloody bags, not her. I should be the one taking charge and keeping everyone safe. I should be the one tending to stuff and making this disaster easier...*not her.*

Damn her for caring.

Damn her for being a better person than I was.

While she'd been off playing explorer, I'd replayed the glance I'd earned down her top. I'd concluded that the scratch on her chest had been from the helicopter harness. And if the cut was that bad, it probably meant she had broken ribs as well.

My suspicions were validated as Estelle dropped her armful of gear, unable to hide her wince and the quick way she wrapped arms around herself.

Christ, what I'd give to be able to leap to my feet and take over.

Conner dropped his armful and came to squat beside his sister. Pippa didn't move in my embrace as he stroked her hair, his eyes bloodshot from tears and stress. "She okay?"

I somehow managed to plaster a smile on my lips, hiding my rage at not being able to help. I was a glorified bloody babysitter. All I was worth. "She's fine. Been sleeping the entire time."

My throat scratched with thirst; I hated the hollowness in my stomach. If I was hungry and all I'd done was sit here, Estelle and Conner must be starving.

I'd done my best to come up with a plan, eyeing the foliage, pretending I knew what I was looking for.

But I had to face facts. I knew crap all about that sort of thing. "That's good." Conner stood. "Sleep will make it easier."

I pointed at the supplies they'd brought. "Been shopping?"

Estelle half-smiled, thanking me wordlessly for not asking hard questions like 'what did you see?', 'where are we?', and 'just how screwed are we truly?'. Those questions would come later—when we weren't in front of two scared children.

Moving toward Conner, Estelle draped an arm over his shoulders. They almost matched in height. In another few months, he would be eye-level with her. "Conner found a convenient helicopter supermarket, didn't you?"

He grinned. A rudimentary splint shackled his wrist; he fiddled with the black ties holding it together. "Sure did."

Pippa's head shot up. I let her go as she squirmed out of my hold and ran to him. "You're back!"

Conner grunted as she wrapped stick arms around him, tears spilling down her cheeks. "I dreamed you were sleeping, too. Never go to sleep, Co. Never. *Promise* me."

Estelle's face crumpled with sadness. I wondered if she had the same thought: that it would've been kinder if they hadn't survived. Was a quick death better than a slow one? Or was the hope of being found justified to warrant starvation and uncertainty? Because we couldn't deny it longer.

We were alone.

Chances of being found were slim—not because of location or remoteness but because of our ability to stay alive until that day happened.

It might only take a few days to locate us...but a few days were too long when we were already hungry and dehydrated with no skills at sourcing food or water.

Shut up.

I swallowed hard, quelling those unhelpful thoughts.

Conner squeezed his sister. "You just went to sleep and woke up. Not everyone falls into the forever kind of sleep, Pip." He brushed aside the hair sticking to her cheeks. "I'm going to sleep at some point. Estelle and Galloway, too. You can't freak out if you wake up and we're resting, okay?"

Pippa sniffled. "But what if you don't wake up? I'll be all alone. I don't want to be all alone. I want to go home!"

Conner looked at me for help.

I splayed my hands. I didn't have experience in child psychology. I didn't know how juvenile minds dealt with death.

However, Estelle saved me once again.

Bending over, she collected two rucksacks and painfully slung them onto her shoulders while somehow managing to hold her ribs. "How about we get out of this shady place and enjoy some sunshine? Fancy going to the beach? We can have a picnic there and see if we can spot any boats."

Christ, she was awesome.

She was a natural and so genuine even *I* wanted to go to the beach.

My eyes locked onto her mouth again. Her bottom lip was plump and pink, drugging me better than any painkiller. If I could stare at her, I could forget the discomfort and our shitty situation. If I could talk to her, get to know her, let her see I wasn't the bastard I pretended to be...I might survive this place.

Conner kissed Pippa's cheek. "Sounds cool, huh? A perfect start to a holiday."

Pippa burst into tears. "I don't want a holiday. I want Mummy and Daddy!"

Conner dropped his stuff, hugging her. "I know. Me too. But we've got each other. And I'm not leaving you."

How old was this kid?

His capacity to hold back his own horror and support his sister astounded me. Estelle too by the way her eyes misted and pride shone on her face. She gawked at the two children as if wishing someone could hug her the same way and utter comforting things.

Come here, I'll do it.

I would gladly hug her, stroke her, kiss her until she forgot where we were.

But that was out of the question and I couldn't make it worse by letting her know just how attracted I was to her. We were the adults here. We had to set the example.

Leaving the two siblings to talk, Estelle came toward me. Her skin paled with pain. "Are you okay?"

"Are *you* okay?"

"I'm fine." She looked as if she wanted to say something else but stopped herself. Cocking her head at the path she and Conner had created, she said, "I think it's best if we rest on the beach. That way people can see us."

"What people?" My tone dripped with sarcasm.

"You can't do that." Her eyes narrowed. "It's up to us to keep them calm. God only knows how long the meagre rations we found in the helicopter will keep us alive. We don't need tears using up bodily fluids and stress burning through calories. Got it?"

I gave her a salute.

She was right but damn if it didn't piss me off that she had to remind me.

Again.

Why was I being such a prick?

I growled, "It really should be me carrying all of that and exploring the island and—"

"Why? Because you're a man and believe in sexism?" She rolled her eyes. "Save it for somewhere that gender actually matters."

Hugging her chest, she took a few steps away. "I'm going to drop this off at the beach. I'll come back for you." Her gaze fell on my leg. "I'll find a stick to splint your ankle like I did for Conner's wrist."

I ground my teeth. "Don't worry about me. I can find one myself."

"Yeah, right. You can barely move." She laughed coldly. "Tell you what, best of luck proving you don't need others to lean on while I drop this and the children off. You have about half an hour before I return. And when I do, be prepared to show a bit of gratitude and drop the arrogant asshole routine."

She left again, traipsing down the path, steadily fading into the green haze and thick foliage. Every inch of me wanted to chase after her, back her into a tree, and show her just how thankful I was that she was here. I'd use my fingers and tongue and—

I groaned under my breath as my cock hardened again.

What the hell was my problem? I couldn't have her like that. And I didn't have energy to waste on lust. She'd offered to help. That was it. Yes, I couldn't walk. Boo fucking hoo. If I wanted to show her how grateful I was, then I had to stop being a dick.

Her voice sailed back, snapping with authority. "Conner, Pippa. Come on!"

The kids grabbed the remaining scattered items by their feet and dashed to catch up. Conner looked back. "You coming?"

I grinned, even though I felt like swearing. "Yep. Right behind you."

"Cool." Taking his sister's hand, they vanished.

The second they'd gone, every emotion that I'd spent the last few years running from suffocated me. Hatred, loneliness, regret, and most of all...terror.

I didn't do well on my own.

But I didn't do well with others, either.

I wasn't hardwired right for society, and suddenly, society had thrown me away. I had no one.

No, that wasn't true.

I had three invaluable people who'd gone from strangers to my entire world.

They were all the company I had.

The only people I could rely on.

My skin itched and the familiar urge to run consumed me.

Come back.

Don't leave me.

I'm sorry.

· ·

"I'm impressed. You're still here."

My head shot up as Estelle returned, minus the kids and whatever supplies she'd had. In her hands rested a large stick. Moving closer, she eyed my leg, slowly dancing her eyes over my crotch, waist, and face.

I couldn't deny having her eyes on me made me hard.

Did she like what she saw? Did she see the real me? The me I'd chained deep, *deep* inside? The me that died the day I became a monster?

I flexed my bicep like a moron, hoping to impress. I made an effort to stay in shape—not because of egotistical reasons but because it was a necessity. Working with timber and building on a daily basis demanded strength and stamina.

Not that sculpted muscles will impress her when I can't bloody walk!

I took a deep breath, doing my best to stay calm. Sitting still, chained to pain and unable to move, hadn't put me in the best of moods. "I thought you'd forgotten about me." I wiped away the copious amounts of sweat from my brow. I didn't relish the thought of moving somewhere where the sun would cook me, but I did crave the ocean breeze.

"It took longer than I thought to find the stick."

"I told you not to worry about it."

"And I told you that you had half an hour to turn off the douche-bag agenda and be nice."

"I'm always nice."

"Ha!"

We glared at each other. Her chest strained and her breaths came in shallow spurts.

I pointed at her chest. "Instead of trying to find half a tree to tie to my leg, you should've strapped your ribs."

"Don't worry about me. Worry about yourself."

"I could say the same about you."

Another stalemate.

Without the kids, the freedom to speak frankly untied the gag around my vocal cords. I let loose. "Who exactly are you, anyway? You're hurt—just as much as the rest of us—yet you've taken control and put yourself in charge. Who made you—"

"I didn't *want* to put myself in charge. Do you think I enjoy this? That I wanted to find myself in a situation where two children lost their parents and now look to me to make it better? If anything, I wish you were—" She snapped her lips together, but her eyes glowed with what she wanted to hurl.

"That I wasn't such a loser and could take over. Is that what you were going to say?"

She tore her gaze away, balling her hands.

I wanted to curse her. All the questions I needed answers to demanded to be shouted, but I couldn't do that to her. Not now. She wanted comfort, just like the rest of us. But she wouldn't find comfort from me because I didn't know how to offer it. All I knew how to do was screw up an already screwed-up situation.

"Look, I'm sorry." Rubbing my eyes, I wished I had my glasses so at least something would be right in my world. I hated the fuzzy lines and shadowy colours. I could make out Estelle's features well enough, but she wasn't in high definition and it strained.

She didn't reply.

Unconsciously, I stopped rubbing and fumbled on my lap for non-existent lenses—so used to taking them off and putting them back on without thinking.

Christ, I can't do anything right.

"Can you see okay without them?"

My head wrenched up. "What?"

She motioned to my face. "Your glasses. I noticed you were wearing them in Los Angles and again in Nadi. I take it they're not just for show but are legitimately required."

She'd noticed a simple thing like that? Was that because she was an observant person or because she'd been drawn to me as much as I'd been drawn to her?

Either way, it gave me relief from the edgy agony I'd been wallowing in. I cracked a genuine smile. "They're not a pompous decoration if that's what you're asking. I literally need them to see."

Her shoulders relaxed a little, but she didn't return my smile. "Are you blind without them?" Her hand came up with three fingers. "How many fingers am I holding up?"

I chuckled. "Seriously? You're right there. I can see you."

"So how many?"

"Five."

Her face fell. I'd stared at her so much I'd already begun to recognise her quirks and facial features. Her mouth formed a worried 'o,' and her eyebrows battled between rising and frowning.

I'd freaked her out.

I laughed harder. "Relax. Three. You were holding three."

"Oh."

"I'm not blind, okay? I know I'm a cripple, but at least you don't have to worry about another disability."

"I wasn't thinking that—"

"Yes, you were. And it's fine." Corrosive frustration filled my tone. "I'd be pissed too if I were you. Having to look after a broken patient when there's so much else to worry about? Dealing with orphans when you don't know how to keep yourself alive? Hell, if I could walk, I'd be running as fast as I could."

"I would never run, no matter how bad things get." Her face darkened. "I'm not a quitter, especially when others are relying on me. And besides, that's not what I was thinking."

It was a joke. A bad one, I admitted. But she'd successfully made me feel like even worse scum than I was.

"Doesn't matter." I flinched as my leg throbbed with renewed pain. "It's what most people would be thinking. But I get it. I annoy you and you want nothing to do with me. I can fend for myself, so you don't have to worry about me, all right? Worry about the damn kids and leave me—"

"Oh, for God's sake." Her hands slammed on her hips. "Dammit, you piss me off."

I froze.

The fire in her eyes, the rosy pink of her cheeks, and the sharp angle of her jaw made me swallow hard. She was beautiful when she was caring and doing her best to reassure, but goddammit, she was exquisite when she was mad.

My heart thundered as she pointed a finger in my face. "Let's get something clear, right now."

I couldn't move. All I could do was stare and do my best not to fall. Fall and fall for this creature who I didn't know but wanted to. Fall for a stranger who looked at me with scorn and irritation. Fall for the only woman on this godforsaken island.

There was no such thing as love at first sight. But I did believe in lust. And Christ, I lusted.

"I am not the type of person you can swear, be nasty, or act like a jerk to because I won't put up with it. I'm not like others who will scream at you when you're being a dick or give you a second chance when you screw up. I'll just cut you off and act like you're invisible. I'll take care of those kids because they need me and I need them to need me to ensure I don't collapse in despair. But I don't need you. I don't need you to antagonise me or get under my skin. I want to help you but only if you'll help yourself and shut the hell up and be nice for a change."

Running her fingers through her hair, blonde strands crackled with static as she forced herself to calm down. "I'm sorry. I don't normally yell." Her face scrunched up as she hugged her chest. "My ribs hurt and you're right. I think a couple are broken. But unlike you, I'm not letting rage get the better of me. This is our life now. We're lucky to be alive. Try acting like you want to survive and we'll get along fine."

Part of me wanted to tell her to go away. Because she was right. About everything. And it was about time someone had the balls to tell me to my face that I should be grateful.

This was a fresh start. No one knew me here. I had no dirty track record or deplorable history. She didn't need to know the type of man I'd been because here I could be someone different.

It was as if a massive boulder suddenly rolled off my back, removing its weight of shame and anger.

I could be *better* here.

I could be anything I wanted.

Estelle didn't move, her eyes never leaving mine.

Wincing, I arched my ass off the forest floor and pulled something out of my back pocket. I'd forgotten it was in there until Estelle took the kids to the beach.

I was going to keep them—just in case we needed them at a later date. I'd even been tempted to take them myself (because I was a weak asshole who put himself first). But I wouldn't hide it. Because right now, this was an olive branch. My first decent thing I'd done for years.

Keeping my fist tight, I held out my hand. "Here. This is for you."

For a moment, she didn't move, but then she leaned forward and accepted my gift. The foil packet fell into her palm.

Her eyes widened. "No, I can't take this."

"Yes, you can."

"No, really. I can't." She shook her head. "Conner or Pippa should have this. Or you…"

"I'll manage and the other two will be okay."

"But—"

"No buts. If you insist on being there for us—even me after I've been a prick to you—the least you can do is take it so you don't have to care for us and be in so much pain."

Estelle clutched the single dose of Advil that I'd bought before boarding the plane in Los Angeles. I'd had a headache and bought the two pills just in case it morphed into a migraine. I had a tendency to get those if I got too stressed and leaving the timber farm where I'd finally found peace stressed me to the max.

I smirked. "Not sure how you'll take them seeing as I don't have any water. But please, I want you to have them."

"Is this your way of apologising?"

"I need to apologise?"

That earned me half a smile.

I chuckled. "Call it a do-over. Can we do that? Take the pills…please."

I fully expected her to refuse. She was the type of person to forgo any benefit to herself and give it to others—I didn't need to spend a lot of time around her to know that—but she ripped open the foil and placed the two tablets on her tongue.

Throwing her head back, she swallowed them dry.

She must be in serious pain to accept them.

Crumpling the packet into a ball, she wedged it into her jeans pocket and came closer. Holding out her hand, she smiled. "I accept your do-over. Let's begin again, shall we?"

I tensed as my fingers interlocked with hers. The same spark and tingle of awareness danced on my skin. She was sun and sin and safety all at once.

Her lips parted as heat ignited between us. She tried to hide the fact she felt whatever it was unfurling intensely; it took every effort not to tug her into my lap and hug her. Just touch her. Yes, I wanted to kiss her but not because the old me was selfish and crude. But because this new me wanted to kiss her with gratitude.

Her gaze darkened as we shook hands. "I'm Estelle Evermore. Pleasure to meet you."

My heart became a dragon, breathing hot fire as she smiled so innocently yet completely seductive.

Did she have any idea what she did to me?

Breaking our handshake, I cleared my throat. "I'm Galloway Oak. Likewise."

"Should we get the simple bullet points out of the way and then head to the beach?"

"Bullet points?"

"Yes, you know. Age, occupation, future aspirations, that kind of thing."

My lips twitched. "Shouldn't we be enquiring what survival skills we bring to the table? This isn't exactly a first date situation."

She stiffened.

Way to go, Oak.

I sighed. "Did that come across as rude? If it did, I didn't mean it to."

She waved it away. "Don't worry. You're right, though. Okay, who are you, Galloway? Give me the abbreviated version so we can get back to Pippa and Conner as friends rather than enemies."

My heart spasmed at the thought of ever being her enemy. I never wanted her to hate me. Not because we were literally the only man and woman in this place, but because something inside already howled at the thought of never being able to talk to her.

The problem with telling her about myself meant a whole lot of censorship. She didn't need to know about me. It wasn't lying; merely self-defence. Besides, I was a better person starting now. None of that crap mattered.

"All you need to know is I find you stunningly attractive and out of anyone in the world to crash land with, I'm glad it was you."

She stumbled.

I grinned. "I take it I just shocked you."

"Well...a little."

"I've decided to use a different approach."

"And what's that?"

"Brutal honesty."

She bit her lip.

"I'm sick of hiding." I shrugged. "Crashing here just reminded me how short life is and I'm not going to waste another second of it."

"Okay…but you do understand that I only want to be friends. I'm not exactly on the prowl for a date."

"Completely understood." I lowered my brow. "Doesn't mean I'm willing to stop at just friends, though."

"You're impossible."

"I've been called worse."

"I can't deal with this right now. We have to get back to the children."

Clapping my hands together, I said, "Fine. Deeper introductions can wait. Hand me the stick and I'll see what I can do about fixing my fucked-up ankle."

She flinched at my curse but didn't chastise me. I hid my smile. Already we were compromising. She wasn't comfortable with me…yet. But I had time. If starvation and dehydration didn't kill us first, of course.

Estelle passed me the stick. Doubt shadowed her face. "I don't think I can set your break here. The ground is too uneven. I need to get you to the beach."

I didn't see the difference, but I let her be in charge. "What do you suggest then?"

"I need to find a way to get you to your feet." She rubbed her ribcage. "Normally, I would just do my best to haul you upright, but I don't think I'd be able to withstand my own pain—let alone you living through the torment."

"Ah well, can't have everything. Don't worry about me."

I had to admit, the very mention of what lay in my future made me sick. Just a simple poke irritated the bone to the point of agony, let alone standing upright.

Regret filled her gaze. "I shouldn't have had those painkillers. You need them more than me."

"Stop that." Temper peppered my voice. "I wanted you to have them. Don't bring it up again."

Her fingers fluttered by her side as she deliberated. My jeans hid the break (apart from the nasty cut on my opposite thigh) but couldn't hide the fact I sweated with pain. The amount of liquid I'd perspired didn't help my rapidly increasing thirst.

I'd never broken a limb before. Was the dull throb supposed to be this bad? When would it fade?

It has to fade.

That was the only way I'd be able to survive and ensured I walked off this island—or rather *limped* off this island.

Estelle murmured, "Wait there."

"Like I can go anywhere."

She jogged into the undergrowth before I could stop her.

Goddammit, this girl.

When I first met her, she'd come across shy and aloof; now, the depth of caring she possessed annoyed me because she made me feel as if I was lacking as an average human being.

Crunching and crackling drifted on the stagnant air.

What the hell is she doing in there?

Visions of a cooling sea breeze and fresh air made me eager to leave the soupy humidity of the forest. The more I thought of relocating to the beach, the more anxious I was to go.

Estelle was gone a while.

She finally returned with two more sticks (not they could be called sticks when they were the size of small saplings) of approximately equal length. One had a kink in it but, overall, was straight, while the other had a bulbous end as if it had been a root system once upon a time.

Passing them to me, she smiled. "Here you go."

My forehead furrowed. "Oh, you shouldn't have."

Stop being an asshole.

I made eye contact. "Um, thanks?"

She crossed her arms. "They're crutches. At least, this way you can move around—or as much as you can on the uneven terrain. They're probably a bit long but we can fix them once we get to the beach."

My eyes bugged. "Seriously? Who are you? *MacGyver*?"

Instead of laughing, her eyes blackened with annoyance. "Instead of belittling my idea, let's go." Grabbing the other stick from beside me, she wedged her tiny frame against mine. "Use one of the crutches and put the rest of your weight on me."

Oh, hell no.

I pushed her away. "No chance. I'll crush you. Look at the size of you."

"I can do it."

"Your ribs can't. No way."

"Those painkillers will dull some of it. I might be smaller than you, but I'm strong." She grabbed my free arm and slung it over her shoulders. Sucking in a breath, her face waxed with pain. "Come on. I don't want to leave Conner and Pippa any longer than necessary. Who knows if their self-control will obey me when I said not to eat the small amount of food we found."

"Food?" My stomach grumbled on command. "Why didn't you say that in the first place?"

She hissed as I gingerly put my weight on her.

I immediately stopped. "This is ridiculous."

"Do you have a better idea?"

"Well, no…"

"Exactly." Tugging on my wrist, she braced herself against the palm tree and yanked upright.

"Christ." She didn't give me a choice. I growled and swore as inch by inch she slid my crippled ass higher up the tree trunk and into a wobbling standing position. My muttered oaths became amplified as my ankle twisted, bellowing with torture. "Fuck me."

"I'd appreciate it if you kept the curses to a minimum."

"You try moving with a broken everything, and we'll see who can keep their speech PG rated."

She snorted. "You're such a drama llama."

I turned rigid. "*What* did you just call me?"

"A drama llama." A smirk teased her lips. "I saw it online awhile back. I thought it was kind of funny."

"Did you seriously just call me a llama?"

"Well, you did say you'd been called worse."

"Not a bloody barn animal."

Wedging the crutch under my free arm, she took a step back. I didn't even notice I'd borne my own weight until she spread her hands in triumph. "First thing for everything. Besides, it worked, didn't it? You're standing. Best news all day."

You can say that again.

I flinched as she wrapped an arm around my waist.

My blood thickened as my heart rate accelerated. Different urges replaced thoughts of pain. I wanted to crush her to me and inhale the faint smell of vanilla. I wanted to lick the salt from her skin and thank her in kisses rather than words.

When I didn't move, she pinched my side. "Come on. Let's go. What are you waiting for?"

"If I told you, you wouldn't want to help me."

Her face tilted up, her eyes wide with questions. "Oh? Try me." She looked so innocent and eager that it took everything to grin with cockiness rather than overwhelming sincerity.

"Try you?" My voice slipped into a caress; my gaze locking

onto her mouth. "I appreciate the invitation, Estelle, but I really don't think I should."

She jolted. "That's the first time you've said my name without it sounding like a bad thing."

Sexual tension catapulted around us stronger, faster, far, *far* more intense than I'd ever felt before. Her arm jerked around my waist.

I slung mine over her shoulders without thinking.

"Want to know what I'm waiting for? Fine, I said I'd be brutally honest. I'll be honest." My head lowered, my lips coming within a whisper of hers. "I'm waiting for a kiss. I don't want to move just in case you realise how close you are to me and run away while I can't chase you."

She panted as I battled with the urge of stealing a kiss or doing what was right and honouring the boundaries of first acquaintance.

I looked up at the tree canopy, exhaling heavily. "You have no idea how hard it is to be a gentleman right now."

She cleared her throat, trembling a little. "I think you're delirious with pain."

I snorted. "Let's go with that if it makes you feel better."

"It does. It definitely does."

"So I shouldn't tell you that I'm hard and I barely even know you? That I haven't stopped thinking about you since I saw you in Los Angeles?" I lowered my head, nuzzling behind her ear. "I shouldn't tell you that I wanted to talk to you the entire flight over or that everything about you makes me happy and sad at the same time?"

The thing with having lacklustre eyesight since birth meant my other senses had heightened to compensate. Her smell (while faint) ripped my innards out and made me want to beg for all manner of things. I wanted her naked. I wanted her laughing. I wanted her far away from me so I never destroyed her perfection.

"Why didn't you?"

I did my best to concentrate. "Why didn't I what?"

"Come talk to me? Answer honestly this time."

I reared back. "You can't guess?"

She held her breath.

And I did the one thing I'd promised myself I wouldn't do. I treated her like a damn object.

Tightening my hold on her shoulders, I brought her body in line with mine. The moment her breasts squashed against my chest, I couldn't breathe and when her lower belly wedged against the aching hard-on in my jeans, it took everything I had not to thrust her against the damn palm tree and forget about civilised rules just so I could have one tiny, delicious taste.

Her eyes widened as she felt what I offered. My hips rolled just a little; my broken ankle growling with torment. "Does *that* answer your question?"

She struggled to speak which clutched my heart and scrambled my thoughts.

"No, not at all."

"The answer is because when I want something as bad as I want you, nothing good comes of it." I chuckled harshly. "I hurt those I love and I have no intention of hurting another."

We both froze at the 'L' word. The depth of connection that came with those four little letters wasn't something either of us wanted to discuss.

I deliberately angled my hips away, holding her at a distance. I needed her to help me walk, but I wouldn't force myself on her any more than I had.

What a douche-bag thing to do.

We'd finally broken the ice, and I'd ruined it by sprouting all kinds of idiocy.

I groaned under my breath, passing off my stupidity as pain.

Estelle leapt into action, taking a step forward. "How about we forget what just happened and head to the beach…okay?"

"Fine."

"Just…let me guide you. Lean on me and use the crutch. I'll do my best to prevent as much discomfort as I can."

You're the cause of most of it.

At least, I managed not to say that out loud.

Nodding, I soundlessly accepted her help. I held her closer than necessary under the guise of using her as transportation. She accepted my closeness without complaint, her fingers tight around my side.

Rearranging the bulbous part of the stick under my arm, I hopped forward hesitantly.

Estelle moved with me, gasping a little as my weight landed then relaxed on her frame.

She didn't speak, so I didn't either.

I forced myself to concentrate, not on Estelle and her sexy-perfect strength, but on coordination and the agony of hobbling on an unsupported broken leg.

Shuffle by shuffle, we traded forest for sunshine.

We made our way to the beach that would become our new home.

I just didn't know how long it would be home for.
If I had known...who knew what I would've done differently.

Chapter Fifteen

....

ESTELLE

......

He loves me. He loves me not. He loves me.
How could a stupid petal tell me the heart of another?
~~He loves me. He loves me not. He loves me.~~
How could I fall for stupid lines stolen from others?
He loves me. He loves me not. He loves me.
~~I don't believe in love.~~ I do believe in love.
But not with him.
Taken from the notepad of E.E., aged nineteen.

...

I SWALLOWED MY fears for the billionth time and kept my fake smile in place.

We're not going to make it.

Yes, yes we are.

I couldn't cry because Conner and Pippa never stopped watching me.

But it didn't stop my runaway wretchedness.

Galloway's eyes were like missiles tracking my every move. My skin still tingled where he'd hugged me to hop through the forest. And I couldn't stop reliving the pressure of his erection on my lower belly. What possessed him to do such a thing? And why didn't I mind nearly as much as I should?

For the past hour, we'd split one muesli bar between the four of us and washed it down with two mouthfuls of water from the bottle in Duncan's backpack. We'd found it when we'd foraged for the other bags, littered like candy wrappers a few metres away from the crash site.

We hadn't found my jacket or Amelia's tote, but we had found the survival kit that the pilot kept strapped beneath his seat.

The food had been heaven-sent and I'd tried to forgo my mouthfuls of water, stating I'd had some from the storm, but Galloway wouldn't accept it. The meagre food hadn't given us much energy—if anything, it had aggravated our hunger and made it worse.

Better get used to it.

After our quick meal, Conner and I had returned to the helicopter and stripped the cabin. We'd hauled back the well-worn leather cushion from the bench seat, three life-jackets, and a piece of mangled fuselage that I envisioned doing something with but had no idea what.

The beach had turned into a wasteland of broken, mismatched items that I hoped would somehow keep us alive.

Sitting on my haunches, I surveyed the spread gear. "We have a few good tools to at least make a shelter."

I think.

I don't know.

Galloway scoffed while Conner nodded hopefully.

Pippa sat quietly with her thumb in her mouth watching everything I did. The intensity of the little girl's gaze threatened to destroy me knowing she looked to me to keep her safe. At least, we'd found her stuffed kitty, Puffin. She hugged him as if he'd squirm away and vanish.

My heart stuttered at the thought of providing basic necessities for them. They were still young enough to believe that adults had all the answers and that was almost as naïve as believing in Santa Claus.

Adults didn't know what they were doing—we were just good at faking it.

But there would be no leeway to pretend here. It was achieve or die. Attempt or perish.

My attention zeroed in on Galloway; sympathy still flowed from the struggle he'd gone through getting to the beach. He'd hated, positively *hated* that I'd seen him vomit while hobbling the last stretch. He'd shoved me away and fallen to retch in a bush.

Not that much came up.

The pain was too much for his system.

He couldn't make eye contact as he finally let me touch him again and guide him the rest of the way. No wise cracks. No surly comments. Just utter silence.

I respected his feelings and didn't say a word, just helped him rest on the sand. Even now, a few hours later, I hadn't brought it up.

Galloway kept his eyes closed, his fists clenched from pain

while his skin alternated between flushing with adrenaline and whitening with agony.

As a group, we weren't doing so well. With my broken ribs, Conner's mangled wrist, and Pippa's bloody shoulder, we were in no state to hammer together a home or hunt for dinner.

It's not as easy as the storybooks.

I had a secret obsession with all things survival. I used to love watching castaway movies and read every book in the genre. I adored the idea of being alone and finding utopia in the most unlikely of places.

But that was before it happened to me.

That was before my comfortable window seat in my apartment with a crisp glass of iced tea became a wild Fijian island with no signs of help.

The characters made it sound so easy. Fishing with earrings, hacking at coconuts with ice-skates. Luck seemed to shine on them.

But us...

Will we be so able?

My eyes drifted over the ragged survivors who'd become my family. We were all too hurt to manage. And if we were too hurt to build and hunt, we would eventually grow weaker and sicker until being rescued no longer mattered.

No...

Launching upright, I held my ribs and marched toward the shoreline. Tears I could no longer stop trickled down my face as I begged the empty horizon for hope.

Please...how do we manage?

How do we drink and eat and create shelter when none of us are healthy enough to try?

Wading deeper into the water, I didn't care the bottoms of my jeans grew wet. I'd wanted to change for hours. We all needed to change. We all needed a shower, a bed, and some subsistence.

Stop feeling sorry for yourself.

At least, no one you loved died.

No, that'd happened a year ago.

I'd had time to adjust.

I looked over my shoulder at Conner and Pippa. They sat together, locked tightly in mutual fear and sadness. However, they still talked, still smiled. And if they could chatter and share the occasional (if not entirely appropriate) joke, then I could definitely be there for them.

Scooping a handful of tepid seawater, I washed my face. The droplets smeared away some of the sticky sweat.

Feeling slightly less consumed with despair, I plodded back up the beach and resumed my position in front of the supplies.

Galloway groaned as he shifted higher, reclining against the fallen log I'd dragged (with help) from the forest edge into the shade of a leafy tree. The dense foliage acted like an umbrella and we'd found solace in the shadows while still able to enjoy the cooler air from the sea.

"Are you okay?"

My smile was brittle. "Of course. Why wouldn't I be?"

Galloway frowned. "I can think of a hundred reasons."

"Yes, well. None of your reasons apply to me."

I couldn't deal with him. Especially after his honesty about how much he wanted me.

Who did that?

We were on a *deserted island*. I had enough to think about.

His eyes burned into me. "You sure?"

"Totally sure. All good." I winked at Pippa.

She rewarded me with a smile.

"Okay, inventory time." I pointed at each item—the only things saving us from extinction. "We have one Swiss Army knife, a clear polyethylene sheet, a small axe that I guess would've been used to chop out the cockpit window in case of an accident—kind of moot if a palm tree spears it instead."

I shuddered as an image of Akin's dead legs filled my mind. "A pair of sunglasses, a baseball cap, a small medical kit with antiseptic wipes and a flimsy needle and thread, a hand-held mirror, a wind-up torch, and a packet of dried jerky with a use-by-date of two years ago."

Turned out Akin had a survival kit but hadn't checked it in a very long time. I wished he'd had fishing hooks and painkillers and a lighter. Just those three things would've made our life a lot easier.

Galloway said, "So…what you're saying is we're fucked."

"Hey!" My head shot up. "Language."

Conner laughed. "It's okay. We've heard worse from our dad."

Pippa nodded. "He liked the word bollocks."

Galloway chuckled. "I'll have to add that to my repertoire."

"Oh, no, you won't."

"Watch me." He glanced at the kids; they shared a conspiratorial smile.

I struggled not to give in. The relief of laughing helped soothe our stress. If a few colourful words provided entertainment, then so be it.

Leaving them to joke, I scooped up the items and tucked them carefully into the black drawstring bag.

Galloway coughed, catching my attention. He didn't speak, but his eyes confirmed my previous thoughts. How could two adults and two children survive in a world where we had nothing?

The obvious answer?

We couldn't.

But we would try so damn hard.

I stood up quickly. I couldn't stay there looking at our meagre possessions anymore. I had to keep moving.

Pippa left her spot by her brother and came to take my hand. "My back hurts and my head feels funny."

My stomach flipped.

Oh, no.

I'd tended to Conner's wrist, but I hadn't looked after Pippa. How could I forget about her bleeding shoulder?

Ducking to her level, I smiled as brightly as I could. "I know how to fix it."

I don't know how to fix it.

"Salt water is good for cuts."

Maybe not seawater though; what with so many critters and algae and germs...

But what was the alternative?

Looking at Conner and Galloway, I forced away my concerns. "Let's go for a swim. We all need a bath, and it will make us feel better."

And, depending on how bad Pippa's wound was, I might have to use the needle and thread a lot sooner than I wanted.

Nausea rolled through me at the thought of stitching up the little girl with no anaesthesia.

"Come on." Not waiting for replies, I untangled my fingers from Pippa's and stomped toward Galloway. I hadn't braced his leg yet because he'd refused to take off his jeans.

Idiot.

What was his problem? He'd pressed himself against me in the woods, he'd come within a whisker of kissing me, and now, he'd gone too shy to let me strip him so I could help.

At least, he'll have to undress to go swimming.

I held out my hand. "I won't ask again. A swim will be beneficial."

Desire glowed in his eyes (I didn't know if it was for me or the thought of the ocean), but he glared at my hand as if it offended him. "I can't stand."

"Yes, you can."

"No. I can't." He glowered at the horizon. "I won't do it."

Crouching, I ignored my ribs and dropped my voice so the children didn't hear. "Throwing up is natural. Your system can only handle so much pain—"

"Forget you saw that."

"I won't because it's nothing to be ashamed of." I moved to his side and passed him the crutch with the slightly wider end. "Come on. Please."

He looked up. For a second, the crackle of connection and lust sprang between us then dispelled as Galloway growled, "Goddammit, you don't play fair."

"I didn't know I was playing, but if it means I win, then great."

"Bollocks."

I laughed despite myself.

Muttering under his breath, he wedged the crutch into the sand and allowed me to duck beneath his arm. Conner dashed forward to help lever him from behind.

It took a lot of pain and effort from all of us, but we finally got Galloway to his feet.

He squeezed his eyes. "This better get easier."

I'd taken my shoes off while we ate and the sugar-soft sand oozed between my toes. "It will. Once it's set and has support, the pain will fade."

I'm lying again. I have no idea if that's what will happen.

"She's right." Conner held up his wrist. "This freaking killed but ever since she tied the stick to it, it feels better."

Apparently, my lies are based on truth.

Pippa followed us like a tiny shadow as Galloway limped and hopped from the shady campsite.

A ragged groan fell from his lips.

He swayed and I quickly pressed against him, allowing him to wrap his arm tighter around my shoulders.

My heart galloped as he trembled.

Holding him reminded me of how much I wasted my life being alone. How much I'd valued silence over nightclubs and preferred conversations with a pen and paper rather than flirting with a stranger.

I'd been alone most of my life, and now, I was alone on an island. And for some reason, the only male of dateable age found me desirable.

The longer we spent in each other's company, the more I saw beneath his mask. He came across as brash with hard edges, but I sensed there was a lot more to Galloway Oak than he wanted to reveal.

Pippa darted in front of us. She spun around with her bottom lip stuck out. "Can I jump in?"

I stopped as the first lap of seawater met my toes. "Think you can take some of your clothes off, so they don't get wet?"

Or is it best to swim in our clothes so they're semi clean?

We all had a few pieces to change into. I'd found my handbag with my nightgown, bikini, and shorts. And Conner had sourced Galloway's messenger bag and his father's rucksack. We had enough clothing to tide us over.

The clothes we'd folded neatly and weighed down with a rock after rummaging through supplies. What I'd really been searching for were things of use: lighters or matches, cell-phones or communication devices (even a flare would've been nice). But Galloway's phone was dead with no charger, and Conner said his mum and dad begrudgingly left their tablets behind so there would be no work distractions.

I have to find my jacket.

I had a phone *and* a charger.

That was our best hope of rescue.

Conner jogged to his sister, peeling off his t-shirt and hopping on one leg to shed his shorts. His actions were awkward with his wrist splint, but he stood proudly in silky *Star Wars* boxers. The satiny material clung to his skinny boy hips.

He nudged Pippa, who'd gone shy. "Come on, Pip. Swimming in clothes is no fun."

She wrinkled her nose. "You're so scrawny."

"And you're just a chicken." Dashing into the lapping waves, he called, "Last one in has to give the other their allowance."

Allowance.

My heart rattled like a moneybox with no change. Those normal things had now vanished. There would be no allowance here. Unless payment in the form of shells were welcome currency.

Pippa squealed, hurriedly ripping off her t-shirt before slipping out of her trousers and barrelling toward the water in just her knickers.

I slapped a hand over my mouth at the nasty gash in her shoulder.

"Oh, my God."

Galloway flinched. "Ouch. That kid has balls not to scream every time she moves."

I couldn't stop looking. Her pearl-white skin was torn apart and angry. "Do you think she'll be okay?"

His answer took a long moment. "I hope so."

My throat clogged with tears.

Galloway's arm tightened around my shoulders. "Hey...it will be okay. *She'll* be okay. You'll see."

I nodded, unable to reply. Shrugging, I wordlessly requested he let me go. He obeyed, loosening his hold and placing more of his balance on the crutch.

I moved down the beach, never looking away from the children diving beneath the crystal water and acting like nothing was wrong.

Everything was wrong.

Including my feelings toward a man I barely knew.

Galloway had the unnerving ability to slip into my thoughts and trickle into my heart. I could cope with him being a bastard but not his sincerity and concern. That would ruin me because I didn't have any more space to care so much when our future was unknown.

"I'm going to join them." Shoving away my nerves, I yanked my black diamante top over my head (which bloody hurt my ribs) and anxiously stepped out of my jeans.

I didn't dare look at Galloway.

Not one glance.

But I knew he looked at me because my skin prickled with heat.

I kept my head high as I waded into the ocean in my black knickers and bra. So what if he saw me in my underwear? I had no doubt he'd see me in all forms of undress over the next few days while we waited for rescue.

The blissful sensation of fresh air after wearing hot denim made me groan with relief. The moment the cleansing water licked up my hipbones, I dropped to my knees on the sandy bottom and disappeared beneath the surface.

I hovered until my mind felt mildly saner than a few moments ago before pushing upward.

My gaze landed on Galloway. Every nerve, stress, desire, and lust exploded into intensity.

He'd managed to strip off his t-shirt, revealing a powerful chest of sculpted pectorals and obliques. The ripples of his stomach shifted with every breath, his skin glittering with sweat.

My mouth fell open as I unashamedly drank him in. I'd found him attractive at the airport. I'd appreciated his height, roguish good looks, and bookish sex appeal with his glasses. But now...holy hell, I wanted him.

I wanted to be reckless and forget our lives were on the line.

I wanted to pretend we'd made it to Kadavu.

I wanted to believe he was an island fling and nothing could harm us.

My fingers tingled to touch him, my tongue watered to taste him.

I stopped breathing as he reached for his fly. My heart became a skipping stone as he unbuttoned and unzipped, loosening the denim to slide halfway down his hips. Black boxer-briefs and the delicious swell of a well-endowed male.

My mouth mimicked dry sand.

Galloway looked up.

I froze.

Instead of smirking at the fact I'd been caught staring, he grimaced and glanced away. The pain he endured shone on his face while his breathing laboured.

From the safety of the water, I knew what would happen. I also knew I wouldn't refuse even though it would cost me more than I had.

He couldn't get his jeans farther down his legs without help.

I shivered. *Don't ask me. Don't ask me to help.*

"Estelle?" His jaw clenched with frustration. He couldn't make eye contact, far too proud to admit he couldn't do it himself.

The alpha vulnerability tore apart my heart.

Dammit.

Balling my hands, I waded out of the water and stood dripping wet before him. "Should I pull or do you want to lean on me while you do it?"

His face contorted with rage. "I don't want your help at all."

Anger filled my blood. "Then why—"

"Because I'm a fucking invalid who can't do anything on his own." Breathing hard, he glanced at the horizon, waves, beach— anywhere but at me. "Just yank them down, all right? Don't make me bloody beg."

I battled with the desire to slap his attitude away and hug him for being in such a demoralizing position. "It's okay. I don't mind." My voice was soft as I dropped to my knees in front of him.

I looked up.

Crap, I shouldn't have done that.

From this position, I had the perfect view of tight boxer-briefs, perfect bulge, sleek chest, and furious man towering over me.

We both turned rigid.

Instincts beyond my control took over. The urge to soothe

him, kiss him, yank down, not just his jeans but his boxer-briefs too, hijacked my nervous system.

Oh, God.

Clearing his throat, Galloway tore his eyes from mine. His fists clenched by his sides.

With slightly shaking hands, I reached for his hips and slid my fingers into the belt loops. Slowly tugging the dense material down his thighs (doing my best to avoid his bleeding wound), Galloway sucked in a harsh breath.

Conner and Pippa splashed behind us but all I could focus on was Galloway and how close I was to a very intimate part of him.

He swallowed a growl as I slid the denim over his knees.

I paused. "You're going to have to bend your leg for me to slip your foot free."

His blue eyes bore holes into mine. "Fine." Holding his breath, he did his best to balance on his good leg. However, he stumbled and his hand landed on the only place he could reach.

My head.

The instant his large fingers clutched my skull, tugging on hair and reminding me what normally happened when a woman was on her knees before a man, my core clenched.

Breathe.

Don't pay attention.

The sexual flush irritated and scared me; I jerked his jeans harder than intended.

"Christ!" He stumbled again, his fingers digging harder into my head as I freed one leg.

We both paused. There was no way he could put weight on his broken ankle.

He came to the same conclusion. "I should've sat down for this."

I laughed, cursing my winged heart. "Well, you can't wear these for the foreseeable future anyway. Just go in the water with them. I'll tug them off once the sea takes your weight."

He scowled. "Why can't I wear them?"

"Because once you're clean, I'm going to make you a splint and jeans won't fit over it."

"Fine." Hugging his crutch like a lifeline, he hopped toward the tide, not asking for my help.

I let him go.

I pretended it was for his benefit, so he could he take back some of his independence even as his jeans trailed after him.

But I really did it for me.

I did it for my heart.
I did it for my sanity.

Chapter Sixteen

••

GALLOWAY

••••••

SCREW THIS DAMN island.
Everything so far had been awful.
Not her, though.
No, not her.
She was the only thing making it bearable.
I wallowed in warm water, wishing I could look away but couldn't.

Estelle had her back to me as she tended to Pippa's cut. Considering I knew nothing about her, I'd already learned so much. I'd learned she didn't have much experience dealing with children. She treated them like adults, talking soothingly but smartly, not dumbing anything down or lying when Conner asked her a brutal question about where we would sleep tonight.

For the record, the stars would be our roof. That should've been my job. I was a builder, for christ's sake. But how could I create shelter when I could barely stay conscious while standing?

I *hated* my weakness. But I had no intention of staying that way. Tomorrow, I would be better, and I would build us a damn fort, even if my ankle continued to be a prick.

I was done being the cripple.

On top of building a fort, I'd construct a raft. I'd somehow figure out a way to build a boat to get us off this godforsaken place. *If they can't find us…we'll sail to find them.*

Estelle also seemed to have an endless well of quiet strength and common sense. We had no medicine for Pippa's shoulder. It would almost guarantee an infection if we didn't stay on top of its cleanliness. But she didn't fret outwardly, merely focused on the now.

It turned my stomach to see the sea turn pink with blood as Estelle sluiced Pippa's wound, but I had to admit, the injury looked a lot better than it had.

The fear of a shark coming to investigate niggled me. Did they have sharks in Fiji?

Once she'd tended and done all she could, Estelle pushed Pippa to neck height in the water, telling her to stay under for ten minutes to let the salt heal. That was the only white lie she told: that the sea would take away her pain and sew her up perfectly.

But who was I to say differently? I felt better with the water cradling my break. If Estelle believed the ocean could cure everything, I wanted to believe in it, too.

Conner swam off, chasing silver fish beneath the surface.

We need to catch a few.

I was starving and thirsty. The snack before (if a few mouthfuls could be called a snack) hadn't achieved anything.

My attention turned to the three necessities of survival.

Shelter.

Food and Water.

Health.

We had no shelter, but I'd fix that (watch me. Break or no break).

We had limited food, and soon, we'd have none.

Our health was compromised.

We would need a miracle to survive.

But how could we ask for another miracle when we'd just lived through one? We were here while three others were rotting beneath the Fijian sun. That was a miracle... *right?*

Tearing my eyes from Estelle (doing my best not to get hard remembering her in her underwear), I looked up the beach at the postcard-perfect view. My sodden jeans dried in the sun and our footsteps led to our sparse camp where salvaged items rested in the shade.

"What are you thinking?" Conner swam up, his arms powering through the water.

My thoughts remained morbid. How much longer would he have the strength and energy to swim and want to talk? Once he burned through his body's reserves, would he still smile, still joke?

When I didn't reply, Conner splashed me. "Know what I'm thinking?" He pointed at the horizon.

The empty, beautiful, cursed horizon.

No islands.

No boats.

No seaplanes.

No traffic or pollution of any kind.

"I think they'll find us. Search and rescue have already left and will be here soon."

Wishing so much to believe in the fairytale, I played along. "Yeah, I bet they're just around the corner, bringing burgers and Cokes, ready to ferry us to our hotel."

Conner's eyes suddenly glassed over. "Even if the hotel came for us, Pip and I couldn't check in without Mum and Dad." His gaze switched to the island and the resting place of his parents. "Is it strange that I don't believe they're dead? That it doesn't feel real."

The sea was shallow and we both bobbed on the bottom with our arms keeping us afloat. "I get that. My mum died a few years ago."

"Did you get over it?"

I deliberated if I should tell him what society expected. The generic 'yes, time heals all wounds and the grief will get easier.' But Estelle didn't bullshit them, so I wouldn't, either. "No, I didn't. When it first happened, I got angry. *Really* angry. I did…something. I hurt my dad." I smiled crookedly. "Don't let that happen. I can't tell you how to deal with the fact they're never coming back, but I can tell you what *not* to do."

"What shouldn't I do?"

"Don't confuse sadness for rage. And don't take it out on those who care the most." I hadn't told anyone that. I hadn't even apologised to my father for being such a screw-up.

My soul crumpled. I'd never had the balls to address what I'd done. And now, I might never have the chance to hug my dad and say I'm sorry. I'd left him when he needed me the most. Not only did he lose a wife, he also lost a son.

Twice.

I couldn't.

I couldn't stay in the sea any longer.

I cut through the water and dragged myself onto the sand.

I did my best to shuffle/hop with my crutch, ignoring my pain, and left the others behind.

I didn't look back.

Chapter Seventeen

ESTELLE

······

~~Life never delivers more than you can endure.~~ *Life has the sickest sense of*
humour.
Sometimes happy. Sometimes
s
a
d.
But always moving forward. The key to surviving is laughing when things get
bad and crying when things get good.
~~*I don't cry enough.*~~
I laugh a lot.
Taken from the notepad of E.E.

...

I SAW HIM go.

How could I not?

I was hyper-aware whenever his eyes landed on me. My ears
strained to eavesdrop on the conversation he'd had with Conner.
And I'd split my awareness between tending to Pippa and what
Galloway was doing behind me.

It hadn't worked very well.

Pippa's forehead mimicked the blazing afternoon sun and her
lips were dry and cracked from dehydration. At least, the sea had
helped; the salt water had turned the edges of her wound from
bright red and crusty to whitewashed and swollen.

Conner struck off after Galloway. Two males—one hobbling
like an ancient warrior and the other dashing after his new idol.

I didn't move, cradled by the tide.

Pippa touched my arm. "I want to go join them."

"Me, too."

I wanted to know what Conner had said for Galloway to storm off, what he kept hidden. I wanted to know so much but doubted I ever would because secrets had a habit of taking up too much space with no avenue for conversation.

Our island wasn't tiny, but Galloway's attitude took up a large section of it, tainting the beach with scorn.

Taking Pippa's hand, I led her from the ocean.

Instantly, the hot sun seared my skin, sizzling the droplets on my spine. I didn't have any UV protection or ways of preventing sunburn. After all, I'd planned to go home. Not some hare-brained idea of going on holiday.

Home.

God, what I would give to be home.

Pippa untangled her fingers from mine and dashed ahead. My eyes fell on our scattered belongings, hating my lack of know-how. How could I turn a few helicopter cushions, plastic wrap, and meagre items into food and shelter?

Galloway had propped himself up against the log, and his temper had faded enough to continue talking with Conner. They turned silent as Pippa and I returned.

Galloway refused to meet my eyes. Something had changed. He seemed more angry and vulnerable all at once. However, he directed his pissy attitude at himself rather than at me for a change.

Wringing seawater from my hair, I said, "I need to set your leg."

"I can manage."

My hands slammed on my hips. I didn't care I stood before him in my underwear. I didn't care that the lace was see-through in places. All I cared about was getting him to accept help without hating the ones doing the helping. "You're an idiot if you think that."

I stalked to the forest boundary and grabbed the long stick I'd found. Conveniently, another tree limb rested close by of equal length and thickness.

Two will be better than one.

Claiming both, I stormed back.

No one said a word as I ducked by Galloway's splayed leg (covered in sand, of course) and watched as I grabbed the Swiss Army knife and cut the rest of my singlet into strips. I mourned the diamantes as they fell into the sand with a lifeless sparkle.

Once I had six strips, I positioned one stick on the right side of Galloway's ankle and shin and the other on the left. With brisk efficiency, I brushed away as much of the annoying granules as I could and ignored the way Galloway's muscles stiffened beneath my touch. When he was as clean as I could make him, I said to Conner. "Come and hold these for me, please."

Conner scrambled up and did as I asked.

Smiling in thanks, I brushed away tendrils of drying hair, and glared at Galloway's ankle. My stomach rolled with what I was about to do.

It'll hurt.

So much.

"Damn."

Galloway flinched. "What is it?"

I pointed at the rough bark of the splint. "That will rub. I need something to wrap around your skin to keep it from getting sore."

"You can cut up my jeans if you want."

"You might need them and they're your only pair."

"You've already seen me in my boxers, Estelle. I hardly think I need to worry about appropriate wardrobes."

I didn't reply, merely kept glowering at his leg as if I could magically remove the swelling, realign the abnormal bumps, and take away his agony.

His raspy baritone filled my ears. "You know...I've never had a woman glare at my ankle as much as you are."

"Zip it."

"Normally, they focus their gaze a *little* higher."

"Stop it."

He smirked. "Just trying to ease the tension."

"I'm not tense."

I stiffened as his hand landed on my shoulder with a possessive weight. My heart leapt into my mouth as he slowly, sensually dropped his touch down my bicep, forearm, and traced the blue veins in the back of my hand. "Could've fooled me."

I shook him off. "Leaves. We need leaves."

"What?" He chuckled.

What the hell am I rambling about?

I'd just blurted something random to combat the power he had over me.

However, Conner came to my rescue. "For padding, you mean? Like you did with mine?"

I latched onto the lifeline. "Yes. Exactly. That's *exactly* what I mean."

Cool it.

You're acting like a ridiculous schoolgirl.

Standing quickly, I winced and held my ribs. I eyed our

umbrella tree with its large glossy leaves. I gathered a few handfuls and rolled them up until they created a cushioning barrier. Sandwiching them between the splint and Galloway's ankle, Conner kept them in place while I tied the first strip of my top around his knee.

Galloway winced but didn't complain as I continued down his leg, fastening the makeshift cast.

When it came time to straighten his oddly shaped ankle, I feared we'd both throw up.

Luckily, neither did.

Only once I'd finished did I sit back and stretch out my back. All things considered, it wasn't too bad. From his knee to his ankle, I'd imprisoned his leg well enough to hopefully heal straight. I hadn't tried to reposition anything. I couldn't do anything about the swelling and obvious breaks in his foot. But I didn't have the expertise to yank or try to realign.

My heart pounded. "How does it feel?"

Galloway frowned. "Not sure…"

It won't work. I'll have to try something else—

He cracked a rare smile. "It feels better. Thanks." His eyes warmed, looking more blue-galaxy than tempest sea. "I appreciate it."

Thank God.

For once, I was able to relax under his scrutiny. "You're welcome."

....

Night-time.

Our first night in the wild.

Well, second if you count our crash and stormy welcome.

The sun had bowed to the moon and the sweltering heat of the day turned to a nippy chill.

In our meagre luggage, we'd found our respective toothbrushes and two tubes of travel-size toothpaste. Cleaning our teeth and swilling our mouths with seawater wasn't ideal, but we all needed a slice of normalcy. We didn't have soap, but for now, we would settle for minty fresh breath.

Galloway and Conner had spent the afternoon fiddling with sticks and the polyethylene plastic, trying to come up with something sturdy to sleep beneath. But exhaustion and pain had finally taken its toll and we accepted that tonight…the Milky Way would be our ceiling and the stars our curtains.

I shivered, huddling in the spare t-shirt Conner had given me. I didn't think my silky nightgown was appropriate, nor would it grant much warmth. My cotton shorts didn't stop sand from slipping into every inch. I craved a shower to rid the sticky salt, a gallon of fresh water to temper my raging thirst, and a comfy bed with feather pillows and the softest blankets imaginable.

The entire day we'd been feeding off each other's energy. But now, daylight had gone, signalling twenty-four hours with nothing to show for it. Our enthusiasm to converse had dwindled to non-existent. Even the piece of beef jerky for dinner hadn't put us in a better mood.

All I wanted to do was curl up and shut off. The introvert part of my personality demanded I recharge away from the others, but the fear of being alone on a deserted island kept me appreciative of the company.

Pippa crawled toward me, her face pinched from crying. "Can I sleep next to you?"

I held out my arms. "Of course, you can. We can keep each other warm." Her tiny form slotted against mine, sharing body heat, and surprisingly, offering comfort. However, she didn't come alone. She clutched her stuffed, slightly damp kitten, wedging him between us.

The cold sand wasn't exactly comfortable, but we'd all scooped four bed-like troughs to fit our individual shapes.

I hugged her hard, kissing her head. "Go to sleep. I've got you." My heart stirred, already falling for the parentless waif.

In the dark, my eyes met Galloway's. We slept facing the same way but a few metres apart. I hadn't consciously placed myself so far from him, but even with the distance, his gaze still managed to splatter my skin with goosebumps.

He didn't say a word, just stared with intense eyes almost opalescent in the night.

He'd done his best to help (offering to go with Conner and me to explore the island again—just in case we'd bypassed civilisation (we hadn't unfortunately)), but his pain meant he was no use to anyone.

He didn't see it that way, though. He saw it as weak. He looked at me as if I'd stolen something by doing my hardest to stay strong. He didn't need to know that when I'd gone for a bathroom break, I'd used the rest of my singlet to wrap around my ribs. He didn't need to know my discomfort or the fear I kept screwed tight like an over shaken bottle of lemonade.

He couldn't erase my injuries, just like I couldn't erase his.

We were in this together, whether we liked it or not.

Sighing heavily, I broke eye contact and settled in my sandy bed. I hated the way grains rubbed on my skin, sticking to my cheeks.

Pippa scooted closer, her tiny body drunk with sleep.

I couldn't move with her draped on me, nor did I want to. Staring at the starlit sky, I did my best to find solace in song writing. Ghostly lyrics and phantom music filled my head, composing a melody, turning to symphonies for salvation.

Tomorrow will be better.
A new day always is.
Mistakes vanish. Tears dry.
Tomorrow will be better.
A new day makes sure of it.

·························

DAY TWO

Tomorrow turned out to be worse than yesterday.

At daybreak, Conner and I returned to the helicopter, grabbing another plastic tarp from a dusty storage compartment and slicing through the seat belts with the Swiss Army knife. The nylon straps I cinched around Galloway's splint, fortifying my flimsy shirt with rigidity.

We'd enjoyed a meagre breakfast of half a muesli bar each, another piece of beef jerky, and the rest of the bottle of water from Duncan's backpack. We had two more bottles from the pilot's supplies and three more muesli bars.

After that…we were screwed.

The aches and breaks from the crash had doubled overnight and muscles seized with day-late punishment. We moved stiffly with no smiles or conversation, slipping quickly into depression.

By afternoon, insects started to bother us: mosquitoes with their preference for blood, flies with their pestilent buzzing, even a few lizards and geckoes made appearances. I wasn't hungry enough to contemplate stewing a lizard, but who knew what time would bring.

Pippa continued to burn up, and Galloway was no better. His ankle had kept him up most of the night and my heart hurt every time he struggled to his feet.

At some point in the night, I'd whisper-asked if he wanted help to go to the bathroom, but he'd never answered, leaving his sharp silence as all the reply I needed.

At least with his splint, he could move slightly easier.

Late afternoon sun beat down on us. No rain clouds danced on the horizon signalling an end to our thirst, and no boats or planes sought us out.

It was another day in paradise.

A paradise that was quickly killing us.

I paced the water's edge, doing my best to figure out a way to survive.

Hunger and lack of water would soon drive us mad.

That's my first priority.

Then we could create shelter.

But first…food.

Striding from the shore, I disappeared into the forest with renewed purpose. The strapping I'd wrapped around my ribs helped and I'd grown used to tensing when I moved to combat the nasty twinge.

Glowering at trees and bushes, I wished I'd studied botany.

What could I eat? What was good and what was bad?

Coconuts littered the ground, but I knew from drinking coconut water every morning in my smoothie that you had to get the juice from the young green ones, not the husky brown ones. The older ones were bitter and not nearly as bountiful in liquid.

Footsteps sounded behind me.

Conner.

His young face tight with worry. "Pippa is burning up. I'm worried."

"She'll be okay. We'll look after her."

"How?"

"Not sure yet, but we will."

I'd checked her back this morning, and (thank God) she didn't need stitches.

When I'd started my health food kick with smoothies, Madeline had sprouted all kinds of medicinal properties that coconut water supposedly held. Something about antioxidants and vitamins. I didn't know how true it was, but I was willing to try anything.

"Want to help me get a few coconuts?"

"If it's food, then yes. I'm starving."

"You and me both."

The mere thought of eating made my mouth water and stomach tear itself into eager pieces. We could have another muesli bar, but I didn't want to use our supplies so quickly.

Heading deeper into the forest, I kept an eye out for animals. The island was sizeable but not that big. I doubted we'd encounter large predators but snakes might lurk in the undergrowth.

A crash sounded, jerking our heads up.

"What was that?" Conner stepped closer to me. For his bravado and gung-ho attitude, he was still just a kid.

A few seconds passed with no other noise.

Swallowing my nerves, I shrugged. "Not sure. Let's find out."

"What?" Conner grabbed my wrist. "I don't think that's a good idea—"

I kept moving, dragging him with me. "Trust me. We have to explore this place. We know humans don't inhabit it, but knowledge is what will keep us alive, not fear. We need to know everything we can." Flashing him a smile, I added, "Besides, we're in Fiji, what bad could happen in paradise?"

He rolled his eyes. "Um, cannibals, sharks…"

"Cannibals?" My smile turned genuine. "What old documentaries have you been watching?"

"I dunno. Stuff."

"Stuff?"

"Yeah, you know. Gruesome stuff. It's better than some stupid video game."

"Wait. I saw you playing on one of those handheld devices. You're going to fib and say you don't like PlayStation? You have to be the only boy in the world, surely?"

Conner scowled. "No, I like it. I just don't believe in it like some idiots do. They think they're some macho soldier after playing *Call of Duty* for a few hours. They think being virtually blown up by a grenade is the worst thing ever, but they haven't watched the History Channel."

Wow, he's a switched on boy.

I assessed him with fresh eyes. "You're pretty cool, you know that?"

"Cheers." His gaze darted from mine to the undergrowth by our feet. A green coconut nestled against the bracken. "Coconut has been found."

I bent to pick it up. "That's what must've made the crash." Peering into the canopy, I shielded my vision from the sun spearing through the fronds. "This tree has a lot of them."

Conner yanked me back. "Another might fall then."

I warmed at his concern.

Allowing him to pull me to a safe distance, I passed the coconut to him. "Tell you what. You hold this and keep an eye out. I want to try something."

"Wait. What are you going to do?"

I darted to the other side of the tree where coconuts didn't lurk above my head. "Watch." Tensing against the upcoming pain, I threw myself into the trunk shoulder first.

My ribs screamed.

Holy crap, that hurt.

The wiry palm shuddered but nothing fell.

"What the hell are you doing?" Conner inched closer.

"Stay back." Gritting my teeth, I drove my shoulder into the tree again.

And again.

Ow. Ow. *Ow.*

By the third shoulder nudge, another coconut crashed to the floor.

"Wow." Conner dashed forward and scooped it up. "Good work."

Rubbing my shoulder, I panted, "We'll need to figure out a better way of doing that."

"I'd say."

Taking one of the coconuts, I headed back to camp. "Let's return to the others. They'll be wondering where we are."

....

"Where are they?" Conner dumped the coconuts by our supplies, peering along the beach. "Pip?!" His voice hadn't deepened yet; it cracked with worry.

My heart raced at the immediate leap of something terrible happening.

The thought was too painful to contemplate.

Conner spun in place, his gaze locking onto the see-through plastic we'd found in the helicopter. Unlike before, where it had been scrunched up on the sand, it was now wrapped around a section of our shady tree. Branches and leaves were imprisoned in the plastic while a funnel had been tied with a piece of my singlet that'd been around Galloway's leg.

What on earth?

I drifted forward, obsessed with its purpose.

Droplets of condensation clung to the inner plastic, rolling hesitantly toward the funnel at the bottom.

Conner poked the plastic with his finger. "What the hell is this?"

"Fresh water, of course." Galloway hopped, with the aid of his crutch, from the forest edge. His face was tight with pain, and his five o' clock shadow had grown thicker overnight.

Pippa dashed forward, holding the unwrapped poncho that I'd stuffed into my pockets.

My pockets!

My jacket.

I froze in place. "Oh, my God!"

Everyone jumped.

"What?" Galloway demanded.

I dashed toward Pippa, kidnapping her hands. "Where did you find this?"

"I didn't steal it. Promise!"

"I know. I'm sorry. I'm not saying that. But it was in something of mine that I can't find. Do you know where it is?"

"That puffer thing you wouldn't let go of?" Galloway's voice wrenched my head up.

I nodded furiously. "Yes, that. My jacket. Where is my jacket?"

"Why, what's so important?"

"Doesn't matter!" I breathed hard, tasting salvation like a sweet, sweet wine.

We could be saved.

This could all be over.

"I lost it in the crash. I couldn't find it—"

"Okay, okay." He held up his hands. "I'm only messing with you. I hung it on a tree a few metres away to dry." He pointed into the undergrowth. "It's not exactly clean—"

I didn't hesitate. "I'll be back." My feet flew, my ribs cried, but for once, I didn't care.

My jacket would send us home.

My jacket held my cell-phone.

Chapter Eighteen

• •

GALLOWAY

• • • • • •

DAMN WOMAN TOOK off like a bloody gazelle, leaping into the treeline.

Conner made to chase her, but I grabbed his wrist. "Not this time, little buddy. Let her do whatever's so important."

I knew what was important.

I'd found her jacket.

I'd gone through her pockets.

I'd found the cell-phone.

For a second, I'd wanted to cry in relief, but when I tried to turn it on…it was dead.

The crushing blow had been enough to put me in a sour mood even though I'd remembered a survival technique that would, at least, keep us with a small ration of water.

If I'd told Estelle about the flat battery—same as my useless, smashed-to-pieces phone—she wouldn't have believed me. Something like that (when you have so much hope pinned on it) had to be seen to be believed.

So, I did the only thing I could.

I gingerly lowered myself to the sand and stretched out my broken leg. My hands shook as I placed the crutch beside me. The shaking wasn't new. I constantly shook. I didn't know if it was from hunger or pain—the two sensations had plaited together and tormented relentlessly. But I did know I was on the brink of a fever and needed to be smart about conserving my energy as much as possible.

Pippa's bottom lip wobbled. "Where did she go?"

"She'll be back soon. Don't worry." I patted the ground beside me. "Come on, sit here."

She shook her head, staring longingly into the forest. Already the kids had latched onto Estelle because she permeated a vibe that said everything would be okay as long as she was around.

With me…they were more likely to get snapped at than hugged.

I told the truth when Estelle asked if the splint had helped. I did feel better. She'd earned my eternal gratitude. But it didn't matter because there was so much bad to overcome before we found anything good.

Thinking of her must've yanked her into manifestation because she exploded from the forest, holding her bronze puffer jacket.

Her face split in the biggest smile. "I found it! We're saved!"

No…we're not.

Slamming to her knees in the soft sand, she ripped open the zipper pockets and scooped item after item. Notepads, pens, handheld mirror, small tube of toothpaste, hair-ties…on and on until finally she tore free her cell-phone.

Shit.

My heart sank for her.

This was going to suck watching her hope disintegrate.

I gnawed on the inside of my cheek as she brushed away lint and pocket remnants. She thought we would be rescued. That we wouldn't have to worry about tree huts or eating raw fish (if we could even catch one).

Estelle wiped away grateful tears. "Thank God, it's waterproof. Otherwise, the storm would've wiped it out."

Like mine.

Even if my battery wasn't dead and the screen smashed into a million filaments, the water leaking from the keypad would've killed it.

With shaking hands, she tried turning it on.

I stiffened.

Don't do it. Don't hurt yourself this way.

Conner and Pippa gathered around her, the air of excitement palpable.

I can't watch.

My shoulders tightened as Estelle made an annoyed noise and Conner sucked in a breath. "Shit, it's dead."

Estelle didn't comment on his profanity. I waited for the trauma, or worse, the epic silent despair that was imminent.

Wanting to console her, I murmured, "Don't worry about it. It was a long shot and it's over."

She looked up. "It doesn't matter."

I ran a hand through my hair. "What do you mean, it doesn't matter? Of course, it bloody matters. Stop torturing yourself and accept the truth. It has no power. None."

Was she well? Had the heat finally cracked her?

My heart knotted into a noose at the thought of her losing it. As much as I hated leaning on her, I couldn't survive without her coherent and completely here with me.

"Oh, really?" She merely smiled and gave the phone to Pippa to hold.

Yep, she's lost it.

Dragging her jacket higher up her lap, she pulled one last thing from a pocket I hadn't seen inside the lining. A passport and credit cards fell unneeded onto the sand. A smug grin tugged her mouth.

Unravelling the device, Estelle smoothed out the wires and angled the black glass into the full path of the sunshine.

Conner bounced on his knees. "Crap, that's awesome."

"What's awesome?" My curiosity billowed with every breath.

"They're so cool," Conner said. "My dad gave me a torch with a solar panel charger for Christmas last year."

Solar charger?

She had a bloody *solar charger?*

Who *was* this woman?

Who was ever this prepared?

"Why the hell do you have something like that?"

Her head snapped up. "I was on tour. My battery didn't last a full day, and I didn't have access to a socket."

"Tour?"

She waved away my comment. "Doesn't matter. What matters is…we have power."

I couldn't.

I just couldn't.

First, she took care of us, setting our breaks and doing everything in her ability to make us comfortable, and then, she had the foresight to pack her pockets with things like solar chargers and a waterproof phone?

I want to marry her.

I didn't care if she said no. I didn't care that she didn't want me. I *had* to have her.

Despite myself, the bitch called hope unwound, reeling me in with tasty bait. Could we be saved, after all?

Stop it.

It was never that easy and coming down from a hopeful high was a bloody killer.

"They're cool, right?" Estelle plugged her phone into the sun-operated charger; the chime of a connected device to an energy source rippled over my skin.

Estelle sat on her haunches as she waited for the phone to come alive.

I'd never been so anxious in my life.

"It takes a long time for a full charge, but I can use it while it's plugged in." Swiping the screen, she waited for the boot-up process.

The kids hovered far too close, their heads in her line of vision and fingers reverently touching the phone. We all waited, unsuccessfully hiding our impatient eagerness.

"Well?" I asked, frustration heavy in my voice.

"Well, what?" Estelle tapped and surfed menu after menu. Her shoulders locked the longer she played.

And I knew.

I just *knew* it wouldn't be our ticket to freedom.

Goddammit, why did I let myself get swept away?

I knew this would happen, yet it still hurt like a blood-thirsty butcher.

Scooting down the log, I lay on my back and glowered at the leaves above. My ankle and foot amplified in agony, but it was nothing compared to the deflating hope inside.

Pippa was the one to point out the obvious. "No signal."

Estelle sighed unhappily. "You're right. No signal."

"Perhaps, we need to get higher." Conner squinted into the bright sky. "There has to be a signal. There are mobile satellites and networks everywhere."

I let them plot the pros and cons of how likely a signal would just magically appear while I sank deeper into regrets. I wasn't helping myself by wallowing, but I couldn't stop wishing I'd been a better person, nicer, more appreciative before crash landing on this godforsaken place.

A burst of energy hurled me upright. "Screw this." I wasn't going to sit there and waste any more of my life. I might not able to fix what'd happened, but I could grant a better night's sleep tonight by erecting some sort of shelter.

It took every reserve I had to brace myself against the sand and use the fulcrum of my crutch to stand upright. I barely made it to the edge of the forest before Estelle dumped her phone onto the beach and rushed toward me.

Taking my elbow, she ordered, "Go sit back down, before you fall."

I shrugged her off. Couldn't she see her concern only made me hate myself more?

"Leave me alone."

She winced, dropping her hand. "You don't have to do this. You need to rest."

I rounded on her. "Oh, I don't, do I? So you're happy to sleep in the elements? Or are you going to use that Swiss Army knife and build a damn mansion? Show me up yet again?"

Her eyes narrowed. "I'm not showing you up—"

"You think caring for us gives you a purpose?" I snorted. "Well, stop being a hypocrite and let me help for a change."

"Hypocrite? How am I a hypocrite?"

Conner sidled up to Estelle, instinctually protecting the woman over someone much bigger than her.

I ignored the kid. "You're hurt yourself. Don't think I didn't notice you strapped your ribcage and gasp every time you bloody move. You expect us to heal and relax but what about *you*?" Shoving her away from me, I pointed at the camp. "Sit down, shut up, and let me do something. I *need* to do something. Let me help rather than treat me like a useless invalid."

The standoff lasted far too long. The glint in her eyes warned she wouldn't give in.

Conner was the saving grace.

He tugged Estelle's elbow. "He's right. My wrist isn't as painful thanks to you, and Pippa's cut is clean because of what you did. Let us look after you in return."

Estelle suddenly slapped her forehead. "Damn, Pippa's injury. I forgot." Flashing me a scowl, she smiled at Conner and dashed to Pippa. "Pip, now that your back is clean, let's put some cream and the Band-Aid on that we found in the medical pack. What do you think?"

Damn woman didn't know how to stop. Her caring for others would only hurt herself in the long run.

It's her coping mechanism.

Mine was to become a complete and utter asshole so people left me alone to self-damage. But hers was the exact opposite.

She was purity while I was filth.

Fine.

She could be my opposite and I would do my best to mirror her goodness—starting with building a shelter.

My voice bordered on a growl. "Want to help, Conner?"

Conner looked up. "Help with what?"

"Dunno. I'll figure it out when I know."

"You really think we can build a house?"

No.

"Yes." I hobbled deeper into the forest. "You coming?"

He followed, laughing wryly. "Broken wrist and broken leg. I don't like our odds."

"I've had worse."

"And how did it work out for you?"

Crap. Worse than crap. It ruined my screwed-up life.

"Perfectly fine." I grinned as if it were nothing. "We're men. Nothing is unachievable."

Conner rolled his eyes. "Okay, we'll give it a go, but don't say I didn't warn you."

Chapter Nineteen

• •

ESTELLE

• • • • • •

I hate you. The sky cries with how much I hate you. The plants die with how
much I hate you. I hate you for leaving. I hate you for dying. I hate you.
~~But that's all a lie.~~
I don't hate you. I love you. That's the truth. The sun rises with how much I
love you. The weather warms with how much I love you. And the potted flower
you gave me the morning you died...it blooms every second with how much I
miss you.

Lyrics: 'Hatred' Taken from the notepad of E.E.

• • •

WE NEVER DID achieve a roof over our heads.

Another night descended and we nibbled on our second-to-last muesli bar and final sticks of beef jerky. Using the small axe from the cockpit, we split open the two coconuts Conner and I had found.

Unfortunately, our technique sucked and we hit too hard, losing the sweet water all over the sand.

I berated myself until my eyes prickled with angry tears. We didn't get to drink the nectar, but at least we were able to share the flesh, scraping the coconut with the Swiss Army knife and pretending it was dessert to round out our lacklustre dinner.

No one mentioned the awful situation of a working cell-phone with no signal. No one could bear the admission that the final nail had been hammered into our lonely tomb.

It was as if it never happened and I hated shouldering the responsibility for taunting them with hope.

The battery on my phone had hit forty percent before the sun went down, and I tucked it safely away for tomorrow's solar charge.

But...what was the point?

The phone had turned into a paperweight. Emergency numbers didn't work. Wifi, data, calls...*nothing*.

Useless.

Just like everything else on this island.

Just like me.

The constant hollowness in my stomach grew worse as hours ticked into days. I'd never gone without food for so long, and already, I felt things shutting down. I rarely needed to pee, and everything was hazy—as if I'd entered a realm where comprehension was blanketed with syrup.

I was lethargic, short-tempered, and depressed.

By the time we curled into our sandy beds (Pippa wrapped in my arms and Galloway refusing to admit he wasn't well enough to build a shelter), I fell into the first sleep I'd had since crash landing.

Not because I was utterly exhausted and my body finally forced me to rest. But because dreams were so much better than reality.

······················

DAY THREE

"I'm sorry."

I spun around, stumbling in shock. "You're awake."

Galloway's hand lashed out, catching my elbow and keeping me upright. "Heard you get up."

I took a step away, breaking his hold (even though his touch was more than welcome). I didn't like the animosity from yesterday and definitely didn't like the sensation of loneliness when he'd left. I had no one else to turn to. We couldn't afford to be angry with each other.

"I'm sorry, too."

His eyes smouldered in the night, his lips twitching into a soft smile.

Some of my fear and unhappiness dissolved. I was so glad to have someone to talk to, even if the topics of conversation weren't normal.

Galloway was no longer a stranger but a friend. A friend I trusted even if I didn't fully understand.

Turning to face the polyethylene he'd wrapped around a few branches of our shady tree (what was that about anyway?), I whispered, "I couldn't sleep."

Glancing over my shoulder, I ensured Pippa and Conner slept without interruption. After my slip into unconsciousness, I'd awoken abruptly, only to find the sun hadn't risen yet.

"Me either." Galloway swayed, his crutch wedged beneath his arm for support. The cut on his thigh had scabbed over, healing faster than the scrape on my chest.

At some point, he'd pulled on a pair of board-shorts with a black and teal pattern. They hid his boxer-briefs but still allowed the splint to stay on.

"How are you feeling?" I hugged myself, doing my best to stay warm. Daytimes were hot but the nights…weren't. If lack of hunger didn't kill us, the swinging temperatures would.

Galloway glanced away. "I'm fine."

"Would you tell me if you weren't?"

A flicker of amusement. "Probably not."

"Such a man."

"I would've expected a worse name than that."

We made eye contact. My heart became a stupid pinwheel. "Oh? What should I call you?"

He shrugged. "I dunno. Idiot? Douche-bag? Those are two."

I let the joviality hover, enjoying the simplicity. "I don't think either of those suit you."

His voice switched to an intoxicating murmur. "What do you suggest then?"

Turning to face him, I cocked my head. I used it as an excuse to stare at him. Stare at his dark brown hair curling over his forehead, the pink sunburn on his nose, and his perfectly formed lips.

My stomach fluttered as his gaze dropped to my mouth.

Everything tightened. My muscles, my core, my heart.

I wanted to bridge the gap between us. I wanted to wrap myself around him, and in turn, have his arms wrap around me, stealing reassurance that tomorrow *would* be a better day.

Joking disappeared as we stood, totally silent, utterly immobile, neither breaking the spell. It was unbelievably stupid to get caught up in desire, but in that stolen moon-sleeping moment, reality vanished and I indulged in guilty, desperately needed pleasure.

Kiss him.

Galloway sucked in a breath as I swayed closer.

I didn't touch him.

No hands or arms or fingers.

Just closed the distance, stood on my toes, and pressed my lips to his.

He froze.

I froze.

The world froze as our lips joined, and I forgot what came

next. I forgot because every thought in my head erupted into a thousand pieces of confetti.

His lips, *oh*…

They were so warm and firm and masculine and…

He tilted his head ever so slightly, the tip of his tongue caressing me. His touch wasn't a seduction more of a question.

What are you doing?

I'd kissed him. It was up to me to decide how the kiss would morph.

Did I kiss him in thanks? In friendship? In desperation for everything I might never see again? Or did I kiss him in lust? In attraction? In hopes of finding my rules on friendship could be stretched to something more?

Galloway bit back a groan as I parted my lips, accepting everything I couldn't articulate. His hand swooped up, capturing the back of my neck. His fingers tightened around my nape, pulling me harder against his mouth.

The possessive pressure undid me; I swiped my tongue into his wet warmth.

And that was it.

He snapped.

His crutch thudded softly to the sand as his arm wrapped tightly around me, lifting me off my feet. A few hops and hobbles and my back wedged against the umbrella tree, my front bowing under the hard lines of his body.

I gasped as his fingers hooked around my hair, tugging my head back, kissing me harder.

Oh, God.

He was everywhere at once. Kissing me with an intensity I worried would devour me.

Don't stop.

His hands ran down my body only to recapture my face. Kissing me harder, faster, wilder.

Wait…

I clung to him, letting him do what he wanted because it gave me the freedom to live in sensation.

Stop.

I couldn't stop.

My lips danced with his; our tongues fought and licked.

Stop!

Lust crushed everything in its path. I melted as Galloway grabbed my thigh and hitched it over his hip. I arched my back as his hand skated to my breast. I moaned as—

"Wait!" I pushed him away, panting hard.

He growled as I removed his fingers from my nipple. The sharp jolt of liquid pleasure almost made me give in. But this wasn't real life. This wasn't some holiday. This was serious.

This can't happen.

Ducking away from the cage of his arms, I did my best to straighten my hair. Conner and Pippa still slept (thank God) and I rubbed my lips to rid the electrical current left by his kiss.

Galloway breathed hard. "What was that?"

I paced in front of him. "I—I don't know."

"You kissed me, remember?"

"I know I did."

"Then why did you stop?"

"Just because I kissed you doesn't mean I was going to *sleep* with you."

"Oh, no? You were pretty keen on the idea a few seconds ago."

The heat throbbing in my core rapidly switched to indignation. "Wow, your ego's pretty big, you know that?"

"That's not the only thing that's big." He winked.

"Really? You're going to treat this like a sleazy pickup?" Infuriation was a smoking fire in my chest. "That's low, Galloway."

"What do you want? An apology for something I didn't start?" His jaw ticked. "Look, I'm aware that there are things about me that aren't...smooth. A lot of me is riddled with flaws. But that kiss...it wasn't one of them. That kiss—" He cut himself off, whistling under his breath. "That kiss was the best damn kiss I've ever had."

I shivered with delight even as I stomped on lust with steel-capped boots. "Doesn't matter. It won't happen again."

"Why not?" His voice was a whip.

I waved at the warming dawn, lapping tide, and empty island. "Because we have much more important things to worry about."

He sighed, bending awkwardly to pick up his crutch. "You're right."

I paused, sensing a trap.

Determination plastered his face as he repositioned himself. "However, this situation is a pretty shitty one. What's the harm in finding happiness to make it bearable?"

My breathing slowly calmed. "You're saying you were *happy* kissing me?"

"I've never been happier."

"Oh."

How can he say that with what's happened?

"You guys are up already?" Conner yawned, rubbing his sleepy eyes.

Galloway and I jumped.

The guilt of doing something we shouldn't stamped a scarlet letter onto my forehead.

Galloway managed to set aside our little indiscretion and act completely normal. "Yep. No sleeping in for us."

Conner swiped his good hand through copper hair, making it stand up in every direction. He needed a bath (we all did), but apart from the dwindling supply of toothpaste and the aid of our ingenious use of sand as soap, we had nothing else to use.

Dragging dirty hair over my shoulder, I quickly plaited it—doing my best to hide that it desperately needed a clean. I couldn't decide if the blonde was darkening with filth or bleaching thanks to the salt and sunshine.

Rolling from his makeshift bed, Conner jumped a few times to get his circulation going. "Damn, I'm freezing."

My eyes flittered to Pippa; she slept in a tight ball with my jacket over her legs. Poor kid needed blankets, not exposure to the sky.

Would it be possible to make some?

It might be possible, but bedclothes were far down the totem pole of importance.

As is making out and all things related to desire.

"It will get warm in about an hour." Galloway pointed at the pinking sky. "The sun is about to make an appearance."

Securing my plait with a hair-tie from around my wrist, my silver and gold bangles jangled. Every second the sky brightened helped switch my attention from kissing to the plastic-wrapped leaves of our tree.

I cleared my throat. "I have a question."

Galloway looked at me. "Which is?"

"What exactly is that for?" I pointed at the funnel and the small catchment of liquid. The leaves were cramped in the tight space and condensation only increased as the day grew warmer.

"It's a lifesaver, that's what that is."

My throat panged with thirst. "It makes water?"

Galloway nodded.

"How does it work?"

"I'll show you." He turned to Conner. "Where did the poncho go that your sister found in Estelle's pockets?"

"I'll get it." Conner jogged toward the baby-blue packet that I'd bought in Texas. He ducked and touched his sleeping sister's forehead before making his way back to us. With every movement, he was very aware of his broken wrist.

Passing the poncho to Galloway, Conner asked, "What are you going to do with it?"

Galloway clutched the packet, using his crutch to hop to a free branch. "Demonstration time." He ripped open the packet and shook out the poncho. Passing his crutch to Conner, Galloway stretched and grabbed an armful of the tree, struggling to wrap the thin raincoat around it.

"Here, let me help."

He gave me a dark look as I tugged the branch, giving him room to secure it. Wrapping it tight, he used another piece of my singlet to tie the ends together at the top.

"Damn, I've run out of ties."

Thinking quickly, I pulled the elastic from my hair and handed it over.

A second passed before he accepted it. Pinching the plastic, he formed another funnel, allowing space for water to slide to the bottom.

The moment it was done, he nodded with satisfaction.

Conner asked, "So…now what?"

"Now, we do nothing."

"But I'm thirsty."

Galloway chuckled. "You and me both, kid."

"What are you doing?" Pippa appeared, her little arms wrapped around her goosebump-decorated body.

I welcomed her against my side. "Making water."

"Really?" Her eyes widened. "Good because I want some."

"Galloway was just explaining how it works." I looked at him expectantly.

"I'm not sure exactly." He cleared his throat. "When wrapped in something non-breathable, the leaves perspire and it condenses into fresh water."

Wow.

I cocked my head. "How?"

"Not sure how. Photosynthesis or something. The man I worked for used this method when we'd forgotten to take the large canteen. We'd gone logging and there were no streams or lakes to fill up our empty bottles. He had some clear tarp in the back of the truck, and after wrapping it like I have, we returned to work. It took a few hours but by the time we stopped for the day, we had enough to keep us going until we got home."

"That's amazing."

"But what if there's an easier way?" Conner asked. "Do you think there's a river or something?"

Galloway looked at me. "Estelle? You guys have explored the perimeter twice. You know this place best."

Me?

Hardly.

Crawling around in the storm then foraging for crutches didn't make me an expert. Yes, I'd walked the coastline, but I hadn't bushwhacked through the dense interior.

Could there be a waterfall?

I wished there was, but I didn't think we were that lucky. I'd seen no mangroves, no soggy ground, no trickle.

Three hopeful faces watched me. I had nothing to offer. "I don't think so."

We fell silent, consumed with hunger and thirst and the desire to find some way off this damn island.

"Anyway." I broke the nasty silence. "Soon, we'll have purified water thanks to Galloway."

He gave me an awkward smile. He couldn't take a compliment. He couldn't allow himself one moment of pleasure for doing something so life changing.

Why is that?

My heart swelled at his self-defacing attitude. "This is huge, Galloway."

He shook his head.

"You just kept us alive as if it's no big deal," I said. "I would never have known how to do that."

He shrugged uncomfortably. "Don't mention it."

"When can I have some?" Pippa reached up and pinched the funnel where a couple of droplets had rolled.

Galloway touched her head. "Not for a while. The tree isn't fast like a tap. It takes a few hours for the leaves to sweat."

My blood warmed as Galloway tucked hair behind her ear. He came across so angry and gruff but beneath that lurked a man I'd caught glimpses of, a man I wanted to know.

He was the man I'd kissed.

He was the man I wanted.

Pippa squirmed. "But I'm *thirsty.*"

"I already said that." Conner slung an arm over her shoulders, careful not to touch her scabbing wound. "Copycat."

Pippa stuck out her tongue. "I'm hungry, too. Did you say that already?"

He patted his concave stomach. "That goes without saying. I

could kill for a lasagne."

"Lasagne?" My eyes widened. "That's your favourite food?"

He nodded. "That and ravioli. I have a thing for pasta."

"Mine is cherries." Pippa tugged my hand for attention. "Cherries and raspberries and blueberries and—"

"Every berry, we get it." Conner rolled his eyes. "Doubt you'll find them here."

"What's your favourite, Estelle?" Galloway's soft voice wrenched my head up. He didn't look away, his gaze intense, as if he could strip aside my outer shell and wrench out my secrets one by one.

"What?"

"Your favourite food? If you could have anything delivered right now, what would it be?"

I bit my lip, flicking through tastes and memories. Once upon a time, my favourite meal was spiced eggplant with grilled halloumi. However, I'd been eating it when the call came about the death of my parents and sister.

I hadn't been able to touch it since.

"Not sure," I hedged. "I guess a good soup with crusty bread is nice."

"*Soup?*" Galloway pulled a face. "Seriously?"

I bristled. "I think we have more important things to do than discuss our favourite menus, don't you?"

"Unless you're suggesting ordering me a massive cheeseburger with all the trimmings, then nope." Galloway's smile taunted, almost as if he could read my annoyance and understood how much he affected me.

Well, so what if he could?

We'd kissed.

We'd liked it.

But now, we had to move on and survive side by side rather than lip-locked.

"I'm afraid I don't have a cheeseburger, but I do have one last bottle of water and a final muesli bar." Smiling at the children, I said, "Let's have breakfast. We can afford to have it now that we have a source of water."

I didn't mention we didn't have a source of food...yet.

My eyes drifted to the twinkling ocean. Beneath the surface lived countless molluscs and crustaceans that could keep us alive. We just had to figure out how to catch them.

Today is fishing day.

And tonight, we would eat something substantial for the first time in days.

Please...

The children cheered, but Galloway shook his head. "This isn't a fix to our dehydration problems, Estelle. It will take all day to get a single pint. Sure, it will tide us over, but we need more."

"Oh." My heart fell. A single pint between four of us...that wasn't enough. "We have two funnels. Does that make two pints?"

"Yes, but it's still not enough." He squinted at the new sunshine. Not one cloud in the sky. Not one threatening rainstorm. "We need rain. But before it does, we need to have things ready to store as much as possible."

Once again, I imagined weaving waterproof baskets.

Don't be ridiculous.

I could barely mend a hole in a sock, let alone weave a water goblet. How would we store it? What could we possibly use?

Galloway followed my concerns. "For now, we'll dig a trench and waterproof it somehow so we can catch large quantities—if and when a storm comes."

"What about the helicopter? We can use some of the metal as a large dish." Conner piped up. "And the life-jackets can line a hole in the sand, too."

A smile split Galloway's face. "Good thinking." Ruffling the boy's hair, Galloway hitched his crutch under his arm. "We'll head over after breakfast and see how easy it is to dismantle the fuselage."

I padded behind them. "Correction, Conner and *I* will head over. You will rest with Pippa."

Galloway spun around. "No way. I'm not being a bloody invalid anymore."

I couldn't breathe as he glowered with blue intensity.

I swallowed. "Fine."

Not fine.

I'd just leave without his permission.

I was the one least hurt.

It was up to me to do the most work until the others healed enough to participate.

We didn't speak as we huddled around our belongings and slowly savoured the last of our food and water.

I licked my fingers, savouring my final mouthful.

That's it.

No more.

From here on out...we would have to hunt.

Chapter Twenty

·····································

GALLOWAY

······

I THOUGHT SOLVING our water crisis would make me feel better about myself.

It did the opposite.

Estelle was so damn grateful it made me feel like swine flu. She'd done so much for us, yet she treated me like a bloody king for the one minuscule thing I'd achieved.

Yes, I'd remembered how to snatch water from thin air. But that wasn't my geniusness—that was my mentor back in the States.

I couldn't take credit.

Estelle was the one who'd cast my leg, Conner's wrist, and dressed Pippa's back. She was the one worrying about us at night, giving us fresh leaves to line our damp sandy beds, trying to forgo her last mouthful of muesli bar so the kids had more to eat.

She was the saint on this island.

Not me.

And for her to treat me like one...well, it pissed me off.

Made me angry.

Made me so bloody livid that I couldn't get over the pain in my system and the break in my ankle to be better for her.

Not to mention that kiss between us.

What the *hell* was that about?

My cock had hardened to a damn palm tree, desperate to get inside her even though I didn't deserve the kiss, let alone anything else.

I accepted my ration of food as Estelle broke apart the last muesli bar and nibbled hers with determination. I inhaled mine in one bite. I wouldn't taunt my system with tiny tastes. It wouldn't do me any better to eat fast or slow.

But I did know what *would* make me feel better.

Being productive and helpful.

My eyes landed on Estelle's exposed arms and legs. She still wore Conner's black t-shirt and cotton shorts. Conner wore similar attire of chequered board-shorts and a grey t-shirt, and Pippa wore a pink skirt and frilly tank top.

Instead of unblemished skin, they were all pink from being in the sun and swollen bumps marked our forearms and legs from mosquitoes.

The freaking bugs had killed us. We didn't have coverage and were easy blood sacks.

That needs to be rectified.

How? I had no freaking idea.

Estelle finished her breakfast and tucked the empty wrapper and bottle into the pile of belongings so it didn't litter the sea. I couldn't tear my eyes away as she grabbed something from her handbag and turned her back on all of us.

I hated myself for watching.

I hated that I couldn't stop my eyes drinking in glimpses of her naked back as she changed from t-shirt to bikini top now the heat had returned.

My cock twitched as she struggled to tie the strings, wrangling with the black material still strapping her ribs.

I was a damn pervert. A pervert who lay on his back giving in to weakness and injury.

Estelle managed to complete the bow, before turning to pick up a few items and forage in the black survival bag the pilot had in the cockpit.

What the hell is she doing?

My leg and foot didn't feel any better and the constant throb made my temper nasty. I'd snapped at poor Pippa when she'd asked a billion questions about the water collector. She'd only been inquisitive, but her questions showed me how much of a fraud I was.

Estelle had given me a stern look, making me feel like scum (worse than scum, the algae infesting scum).

Self-pity was an ugly monster, and I wanted it out.

I *needed* it out.

The urge to walk, jog, *run* overwhelmed me. But I couldn't. And even if I could, it would be insane to exercise beneath the hot sunshine with no food or water.

Conner stood, brushing his hands on his shorts. "Gonna use the little boy's room."

He vanished into the undergrowth, reminding me another task awaited. We had to dig a latrine; otherwise, the bugs would be ten times worse.

"We'll leave when you're done," Estelle called after him.

Conner paused. "Leave?"

"Yes, to the helicopter." She held up the Swiss Army knife and axe. "We'll unscrew some panels so we're prepared for rain."

Oh, hell no.

"Wait a goddamn minute." I hauled myself to my feet.

Shit...

The beach swam with agony. I wanted to punch a tree and vomit at the same time.

Estelle didn't come to support me, backing away instead into the forest. "I told you before, Galloway. You're not well enough—"

"I'm *perfectly* well enough."

Her fingers tightened on the weapons. "No, you're not. Be reasonable. You're borderline feverish. Your ankle is giving you grief. Conner and I can do this. We'll be back a lot quicker than you would be. The walk alone would kill you."

My nostrils flared. "Way to make me feel completely useless, Estelle."

Goddammit, did she have to take every task away from me?

"You're not useless." She pointed at the umbrella tree. "You've provided us with water, for goodness' sake. You've guaranteed we'll survive a few more days."

I shook my head. "I should be the one going back there—"

Don't make me say it out loud with the kid present.

Conner had disappeared but was most likely in hearing distance. And Pippa, she already had a healthy dose of wariness around me.

Not that I blamed her.

But things needed to be discussed...dealt with. Horrible things that no one should have to do.

"Estelle," I growled. "You can't go. I'm the one who—"

"Who what? Needs to drag heavy pieces of fuselage back? How exactly? You have a crutch; you can't carry large items with one hand. That won't work."

She's right.

I didn't care that she was right.

This was about me being her equal. Me being *worthy.* Me showing her I was strong enough for her to lean...reliable enough to deserve her trust.

And something else entirely.

"I'm not talking about that."

Her eyes narrowed. "What *are* you talking about?"

I glanced at Pippa. "Not suitable for—"

She jammed her hands on her hips. The flat muscles of her stomach peeked below the black strapping on her chest. "You started this argument, Galloway. So finish it. Why should you be the one to—"

Bloody hell.

"The bodies, all right?" Breathing hard, I hissed, "The non-survivors. Unless you've forgotten, seven of us landed here and only four of us live on this beach."

Pippa pulled her legs up to her chin, wrapping her arms around them. She didn't speak but awful comprehension filled her face. I wished she were slightly younger so she didn't have a clue what I spoke about.

Estelle stiffened.

She had forgotten.

I lowered my voice. "It's best to deal with them now..." *Before they start decomposing.*

Her eyes flittered to Pippa, tears welling.

Gritting my teeth against the pain, I hopped over to her. My lips grazed her ear. "If we're here for much longer, the kids will stumble onto their parents eventually. Do you want them to find them like that? Decomposing? Rotting in the—"

She jerked away. "I get it. Okay? I don't need to hear any more."

"No, you don't. You also don't need to go in there on your own. Someone needs to deal with it, and it isn't you or Conner."

She stared at the ground, her face turning slightly green. "You can't do it on your own. I'll help you."

I grabbed her elbow. "Listen to me and listen good. There is no way you want to deal with a bloated body."

She tried to shake me off, but I didn't let her go.

My voice turned to a growl. "You're not helping me. Got it? You've helped enough."

She sucked in a breath.

I had no right to be angry with her, but I didn't want her scarred for life. Once you'd dealt with something like that, you couldn't delete it. I'd seen my mother. I'd seen another corpse after. And both times, the remains hadn't been exposed to high humidity or sunshine. It hadn't stopped the white-blue skin and dead eyes from haunting my dreams, though.

I sighed heavily. "Promise me, you'll obey."

"*Obey* you?" Her face pinched with rebellion.

"Yes. Promise me."

"We need those pieces of fuselage."

My teeth ground together. "You're not going to give up, are you?"

"They're already dead. We're not. If returning to the helicopter ensures we stay that way, then I'll do whatever needs to be done—decomposing corpses or not." For her brave talk, her body trembled with horror.

Once again, we were in a stalemate.

I let her go. "Fine. I won't stop you from going to the chopper. Get what you can and come back. Immediately."

She sniffed. "In return for what?"

"You don't take another one of my tasks away from me. That's my job and mine alone."

Her shoulders tensed, but finally, she nodded. "Okay."

Conner appeared in the treeline, frowning at the way we stood huddled together.

Estelle exhaled as tears faded from her eyes. "I agree. As much as I want to keep you resting, I don't have the strength to deal with a burial." Her gaze softened. "Thank you for wanting to protect me. I hate the thought of you doing it alone—I don't even know how you'll manage—but I promise I won't try to do it myself."

A certain kind of relief filled my chest. "Thank you."

We shared a smile.

My heart coughed.

I wished we'd had a different topic to discuss.

I wished I didn't have a date tonight with a fuselage-spade and three graves.

I stepped back. "If you're not back in an hour, I'm coming after you. Broken limb or not."

Chapter Twenty-One

. . . .

ESTELLE

. . . . . .

I'm loneliness personified. I'm without a map or directions.
~~I want to wallow.~~
I don't want to wallow.
I'm breathing exemplified. I'm a girl who's finally found her path.
Taken from the notepad of E.E.

. . .

"THIS IS TAKING *forever.*"

"Quit your moaning." I stuck my tongue out at Conner, even though it took every last reserve I had to joke. The past few hours had really hit me. The constant hunger switched my common sense to scattered thoughts, strength to weak muscles, and the unbearable desire for food to madness.

I'd never been so *hungry.*

Never been so eager to *eat.*

But that wasn't the worst part.

It's death.

I'd kept my oath to Galloway and ensured Conner obeyed, too.

We didn't go around the front of the helicopter where Akin's corpse lay.

However...just because we couldn't see him didn't mean we didn't know he was there.

Only a few feet away.

There.

Dead.

It didn't stop the smell.

The gut-wrenching, nose-melting, soul-destroying smell.

We'd retched a few times as the island breeze wafted a particularly strong odour in our direction.

Galloway was right. The bodies needed dealing with.

But for now, we worked in stench and did our best not to focus on the cause.

Taking a deep breath, timing it with fresh air coming from the south, I looked over my shoulder at the two metal sheets we'd managed to hack off. "Keep going. We're almost done." It'd been painstaking work and the tips of my fingers were blistered and sore. But we'd achieved more than I thought we would.

The Swiss Army knife screwdriver didn't fit perfectly into the fixings and the aviation rivets meant our tools were completely inadequate. The axe came in handy to smash some areas but didn't help with the larger panels. We'd been limited to smaller pieces of the tail where the crash had already done a lot of the breaking apart for us.

"I'm starving," Conner muttered, licking his lips. "I don't think I'll be able to last much longer without food."

His fear was my fear, poisoning my heart.

My head pounded with dehydration; my mouth no longer had lubrication. We were demanding our bodies to do too much without putting any fuel back in.

We can't go on like this. Not if we want to survive past a week.

But I couldn't agree with him. I couldn't spill my terrors to a thirteen-year-old boy. Not when I was supposed to be his guardian.

I forced a bright smile. "The minute we're done, we'll go fishing. How about that? We'll catch something. Stranded people always do."

Conner rolled his eyes. "With what? I don't see any hooks or rods."

"Doesn't matter. We'll manage."

"Whatever, Estelle."

Conversation faded as we turned our attention to the final piece of fuselage. The crash had dented it. The indent would hold a few litres …when the rain hit.

My mouth tried to water at the thought of quenching my unquenchable thirst. But saliva was non-existent. The thought of drinking tree-created water when we returned to the beach was the only thing keeping me going for the past two hours.

The first thing Conner and I had done was scrounge for any remaining edibles. We'd been stupid with how quickly we'd consumed our rations. And probably even more stupid by wasting the last dregs of energy on stripping a helicopter that wouldn't replenish the nutrients it took to demolish.

But there was another reason why I was eager to get as many

pieces as possible. Yes, we needed the metal to somehow turn into water catchments (if and when a raincloud arrived) but if we arranged the fuselage into S.O.S on the beach, we might attract a plane.

Not that any have been close since we arrived.

"Yes!" With a final yank, the screw I'd been working on popped off. "Got it."

Conner squatted, picking up the fallen fixing, and adding it to my pile. I'd meticulously kept hold of the ones we'd undone, just in case they could be used for something.

Like what, exactly? You plan on building a home on a deserted island?

I ignored my snide thoughts.

Last week, I would've scoffed at the mere mention of saving such things, but now…everything was an asset, even if it didn't seem that way.

Conner placed the metal on top of the others and disappeared back into the cabin. He returned with a coarse piece of rope, no doubt used as bracing for packages.

I tucked the leaf-parcel I'd wrapped around my screws into my shorts pocket. I didn't ask what he was doing, giving him free rein to think outside the box.

With intense concentration, he secured the rope around the jagged edges of the metal and tugged.

The entire pile slid toward him.

He looked up. "What do you think? I don't know about you, but the thought of carrying all this stuff to the beach? I don't have the energy."

My shoulders rolled in relief.

Thank God.

I'd been dreading that part. "I know *exactly* what you mean."

His face whitened with concern. "I feel strange. My eyesight's wonky, and I struggle to concentrate. Is that normal?"

"It is when you're severely dehydrated and hungry."

He looked off into the distance. "We need more food."

I nodded, swallowing at the mammoth task of such a thing.

We need to be rescued.

Stepping away from the wreckage, something cracked beneath my flip-flops. I looked down, expecting a snapped twig but something glinted beneath the dirt. "What on earth—"

Conner watched me as I bent over and picked up the item.

My heart instantly hammered. "They're Galloway's."

"He wears glasses?"

Unobservant teenager.

My fingers trembled as I smudged the broken eyewear with my thumb. "Yes. Not that he can wear these anymore." The black frame that'd cradled his celestial blue eyes had been demolished. One lens had shattered but the other had survived intact (although extremely dirty).

"So he's blind without them?" Conner asked. "He seems to see okay."

"It's not like that. He can see. He can do everything a normal person can; it's just slightly out of focus."

Conner wrinkled his nose. "Ugh, that would suck."

"Yep." I turned the glasses over, seeing if there was any way I could mend them. Unfortunately, with the bridge broken and one lens unusable, he'd have to use the glasses as a monocle.

Or…they can be used for something else.

Hope exploded inside.

Hope linked entirely to survival. Hope that could attract attention. Hope that would make our evenings beneath the star-peppered sky more bearable.

Why didn't we think about it before?

"Fire."

"What?" Conner frowned.

"We don't need a lighter. We have something that will work just as well." I smiled at the burning sunshine.

Conner didn't speak as I marched past him, heading in the direction of the camp. "Come on. I want to get back. I want to try before it's too late."

Silently, he followed, pulling his newly fashioned sleigh, leaving the pungent whiff of death behind us.

Chapter Twenty-Two

. . . .

GALLOWAY

. . . . . .

I COULDN'T DO it.

Yes, I was in pain. Yes, I could barely move. Yes, I had no energy what-so-bloody-ever. But Estelle was working, trying, doing her best to keep us alive.

She thought I'd obey and rest while she worked?

Fat chance.

She didn't know me at all.

There was no way in hell I would be a lazy slob while she killed herself doing things *I* should be doing.

My thoughts smashed into one another like a nasty pile-up. I'd sorted the water issue. We had enough to stay breathing—not enough to quench our thirst—but enough.

Shelter wasn't something I could manage at the moment, no matter how much I hated admitting that.

So, that left hunting.

I couldn't swim, so I couldn't fish. I didn't have a net or any way of trawling the shallows for smaller sea life. I didn't have a spear because Estelle had run off with the only knife and I couldn't make a sharp point without one.

My options were limited.

But I couldn't sit there another damn minute.

If I can't hunt. I'll forage. There must be something to eat on this bloody island.

Marching (okay, hopping with my crutch) to my messenger bag, I grabbed the bottom and upended it. A no-longer-working iPod fell out, along with my sketchpad with business logos that I'd been working on, earplugs from working in the lumberyard, my passport, and a packet of chewing gum.

If by the luck of some deity I *did* find something to eat, I needed somewhere to store it. I wouldn't waste my time finding something and having no way to cart it back. Because as ravenous as I was, it wasn't just me I had to feed. There were four mouths, and two of those were entirely reliant on Estelle and me.

Pippa looked up as everything I owned scattered on the beach. "What are you doing?"

Slinging the satchel over my shoulder, I repositioned my crutch and began the arduous, agonising journey from soft sand to water's edge. "Finding some food. Want to come?"

"But Conner told me to stay."

I held my hand out, smiling with invitation. "You'll be with me. I'll look after you."

Her gaze flickered from me to the trees.

Any sign of her fever or infection had disappeared—thankfully, her young genes had been strong enough to fight.

"He'll be a few hours. You don't want to wait that long, do you? You'll get bored."

She kicked the sand with her bare toes. "I guess not."

"Imagine how excited Conner will be if he comes back and we've found dinner. Would you like that?"

Her face brightened. "Dinner? Can I have chicken strips and mashed potatoes?"

My heart sank. If I did manage to find food, the chances of it appealing to the kid's taste buds were zero. Not to mention, we'd have to eat it raw.

Unless I can perform the 'rub two sticks together and create fire' trick.

"I don't think we'll find that, but it will be food and give you energy." I smiled. "Come on. Let's go."

Pippa didn't argue, skipping lightly on her feet to join me. She didn't try to hold my hand, which I was grateful for, as I needed both to manhandle my crutch and not face-plant. I couldn't put any weight on my broken ankle and the action of leaning, hopping, leaning, hopping took far more energy than a simple stroll.

It got easier as we traded the soft sand for hard. I sighed in relief as the tide lapped over my foot with lukewarm water.

Pippa kicked in the shallows, keeping her head down.

The expanse of beach existed before us. I kept going. I had no idea what I was looking for, but hopefully, we'd come across some shallow pools that trapped sea life at low tide.

Over the past few days, I'd studied the ocean and the tide ebbed and flowed by a few metres, silently creeping up the beach before retreating in apology.

The sun beat down and I cursed that I hadn't had the foresight to grab the baseball cap from the pilot's kit. Pippa's long hair protected the back of her neck, but her brow and nose slowly grew red as we continued down the beach.

"What are you looking for?" she finally asked.

Sweat rivered down my back and my needs spread equally between food, water, and throwing myself head first into the ocean to cool down. "Anything we can eat."

Her pretty face scrunched with eagerness. "Like what?"

"Like…" I pointed at the sea. "Like fishes or lobsters or crabs or anything really."

I'm not good at this educational stuff.

"Crabs? I saw one that lived in a shell in my friend's house. She had a tank with a bunch of them." She twirled her fingers. "I don't remember what it was called, though."

That one I do know.

"A hermit crab."

"Yes." Her hair bounced as she nodded. "Where do other crabs live if they don't have a shell?"

I stopped, brushing my hair from my forehead and cursing the thickening beard on my chin. A few days' stubble itched like crazy. I hadn't packed a razor in my hand luggage for security reasons and craved a blade to get rid of the growth.

"They hide under rocks and sometimes bury themselves in the sand." Looking at our feet, I used the end of my crutch to dig into the wet granules to demonstrate. Maybe, I'd get lucky and uncover a few edible critters. However, the thought of eating the liquid meat with no way to cook them wasn't appealing—no matter how hungry I was.

Pippa dropped to her haunches as I swirled my crutch and made a hole that immediately filled with seawater. "I don't see one."

"No, they're very sneaky. They probably knew we were coming and tunnelled under us."

Pippa giggled, poking the hole.

I kept my crutch away from her petite fingers.

Air bubbles popped in the watery depths. I peered closer, just in case a crab did appear, but nothing scurried to the top.

Damn.

Pippa's fingers disappeared into the sand, her tongue sticking out. "I think I feel something."

Just debris or driftwood.

I had no hope it would be anything worthwhile, but I praised the girl as if she'd found the Titanic. "Really? Awesome. Can you pull it out and show me?"

Her face tightened with determination. Her second hand disappeared in the hole. Her toes planted and she rocked backward, using her inertia to free whatever she'd grabbed hold of.

She fell backward with a splat, holding up her prize. "Here."

Holy crap.

Adrenaline drenched my system as I gently accepted the nondescript shell of a clam.

A clam!

"Wow, great find, Pippi."

She giggled. "That's not my name."

I waggled my eyebrow. "It is now. Pippi Longstocking. Did you ever watch that show?"

She shook her head.

"Neither did I, but a girl I once knew did. She braided her hair with wire and made pigtails stick out the side of her head."

"Eww." Pippa wrinkled her nose. "If you can call me that, then I want to call you something."

"You don't like my name?"

She paused. "It's long."

"All right." I tapped my fingers against my lip. "Well, you choose. Whatever you want."

Seconds switched to a full minute while intense deliberation tightened her face. "G."

"G?"

She nodded. "G."

I'd had a few abbreviations of my name growing up. Gal, Gallo, Way-wasted. But never G.

I kinda like it.

I shrugged. "G, it is."

"Good." She sniffed with authority as if my identity had just been switched by the queen herself. Then, as if the topic completely uninterested her anymore, her attention fell to the mollusc in my hand. "Can we eat it?"

The very mention of eating made caveman urges rise and demand I smash the innocent creature apart and suck its meat straight away.

If I had the damn Swiss Army knife, I could get into it.

I looked at my crutch. I could smash it open…but then it would be covered in sand. As much as my body demanded to feed, I wouldn't waste it. Not if it was the only one we found.

"Yes. We can. But before we do…let's see if we can find some more, yeah?"

She pouted. "But I want to eat it now."

"Me, too. But we can't forget about your brother or Estelle, can we? That wouldn't be fair."

Her stomach growled, a wildness entering her gaze. She couldn't tear her eyes away from the clam, but slowly, she switched from feral monster to empathetic girl. "I guess."

Hopping forward, I dug another hole with my crutch. "I'll dig and you search, okay? I can't bend down."

Seeing as she was soaking from landing on her butt, she crawled on all fours to the new hole and stuck her hands in it.

I didn't breathe as she foraged.

A few moments later, she squealed with delight. Yanking her hands up, she presented another clam.

If I could've moved, I would've grabbed her and danced around like a crazy idiot. Instead, all I could do was pat her head and swallow back my happiness. "Good work, Pippi."

She grinned. "One for me, one for Conner. We need one for you and Stel."

"Stel?"

"Yes, she told me I can call her that."

I hated the jealousy that a little girl was given a nickname to use when I'd kissed Estelle, wanted her, and been kept at arm's length.

I had nothing to offer her.

But now…Pippa and I had found hope.

I'll show her that I'm better than what I portray.

Looking at the expanse of beach, I murmured, "Come on, Pippi, let's get dinner."

....

Smoke.

Something's on fire.

My hobbling became a painful mismatch of shuffle-hops. "Pippa, run ahead. Make sure the camp is in one piece."

"Conner!" She took off, her entire body saturated from clam digging.

We weren't far from home, but the fact I couldn't run drove me insane!

Pippa would beat me but what the hell could she do if something *was* on fire?

We'll lose everything.

Everything we couldn't afford to lose.

I followed as fast as I could. The messenger bag dripped down my thigh from excreted seawater from the clams.

Nausea from moving too quickly mingled with starvation as I cut across the soft sand.

Instead of stumbling onto a scene of carnage where the sun had somehow incinerated our belongings just for the hell of it, I slammed to a halt as Conner grabbed Pippa in his arms and danced with her.

Estelle laughed, waving a palm frond with fiery ends.

"What the *hell* is going on?"

I couldn't decide if I was impressed, grateful, or pissed off that, once again, Estelle had made me look like an idiot. She'd conjured fire. She'd created heat and cooking facilities and—

Goddammit, who am I kidding?

I wasn't falling for this woman. I was absolutely bloody besotted.

Where had she come from and how the hell did I make her mine?

Conner clapped his hands, his face rosy and flushed. "Fire! We made fire!"

For a second, I ignored the massive implications of such a marvel and peered at Estelle.

Had she obeyed me? Had she avoided going near the dead? However, nothing haunted her gaze or tainted her voice. Her eyes glittered as she spun like a dancer, holding her burning frond aloft. "We did it! We created fire!"

"I can see that." My gaze leapt to the sleigh-like contraption by our belongings. Not only had they succeeded in something wondrous, but they'd also carted back items that would extend our likelihood of survival.

I wasn't besotted; I was infatuated, intoxicated, completely and utterly blown away by how incredible this island-wrecked woman was.

My heart pumped like an out-of-control locomotive complete with coal smoke. I couldn't take my eyes off her as Estelle tossed the burning plant into the fire and wiped the back of her hand on her cheek, spreading soot over her skin. "You're back. We were worried."

Conner bounced up and down. "Fire. Fire. *Fire!*"

I fought my smile. I didn't know why. I was just as excited as he was. But somehow, I felt excluded. Like I'd never be worthy of Estelle because she had no need for me when I had desperate need for her.

Stop being such an idiot.

Estelle made her way to me, pulling something from her

pocket. The tanning skin of her arms and face clutched me around the throat.

Hell, she's beautiful.

And smart. And brave. And strong. And so goddamn selfless.

"Here, I found something that belongs to you."

"Oh?"

She took my hand. My skin charred beneath hers, zinging with attraction and desire. She sucked in a breath but didn't look up, avoiding the sudden intensity between us. Uncurling my fingers, she placed half of my glasses into my palm.

There goes my ability to see clearly on this island.

I chuckled to hide my disappointment. "They didn't survive the crash too well."

She cringed. "I'm sorry. They're not useful to you anymore, but they're by far our most precious item."

I looked over her head at the crackling, cheery blaze. "You used them to make that."

"Yep." A smile stretched her face. "It took a few goes but Conner helped. The sun truly is a wondrous thing."

I had no response. Just awe. Awe and lust and amazement and…I could go on and bloody on.

Her gaze fell to my bag. "What did you guys get up to?" She glanced over her shoulder. "And why is Pippa soaking wet?"

"Uh, I have a good reason for that." Unhooking the bag from my shoulder, I passed it to her. "It so happens your fire attempt couldn't have come at the more perfect time." My heart warmed as she took the weight of the heavy bag with surprise. "Otherwise, we would've been eating these raw, and I can't imagine that would be nice."

Her mouth fell open as she lifted the flap. "Oh, my God." Without warning, tears burst from her eyes and she dropped the bag. Leaping toward me, her arms slung over my shoulders and her lips graced my stubbled cheek. "*Thank you.* Thank you, thank you, thank you."

Shit.

My arms snapped around her. My balance teetered in her sudden embrace but *nothing* would make me let go of her. I buried my face in her hair, inhaling the faint scent of salt and sunshine and castaway. There was no hint of shampoo or perfumed products anymore.

I was glad about that.

This way, I got to smell the real Estelle, and she smelled goddamn gorgeous.

My arms banded tighter.

She gasped as my nuzzling turned to kissing. I knew I shouldn't but she'd just thanked me as if I'd changed her life. She'd made me feel so damn good when *she* was the one who'd created a miracle. The fact that she didn't resent me. That she accepted me, limp and all. That she didn't try to pry into my unsavoury background. That she liked me for *me* even in our imperfect circumstances.

I could never repay her for that.

That kindness.

That generosity.

That faith.

I kissed her collarbone, breathing softly with restrained need. "You're amazing."

She shuddered as I licked her ear lobe. Salt exploded on my tongue, snarling my stomach for more, confusing itself on food it could eat and passion it could only torment with.

It took a lot of effort but I managed to let her go. My cock had thickened and I subtly placed my free hand in front of my board-shorts. "What do you say we cook these babies and eat?"

Her smile was pure bliss. "I say that's the best plan I've ever heard."

"I've got a better plan—after food, of course."

Her eyes hooded. "Oh?"

"I can't tell you."

"Why not?"

"Because my plan isn't exactly approved by you." Mindful of being watched by Pippa and Conner, I murmured, "It includes finishing what we started. The last time we kissed, I didn't want to stop, and you had no intention of letting me continue."

Her breath picked up. "You want to kiss me?"

My stomach clenched. "More than anything."

"More than clams for dinner and fresh water from your invention?"

"More than lobster tails dripping in butter."

She moaned dramatically. "Well, I don't know. That's a hard choice. I do really love lobster."

I growled, playing along. Knowing we could finally have a decent feed put all of us in a happier mood. "What if I promised you'd like me better than lobster?"

"That's a big boast to make."

"I never break my promises."

"Is that a challenge?"

I leaned closer, our noses almost touching. "Do you want it to be?"

"A challenge of letting you kiss me?"

I shook my head. "No, a challenge of making you fall in love with me."

Chapter Twenty-Three

••

E S T E L L E

••••••

A door closes, a window opens.
A window closes, a car arrives.
A car stops, a plane flies.
A plane lands, a helicopter soars.
A helicopter crashes, life ends.
Life ends, a new world begins.
A new world ends, a person evolves.
A person evolves and finds

~~*fear*~~
~~*terror*~~
~~*hunger*~~
~~*questions*~~
~~*desperation*~~
~~*struggle and strife and sadness*~~
true happiness.

Taken from the notepad of E.E.

•••

MY SKIN BURNED.

Not from too much sun or getting too close to the fire.

But from *him*.

I burned.

Everywhere.

Galloway's lips still tormented my flesh, even though minutes had passed since he'd kissed my neck, my collarbone…my ear.

I was starving.

For both food and him.

I was confused.

For both help and privacy.

I was hurting.

For both rescue and desire.

Two extremes.

Both as strong as the other.

"No, a challenge of making you fall in love with me."

Galloway's voice repeated over and over, spindling my heart until it became a blur.

Who felt like this? Who willingly let sex fill their mind when they'd been helicopter-wrecked with no way of being free?

Me, apparently.

I'd become someone I didn't like. Someone who let her needs control her rather than common sense.

My stomach growled, taking centre stage with rumbling cymbals.

At least, I had another need. One more acceptable in our current condition.

Hunger.

I couldn't stop looking at the messenger bag full of delicious clams. My body demanded I fall to my knees, crack open a shell, and slurp out the raw meat that very second.

But no matter how it pressured me, the other type of starving never let me go.

The sexual type.

A desperation that had no business here. I had to focus on staying alive. How was my body even capable of wasting energy on such silly things? Why did my heart torture itself whenever Galloway looked at me? And why, when faced with a bag full of dinner or a man who promised he'd make me fall in love with him, did I want him more than food?

He made me glow.

His eyes held rescue and freedom and safety, placing me on a pedestal I had no right to occupy.

He looks at me as if he's unworthy.

I trembled as my thoughts careened. Who was he? What was his story? Why did he remind me of a fallen seed: closed off and unapproachable on the outside but bursting with the most beautiful ready-to-bloom oak tree on the inside?

Stop it, Estelle. This isn't scripture for your notebook. This isn't a song. This is real life. Pay attention and survive it!

Galloway moved away, a sad smile on his lips. Sad? Why was he sad? He'd just admitted he was up to the challenge of making me *fall in love with him.*

Here.

On this island.

He spoke of finding love amongst palm trees and empty beaches.

So why did the frown never leave his forehead? Why did the darkness never leave his eyes?

Stop it!

"So…how did you create this cheery blaze?" Galloway asked, slapping Conner on the back as he hobbled past. His eyes locked onto the salvaged fuselage, plans already forming on his face like blueprints.

Conner winked, exuding happiness. And he should be happy. We had water to drink, food to eat, and fire to cook with.

This was a trifecta of happiness.

"With your glasses, geek boy." He ducked as Galloway ruffled his hair.

"What did you just call me?"

"Geek boy. And we didn't have a lighter, so your glasses had to do."

"So my glasses were a consolation prize."

"What would've been first place?" Conner asked.

"A lighter. But I'm not a smoker."

I drifted forward, nabbing Pippa as she beelined for the clams. Her eyes seemed too big for her face, hungry hungry hungry.

I cracked a cynical grin. "Funny how a habit that would've killed you in the future might've saved us today."

Galloway smiled. "You have a point." We shared another heated look.

He watched me as if I were some mystical creature, not a girl who had no idea what she was doing. Everything I'd achieved so far was from pure luck and determination—not skill.

I hugged Pippa, using her as my shield. "We should eat."

"Yes. Food." Pippa squirmed out of my arms, plucking two clams and bashing them together.

I glanced at our dwindling woodpile. Now that we'd created the fire, we had to keep it fed.

Ourselves, too.

I pinched the clams from Pippa's eager fingers. "You can't eat them raw, Pip."

Pippa strained to take them back. "They're mine. I found them first." Her angry eyes met Galloway's. "I did, didn't I, G? Tell her. I want them."

My head whipped up to stare at Galloway. "G?" My heart flurried. "You've already earned a nickname?"

He half-smiled. "Not gonna complain. Besides, I gave her one first."

Something warm spread across my insides as Galloway smirked at the little girl. "Want to tell them what it is or shall I?"

"No!" Pippa shouted; a mixture of pleasure at being singled out and mock-annoyance for sharing her secret. "Only you can call me it." Her eyes flashed to her brother. "Co will only ruin it."

"Will not." Conner shook his head.

"Will, too."

Galloway gruffed, "Fine. Pippa's nickname is mine and mine alone."

The girl beamed as if she'd been given every toy she'd ever wanted.

The warmth inside me spread into hot heat.

He'd given Pippa something so precious. He'd taken her mind off the loneliness of being an orphan and the fear of being stranded.

He continually surprised me. One moment he seemed as if he couldn't stand the children. The next he acted as the perfect father and friend.

Galloway hopped up the beach and awkwardly grabbed the dented piece of fuselage that resembled a witch's hat. "Perfect."

I moved closer, giving up at preventing Pippa from rummaging in the clam bag. "Perfect for what?"

His face pinched in pain as he hobbled back and placed the piece of metal directly into the fire. The burning wood separated for him as he used his crutch to tap the metal into position, half in the fire, half on top of it.

"What are you doing?"

Instead of answering me, Galloway gave orders, "Conner, go grab some seawater. Use the empty bottles from your dad's backpack."

Conner flinched at the reminder of his dead parent but charged off with the three bottles in his arms. He came back just as quickly, his forearms and legs dripping wet. "Now what?"

"Fill up the pot, of course."

A pot.

God, I'm an idiot.

How else did I think we'd cook the clams? "You're a genius."

Galloway cringed. "No. I'm not."

"You are. Here I was thinking of opening the shells and spearing them onto sticks."

"That way would work, too."

"Your way is much better."

He scoffed but didn't reply; his eyes locked on the water-filled metal. "We'll wait for it to boil then put the clams in. It would be better with fresh water, and I dread to think how salty they'll be, but beggars can't be choosers."

Warnings of raw shellfish and food poisoning ran through my mind. "How do we know we can eat these?"

"They're fresh so that shouldn't be a problem." Galloway's forehead furrowed. "My plan was to boil them like mussels and only eat the ones that open."

"Sounds reasonable."

"Once it starts to boil, toss them in. Conner and I will be back." Galloway made his way laboriously to the treeline.

Nerves fluttered. "Wait. Where are you going?"

Conner chased after him. "Yeah, where are we going? I'm starving. I'm going to pass out if I don't eat something soon."

Galloway bent over and picked up a piece of fuselage. "You'll see. I need your help." Passing the piece to Conner, he grabbed another and entered the forest.

I let them go.

I didn't really have a choice but curiosity niggled. It wasn't like me to want to be with someone. Normally, if a person left, I was glad. I willingly let them go as it meant I could regroup and find peace that I couldn't find in company.

But Galloway was different.

The moment he'd disappeared, I wanted him to return. I felt better when he was around. More alive. More certain. More awake to every sensation.

My tummy clenched as I relived the kiss we'd shared.

His challenge of making me fall in love with him might not be as big a feat as he thought.

And that terrified me.

Pippa tugged my hand. "The water is bubbling."

Pushing Galloway from my mind, I beamed. "Excellent. Want to help me put the clams in?"

She bit her lip, nodding with utmost seriousness.

"Be careful, it's very hot." I was wrong to let a child tend to an open fire with boiling water. But this wasn't an ordinary kitchen in an ordinary world. This was survival, and everyone had to grow up fast.

Together, we ladled handfuls of the white and orange shells into the boiling water. A few hot splashes singed my knuckles and my legs burned from being so close to the flames.

A strange banging came from the forest, over and over.

What the hell are they doing?

Once the last of Galloway's haul was tucked nicely in the water, I sat on my haunches and high-fived Pippa. "Great job."

She grinned.

"Did you really find all of those?"

She grinned wider. "Yep."

"All forty-two of them?"

"Yep!"

I exaggerated my awe. "Wow, that's amazing!"

She swivelled her foot in the sand with sudden shyness. "Will it be enough?" Worry etched her young skin. "I'm so hungry. I want them all."

"It will be enough for tonight. But tomorrow, we can all go and find lots more. How about that?"

Along with an armful of coconuts so we have additional liquid.

She pondered for a moment. "Can I find them with G?"

G.

My heart turned into a tambourine, shivering with a happy tune. "Of course. We'll team up. You and G against Conner and me. We'll have a race."

"I'll win."

"Oh, I have no doubt." I tickled her tiny chest. "You're the wonder gatherer. Clam extraordinaire."

She giggled.

"Don't tell her that." Conner appeared with the two pieces of fuselage. They were almost as big as him. How he managed to cart them when running on dregs of energy and protecting his broken wrist, I didn't know. "It will only go to her head."

Pippa stuck out her tongue. "You'll see. I'll win. I'll find all the clams and you won't have any."

Conner blew a kiss at his temperamental sister. "But you'll share with me, right?"

She crossed her arms. "Nope."

"Oh, come on, Pip. You have to." He waggled his eyebrows. "You love me. You wouldn't let me starve, would you?"

Galloway chuckled, following Conner with a lot less grace than he left with. His forehead glistened with sweat, his back rolled, and he hopped with a wince.

What the hell had he been doing?

Galloway muttered, "She won't let you starve. Will you, Pippi?"

"Hey. You said you wouldn't tell!" Pippa's eyes glowed with indignation.

Galloway didn't look well as he forced himself to act shocked and contrite. "Whoops, sorry. Oh well, your secret is out. But it's safe with Estelle and Conner. Isn't it, guys?"

We all nodded. "Of course. Cross our hearts."

Conner and I laughed as we both drew a cross on our chests at the same time.

Galloway attempted to chuckle but everything about him echoed agony. He looked worse than when I'd found him leaning against the palm tree with his broken ankle swollen and useless.

Leaving my post by the boiling clams, I moved toward him. "Are you okay?"

He didn't make eye contact. "I'm fine."

"Oh, my God." I snagged his free hand. "You're bleeding." Cuts marked his strong fingers. A nasty gash split his palm. "What were you doing?"

"Making something."

"I doubt it was important enough to kill yourself over." I counted five cuts on his left hand alone. "We'll have to look after these."

"Later. Let me go, woman."

I had no choice but to follow him to the plastic-wrapped branches where Conner had dug out a small trough in the sand directly below the funnel. The plastic was tight with collected water.

My mouth begged at the thought of a glass of ice-cold H20

Galloway nodded in approval. "Great, now put the catchment down."

Conner did as he was told, wedging the fuselage into position.

Once it was in place, I understood what they'd been doing. What the rhythmic banging had been. "You made that?"

Conner looked up. "Yep. Well, Galloway did."

"How?"

"With a rock and a lot of elbow grease." Galloway leaned heavily on his crutch. "Do the other one, Conner."

Conner climbed to his feet and repeated the process, digging a hole to keep the trough upright and wedging the metal into position beneath the burgeoning funnel. The metal had transformed into a pockmarked container with sloping sides and a big enough surface area to hold litres of water. Our own personal reservoir.

Is it safe to drink out of metal from an aircraft?

Worry tainted my joy. Who knew what the metal was coated with or what nasty chemicals would seep into our water supply.

But like Galloway previously said, 'beggars can't be choosers.' It was this or no water or cooking facilities.

I choose this.

Regardless of the consequences.

Once secure, Conner stood and Galloway held out his hand to me. "Swiss Army knife, please."

I pulled the lifesaving tool from my short's pocket. Pressing it into his palm, I suffered another electrical jolt as his fingers brushed mine.

He smiled (more like grimaced) in thanks and hopped toward the plastic. He cursed under his breath.

I stepped forward. "What's up?"

He spun the knife in his grip. "To extract the water, I either have to unwrap the tree which would potentially lose a lot of liquid or cut the funnel and pour out the gathered supply. The only problem is once it's cut, the water won't gather as there'll be an air gap."

My mind raced with solutions.

I yanked off my second-to-last hair-tie from around my wrist. "Can you secure it with this?" I looked at the metal container below. "It doesn't have to be strictly water tight, right? The droplets that escape will be caught."

I didn't mention the fact that the sun would dry up any liquid almost as fast as they dripped. Now was not the time.

Galloway said, "You're right."

"Great." I passed the tie to him. "All yours."

He eyed my tangled blonde hair. "Why haven't you been putting your hair up? Aren't you hot?"

My skin danced beneath his gaze, loving the way he studied me and terribly self-conscious, too. I had no makeup on. No beautification of any kind. He saw me at my worst—my sun-bleached, windswept, island-crashed worst.

Oh well, he can't see all that well.

Perhaps, he'd missed the salt-tightness of my skin or the shininess of greasy hair.

What an awful thing to think.

It must be horrid not being able to see with clarity. I wished he *could* see me. See the honest to God's truth of who I was so there was no denying he'd accepted me for *me* and not some hazy, unfocused version of what he wanted to see.

I couldn't hold his gaze anymore. "My hair is the only sunscreen I have for my shoulders and neck. I'm hot, but at least I'm not as badly burned as I would be if I tied it up."

Having earned his answer, he turned away and poised the blade over the end of the funnel. I moved closer, taking his crutch as he balanced and pinched the plastic.

With utmost care, Galloway nicked the bottom. Instantly, a stream of collected water poured into the awaiting metal below. A few droplets splashed onto the sand, absorbing instantly, but the majority made the most satisfying splash.

"Crap, I need a drink." Conner fell to his knees. "One taste. Please?"

Galloway growled, "Grab the bottles and fill them up. We can't be stupid with the small amount we have."

Conner obeyed instantly. Galloway hadn't been angry, but he did command a certain kind of reverence.

While Conner carefully held the empty bottles in the trough, filling them one by one, Galloway and I moved to the poncho collection.

With bleeding hands, Galloway nicked the funnel, and once again my heart leapt at the delicious flowing water. It took every willpower not to face-plant and slurp up every drop.

Galloway secured the funnel with my hair-tie and swiped sweat off his forehead. The sun had just set, leaving us in twilight. "Well, that's that."

Pippa darted over as Conner screwed the caps on the bottles. Yesterday, they'd been empty, and I'd been at a complete loss how we'd ever refill them. Now, they held life-giving liquid.

I would forever be grateful to Galloway for giving us that precious reprieve.

We weren't dying anymore.

We would survive long enough for rescue to find us.

Because of him.

He'd created water from nothing and found food from nowhere.

Compared to what I'd contributed, that was *everything*.

Conner and Pippa immediately shared a bottle, swigging mouthfuls, groaning with contentment.

Galloway took the other full one and passed it to me. I shook my head, forcing it back to him. "No, you hurt yourself making this possible. Please, I insist."

He looked as if he'd argue, so I took matters out of his control. Snatching the bottle, I unscrewed it and held it to his lips. His eyes widened as he watched me with blazing awareness. Slowly, his lips parted and allowed me to tip the bottle so water cascaded into his mouth.

Something hot and fierce sprang between us.

Something so intimately sexual about feeding another.

Something so raw and primal.

My core melted at the thought of replacing the bottle with my lips and kiss kiss kissing him. Kiss him so hard. Kiss him so gratefully. Kiss him just for the sake of being alive and being able to kiss him.

His hand came up to curl over mine, steadily draining half the bottle before tugging and guiding the rim to my mouth. Completely bewitched by him, I opened and never looked away as he tipped my share down my throat.

I moaned.

How could I not?

The water was too warm, slightly plasticy, and held a faint taste of evergreen but it was the best, most delicious water I'd ever had. And the fact that the most courageous, mercurial, complex man had sourced and fed me every drop made my heart sing with possibility.

I didn't know who ended the spell, but the bottle switched from full to empty and we were down to one.

I could've drunk ten more.

But for now, it would have to do. The throbbing headache from lack of hydration faded a little as my body greedily accepted its gift.

I licked my bottom lip, savouring the final taste. "Are we ready for dinner?"

The children fell dramatically in the sand, holding their grumbling stomachs. "Yes! Feed us."

I laughed.

Galloway flinched as he inspected his hands.

I'll take care of him after we've eaten.

Together, we headed back to the pot of cooked clams.

As the sun set on our third day, I vowed that tomorrow would be better because today was better than yesterday and this week was somehow better than the last—even though it was so incredibly different.

Our lives had changed so much, but we'd found we could survive it.

"You did a really good thing today," I whispered as Galloway tore open the shell of a steaming clam and slipped it into his mouth.

The children devoured theirs. The food hit my stomach, spreading its happy welcome through tired, starving muscles, and little by little, smile by smile we left the shadow of death.

He looked at me but didn't speak. But his gaze said a thousand things.

We *did a really good thing.*

We can do this.
Together.

Chapter Twenty-Four

GALLOWAY

THE SMELL WAS what killed me.

The rotting, sickening stench.

My hands ached from using a rock to hammer the fuselage, the cuts on my fingers stung, and my ankle...crap, my ankle felt ten times worse.

All I wanted to do was sleep.

To rest.

To heal.

The clams had scratched the intolerable itch for food and the third shared water bottle had tempered my thirst for a time.

But I'd meant what I said about Estelle avoiding the dead. I didn't want her or the children going anywhere near them. It was bad enough Conner and Pippa had seen their parents after the crash.

It would be million times worse if they saw them now.

I stood over Akin.

His neck had broken. The sudden arrival had sent him smashing through the cockpit windscreen. A spider crawled from his nose and his black hair was matted with dried blood.

Christ.

The moon barely made it through the canopy. There were no rainclouds, no hint of a storm. Fiji was supposed to be tropical, but for days, we'd had no rain.

Luckily, my imperfect eyesight wasn't too much of a hindrance. All I needed to see was the silhouettes of trees and enough illumination to dig three graves before the sun came up.

I groaned under my breath.

How?

How exactly are you going to do that? You're hurt beyond hell. You can't bend. You can't dig.

As a guy (the only guy older than thirteen), I had to man up and protect the others. But what was the use in wanting to do what was necessary when my body point blank said to get screwed?

I took a deep breath, trying to calm down. Standing with a dead body gave me the damn creeps.

Get it together. You need to work fast.

I didn't know the time. Probably not too late as we'd fallen drowsy after our meal and retired. For the first time, we settled into our dug-out leaf-lined beds and were warm thanks to the fire.

Perhaps, I'll have to wait until I'm healed.

I rolled my eyes. Eight weeks minimum before I had full use of my ankle and foot again and that was only if they healed correctly. I couldn't wait eight weeks. The bodies would stink out the entire island by then.

We might be found before that happens.

We had a fire now. A way to signal. We had enough resources (hopefully) to keep us alive until that day.

But as much as I wanted to believe that in eight weeks I'd be somewhere where indoor plumbing and supermarkets reigned, I didn't hold my breath.

I'd stopped believing in miracles unless I had the power to grant them. And I had no power to guarantee a rescue.

Not until I'm well enough to build a raft.

The only option I had was to suck it up and get it over with.

Pain or no pain.

Hobbling, I moved closer to Akin. His skin was purple-bloated with congealed discoloration. I gagged as I grabbed his wrist and hauled him from the helicopter windshield.

The squelch of his body sent repugnant disgust rippling down my spine.

I had to let go.

I had to clamp a hand over my mouth.

I had to stop this.

I can't stop.

Gritting my teeth, I picked up the smaller piece of fuselage Estelle had salvaged and looked for a clearing to dig.

How the hell are you going to do this?

Ask the corpse to kindly bury itself?

Goddamn tears sprang to my eyes. In the days since we'd crashed, my temper shielded me from the helplessness inside. But here, in the middle of the night, in the middle of a forest, in the middle of nowhere, I couldn't hold it back anymore.

I needed help. But was too bloody stubborn to ask for it.

I sniffed, pinching the bridge of my nose.

Do. Not. Dare. Cry.

My eyes burned but I managed to shove aside my need for someone, *anyone*, to tell me things would work out and keep it together.

I bent over to grab Akin's wrist.

"Stop."

My torso twisted toward the soft command. My leg screamed at the extra weight I placed on it.

Then anger blocked everything out but *her*.

Estelle.

The woman who'd blatantly disobeyed me.

"What the hell do you think you're doing?" I spun around, doing my best to shield her from the body.

Her gaze zeroed in on him anyway, her face contorting. "You were gone when I woke up."

"That was the plan."

"You can't do this on your own."

"Watch me."

"That's the thing. I don't want to watch you. I want to *help* you." Drifting closer, the moonlight cast her blonde hair into platinum. "Don't ask me to walk away. Not when I just saw—"

My blood stopped flowing. "Saw what?"

She swallowed. "Saw how much you're hurting…inside as well as out."

I turned my back on her. "You didn't see anything. I'm fine."

She didn't say a word. My scalp prickled from her presence.

Straightening, I growled, "Go away, Estelle."

"No."

"Do it. Before I get pissed."

"You're already pissed."

My growl became a snarl. "Estelle…goddammit."

Let me shield you from this. Let me take the horror so you don't have nightmares.

I already suffered bad dreams from what I'd done. This was nothing compared to those.

She came closer, placing her hand on my shoulder. It could've been condescending but the way her eyes filled with understanding turned it into a caress. "Listen to me. I'm not leaving. You can swear and curse but the fact is, you can't make me leave."

My hands curled. "I could with force."

"You could." Her fingers massaged my flesh, granting comfort and relief to crash-bruised muscles. "But you won't. Because as much as you don't want to admit it, you need me. You can't do this on your own, and I don't expect you to."

She gave me the sweetest smile. "Please...let me help."

I had two choices.

One, continue to waste night hours and my dwindling energy on forbidding her. Or two, accept that I did need help and trust she had what it took.

She knew my answer before I spoke. Knew in the way my shoulders slumped, my eyes closed, every ounce of anger drained into the dirt.

"Thank you, Galloway."

My eyes snapped up. "Never thank me for letting you do this. *Never*, do you hear me? This is a thankless task and shouldn't be done by anyone, let alone you."

She touched my hand wrapped around my crutch. "Nothing is thankless. No matter what it is. Someone always appreciates it."

"That's not true."

"It is." Her voice was a soft melody. "A rubbish collector, for example. A thankless task for him. Dirty, smelly, a stigma attached to his profession. But every bin he collects, every removal he does, a house owner is grateful. They might not consciously thank him, but they *are* thankful."

I huffed. "They're alive to appreciate it. Big difference in this case."

"How so? Conner and Pippa aren't aware of what you're doing, but they're grateful regardless. You're saving them heartache and pain. It's best that they don't know because their thanks is worth a thousand more because you did the right thing."

I couldn't win with her. She was so wise, so calm. The exact opposite of who I was. Was it possible to develop such intense feelings for someone so quickly? Was it our situation—stuck on an island and all alone?

Either way, I never wanted to be apart from her.

I reluctantly gave in to her reasoning. "I accept what you're saying but you got something wrong."

"Oh?"

"You said me. What *I'm* doing." My heart beat faster. "You mean us. What *we're* doing."

Her smile glowed like the moon. "I'm glad you've come around. Now...let's get started."

....

I swayed on the beach, holding my crutch with all my strength because if I didn't, I'd splat head-first into the sand. Estelle stood beside me, our skin on fire with proximity but not touching.

We didn't say a word as the tide slowly crept higher the brighter the sky became.

Sweat had drenched and dried on my skin. Estelle's had done the same. Her hairline was damp, her cheeks flushed, her movements achy and overused. She'd done so much. I would never be able to repay her.

Her suggestion had saved me work I couldn't have accomplished on my own, and together, we'd ensured the island was dead free and the children would never see what a child should never see.

Amelia and Duncan Evermore were almost gone. We couldn't give them the send-off they deserved, but they would always be remembered.

Estelle's head suddenly landed on my shoulder. Her blonde hair draped over my back, tickling my bicep and forearm. "They're at peace."

I didn't respond.

The three bodies in front of us lay on their backs, their hands tied together in prayer, pebbles placed on their vacant eyes, and rocks inserted into their clothing.

We'd taken anything that might be of use. A pen engraved with Duncan's initials for Conner, a gold tennis bracelet from Amelia for Pippa. We removed the wedding rings and decided to use them as a memorial. We'd already painstakingly carved their names on a piece of driftwood and attached two plaited pieces of flax to hold the rings.

Akin lay beside the Evermores, together but apart. Would his family be searching for him? Would they know how to find us? Or had any hope of being found died the moment we stepped aboard a helicopter without a working Emergency Locator Transmitter?

Slowly, dawn crept closer as did the tide. The bodies went from being lapped gently to slowly consumed, their legs vanishing beneath the surface, followed by their chests and faces.

It had been Estelle's idea to use the ocean.

The island soil was rich and fairly simple to dig, but tree roots and obstacles didn't make it easy. After a few minutes of trying, Estelle had asked me to trust her, and together, we found Amelia and Duncan and respectfully, painfully, so, so slowly dragged them to the opposite side of the island.

Our pace had been a gait between a hobble and a lurch, careful not to damage the dead any more than they were. The causes of death had been easier to see the lighter the sky became. Duncan had perished from a broken neck like Akin, and Amelia had bled out from a piece of metal cutting her carotid artery.

The beach on this side was rockier than on ours. A steeper slope to the water with sparse undergrowth. By weighting the bodies down, they would sink and be dragged along the ocean floor as the tide took them farther out to sea.

There was a risk they would eventually make their way to our side of the island. However, the teeming sea life would help with that. Crabs and fishes, sharks and crustaceans, the creatures would live another day by the grace of one of our dead.

I wanted so much to sit. To lie down. To close my eyes and slip into sleep with Estelle in my arms.

But we'd made an unspoken agreement to be there until the end.

So we stood as the night gave up its cloak of black and the sea slowly devoured the dead. When we could no longer see them through the water's surface, Estelle raised her head from my shoulder.

Her voice was haunting in the dawn. "Rest in peace knowing we'll look after your children. We'll love them. Care for them. Make sure they grow and eventually find rescue off this island. Akin, we promise to let your family know your final resting place. Goodbye."

Silence fell.

Should I say something?

But what?

I didn't know the first thing about eulogies. I hadn't given one at my mother's funeral because I hadn't attended. I didn't know how to say goodbye.

Estelle saved me from the task by turning and clambering up the beach. She turned to look back. "Are you coming?"

Every part of me shook but I nodded. Slowly, I hauled myself up the sand, crutch and hop, crutch and hop. One lumbering step at a time, following the woman who made me a better person just by smiling at me.

Together, we returned to our furnitureless home.

Together, we stripped off our clothes and waded into the fresh ocean and washed away the remnants of the night—washed away the smell, the memories, our old life.

Together, we looked forward to the future.

Chapter Twenty-Five

ESTELLE

~~I'll die on this island.~~
I'll survive on this island.
~~I'm afraid.~~
I'm no longer afraid.
~~I'm alone.~~
I've found someone worth fighting for.
Taken from the notepad of E.E.

...

DAY FOUR

THE CHILDREN KNEW.

After our swim, Galloway and I set up the driftwood memorial at the base of our umbrella tree. The pen and bracelet taken from their parents were placed by their respective heads for when they woke, and the wedding rings glinted in the sunshine, clinking together in the muggy breeze.

When the children woke, their melancholy blanketed the campsite. They didn't speak, merely hugged their tokens and sat in vigil to say goodbye.

No one mentioned what we'd done. An unspoken bond that their parents were gone and all that mattered was their memory.

The day followed much like the last.

Water collected over the course of the day, the leaves graciously donating liquid the hotter the sun became. After a brief nap in the shade, Galloway mentioned he would go clam gathering. But when he went to stand, he couldn't.

He'd done as much as he could.

His body had reached an impasse.

The self-hatred and curses he layered upon himself broke my heart. He needed to be kinder to his body and mind if he was ever to find true happiness.

I brought him water and kissed his brow with sweet sincerity. He held my hand, whispered his thumb over my knuckles, and looked at me as if I was an angel, begging for salvation.

I wanted to fall into his eyes and forget. I wanted to curl in his arms and remind him that he wasn't alone.

But there was too much to do. Too many tasks to complete in order to stay alive.

Leaving him to heal, I organised the day even though I hurt all over. My ribs hadn't let up their torture and my back ached from dragging corpses all night. I never, ever, *ever* wanted to do something like that again.

Galloway was right.

Some things, you should never have to do.

No one had the energy to arrange S.O.S out of logs and fuselage; we subconsciously agreed the fire would be our signal.

And as much as we wanted to rest...we couldn't.

If we didn't forage, we didn't eat. And I was more able than Galloway was today. Tomorrow, I might have to lean on him. I didn't mind sharing duties. If only he could understand that.

Pippa and Conner came with me when I announced a scavenging trip. Together, we found twice as many clams as the day before. Galloway's messenger bag groaned beneath the salty weight.

I was careful not to lead them too close to the other side of the island, and once we'd collected all we could carry, we returned to the beach and gathered more firewood and fresh coconuts.

Once our chores were complete, we rested around the fire, and ate a simple fare washed down with evergreen water.

We said goodnight to yet another day in deserted paradise.

....

DAY EIGHT

The sun seemed intent on chargrilling us from the moment it crested on the horizon to long after it fell into the sea. The children were lethargic and suffered borderline heatstroke.

We spent most of the day bobbing in the tide, trying to stay cool.

If anyone noticed us, swimming in a mismatch of t-shirts and slovenly clothing, they would've laughed at our ingenious ways of staying free from sunburn.

Galloway wore the baseball cap while Pippa and Conner found

their own straw sailor hats from the clothing Amelia had packed for them. I wrapped my gold negligee over my head and drenched it with seawater, ensuring as much as possible shielded my face. It'd taken a lot of convincing, but Galloway insisted I wear the only pair of sunglasses as I didn't have a hat.

At least, spending all day in the water meant I was able to sand-scrub our clothes and do my best to get them clean.

Dinner consisted of clams and coconuts washed down with restricted allotments of water.

At the end of the day, I slipped into my dug-out bed, toasty warm by the crackling fire. Drowsy, I stared at the clear horizon and begged for rain. I prayed to every god to grant us a reprieve from the dry spell. Our limited water collection from the trees kept us alive, but we *desperately* needed more.

Every night, the urge to be greedy and keep all three bottles for myself turned me into a horrible person. I craved the luxury of a fresh-water bath. Of washing away the salt and sand from my skin. I dreamed of gallons of crisp water raining from above; I fantasised of ice cubes and air-conditioning.

I imagined we were rescued and this was all over.

But that was all they were: dreams, fantasies, imagination.

We went through the motions.

We ate but slowly lost weight.

We drank but slowly died from dehydration.

And we interacted less and less, growing quieter as the hours plodded on.

We'd survived longer than originally thought.

But we hadn't been rescued.

Not one engine on the horizon. Not one flare of hope.

Our limited supplies of toothbrushes and meagre possessions gave us a little wealth but in the scheme of things…we were destitute.

We'd explored and trekked and plotted and planned.

But we were alone.

And our temporary measures at clinging to life weren't working.

DAY TWELVE

My taste buds craved anything else but clams.

It'd been twelve days; I needed variety. Nutrients. Vitamins from a range of food not just one salty morsel.

We'd tried to snare the occasional lizard that ventured too

close. We swatted at mosquitoes that turned us into a meal. We eyed seagulls flying high. And we resorted to hunting tropical bugs and panfrying them on rocks. The crunchy critters tasted disgusting, but at least it offered a small amount of protein.

Our qualms over what society deemed acceptable quickly shredded the longer the days stretched. My stomach constantly ached along with a dehydrated throb behind my eyes.

The hottest part of the day was reserved for rest, but the remaining hours were dedicated to remaining alive for one more day.

One more morning.

One more night.

One more chance of being found.

Yesterday, Conner had earned a lashing from my tongue. He'd taken it upon himself to swim offshore, far, far, farther than his young body should. I hadn't noticed until it was too late, his head bobbing in the turquoise drink.

Galloway cursed like a pirate when the dripping, broken-wristed boy finally waded back to shore. But Conner merely straightened his back and said someone had to try. Someone had to swim out to the reef-break and see if there was another island close by, a ship hidden behind an inlet, some sort of hope that we couldn't imagine.

But just like our island…there was nothing.

We were in a snow globe. The centre figurine surrounded by invisible walls.

We faded into despair after that.

Conner didn't mention rescue again. And Galloway erected impenetrable partitions around his soul. Pippa was the only one who spoke, but the childish belief that things would work out faded quickly as repetitive sunrise and sunsets stole us into an unsurvivable future.

I sang snippets of my songs-in-progress to lull her to sleep. I stole precious moments to scribble in my crinkled notepad, outlining sonnets that would never be heard.

With nothing else to do, the children kept themselves occupied—building an occasional sandcastle, swimming where I could keep an eye on them, and napping in the shade.

We'd all lost weight.

Galloway's cheeks were gaunt but that was from agony as much as the lack of food. His facial hair grew thicker every day, the same chocolate brown as his head.

My hipbones steadily made themselves known and the broken

ribs I kept strapped slowly protruded from my flesh.

We needed to fish. To learn what other food we could find. We needed to think long-term, rather than pin our hopes on a fantasy of rescue.

As the sun slowly set on yet another day, we shared the collected water like we did every night, and settled in to rest. Once darkness fell, there wasn't much to do apart from sit around the fire and talk.

But tonight, we couldn't even do that.

We didn't have the energy to form conversation.

Galloway curled up in his bed, finally succumbing to his body's need to heal and his incorrigible mood. The children decided to dig a bed together, falling asleep in each other's arms. And I stared sleeplessly, long after they'd left me for dreams.

Ever since we'd put up the memorial cross and given the children the bracelet and pen, they'd been closer. Less argumentative and more compassionate. They'd grown up faster in a few days than in years of their happy childhood.

Unable to lie still, I pulled out my cell-phone. I kept it hidden as I couldn't stomach the looks of despair whenever anyone looked at it. The screen came to life, bright in the dark, fully charged thanks to my solar charger.

I tried again to find rescue. Scanning and searching for any hope of connection. I dialled the emergency number in all its variations, listening for anything but the empty silence of unsuccessful outreach.

Silent tears cascaded down my face. Sniffing quietly, I brought up the calendar app and rubbed the sudden ache in my chest.

Yesterday, I had a lunch date with Madeline.

The day before, I had a vet appointment for Shovel-Face and his yearly check-up.

Next week, I had a Skype conference with my agent to discuss the songs I'd agreed to pen and perform for my producer.

A life waiting for me to return.

A life thinking I was dead.

I can't look at it anymore.

Closing the app, I switched on the camera. I didn't dare flick through the gallery and torture myself with pictures of the trip in the USA, of funny faces with Madi, and landscape panoramas of the crowds who'd come to hear me sing.

I merely opened the camera, switched it to night mode, and stood.

Silently, I catalogued our beach. I imprisoned heart-splintering pictures of Conner and Pippa sleeping back to back. I guiltily snapped images of Galloway, slumbering with a frown permanently on his face.

I took photos of the moon.

Of the sea.

Of the beach.

Of shells.

And a selfie of me with the campsite behind.

I liked to think I took it so I had evidence when we were found. A picture to discuss with Madeline when she begged for tales of my castaway days.

But the truth was, I took it to monitor how I fared over the next few months.

I took it knowing full well that if we didn't eat better, drink more, and figure out a way to survive, the selfies would slowly show a young music-writer with hazel eyes and long blonde hair turn into a haggard, skeletal woman walking quickly into her grave.

I didn't want that.

I won't let that happen.

I had Galloway and the children to fight for.

We would find a way.

We have no choice.

Chapter Twenty-Six

. . . .

GALLOWAY

. . . . . .

DAY SIXTEEN

I WOKE UP drowning.

My muscles hauled me into a sitting position; I opened my eyes to a bloody miracle. "Estelle!"

Estelle flew upright, her eyes wide and unfocused from sleep. Understanding registered instantly, and the brightest smile I'd seen in days spread across her lips. "Oh, my God!"

"Get whatever you can." I hurried upright, wincing against my break.

Conner and Pippa sprang to their feet, dancing in the phenomenon.

Rain.

Delicious, *precious,* drinkable rain.

Fat raindrops exploded on our skin, washing away the salt for the first time in weeks.

"Yay!" Pippa squealed, holding her face to the sky. Her tongue flicked over her chin, slurping as fast as she could. "More! *More!*"

Conner whirled around with his arms spread. "Yes!"

Estelle bolted to the forest edge where we kept our clothes and belongings. We still hadn't built a shelter. We hadn't needed to. The fire kept away most of the bugs and chilly nights and the sky had been dry up till now.

It'd been a blessing not to have to build and struggle with my broken limb. But now, we paid the price as everything we owned was drenched.

The sand pockmarked with raindrops, slowly darkening the harder it fell.

The fire hissed and spat, fighting to keep burning.

Part of me wanted to protect it. To cover the blaze so it didn't go out. But we had my glasses. We had the sun. We could rebuild it.

"Grab whatever you can and store as much as possible." I looked for items of use. We'd already dug holes and lined them with deflated life-jackets. We'd been prepared for this for weeks.

Estelle flew past with the three bottles we drained every night, planting them securely in the sand.

Conner dragged a piece of fuselage that would eventually lose its contents as it had no sides, but as a quick gatherer to drink from, it would do.

Pippa grabbed the pot we used to boil clams, tipped out the seawater, and held it in her skinny arms to the sky. "Fill it up. Faster!"

I laughed as Estelle looped her arm through mine. She kissed my cheek. "I've been dreaming of this to happen. *Begging* it to."

My body came alive beneath her touch.

I was stupid to keep her away from me. For days, I'd avoided her, refusing to talk, letting every moronic excuse turn me into an ass.

I'd been miserable—we all had. Why had we segmented ourselves off from one another? Things were so much more bearable when fought side by side.

I'm sorry.

I wanted to apologise, but she wouldn't understand. She wouldn't understand that I wasn't just apologising to her but to myself, my past, the circumstances that'd made me this way.

I trembled with desperation as her eyes glittered brown and green. I dragged her closer, wrapping my arm around her waist.

Ever since dealing with the dead, we'd been linked. Despite our days and nights apart, I was achingly aware of her. I hadn't tried to kiss her again, but it didn't mean my heart didn't leap whenever she was near.

I needed her with an inferno that licked every part of me but my need was more rounded now. I no longer wanted the quick satisfaction of sex but the full-bodied joy of connection.

I fell into her eyes.

Instantly, the joy of the rain disappeared and desire ignited on her face.

She looked at my lips.

She stopped breathing.

I couldn't stop myself.

My hand crept up her back, tracing the beads of her spine that were more pronounced than before. Silently, I cupped her nape. "Do you remember my challenge?"

"Yes."

"And?"

"And?"

"What do I have to do to make it come true?"

Her cheeks pinpricked with heat. "To make me fall in love with you?"

I nodded. My throat dry like ash. My heart imitating the booming thunder.

She'd kissed me the first time. She'd taken me by surprise.

This time.

I kissed her.

My head dipped down; hers tipped up.

My lips parted; hers fluttered open.

My nose brushed hers; she sighed softly.

My arm summoned; she came closer.

And our lips...they met.

She *whimpered.*

She undid me, claimed me, owned my very soul with that whimper.

My tongue licked her; she licked back.

My head tilted; she mimicked.

Our lips turned from touching to embracing. Our tongues danced, heat bloomed, and the kiss turned into a meal of desire.

"God, I want you."

She moaned. "You have me."

"No, I don't."

"Yes. Yes, you do. Believe me. You do." Her breathless voice wrapped around my cock, pounding my need into something I could no longer fight.

Rain mixed with our kiss, diluting her flavour. "It's raining."

She nodded.

"Is the sky weeping or happy for us?" My lips trailed from her mouth to her ear. "Are the clouds sanctioning this or forbidding it?"

Her fingers curled on my t-shirt (the very same one she'd washed with sand and kept as sanitary as possible), pulling me tighter toward her. She whimpered again, and this time, she stole one, twenty, a million fragments of my heart, placing them in her bikini top and stealing them forever. "It's raining because the sky wants us to survive."

"And what of my challenge?"

"What of it?"

I bit her throat. "You know what I want."

Her heart drummed against mine, our bodies as close as we could get. "What if I said there is no challenge. That whatever you're doing…it's working."

Whatever I was doing? I wasn't doing enough. I'd reached my limit mobility-wise, and spent my days hobbling or resting. I was of no use to her.

To say there was no challenge; that she was falling for me just as surely as I was falling for her.

Christ.

I kissed her again.

Hard.

Fast.

Brutal.

She matched me lick for lick, turning a simple kiss into a complex sin.

Breaking apart, she breathed, "I'm glad it's you on this island. I'm glad it's you beside me."

I had no defences left. All I could do was cling to a raft of wishes and potential possibilities. Potential possibilities of actually winning her, of seducing her, of calling her mine.

"Eww, what are you guys doing?" Conner's hair was plastered to his head.

We pulled apart.

"Nothing, silly." Estelle recovered first. With a quick glance, she jogged down the beach and took Pippa's hand. They danced around the pot, filling quickly with water. Pippa's back had scabbed and scarred, slowly erasing the method of how we'd arrived.

"Come on." Grabbing the discarded coconut shells, I gave one to Conner and hopped down the beach to my stranded family.

Scooping the half-shell into the pot, I filled it to the brim with drinkable liquid. Holding it aloft, loving the way the heavens drowned us, I said, "To us and surviving."

Everyone followed suit, filling up their fancy goblets and toasting.

"To rain and drinking."

We drank. Fast. And repetitively.

We drank as quickly as the rain refilled.

We drank until our stomachs bloated.

We drank until we replaced every hydration.

And *still* it rained.

It poured and stormed; lightning flashed and thunder boomed until midnight turned to midday, and our island glittered with droplets in the new sunshine.

• •

"What are you doing?"

Estelle hid something behind her back, guilt washing over her face.

Three days had passed since the storm and we'd finally dried our clothing, relined our beds with fresh leaves, and grown accustomed to having a reservoir of water where we could drink when we wanted without waiting for the trees to provide.

Our supply wouldn't last forever, but for now…we were reckless with our thirst and drank often.

"Nothing."

I hauled myself to my feet. I'd spent the morning plaiting flax into rope. I had a plan to put a roof over our head and four walls around our bodies, but in order to do that, I needed something to build with. I didn't have screws or nails (the ones from the chopper wouldn't work), so rope would have to do.

Once I knew how to create using island fare, a raft was on my agenda.

"It is something. Show me." I hopped toward her.

"Don't. Forget it. It was a stupid idea."

"No, show me." I moved as quick as I could, hoping she wouldn't dart away. Holding my hand out, I glared until she pulled whatever she was hiding and placed it into my palm.

My heart wrenched to a stop. "Your phone."

She nodded.

"Did you manage to call someone? Is that what you're doing?"

Her eyes widened, filling with apology. "No. I've tried every night and nothing."

"Then why torture yourself?" I ached to comfort her. I would never say it aloud, but here, on this island, even with the trials of surviving and the fear of what would happen, I was happier than I'd been in a long time. The thought of Estelle pining for a life where I wouldn't be welcome hurt me a lot more than I could admit.

Since our kiss in the rain, we'd kept our distance. Partly for the children's sake, but mostly because, if I kissed her again, I wouldn't be able to stop.

And Estelle wasn't ready for more.

She wanted me; I knew that. But she was hesitant about how far to go. I hadn't figured out why yet, but I respected her desire for slowness.

"That isn't what I was doing." She flinched as if telling me her secret physically pained her.

"I don't understand."

She dropped her head. "Go to the gallery. You'll see."

Propping myself up with my crutch, I navigated the menu and pulled up the pictures. My mouth fell open as the first image exploded in vibrant pigment. "Why did you do this?"

I'd expected images of her past life, perhaps photos of a past boyfriend (who I would like to murder) or friends who thought she was dead. Not this. Not...*me*.

"Why?" Her eyebrows rose. "Why not? Isn't that what humans do? We store memories to look back on later. Happy, sad, it doesn't matter. We gather them for future use."

"That's what you're doing?"

She shrugged. "I don't know what I'm doing. I don't know if we'll ever get off this island, and I don't know how much longer my phone will last, but I wanted to honour whatever we lived through with the same cataloguing as I would any other adventure."

"By taking pictures of us?" My hands shook as I scrolled. She'd taken photos stealthily: me plaiting rope. Conner and Pippa crouched on their haunches, digging for clams. A selfie of her with the helicopter crash in the background.

I paused on the one of me sleeping in the dark. My beard had grown in, and I looked in pain even as I slept. "When did you take this?"

"The night before the rain came."

I switched to the selfie of her standing alone on the beach— the moon etching her in silver and the shapes of us sleeping in the background. It was a haunting image. It sent shivers down my back.

"Wow."

She tried to take it back. "Anyway, it was a bad idea. I didn't mean to upset you."

"Upset me? Why would I be upset?"

"Because I took pictures of you without your consent."

I chuckled. "Estelle, knowing I mean enough to you that you want to photograph me for future memories is the nicest thing I've ever heard."

She blushed. "So...you're not mad?"

"Why the hell would I be mad?"

Her lips twitched. "I just said why."

My insides warmed as fresh desire thickened my blood. My gaze locked on her mouth. "Christ, I want to kiss you again."

Her throat worked as she swallowed. "You can't. The children are right there. I don't want to have to explain—"

"They're not newborns, Stel. They get what kissing is."

"Yes, well. I just…I want them to be happy. It's too soon after their parents' death. Change isn't good for them." She trailed off, tucking sun-bleached blonde behind her ear. "Just…give it time. Okay?"

My heart hurt but I grinned. She didn't notice I'd used her nickname. And I didn't let her see how honoured I was to use it. I was allowed. Even though I'd done nothing to deserve it. "That I can give you. What other commodity do we have but time?"

She laughed, but it was forced. "Thank you."

"Don't mention it."

Looking away, I flicked the phone from gallery to camera and tapped the video recorder. "Now, how about instead of taking sneaky pictures, we do this the right way?" Holding the lens up, I captured her beauty. Freckles had appeared on her nose and the salt and wind had banished any hint that she'd been a city girl, replacing her polished smoothness with survivalist edges.

She laughed, covering her face. "What are you doing? Get that thing away."

"No chance." Hopping backward, I called, "Conner, Pippi. Home movie time." Scanning the phone their way, I captured their white smiles, skinny bodies, and feet splashing in the tide.

"Movie? Can I be the Incredible Hulk?" Conner tried to commandeer the phone.

"I want to be a princess." Pippa twirled.

Looking at Estelle, I said quietly, "Starting today, let's document every little thing that matters. Be it rain to drink or a fish to eat…or a kiss to pleasure. Let's be grateful for what we have."

I zoomed in as Estelle stared at me with a thousand emotions in her gaze. The camera picked up flashes of brown and green, twisting my stomach into a hundred knots.

Slowly, she grinned. "I'd like that."

"I'd like it, too," Pippa said. "Will we be on TV when they find us? Will they use our movies?"

I stiffened.

Who knew what the footage would be used for? Perhaps, it would be used as evidence of how a bunch of ordinary, society-spoiled people endured the elements.

Or…

Maybe the videos would be found many years from now, washed up in a bottle, a message to the outside world of four castaways who didn't make it.

Chapter Twenty-Seven

....

ESTELLE

......

Don't fret when fate forbids you. Don't cry when life doesn't listen. Be brave and trust that you will survive. Be strong and never give in.
Never give in.
Never...give...in.
Lyrics for 'Never Give In' Taken from the notepad of E.E.

...

FOUR WEEKS
(September bleeding into October)

COCONUT, CLAMS, AND water.

Coconut, clams, and water.

I'm sick to death of coconut, clams, and water.

We'd done our best to supplement our diet with insects and an occasional lizard but even starving, there were limits.

Despite the lack of variety, my body still functioned, my period came and went, the children grew, and life aged us.

I craved fish. Something robust and meaty. Up till now, no one had been physically able or skilled enough to catch any (and we'd all tried, on numerous occasions).

I sat with my arms wrapped around my legs, resting my chin on my knees as the world woke up.

Four weeks and counting.

We'd survived this long doing what we knew. But fear kept us from trying anything new. Along with our unsuccessful attempt to spear a fish, we'd done our best to catch a seagull that'd landed to inspect our quickly growing pile of clamshells.

But we'd failed.

We were slowly starving from sameness.

To make it worse, the clams were getting harder and harder to find. Every day, we had to dig a little deeper, wade out a little farther. We'd exhausted our supplies, and now, we didn't have a choice but to push ourselves to find alternatives.

The sun appeared on the horizon, spreading its pink glow across the ocean. My eyes drifted to the sea. Below the surface existed plenty of food. However, we had no fishing implements, no way of catching the slippery devils.

We need to change that.

It was time for the next stage. Evolve or die. Life wasn't kind to those who didn't help themselves.

My ribs and chest were mostly healed and nowhere near as painful. Conner had taken the strap off his wrist and claimed he could use it with only a small twinge, and Pippa's shoulder had scarred neatly.

Galloway was the only one still unwell. His ankle gave him grief. He couldn't move without his crutch. He pretended he was okay, but I could tell he was lying.

He glared at his leg, cursed his disability, acted as if he'd sooner chop it off than wait for his body to fix.

For a week now, I'd had the horrible thought that perhaps his shin, ankle, and foot would never heal properly. What if his bones were crooked and no matter how they knitted together, he would always limp?

Don't think that way.

I bit my lip, resorting to a habit I'd begun and couldn't stop. I gnawed on the sides of my cheeks, too, slowly eroding the flesh with stress. My teeth constantly felt furry as the toothpaste had run out and our toothbrush bristles slowly softened with use.

Last week, I'd taught the others what Madeleine had shown me when we'd gone on a double date and a seed from dinner wedged into my teeth. When Madi had taught me, I'd been in awe of the simple (but frankly rather gross) suggestion.

Hair.

A girl with long hair could tweak out a strand and use it as dental floss. Every night, I pulled a few free and passed them to Conner and Galloway. Pippa used her own, and together, we did our best with dental hygiene.

Soap had become seawater and sand and the sun kept us so hot that we sweated freely without smelling. As far as cleanliness went, we'd adapted. Even my hair had balanced in oils and no longer looked greasy but salt-sprayed and crinkled with sun-encouraged curls.

Sunburn was also avoided as we managed to stay in the shade at the height of the day and covered up when we had no choice but to be at its mercy.

Our way of living had advanced, our friendship deepened, our family group wedged firmly in my heart.

I loved them.

I couldn't deny it.

I loved Pippa with her steely temper and quick-fire questions.

I loved Conner and his teenage need to prove himself.

And…

I loved Galloway.

I loved the way he dropped what he was doing if the children summoned him. I loved how he watched them sleep when he thought I wasn't watching. I loved the way he left hibiscus flowers for me in the mornings when I went to collect firewood. I loved the way he made me feel as if everything he ever needed dwelled right inside my soul.

And I loved the way he spoke of grand plans of building a raft and sailing us to freedom—even though we'd had many conversations about how suicidal that would be: leaving the safety of land to bob around an ocean with no navigation or propulsion.

Ignoring logistics, Galloway was adamant he would rescue us.

And because of that…I loved him.

But was I *in* love with him?

Was it love with a use-by-date? Would it fade the moment we were found and returned to separate worlds? Was it love born of survival or truth? Or perhaps was it our circumstances and the fact that I'd have no one without him? Or was it providence…fate?

Despite perpetual hunger pangs, my body constantly desired him.

I'd wake from a dream with resonating clenches from a sleep-enjoyed orgasm. I'd excuse myself and swim when my turned-on wetness threatened to be noticeable on my cotton shorts.

He drove me insane; he drove me happy. He made me want to care for him while accepting his care in return.

Was *that* love?

I'd lost everything and been dropped in the middle of nowhere with strangers. Strangers who'd become the most important people in the world.

I love them.

And because of that, I wouldn't let them perish from malnutrition.

I had to do something.

Today.

Unwinding from my position, I shrugged out of my black t-shirt and slipped down my shorts. Skinny-dipping wasn't normally done, but everyone was asleep and I didn't want to wear wet clothes once I'd finished.

Wading into the warm tide, I exhaled as I dropped below the surface.

The current flowed around me, some cool, some hot, all of it gentle and protective. Swimming bare allowed the sinful sensation of water against my sex and nipples. I felt naughty. I felt turned on. I felt beyond ready to invite Galloway to take the next step.

He'd been the perfect gentleman the past few weeks. Never pushy, no matter how much lust crackled between us.

Swimming upward, I took a deep breath and floated a few metres before scooping a handful of sand and scouring my body. The exfoliation method kept my skin super soft, but without moisturizer, I had to accept the tightness of having no age-defying protection.

Along with growing closer to my crash-mates, the island had become a friend, too. A living entity that provided for us, sheltered us, and ultimately kept us trapped.

It was a prison and salvation all at once.

Why haven't they found us yet?

Where were we? Was Conner right with how many uninhabited islands there were? Was it possible to vanish in this day and age?

Obviously, it was.

We were living proof.

In the month we'd been here, not a single boat or plane had passed by. The ocean was silent as if the world had ended and we were the only ones remaining.

Ducking for another handful of sand, I scrubbed my hair and reclined in the water to rinse it out as best I could.

Cleaned, I paddled back to shore.

Wringing my hair out, I left the sea and shook out my t-shirt to get dressed.

The air evaporated droplets from my skin, and I was ready to face the quest of finding more food.

Pippa barrelled down the beach just as I hauled my shorts into place. "You went swimming without me."

I bent and hugged her. "You're up early."

"I know. I had to pee."

I was probably the only person alive who loved the fact she

had to pee. It meant she had enough water to drink and her body wasn't dehydrated. "Well, you can always swim now. I'll watch you if you want."

She shook her head. "I'm good. I'm too cold." Rubbing the goosebumps on her arms, she reminded me that sleeping on the chilly sand wasn't preferable even if we did have a fire.

She cocked her head, her copper hair turning a light auburn the longer we lived beneath the sun. "What were you doing?"

"Ah…I can't say. It's a secret."

Her childish face scrunched up in frustration. "Tell me. I won't tell anyone."

Another reason I loved the children: they made me make an effort rather than waste away begging for rescue.

If Pippa and Conner weren't here, Galloway and I would probably have resorted to grunting barely uttered syllables, unwilling to converse.

We might not talk, but we'd have lots of sex. Lots and lots *of sex.*

We'd probably never leave our sandy beds, utterly addicted to indulging in an activity that felt so good versus a life of drudgery.

How do you know it would feel good with him?

I hid my smile. Oh…I knew. I'd seen him in his boxer-briefs. I'd stolen glances as he stretched in the morning and the delectable muscles of his chest rippled with power. And his kisses….no one could kiss like that and not be good in bed.

"Tell me," Pippa moaned when I didn't reply.

I pressed her button nose. "Well, if you promise to keep it a secret. You've caught me. I'm really a mermaid and just came back from visiting my father King Trident."

Her mouth fell open, literally smashed into the sand. *"Really?"*

The childlike awe on her face made me happy and sad. Happy that I was able to grant some magic and sad that it was all I could offer.

"Yes, and if you're very good, he said he'd come visit you someday."

Suspicion chased away her belief. "Are you sure?" She poked my leg. "Where's your tail? I've never seen you with a tail, and we swim lots and lots."

I didn't know if I should keep up my fib or shatter her imagination with the truth.

So I did neither.

Brushing past her, I headed up the beach. "Come on, time for breakfast."

"Hey, wait."

I cringed against having to tell her the truth but she shot in front of me and pushed out her bottom lip. "Can we have rabbit food?" Pointing at the camp, she added, "Puffin is sick of clams."

The mention of her cuddly toy fluttered my heart. "Wait. He's sick of clams, or *you're* sick of clams."

"*I'm* sick of them." Her face brightened. "But rabbit food would be good."

"What on earth is rabbit food?"

"That's what Daddy used to call it."

I frowned. "Salads and veggies and things?"

She nodded.

"What's your favourite veggie?"

She contemplated before answering. "Celery sticks."

I couldn't hide my surprise. "Celery sticks?"

"Yep with dip and stuff."

I pushed aside my dripping hair. "I would've expected you to say you hated veggies and wanted chocolate."

Pippa made a gagging noise. "Eww, no. I'm allergic to chocolate. Makes me itch and swell."

Allergic.

Allergy.

My brain exploded with what the word meant.

Of course!

An allergic reaction was the body's way of saying we couldn't eat something. It wasn't packets telling us ingredients or companies manufacturing food.

It was millennia of trial and error. Eat something and see the results. Try something and...see if there was a reaction.

Grabbing the little girl, I kissed her. "You're a genius."

Dashing up the beach, Pippa followed.

I held up my hand. "Stay here. Tell the others I won't be long."

The fire crackled, smouldering a little as it begged for new wood. The A-frame we'd fashioned with branches and Galloway's rope guarded our belongings on the forest edge. The shady shelter was handy during the day, but it wasn't practical to sleep in.

It was too small.

Moving past Galloway, he continued sleeping. Conner, too. Along with getting used to sleeping outside, we also slept deeply. As if living in the wide open vastness drained us faster than elsewhere.

Not looking back to see if Pippa obeyed, I slipped on my flip-flops and dashed into the forest.

My feet had grown tougher the past weeks. The hot sand

scorched my soles and pricks from twigs leathered my delicate skin. But today, I didn't know how far I would have to go. And I didn't want to have to turn around before I was ready.

This could royally backfire.

I shoved the thought aside. I didn't worry that I might die if I chose wrongly. That I might suffer tummy cramps and embarrassing after-effects of eating something my body didn't agree with.

Because if I did this and it worked...

Food wouldn't be so hard to come by.

Dashing to the first bush that looked innocuous and tasty, I tore off a leaf and brought it to my mouth.

"You can always test food another way. Care to answer what way that is?" My old biology teacher's voice popped into my head. God, it'd been so long since I'd done biology—ever since I changed my mind from being a vet because I couldn't stomach the thought of cutting up animals even if it was for their own good.

What had Professor Douglas said? Something about not eating it but...

The teacher tapped the blackboard. "Don't eat it. That's entirely too dangerous. Rub it on your skin first. Your body will let you know if it's safe or not."

Of course.

Doctors did that for new drugs and ointments. Before full use, they recommended a scratch test and a twenty-four hour wait.

I straightened out my left arm and dragged my fingernail across the underside.

Pain flared but I didn't draw blood. I scraped deep enough to make my skin pink but not deep enough to do damage. I crushed the leaf between my fingers and rubbed it over the scratch—dousing my skin with foreign flavours.

If I remembered correctly, if in twenty-four hours my skin was hot or puffy, my body had rejected the leaf and it wasn't safe to eat. However, if there was no reaction, it was okay to take to the next level and sample by eating.

My stomach growled at the thought of devouring something new.

Drawing an *X* on the soft mulchy ground, I moved toward another bush. This one smelled vaguely of thyme. Repeating the process, I scratched the inside of my right arm and smudged the pungent leaf over the irritated skin.

This time, I left an *X* with the Roman numeral *I* beside it.

Let the wait begin.

It would be the longest twenty-four hours of my life.

I stared longingly at the other undergrowth. If I tested each one tonight, then by tomorrow, I could have a smorgasbord of things to cook. But then, I wouldn't know which set off a reaction if I suffered.

No, this is the only way. Two at a time and no more.

Striding back to camp, Galloway and Conner had woken and Pippa had filled the water bottles to share. My adopted family looked up as I returned.

"Where have you been?" Galloway's intense blue eyes narrowed. "Pippa said you just ran off."

"Oh she did, did she?" I scowled at Pippa, faking annoyance. "I hope she didn't tell you anything else."

The little girl shook her head. "Nuh uh. I did what you said. I waited and told them you'd gone. That's it."

My lips curled at how literal she was. She hadn't quite captured the knack of sarcasm yet. "Well, I'm glad that you kept my *secret* about you know what and where I was with you know who this morning."

A smile split her lips, catching my mention of our magical moment of mermaids.

"Wait." Conner poked his sister. "What secret?"

Pippa stuck up her nose. "Not telling."

"Go on, Pippi. You can tell us." Galloway joined in, tickling the girl, making her squeal. "Not going to stop until you tell us."

I laughed, moving to sit close by.

Galloway didn't let up, drawing giggles and happy noises from her. To her credit, she didn't break and she managed to escape Galloway's hands and run.

I opened my arms. She barrelled into me, her tiny body trembling with exertion. "Never. I don't tell secrets!"

I kissed her cheek. "Good for you, Pip. You tell 'em you're not a tattler."

Her happy smile undid me. The fact she'd found some sort of joy here…that was priceless. Suddenly, her arms wrapped around my neck; she buried her face in my hair. "I love you, Stelly."

Tears instantly sprang to my eyes.

She loved me.

My hug turned to steal; I crushed her to me. "I love you, too, Pippi."

My eyes drifted over her head, meeting Galloway's. He stood with every complex severity of our situation along with a faraway wish on his face. His mouth pursed, eyes bright, chin cocked with emotion.

I fell.

Staring at him.

I fell.

Harder and harder, deeper and deeper.

The way he watched me. The way he made me feel.

I couldn't deny what my heart and body wanted any longer. I couldn't lie that I wasn't terrified of what I felt for him. This wasn't an opportunist fling because of our circumstances. It was a true connection between two people who happened to be thrown together by fate.

Galloway left Conner, moving toward Pippa and me.

Goosebumps broke out. I couldn't breathe as he moved smoother than he had in weeks, putting a little bit of weight on his broken ankle before transferring to the crutch. We didn't speak as he kissed Pippa's hair and pulled her away from me.

The little girl went, her brown eyes glowing. Galloway bent and whispered in her ear.

I couldn't hear what he said, but she nodded and headed to Conner. Her brother welcomed her, his smile scripted just for his younger sibling.

Holding out his hand, Galloway waited until I put mine in his. Jerking me onto my feet, his bicep tightened, intending to pull me into him.

My lips parted, preparing for a kiss. My heart danced a furiant, expecting a bolt of passion.

But his eyes dropped from my face to my arm.

My *red and scratched* arm.

He froze. "What's that?"

Shaking myself from my sexual stupor, I frowned. "What?"

"That." Untangling his fingers from mine, he grabbed my wrist, twisting my arm for a better view. The sunshine shone directly on my self-inflicted injuries—red and long, irritated and green-stained.

I slapped my palm over it. "It's nothing. Don't worry about it."

"What do you mean it's *nothing*?" His voice was deceptively soft. "It's not nothing. It needs to be treated."

My heart raced for an entirely different reason. "Ah, well…it's not that kind of wound."

He imprisoned me in his gaze, waiting for me to dig myself further into a hole. When I didn't continue, his fingers tightened on my wrist. "Explain…"

"It wasn't an accident, okay?" Tugging, I freed myself and hid my arms behind my back. "It's a trial."

"A trial?" His eyes narrowed. "What sort of trial."

"Don't worry about it."

"Like hell, I'm not going to worry about it." He leaned closer, anger glinting. "What are you up to?"

I blew salty bangs from my eyes. "We need a better diet. I remembered my teacher saying the best way to see if something is edible to do a scratch test."

His eyes bugged. "And you thought that was a good idea?"

"Well, yes." I shrugged. "We need other things to eat, and unless you've studied botany and know what plants are okay, this is the only way I can think of."

He stared blankly then livid temper coloured his face.

I flinched, waiting for the blow-up. Instead, he snagged my wrist and yanked me toward the forest edge.

"Hey." I tugged.

"Be quiet." Hopping in an angry hobble with his crutch, he didn't let me go as he dragged me past the children. "We'll be back. Adult time."

Conner rolled his eyes. "Adult time….riiigght."

Pippa wrung her hands. "Don't be mad at her." Her eyes flickered between us with worry. "Please?"

I smiled, fighting the uncertainty in my blood. "He's not mad, Pip. I'm just going to show him which plants I tested. He's happy at the thought of rabbit food. Aren't you, G?"

Galloway's fingers tightened. "Yes. Exactly. Don't worry, Pippi."

Pippa nodded. "Okay..."

With a final look at the children, Galloway stole me into the treeline.

Chapter Twenty-Eight

....

GALLOWAY

......

OF ALL THE hare-brained, stupid, idiotic, *crazy* things to do.

I can't believe this.

I didn't want to believe she would willingly hurt herself and run the risk of a serious allergy, all so we had a better bloody diet.

"Galloway, stop." Her fingers touched my forearm. "You'll hurt yourself if we go any farther."

Hurt myself?

I couldn't do it.

Didn't she get it?

Didn't she see how goddamn stupid that was? How dare she put herself in harm's way without telling me? What if something happened to her? What if whatever she'd tried *killed* her?

My temper exploded.

Letting her go, I rounded on her.

Her eyes bugged as she stumbled backward for every hop of my crutch. "Galloway, it's nothing…honestly."

"You don't get it, do you?"

"Get what?"

One step.

Another.

"That wasn't your call to make."

She frowned. "It's my body. I can do what I want with it."

My fists curled. "Wrong."

"Whatever. You can't tell me what I can and can't do."

I bared my teeth. "Think again, Estelle."

"I don't have to think. I *know*." She pointed a finger in my face, still retreating as I backed her into the tree. "Just like I can't stop you from overdoing it when you should be resting. Just like I can't stop anything that might happen to us on this island."

I didn't reply, just kept pushing her. She wasn't watching where she was going. But I was. And I wanted her flush against the tree so I could teach her a goddamn lesson.

"I'm going to lay it out for you so listen closely."

Colour spotted her cheeks. I didn't know if that meant she was angry or embarrassed or turned-on.

I don't care.

My voice turned into a snarl. "First, you belong to me. To *us*. Me, Pip, and Conner. Everything you do affects us. That includes stupid things that you think benefit us but only benefit you."

"Me?" Her eyebrows disappeared into her hairline. "You think I *want* to have an allergic reaction?"

"I think you want to be the goddamn hero."

Her lips pulled back. "That's *it*. I've had enough of you." Shoving my chest, she grunted as I didn't move. "You can't speak to me that way. You don't know me. You don't know what I'm trying to do. You don't know what I think or how I feel—"

"You're right." I pushed her shoulder, crushing her against a tree. "I don't. But I do know how *I* feel. I know what would happen to us if you died from some asinine attempt at looking out for us."

My voice hissed. "Want to know what would happen? It would fucking *kill* me. That's what would happen. You're the only reason why any of us are coping in this godforsaken place. You're the only reason why I get up in the morning even with my ankle bloody screaming." I panted. "You're the reason why I'm in so much goddamn pain."

"Don't blame me for your discomfort, Galloway. I did my best to splint your injury. I never said I was a doctor and knew how to fix—"

"Shut up and listen." I slapped a hand over her mouth, doing my best to ignore the delicious puffs of breath on my knuckles and the slight dampness of her lips against my palm. "I haven't finished."

Now that I'd started, I couldn't stop. I hated spilling such things. But my mouth wouldn't shut it. "Christ, Estelle. Don't you see? These weeks have been torture. I've kissed you. I've tasted you. I've slept beside you every night and I'm not allowed to touch you."

She was mute, wide eyes glistening.

"I know you want me, too. I see it in the way you watch me, care for me, make me feel like I'm worthy. But you're afraid of me." My hand slid from her mouth to her cheek, grazing her bottom lip with my thumb. "What are you afraid of that you'd rather scratch yourself with an unknown substance than dare to be alone with me?"

The fight between us paused, swirling with passion and questions.

Her chest rose and fell, agitated and primed for a fight. Retorts gleamed in her gaze and I waited for her to shove me back, scream some backhanded comment, and storm off.

But...she didn't.

She stayed against the tree, watching me.

The fight switched to lust. Insane, *undeniable* lust.

I could barely speak; it came out more like a feral growl. "If you can't answer me, then you should probably run."

She sucked in a breath. "Run?"

"You're not safe with me. Not right now."

She stopped breathing but didn't move.

My cock thickened, my heart thundered, and every molecule turned heavy. "Too late."

My hand darted from her cheek to the back of her neck, yanking her lips to mine. "Don't you dare hate me for this."

She stiffened the moment we kissed; her fingers scratched at my t-shirt, her legs squirming for purchase.

But I'd reached my limit.

She was mine. And she had to be taught that her life wasn't hers anymore. She didn't get to decide what risks she took. She owed me because she was the only person to look inside me and see redemption.

I didn't wait for her to submit. My tongue darted past her lips, taking what I wanted, no *needed*. I needed her. I needed her so damn much I felt unhinged. Dangerous. Not entirely human.

She moaned as I slammed her against the tree, sandwiching her body with mine.

The kiss turned ravenous.

Something inside her switched and she returned my violence, sweeping me away by the righteous feel of having her in my arms, her scent in my nose, and taste in my mouth.

She was so sweet.

So hot.

So wet.

So alive.

Stay alive, Estelle.

No matter what happened on this island, I needed her to stay alive. I was sick to death of being her friend and respecting the boundaries she'd drawn.

"I need you." My lips worked faster, kissing harder.

Her hips rocked, pressing her lower belly against my steel-hard erection.

She didn't verbally give me permission, but her body did. Christ, how it did with mews and groans, trembling and arching into my touch.

"I'm so bloody mad at you." I nipped her.

She groaned as I threw away my crutch and slipped my hand beneath her t-shirt. I shuddered as I palmed her bra-less breast.

"So, so mad."

A smile teased her lips. "Is this your way of showing it?"

I kissed the smugness from her mouth. "No, this is how I force you to obey me and not be so stupid in the future."

"Obey you?" Her breathing accelerated as I rolled her nipple between my fingers.

"Always, just like I demanded before."

The softest sigh escaped her as I pressed my cock along her body. I throbbed for a release. Already my spine tensed with an impending orgasm and my balls tightened to marble.

"I'm going to teach you a lesson."

Her head fell back as I kissed my way along her chin. Pinching her nipple, I inserted my free hand down the front of her shorts.

She bucked as I touched her where I'd been dying to touch her for weeks.

"Wait…"

I sucked her bottom lip as I fingered her. "No."

"I'm…I'm pissed at you." Her legs opened for me. "Stop…" Her head fell forward as I inserted my index finger inside her.

Languages didn't mean a thing to me anymore. All I conversed in was how incredible she writhed on my finger, how wet, how hot, how eager. Curling my touch, I pressed my thumb against her clit. My head angled, kissing her, driving my tongue in time with my finger.

I coaxed her to give in to me. I forced her to forget where we were, what had happened, and just live in the moment. This intoxicating, sexual moment.

Tearing her face from mine, she half-heartedly tried to stop me. Her fingers looped around my wrist, tugging away from her shorts.

I shook my head. "No. You want this. Same as me."

"Not like this."

"Not like how?" I stole another kiss, dragging a moan from her as I inserted a second finger.

It took a long moment for her to reply.

Her eyes squeezed as her hips rocked against my hand. "Not as a punishment."

"Punishment?" Her pussy clenched around my touch. "This isn't punishment, Estelle."

Her eyes opened, blazing into mine. "What would you call it?"

I nuzzled into her hair, pressing upward and driving into her soft body. "I'd call it the opposite of punishment."

She struggled.

I couldn't let her overthink this. Who knew if she'd ever let me get this close again. Abandoning her breast, I grabbed her chin. "Kiss me."

"No." Her eyes fluttered as I fingered her faster. "Kiss me like you're sorry. Kiss me and promise you'll never do anything like that again."

"I'll promise nothing of the sort."

"Fine. I'll make you agree to a different kind of promise."

Her eyes flared as my fingers shifted from teasing to demanding a response.

"I'm going to make you come. And when you do, that's a contract between you and me that you'll do everything in your power to stay safe. You won't be reckless..." I thrust with both fingers. "You won't be heroic..." I massaged her clit. "And you'll let me into your goddamn heart because you're already in mine." I pressed my erection against her thigh as my fingers dove into her pussy.

She bit back a moan as I forced her body to respond. A flush of wetness covered my hand and the clutching of her delicate muscles increased the higher I forced her.

"Stop." She raised her heavy-lidded gaze, cursing and begging at the same time. Her tongue licked her lips, aroused and annoyed and so bloody beautiful I couldn't stand it.

"No, I won't stop."

"G..."

"Never. Not until you come."

"I won't—"

I grinned as her legs turned to jelly and her weight slouched against mine. Her forehead slammed on my shoulder. I propped her up and kept fingering her. My wrist ached. My spine tickled with sweat. And my cock begged for attention.

But this wasn't about me.

This was about Estelle.

And I wanted her to find a smidgen of pleasure, right here,

right now.

Tilting her face toward mine, I took possession of her mouth again. Our lips danced, our tongues duelled, and everything I never let myself hope for came true.

Estelle responded, kissing me back with ferocity.

I was completely at her mercy. I might be the one touching her body, drawing physical desire. But she was the one touching my soul, wrapping strings around my heart and fastening me to her forever.

I groaned as her sex rippled over my fingers. I couldn't stop my hips rocking against her hip. "Feel that?" I kissed the corner of her mouth. "Feel how much I want you?"

She moaned.

"You own me, Estelle. How can this be about punishment when you can feel how much I want you, the depth of what I feel for you?"

I traced the shell of her ear with my tongue. "Let me give you pleasure. Please…. Please allow me do this one thing for you, after you've done so much for me."

She tensed, her thighs tightening against my hand. But her inner muscles turned to liquid, heating for me, accepting what I gave.

"Oh…" Her face scrunched up. "Oh…my God."

"That's it." I worked faster, thrusting and dying in desperation to replace my fingers with my cock. Only a few pieces of sun-bleached material stopped me from taking her.

She would let me.

I think.

But I didn't want to push her too far, too fast. I wanted her to know this wasn't just about sex for me. This was about trusting me to keep her safe. This was about standing against survival side by side. This was about becoming a team—more than a team—soul-mates.

"Yes." Her sharp teeth clamped on my collarbone. "Don't stop. *Please*, don't stop."

"I'll never stop." I wanted to kiss her again. I wanted to run my hands along every contour of her body.

I needed air.

I needed to come.

I needed to get away from her before I damaged our relationship by forcing her to give more than she wanted.

But how could I let her go when her arms trembled, clutching me. When her breath gasped, fighting the pleasure I granted. And how could I possibly stop touching her when the dam broke and she came.

Her tiny cry echoed with the depth of how far she unravelled. Her spine jerked as her hands scratched me to stay upright. Wave after wave flowed over my fingers.

I held her long after they stopped.

Once she'd come, she didn't try to move away. She didn't wriggle for me to remove my hand.

We merely stood there, glued together, breathing hard, hearts beating harder, and recognised what we couldn't say.

This *was* a punishment.

For both of us.

For her because she let me take something that she hadn't been willing to give. And for me because now, I wanted her every second of every damn day and I didn't know if she'd let me.

I sucked in a shaky breath, cursing my raw emotions.

I wanted to stay hugging her until the world stopped spinning, the pain stopped throbbing, and rescue came to find us.

But that would never happen.

Slowly, I removed my fingers and wiped the silky moisture from her pleasure on my thigh.

She didn't make eye contact.

Taking a deep breath, she stepped away from me. She paused as if wanting to say something but then shook her head.

She broke into a jog and vanished into the forest.

Chapter Twenty-Nine

ESTELLE

••••••

~~*Life takes more than you can give. But only because it knows you better than you know yourself.*~~
Life takes more than you can give. But only because it pushes you to be more than what you are.
But he…
~~*He took something from me and I can never take it back.*~~
He took something from me and gave me something so much more valuable in return.

Taken from the notepad of E.E.

…

FIVE WEEKS

    LIFE WAS HARD and dolorous and confusing and messed up in a thousand different ways. I was a smile living in a frown, hiding my somersaulting emotions through polite veneers.

Every day, I kept avoiding what'd happened between us in the woods. And every day, it grew more awkward.

But we kept going.

Kept enduring.

Kept believing that one day soon a boat would pass by or a plane would fly over. Anything to get us off this island and away from the maddening lust and hardship.

We'd returned to the crash site hoping to gather whatever fuel we could from the broken gas tanks for the largest signal fire we could muster. However, they'd bled dry over the past weeks, soaking into the soil. There was a chance the foliage around the chopper could catch fire, but even if it did, it was buried in the forest and would have to burn for a while to be visible. Plus, we needed the helicopter. It still held supplies that could be of use…depending on the length of time we remained.

As the days stretched on, we embraced our certain tasks. Galloway flat-out refused to discuss my need to find more food. Only one of my scratch tests had swelled with an allergic reaction, meaning the bush marked *XI* was safe to eat. Whenever I tried to bring it up, he shot me down like an arrogant asshole.

I knew he was only looking out for me. I knew he wanted me and tried to protect me and possibly dreamed about making love to me (like my constant dreams about him). But there was a potential food source. We were starving. And I didn't know how much longer I could agree to keep the peace by not eating it.

A few days ago, we'd found a black and white banded sea snake that'd washed up on the beach. Conner had come across it while collecting clams. He'd poked it with a stick, giving me a damn heart attack.

Galloway had studied it, deemed it fresh (how would he know?) and gutted and skinned it. He tossed the head back into the sea and the body became our dinner. I'd sniffed the meat to make sure it wasn't rotten, and Galloway decided it was much more appealing to eat a dead sea-creature than a sampled and half-verified plant.

Men.

I couldn't understand his logic.

At all.

Not that it mattered, because the flesh of the snake (stabbed on a stick and roasted over an open fire) had been a delicious delicacy (even for a vegetarian).

Conner and Pippa had sounded like a rabid carnivores. Moaning with each mouthful, sucking their fingers, so grateful to have a decent meal for the first time in weeks.

The next day, Conner disappeared into the forest, returning with a stick half as thick as his arm and almost as long as he was. He and Galloway spent all day carving the end into a nasty spike and hardening it in the fire.

To his credit, Conner took it upon himself to hunt. Inspired by the sea snake, he waded into the ocean, his arm raised to strike, his spear deadly in the sun.

For two days, he attempted to spear anything that moved. No fish, manta ray, octopus, crab, or eel was safe. However, no amount of willingness or hours spent glaring for prey granted him luck.

All he earned for his troubles was sunburn and wrinkled extremities from spending all day in the sea.

Yesterday, he'd traipsed back, sopping wet and pissed off—

unsuccessful again—but with an odd-shaped prey harpooned on his spear.

A starfish.

Poor thing.

Conner had dumped it by the fire with full intention of devouring it. However, Galloway had instantly forbidden it.

He was right to do so.

I'd actually tried starfish once at a sushi restaurant. Knowledgeable chefs with experience in culinary specialities like urchins and puffer fish had prepared the dish. A cook with expertise needed to prepare all three delicacies as some elements were toxic.

It hurt that he'd killed a creature we couldn't eat. It hurt even more to throw away fresh food. But we didn't know the repercussions of such a meal. It didn't make sense to risk it…no matter how much we wanted diversity.

We'd survived this long by being smart; we wouldn't let our stomachs lead us to an early grave.

While Conner turned into a spear-thrower—single-mindedly focused on his task—Pippa suffered a relapse with her grief. She lost interest in everything, preferring to spend the day beneath the umbrella tree, stroking her mother's ring and bracelet, weeping herself to sleep.

I tried to be there for her.

I did my best to hold her and let her know she wasn't alone. But that was the nature of death; the ones left behind had to continue living but occasionally the memories stole us, and no matter how much time passed, no matter how many hugs were given, it couldn't stop sadness from winning.

As life crawled onward, I turned to my own activities. My hands became sore from plaiting flax rope as I focused on making as much as possible.

Once Galloway could move around without hopping (if that day ever came), we would have supplies ready to build. We could finally have shelter.

Not that we suffered too badly in the open-air home we'd become accustomed to. But a roof would be nice when the rain came.

A few weeks ago, I'd offered to build. I'd argued that Galloway could give Conner and me instructions and we would be his labour.

Fat lot of good that did.

Galloway vibrated with self-loathing, masking it with rage. He would've bowed to the idea if I'd pushed (I knew that), but I couldn't do that to him. I couldn't strip him of his worth.

I still didn't know much about him. I didn't know his likes or dislikes. I didn't know why he carried such a curse around his shoulders. But whatever it was, it didn't let him find peace and I couldn't stress him further.

Hopefully, we would be rescued soon and shelter would be moot; and if we didn't, well, we only had time.

Lots and *lots* of time.

We would make a house…eventually.

The island kept us both bored and never able to rest. Bored because hours stretched from dawn to dusk where the usual chaos of life wasn't there to keep us occupied. There was no TV, no books (my e-reader and Conner's hand-held gamer didn't survive the crash), no bars or social media. My phone provided some entertainment with saved movies I'd loaded before my flight, but we learned how to relax in silence rather than commotion.

For four people living together, we remained strangers for the most part. Conner and Pippa clammed up whenever I asked about their old life because it hurt too much to talk about their parents. And Galloway had a perpetual sign warning personal questions were off-limits.

We didn't take time to speak or chat or play games. We'd been here five weeks, yet we weren't entirely comfortable with each other. Galloway suffocated in his secrets. The children alternated between being young and swimming happily to staring into space where nothing and no one could reach them. And I languished in fear over what had happened to my world. Was my cat being cared for? What about my recording contract? Was Madeline okay? I hadn't sorted out a will and had no beneficiaries to make it easy on whoever annulled my life.

We each had demons, and unfortunately, we dealt with them alone.

We have to talk to one another.

It wasn't enough to be island companions; we had to be what we *were*.

A family.

Orphaned.

Lost.

Forgotten.

I shook away my thoughts, my eyes flicking to the forest behind me. The sun had set, but it wasn't late. Pippa and Conner had gone for a walk, and Galloway sat carving another spear. His hands flashed white in the darkness, his eyes narrowed with the small amount of illumination coming from the fire.

That was another thing I couldn't get used to: the dark.

We had a torch from the cockpit, which never died thanks to a windable charge. The beam of light was handy when we used the latrine in pitch black.

I'd dug the facilities a week into our stay, doing my best to keep it downwind and far enough from the camp not to attract smells or insects. We kept a mound of sand beside it to act like a flush, and leaves functioned as another use rather than just a potential food source.

The only other form of light we had was my phone. The torch app had come in handy a few times, but I missed the ease of pressing a switch and harnessing brightness. I missed the convenience of being able to see, regardless of the hour.

I'd taken a lot of things for granted, but most of all, I missed Madeline's friendship. I missed her easy laugh. I missed the way she pushed me when I needed to be pushed and gave me peace when I'd reached my limit. But most of all, I missed her advice.

Along with every major event in my life, she'd been there when I broke it off with Todd after four years of mental abuse. He'd never touched me, but his mind manipulation turned me into more of a social phobe than I naturally was.

Her advice had been key to me leaving. And if she was here, she'd give me no choice but to deal with the tense awareness between Galloway and me.

She'd force me to answer the ultimate question: did I lust for him or did I love him? And if I loved him…what did that mean? What could it mean on an island like this? What if we were never found? What if we had sex and then hated each other? It wasn't as if we could vanish and never see each other again.

Our survival relied on our linked resources. It wasn't safe to jeopardize all of that.

Is it?

Sighing, I rubbed my eyes and stood. I needed a walk, and a few days ago, I'd come across a clearing in the forest where a thicket of bamboo grew. Long and thin and strong. I loved to listen to the rustle of their skinny leaves as the breeze made natural music.

I'd also found a cloud of butterflies hovering in the middle of the thicket, dancing like papery short-lived angels.

It relaxed me.

I need relaxing.

Ever since Galloway had caught me taking pictures on my phone, we'd shared the creation of memories and often recorded parts of our new life. We had home movies of fishing and digging and diary moments with no censorship on the mental toll and weighty depression that tarnished everything.

It helped…admitting such things. I was happy to share the device. However, I had one secret I didn't want him to know.

My notebook and lyrics.

My music was for me. Not him. Not the children (apart from the occasional lullaby for Pippa). Not for anyone. Scratching melodies and forming singable patterns was a therapeutic activity I wanted to keep hidden.

Not that my pages were immune to the hardship of the island.

With every rainstorm, my notebook grew damp, smearing verses, and washing some ink away entirely.

My bare feet slipped over the cool sand as I reached into my bag and hid my notebook in front of me. Staying as inconspicuous as possible, I headed away from the camp.

I wanted to compose but not around him.

He wouldn't understand the confusion inside me and I had no intention of telling him—not when he refused to tell me anything about his past. All I'd learned was he'd been on his way to Kadavu to build homes for underprivileged locals as part of a charity.

The fact he could build told me he was in that profession and the knowledge that he'd donated his time told me he was either a selfless human being or someone who had to atone for something.

Either way, I'd never know because he would never tell me.

"Where do you think you're going?" Galloway stopped carving his spear, his eyes catching blazing tendrils from the fire.

Damn.

I wasn't as discreet as I hoped.

Keeping my book hidden, I paused. "Going for a walk."

"To find Pippa and Conner?"

I kept my back to him, looking over my shoulder. "No, just…to clear my head."

"You can't clear it here—" He glanced down. "With me?"

The anxious, unfinished situation between us sprang deeper, demanding closure. For a week, we'd used the children or talks of island life as a way to avoid a messy confrontation.

I was just as guilty as he was for pushing it under the proverbial rug.

But I wasn't ready to deal with it.

I didn't think I'd ever be ready.

Don't do this…

His hands curled on the half-carved spear. "Estelle…you can't keep avoiding me."

"I'm not avoiding you."

"Bullshit."

Yes, well, you made me come. You took pleasure and layered it with punishment.

"It's not bullshit. I'm not avoiding you. I've just been...busy."

I flinched, hating the way my voice wobbled and chest emptied into a cavernous ache.

Neither of us spoke for a moment.

He cleared his throat. "We need to talk."

My heart swooped. "No, we don't."

"How about I make this easy for you?" He shifted, his splinted leg rustling in the sand.

Every day, he seemed slightly better. He hobbled now rather than hopped, but the injuries still hadn't healed.

"For the first time, we have the camp to ourselves. We can be honest. No cryptic talk, no games. I need to speak to you, to clear whatever the hell is going on between us, because this—" He waved at the space between him and me "—is not working."

I sighed heavily. My fingers clutched my notebook, dying to run away and ignore him. What could he do? Chase me?

Turning to face him, I kept the book behind my back. "Well, we're alive, and it's been five weeks, so something has to be working."

"You know what I mean."

I widened my eyes deliberately. "Truly, Galloway, I don't know what you want from me. You said it perfectly the other day when you had your hand down my shorts." I blushed when his mouth parted, and he licked his bottom lip. "You know I want you, but you're right, I'm afraid of you. And fear should never be part of a relationship."

"Wrong," he growled. "It should have everything to do with it."

"What?"

He watched me beneath hooded eyes. "You don't fear me, Estelle. You fear what I can make you *feel*. If you didn't feel when I touched you, then there wouldn't be anything between us. And there *is* something between us. Something that deserves to be explored."

I hated that he was right. I hated that he could see right through me and didn't give me anywhere to hide. I'd tried so hard to ignore him. I forced myself to forget the delicious sensation of his fingers inside me. I downplayed the epic release under his control. And I definitely didn't let myself dream of stealing him into the forest and finishing what he started.

I wanted him.

So, so much.

But he was right. I was frightened. For reasons I still didn't understand.

Galloway looked into the fire, granting me a brief reprieve from his gaze. "I don't know anything about you, Estelle. You won't talk about where you're from or who you are. You won't let me in. But this is our life now. We don't know how long we'll be here. And I'm sick to bloody death of lying in bed at night so damn hard from wanting you and not knowing where I stand."

His English accent. His words. They dripped like morphine through my blood, blocking my concerns.

My temper hissed. "*I* don't tell you stuff? What about you? Whenever I ask the simplest question you shut me down. Don't be hypocritical, Galloway, it doesn't suit you."

I would never tell him I understood his pathological need for secrets. I wasn't comfortable sharing pieces of myself, handing over my history, and willingly opening my world to another's criticism. I respected his need for space because I demanded the same.

Besides, I already know more than he thinks.

"Hypocritical? You want to play that card?" He bared his teeth. "Fine. Let's focus on who's the *true* hypocrite, shall we?"

My mouth fell open. "You can't mean me."

"Got it in one."

"How?"

His eyes narrowed. "You kissed me first, remember? You're the one who started this."

"That kiss was a mistake. We'd just crashed and were so thirsty we were a day away from dying. Excuse me if I gave into a spur-of-the-moment decision to have some happiness before I died."

"And it was a bloody amazing kiss." His hands tightened on his spear. "Do you deny it?"

I gritted my teeth. I wanted to deny it. If I did, it might put an end to this ludicrous conversation. But I'd never been a liar. I ran, yes. I hid, yes. I went out of my way to avoid a fight from anyone. But I'd never been a liar.

I hung my head. "It was good. That I can't deny."

"And the other day, when I made you come. Didn't that feel equally amazing?" The smugness in his tone irritated me.

My hackles rose. "Besides the point."

"No, it's *the* point. Answer the question. Did you or did you not like what I did to you?"

How dare he put me on the spot? What if Pippa and Conner could hear us?

"Galloway, stop—"

"No, I won't stop. Not until you put me out of my goddamn misery."

I breathed hard. "How?"

"Tell me the truth."

"What truth?"

"Can I have you or not? Will you let me take you to bed? Will you give in to whatever links us and put us both out of pain, or will you be stubborn and continue to avoid me?"

Keeping my notebook a secret was forgotten as I brought the pages in front of me and hugged it. I squeezed it as if the answers Galloway demanded could be found in its lined papyrus. "I—I don't know what to say."

"Do you want me or not? Simple question. Simple answer."

I sucked in a breath.

Nothing was simple about that. It was layered with commitment and the strength of putting my heart on the line when nothing was assured about our future.

"I don't know." My voice was a moth, fluttering and soft.

"Yes. Yes you do, Estelle." Galloway propelled himself upright, grabbing his crutch and hobbling closer. "Tell me. Right now. Yes or no."

"Yes or no to what?"

"To *us*, goddammit!"

I looked at the moon-silvered beach, fearing Conner and Pippa's return. "I can't answer that."

And don't ask me why because I don't know why.

I wanted him. I feared I might be in love with him. But I wouldn't let myself be any weaker than I already was. If I let him consume me, how would I survive if he died? How would I cope if he got sick and I couldn't heal him? How would I continue living *here* (in the epitome of loneliness and seclusion) if something happened to him?

No. It was too much. I had to remain a safe distance.

Care for him.

Love him.

But not fall *in* love with him. Never give him my heart because it would destroy me.

"Yes, you can. It's easy." He hobbled closer. "Nod for yes or shake your head for no." His free hand went between his legs, cupping the long erection visible in his board-shorts. "Let me know if you want this...want me." His jaw clenched as he thumbed the crown. "One little word, Estelle, and you have me. I'll let you command me every damn day we're on this godforsaken island and every day after. Just...say the word."

My breath vanished as if he'd stolen every inch from my lungs. I took a step back as he kept moving forward. Was he asking me to go out with him? Was that what this was? Was he expecting me to agree to a relationship with dates and anniversaries and...holy God, potential marriage? Or did he just want a screw-buddy to roll around in the sand until we were found or finally succumbed to death?

It hurt that my heart leapt at the former option.

I wanted commitment and someone to call my own. But not here where he would become everything and more to me. We would smother each other. We would fear our existence worse and worse the more we had to lose.

"I can't give you what you want." I shook my head. "Besides, it doesn't have to be that way."

"What way?"

"Demands and ultimatums."

"Yes, it does. Don't you get it? I can't keep hoping that one night you'll slip into my bed and kiss me again. I can't stop dreaming about your lips on mine or my fingers in your body. I want you, Estelle. No, I *need* you. And until I know where I stand, I can't turn the hope off."

He looked at me with such anger but also such a plea. He yelled but I held all the power because, unless I agreed, he couldn't have what he wanted.

He was pissed off that he had to give me the choice. I was surprised he didn't ignore my protests and claim me anyway.

I'd let him.

I shuddered at the truth. I'd not only let him—in a way, I wanted him to. He'd take the responsibility from me, and I'd have no choice but to fall and fall and hand over my life forever.

"I—I—"

Do it. Stop fighting. You like him. You want him every second of every day. What the hell are you waiting for?

Life was too short for nonsense. The fear of the children seeing us was inconsequential—they were old enough to understand. The terror that I'd give him my heart, only for him to die and leave me was unsustainable because that possibility existed in the biggest metropolis or on the tiniest island. And the idea that one day we'd be found, only to be broken-hearted if Galloway decided I was nothing more than a castaway fling wasn't enough to refuse temporary happiness.

We could be together.

We could bring each other pleasure.

We could have so much more in each other's arms than we did apart.

I took a step closer, my eyes locking onto his.

His back straightened, feeding off me as my decision formed stronger and stronger.

Yes, I wanted this.

Yes, I wanted him.

I wanted his kisses. His touch. His whispers. His caresses.

I wanted his body inside me. I wanted to fall asleep in his arms. I wanted to scream with pleasure as I came. And I wanted to bask in lust knowing I could do the same for him. "Galloway…"

He froze. "Yes or no, Estelle. If it's yes, you'd better be ready to have me because I can't stand another second."

We deleted another metre between us.

Two more left.

Barely anything at all.

My tummy flipped in anticipation.

"I—I want you."

His eyes snapped closed. "Thank hell for that."

He took another step. A single metre barricaded us.

My skin came alive, begging for his touch.

He would be happy with me. I'd give him safe harbour to relax and stop judging himself. He would find value in his worth by the way I held him, thanked him, and looked into his eyes as he slipped inside me.

Our bodies would join.

He'd thrust into me.

And every time he orgasmed—

I slammed to a stop.

No.

No, no, *no*.

Galloway tensed. "Whatever you're thinking, stop. You'd made up your mind. It was yes, Estelle. I saw it in your eyes. You were going to say yes."

I backed up. The one metre returned to two. "We can't."

"Can't?" He glowered. "Can't or won't?"

"We can't." I hung my head. "You've been honest with me, so I'll be honest with you. I want you. You know that. The thought of giving you everything that I am terrifies me, but I'd happily trade my stories for yours. I want your hands on my skin, your tongue in my mouth, and your body—"

He groaned, "Then do it. You have me." His hand stretched out, his fingers imploring me to take them. "Please...come here."

Looking at the sand, my voice slipped into sadness. "But none of that matters. I dream about having you, but that's all it can ever be. A dream."

"What?" His face contorted with rage. "Why the hell can't it be a reality if you want me as much as I want you?"

Raising my eyes, I couldn't believe how much I missed the modern world. How much I would've given to have a pharmacy close by or a doctor for prescriptions. But he didn't get it.

Orgasms meant combined pleasure.

Cum meant combined DNA.

Sex meant combined genetics.

I could get pregnant.

I might give birth on an island with no help.

I could die delivering, or worse, whatever infant we created could perish.

There were no safeguards. No fail safes. Eventually, no matter how careful we were...we'd slip and suffer the consequences.

I wanted children...eventually.

But not here. Not like this.

Not when we're so unprepared.

Sex had gone from the most tantalizing promise to the most abhorrent curse.

Tears trickled down my cheeks. "Let it go, Galloway. My answer is no. And it's final. I'll be your friend. But that's all I can offer you."

I couldn't stay for the repercussions.

Clutching my notebook, I ran.

••••••••••••••••••••••••••••

I didn't run to my hidden patch of bamboo. I didn't run to the beach to write by moonlight. I swam with guilt, overrun by emotions that wouldn't stay imprisoned in mere words. Instead, I bolted into the woods, into the green maze that could give us so much more than what we let it.

With tears running down my cheeks, I found the bush I'd marked *XI*.

I looked over my shoulder.

I cursed myself for denying what I wanted, refusing Galloway, running away from whatever happiness we might've had—all because I was too afraid.

I was weak. I wasn't worthy.

I had to make up for what I'd done.

And this was the only way I could think of.

With shaking hands, I tore off a leaf and stuffed it into my mouth. I should've taken the tiniest of bites. Let my system solve the question if it was edible.

But I didn't.

I couldn't give him my heart, but I could keep him alive.

I couldn't sleep with him, but I could give him something to eat.

I disobeyed his commands not to be reckless. I willingly went behind his back because I had no choice.

I'd just broken something good between us.

The least I could do was try to fix it.

I chewed the leaf and swallowed.

The bitter taste lingered on my tongue, warning me I wasn't used to the flavour.

My body wasn't savvy on the nutritional value of such a thing.

It could backfire. It could be painful. It could hurt.

It doesn't matter.

Tearing off another, I ate quickly.

I ate another.

And then three more, ensuring my system had no choice but to accept the foreign food or expel it.

Either way—be it sickness or good health—I'd done what I could to make up for the worst decision of my life.

I'd said no to Galloway. No to him looking after me. No to hugs and kisses and love.

I'd walked away from him and eaten what he'd told me not to.

He would hate me now.

And I'd live with the consequences.

Alone.

Chapter Thirty

GALLOWAY

WHAT THE HELL?

What the ever living goddamn hell?

I let her go.

I'd fought for her. I'd asked her to reconsider. And she'd shot me down. I wouldn't chase after her like a damn Labrador. I'd tried to win her and failed. That was as far as I was willing to go in terms of handing over my balls to a woman who was so damn contrary she didn't know what she wanted.

She wanted me as a friend?

Fine.

I'd be her friend. I'd be her acquaintance. I'd be nice when spoken to. I'd be courteous when dealt with. But besides that, forget it.

I'd had some stupid notion that Estelle would accept me. That she'd ignore my mistakes and flaws because of who she saw inside. I'd hoped I could finally find peace knowing whoever I'd been before no longer mattered because Estelle made me better.

But I was wrong.

She knew.

She could tell.

She'd guessed I was no good. Someone not to fall for. Definitely not someone to get physical with.

She'd seen I was bad news. And I couldn't bloody blame her for running.

That's it, then.

No matter how long we lived on this island, at least, I knew my place.

I was her friend.

I would protect her, care for her, tend to her needs, and do my best for the kids and our future.

But anything else, I couldn't do.

As of right now, every desire and trickle of lust would be shot down and destroyed.

I refused to live a life trapped in paradise with a woman who didn't want me.

My heart couldn't take it.

My body couldn't stand it.

The hope I'd stupidly clutched onto was dead.

Chapter Thirty-One

ESTELLE

. . . . . .

~~Love is a complicated entity.~~ Love is the worst affliction imaginable.
I'm no longer myself. Love changed me.
I'm no longer happy. Love ruined me.
I'm no longer alive. Love killed me.
I'm no longer breathing. Love consumed me.
Taken from the notepad of E.E.

. . .

SEVEN WEEKS

I'D COUNTED EVERY minute of every day for two weeks—waiting, expecting, *hoping* Galloway would lose his courteous kindness and demand a different answer to his question.

But he never did.

My secret about eating the leaves hung on my soul like iron shackles. I wanted to tell him what I'd done. I wanted to share the good news that I'd had no adverse reactions. My digestive system had accepted the island salad, and we might have another source of nutrition.

However, because an experiment had to be conducted over and over to ensure correct results (and because I didn't trust the first success) I ate it again.

And again.

In between the days of physically eating the leaf, I did four more scratch tests with different foliage. Out of the four, only two had swollen. The allergies had been painful and burned rather than itched. The most recent came from a plant with large, lily-pad like leaves. I'd scratched myself with no reaction, but when I'd eaten the leaf, I'd been violently sick. The sharp tang of bitter iron stayed with me for days, and it was only because of a sudden bout of helpless anger that I attacked the plant, ripped it from the soil, and found the tubular crop below.

It was familiar…like sweet potato or…

Stroking the muddy root, a vague memory returned: taro. Instantly, I discounted it as I remembered it was poisonous if not cooked correctly. I wasn't entirely sure on its preparation and was scared of the risks…but what if it turned out to be a staple like potatoes? The fibre and carbohydrates would be a godsend to our diet.

I wanted to tell Galloway. I wanted to ask his opinion.

But I couldn't.

I'd learned from the last scratch test not to let him see what I was doing and chose a different place to my forearm for further testing. My hipbones were a good selection. Thin skin, easy to irritate, and hidden away from view.

I kept a t-shirt and shorts on over the course of the two days that a particular swelling took to disappear.

I'd eaten another slightly denser leaf last week, testing the hypothesis from scratch to consuming. And apart from a small twinge in my gut, I'd been fine. However, that couldn't be said for another sample just a few days ago. That had twisted my insides with agony, dispelling itself with overwhelming cramps.

I'd been weak for a few days, doing my best to hide my affliction from the children and Galloway.

Every day, we ate clams and coconuts washed down by rainwater, and every day, I wanted to bring out the approved leaves and taro and announce a new element to our menu.

But something held me back.

I wanted to try again and again to make sure it was safe. I wanted to use myself as the guinea pig so when I did reveal my findings, Galloway had no choice but to accept it was a good decision.

I'd been terrified of returning to camp the night I left him with my final decision. I'd left it as long as I could before returning with my eyes downcast and guilt heavy on my spine.

But he hadn't pounced and made me reveal why I'd turned him down. He didn't yell or shout. He'd merely smiled when I placed a log on the fire and slipped into bed. The children had already returned, and Pippa was fast asleep with my puffer jacket thrown over her shoulders.

Conner had waved as I lay down, blowing me a kiss goodnight.

I'd caught it, barricading my soul from clenching with pain.

I didn't dare look at Galloway, but as I lay staring at the stars, his voice whispered across the sand. "Friends, Estelle."

Instead of being relieved, my heart broke, and I sniffed back tears. "Friends, Galloway. For life."

Ever since that ceasefire, we'd gotten on with our lives. Conner had become better with his spear, and he'd managed to catch three fish over the course of two weeks. The first had been a bright parrotfish that barely fed the children with its bony flesh and tiny fillets. The second had been a silver thing with spines that'd made Galloway bleed as he gutted it. And the third had been the largest—a species of reef fish I didn't know the name of, but tasted like the ocean and turned flaky when cooked.

The past few nights, Conner hadn't been successful, and we'd resorted to clams and coconuts (our version of rice and chicken). Meanwhile, I worked on another project to keep me busy.

We still didn't have shelter, and I'd reached my limit of sleeping on the cool sand. By day, our umbrella tree kept us safe from the sun, but at night, even the fire couldn't turn damp grains into a comfortable bed.

I'd tried to make a blanket a few weeks ago. After watching Galloway and Pippa plait metres of flax rope, I'd modified the idea and weaved larger pieces together. However, the plant material had been too dense and unbendable. Not at all useable as a blanket.

It wasn't a complete loss.

The stiffness of the weave meant it became a handy covering to sit on and we'd each taken turns to sleep on it to see if it would be better.

However, after a sleepless night, we all agreed it was too rough with prickly edges.

I hadn't given up and a fresh idea came to me after glaring at the mat, wishing I had some wool or cotton. Every material I craved was natural with manmade manipulation, to turn it from its original state (sheep's wool to decadent spun colours and silkworm cocoons into satiny dresses). I didn't have sheep or silkworms, but I did have something I could weave together; I just had to figure out how to make it softer.

"Whatcha doin'?" Pippa looked over my shoulder as I shredded more flax into the saltwater I'd gathered in a fuselage tray. I'd wedged the trough by the water's edge where the sun beamed the hottest.

"Hopefully making a blanket."

Pippa wrinkled her nose. "How?"

"Not sure yet." My pile grew bigger as I continued to shred.

Once I had enough strips, I pressed on the plant matter, drowning it. My hands revelled in the feel of warm liquid after the sun had heated it. The ocean was bath-warm and did perfectly fine for washing every day, but I missed hot showers and instant electricity for boiling water.

Coffee.

God, I missed coffee.

Caffeine in general.

For a few weeks after the crash, I'd had a caffeine headache that had nothing to do with dehydration.

I found it strange that I didn't crave fast food, but I did mourn the ability to go to a store and buy ingredients for anything I wanted. I was a vegetarian, so eating meat was never my thing, but spices were. Cumin and paprika and cinnamon. We had salt now (thanks to our coconut shell of evaporated seawater) but nothing else. No mint or sage or coriander.

No sugar.

God, I missed sugar just as much as I missed coffee. I couldn't deny I had a sweet tooth.

I smiled, nudging Pippa's shoulder with mine as she poked the drenched flax. "You're allergic to cocoa but what about sweets like marshmallows and things? Do you miss them?"

"Yes, I love gummy bears. Mummy rarely let me have them, though."

The sun had kissed every inch of Pippa's body a nutmeg brown. Most days, she ran around topless in her white knickers (well, now grey from swimming and no bleach). I'd tanned as well but not as much. Being blonde, I burned instead, but my hair had turned almost white thanks to always being in the ocean.

Galloway was the only one whose hair colour hadn't noticeably changed. It'd stayed a delicious dark chocolate, demanding my fingers to run through it.

He was so handsome. So wild and untamed, becoming sexier the further society slipped away. His beard framed his perfect lips, taunting me to kiss him, and his blue eyes only grew brighter the more he tanned.

His muscles had become even more defined as we all lost body fat, turning to sinew and skeleton. But his hands...they intoxicated me the most. Was it because two of his fingers had been inside me? Or was it because of the visible veins disappearing up ropy forearms?

Everything about him turned me on. The daily battle was real.

Not to mention, a second period had tormented me the past

few days. I'd always been irregular and the fact I had no sanitary products meant those days were the worse. Leaves could only do so much. (Let's just say, laundry day turned into laundry hour and I stayed alert when I swam, just in case of sharks).

I hate being a woman.

I squeezed the flax, wringing out some of my frustration.

"G said he'd show me how to make a necklace out of fish bones." Pippa beamed. "You want to learn, too?"

He knows how to do that?

My heart fluttered. Galloway...*sigh*. He'd gone out of his way to entertain the children, making me want him almost as much as I wanted sugar and coffee.

No, I want him more than that.

I squeezed my eyes.

Stop it.

"I'd love a lesson...if it's okay if I join."

"Yep."

"It's a date then."

Drying my hands on my legs, I pushed upright.

Pippa followed, her body nimble and naked chest showing a skinny girl who needed to put on a few kilos.

Are we malnourished?

Will my periods vanish the longer we stay?

How long could a human body function before vitamins and minerals depleted to dangerous levels?

"That's it?" She pointed at the flax. "Are you going to drain it?"

"No, I'll let the sun and water rot it a little."

"Rot?"

"I'm not sure that's what I want to happen. But I need the structure to break down, so it becomes malleable. Rotting is the best idea I came up with."

"And the salt water will do that?"

"Who the hell knows?" I threw my arm over her shoulders. "I guess we'll find out, won't we? Now, let's go find G and play with fish bones."

Chapter Thirty-Two

GALLOWAY

· · · · · ·

EIGHT WEEKS

WAS IT POSSIBLE to hate everything but be grateful at the same time?

I hated clams, but I loved them because they fed us.

I hated the evergreen-tainted water from the trees, but I loved every droplet because it quenched my thirst.

I hated the sand, the sun, the waves, the island, the calendar on Estelle's bloody phone marking every day we'd been missing, but I loved them all because I was alive to see them.

And I hated Estelle...but I loved her, too.

Damn curse.

Damn woman.

I'd done what I'd promised and locked away every desire and craving I had for her. I treated her like the best friend I never had. I went out of my way to be kind and courteous and how did she repay me? By watching my every move with lust dripping from her pores. She licked her lips if I stripped in the hot sun. She sucked in a breath if I accidentally brushed past. Her body sent message after message to take her.

She infected my dreams, my thoughts, every damn moment.

It wasn't fair.

I suffered a permanent case of blue balls and deliberately sat farther and farther away from her at meal times and during chores around the camp.

But it didn't help.

There was no ignoring the heat in her gaze or the begs in her body.

But she'd told me no.

And until she told me yes, she could keep staring, keep hurting both of us. I'd tried to make her accept me, and she'd turned me down. If she wanted me…it was her turn to do the grovelling.

Conner groaned as his spear flew sideways down the beach. If the kid wasn't in the ocean hunting fish, he was on the sand practicing.

Today was no different.

My leg itched and I wanted the splint off. If I were honest, I'd wanted it off the day Estelle had put it on. But I didn't dare remove it. I was too chicken to see if the break was still abnormally crooked.

I'd become used to estimating the time with the placement of the sun, and I guessed it was threeish. Estelle and Pippa had disappeared to find firewood, and I was sick to death of plaiting rope for a house I still wasn't physically ready to build.

Screw it.

Hauling myself up, I grabbed my walking stick. Last week, I'd chopped my crutch in half so I could use it as support rather than a second leg. I'd disposed of the end, keeping the bulbous root for a convenient handhold.

Hopping toward Conner, I was grateful the sharp pain had turned to an aching throb and was tempted to put more and more weight on my ankle.

Don't be an idiot.

In my heart, I knew it hadn't healed. If I rushed it…it would only backfire.

Conner swiped his long, sun-turned hair from his eyes as he jogged to collect the spear and return to his starting spot. He frowned as I patted him on the shoulder and kept hopping toward the water's edge. "Come on. I have an idea."

He immediately ran after me. Shirtless, his chest had filled out, straining to become a man even on limited food. "Hunting?"

"Yep."

"But the fish aren't around at this time. They'll be back to feed in an hour or two."

I smirked. "Been staring at them so long you know their dates and appointments, huh?"

He scowled. "If only that knowledge came in handy and let me catch the bastards."

"Language."

He snickered.

I let him swear. After all, if we couldn't curse here…where could we? Estelle and her need for verbal purity be damned. "Well, let's try for something else." The thought of a cheeseburger with all the trimmings once again tormented me. I missed flavour. I missed lemon zest and mayonnaise. I missed garlic and barbecue sauce. Everything that made boring food awesome was missing in our bare essential pantry.

My crutch sank into the wet sand as I traded dry land for lapping waves. Wriggling my toes in the water, I glared at the turquoise sea. Our turquoise prison. "Let's see what else we can find."

"Like what?" Conner splashed beside me. He'd become part water nymph with how much time he spent in the salty realm.

I shrugged. "Not sure."

His eyes fell on my splint. "Can you swim with that?"

He knew the answer already. We'd been on this island for two months, and I'd yet to wade out of the shallows because I couldn't kick with the cumbersome weight.

His voice lowered. "Do you think you should rest it more? I mean, you've never just lay down and let us do the work. What if it's not fixed—"

I cut him off. I couldn't stomach that conversation. "I can rest when I'm dead, and I have no intention of dying on this island. Broken bones won't stop me from doing what I need to do."

"Doesn't matter anyway." Conner stabbed his spear into the crystal water. "The reef isn't that far. It only comes up to my chin, so you'll be okay. You won't have to swim." He squinted in the sun, assessing my height. "You can be on spot duty. If you see something, yell and I'll catch it."

I cracked a grin. "All right, Aqua Boy."

He rolled his eyes. "I want a cooler nickname."

"Can't get a nickname unless you earn it."

"I've earned it."

I waded deeper. The density of the water fought the floatable properties of my walking stick.

Don't need it in the water anyway.

Twisting, I tossed the support up the beach and out of the wave's grip.

"Ready?"

Conner smiled. "Ready."

"Let's see if we can get you a cooler nickname than Aqua Boy." The sun bounced off the surface, blinding me. Every day, I mourned the loss of my glasses. I was sick to bloody death of straining to see and living with a permanent haze. Would I ever see Estelle in high definition again? Would I ever be able to look into her eyes and see hazel swirls and not a mist of muddy colour?

That's besides the point.

She'd never let me get close enough. She wanted me but for some reason turned me away. I wasn't going to keep begging.

Limping through the warm water, I said, "Keep your eyes open for anything on the bottom. That'll be easier to catch than fish at this point."

"Good because I suck at catching fish."

"You don't suck."

"Do too." His jaw clenched. "But I'm gonna become great. Every day, I want to catch a fish for each of us. Four fish a day. Watch me. It will happen."

I sucked in a breath as the water crossed my waistline, reaching for my chest. "I have no doubt."

"Strange that I want them so bad when I don't even *like* fish." My eyes widened. "You don't?"

He pulled a face. "Hell, no. They're gross."

I chuckled. "Believe me, if you never get off this island, you'll start to like fish."

Conner froze at the reference of never being free but stuck out his tongue and played along. "No, I won't."

"Believe me, you will when there's nothing else to eat."

"You found clams, and they aren't too bad."

"Yes, but we have to vary our diet; otherwise, things like scurvy happen."

Conner ducked under the water to wet his hair. "Scurvy? Is that like the bleeding gum thing pirates used to get?"

I laughed. "Where did you learn that?"

"Playing *Assassin's Creed.*"

"Of course, you did." I kept moving. "And to answer your question, you get scurvy from lack of vitamin C."

"Well, sorry to say I don't see any oranges growing around here."

"Vitamin C comes from many places, but you're right, that's one source." Out the corner of my eye, I spotted a flash below the surface. Lunging forward, I snatched Conner's spear and stabbed it into the sand.

An awful squelch and crunch of something living ricocheted up my arm. "Got dinner."

Conner shoved his face underwater (as if he could see without goggles). Spluttering, he said, "What? What is it?"

Whatever it was wriggled and fought. "Not sure." I couldn't make it out through the rippling ocean and my shoddy eyesight failed me once again. Whatever I'd harpooned wasn't happy about it.

Sand swirled from the depths.

Conner squeaked, lifting his feet off the bottom. "It's fighting pretty good."

My arms bunched as the spear shifted to the left, moved by whatever I'd stabbed.

"If I pull up, it will escape." I frowned. "We need to get it to the surface somehow."

"What do you want me to do?"

I ran through the scenarios. We couldn't use our hands—just in case it was venomous. And we had nothing else. Inspiration struck. "Run back to the camp and grab the piece of metal we use as a spade."

Conner didn't need telling twice. He swam off in a breaststroke, beaching himself and tearing up the sand.

I stood there, fighting with the creature below, waiting for him to return.

He didn't waste time. Bolting back with a smaller piece of fuselage, he dived into the water and popped up beside me. "Here you go."

"Use the metal and go down there and wedge it beneath it."

"What? Hell, no. I'm not doing that."

I laughed. "Just testing your manliness." If he'd agreed, I would've forbid it. What sort of father figure would I be if I made him fight with an unknown sea monster? "The look on your face means you'll forever be known as Aqua Boy."

"You suck." Shoving the metal at me, he wrapped his hands around the spear. "New deal. I'll hold it while you go down."

"Good plan." I let him take control.

The moment I let go, his face shot white. "Damn, it's struggling hard."

"Don't let it escape." I brushed hair away from my face, preparing to dive under. "Stay leaning on it. Got it?"

He nodded.

Taking a deep breath, I shot beneath the surface, blinking in briny water. I couldn't see crap, but something blurred and wriggled like a demon on the seafloor. Doing my best to fight buoyancy and swim with a splinted leg, I stabbed the sharp tip into the creature, trying to put it out of its misery before wedging the metal into the sand beneath it.

Is it dead?

Something slimy wrapped around my wrist.

Shit, not dead.

I swallowed a mouthful of water and shot upright.

Conner fought the creature, his face dripping wet. "Now, what?"

Rubbing my wrist, I made sure I hadn't been bitten or stung. The slime and suckers said we'd stabbed an octopus.

Lucky us.

Hopefully, it wasn't a blue-ringed bastard. Those were dangerous and definitely not edible. "I'm going down again. I'll raise the metal while you move with me, okay? We'll keep it pinched between the two. Just move when I push."

He swallowed hard. "Got it."

Taking a breath, I dived again, fighting revulsion as the prey instantly wrapped around my wrist. Ignoring it, I pushed upward, signalling to Conner to rise with me.

He did as planned, slowly pulling the eight-tentacle animal from the depths.

The closer I got to the surface, the more my skin crawled. The octopus wrapped three, four, five sucked arms around my skin.

At least, Lady Luck decided to give us a break. The flesh of our prey was slimy-grey, not bright blue circles.

Conner squealed as our meal erupted from the sea, wriggling in its multiple-armed glory.

The suckers remained glued to my arm, but its head and nasty beak were pinned against the metal.

Struggling a little with its heavy weight and flailing body, I took the spear and kept the octopus safely pinioned. "Good job. Let's go."

Wading back to the beach, I caught sight of Estelle as she appeared with Pippa from the treeline. Afternoon sun glowed on her face, hardening my cock despite my resolution to avoid everything to do with her.

There was something about her.

Something I couldn't ignore.

I just hoped she couldn't ignore it, too.

Because I didn't know how much longer I could keep my promise to be her friend.

....

"We come in peace." Conner pranced ahead with the dead creature aloft.

We'd taken the time to kill the octopus down at the water's edge and wash off the natural slime and too-late-to-be-effective ink.

The girls (who had their heads bent together weaving the flax

Esselte had boiled in the sun for a week) looked up.

"Eww!" Pippa sprang to her feet, backing up. "Get it away."

Conner laughed, dashing forward to taunt his sister. "What? Never seen an octopus before?"

"No!" Pippa darted behind the umbrella tree. "Co, don't!"

Conner didn't listen, chasing her and waving the eight-suckered sea life in her face. "It's gonna get you, Pip!"

"No!"

"Conner, stop harassing your sister." Estelle set down her work and stood, massaging the kinks in her back from working with no table or chairs.

The past few weeks things I'd taken for granted became sorely missed: a table to write on, chairs to recline in, utensils to help us resemble human beings rather than sand dirty savages.

I missed light switches and air-con and flushing toilets. I missed cars and radio and internet browsers. But I also missed simpler things. I missed the silence of a house when all the doors were closed. I missed the comfort of having a roof and walls protecting me from the outside. Here, the slap of the waves was constant, the buzz of mosquitos never far away, and the breeze we could never escape was part enemy, part friend.

Estelle's gaze dropped to my soggy splint. "How was it swimming?"

"Useless. I think it's time to come off."

She pursed her lips. "You might be right."

I stiffened. First thing I'd be right about, according to her.

I wanted it off. I could've done it myself many times over, but I didn't because of some stupid reason.

A reason that would never come true.

I want her to do it.

I wanted her fingers on my thigh. I wanted to make her touch me because God knew she wouldn't touch me otherwise. She hadn't even changed the leaf-padding in the weeks it'd been on…deliberately withholding care from her patient. A patient who'd reached the end of his patience. A patient who wouldn't be able to stop if she ever *did* touch him.

In two months, I hadn't been touched. It wasn't something that'd ever crossed my mind that I needed…but hell…I did.

The kids weren't cuddly. Pippa got her needed affection from Estelle, and Conner was happy with a fist-bump rather than an embrace. And Estelle got her hugs from Pippa and the occasional one from Conner.

What did I get? Nothing.

Bloody nothing.

I'd never been a massive hugger—only hugging those I truly cared for. My dad earned his fair share, and my mother was smothered in them toward the end.

But apart from that, I kept my physical contact to a minimum—even when I'd had no choice with what happened after my mum's death, I didn't seek out any more than I had to.

But Estelle?

Living with her. Sleeping by her. Watching her. Being the best goddamn friend I could be to her.

It was killing me.

Every damn day, I died a little more. I craved a little harder. I dreamed a little deeper.

I'm pathetic.

I'd given my heart to this woman, against my wishes and common sense, and slid further down the slippery slope into love-lust. And she didn't love-lust me back. Not the way I needed her to.

Hey, that was life. We crashed landed. Why did I ever think I would find a silver lining?

When I didn't respond, she returned to massaging her lower back.

"Want me to get that for you?" I smirked, hiding everything I would never say.

She smiled softly. "I'm good. Thanks, though."

She didn't even want a platonic massage from a friend.

Why do I even bother?

I moved away. "Conner." My bark came out firmer than I'd intended. "Give me that damn animal and give Pippi a break. Let's make dinner."

Dinner.

Thank hell for something other than clams.

Pippa charged to my side and curled her arm around my hips. "Don't let him touch me with that."

Having her little body snug against mine hurt my blackened heart. Ducking to her level, I crushed her to me. I didn't care if I came across as a psycho. I just wanted a hug.

She froze, not used to such embraces from me. Tentatively, she squeezed me back. Her lips smashed on my bearded cheek. "Love you, G."

I ruffled her hair. "Love you, too."

Estelle watched the entire thing.

Let her watch.

Standing, I didn't give on that it hurt just as much when Pippa left as it had when she'd hugged me. I was in a weird headspace and needed some time to sort my mess out.

Grabbing the octopus from Conner, I hobbled to the fire and unsheathed the Swiss Army knife.

Estelle followed me. "How on earth did you catch that thing?"

"Teamwork."

"Is it safe to eat?"

"Safe as any squid you've ever had." I struggled to sit down. I couldn't wait until I could bend and not have to put my leg straight out in front of me with the damn splint.

"We're going to eat that?" Pippa's eyes widened. "But it has tento—tenta—tenttoplicles."

"They're called tentacles and yes. It's delicious." I laughed as she scrunched up her face.

Conner poked the dead animal on my lap. "It's going straight in my stomach. Don't care what it tastes like. I'm starving."

I grinned. "Proud of you, Co. We'll have a feast tonight thanks to your hunting skills."

He opened his mouth to argue, but I shushed him. The logistics didn't matter. He'd worked hard, and this was his triumph, not mine.

Infectious anticipation spread through the camp, turning everyday drudgery into excitement. Everyone crowded around me as I used the knife to cut off the head. Next, I cut the eight tentacles into sections and handed them over to the children to take to the sea to wash.

It needed to be tenderised, but I couldn't be assed. And I was sure there were many ways to cook such a delicacy, but all I could come up with was kebabs.

Once cleaned, I skewed the rubbery meat onto four sticks and passed them to my stranded family. "Dinner."

Estelle smiled gratefully. "Thank you."

"Don't thank me. Thank Conner."

She redirected her smile. "Thanks, Co."

He glanced at me before grinning. "No sweat."

Instead of taking a place by the fire, Estelle's eyes clouded, looking behind her at the undergrowth.

What's her problem?

"You know what?" She passed her octopus stick to Pippa. "You cook for me. I'll be back in a moment."

"What? Why?" I stood awkwardly, brushing sand from my ass. "Where are you going?"

"Umm, nothing. Just…give me a sec." She padded up the

beach and into the trees.

I stared after her. Either she had to use the facilities or there was something she wasn't telling me.

Who was I kidding? There was a *lot* she wasn't telling me.

I tried to put it out of my mind while the kids shoved their kebabs into the fire and I taught them the best way to chargrill an octopus, but I couldn't.

I hated that she hadn't opened up to me. I hated that I still knew nothing about her.

That's because the price of her past comes with demanding yours.

And I wasn't ready to spill that can of dirty worms.

Finally (not that much time had passed) Estelle returned, slightly sheepish, slightly afraid, but mostly defiant.

I frowned. "What do you have behind your back?"

She came forward, still keeping it hidden. "Now...before you spaz out, listen to me."

My spine stiffened as every muscle seized. "Spaz out? Why the hell would I 'spaz out?' I don't *spaz out.*"

She pinned me with a 'yeah right' look. "Because you're protective and won't like what I'm about to say."

My fist curled tighter around my stick. "Go on."

"A couple of weeks ago, I ate one of the leaves that passed the scratch test."

I sucked in a breath. Christ almighty, she had a death wish. That was all I could think of because eating foreign material was a sure way to kill yourself.

I couldn't speak.

Estelle took that as a sign to keep going. Pulling a haphazardly woven basket from behind her back, she revealed a thicket of mismatched leaves.

More than one type.

A damn salad full with some knobbly looking potato things hidden below.

I glowered. "How many?"

She ducked her eyes. "Four so far." Glancing at the kids, she added, "I've sampled each one every day for the past week to see if my system could handle it long term. I wouldn't give anything to you guys unless I was sure it was edible." She shrugged, seeming smaller and less certain. "We needed something to supplement our diet with...well, now we do."

I wanted to throw my damn octopus stick at her. I wanted to grab her and kiss the bloody daylights out of her. I wanted to scream and yell and get on my knees and thank her for being brave enough to do something so selfless.

"I can't believe you." My growl hid my true thoughts. "I can't *believe* you went behind my back."

She flinched. "I know. I'm sorry. But I was willing to take the risk. Like I said, it's my body—" She cut herself off, rolling her shoulders. "Anyway, I figured we have a great dinner tonight, so let's make it even better with a salad. And if we can figure out how to prepare the taro…that's another element of food we can enjoy."

"Yay!" Pippa jumped up and down. "Yum. Gimme." Her hand disappeared into the basket, and before I could yell, stuffed a few leaves into her mouth.

"What the hell did she just eat?" My question was for Estelle, but Pippa answered with her mouth full. "Rabbit food."

Estelle looked at me from beneath lowered eyes. "It's sharper and more bitter than what we've eaten before, but we'll get used to it. Not to mention, there's an endless supply if we grow to like the taste."

"I like it." Pippa reached for another handful. "I like it better than clams."

Conner wrinkled his nose but accepted a glossy leaf as Pippa practically shoved it in his mouth.

He chewed hesitantly.

I waited until he swallowed. "Well?"

He raised an eyebrow. "Not as bad as I thought."

Pippa rushed to grab the salt and a few coconut shards that we'd sliced that afternoon. Sprinkling the white flesh over the salad and a small pinch of seasoning, she grinned. "Mummy taught me everything tastes better with salt."

What an odd kid.

Estelle caught my eye. She wouldn't relax until I gave my permission. And when she looked at me that way, how could I not give it?

She played every chord on my heart like a damn maestro.

Shedding my annoyance, I nodded. "I won't forgive you for doing something so reckless behind my back. But I won't refuse to eat it if you say it's safe. I trust you and won't waste your sacrifice."

She exhaled with huge relief.

Having her emotions tied intrinsically to my happiness was yet another hint that she'd lied about only wanting to be friends.

Well, she knew where I lived if she changed her mind.

Forcing a grin for the kids, I clapped. "I guess tonight's menu no longer just features an octopus.

"Let's tuck in."

Chapter Thirty-Three

∙∙∙

ESTELLE

∙∙∙∙∙∙

∙∙∙

<u>**TWELVE WEEKS**</u>
(December)

ONCE WITHIN A song, a girl had everything stripped away in an instant. But in nothing, she found the value of something far more precious.

The night we had octopus was a changing point for us.

Galloway never mentioned me sampling the foliage for food and never refused the leaves I deemed fine to consume. We soaked the taro for a few days and tossed away the water before double boiling to ensure whatever toxins existed were no longer harmful.

Trial by trial, knowledge by knowledge, we all learned new skills. It wasn't a conscious decision (although I did my best to advance my understanding on a daily basis) but evolution taking control to ensure our survival.

Things I'd never paid attention to suddenly became useful: the skinny vines hanging like streamers in the trees became natural string. The large taro leaves became handy pouches and coverings for our slowly growing larder of food. We threaded the vertebrae and discarded bones from our dinners on string to create wind chimes, composing music in the breeze, or slightly morbid jewellery for Pippa.

The island had stripped everything away, but in return, it'd given us new choices. Choices that held so much more importance than internet browsing or television channels.

Here…our concerns had whittled down to one: *surviving*.

As long as we achieved fire, warmth, food, and companionship…we were winning at this new life. No matter the stress of abandonment and constant wondering if we were lost forever, we had each other and that was priceless.

Conner's success (thanks to Galloway) with the octopus, invigorated him to keep improving his spearing skills and most days (admittedly after hours of lunging and sometimes defeat) he came home with a fish.

If he wasn't so lucky, he returned with other morsels. He produced an eel last week, which was almost as terrifying as the dead sea snake, a large crab two days ago that gave each of us a mouthful of delicious flesh, and yet more clams.

Between the food from the sea and the salad from the forest, we curbed our hankering for variety, but we couldn't confuse our taste buds into wanting more flavour.

I *craved* seasoning other than salt. I would've given away every basket I'd woven just for a bottle of peach iced tea. I'd even donate my semi-successful flax blanket for a heavenly sip of chilled apple cider.

The other night, Galloway had been discussing the children's birthdays as Pippa was turning eight soon. He'd let it slip that his was only a few weeks after hers.

I'd hoped rescue would be their gift. However, if fate wasn't that kind, I had plans to make the softest, comfiest blanket I could for both of them.

My technique of rotting the strands until they were pliable worked. The overall result gave us something to drape without being stiff and scratchy. And I'd already thought up new ways on how to refine the concept with scraping the filaments before soaking, thrashing them, bruising them. Experiments that would hopefully yield something better.

Apart from the overheard conversation, we didn't discuss our previous lives often. Some unspoken agreement existed that those memories would only depress us, and for now…we were different people (stranded, wild, and entirely dependent on the land) and no longer city dwellers with bankcards or phone numbers.

It didn't mean I stopped believing in gift giving and appreciation. The past month, Galloway had morphed from my friend into my confidant, rock, and brother. The way he watched me with cobalt-blue arrows ensnared my heart until it beat only for him.

Most days, he hid his dark pain, smiling and interacting, showing only a muscular islander with long chocolate hair, sable eyelashes, and a mouth that entranced me whenever he talked.

But some days, he looked as if he'd been up all night drinking, hung over with whatever he'd done in his past, buried beneath guilt and disgrace. Those days, I fell for him more. Because those days made me see the truth.

He wasn't just a man. He wasn't the tatty clothes he wore or the unkempt emotions he hid. He was mine. And I wanted him more than anything.

But not once had he forced me to face my feelings. He no longer avoided me. He chatted with me, laughed with me, discussed new ways to harvest water and store supplies. He walked with me (or rather limped with me) on nights I wanted to stroll with no messy undertones and helped with chores with no anger or hidden contempt.

He was the perfect gentleman.

But one thing was missing.

I wasn't proud of my actions. I hated myself for turning him down with no explanation. But I couldn't help it. I'd denied myself what I wanted. Not because of some stupid decision, but because of a bonafide fear of getting pregnant. Despite the length of time here, my periods hadn't stopped. I could still give birth.

Maybe once they stop?

But they might never stop. We might scavenge and hunt enough that my body never ceased being fertile.

Galloway didn't know my fears, and my terror didn't stop me from growing wet or watching him every second I could. Some mornings, I'd pretend to be asleep just to catch a glimpse of his morning erection as he stood. I gawked when he came out of the ocean in his black boxer-briefs, and one day, when I'd been in the tide with Conner and Pippa and he'd been on his own up the beach, I'd caught him naked, slipping commando into his board-shorts. The size and shape of him had clenched my core until I could've come with the slightest touch.

The throbbing desire drove me mad. I became tongue-tied whenever he was near because all I could think of was sex, sex, *sex.*

I'd tried to hug him the night we ate octopus and told ghost stories around the fire. I'd gathered the courage to touch him as a friend and hoped I was strong enough to keep it platonic.

But when I'd leaned in, he'd backed away, pouring acid on my wounds with a small shake of his head and a glow in his eyes that destroyed me.

Friends to him was no touching, no spilling of secrets, no talking of our pasts or dreams. Friendship to him was plodding through life, making tools for the camp, and ensuring we had enough food for another day.

I grieved for the ruined opportunity but stood firm on not risking our livelihood.

So far our existence worked. The sun shone and our island kept us provided for.

However, that wasn't the case the past few days.

The sun had vanished, swallowed up by gunmetal grey clouds and a constant drizzle. Everything we owned became saturated—including ourselves—and we had nowhere to go for shelter.

Last night, we'd tried to sleep in the forest, hoping the trees would protect us, but it was useless.

During daylight, we did what was necessary: collected rainwater, hunted for another day's ration, and carved a few twigs into chopsticks so we'd finally have utensils to use after so long with just our fingers.

But none of it made us happy.

We existed in foggy soup, lethargic and sad, staring at the sky, begging the sun to return.

My phone wouldn't charge because there were no solar rays, so we had no distraction or photo entertainment; our emotions turned downtrodden. Would we ever get off this piece of dirt? Would we ever live in a city again? Would Conner and Pippa ever come to terms with their loss and live a normal life with school and friends and parties?

I spent most days by the water's edge, glaring out to sea, battling with depression and the constant swinging emotions of incurable positivity and debilitating wretchedness.

Everyone was so brave. I hated that I was weak enough to miss home, miss toilets and roofs and restaurant-cooked meals.

Desolation built slowly but surely, drawing power from my desire to keep going. I wasn't proud to admit it, but some days, I wanted to throw myself into the ocean and swim

swim

swim.

Swim until I found someone to save us and pretend none of this was real.

But I couldn't.

I had children who relied on me, and it was their blind faith that Galloway and I could protect them that stuffed the cloud of grief back into its padlocked box and allowed me to smile and create and pretend that this was just an adventure and not the rest of our godforsaken lives.

I did my best to teach the children on the afternoons when we rested beneath our tree. But I hadn't applied myself at college and Galloway was cagey about his education. We weren't scholars and I failed in teaching algebra and trigonometry when I barely remembered my own schooling.

I groaned, doing my best to get comfortable in the damp sand. The day had ended and the sky had darkened. The stars couldn't shine, hiding their brilliant sparkle in the mist.

My bones ached and our fire spluttered and wheezed as drizzle did its best to slowly suffocate it.

For two days, we'd barely moved from the meagre warmth of the flames, waiting for the weather to switch and greyness to pass.

I'd had enough.

We couldn't let sadness infect us.

Once we did, it would be all over.

"Come on." I stood up, swatting at my sandy legs. "We're doing something."

Pippa threw a hand over her eyes, lying on her back. "I don't wanna."

"Too bad. We're going to."

Conner sat up, rubbing his face. "Do we *have* to?"

"Yes. Up."

Galloway groaned. His hair covered one eye and his lips glistened with every sinful thing I wanted to do to him.

I expected an argument, but he levered himself up and grabbed his walking stick. "Come on, guys. What's the harm? Got nothing better to do."

In a mixture of grumbles, everyone climbed to their feet and swiped wet hair from their foreheads. Silently, they followed me to the water's edge a little way away from the camp.

I didn't know where I was going. I had no clue what I was doing.

Please…let me come up with something. Something therapeutic but fun.

In the weeks since the crash, we'd formed some resemblance of fun. We'd played games, told jokes. We'd scratched tic-tac-toe, a checkers board, and rudimentary snakes and ladders in the sand. For pawns, we used twigs and shells, letting the tide wipe our game board away whenever it crept up the beach.

I stopped.

That's it!

Everyone slammed to a halt.

"So…what's the big idea?" Conner frowned. "Come on, Stelly, I want to go back to the fire."

"Stop whingeing." I marched to Galloway and stole his walking stick. "May I?"

He let go of it instantly, avoiding my fingers as if I was contaminated. "By all means."

His leg had healed enough that he could stand without support.

His splint needs to come off.

Wasn't a normal cast about six to eight weeks (depending on how bad the break was, of course)? His had been on for twelve. I was surprised he hadn't taken it off yet.

What if he fears the same thing I do?

The fear that he still limped, not because of the obstruction around his leg, but because of his body's inability to heal properly?

Don't be ridiculous. He'll be fine.

He *had* to be fine.

I couldn't…I couldn't cope if he wasn't.

Swallowing those thoughts, I strode away and used the end of his stick to scratch into the sand. Mist and sea spray dampened my holey clothes. I was miserable and low but my mother had taught me this trick. However, she hadn't shown me on the beach; she'd shown me in a field where the wind was the eraser and not the ocean. But it worked, that much I knew.

Everyone crowded around me.

The songwriter part of me had an outlet for my emotional troubles. I found solace in scribbling sonnets when no one was looking. Each time I jotted something down, I felt a little lighter, a tad calmer, more able to deal.

I had that outlet. But what did Conner, Pip, and Galloway have?

"What are you doing?" Pippa asked, her hair tangled like a kelpie.

I smiled. "Something secret."

"Doesn't look secret." Conner crossed his arms.

"Well, it's magic then."

"Doesn't look like magic, either."

I scowled at the teenager before scratching more words. He'd been getting argumentative as the calendar inched onward. "Just wait. You'll see."

Biting my lip, I manhandled the large stick-pen and finished my design. My heart skipped a beat as I stepped back and bumped into Galloway.

He stiffened but didn't move away, letting me catch my balance. His body was warm (so much warmer than mine) and the same electrical charge flowed from his skin, lighting up dormant cells, turning my blood into a heated pathway of need.

My insides clenched and melted at the same time.

I gave him a fleeting smile. "Thanks."

He cleared his throat but didn't reply.

Pippa read what I'd carved into the sand: *"Give me your worries and I shall make them disappear."* Her brown eyes met mine. "What does that mean?"

"Ugh, I'm not interested." Conner's hair stood up in all directions as he shook his head. "It means a counselling session, Pip. And we don't need one of those."

Is it puberty turning him into a brat or the lack of sunlight and endless drizzle?

I held my frustration…barely. "Just go with me, Co. You don't have to question everything."

"Yeah, I do. I know about this stuff and I'm not playing."

"It isn't a game."

"Don't care."

My eyebrows rose. "How do you know about counselling, anyway? Why would you know about that stuff?"

He shrugged, full of blustery blasé, but his gritted teeth hinted at glass-sharp memories. "My parents went to a marriage counsellor. I overheard them doing homework exercises and 'sharing their worries' so they could be happy again."

The memory of Amelia and Duncan Evermore didn't fit with the description of a strained couple. But no one truly knew the inner workings of another's life.

Pippa sucked in a shaky breath, her eyes filling with tears. "I miss them."

Immediately, my arm lashed out and snuggled her against me. "And you're allowed to miss them."

She wiped her nose on the back of her hand. "When will it stop hurting?"

My heart broke. "No one can tell you that, Pip. It's a time thing."

She stared at the sand, her little shoulders quaking.

"So how does this work?" Galloway's voice blanketed my soul, gracefully planting himself on my side of the argument. "What exactly are we meant to do?"

I looked up.

His gaze was locked on Pippa, despair and helplessness on his face. As much as he pretended to be unaffected by the children, he adored little Pippa. And the fact she grieved and he couldn't do anything about it…it drove him wild.

Knowing he had such capacity to love drove me wild in return.

Why am I staying away from him again?

Why did I sleep alone when I could sleep with him? Why did I punish myself with no contact when I could touch him whenever I wanted?

My reason seemed less and less a deciding factor and more and more like a pesky nuisance.

I cleared my throat, forcing my jackrabbit heart to calm down. "I'll show you."

Galloway cocked his head. "Show us what?"

"The magic of washing our worries away."

Conner groaned dramatically but didn't leave. For all his 'I'm too cool for this,' he was still young enough to value togetherness and joint activities.

I see through you, Conner.

Stepping forward, I held the walking stick ready to write. Everyone fell silent as if I truly had the ability to conjure a spell.

I wished I did.

I wished I had a wand where I could manifest a boat and sail away. Or whimsically wish for a plane to fly home. Or pluck a phone signal from the sky and call for help.

I wanted to see Madeline. I wanted to hug Shovel-Face. I wanted to buy contraception so I could jump Galloway and not be afraid.

But I wasn't a witch and this wasn't that sort of magic.

Ducking to look into Pippa's eyes, I murmured, "What are you most afraid of?"

She flinched.

Galloway growled, "You really think that's a good question to ask?"

I hushed him. I had doubts, but this had helped me. If it helped Pippa, then I was willing to take the risk.

Pippa glanced at her brother, silently asking for help.

Conner splayed his hands, but his face was encouraging. "Go on, Pip. What are you most afraid of?"

She scuffed her toes in the damp sand. "You won't make fun of me?"

Conner pointed at his chest. "Me? No, I promise. Cross my heart and hope to die."

Pippa jolted at the word 'die'. I had no doubt that those three little letters had been irrevocably tainted for her.

Finally, she filled her lungs and announced, "I'm afraid of sleeping."

Everyone jerked.

Sleep.

The black recharging shroud we needed and loved had become her personal demon.

I remembered Pippa's terror at us going to sleep and never waking like her parents. But I didn't know she still suffered. Motherly instincts wanted to tell her not to be afraid. That sleep was one of the safest things a person could do. I wanted to remind her of the beauty of dreams and rejuvenation of the best nap in a patch of sunshine.

But that wasn't for me to do. That was for her to remember.

"You're very brave admitting that." I kissed her forehead. "Now, I want you to write that in the sand."

"Why?"

"You'll see."

"I don't know how to spell sleep."

"I'll help you."

Together, we traced wonky cursive in the wet beach. The sentence came alive before us: *I'm afraid of sleep.*

I also added the line: *but after tonight, I don't need to be afraid anymore.*

Once the last word had been finished, Pippa let go of the walking stick and I motioned for Conner to come closer.

He did, although reluctantly.

"Now, it's your turn." I passed him the pen. "What are you most afraid of?"

He shuffled on the spot. "Uh…that I won't be able to play tennis again because of my wrist."

I wanted to ask about his tennis past. He'd mentioned he played over the course of our island imprisonment. We'd even attempted to play cricket with sticks for wickets and a log for a bat. I loved learning about him because it brought him to life, all while Galloway remained in the shadows unwilling to share.

Was Conner right to worry? In the tasks around the camp, his wrist seemed strong and useable. But who knew if the bones had knitted correctly—just like we'd never know with Galloway's leg.

Stepping to the side, I waved at the sand beneath Pippa's

sentence. "Good. Write it down."

Giving me a sideways look, he took his time, indenting the pristine sand with jagged lettering. Once done, he shoved the walking stick at Galloway and moved away.

I sucked in a breath as Galloway's fingers tightened around the wood. I had no idea if he'd play along. This was a testament to how far he was willing to go to avoid anyone knowing who he truly was.

As seconds turned into long moments, my palms sweated. I opened my mouth to excuse him, but suddenly he lurched forward, shoving the stick into my hands. "I won't be able to duck low enough to write." His gaze smouldered. "You'll have to write it for me."

I froze, cursing the way a simple phrase undid me.

"Okay…"

Poising below Conner's penned confession, I waited.

Galloway took his time before muttering, "I'm afraid of never being able to apologise to those who most deserve it."

The cryptic reply echoed in my head long after I'd scratched it into existence.

What did he have to apologise for and to whom? Why couldn't he open up to me and share whatever it was that ate at him?

"Your turn." Pippa tugged my wrist. "What are you most afraid of, Stelly?"

I bit my lip. So, so many things.

I'm afraid that I want a man for all the wrong reasons.
I'm afraid I'll never get off this island.
I'm afraid I don't want *to get off this island.*
I'm afraid I don't know who I am.
I'm afraid I don't like who I'm becoming.

So many to choose from but I chose the one closest to my heart. Sighing, I wrote my fear below the others. *I'm afraid I'll lose my voice, and once it's gone…I'll never get it back.*

It meant so many things and was just as cryptic as Galloway was. It meant I was afraid of losing my backbone and never having the guts to chase what I wanted. It meant I was afraid that my song writing and music ability would dry up beneath the Fijian sun.

Galloway caught my eye but didn't say anything.

We all stood there, reading the four sandy admissions.

Conner broke the silence. "Now what?"

"Now, we go to bed."

"Huh?"

"In the morning, you'll see. Trust me." Pinching Pippa's cheek, I added, "It's magic, after all."

We all turned to return to camp, but at the last second, Galloway hobbled back and wrote one last line in the sand. Turned out he could do it himself, faintly scribbling his extra fear.

Conner and Pippa waited patiently while my heart pounded. Would this be the first glimpse into Galloway's thoughts? The first time I'd learn what he was feeling because he damn well sure never talked about it.

Turning his back on the script, he hobbled past us, leaving us to catch up. The children dashed ahead, but I couldn't stop my curiosity. Taking a few steps back, I stood over his words and tears filled my eyes.

I'm sick of not knowing if I'm healed or disabled for the rest of my life. I want my splint off so I know either way.

I looked at him making his way slowly up the beach. He didn't look back. He didn't make eye contact or give any glint that he wanted to discuss.

Not that he needed to.

It was perfectly self-explanatory.

His fear was genuine. His terror was tangible.

And it wouldn't be the tide that made his wish come true.

It would be me.

Chapter Thirty-Four

∙∙

GALLOWAY

∙∙∙∙∙∙

TOUCH.

She finally touched me.

And I let her.

Her fingers were hypnotically soft; moving over my face, across my lips, lingering on my throat.

My body instantly hardened.

I reached for her, but the touch dropped lower, across my sternum, along my lower belly, feathering on my hipbone to my thigh.

My cock stood up, begging to be granted the same treatment, but the touch vanished, tugging on something around my leg.

My teeth snapped together as the frustration I'd been fighting for months boiled over. Lashing out, I connected with hair.

Not a faceless face or dream-figmented breasts.

Hair.

Real.

My eyes flew open.

The dream ended.

And I shot upright only to slam back down again when I noticed it *wasn't* a dream.

Estelle bowed over me. Her knees against my thigh, her fingers unbuckling the seat belts and fabric ties around my splint.

I sucked in a breath, whisper-hissing in the dark. "What the hell do you think you're doing?"

Her eyes flashed then skittered across the camp to Pip and Conner. They slept in individual beds tonight, not needing each other's support from the lonely memories of being parentless.

She froze. "I'm doing what you want."

"What *I* want?"

A Technicolor porno unravelled in my head. What I wanted was her mouth on my cock. What I wanted was her straddling my hips and me thrusting into her tight, hot heat.

What I wanted was *her*.

A thousand times *her*.

I gritted my teeth; balled my hands. I did everything I could to fight the undeniable urges volcanoing in my blood.

"Estelle, I suggest you move away from me."

I gave her a warning.

I was a gentleman.

If I touched her now, kissed her, fucked her…it would be her fault for coming too close when she knew the uncrossable boundaries between us.

"Just tolerate me for a few seconds and then I'll be gone." Her eyes dropped back to my thigh.

Tolerate?

She thought I couldn't *tolerate* her?

Shit, I was in love with her. I spent my days falling more and more into goddamn love with her, and she thought I could barely tolerate her?

Stupid, stupid woman.

I couldn't do it.

I sat up to push her away but the last band of my splint came away and the two sticks clunked to the sand, freeing me.

I groaned in relief. The support had kept my ankle straight, but hell, it'd been heavy and uncomfortable.

She smiled in the darkness. "Feel better?"

I'd feel better with you lying on top of me.

I swallowed, nodding tightly. "Yes. Now, go away."

Even as I said it, her eyes fell from my mouth to the raging hard-on between my legs. My heart waged war on every other organ. "Estelle…"

"Yes?" Her normal breath turned into tormenting pants.

"Get away from me."

Hurt clashed in her eyes. She dropped her head. "I'm sorry."

"I don't know what for. But it's time for you to leave."

"I'm sorry for what I said that night."

"What night?"

I knew exactly what night. The night she told me she wanted nothing to bloody do with me.

Her gaze flashed. "You know what."

I chuckled caustically. "Oh, you mean the night you said you didn't want me? That night?" I brushed aside my long hair. "Don't worry about it. It's fine. I'm over it." Sitting a little higher, I growled, "Goodnight."

She didn't move.

For a bloody age, she didn't move and everything inside howled to grab her. I had the control of a priestly saint not to fist her hair and kiss her—regardless what she said before.

But I didn't.

Because I respected her.

And this island was too damn small to make a mistake with our friendship.

Because if I did kiss her, it would be a mistake.

And I'd made enough of those to last me a lifetime.

Finally, she moved. But not in the fashion I expected and needed. Oh hell no, her hand glided from her lap to my cock.

I jolted as if she'd shocked me with a hundred volts of power. "Goddammit, wha—what—" I couldn't finish my sentence.

Her fingers stole my vocabulary as they wrapped sensually, possessively around my erection.

My back arched and I fell backward in the sand, giving everything to her because she'd finally touched me. Finally willingly, on her own damn merit, touched me.

This was a dream. I hadn't woken up yet.

I'm still sleeping.

This wasn't real. It *couldn't* be real.

I'd wanted this with every atom in my body. I didn't deserve to get what I wanted. Estelle would never touch me without the secretive boundaries of slumber. Why should I push away a fantasy when it brought fleeting happiness?

I shouldn't.

I won't.

Her hand moved toward the Velcro of my board-shorts, ripping apart the fly and pushing her hand into my underwearless crotch.

The kids.

Screw, the kids.

This was a dream…and if it wasn't…they could watch, for all I cared. My sainthood had been revoked, and I was nothing but raging blood and throbbing pressure and hissing fuse to the largest explosion in history.

Estelle *touched* me.

And her fingers felt a thousand times better on my naked flesh. Stars burst behind my eyes as she stroked my length.

Her touch caused paralysis. Her touch caused every sense to

belong to her.

Only her.

Some part of my brain that was still human tried one last time to stop whatever she was doing.

I garbled nonsense, I half-heartedly shifted my hips, but her long hair tickled my exposed belly as she shook her head.

"No…no more thinking. Just relax. Let me do this for you." Her lips whispered over mine as she bent over me, her hand working up and down, swirling around. Her thumb, *shit*, her thumb, found my crown, pressing hard on the sensitive tip, stealing the moisture she found there and smearing it down the shaft. "Let me return what you did for me."

Fantasy.

Nightmare.

Hallucination.

Or was this death? Some cruel joke by the devil before sending me packing to Hell?

My left hand clutched the sand as I rode out the most intense hand job I'd ever experienced while my right thrust into her hair and smashed her lips against mine.

I needed this. I needed to come. So. Damn. Badly.

I'd serviced myself a few times over the past few months but that had been a necessity to rid the heavy ache in my balls. But this…hell this was pure utopia.

My breathing turned ragged as Estelle's hand worked harder. She wasn't messing around. She wasn't there to tease me. She was there to make me come. Fast and efficient. A donation.

A charity orgasm.

If I weren't so far gone, I would've hated her for that. I would've pushed her away—no matter how incredible she worked me. I wouldn't have put up with such underhanded manipulation.

But I wasn't in the right head space.

I'd fallen for a girl who didn't want me and barely accepted my friendship. If she wanted to pity hand-job me, then fine, I'd take what I could get.

My hands clutched her hair, kissing her harder, deeper, giving up and thrusting over and over into her palm.

She let me.

Her fingers tightened, giving me the perfect noose to jack off into. Her thumb swirled around my crown and her spare hand vanished between my legs to play with my balls.

Everything she did was utterly perfect. It was as if she'd been born knowing my code. That she'd hacked every part of my anatomy and owned me.

"I love touching you like this, G." Her whisper fed my starving lungs.

I couldn't hold off anymore.

Every muscle jerked, tightening to the point of cramp.

My balls became bombs; my cock the cannon.

I came.

And came.

And *came* all over her hand and my stomach.

I trembled and twitched as she kept going, milking my extremely sensitive body. I grabbed her wrist, stopping her.

Breathing hard, I slowly came back to earth and opened my eyes.

I stared at her.

She stared back.

No words were spoken but we knew.

We knew that this couldn't be ignored.

Wordlessly, she stood, rinsed her hands in the fuselage we kept topped with seawater and crawled into her bed.

She went to sleep with her back facing me.

But I stayed awake until morning, alternating between shock and sedation. Thankfulness and plotting.

All rules were broken.

She said it was returning the favour.

I called it asking for trouble.

She'd been the one to touch me.

Now, I would be the one to touch her.

Chapter Thirty-Five

ESTELLE

. . . . . .

I buckled. I submitted. No, I gave in.
Feeling you come apart. Watching you fall apart. Listening to you break apart.
~~*It makes me want you so much more. Too much more. Terrifyingly more.*~~
I failed. I lost. No, I finally let myself win.
Taken from the notepad of E.E.

. . .

WHAT WAS I thinking?

The sun had risen an hour ago, and still, I slept on my side, facing away from Galloway. Every time I thought about what I'd done in the dark, my body flushed, my nipples ached, and the tingle of a desperately needed release drove me insane.

The way he'd given in to me.

The way he smelled of cedar and liquorice even though he hadn't used shampoo or aftershave in weeks.

The way his muscles trembled and body hardened and eyes fluttered and lips kissed and hands clenched and breathing stuttered and *and*...

An arc of desire throbbed in my clit.

I shuddered, curling into myself with need.

I'd given him pleasure. I'd taken pleasure from giving him pleasure.

But now...now, I suffered.

I was more turned on than any point in my life. I could barely move without my thighs pressing together and my hips rocking to find relief. I could barely breathe without my breasts rubbing my t-shirt and my nipples sparking with ten thousand demands to be touched, sucked, bitten.

My brain was useless. My body was obsessed. I had to. I had to. I *had* to find relief.

I wasn't Estelle. I was female. I was sex.

And I wanted, wanted, *wanted.*

With every inhale, I promised myself the freedom to spin around and beg Galloway to take me. With each exhale, I broke every vow and huddled tighter in the sand.

You can't.

I couldn't remember why.

But I couldn't execute the day, talk to the children, or pretend to be normal in this state.

Hurling myself out of bed, I kept my back to Galloway and fled into the forest.

I ran and ran until I was far enough from the camp and sprawled against the bamboo thicket I'd adopted as my writing nook. My cotton shorts came down. My hand disappeared into my wetness.

And I fingered myself all while my thoughts belonged to Galloway.

Galloway.

Galloway.

Galloway.

Chapter Thirty-Six

GALLOWAY

SHE RAN.

I saw her. I watched her. I didn't move as she bolted from her bed and into the forest. She had a habit of disappearing into the trees for reasons I couldn't fathom.

But this reason...I understood completely.

I knew what she was doing.

I pictured exactly how she would look.

And I grew hard all over again knowing she had to relieve herself from the need compounding every day between us.

After last night, after what she'd done to me, she couldn't deny it anymore.

She wanted me. Far, far more than she let on.

She'd put me out of my misery for a few hours. One day (hopefully soon), she'd let me put her out of hers. And when that day came, I'd take my time. I'd tease the hell out of her before finally transporting her into heaven.

I didn't say a word when she returned, face flushed, and breasts swollen in her black bikini top. I pretended I didn't notice the damp spot on her cotton shorts or the way she washed her hands guiltily in the sea.

I let her believe I didn't know.

After breakfast of coconuts, a salted fish from yesterday, and some cooked taro, Estelle guided the children to the water's edge where we'd scratched our messages into the sand.

I took my time, limping after them with the aid of my walking stick.

Estelle might've given me the best orgasm of my life last night and removed the annoying splint, but she hadn't been able to save me from the heart-destroying conclusion.

My ankle hadn't healed properly.

The ache in my bones hurt every time I put weight on it. An odd bump remained where the joint had broken and I couldn't deny it anymore.

I could walk, but I might never run.

I could move but not without the aid of a walking stick.

I was a damn invalid and nothing in the world could change that.

Pushing my anger and grief away at never being whole again, I caught up with the others, looking for the messages.

Only...they'd vanished.

The tide had wiped the slate clean, leaving behind a virgin beach with no marks, no terrors, no confessions of any kind.

Pippa turned to me with her forehead scrunched. "Where—where are they?"

I grinned, hiding my depression at my disability and playing up Estelle's party trick. "It's magic."

"No, the tide washed them away." Conner pouted, clearly unimpressed with the game. Pointing at my leg, he added, "Hey, you removed your brace."

"Yep."

That topic wasn't for young boy's ears. He could see it was off. End of story.

Estelle flinched. "You're right, Co. But that's what the ocean does. It washes away the bad and brings only good."

"I don't get it." Conner squinted in the new sun. Overnight, the drizzle that'd haunted us for days had finally broken; we all slowly thawed out and dried off.

Pippa stuck her thumb in her mouth, something she'd started doing a few weeks ago, reverting to childlike behaviours.

Estelle gathered her close, hugging her tiny head against her side. "It means those fears...they're gone. Don't you feel lighter? Knowing that you don't have to be afraid of sleep anymore?"

She tensed. "I don't know."

Estelle looked at Conner. "Don't you feel better knowing you don't have to worry about tennis anymore?"

He shrugged. "I guess."

Her eyes landed on mine. "G?"

I waited for her to bring up my leg and recently removed splint, but she surprised me by bringing up my other fear.

"Don't you feel better knowing whoever you want to apologise to no longer needs to know you're sorry. That whatever it is that you've done has been forgiven?"

I laughed coldly. I couldn't help it.

If only she knew what I wanted to apologise for…then she wouldn't be so sure a high tide could fix it.

Her face turned an odd shade of crimson.

Swallowing my morbid chuckle, I nodded. "You're right. I feel a lot better."

Not at all. But thanks for trying.

She cocked her chin. "Well, I don't know about you guys, but I *do* feel better."

The defiant way she held herself sucker punched me in the heart.

"I was afraid I'd lose my voice, lose my ability to write songs, and fail at my love of putting tragedy onto paper. But I don't have to worry anymore because lyrics are a part of me as much as my heart beats and my blood flows red."

Wait…write songs?

She was a poet?

A singer?

How did I not bloody know this?

Same reason why she knows nothing of you—you're a self-centred asshole who refuses to share.

Pippa slowly smiled, her face filling with awe as she let Estelle's promise gain power. In her childish, whimsical mind, it was entirely possible for her fears to be swallowed by the ocean, her safety guaranteed by the waves, and her life guarded by merfolk and fantasy.

I was glad. Happy for her. Relieved that her little heart would be lighter.

God knew, she needed it.

The messages in the sand hadn't done what Estelle had intended, but it taught me something. Her visiting me in the night. Her touch on my body. Her lips on my lips.

She'd shown me what a hypocrite I'd been.

I hurt because she wouldn't touch me. Wouldn't let me touch her. I hated that she kept me at arm's length physically.

But I'd done the same to her. I'd barricaded my emotions. I'd buried my past and locked up my secrets. I'd cut her off emotionally.

My shoulders sagged as an even more heart-destroying conclusion found me.

If I was to earn Estelle's permission to finally have her, then I had to give something of myself in return. I had to be willing to share.

I had to be willing to let her in.

I had to be willing to let her judge me for herself.

Chapter Thirty-Seven

. . . .

ESTELLE

. . . . . .

Time is measured more than in minutes and hours. Time is more complex than dials on a wall or hands on a clock. Time is contrary.
Twenty-six years, I'd been alive. Two years, I'd been a successful songwriter singer. Three months, I'd been island-wrecked. Two weeks, since I'd touched him.
So why did two weeks feel longer than every year I'd been breathing? Why did three months seem like an eternity?
Taken from the notepad of E.E.

. . .

<u>FOURTEEN WEEKS</u>

SOMETHING CHANGED IN Galloway the night I'd touched him.

He thawed a little. He smiled more. He made an effort to converse.

In the beginning, I'd been wary—looking for a trap. Then I'd been besotted, drinking in everything he let slip. His revelations were nothing earth-shattering. But I valued him opening up to me, to us. I finally believed we could become true friends and not standoffish survivors.

I learned he didn't like hard liquor but loved craft beers brewed right. He didn't like large cities but loved working in wide open spaces on his own. He got headaches when he was stressed. He suffered from claustrophobia. He was an only child and his dad was still alive.

Such simple things but I hoarded each one as if they were the key to unlocking him. Unfortunately, the more I learned about him, the more I wanted him.

My trip to my bamboo spot to pleasure myself became a regular occurrence and the desire to orgasm never stopped tormenting me.

I knew what I needed.

Him.

But no matter how many invitations I gave him: lingering glances, fleeting touches, desperate wordless hints to take me.

He never did.

He permitted my fingers to touch his when we cooked together. He allowed my thigh to rest against his while we carved bowls from coconut shells and weaved another blanket to sleep on.

Yet, he never accepted my solicitations.

He did, however, throw himself into building us a home.

Ever since the week of dismal dusting of rain and shadows, he'd announced we'd waited long enough for a roof over our heads.

Now his splint had come off, he moved more, but he couldn't hide the anger at not having a fully healed leg and ankle. He limped (he tried not to), but his body was broken and there was nothing we could do.

It didn't stop him from working with Conner. Together, they slowly dismantled the helicopter's rotor blades with the aid of rocks and axe, smashing them free from the mast and dragging them through the forest to our beach.

It took them three days to get the two rotors to the sand and another afternoon to dig deep enough holes to ensure the blades stuck proudly from the beach like joists for a wall.

We only had two, but it was better than nothing.

Galloway took his time.

He asked for a page from my notebook and scribbled calculations and schematics, coming up with a draft for our island house.

Once the blades were sturdy and the markings for walls and entrances were drawn by our toes in the sand, I took Galloway to my private zone with the bushes of bamboo.

His eyes lit up. His hands twitched to touch me. And my heart knew if Conner and Pippa hadn't been with us, he would've kissed me.

And if he'd kissed me, I wouldn't have let him stop.

Pregnancy or no pregnancy.

With the axe, he hacked away bushels of long, strong stems, carting them back to begin the arduous task of erecting walls.

Conner turned out to be a perfect protégé.

Pippa and I took over hunting while the boys spent every

daylight hour hacking, splitting, tying, and constructing.

Pippa, apparently, was the chosen one with fishing. She wasn't strong enough to use the spear, and I had no coordination. But together, we used my tatty t-shirt and a Y-shaped frame to drag the material through the water and catch the smaller silver fish in the shallows.

She became so fast, she could tickle them from the water with her bare hands.

The first meal with the smaller fish had been awful with crunchy scales and bones. But every inch of the creature (minus the entrails and head) was nutritional. The calcium from their bones, the protein from their flesh. Nothing went to waste, and slowly, we invented new ways to cook.

While the boys steadily turned our roofless camp into a home, Pippa and I experimented with menus. We forced ourselves to think outside the box. We wrapped fish fillets in leaves (like nature's tinfoil) and broiled in charcoal. We pan-fried on rocks and buried pockets of ingredients in hot ash.

Some trials worked and others didn't. But we never stopped trying.

One afternoon, we shredded three coconuts, warmed some water, and pounded the mixture together. Once a gooey paste, we wrapped it in a purple muslin scarf we'd found in Amelia's tote. Squeezing the goo as tight as we could, we painstakingly drained the concoction and made coconut milk.

We used the white liquid to boil crabs and fish, and dinner had never tasted so decadently delicious.

Little by little, meal by meal, we were adapting, evolving.

Soon, we wouldn't recognise ourselves.

Soon, we would be ruined for any rescue.

Because as we adapted and evolved, we found more and more happiness in the simplest of things. We gradually, grudgingly accepted that this was our home now.

And we might never be permitted to leave.

....

SEVENTEEN WEEKS

Christmas came and went.

We didn't celebrate.

I took photos on my phone and recorded a home movie of the progress of the house, but I didn't tell the children the date.

After all, the essence of Christmas was celebration and gratefulness.

We were grateful but not celebratory. We would wait until we were found to honour the day of gift giving and happiness.

"Are you awake?"

I jolted, curling up in the flax blanket I'd made. We each had one now. It wasn't exactly warm, but it did grant a resemblance of comfort. "Yes." I paused, breathing shallowly, waiting for Galloway to follow through. When he didn't, I whispered, "Why?"

Shuffling sounded as he sat up. I looked over at him, glancing quickly at the children to make sure they were sleeping.

Three nights ago, Galloway had insisted we all move farther down the beach. We'd grumbled, but it was strictly temporary. The house was almost done and he wanted to add the finishing touches without us seeing the end product.

The inconvenience of sleeping in a more exposed area on the beach and not being allowed to return to the camp was overshadowed by the excitement of moving into our new abode.

Not to mention, the change of location had acted like a holiday. Lightening the moods of Pippa and Conner, making my heart sing as they played together and laughed more than they had in weeks.

Galloway murmured, "I think it's time I told you something."

My heart stopped. "Tell me what?"

He rubbed his face. "Everything."

I sat up, kneeling in my sandy bed. "Okay…"

Raking both hands through his hair, he gave me a crooked smile. "I'm not ready. I don't think I'll ever be ready. But I can't keep it from you anymore. The past few weeks, talking with you, sharing small pieces of who I am, I'd forgotten how nice that is. Nice to be known."

"I've enjoyed it, too. I'm honoured that you trust me enough to tell me."

His blue eyes glowed. "I don't just trust you, Stel. It's gone far beyond that."

I looked away, unnerved by how much emotion he stared with.

"I need to tell you because I want more from you. Being your friend…it's not enough." His voice deepened to a heavy rasp. "And I don't think being friends is enough for you…either."

My lips parted. This was my moment. The moment when I fixed what I'd broken. If he were brave enough to finally tell me what haunted him, I could be honest and tell him why I was terrified of sleeping with him.

The words danced on the tip of my tongue.

No, it's not enough.

You're right; I want you so much I can barely stand it.

But something held me back. A weakness. A fear. My own stupid indecision.

I ruined it for the second time. "I—I like being your friend, Galloway."

He stiffened. "That's it?"

"Is that not enough?"

"Can you honestly say that it is?"

My heart ceased beating. "I can't answer that question."

"You know what, Stel? You really are a piece of work." He chuckled coldly. "This past month, I've gone out of my way to open up to you—let you see that I'm worthy enough of one sliver of your affection. But nothing is good enough for you."

"Wait." I flinched. "That's not true."

"Yes, it is."

I shook my head. "Galloway, you have it all wrong. I want you—"

"You know what?" His hand shot up to silence me. "I don't need to know. Whatever it was that I was going to tell you…it's not important."

Throwing himself back into bed, he rolled over.

Tears tickled my eyes. "Galloway…"

He didn't turn around.

I hugged my blanket closer. "G?"

Still, he ignored me.

For an age, I waited for him to give me a second chance.

But he never did.

My back ached as I finally accepted what I'd done. "I'm sorry." Slowly, I slid from kneeling to lying, staring at the stars above. My tears escaped, rolling down my cheek with salty sadness.

Tell him!

Sit up and tell him how much you want him. Tell him what scares you. Be honest!

But my muscles locked with a hundred anchors of doubt. We'd been each other's lifeline for so long that my fear wasn't just about pregnancy anymore. What would happen if sleeping together destroyed the limited friendship we'd found?

What if he hated me afterward? What if he swam off the island and left me because I wasn't what he wanted…after all?

I squeezed my temples, willing my tears to cease. We lived the simplest existence, constantly dodging death's grip, finding joy in the basic of activities, yet I couldn't find the courage to admit that, yes, I was in love with him, yes, I wanted him with every fibre of my body, and yes, I would bind myself to him on our island, in a city, or on any place on Earth.

But I didn't.

The moment was gone.

The breeze brushed away the tension with combs of wind and the beach exhaled unhappily.

Why did I do that?

Why was I so afraid?

Dawn broke and the sun rose and I still didn't have an answer.

....

The next night, I followed the sandy trail toward the shore in total darkness.

I needed to breathe. Just stare at the waves and demand answers they couldn't give.

A ball of sorrow lodged in my throat. That ball of sadness was never far away—how could it when we were marooned and forced to shed the glamour and pampered ease of living in a city? How could it when I'd once again screwed up where Galloway was concerned?

No matter the accomplishment we'd achieved from shedding the glitz of modern conveniences and learning how to gather and create, hunt and prepare, it was nothing if I couldn't balance happy relationships.

He hadn't talked to me all day.

We'd gone about our tasks. We'd prepped and ate and swam and drank. And not one word. Even the children had been quiet, sensing something wasn't quite right between us.

The icing-sugar sand slipped through my toes as I moved closer to the lapping sea. The world continued on, regardless of night and day, but there was a difference when darkness replaced sunshine. Things shed their harsh reality and became magical, mystical. The blue of the ocean became silver-black from the moon. The palm trees became ghostly sentries keeping us sheltered. And the universe as a whole cocooned us with galaxies we could only dream of visiting.

I peered into the gloom, looking for Galloway. After not talking to me all day, he hadn't come to bed, working all hours to finish the house.

I wanted to chase after him and apologise. Finally come clean as to what terrified me and how refusing him carved pieces out of me until I was hollow with want.

But I didn't.

Because my reasoning was weak and made no sense. He'd

curse me for not telling him sooner and giving him the chance to solve the issue instead of hiding it from him.

Sitting on the sand, the cool dampness soaked through my shorts. I looked at the starry horizon.

"Am I going to die here?" My whisper kissed the moon. "Will I die and never see Madeline again? Will I forever be mother and protector to two children and never be allowed to submit to the man I've fallen in love with?"

I held my breath as my questions threaded with the wind, dispersing each vowel in different directions.

North, south, east, west.

No answer from the useless compass.

No premonition.

No extra splash from the waves or twinkle from the stars.

Nothing.

I didn't know how long I sat there mourning my life, my future, my present, but after a while, the melancholy in my blood turned to anger.

I'd survived.

I'd nurtured two small humans. I'd healed a fully grown man. I'd proven my self-worth over and over again.

And I had no one else to blame but myself for not having Galloway.

What am I doing?

Shooting to my feet, I waded into the water, welcoming the warm liquid to lap around my calves.

The sea was abnormally low tonight. We'd all become rather indebted to the tide. It washed away our dreams, our fears, our wishes. Every message we wrote in the sand was soothed by the briny waves.

Kicking the water, droplets rained around me. Back in society, I'd lost the ability to feel pride of accomplishment and beauty in small things, brushing them under a rug of indifference and the endless desire for more. More wealth, more safety, more friends, more love, more, more, more.

But here...our world was simplified. We no longer had to compete with one another; we survived because we fought side by side. We no longer felt envious of another's happiness because day after day, we garnered joy for staying alive in a hostile world.

The simple pleasures of feeling sand through my fingers or seeing rainbows in droplets had made me full again. The muse for my song writing had become a vicious mistress, driving me to find inspiration in the randomest of places.

Looking toward the camp, something caught my eye. Indents in the sand, lettering scratched by a twig, just waiting for the sea to wash its secretive confession away.

I frowned.

That's strange.

Pip and Conner hadn't wanted to do the messages tonight, opting instead for a large bonfire to commiserate the number of months we'd been here. The calendar on my phone helped us keep track, but it also kept us very aware of how long it had been.

If they didn't write them, then who…

Wading out of the water, I drifted closer.

The honest scrawl slipped down my throat and yanked my stomach from its home.

I'm hurting. I'm angry. I want the memories of what I did to leave me alone. I want to be a good person again. I want her so fucking much. I want to taste and touch. I want to lick and stroke. I want to be off this goddamn island so I might stand one chance with her.

I hugged myself as my heart lost its flying feathers and plummeted.

I'd done this.

I'd hurt him.

Over and over again.

The tide wasn't close to wiping away the words or the passion dripping from them.

Sucking in a breath, my nipples tingled at the ferocious need permeating the penmanship.

Galloway wanted me.

I had the power to make him happy. I could help him forget whatever he'd done.

This was no longer about me.

It was about him.

Chapter Thirty-Eight

•••

GALLOWAY

••••••

FIVE YEARS BEFORE THE CRASH

"I, GALLOWAY JACOB Oak, swear that the evidence I shall give will be the truth, the whole truth, and nothing but the truth, so help me God."

My hand shook as the defence attorney removed the bible from my reach, sneering with disdain. He'd already judged, condemned, and ruined me.

I was screwed.

My eyes flickered to the jury where the faces of all ages, ethnicities, and religions stared back. Each one held a key to my freedom, but not one of them would give it to me.

And why should they?

I didn't deserve it.

Not in the eyes of the court anyway.

In the eyes of my mother…well, I knew she would've been grateful if not sad for what I'd become.

The attorney paced like a jackal in front of my witness box, linking his fingers pompously. "Now, Mr. Oak. Answer clearly and precisely for the court so there is no misunderstanding. Did you or did you not kill Doctor Joseph Silverstein?"

I glanced at my father. I straightened my shoulders. I prepared to throw my life away.

Not that I had a life left.

I was a murderer.

"Yes. Yes, I killed him."

•••••••••••••••••••••••••••

BLOODY NERVES DROVE me mad as I waited for the others to join me.

I'd had four days to perfect our home on my own. Even

Conner hadn't been permitted around the camp while I finished it. He'd been as integral to the creation as I had, but I wanted the final touches to be special for him, too.

Hence the banning.

I stood by the fire, critiquing the building we'd created from flax rope, bamboo, and helicopter rotor blades. It wasn't fancy, but it was fairly large and substantial enough to withstand a storm or two, but not a typhoon if one of those decided to make our life even more hellish.

It'll leak.

I scowled. That part was unavoidable. The roof was flax fronds layered tightly together and the open holes for windows merely had a woven mat secured to the wall to roll down. It was the best I could do without waterproof tiles or glass.

I heard them before I saw them.

I crossed my arms and waited as Pippa's giggle and Conner's voice drifted around the bay.

Last week, Conner's voice had dropped a few octaves, leaving behind boyhood for puberty.

I was proud of that.

Proud that we'd all signed a death warrant the night we'd crashed, yet we hadn't succumbed. Pippa was happier than she had been in a while, Conner was adapting, and Estelle had somehow grown more bloody beautiful.

She'd lost weight—like all of us—but her bone structure only stood out more. With tanned skin and bleached white hair, she truly looked like an island seductress.

My heart wrapped itself around my ribcage as she appeared on the edge of camp. The children trailed behind her. She walked quickly, eager to see what I'd done.

My mood bounced between pissed off and inadequacy. Pissed because we still hadn't cleared the air between us and inadequacy because as hard as I'd worked on our new house, it had its flaws.

Many, many flaws.

It wasn't perfect, and to me, every issue and mistake was blatantly obvious.

What if she refused to live in it?

Her lips twitched into a kind smile, her eyes full of sorrow for the emotional gap between us. It was hard having a silent fight when it was just you and two kids on a damn island.

Unless someone was willing to clear the air it became harder and harder to stomach. I knew I'd been in the wrong. I'd jumped down her throat after she'd been nothing but forthright with me. It wasn't her fault she lied about wanting nothing more than friendship—regardless what her body said.

Her eyes drifted from mine to the house.

She froze.

Her mouth fell open.

Tears sprang to her eyes.

My heart thundered, expecting her to rush toward the dwelling and step inside for the first time.

But she didn't.

She ran straight toward me.

Her feet kicked up sand and when her arms clamped over my shoulders, I couldn't stop my body's insane craving for her. My fingers dove into her hair, and I didn't know who did it.

Her or me.

It didn't matter.

One moment, we were separate.

The next, we were one.

Her lips collided with mine.

Her tongue welcomed me.

Her taste exploded everywhere.

And I swore right there and then that I couldn't do this anymore. I couldn't hold a grudge. I couldn't be angry. I couldn't hate her for not accepting me.

Our fight dissolved. The distance between us erased.

Her kiss was like slipping into comfort and forgiveness all at once.

A groan caught in the back of my throat as her breasts pressed against me. Intensity thickened and heated until I worried I'd incinerate in her arms. I wanted to run my hands down her body, pluck her from the sand, and carry her into the first home we'd had in months. Cradle her in four walls and make love to her with a roof above our heads and privacy hiding our secrets.

Her teeth caught my bottom lip, dragging me closer for one last second.

Then, it was over.

She pulled away, dropping her eyes. "Um…somehow my scripted thank you became—"

"The best kiss since the first one you gave me?"

She blushed. "Yes…well. Sorry."

I wouldn't let her get away this time. Not again.

Cupping her chin, I forced her gaze back to mine. "There's nothing to apologise for."

She sighed as if a terrible weight had been lifted.

"Wow!" Pippa squealed as she ran ahead, disappearing into the only habitat on the island.

"Hey, wait for me!" Conner charged after her.

Estelle laughed. "I guess it's inspection time."

I didn't want our moment to be over, but the ceasefire between us was an enjoyable place to dwell until we had more time to be open.

Considering we lived together…we rarely found time to just be and talk. Staying alive demanded a lot more effort than I'd ever imagined.

But we're alive…and that's all that matters.

Heading toward the top of our camp, I brushed my shoulder with Estelle's.

She shook her head, wonder on her face. "I can't believe you were able to create this."

I squinted at the house, doing my best to see past its faults. The ratty flax knots and knobbly bamboo. Unstraight walls and basic layout. It was better than a tent…barely. "I just wish it could've been better."

She wrenched to a halt. "What do you mean, *better*? Galloway, it's perfect."

I shrugged. "Next one, I'll fix the issues."

"I don't want a 'next one.'" She scoffed. "I want this one."

I grinned. "Good job, you're stuck with this one for a little while then, huh?"

Her smile broadened. "I guess so."

I'd already drawn up blueprints for my next creation, and it wasn't a house. I wouldn't tell her, but my upcoming project was something floatable so we might have a chance at freedom.

In the months since we'd been stranded, not one aircraft, helicopter, or boat had been close enough to hear or see us.

We'd fallen through a tear in the map and no one knew where we were. It was up to us to find a way to be found.

"Come on. I want the grand tour." Estelle dug her toes into the sand, moving faster.

I refused to use my walking stick any more than necessary and today was a day without it.

Gritting my teeth, I fought through the ache and did my best to hide my limp. She didn't say a word as I moved with her, closer and closer to the house.

My fingers itched to touch her. Normally, I would fight the urge, but this time…I didn't deny myself.

My hand curled around hers, holding loosely to give her the

opportunity to pull away.

She didn't.

Her grip tightened around mine, and together we entered our home.

The second her toes left sand and hit bamboo flooring, she bounced in place. Her black bikini top jiggled as her breasts moved; her cotton shorts bravely stayed up even with a few holes on the waistline. "It's amazing."

I'd painstakingly spliced, tied, and flattened the hard-wearing bamboo to finally have a floor that didn't resemble a beach.

Conner and Pippa had already claimed their beds.

Their bright faces beamed. "You made us our own room." Conner shook his head. "Wow, man. Thanks."

It'd taken many hours of not having him there to help, but I'd inserted a few partitions in the house to make it more private. There were no doors, but Conner had his own spot with a partition blocking him from Pippa. It would be simple to remove the flax frond wall if they wanted to be together, but this way…they could have a normal sibling relationship without encroaching on each other.

Estelle drifted to the right where I'd put our wing.

Ours.

Only if she accepts me and stops fighting whatever exists between us.

I'd done the same thing on this side.

Another temporary wall separated her sleeping space from mine, but I hoped in time, we could reposition it to block the kids off and have our own private bedroom to do whatever we pleased away from the attentive eyes of youth.

Her fingers trailed over everything. From the natural walls to the fully stocked beds with a thick layer of fresh leaves to make a comfortable, warm, and no longer sandy resting spot. I'd arranged Estelle's blankets just like a hotel would and even placed a tiny white flower on top. All that was missing was chocolate wrapped in fancy gold paper on the pillow.

The window holes let light in and a gentle breeze, keeping it cool while the shade finally gave our eyes a rest from the glare of fiery sunshine.

The middle of the house stored the cups and bowls we'd carved from coconut shells, the necklaces Pippa had made from fish vertebrae, and countless tools we'd adopted to make our life easier.

Shelving held the Swiss Army knife and axe, safe and ready for use whenever we required. We even had stored food, mainly salted fish with another bowl holding a variety of leaves and taro, along with a piece of fuselage hammered into a deep catchment holding fresh water.

We didn't have a card house that would blow over like dominoes. We didn't have a tent or lean-to. We had roots. *Foundation.* And for the first-time since we crashed, I truly took stock of what we'd achieved and how far we'd come from city dwellers to wild islanders.

We'd created this from nothing.

We'd forged bonds and skills through hard work and determination.

We'd become more than we ever thought we would.

I'm happy.

My heart shone like a torch as Estelle twirled in the centre of the house, smiling at the roof above her head. Watching her relax and throb with gratitude crucified my desire.

I was happy.

But I could be happier.

And I couldn't wait any longer to find the ultimate paradise.

I wanted.

I needed.

Her.

Chapter Thirty-Nine

ESTELLE

••••••

~~I've been an idiot.~~
I'm the question mark on a question too hard to ask.
I'm the pause behind the sentence too hard to hear.
I'm the ellipses trailing on the confession too hard to read.
I'm the breath waiting to speak the truth too stupid to believe.
Taken from the notepad of E.E.

•••

WORDS COULDN'T DESCRIBE how singular and special such a simple thing like a roof was.

It wasn't perfect.

It wasn't airtight, rainproof, or even safe from bugs, but it was a roof and that was indescribable.

Waking up after our first night in our new home made me happier than I'd been in years. Happier than being on stage and performing to countless listeners. Happier than signing a million-dollar contract with my producer.

I'd kissed Galloway.

The air had cleared.

Tonight, I would tell him that I truly wanted him and finally indulge in the pleasure I'd denied both of us.

I shivered at the thought of touching him again, kissing him, finally feeling him thrust inside me.

Joy was hard to quantify, but I couldn't remember being so happy as I left the house and prepared a breakfast of crab and fish for my still slumbering family.

Sighing peacefully, I glanced at the ashes smeared on the lintel over the doorway. The children had used the soot from the fire last night to name our castaway habitat.

The name wasn't relevant or unique. Just a play on sounds that worked perfectly.

BB-FIJI

Bamboo Bungalow Fiji.

The ash christening would be washed away as soon as another rain shower arrived, but for now…the dark smudges told a story of people who'd finally found contentment in terrible adversity.

....

Lightning flashed out to sea, far enough away from us that it didn't spark fear and send us running, but close enough to threaten that the storm might change direction and come toward us.

If rain hit, we would restock our dwindling water supplies, and for the first time, be semi-dry thanks to a roof and shelter.

I actually wanted it to rain. I wanted the blissful euphoria of lying in bed, listening to the droplets and not be in the midst of it.

"Do we have time to finish?" Conner eyed the horizon. The sun had set and once again another night had fallen.

Tonight was New Year's Eve, and once again, I didn't share the date. Our goals and resolutions wouldn't change.

Surviving.

That was our ultimate and only purpose.

Our old city rhythm had well and truly become history. We had no alarm clocks or rush-hour traffic; no bills to pay, no stress of social niceties. We worked harmoniously, ate happily, and kept busy throughout the day. This new rhythm snuck up on us so sedately, we didn't even notice it'd happened.

Galloway and I had smiled and found every reason we could to touch one another while performing our tasks. Every brush and whisper sent desire cycloning inside me, spiralling with strength until a tornado billowed in my soul.

Tonight.

Once the children were in bed.

Things would finally be resolved between us. Being together would be our celebration and welcome of a new year.

"We have a few hours before it comes this way, I think." Passing Galloway's walking stick to Pippa, I added, "If it even swings this way. It might stay out to sea."

Pippa took the stick, chewing her bottom lip. "I hope so. I don't like thunder." She shuddered. "Reminds me too much of the noise when we crashed."

Galloway smiled softly. "You too, huh? Thought that was just me."

I had no doubt he didn't mind thunder—but the fact he was

willing to come across as a scaredy-cat to support her made my body melt.

Over the past month, the message writing had become an integral part of our nightly routine. Some nights, we didn't bother, but it'd become valuable in a strange way. We focused on different things: fears, wishes, favourite hobbies, ultimate experiences, what we missed most.

Tonight, the theme was gratefulness.

I pointed at the sand. "What are you most thankful for, Pip?"

She bent over, doing her best to scratch out two simple words. *I'm alive.*

Coming from such a tiny, orphaned girl, it was one of the most touching things I'd ever read.

An angry thunderclap boomed on the horizon. Perhaps the weather was heading our way, after all.

She jolted but bravely handed the stick to her brother.

Conner took it, quickly etching his sentence.

His was no better for my heartstrings. *I'm grateful for Galloway, and the skills he's shown me. I can build and fish because of him.*

"That's all on you, Co." Galloway hugged the boy. "You're a great student."

Conner grinned, his tanned face lighting up. "It helps that I like my teacher."

Pinching the stick, Galloway scrawled: *I'm grateful for the sun reminding me that every new day brings a better tomorrow.*

My heart no longer had a normal beat around him. It spiked and flopped and sparked and galloped. His comment made it do all four.

With hooded eyes, Galloway gave me the walking stick.

I blanked.

I'm grateful for life.

I'm grateful for who I am.

I'm grateful for tonight and what will happen.

In the end, all I wrote was: *I'm grateful for every moment because without them, I wouldn't be living at all.*

Another boom of thunder jerked our gaze skyward.

"Um…maybe we should go inside?" Pippa tugged my shorts, hugging Puffin, the kitten. I smiled at how delicious that sentence was. After so many months, we actually had somewhere to call inside. A shelter to protect us.

I looked up at Galloway, hoping he saw how grateful I was. How grateful I would *always* be.

That's what I should've written.

I'm grateful for you.

Always.

Another fork of lightning.

Conner broke from our group, peering at the shoreline. His hand came up, pointing at something in the tide.

Something large, black, and sinister.

"What's that?" He took a step closer. "Something's crawling out of the ocean."

"What?" Galloway spun around. "Where?"

A black blob slowly lifted itself from the waves, making its way inch by inch up the beach. "What the hell is that?" Galloway moved with Conner, closer and closer.

I didn't want them to get too close, but if we didn't investigate, we might be worse off. Knowledge was key on this island.

"I don't like it." Pippa stole my hand. "What if it's not friendly?"

I squeezed her fingers as another black splodge appeared, following the first.

Then another and another. "I'm sure it's fine, Pip. But let's get closer and see."

The little girl fought my pulling, but I didn't let her go. Circumstances like these—when facing a new challenge—were best done together.

Galloway suddenly laughed. "Holy crap."

"That's so cool." Conner ran toward the closest blob, his fear completely eradicated. "How awesome is this?"

Galloway jogged (with a slight limp) after Conner. Together, they hovered over the creature hauling itself up the beach.

"What? What is it?" Pippa strained to see.

My eyes finally made sense of the non-descript animal. "I know what that is."

Pippa squirmed to chase her brother. "What is it?"

Galloway turned to grin. "They're turtles. Lots and lots of turtles."

I gaped at the carpet of turtles making their way up our stretch of sand.

After months of being on the island, we hadn't seen any creatures apart from an odd lizard, snake, and occasional seagull. However, we'd suddenly become a zoo. "What are they doing here?" More black shapes hoisted themselves from the warm water, coming to meet us with a sheer mindedness that gave me goosebumps.

"I'm not sure." Galloway left Conner crawling beside the

leader, and returned to my side. "Perhaps to mate?"

The word mate and the implication of what that entailed twisted my tummy.

He cleared his throat as the silence between us became heavily potent. "Or to lay eggs. They do that on land."

Pippa freed herself from my hold. "I like turtles." Taking off, she headed for her brother, her stuffed kitten dangling in her hand.

Galloway and I tensed. We weren't alone, but there was enough distance to conjure the same electricity and jolting awareness demanding to be acted upon.

We kept our eyes trained on the children, even as our hands stretched out and our fingers interlocked without a word.

The second we touched, I ceased to breathe. I became nothing more than neurons and hormones, desperate to finally claim him.

Pippa tried to push past Conner. "Is it a turtle? I want to touch the turtle."

Conner caught her as she darted around him. "Wait, you have to be gentle, Pip."

She stuck out her tongue. "I *am* gentle, noodle head."

"Noodle head?" Galloway snickered, catching my eye. "That's a new one."

Over the past few months, the children had hurled obscenities, slowly becoming more and more creative. Any word, if said in the right connotation, could become a surly curse.

I should know. Galloway was a master at muttering simple phrases but with rage that painted my cheeks.

"Come on, we better supervise." Galloway tugged my hand, and together, we caught up to Pip and Conner, sharing in their excitement.

Respectful of the creatures, we didn't talk loudly. Preferring to watch the giants of the sea trade the grace of swimming for manual labour of flippers on sand.

The thunder slowly stopped its threatening rumble, heading away while the turtles took their time climbing ashore.

We paced beside them patiently. I counted eight, with more appearing behind us.

A few minutes later, as more arrivals appeared, Galloway said, "There has to be close to sixteen or so. What were the odds that their nesting ground was our tiny island?"

I didn't know how that made me feel. Awed that we had the honour of being the birthing safety of such ancient creatures or extremely sad that it was far enough away from human and predators that their age-old process hadn't changed.

How long had this island been untouched, unnoticed? How much longer would it remain so?

Another month?

Two?

A year?

Was it possible to go our entire lives in this day and age and never be found?

My throat closed up as my thoughts careened down a chute of depression.

Balling my hands, I forced sharp nails into my palm.

Stop that. Galloway is stronger now. We have a home.

Soon, we would be free to look at methods of leaving on our own merits. We no longer had to wait for nature to heal us. We could find our own way back to society...somehow.

"What are they gonna do?" Conner whispered as the lead turtle stopped a couple of metres from the treeline. Soft sand glistened in the darkness as large flippers scooped and flung a shower of grains over its shell.

I waited for Galloway to mention mating (had the children had the sex talk before the crash?) but he paused.

Scratching his beard, he frowned. "Um, how much do you guys know about the miracle of life?"

"Miracle of life?" Conner snorted. "Come on. I'm thirteen. I know what fucking is—"

"Ah, ah, ah!" Galloway slapped his hand over the boy's mouth. He narrowed his eyes at Pippa. "I don't think we need such talk in front of ladies, do you?"

Conner pulled away, his smile cocky that he knew something Pip might not.

The little girl blinked in confusion, never taking her eyes off the line-up of hole-digging turtles. "What are they doing? What's fucking?"

Conner snorted.

"Great," I muttered under my breath while Conner poked his sister with a smug smile. "They're making babies, Pip."

"Babies?" Her eyes popped. "How?" Her angelic face swivelled to face Galloway. "Tell me."

Galloway chuckled. "Oh, hell no." Pointing in my direction, he added, "You're up, Stel. Girls stick with girls...remember?"

I rolled my eyes. "Gee, thanks."

"You're welcome."

Pippa hugged her kitten. "Mummy told me that daddy somehow put me in her stomach, but I didn't understand how." She pointed at the closest turtle. "Is that how it happens? By digging a hole?"

I struggled not to smile or laugh inappropriately at the thought of telling her exactly what men and women do. If we never got off this island, she would never experience the heartbreak of first love or the pain and incredible pleasure of losing her virginity.

Unless she turns all Blue Lagoon *and fancies her brother.*

I shuddered at how gross that would be.

I remembered my teenage years with crystal clarity because it'd been a time of insanely epic highs and violently depressing lows. My ex had been bad news, but it'd taken me too long to figure that out.

Draping my hair over my shoulder, I said, "Turtles are different. They lay eggs—like chickens. Unlike chickens and the eggs we eat, if a male chicken is affectionate with a female, the eggs turn into baby chicks."

"Okay..." She didn't tear her gaze from the ever-expanding nest the turtle made. I sighed in relief; glad she didn't delve into what 'being affectionate' entailed.

There was time for that. Time for me to come up with a better sex lesson than the one my mum gave me.

She'd petrified me by teaching how to put a slippery condom on a banana. My eleven-year-old fingers fumbled, and I'd ended up with lube and a rogue condom flying into my eye.

Pushing away the recollection, I carried on. "If memory serves, turtles return to land once a year to lay and then leave the eggs to fend for themselves."

"So...they're making lots of babies?"

"Technically, yes."

Pippa's eyes widened. "You mean...we'll have turtle babies?" Her teeth shone in the gloom. "When? When will they be born?"

"Technically, they won't be born. They'll hatch."

"Okay, hatch. When?"

I looked at Galloway. "Any idea?"

He raised an eyebrow. "Nope."

I didn't have a clue. I had no idea what the gestation period was for a turtle egg.

Pippa waved her question away in favour of a much more important one. "Can I keep one—when it hatches? I want one as a pet."

I laughed. "I don't think a wild animal would appreciate being kept for your enjoyment."

She pouted. "But I'd feed it and bath it and take it for walks."

Conner ruffled her hair. "Turtles don't walk, Pip."

"Do too." She pointed at the sand spray as the hard-shelled creature continued to flap deeper and deeper into the beach. "It walked here from the sea, didn't it?"

Conner crossed his arms. "I'd hardly call that walking."

"I do."

His forehead furrowed, preparing to tease. "All right…what do they eat?"

Pippa paused, beseeching my help.

"Don't look at me. Seaweed?"

Galloway cleared his throat. "I think, depending on the breed, squid and fish, anemones, shrimp…anything they can find in the reef."

Pippa's shoulders fell. "We can barely catch those for us. I guess fishing for a turtle would be hard."

Something broke inside me. I hated to see her crash from such a happy place. I whispered in her ear, "We might not be able to train a wild animal to be a pet, but if we make it comfortable and protected, it might hang around on its own accord."

She sucked in a breath. "Really?"

"We can try."

She bounced on the spot. "Oh, yes. Please. I want to try."

I knew I shouldn't, but I indulged in the whim. I missed my cat. I missed having something to cuddle and stroke.

You'll have Galloway soon enough.

Galloway's lips quirked, almost as if he'd followed my train of thought. We shared a look—laden with lust and attraction.

My cheeks heated as I dropped my gaze.

Even if we did manage to come to terms with the chemistry between us, it wasn't the same as caring for an animal. I adored the thought of something friendly and alive to pamper. "What would we call it?"

"Flipper." Pippa smiled. "Or Fish. I haven't decided."

"Fish?" Conner pulled a face. "Stupid name."

Pippa whirled on him. "Oh yeah. What would *you* call it?"

Conner puffed out his chest. "Raphael, of course. From the Teenage Mutant Ninja Turtles."

Pippa rolled her eyes. "You're such a boy."

"Thanks for noticing."

Galloway drifted off, selecting a spot of sand to sink into a sitting position. We'd all become intrinsically linked in the months we'd lived together. Where one went, the others normally followed.

If we had separate tasks, we were always aware of space between us, time apart, and suffered an almost sixth sense if either of us needed help.

I didn't know if it was from our forced closeness or because we had no distractions—no outside influences and no other interaction. Either way, the bonds were like ropes, keeping us connected with knots and pulleys.

Without thinking, Conner, Pip, and I joined Galloway on the beach. Shoulders touching, our little bubble of safety was complete.

Together, we fell quiet, watching the turtles dig and prepare, revelling in the beauty of nature.

Chapter Forty

•••

GALLOWAY

••••••

THREE YEARS BEFORE THE CRASH

"DID YOU DO it?"

I looked up from my day on cleaning dishes. Two years, eight months, and sixteen days behind bars. I didn't want to think how many dishes I'd cleaned in that time.

Bruce cocked his head, his arms covered in soapy bubbles.

Every day he asked that question. And every day I gave him the same answer.

"Yes."

"And you admitted that in court?"

"Yes."

"And your sentence is life?"

"Yes."

"For killing a crooked doctor?"

"Yes."

"Who'd killed a minimum of twenty-two people—that they know of—through malpractice and malicious intent?"

My hands curled. "Yes."

I waited for the same thing that always happened after I'd answered his questions. Bruce shook his head, his eyes glowing with anger on my behalf. "Life is so fucking unfair."

All I could say was, "Yes."

•••••••••••••••••••••••••••••

DAWN TAINTED THE horizon.

The stars refused to give up their velvet darkness, fighting against the ever-lightening sky. But no matter how bright they burned, they fought a losing battle.

And the turtles somehow knew.

All night, we'd watched them dig and position themselves over their crudely made nests. One by one, the shelled creatures settled in to deliver hundreds of leathery eggs until a mound of potential life forms puddled in the sand.

The leader finished first, flapping and scrapping until she covered her loved ones, ensuring the vulnerable eggs were protected by a natural blanket.

My back ached from sitting, and Conner and Pippa succumbed to tiredness a couple of hours ago, resting their heads on Estelle's and my shoulders, snoozing and snoring, refusing to go to bed where they would be comfy.

The turtles finally deemed their eggs safe and pushed off toward the ocean.

Estelle yawned, raking her fingers through her hair. Her nipples hardened beneath her black bikini, teasing me with the perfect shape as she stretched.

My cock twitched and everything I wanted to say collided in my head. I'd planned to put everything out in the open tonight.

But that had been before the turtles.

My eyes shot to the sky, contemplating the time left before a new day stole whatever privacy we might find.

It's still possible.

We still had time. Time to give into each other. Time to stop bloody fighting the inevitable. Because one thing I was sure of, I was in love with her. Irreversibly, indescribably, completely, madly in bloody love with her.

Estelle caught my attention. Her voice mimicked a husky whisper. "You tired?"

"Not in the slightest." I lowered my eyes. "As far as I'm concerned, the night hasn't ended yet."

The pulse in her neck hammered as she swallowed. "Oh?"

"It's not over, Estelle. Not until we talk."

Colour painted her cheeks. "You just want to talk?"

My heart pounded at the shy desire on her face. "Do *you* want to talk?"

"I think…I think talking might be secondary to something else I had in mind."

Christ.

I stifled my groan. "Goddammit, Estelle—"

"Hey…you said you'd wake us when they were leaving." Conner pushed off my shoulder, rubbing sleep from his eyes.

He shook Pippa. "Wake up, Pippi. They're going."

Pippa jolted upright. "Oh, no. I don't want them to go."

I laughed quietly, never looking away from Estelle. Damn kids and their interruptions.

She smiled, understanding exactly what frustrated me.

For once, we were on the same wavelength.

Long may it last.

Rubbing aching muscles, we all stood and followed the turtles down to the water line. Not one of them paid us attention. We weren't important, apparently.

Conner reached out to touch the closest one.

I held him back. "Don't disturb her. You don't know if it will break whatever schedule they're on."

Estelle agreed. "He's right. We can watch but don't interrupt."

Pippa's face softened as the first lumbering beast hit the sea, immediately transforming from uncoordinated oaf to graceful swimmer. "I've changed my mind."

Splashing a little, the turtle floated for a second in bliss. Happiness at her bulky weightlessness obvious after a long night.

Estelle asked softly, "Changed your mind on what?"

"What I'll call my baby turtle."

"Oh?"

Pippa's face melted with affection. "I want to call mine Escape."

I froze.

Damn kid had the power to make me choke up and want to build a bridge back to society all at once. She was so brave, so aware. I often thought she didn't truly understand our situation because of her age.

But she understood everything. She understood too well.

Estelle gathered her close, kissing the top of her head. "I think that's a brilliant name."

"Know why?" Pippa hugged her stuffed kitten.

Don't.

I didn't think I could stomach more of her desolation.

"Because they can swim and escape while we're stuck here."

I sucked in a breath.

Even Conner remained quiet with no quip or tease.

We stood there as time ticked on, saying goodbye as each turtle vanished into the aquamarine tide, leaving only their tracks, flipper marks, and newly dug nests.

When the last had disappeared and the sun had risen enough to scatter away the stars, Conner laughed loudly. "I just realized something."

We turned to face him.

I asked, "What exactly?"

He waved at the empty beach. "We had years' worth of food and we just let it go."

Pippa gasped. "You can't mean—"

"How could you—" Estelle's voice dripped with disbelief. "I could never—"

Conner grinned. "I know…but still."

I hid my thoughts behind a careful mask. The moment the first turtle arrived, I'd thought the very same thing. Food…copious amounts of food. We could kill a few, salt and preserve it, and use their shell for numerous things.

We wouldn't have to fish or hunt for a while.

But the instant I'd considered it, I'd discounted it. It would've come down to me to kill and prepare it and…I didn't have that in me anymore.

Not after what I'd done and the price I'd paid.

I'd killed for the right reasons. I'd killed a bad person.

But it didn't mean it hadn't screwed me up inside. If I could barely tolerate eradicating someone who deserved his fate…how could I handle slaughtering an innocent animal about to grant life?

Pippa squealed and hit Conner with her stuffed toy. "You're a butthead."

"And you're a fish scale."

"Am not."

"Are too."

He struck out, tickling her in the perfect spot to make her explode into giggles. Slapping him away, Pippa charged away.

Conner chased after her.

"Well, seems like the lack of sleep hasn't deterred their energy levels." Estelle drifted closer. The tide lapped around our ankles and my skin heightened to smouldering sensitivity.

I couldn't stop staring at her, caring for her, killing myself slowly with desire for her.

She annoyed me and confused me but something about her also soothed, healed, and centred me. She erased my festering past, heinous guilt, and monstrous rage at injustice.

Prison bars might no longer cage me, but the ones around my soul did. However, Estelle had the power to blow apart the lock, decimate the gate, and hand me the keys to fight for my freedom.

My lips ached to kiss her. My body strained to hold her as if she was the perfect ending to my unhappy tragedy. My body wanted her (that I couldn't and wouldn't deny), but my lust went deeper than that. Deeper than bone and flesh and it was those reasons that bloody terrified me.

I wanted her; not because she was the most incredible woman I'd ever met (a non contestable conclusion) but because of what I wanted to give her in return.

I wanted to give her *me*.

Everything.

The good, the filthy, and the fuckedupness.

But what right did I have to take so much and force her to take me in return? She deserved someone so much better than I was. Someone whole…

My mind quietened as Estelle's gaze met mine.

Suddenly, my worries didn't matter.

The only thing that did was the fact that dawn was only moments away.

I wouldn't let another day disappear without doing what I needed.

It was now or never.

Grabbing Estelle's wrist, I hollered up the beach. "Conner, Pip. Go back to the camp. Relax, nap, do whatever the hell you want. But do not come to the other side of the island. Do you understand?

Estelle and I need to discuss something."

Chapter Forty-One

ESTELLE

What is life? Is it a breath or a smile or a marriage to the perfect mate?
~~What is fate? Is it a predestined script or a fluke in time or the apex of chance~~
~~and circumstance?~~
What is death? Is it everlasting sleep or forever loneliness from those you love?
I don't know what life is. I don't know how fate works. But I do know death.
Death is found in pleasure.
Death is found in sex.
And the ultimate death is found in the purest of orgasms.
Taken from the notepad of E.E.

...

WHAT IS HE doing?

What am I doing?

What the hell was going on?

Galloway hadn't uttered a word but every footfall held entire conversations with their thunderous intent.

I'm done.

I can't stop it.

I don't want to stop it.

His fingers branded my wrist with fiery irons, and his limp was ignored in favour of storming through the wooded area to the tip of the island where the beach met ocean almost by the treeline, no matter high or low tide.

Breathing hard, he let me go, dragging both hands through his hair before pinching the bridge of his nose.

For a second, he didn't move.

I didn't move.

But then he spun to face me, his eyes more alive than I'd ever seen, his heart more visible than I'd ever hoped.

"Estelle."

I waited for more.

It never came.

"Galloway."

His gaze searched mine. Uncertainty fogged their depths like a tropical storm. His hands opened and closed by his sides. "I'm not going to hurt you."

My lips parted. "I didn't think you would."

"Good because I would *never* hurt you. Ever. Do you understand?" He took a step closer.

My toes glued themselves to the beach. "I—I understand." His blue eyes turned into torpedoes tearing into me, whizzing around my body.

"No matter what you read, who you speak to, what my past indicates...I. Will. Not. Hurt. You."

Goosebumps broke out like a cape of worry. "I know that, G. Why...why are you saying this?"

His throat worked as he forced back the discomfort and anger he never managed to shrug off. "I just needed you to know that. That I'm not all bad." He splayed his hands. "Actions don't define us. Isn't that what some stupid quote said? Well, I don't agree. My actions do define me, and I can't get away from that definition, no matter how hard I try. I don't want it to ruin what we might have. I don't want you to hate me—"

I stepped forward, the sand whisper-hissing beneath my feet. "Galloway...stop." I stopped within touching distance, within kissing distance. "I could never hate you."

"You could. If you knew what I was."

"Wrong." My hair slid over the bow in my bikini, tickling my back. My hand hesitantly landed on his chest. Immediately, his gonging heart slammed into my fingertips. *Thud-thud, thud-thud.*

He sucked in a breath, covering my hand with his.

I struggled to focus on words when all I wanted was his touch. "I know I could never hate you because I know who you are. This island doesn't allow us to hold secrets, no matter how hard we try. I know you've done something. And I know it was something big. If you want to tell me, you don't need to be afraid that I'll turn away from you. I'd never judge you that way. But if you don't want to tell me, then don't be afraid that your past will ruin your future. I don't know if we'll ever get off this island. But what I do know is I'd like you to be in it. No matter where we end up."

His body tensed as if Medusa herself had frozen him. "I want you, Estelle."

"I know." My voice thickened. "I want you, too."

"So you don't want to run?"

"I don't want to run."

"That night I asked you if you wanted more than friendship. You said you didn't." His voice lowered. "Did you lie?"

"Yes." I struggled to admit. "You were right. I don't just want to be your friend."

"You want me more?"

I blushed. "Do you really need to ask? The night I took your splint off...I haven't stopped thinking about it. I wish...I wish..."

His eyes narrowed. "You wish?"

"I wish I hadn't stopped." I licked my lower lip. "I wish I'd taken your hand and led you away from the camp to finish together. I want you, G. I'm sick of trying to deny it."

I didn't make a sound as his lips touched my hairline. His breath warmed my scalp. And his body unravelled every fear and restraint I had left.

Sighing heavily, I gave into him, melting into his embrace.

"I've never wanted anything as much as I want you." He kissed my eyelids. "Never been so bloody desperate to be with anyone as much as I am with you." He kissed my cheeks. "I'm going to have you, Stel. I'm going to claim you, satisfy you, corrupt you." He kissed the corner of my mouth. "I'm going to seduce you, and once you're thoroughly seduced, I'm never going to let you leave me."

His gaze shot bullets into my mind.

"Can I kiss you?"

My lips tingled in invitation and surrender. "I feared you'd never ask."

His height towered over me, but his neck bent with grace and purpose, bringing his mouth to mine.

Every cell relocated in my lips, transforming into mirrors and prisms, desperate for his reflection.

He paused one final time. "I won't be able to stop."

"I don't want you to stop. Not this time."

A moan caught in the back of my throat as my breasts pressed against his chest. The tatty grey t-shirt he wore was sun-faded and wave-ruined, but he'd never looked more handsome. Everything— from his overgrown sorrel hair to his soft beard and stark cheekbones.

I'd never been so attracted to anyone.

"You're beautiful," he murmured.

"So are you..."

He kissed me.

His lips were softer than rabbit fur, softer than satin pillows. Kissing Galloway was like snipping the anchors holding me on earth and floating in utter sweetness.

But then his hands came up and captured my cheeks. His feet came forward and imprisoned my body. And his lips lost their soft sweetness, turning into something entirely lost.

"G—" I panted as his kiss became stronger, faster, wilder. The taste of desperation laced our senses while our tongues tried to memorize every slippery sensation.

The explosion of liquorice and musky passion drugged me until my fingers scrambled at his clothing, dying to touch his flaming skin and put an end to my self-inflicted misery.

I moaned as he clutched me harder.

I cried out as his teeth replaced his lips, nipping their way from my mouth to my throat.

My back arched, my body swayed, giving up all control. I didn't want to fight. Not anymore.

But then, we were moving.

Galloway's fingers tugged my bikini top, freeing the black triangles, pulling the useless apparel away from my sex-swollen body.

His mouth tore away from my neck, his eyes transformed into blue-silver beacons matching the sunrise for spectacular beauty.

I followed his lead, gasping as the warm tide washed away the sand on my feet, quickly licking up my calves.

I shivered as Galloway bent his knees and took my nipple into his mouth. My hands flew up, fingers threading like music notes into his hair, holding his face close.

His teeth nipped, my body turned liquid, matching the waves with moisture. And something happened, something that had never happened before.

I lost sense of time, of space, of right and wrong.

I forgot about Conner and Pippa and the crash and the island and the fact I might never see my home again.

All I knew, all I cared about, was the trembling, aching man in my arms and the magical ability our bodies had to delete everything with pleasure.

Letting me go, Galloway tore off his t-shirt and yanked at the Velcro holding his board-shorts. He was nothing but heat and crazy and yearning. But beneath his molten smoulder, he looked at me as if I'd broken yet another piece of him. I'd shattered whatever walls he'd erected and stood in the rubble of his mind. He looked broken but also cured.

I fell and fell.

I fell from disaster and found salvation in his hold.

His erection sprung free as he kicked his board-shorts to languish on the tide's surface. He was past caring for the safety of his limited wardrobe. "Come here." His arm snaked out, lassoing me to his body as his fingers unthreaded the black bows on my hips.

The final piece of my bikini came away, and we stood before each other, painted with russets and apricots of the new sun.

I licked my lips as he hoisted me up. Instinctually, my legs wrapped around his hips, pressing myself against the hardness I desperately wanted.

The thought of condoms and contraception flickered and snuffed out. If we did this, we wouldn't do it with prior conversation of past lovers or health history. We did this out of trust and agreement that we came together bare—both body and soul.

His muscles bunched where he held me, his face tortured with patience and want.

This wasn't the time for long sensory overloads. This was the time to feed our ravenous hunger and give in.

Holding his gaze, I reached between us and grabbed his cock.

He jerked, biting his lip.

Our eyes screamed everything we couldn't say as I silently arched in his hold and positioned him at my entrance.

His jaw sewed tight as I achingly slowly slid onto him. My legs spasmed around his hips, my vision spluttered to greys and shadows as the blissful joy echoed from my core.

I'd never felt so in control and so controlled in all my life. Never felt so full and empty.

When I'd taken as much as his length as I could, I paused.

But he didn't let me stop.

His large hand landed on my hipbone, gently pushing me the final inch, pressing past pleasurable pain, inserting more than just his body but his heart into my chest, too.

We stood quaking with the tide lapping around us, our breathing the same torn rattle.

As much as I didn't want to break the mood, I had to give one tiny instruction. I'd accepted that I was wrong to stay away from him. But I wasn't wrong about my fears. Pregnancy could never happen. We could find happiness together, but that was where our coupling had to end.

Holding him close, I whispered in his ear. "Love me, take me,

I'm yours. But don't come in me."

His body jolted; his eyes searched mine. Understanding followed swiftly and his cock twitched inside.

We groaned together, and he surprised me by pressing his forehead to mine and thrusting up. "I promise."

My heart shed its final prison, becoming a crazed winged creature desperate for him. Knowing he would help me prevent a future of dreadful uncertainty allowed me to fully relax since we'd met at the airport in Los Angeles.

Because even then, I'd known. I'd felt his soul casting its lure to tempt mine. I felt the barbed hooks making their way slowly into my psyche, webbing our lives together, whether we wanted them to or not.

Stumbling forward, Galloway slammed to his knees in the water. A pained grimace showed the action wasn't planned but part of the weakness of his ill-healed ankle.

Water splashed, filling our mouths with salt.

But it didn't stop or dislodge us.

Hauling me onto the wave-lapped shore, Galloway lay me down, baptising me in seawater as his hands clutched the beach on either side of my head and thrust up.

Everything dissolved.

My legs opened.

My fingers clutched.

And my body beckoned him deeper.

"Christ, Estelle." His mouth found mine and together we rode, splashed, and claimed, rocking to the same despairing rhythm, our tongues mimicking our bodies, our mutual want ensuring our rise to the pinnacle flew rather than swam.

Thrust after thrust, I spooled tighter into a galaxy waiting to supernova.

Thrust after thrust, my fear about him coming tainted my pleasure.

And when a growling groan spilled from his lips and his back turned to stone and his features set in quartz, I panicked.

"Stop!"

He didn't.

His lips claimed mine again, orchestrating my body to ignore repercussions and only live in the moment. To come with him. Because he was seconds from coming undone.

"No!" I screamed, my heels kicking his back.

His hips stopped pistoning, his eyes round with fear. "What? I won't hurt you. I promised I wouldn't hurt you." Rage replaced the stunned terror. "You said you believed me!"

My breathing turned wet with swallowed tears. "I promised? *You* promised. You said you wouldn't come inside me."

His eyebrows shot into his dark hairline. "I wasn't. I wouldn't."

"You were about to."

Babies and pregnancy and complications.

My passion bubbled into panic.

"I wouldn't go back on a promise, Estelle. I was about to pull out."

I shoved his shoulders. "Well, pull out now. I can't—I can't do this."

Wrong thing to say.

Heavy shoplifter-proof shutters clanged over his eyes. Without a word, he moved his hips, withdrawing the hard deliciousness from between my legs. Sitting on his knees, he scowled. "Happy?"

Scrambling up, I hugged my knees, feeling ridiculously stupid and horribly naked. "No. I'm not happy. I know I just ruined it. But I'm sorry. I can't...I can't—"

"I wasn't going to come in you, Estelle. You told me not to. I would've obeyed."

I had nothing to say.

I was stupid to jump the gun and ruin something so perfect.

But it was ruined, and I didn't have the strength to salvage it.

Not today.

Unfolding, I stood, fighting the urge to cover myself. "I'm sorry, Galloway." Turning my back on him, I scooped my sodden bikini floating like a black stain on the water and purposely didn't look back.

Chapter Forty-Two

• •

GALLOWAY

• • • • • •

I RUINED IT.

Just like I ruined every other good thing in my life.

That night, I lay in bed agonising over how I could've prevented the awful ending after the best sexual experience of my life.

Estelle was everything I wanted. It wasn't just because she was the only woman on the island. It wasn't just because I found her attractive and smart.

She was my person.

The one perfect creation just for me.

And the knowledge that I'd upset her by doing something she didn't want me to do.

It bloody *killed* me.

I'd tried to talk to her once I returned to camp. We had all day to clear the air and sort out how to fix what was broken. But Estelle threw herself into taking care of Pippa and Conner. She gathered firewood, stoppered containers full of fresh water, fried silver fish in coconut milk, and garnished the dish with fresh salad and toasted coconut shards.

By the time the moon kicked the blazing sun from its throne, lack of sleep from the night before with turtle watching, and the stress of upsetting Estelle, I fell into a restless sleep on my side of the partition wall.

All night she didn't come to me. She didn't crawl around the flax barrier or cuddle into my side.

The next day was just as bad.

Strained and unnatural smiles. Sugary words and polite conversation painted over the truth of what we needed to say.

It was God-awful.

The worst day of my damn life.

But with the magic of hindsight, it wasn't the worst.

Not really.

I'd thought the crash was bad. Being stranded. The fear of survival and never being found.

Turned out, it could get worse.

And it was coming for us.

We just didn't know it.

Chapter Forty-Three

. . . .

E S T E L L E

. . . . . .

Fortune favours the fortunate. Bad luck favours the deserving.
The world has its favourites, just like every man, woman, and child has theirs.
We have our favourite person, our favourite food, our favourite memory.
And unfortunately, the universe has its favourites, too. And for those who don't
play by its rules, misfortune and bad luck reigns.
I thought I was one of the favourites.
Turns out, I was wrong.
Taken from the notepad of E.E.

...

BAD LUCK COMES in threes (or, at least, that was how the expression went). Our luck—what with crashing and being left to our own devices for four months—might be slightly skewed. However, it felt as if the universe didn't like us very much with the week that followed after I slept with Galloway.

First, there was Conner.

The day after my disastrous tryst, Conner collected his fishing spear like every other day and went to spend the morning chasing breakfast, lunch, and dinner.

He'd become so proficient, I no longer worried about him swimming out of his depth or stabbing himself accidentally. The reef around our island protected us from crashing waves and the calm atoll was as safe as a chlorinated pool for a seasoned hunter.

For a few hours, I weaved another blanket with Pippa to replace my first attempts and restocked our firewood. I smoked some more coconut shards on a flat rock in the fire, set a cauldron of water to boil for a clam salad lunch, and even managed to find ten minutes to scribble a phrase or two in my notebook while no one was looking.

But then…

Calamity happened.

Turned out the reef wasn't as safe as a pee-filled paddling pool. Not as secure as a pool with pretty mosaic tiles on the walls.

A pool didn't house enemies.

Pippa saw him first.

Dropping the thin vine she'd been decorating with fish skeletons, she squealed and charged down the beach to her limping, gasping brother.

Oh, my God.

Galloway, who'd returned from the crash site to salvage an extra piece of fuselage, threw the axe into the sand and took off after her. Limping/jogging, he only wore his board-shorts, ignoring screams from his own body to focus on the boy who'd become our son.

Please...no...

"Conner!" I charged after them.

My feet flew in the soft sand, hurtling me to all fours just as Connor collapsed into Galloway's arms.

"I've got you." Galloway lowered him to the beach, cushioning Conner's back on his chest.

My eyes zeroed in on Conner's right leg as it splayed out. His normal brown skin was puckered and white with a wickedly red puncture on his instep.

"No! Conner. No!" Pippa tried to grab him, but Galloway pushed her back. "Pip, don't. Let me deal with it."

Conner moaned, smiling weakly at Pippa. "I'm okay, Pippi. Don't—" Agony cut him off; he buried his face in Galloway's chest. "Make it stop. God, make the pain stop."

I shook as if a magnitude ten earthquake replaced my heart. Grabbing Pippa, I stopped her clutching Conner and wiped at her tears. "Shush, it's okay."

"It's not okay!" Her wails lifted until the sound echoed off the palm trees. "Conner...please." She cracked in half, turning in my arms and sobbing on my shoulder.

I rubbed her back, doing my best to soothe her while terror tore at my soul.

"What happened, mate?" Galloway cuddled Conner close, wiping away his sand-filled hair. "What's up? Tell me what hurts."

Conner opened his mouth to speak, but he retched instead. Galloway repositioned him so he could vomit on the beach. He never stopped murmuring comforting things while Conner gave into the nausea and toxins coursing through his blood.

Pippa's tears turned into rivers; she squirmed from my arms

and grabbed Conner's hand. "Don't go to sleep, Co. *Please* don't go to sleep."

I wanted to calm her—she'd put herself into hiccupping shock soon—but my panic for Conner turned me ruthlessly focused.

I nudged her away. "Pippa...I need to look at him, okay? I'm going to make sure he doesn't go to sleep."

Don't promise something you can't deliver.

My teeth clacked together.

Pippa fought, but she didn't match my strength. In the back of my mind, I hated myself for treating her so cruelly, but she was alive.

Conner was dying.

Shuffling closer, I met Galloway's eyes. His cheekbones stood out starkly; his panic threading a dark blue through his turquoise eyes. He nodded as I cradled Conner's foot, inspecting the wound.

Gritty sand stuck to the blood trickling from his injury, but nothing looked as if it'd lodged inside. The tiny hole already wanted to close, clogging with debris. "Do you remember what happened?" I palpated his foot, wincing at his hot, hot flesh.

I racked my brain for what could've done this.

"I didn't...see it." Conner wheezed, holding his chest as if suffering an asthma attack. "I thought it was...a rock."

"Well, you're okay now, Co. Take your time." Galloway stared worriedly as Conner's lips turned bluish. "Don't try to talk too much, buddy. Just give us the basics."

Tears lived in my fingers, my toes, my heart but none dared torment my eyes. I remained dry-gazed and focused.

Conner was ours. I wouldn't let him die. I wouldn't let anyone I loved die again.

My parents...my sister. They'd been taken from me. Fate wouldn't take my second chance at a family.

We. Will. Not. Die. Here.

My childhood warnings exploded to mind. Living in Australia, we were drilled about poisonous creatures, snakes, spiders, and jellyfish. We knew before we could walk how to wrap something tight around a bite and who to call for antidotes.

After all, we lived in a country where ninety percent of the world's deadliest animals resided.

"Estelle..." Galloway's voice wrenched my head up. "What—what could it be?"

Conner went rigid in his arms, gasping for breath.

Shit!

He said a rock.

Something he'd stepped on.

Something spiny and poisonous and…

Think!

Numerous fish were venomous. Scorpionfish, dragonfish…but only one looked like a pebble.

"A stonefish."

Galloway flinched. "Stonefish? Aren't they…" He stopped himself, but the word hung in the air.

Deadly.

I swallowed hard. "Not if the dose was small enough. Not if it's on an extremity and not on the chest or throat." I did my best to sound knowledgeable and confident, but inside…inside, I was a little girl screaming for her parents to fix this.

Pippa bawled harder. "Don't die, Conner! *Don't.* Don't go to sleep." Hurling herself onto Conner's chest, Galloway stroked her hair while never letting go of her brother.

The little boy looked sick and terrified, his eyes round and white skin shining with sweat.

"What can we do?" Galloway glared at me. "Estelle…think, goddammit."

"I—I don't know."

Liar. You do know.

At least…I think I did.

Memories slowly smashed through rusty locks, bowling through cobwebs and age-tarnished recollections. The longer I thought about school lessons and motherly chiding, the more I recalled what to do.

Somehow, Galloway sensed that. He turned to me to heal the boy we'd fallen in love with. As an Englishman, living in a country where the deadliest animal was a badger, he had no expertise.

But I did.

I can do this.

Fake confidence became real as my nursing skills slipped into regimented actions.

Pulling Pippa away (again), I bowed over Conner. "Co, I know it hurts and I'm going to help you. But first, I need to know how long you stood on it for. Do you remember?"

His face scrunched up. "Only a second. I stepped, it hurt. I jumped."

"That's good, right?" Galloway's voice bordered rage and anxiousness.

I hope so.

I nodded. "That's great."

He has a much better chance of surviving.

"Wait here." Bolting up the beach, I thanked heavens that I'd already put the water on to boil for lunch. It'd reached temperature, bubbling away in its fuselage container. My memory of how to treat such a sting was rusty at best, but I remembered something about hot water—as hot as the injured could stand (sometimes as high as boiling)—and drawing as much of the poison out with scrubbing and disinfecting.

Grabbing a coconut shell, I scooped boiling water, grabbed the Swiss Army knife, a new coconut from the storage pile by the umbrella tree, the severely lacking medical kit from the cockpit, and a torn piece of clothing we kept for cleaning.

Hugging my possessions, and doing my best not to slosh boiling water on my fingers, I flew back to Conner.

Landing on my knees, my knuckles scalded as I carefully wedged the dripping coconut shell in the sand.

Pippa once again sprawled over her brother, bawling.

Frustration bled through my voice. "Pippa, darling, I need you to let go of Conner." I pushed the terrified girl. "Galloway, I need you to put Conner flat on his back."

Without a word, Galloway obeyed, relinquishing Conner to the sand and tugging Pippa into his arms to keep her away while I worked.

Forcing a smile for Conner's sake, I bent over him. "This is going to hurt, but I promise the pain will get better. Okay?"

His tiny fists clenched; his nostrils flared. But he nodded like a World War I trooper behind enemy lines. "Okay."

I kissed his forehead. "Good boy."

Moving to his feet, I tested the water. It wasn't boiling anymore but was still too hot. But we had no antibiotics; nothing to fight whatever battled in Conner's nervous system. I'd rather burn him than let him die from anaphylactic shock.

"Take a deep breath."

Stealing his foot, I placed it into the hot water.

He screamed.

"What the hell, Estelle?" Galloway shouted.

Pippa squealed, her sobs turning to hysteria. "Stop it! Don't hurt him!"

Anxiety and horror at causing more pain made me snap. "Shut up. *All* of you. This is what has to happen." I pushed his foot back into the water. "Please, Conner. Be brave."

He moaned and thrashed, but his strong little heart gave him the courage to keep his foot in such fiery hotness. The moment I knew he'd keep it there, I turned to the medical kit and wrenched open the second-to-last packet of disinfectant swabs we had.

Wrenching his foot out of the water, I scrubbed his wound hard.

I ignored his screams and tugs to pull away. I braced myself against the disbelieving look from Galloway as I deliberately hurt the poor boy.

But I did the right thing.

I was helping.

So I kept scrubbing, hard and fast, using my fingernails where needed in the wound to ensure nothing remained.

Conner retched again, holding his stomach as the cramping began.

More memories returned of what he would go through. The next twelve hours would be a terrible nightmare: tummy cramps, breathlessness, weakness, headache, diarrhoea, vomiting, paralysis, and even skin peeling from the infected area.

But that was only if he had a full dose.

A minor sting would bring him immense agony with a peaked fever for the first hour or two…after that, it would start to fade.

Hopefully.

Please…please let this work.

Conner passed out before I finished cleaning, and Pippa turned almost catatonic with tears.

My own tears threatened to wash me away, but I blocked everything out and focused on holding Conner's foot in the scorching water before sluicing it with fresh coconut juice (for whatever antibacterial and antioxidant properties it might have).

The rest of the day was the longest I'd ever lived. I remained nurse to Conner, flitting around him like a nervous hummingbird while Galloway turned into nightmare-fighter and tear-protector for Pippa.

She dozed and woke up screaming. She cried and passed out from tiredness.

Poor thing had it worse than Conner did because at least he passed out from pain and let his body heal without being conscious.

It didn't matter if he was awake or sleeping, I never left his side.

Galloway and I shared numerous looks, gradually fading from horror at possibly losing him to accepting relief as Conner slowly got better.

My calculations were right.

Conner was stung at one p.m. on Saturday (thanks to my

phone and its steadfast ability at telling time, even if it couldn't catch a signal). By one a.m. on Sunday, Conner was over the worst, and he fell into a deep, dreamless sleep.

....

Three days passed and my entire attention remained on Conner.

I didn't have time to wonder if Galloway and I would be okay. I didn't contemplate the fact we hadn't come or how thick the unspoken discussion hovered around us.

All I could focus on was Conner.

Galloway and I were okay. We were friends. We would work through a bad experience and move on. Sex wasn't everything. And besides, I loved him so much more than that.

But for now...he didn't need me.

Conner did.

Luckily, he healed quickly. The skin around the sting didn't peel, but it did stay bright red (from the poison and the burning water) but that didn't stop him from growing quarrelsome and wanting to head back out to fish.

Galloway and I flatly forbid him, and Galloway took over, bringing home another octopus and a large eel that strangely tasted like chicken (just like everyone said). My vegetarian preferences had been put on hold in favour of my belly earning a full meal.

Pippa stopped crying whenever Conner went to sleep, and Conner spent most of the day teasing her for causing so much fuss when he was ill. She was wary, not trusting his return to health, as if expecting him to die at any moment and pull a terribly cruel joke on her.

Because of her nervous terror, she never left his side, plastering herself to him wherever he limped to the bathroom and pestering him when she insisted on eating almost in his lap.

Conner rolled his eyes and poked and joked, but he never once snapped at her to leave him alone. He understood how terrifying it had been for her.

After all, he'd lost his parents, too.

Pippa was all he had left.

Despite the passing days and Conner steadily growing stronger, Pippa regressed into sucking her thumb again.

We'd all been through an awful ordeal. But at least our family was still intact.

Late at night, sleeping in my bed and feeling grateful for what we'd achieved, it sucker punched me with realisation of just how insignificant we were.

Against all odds, we'd made a home here. We'd learned how to forage and hunt. We'd educated on how to build and create. And yet…we were so vulnerable to Mother Nature and her creatures.

That reminder stole the rest of my naïvety that we would one day be rescued and go home. Ever since the crash, I'd believed that as long as we kept going, kept trusting that we would be found, that everything would be okay.

But that was a lie I could no longer believe.

The chances of rescue became more and more irrelevant every week. We were living on borrowed time.

Hard-earned time.

Time that wasn't kind nor had any intention of giving us a break.

We'd all healed from our crashed arrival, but it didn't mean we wouldn't suffer other injuries, illnesses, mistakes, and consequences.

We wouldn't come out of this unscathed. No matter how much we might wish.

We were on the brink of extinction.

And we couldn't let our guard down.

Ever.

....

Bad luck visited us a second time.

This time…it brought hazardous weather.

On the fourth day after Conner's accident, the clouds galloped over the sun in the late afternoon, blanketing our island with false darkness. The wind sprung from nowhere with the clamouring hooves of thunder and lightning forked as if Zeus himself waged war on his brother, Poseidon.

Our task of cooking dinner was put on hold as rain droplets the size of school buses fell in a heavy sheet a second later. We all dashed into the home Galloway and Conner had built and gnawed on coconuts and salted fish as rabid winds snapped and masticated our roof, tearing away our window coverings, boring a hole for an impromptu skylight, and threatening to destroy the walls.

Once again, the storm reminded us (just like the stonefish had) that we were insignificant; entirely unsubstantial and dependent on the mercy of whatever the world wanted to give.

Memories of the helicopter crash kept us somber. The tally of how many days had passed since we'd been protected by glass and metal, rather than bamboo and flax, repeated with sorrow.

We huddled together beneath a spare blanket, each consumed with thoughts of loved ones back home and the fact that they would never know we were alive…or dead, if we didn't survive.

It was a long night.

Luckily, as Fiji slowly lightened, the squalls gradually quietened. The walls held and the sky grew bored trying to kill us.

By the time we climbed from the relative safety of our bungalow, dripping wet, with the mammoth task of patching up our home and food stores, we left optimism behind as we surveyed our island.

Everywhere, the sand was littered with flotsam. A jumbled hodgepodge of broken rubbish, regurgitated by the ocean. Seaweed slithered on the white sand like entrails of a giant squid while plastic shopping bags from purchases long ago fluttered in the trees.

We didn't say a word as we drifted to the shoreline, collecting useful items given through the charity of the storm.

By the time we'd sunburned and needed to retreat from the noonday heat, we'd collected a broken deck chair that'd been on the ocean bottom for decades (judging by the barnacles on its rusted frame), an empty oil barrel, a few dead seagulls, rotting fish, and a tangled green fishing net.

Apart from the carcasses of dead creatures, every inch of the marine litter would be given a purpose.

Somehow, bad luck had tried to ruin us but the opposite had happened.

We'd been given things that we didn't have before.

Things that would increase our lifespan for the better.

Instead of always being known as the night from hell, it was christened Christmas morning. The holiday season might've been delayed by a few weeks, but Santa had finally found us with his sleigh and reindeer.

....

Even though happiness had come from a night of disaster, I still couldn't shake the memories of what it'd been like when we were first stranded.

The first panic.

The first helplessness.

The first prayers for salvation.

I'd forgotten the depth of craving for home or the endless begging for a rescuer. Time had adapted us and along with physically becoming able, our thoughts had evolved, too. Days passed where I was *content*. Weeks even.

I was happy with our life and consumed with lust and need for Galloway.

We'd all become guilty of forgetfulness. And soon…who knew what the word home would mean. Would this island become home?

Would this wild existence become preferential over the rat race of society?

I didn't know.

I didn't know if I *wanted* to know.

Because if this *did* become home and our mismatched bandits became a real family…what did that mean for future goals? Did we never try to leave? Did we accept that this was our fate and plant roots more permanent than the ones we already had?

I didn't have the answers and, a few nights after the storm, when no one was around to see my betrayal, I tore out a page of my notebook with simple lyrics to a song I'd written in my darkest days on the island.

I rolled the parchment.

I stuffed it into one of the plastic bottles donated by the sea and tossed it as far as I could into the tide.

Messages had been what brought me to this place.

Perhaps a floating ownerless message would be the one to set us free.

·······················

The third bad luck strike wasn't so much our doing or the world trying to kill us…but more of a forgotten date that ruined a little girl's joy.

Pippa turned eight.

And we didn't celebrate.

It wasn't until her sniffles, a week after the monsoon, made me crawl out of bed and go to her that she told me. Holding her in the dark, she broke down, unable to keep a brave face anymore and told me the most awful thing.

She'd had a birthday and not told anyone.

And Conner, being a typical teenager, forgot.

We were so far removed from celebrations and anniversaries that I hadn't even thought to plan.

Poor thing.

When we'd first arrived, Conner had mentioned Pippa turned eight in a few months. However, I'd never asked the date because I'd believed we'd be with our respective families long before the party. What was worse was…I doubted I would've remembered if he *had* told me. My brain wasn't exactly my friend these days.

But I was wrong.

The months had passed, and we were still here.

And no one had made a fuss of such a precious girl.

I cuddled her harder, pouring as much affection as I could to make up for our error. Pippa had tried to be brave, not wanting to make a fuss because she was old enough to understand that our circumstances were different now but still fanciful enough to wish for a perfect soiree.

Galloway caught me rocking Pippa to sleep just before dawn. Our attraction and unfinished business stretched to wrecking point.

My nipples tingled. My core liquefied. And everything inside me wanted to hold him, apologise, and forget what'd happened. Pretend we'd never given in, never screwed it up, and try again with a clean slate.

Why can't I do that? Why can't I go back in time and do better?

But I couldn't go back. I could only fix forward.

"I'm sorry," I whispered.

He smiled sadly. "Nothing to apologise for."

Somehow, after days of cross tension, it dissolved...just like that.

Our relationship transcended miscommunication and mistakes. It was more mature than snippy arguments and cold shoulders.

I'm so very, very lucky.

Leaving his bed, he tiptoed toward us. His limp stabbed my heart with a thousand love-filled regrets. Slowly, he bent and kissed the top of my head. "Next time...trust me."

He wants a next time...thank God.

His blue eyes glowed. "If I make a promise, Estelle, I keep that promise. And I promise I'll do whatever you want. I'll kiss you however you need. I'll make love to you no matter your fears."

He captured my lips with his.

The kiss was soft and stolen. His touch sent pinwheels of togetherness through my blood.

I sighed into his mouth.

Licking me softly, he moved his lips, trailing warm kisses across my jaw to my ear. His breath was sinfully hot as he whispered, "I'll make you come over and over, Stel, but if it means I'll never have the pleasure, then fine. I can live without if it means you live with more."

His gaze found mine again. "You don't have to be scared of me or of being together...promise me you won't keep us apart."

There was so much to say. So much to admit and so much apologising to do.

But now was not the place.

Tasting him on my lower lip, I murmured, "Tonight. Can we go somewhere and talk."

A half-smile danced across his face. "Talk?"

"Talk...for now." I blushed. "But who knows what will

happen when I get sick of speaking."

He chuckled. "Fair enough. It's a date."

A date.

A delighted shiver ran down my spine.

I hadn't been on a date in forever. And now, I had one with the sexiest, most amazing man I'd ever met.

I'm beyond lucky.

Once again, I found myself slipping. After tossing my bottled message into the sea, I'd noted where and for how long I forgot that this existence was only temporary and not something I wanted.

I didn't know if I should be happy or sad that I had more moments of contentedness (from watching Pippa playing with the broken deck chair, Conner unravelling the fishing net, and Galloway patching up the roof while shirtless) than I ever did while staring out to sea, waiting for a boat or plane (a habit we all did but somehow, had become less poignant and more inconvenient) to find us.

Dropping his eyes, Galloway whispered, so as not to wake Pippa, "What's wrong? Nightmare?"

White-blonde hair fell over my eye as I looked down at her. "It was her birthday yesterday."

The pain and anguish on his face stitched up my heart until it burst with blood-soaked strings.

"Bloody hell. I remember how important birthdays were at that age. God, we royally screwed up."

We.

As in…*us*…her parents.

I knew she wasn't ours biologically, but fate had given her to us. She was ours now. Conner, too. No matter what happened, I wouldn't let them go.

Galloway ran a hand over his face, shedding any remaining sleepiness. "We'll fix it."

"How?" I stroked her hair, never breaking the trance I'd put her in. "We don't have any presents, no cake, no friends to invite."

He stood to his tall height, ideas blazing in his eyes. "Leave it to me."

"But—"

"No buts. I'll fix this." He left without another word, slipping wordlessly into the dawn.

Chapter Forty-Four

GALLOWAY

I WAS AN only child, but that didn't mean I didn't know how to throw a party.

Back in the day, I was the quiet kid at school but the one everyone turned up to his shindigs. My parents had always encouraged my popularity by ensuring I had brothers and sisters in the form of friends, even though they'd tried for another child and failed.

And I didn't take their efforts for granted.

I hosted like a king.

I mastered the art of small talk.

I bridged the gap between cliquey groups and hard-to-break gangs.

But that was before I went to prison. The day the lock slammed shut, my willingness to reach out to others and find friendly ground disappeared.

I thought I'd lost the desire forever. But that was before Estelle crashed into my life (literally).

Glancing at the pinking sky, I estimated I had a couple of hours before sunup. Estelle would keep the kids in bed and I would do my best to give Pippa the best eighth birthday she could ever have.

Sweat ran down my naked back as I ducked into the hut and froze at the heart-twisting sight of Estelle fast asleep wrapped around Pippa while Conner slept at the bottom of his sister's bed like a small tabby cat.

Despite puberty hitting and Conner's hormone swings (not to mention the body odour as testosterone kicked in) he was still a caring brother who would give anything to protect his flesh and blood.

Just like I'll do anything to protect Estelle.

Chugging some water from one of our always-full bottles, I cleared my throat.

One by one, three pairs of eyes opened, harpooning my chest and ensuring I would never be free of these people.

Clapping my hands, I smiled at Pippa. "Can the birthday girl please follow me? I think there might be a surprise for her outside."

Instantly, Pippa's tanned, skinny face lit up like a damn survival flare (if only we had one of those).

She leapt from Estelle's embrace and charged toward me. "Really? What?"

"You'll have to wait and see, impatient Pippi." I wrapped my arms around her, scooped her up, and carried her outside.

"What is it? Where?" She bounced in my arms.

The extra weight and uncoordinated balance hurt my barely-healed bones. My shin was the one part that felt semi-ordinary. The bone had a bump but it was strong. My foot was still mottled with bruising, but at least, the metacarpals had healed enough to wriggle my toes (ignoring the ache, of course).

However, my ankle was a bitch.

It'd knitted together but not correctly. It wasn't perfectly straight and the joint where my leg became my foot wasn't normal. I didn't let Estelle know how badly it hurt to have something so broken—not just temporarily but permanently.

I could walk but not run. I could move but never fly.

I was damaged goods.

But despite the ache every time I put weight on it, I wouldn't put Pippa down for all the diamonds in the world.

Squinting against bright sunlight as I stepped onto the beach, I said, "First, let's start this party off with a bang. What do you say?"

Her response was slapping a wet kiss on my scruffy cheek. "I say yes!"

I couldn't move for a moment. Her tiny lips stole every motor control.

Footsteps sounded behind me as Estelle and Conner joined us in the hot morning.

Estelle wore her black bikini (which threatened to make me hard remembering the night I'd taken it off her) and Conner opted for his shorts with a baseball cap. All of us had stark hipbones, angular ribs, and the elongated skinniness of no fat reserves.

But to me…they were beyond beautiful.

Putting Pippa down, I turned to the largest bonfire I'd ever created. I hadn't lit it, but it was stacked and ready, symbolising the start of a new year of her life.

Turning to the group, I held up an already flaming stick from the fire pit we never let go out. Passing it to Pippa, I said, "Go ahead, birthday girl."

She took it, her face dancing with flames. Carefully, she shoved the stick in the heaped twigs and branches, doing what I taught her when dealing with fire and dangerous things.

She was more responsible than any kid her age.

She could make a brand new blaze from my broken glasses (I'd taught the kids just in case anything ever happened to Estelle and me) and she could fish better than any angler. Plus, she'd learned from Estelle how best to trial food and prepare new edibles to avoid gastric complications.

I'm so damn proud of her.

Of all of them.

The fire crackled and spread, greedily transforming dormant fuel into heat and light.

Estelle came closer, looping her fingers through mine.

I hissed a little at the wound on my palm.

Narrowing her eyes, she held up our linked hands and gasped. "You're bleeding."

"It's nothing. Just a nick."

"Now what did you do? You're always blooming bleeding."

"Blooming?"

"Don't change the subject. How did you do this one?"

Her concern avalanched me in love. I kissed her. "You'll see."

Her face scrunched as if to argue, but then she softened, trusting me.

Trust.

An intangible emotion that carried no price or guarantee but was the most valuable thing a person could earn.

The rest of the morning passed in an idyllic cloud as I guided Pippa around the beach to sandcastles engraved with Happy Birthday, seaweed streamers on trees for decoration, and even a shell pile with eight small sticks acting as a birthday cake and candles for wishes.

In the damp sand, I'd scratched good tidings and what I wanted to come true for her. I gave her a knotted vine bracelet that I'd hastily made as one of her presents, and when we finally sat down to eat a breakfast of clams and roasted crabs, Pippa complained her cheeks ached from smiling and proceeded to make my life complete when she announced it was the best birthday she'd ever had.

Estelle couldn't stop touching me. Her eyes burned with desire and her bikini top failed to hide the hard pinpricks of her nipples.

She wanted me.

I wanted her.

Our failed coupling was forgotten.

Sitting beneath our umbrella tree, we all relaxed in the shade. Sliding my arm around Estelle's sun-warmed waist, I hugged her close. "Tonight. Once the kids are in bed, come find me in the bamboo grove."

She sucked in a breath as I kissed the sharp lines of her collarbone. It was my favourite part of her. The one area of her body that made me so damn hard. Sure, I loved her tits and ass, but there was something so femininely sensuous about her collarbone, looking like wings beneath her skin.

She nodded quickly as Conner threw a crab claw in our direction. "Like you said…it's a date."

My cock twitched in happy anticipation. "You damn well bet it's a date." Letting her go, I focused on the teen. "What was the flying food for?"

Conner squinted. "Oh, I dunno. For doing all this for Pip. For being the best uncle ever and for raising the bar high for when I turn fourteen. I expect the same treatment."

Estelle shuddered beside me. I didn't know if it was pride for me earning the title of Uncle or the fear that we would still be here when he turned fourteen. We'd already been here for too long. How much more time would pass before we were found?

Chuckling to ward off such thoughts (confused that they weren't as depressed as they should've been), I called Pippa over who was playing with the pile of shells I'd made into her birthday cake. "Pip. I have one last thing for you. Do you want it?"

Her copper hair caught the sunlight, looking as beautiful as burning fire. "Yes."

"You sure?"

"Yes! Very, very sure." She dashed to stand in front of me. "Please? Please, can I have it?"

Swallowing my smile, I joked, "I dunno. Have you been a good girl?"

The best. I couldn't ask for more if you'd been custom born for me.

"Yes. At least…I think so."

"Don't give it to her, G. There's room for improvement." Conner chortled, choking on a piece of crab.

Serves him right.

Pippa scowled. "Hush up, Co. I've been good. Haven't I, Stelly?"

Estelle pointed at her chest. "You're asking me? I think it's up to G to decide. After all, he's the one with the gift."

I couldn't stop laughing as Pippa draped her arms around my shoulders and kissed my cheek. "Please, G? I've been good, and if I haven't, I'll be better if you give me my present." She kissed me again. "I promise, promise, promise."

"Fine. Begging isn't necessary." Pulling my surprise from behind my back, I handed it to her. I hadn't wrapped it...not that we had any pretty paper to wrap with. But I hadn't bothered with a leaf or anything.

Maybe, I should've.

Crap, I really should've wrapped it.

Nerves fluttered in my gut. I'd done my best. I'd sharpened the Swiss Army knife and spent most of the morning trying not to screw up.

It wasn't pretty.

It wasn't perfect.

But it was the best I could do...for now.

I tensed, seeing every flaw on the copied face of her favourite stuffed kitten, Puffin.

"Oh, my..." Pippa smoothed the carved creature in her hands. "It's amazing!"

Hardly.

But the gratefulness in which she accepted my haphazardly rudimentary gift threatened to unravel what resemblance I had left as a man. A convicted man. A felon.

For so many years, I'd allowed only hate and anger to control me. Now, here in a different type of imprisonment, I found love and hope fuelled me with no greater power.

I smiled. "Happy Birthday, Pippi."

Estelle gasped. "Galloway..." Her eyes watered. "That's...it's beautiful."

"*Pfft.* It sucks. But it's my first attempt. Next one, I'll do better."

"You always say that. And I keep saying that I love your first endeavours."

Love.

My heart skipped a beat at the thought of ever earning such feelings.

"I don't want a second one." Pippa hugged the wooden figurine, complete with indented tail and carved whiskers. "I want this one. I love it." Pippa rained my cheeks in kisses. "Thank you, thank you, *thank you*. It's perfect."

I laughed, waving her away. "Well, I'm glad you like it. You're welcome."

She took off, parading it in front of Conner, doing her best to make him jealous.

Connor had a point. What the hell could I make for the teen when he turned fourteen? He wouldn't exactly settle for a crappily carved kitty.

Estelle snuggled closer, her lips brushing my ear. "*That's* how you cut yourself. Carving that?"

I nodded, flushing with heat. "Yep."

"I love it, Galloway. Seriously. You made her so happy today. Thank you." Her finger tipped my chin, guiding my face to her. I obeyed the fluttering touch, bowing my head to kiss her.

We kissed for a long time.

We kissed for the shortest time.

But I fell just as hard regardless.

I loved this woman.

And I didn't know how much longer I could avoid telling her.

I didn't know what held me back. She already knew the depth of feelings (how could she not with the way I watched her) but I wanted the moment to be perfect. I wanted her to know that I didn't just love her for being here but because she was mine forever.

Tonight.

Perhaps tonight, I would finally be able to tell her.

....

For the rest of the afternoon, Pippa played with her carved cat, now named Mr. Whisker Wood, and Conner invented a new relay game where they chased each other on the beach, swam in the ocean, and flew through the sky like birds rather than stranded children.

The sun glided across the sky, illuminating us with happiness before finally descending and snuffing itself out on the sea-owned horizon.

As dusk turned to darkness and dinner was eaten and cleaned away, Estelle stood and looked at the tired children with such love in her eyes, I swore a cluster of planets existed in her gaze.

It was more than just love. It was contentment. Satisfaction. Fulfilment.

Who would've thought such things existed in the middle of nowhere.

We were all drowsy from eating, and my eyes turned heavy.

However, the moment the kids were asleep, I had grand plans of what I would do to transform the bamboo grove before Estelle joined me.

I had a gift for Estelle, too, and it wasn't just in my shorts.

Estelle shifted, pushing herself up onto her elbows and shaking her hair over her shoulders to tangle in the sand. She looked like a mermaid who'd climbed from the ocean for one magical evening. She looked otherworldly…like she would vanish just like every other mythical creature in the storybooks.

Scooting into sitting position, she twirled her fingers.

She's nervous…why?

Keeping her eyes down, Estelle murmured, "I have one more gift for you, Pip. If that's okay?"

Pippa sat up from sprawling on the flax blanket by the fire. Her little face turned solemn. "You're going to sing for me?"

My heart stopped beating.

Ever since Estelle let it slip that she was a songwriter, she'd refused to tell me more, constantly changing the subject as if it was unimportant to our current situation. But I wasn't above admitting I followed her sometimes when she thought she was alone. I saw her scribbling in her notebook. I listened covertly when she hummed certain lines and sang gentle lullabies to send the kids to sleep.

I stole her secrets one by one until I knew how passionate she was about music. And what a talented singer she truly was.

Not that I could tell her.

I wasn't supposed to know.

To hear her finally give up this part of her coveted life would be the greatest gift.

Estelle clasped her hands, unsuccessfully hiding her shaking fingers. "Yes, if you'll let me."

Pippa dug her heels into the sand, hugging her knees. "I'd love it. Please."

"Do you want a song you know or an original?"

Pippa chewed her bottom lip, full of seriousness. "Could you sing one about me? About us?"

I couldn't move as Estelle glanced at me before straightening her spine. She looked petrified but resolute as if she'd hidden this part of herself for too long and no longer could.

Sing for me.

Please, God, sing.

"I can. The lyrics belong to a song I've tentatively labelled Sand Solitude. I can sing that if you want."

Pippa shifted to her stomach, resting her chin on her upturned hands. "I'd like that. Pretty please, sing that one."

Conner mimicked his sister, holding his face to listen. "I'm down with that one, too. Rock on, Stelly."

Estelle smiled tightly, her concentration inward.

I, on the other hand, couldn't move, locked into my recline with my legs splayed and elbows dug into the beach behind me. I had an awful fear that if I moved, I'd spook her and she wouldn't sing.

I need her to sing.

Already, my cock twitched at the epic joy of finally hearing her. I'd be in huge trouble before the song was over.

I wanted her beyond anything.

If she sang for me…I doubted I'd be able to stand for a month.

For the longest second, she didn't move.

But then, heaven happened.

She closed her eyes and let herself come alive. She transformed from the girl I'd fallen in love with to a goddess framed by fire and marked by ambrosia itself.

Her husky voice held the melody better than any instrument, so fresh and pure, so dark and sexy. Lyrics and verses tumbled from her mouth, wrapping around us like our green fishing net, capturing us forever.

In that single moment, there was no place on earth I would rather be.

"Once there was a little girl who played upon the shore. Her parents loved her deeply, her brother so completely, and her world was magical more and more. Once there was a young girl who crashed upon the beach. Her past no longer relevant, her old life beyond negligent, and her world now full of prayers and beseech.

But there she found salvation.
In the form of unwanted vacation.
By a man sworn to damnation.
And a woman with no foundation.

Once there was a little girl who swam within the waves. Her smiles hardly changing, her happiness darkly raging, and her world now black and brave. Once there was a young girl who flew above the earth. Her soul was free, her future at sea, and her world vastly different in wealth and worth.

But there she found salvation.

In the form of unwanted vacation.
By a man sworn to damnation.
And a woman with no foundation.

Once there was a little girl who harnessed hell itself. Her past long forgotten, her
will never rotten, and her world full of tempest and war with herself.
Once there was a young girl who fought against death for life. Her soul will
survive, her future will revive, and her world will finally be free of hardship and
strife."

And that was how Estelle stole everything and made me hers.
For eternity.

Chapter Forty-Five

ESTELLE

My world changed from notes and quavers to flesh and sinew.
I'm no longer defined by music, but by the days I spend alive. I'm no longer
afraid of stepping from the pages and living. ~~Truly living~~.
I'm no longer interwoven with fear but standing free with my pockets bursting
with possibility.
My heart is the drum, my feet are the chords, and my fate is my finest melody.
Taken from the notepad of E.E.

...

ONCE WITHIN A song, a woman who trusted in nothing finally
found the strength to stop doubting everything.

"G?" I smoothed my gold negligée (the one piece of clothing
not tatty and sea-faded) and cursed my fluttering heart.

This is ridiculous.

I lived with the man. I cooked, I laughed, I joked, I argued, I
survived with him by my side. He knew what I looked like tired and
cantankerous. He knew my smiles and tears. He knew me in torn t-
shirts and boring bikinis.

Just because I'd dressed up and done my best to pinch some
colour into my cheeks and plaited my hair with the same flowers he
laid on my breakfast every morning didn't mean this was any
different to everyday living.

So why does it feel so completely scary?

If it wasn't any different…why did my heart jackrabbit and my
breath come shallow?

Because it is.

We'd had sex before. This wasn't new. I'd seen him naked.
He'd been inside me.

But this…it had a whole new level of romanticism and

connection.

My flip-flops stopped making a sound as I drew to a halt in the bamboo grove.

Galloway had vanished after dinner, leaving me to tidy up and get the children to brush their teeth (with well-used toothbrushes), rinse their faces, and climb into bed.

He'd told me to meet him here.

I had no idea what to expect.

I jumped as a twig cracked in the dark. My eyes flared in the gloom, doing their best to see. "Galloway?"

He smiled, coming from the darkness to gather me in the tightest embrace. "You came."

We shared a brief kiss. "Of course. Why wouldn't I?"

"I don't know." He let me go. "Lots of reasons."

Stalking forward, he took my hand and guided me into the magical grotto he'd created. Not only had he layered a few of my flax blankets on the ground with a couple rolled up for pillows, but he'd also gathered coconut shells and captured fire in their half-round shapes for illumination. The flickering lights surrounded us with warmth while the wind-up torch from the cockpit wedged in the bamboo stems to create an up-lit effect. The spooky shadows of the skinny, sensuous leaves seemed like an intricately woven bed-head.

"Wow, G…this is amazing."

He chuckled. "I had grander plans, but they didn't quite work out. This will have to do, I'm afraid."

Tugging his fingers, I wrenched him to a stop. "This is perfect. I can't thank you enough."

Spinning to face me, he met me in the middle of the flax blanket. My skin sparkled as his eyes glowed with lust. My breasts grew heavier and everything inside me awoke, stretched, and liquefied in preparation for whatever he'd planned.

I had no idea what he intended to do. But I was certain of one thing. I wasn't leaving without pleasuring both of us. We would make love, we would orgasm, and I wouldn't freak out like last time.

I'll trust him.

Not being with Galloway would be the biggest mistake of my life.

He was the answer I was supposed to find. And that was far more important than the stressful words of 'unwanted pregnancy'. Life was too short to refute happiness. Life was far, far too short to say no to love.

Galloway's lips parted as his eyes drifted to my mouth. "I wish

I had a fancy restaurant to buy you dinner. I wish I had a bottle of champagne to toast whatever dreams you chase. I wish I could take you out, Estelle. To spoil you like you should be spoiled."

"You *are* spoiling me."

He rolled his eyes. "All I see is hard ground, dark forest, and entrapment on an island in the middle of nowhere." His fingers slinked into my hair, dragging me closer. "You deserve so much more."

His head bowed; his mouth found mine.

My toes tingled as his tongue slipped dominantly but sweetly to taste me.

I expected a welcome kiss. An appetizer of a kiss.

But somehow, the chastity between us snapped and we lost each other.

He kissed me.

Oh, *God*, how he kissed me.

His tongue didn't hesitate. His lips didn't retaliate. He kissed with grace and passion all at once.

His arms bunched tighter. His erection throbbed harder. And his groan resonated in my ears like perfect thunder. His fingers tightened, drifting to my nape. His body pressed against mine and the heat between us billowed into sunshine.

For the first time, we were free to be ourselves. No children. No pretences. Nothing but time and desire.

Our heads tilted in a dance, our breath mingling, our souls dancing as our connection transcended that of a simple act.

This kiss was power.

This kiss was togetherness.

This kiss was everything I was looking for and everything I didn't know I'd been missing.

It went on and on.

Our desire built and built.

I was seconds away from ripping my nightgown off, undoing his shorts, and begging him to take me.

But he stopped.

The open-mouthed connection severed as he kissed the corner of my lips, my cheeks, my eyelids, and ended on my hairline.

His erection stood upright in his shorts, straining against the material. He hadn't changed his board-shorts (he only had one pair), but he'd slicked back his long hair and shrugged into a grey t-shirt.

To me, he'd never looked more handsome or more tortured.

His breathing was fast as he rested his forehead on mine.

"I'm—I'm sorry."

"What for?"

"For getting carried away."

"I liked being carried away."

He smirked. "Oh, really? You're happy to forgo the date and jump straight to the good stuff, huh?"

"What if I said I did? Would that make me too easy?"

Our eyes locked, humour and lust equal emotions. "I would never call you easy, Estelle."

"Too forward then?"

"I wouldn't call you that, either."

"Even if I do…this?" My fingers latched around his erection, stroking him through his shorts.

His eyes snapped closed. A heavy groan fell from his lips. "Christ, that feels good." His hips rocked into my palm, requesting more and giving himself up all at once.

A full body shiver took me as I pressed my thumb against his crown and kissed his chin. "I think we can forgo the date."

His face lowered so I could reach his lips. "You sure? I don't want you to feel taken advantage of."

I laughed softly, squeezing his shaft. "I think you're confused with who is currently getting taken advantage of."

His chuckle landed in my hair as he squeezed me tight and guided me to the flax blankets. Spreading out, he splayed on his back, tucking me into his side.

I never stopped stroking, revelling in the way his muscles bunched and jaw clenched. "I love having this sort of power over you."

"Woman, you've had this power over me all along." His eyes closed as I squeezed a little tighter. "You just didn't pay attention."

"Are you saying I'm unobservant?"

"I'm saying you're everything I've ever wanted."

His confession froze my hand.

I struggled to know what to say to that.

You're everything I've ever wanted, too. You're everything I'm terrified of. I loved him. I was *in* love with him.

The words danced on my heart, desperate to be said. But was now the right time? Did I say them before sex and mess it up or during sex and turn it into something more than what he was ready for?

I swallowed hard as his large hand captured my cheek, guiding me back to him. "I want you to know something."

His past?

His secrets?

Everything he kept from me?

I nodded, not saying a word in case he changed his mind.

Slowly, he exhaled. "If we were in a city, I would've tried too hard and probably turned you off by being a jerk. First date conversation would've included talk about the weather, travel, my architectural background, and anything I could pry from you. But that would be where my willingness to open up would end. I wouldn't tell you how bloody gorgeous you are by firelight, moonlight, sunlight—hell, by any light. I wouldn't tell you how much I wanted to talk to you even when we first met. And I definitely wouldn't tell you that there's something in my past that I'm not proud of, that I hate myself for, and that I'll pay for the rest of my days. I'm not ready to tell you what that is, but I *am* ready to show you that it has shaped who I am. And who I am now is a lot different to the man you first saw on that plane."

He never looked away as his voice slipped into a murmur. "I'm a different man because of you, Estelle. You taught me how to forgive myself for things I can't control. How to step up and stop wallowing in self-pity, guilt, and hate. Those things will forever be a part of me, but with you in my life, I can have other things, too. Things like love and happiness and a family I never thought I'd deserve."

His lips found mine in an urgent, viscous kiss. "I guess what I'm trying to say is I love you. I bloody love you. I've loved you for months and to finally be able to tell you. Hell, it's the biggest weight off my heart."

I couldn't breathe. Tears shot to my eyes.

I didn't know what he'd done but none of that mattered here. It didn't matter because his actions had redeemed his past mistakes. He cared for us, protected us, and if that didn't make him worthy of my trust and affection…then nothing did.

I wanted to speak but he wouldn't let me interrupt. Pressing his finger over my mouth, he shook his head. "That isn't some ploy to get you to repeat the words or a pity party to make you fall in love with me. I just had to tell the truth after living in lies for so long."

I am.

I *am* in love with you.

Lying flat on his back, he sighed. "There, I said it. I hadn't planned on dumping it all in one go, but so far, tonight isn't going how I'd planned, so I don't care anymore. I love you. I needed you to know that." He gave me a shy smile. "And now, you do."

"Galloway, I—"

Nerves shot him upright and he hovered over me. His eyes searched mine and then he was gone, sliding down my body to settle between my legs.

I stopped breathing as a half-smile decorated his face.

His hands slowly pushed my negligée up my hips. "Can I?" His fingers undid my bikini bows, releasing the swimwear protecting my modesty.

I never wore underwear anymore. There was no point. A bikini was much more practical, even in times like this.

"Don't you want to hear what I have to say?" I whispered as his fingers tickled my hipbone, ducking to the soft, private flesh of my sex.

"Do you *want* to tell me?"

I nodded, biting my lip as the tip of his finger entered me.

His face darkened as he found how wet I was. His touch pushed upward, curling to press against the sensitive spot inside me. "Tell me after."

"After?"

He smiled harshly, his face hovering over my core. "After."

I cried out as his tongue slicked over my clit. My back arched, completely unsuspecting such hot, wet bliss.

His eyes pinned me down, licking me again. "I've been wanting to do this forever."

I moaned.

Words.

What were words when his tongue adored me?

His mouth cupped me, warming, burning; his tongue drawing tantalizing circles on my clit.

"Oh, God—"

His voice was muffled, but his commanding growl arrowed my heart. "Touch me."

His order bypassed my brain; my body obeyed instantly.

My hands dove into his thick dark strands, looping them tight. Even with months of seawater and sunshine, the texture was soft and smooth. Different colours shone in the fire around us: sable and chocolate and bronze.

My hands petted hungrily as his tongue worked faster, harder, stronger.

My mind shot to white noise. He became the most important person in my universe.

Him.

His tongue.

The tornadoeing pleasure conjured by his touch.

My spine tickled with euphoria, warning a release could explode within seconds.

I was lost in the shocking sensation from his devilish tongue lapping with determination and skill.

His one finger became two, turning to masters of ecstasy.

He wanted one thing from me.

He'd given me his truth, and now, he wanted mine.

He wouldn't let me speak. But he would let me show him.

And I would show him.

I'd show him again and again and *again*…

And…

Oh!

I came.

My shoulders flew off the ground as my hands yanked on his hair. My body quaked, his fingers thrust, and his control over me never ceased.

His tongue soothed me as my tremors became spasms and spasms turned to aftershocks and aftershocks diminished to tormenting ripples.

I hadn't come in so long (unless I counted my own ministrations), and I doubted I'd be coherent for anything but lolling on the blanket and fading into heavenly obscurity.

His chin glistened as he prowled up my body. My pleasure marked him, and for the first time, I noticed he didn't have a beard anymore.

He'd shaved.

How did he shave?

I hadn't noticed.

How did I not notice?

Probably because I was more in love with *him* rather than what he looked like. I saw past physical and saw only spiritual.

I adored him no matter what fashion statement or wardrobe he wore.

"I love how wet you are for me." He hovered over me, his arms bunched with his weight. "I love everything about you, Estelle." His tongue swept into my mouth, sharing my flavour, telling me animalistically that he owned me now and I couldn't do a thing about it.

Not that I would argue.

Ever.

"Will you let me tell you now?" I stretched, taking advantage of being pampered like a queen.

Galloway's eyes dropped to my chest where my nipples

indented the gold silk of my nightgown. "Tell me what?"

"Tell you that I love you."

He sucked in a harsh breath. "You're not just saying that?"

"I'm not just saying that."

"You love me?"

"I love you. I'm in love with you. I fall more for you every day." I fanned myself dramatically. "And after that…well, I think you own my heart completely now."

His face shattered. That was the only way I could describe it.

He stole my lips, kissing me with ferocity and kindness. Brutality and tenderness. He accepted what I said but doubted it at the same time. "You've just made me complete, Stel…but…do you think we're stupid? Stupid falling in love here, now, with no idea what our future holds?"

I blinked. "You're saying falling for each other is…inconvenient?"

"No, I'm saying it's the only thing keeping me sane."

"Well then, I think it's a perfect time."

His eyes turned to furnace-hardened sapphires. "I'll never hurt you. *Ever.*"

"I know that, G."

"And I'll never stop loving you, now that you're mine."

"I'm holding you to that."

He kissed me again, teasing me into temptation where I forgot how to speak or move. However, I grasped a tiny bit of coherency to reach between us and rip open the Velcro of his shorts. Grabbing his hard heat, I stroked him.

I wanted to repay the favour.

I wanted to taste him.

But something delicate and fragile existed now. Almost as if he struggled with accepting my heart and desperately wanted to claim it forever. Even if our circumstances weren't ideal.

Some might say finding love in disaster was doomed for failure.

I believed it only made us stronger.

And besides, he didn't have a choice.

I was his.

I think… I've always been his.

"I want you inside me, G."

His gaze was so intense it hypnotised me. "Are you sure?"

"I'm sure."

"And you trust me?"

"I trust you."

"I promise I'll pull out. You don't have to be afraid."

"I know."

Nodding as if accepting my conditions, he sat up and ripped off his t-shirt. In the same fluid movement, he shoved down his shorts and kicked them away.

Naked.

Galloway was a beautiful man. His height, his bearing, his face and smile and body, even his intensity was mesmerizing.

But naked.

He was as sublime as a god.

My eyes drank him in as he reached for my nightgown and pulled it up my body. I didn't say a word as he waited for me to arch and help him slide it over my arms.

Once the gold silk was tossed to the side, he bit his lip and gently rolled me onto my stomach. "You're so beautiful, Estelle." His mouth landed on my shoulder blades, kissing each bead of my spine.

The first suspension of my bikini top around my neck untied, followed by the one around my ribcage. Leaving the slaughtered triangles on the ground, he rolled me back to face him, capturing me in his gaze.

His large hands drifted from my collarbone to my breasts.

Cupping both, he breathed heavily as I moaned beneath his touch.

He touched me hesitantly, but somehow, it was perversely erotic, as if he were a virgin touching a woman for the very first time.

I knew differently. I knew by the mastery of his tongue and magicianery of his kisses that he wasn't inexperienced. And yet, he shed every inch of his past to meet me unencumbered and pure. Giving himself completely to me.

His gaze turned heavy-lidded as I pressed more of myself into his touch. His hair hung around his face, looking piquantly provocative and as wild as the island that'd become our home.

The longer I stared, the more I noticed the shadows in his eyes had faded. Whatever haunted him couldn't find him here...with me. I would protect him from his pain.

"God, I want you."

I placed my hands above my head, offering myself to him. "So take me."

"How can I get used to this?" His fingers twisted my nipples before cascading down my noticeable ribcage. "How can I hope to breathe after inhaling you? How can I hope to taste after licking you?" His nose nuzzled my throat. "How am I supposed to live after having you love me?"

I trembled with the weight of his admission.

Sex had never been so potently heavy for me before. So intrinsically weaved with emotion as well as bodily satisfaction.

This wasn't sex.

This was love.

Pure, untainted love.

"You'll never have to find out." I licked my lips. "Galloway...I need you."

"You want me inside you?"

My body quickened. "Yes, please." I opened my legs, readjusting our bodies so his hips slotted perfectly between them.

"How do you want me?" His face tightened with concentration as I fisted the base of his erection and guided him to my entrance.

I wriggled as he denied my manipulation, panting as his crown smeared my wetness. "No...tell me what you want first."

"I want you."

"*How* do you want me?"

I frowned. "Stop teasing me, for one."

He chuckled, sliding an inch inside me.

I moaned.

Loudly.

"Do you want it like this?" He pushed possessively into me, sheathing himself with the sweetest claiming I'd endured.

"Or do you want me like this?" He pulled out, only to thrust back with fierce tenacity.

"Both. I want both."

He rolled his hips, brushing my swollen clit, sinking entirely inside me. "Whatever you want...I'll give you."

"Oh...please..." My eyes flickered closed as he thrust slowly, quickly, deep and shallow.

The flax below my spine cradled me from the rough ground, but it didn't stop the hardness keeping me in place beneath him. I couldn't move. I didn't *want* to move. I was his to take and control.

My body revved to life, my heart racing, my sex clenching. "Give me everything."

Grasping my wrists, he kept them pinioned above my head, clutching me with white-knuckled force. "I'll give you everything. I'll never stop giving you everything."

His hips thrust fast and hard, relinquishing the slowness for an inexhaustible pace. Biting pleasure and pure indulgence washed with every rock.

I loved every exquisite sensation. Every fullness of him inside me. Every exhale of his restrained desire.

I was so turned on; I couldn't control my whimpers.

His fingers never loosened on my wrists and his lips devoured mine only to nip and bite at my throat the faster he drove into me.

I loved how he'd taken me with tenderness but swiftly lost control, growing rougher and meaner the more lust consumed.

Visible veins coursed in his arms as he held me prisoner. My legs spread for his pleasure and his cock swelled larger inside me until I bruised with delectable pain.

We were stripped to a level of basest needs. We left the human race and became beasts.

"Christ, Estelle." His groan was guttural in my ear. "Come. I need you to come." Letting my wrists go, his hand shot between us, his fingers pinching my clit.

The climax he'd given me made me extra sensitive and slightly sore, but I couldn't avoid his orders.

He pressed me hard, thrusting in time with the swirling circles.

I lifted my hips to meet his.

"That's it." He stretched me, filled me. "I want to feel you come, Estelle. I *need* to feel you come."

He fit me so perfectly. So completely.

Oh, yes. There, there, there.

"G…" I gasped. "Don't stop…don't stop."

"I'll never stop." He gripped my nape with one hand and clamped the other on my hip. "You're so damn sexy. So sexy. I'm going to come soon. You need to, so I can."

Fear tried to yank my fuzzy mind back from the precipice.

He couldn't come.

Not inside me.

But it was too late.

He shoved me off the cliff, catching me as I plummeted with rhythmic waves and crashing bliss. The moment I peaked and crested, he pulled out.

Sitting on his knees, he fisted his cock and thrust. "This is what you do to me, Stel." Mindless in his desire, Galloway grunted as every ridge in his stomach danced with firelight. The muscles in his neck stood out as his head tossed back and he came.

Spurts of white. Spurts of pleasure. They arced through the air and splattered on my lower belly.

I moaned as my body clenched, completely bewitched as he flinched and jerked, milking the dregs of his orgasm.

Slowly, he began to breathe again, piecing himself back together.

It was a wondrous thing, witnessing the true man behind the mask. He was stripped and naked in every sense, but breath by breath, he hid his secrets once again.

Collapsing to his side, he tugged me close. Our sweat-sticky bodies moulded together as he pressed his lips to my brow. "Thank you. Thank you for trusting me."

Hot island air lapped around us as the residual liquid of his orgasm glittered on my stomach. I had trusted him. And he hadn't broken that trust.

I kissed the small coin shaped birthmark on his chest. "Thank you for keeping your promises."

His arm tightened. "Always."

I sank into relaxation, boneless and sated. "Always?"

He chuckled, the sound bouncing around my chest. "You think I'll be able to leave you alone now? After that?" He looked at the stars through the canopy. "No way. I've been addicted to you since we got here. Now that I've been allowed to have you, there's no way I'm letting you go."

I shivered with happiness. I hadn't allowed myself to notice just how deviously charismatic Galloway was. How his moods affected my moods. How his charm was dark and sharp but his will to please took over his own desires.

I love him.

So much.

Unable to hide the chasming depths of emotion, I teased, "It sounds like I'm going to be busy."

He smirked. "Does that bother you?"

"Not at all."

His knuckles brushed aside the hair stuck to my cheek. "I've been hard for you for so long, Estelle. Half-crazy, no, that's a lie, *totally* crazy with wanting you." His turbulent eyes turned a deeper darker blue. "I know I can't lose control with you. That I'll never come inside you. But being with you is the best place on earth for me."

I removed his hand from my cheek, guiding him seductively down my body.

He sucked in breath as I splayed his touch over my breast.

He arched an eyebrow. "Again?"

I nodded.

My fingers explored between us, finding his warm cock. Already, he was semi-hard, reacting to my demands for a second course.

His lips twitched as he rolled my nipple. My hips rocked without my permission, seeking something, seeking him.

"Where have you been all my life?" He kissed me softly.

"Waiting."

"Waiting?"

"Waiting for this." Stretching, I gave him everything I was. "Waiting for you to find me."

"And now that I've found you?"

"You're mine."

"Forever?"

"Forever."

Chapter Forty-Six

GALLOWAY

. . . . . .

FEBRUARY

ESTELLE was a sorceress.

Pure and simple.

Being with her tamed the tempest in my soul, while life deleted my past and skewed all conception of normal.

What was conceived right, suddenly became wrong.

What was wrong, miraculously became right.

And where danger and death used to reign, now happiness and hope became stronger.

That was the island for us.

That was Estelle for me.

After the most insanely incredible night in the bamboo grove, life sped up. Without thinking, we all slotted into our place in this new world and stopped fighting it. And once we did…we no longer struggled as much.

Sure, there were days when loneliness became overwhelming.

When the drizzle became depressing.

When the constant heat became debilitating.

Some nights, we still stared out to sea, begging for a plane to pass. Some mornings, it was hard to get out of bed, faced with yet another day of momentous gathering, hunting, and island living.

But for every dark day, there were bright ones.

For every tear, there were smiles.

For every argument, there was laughter.

We used our time wisely, slowly increasing our skills and building bigger and better things. We educated ourselves not by text books and professors but through nature and trees. And slowly, our mental and physical capabilities adapted to our new place.

I would never admit out loud that I'd accepted this as my home, but in my heart, I couldn't deny it.

This was my place. My safety. My chosen sanctuary.

And it filled my soul with gratefulness that I'd somehow found it.

After I'd admitted to Estelle that I needed her as much as we needed the rain to survive, and she'd admitted that she was in love with me, our sexual tension only increased rather than dispersed.

I took her often.

She took me often.

And in each other's arms, we found paradise.

As my body slipped into hers, and her breath entered my lungs, and her kisses captured my lips, I healed more than I thought possible.

Somehow, she gave me the permission to release the hate for the past I'd suffered, she granted forgiveness for what I'd done and soothed every screwed-up emotion I had left from the trial.

My ankle might never heal completely but with Estelle in my world...I began to think my soul just might.

....

MARCH

The marine debris that'd blown into our lives, thanks to the major monsoon, slowly became fundamental to our existence.

We'd repaired the deck chair with sticks to replace its broken frame and the barnacles were chipped off to reveal a sad, rusted chair that was just as abandoned as us.

The plastic bags added to our tree-water collection, and we now had multiple funnels keeping us hydrated even if the rain was sparse. Even the green fishing net had been repaired and untangled, cutting our spear fishing time in half.

Conner was the one who wielded the net, wading out to the reef and dragging it behind him as he swam for shore. Sometimes, he failed to catch anything, but most of the time, he scooped up enough fish, an occasional handful of prawns or a squid or two, that we never went to bed hungry and even had leftovers to salt and preserve.

Estelle continued to sample leaves, seeds, and the occasional beach nut for allergic reactions, and she and Pippa slowly built our larder to resemble a fully stocked pantry rather than a sparse island habitat.

Some nights, we'd even vary our seafood diet with an

occasional lizard. However, nothing could beat the beauty of figuring out how versatile ash was.

Ash from our constant fire dotted the campsite from popping wood and swirling winds. Slowly, we noticed ants stopped claiming our food as often. Before, we'd leave an open coconut or fish ready to smoke by the fire, and within minutes, it would be black with damn ants. However, with the white ash sprinkled around, they avoided the temptation.

I had no idea why.

We also noticed (completely by accident—thanks to the kids rolling around in a game of wrestle) that smearing ourselves with ash at night kept the mosquitoes away.

Estelle became obsessed with finding other uses. Trial and error showed if she steeped and strained the ash, it became a natural laundry and stain detergent. She used the liquid to wash her and Pippa's hair and even sprinkled the stuff in our home to prevent as many creepy crawlies as possible.

And it worked.

The bugs had been a constant pain in the ass, but who knew ash was a natural repellent?

Along with nature slowly giving up her secrets, the imminent scare of not having enough to eat faded. Our injuries were no longer a detrimental deterrent, and being free from such a harsh master like hunger meant our time was free to try other things.

Things we hadn't dared attempt because of injury, uncertainty, and frankly…the impossibility of such a task.

A life raft.

Estelle and I had had many conversations about what was attemptable and what was not. Estelle played the Devil's Advocate—pointing out how suicidal it would be to bob around with no compass or destination. She pointed out lack of water and food and shade. She layered complication upon complication:

We weren't just two people; we were four.

The raft would have to float securely with no chance of tipping over.

The children could swim, but if we capsized, the life-jackets had holes and wouldn't inflate.

What would we do if we were washed out farther to sea with no islands to cling to?

There were so many unknowns.

It terrified both of us.

But on the other hand, I played Promoter of the Cause:

We weren't two people; we were four. Therefore, we had more

hands to paddle, more chance at travelling farther, more hope at finding civilisation.

The raft would have to float securely, and I wouldn't leave our island until I was sure it was seaworthy. I would create storage for food and water. I would build a canopy for shade. (I didn't utter how heavy such a vessel would be or that I had doubts it would float).

As for not having life-jackets—that was a drawback but not a deal breaker.

The only thing that sat in my gut like undigested rocks was the thought of losing against the tropical currents and being claimed by the ocean just as Estelle said.

If a rip took us, we wouldn't be strong enough to stay in the archipelago of Fiji. However, that chance only existed if we lived on the outskirts of the three hundred plus islands and weren't (by some slim chance) slap-bang in the middle of other inhabited homes.

Despite our many discussions, the drive to protect my family never left, and one day, I couldn't wait any longer.

I enlisted Conner's help, and together, we hacked as much bamboo as we dared (leaving plenty to regrow) and spent our time shredding the stringy bark found on the creeping yellow flowers by the beach line and knotting vine and flax rope to build with.

I was an architect not a boat engineer. I didn't know buoyancy requirements or how to make wood watertight. As much as I hated to admit it, I wouldn't be able to build a yacht. But I could build a floating platform. And with transportation, we might be able to unlock the vast prison gates keeping us stranded and find something that could save us.

Conner and I worked steadily but not stupidly.

Some days, we worked from sunup to sundown. But some days, we took off, swimming in the ocean, indulging in naps beneath our umbrella tree. And not once did anyone mention the unmentionable that if we did this; if we willingly sailed away from our island, we would never come back.

If we found rescue, we wouldn't know the coordinates to return to. If we didn't find rescue…we'd die a lot sooner than we would if we stayed.

Those thoughts kept me up far too many nights.

....

"They're hatching! Come quick!"

My head wrenched up from Conner's excited shout. I placed the Swiss Army knife on the log I was leaning against while doing my best to carve a plaque to hang above our bungalow.

I'd taken the day off from raft building to spend the day doing odd jobs around our home. The roof needed an extra flax or two, the flooring a replaced panel, and our hut still needed an official title.

Pippa tore after her brother, sand flying like smoke from her fast feet. All day, the sun had played peek-a-boo with the clouds, granting us some much-needed shade and the freedom to work outside—to air our bedding, take stock of our salty reserves, and swim without fear of our skin peeling off our faces from sunburn.

However, it also meant that Estelle's phone hadn't charged, which apparently wasn't a good thing the way she yelled in despair and tossed the dead device onto the flax blanket beneath the umbrella tree.

Jogging to catch up with her as she sprinted after Pippa and Conner, I asked, "What the hell is going on?"

"Didn't you hear him? They're hatching."

"What's hatching?"

She threw me an incredulous look. "Seriously? You've forgotten already? Even with what we did after we watched the turtles lay their eggs?"

My body warmed.

I flashed her a smug smile. "When you put it like that, I *completely* remember." I tried to grab her mid-jog, but she shied away. "We can relive that night if you're up for it. Minus the bad ending, of course."

Ever since that night, she'd trusted me. I'd been inside her more times than I could count and not once had I come in her body.

I wanted to more than anything.

I wanted to finish while feeling her clench around me.

But I also didn't want to get her pregnant.

Not because I didn't want a baby (my ideals on children had changed drastically in the past few months), but because I was bloody terrified of Estelle going through that with no medical assistance or specialist care.

She swatted my hand away, changing direction to the vegetation where the turtles had chosen for their nests. "Do you always think with that part of your anatomy?"

"When I'm round you? All the time."

She rolled her eyes, but I could tell she was secretly pleased that I wanted her so much.

And it wasn't a lie.

Whenever she was around me, whether it be chopping wood

or gutting fish, I couldn't help my cock reacting to her lithe figure and long white-blonde hair.

"Oh, my God. They're so cute!" Pippa squealed, jumping up and down.

We slowed, steadying our breathing as we arrived at the nest where tiny shelled creatures did their best to unbury themselves with the aid of ungainly flippers.

Conner sat on his haunches. "Whoa...that's kinda cool."

One by one, hundreds of the damn things erupted from the ground in a stampede.

Estelle couldn't tear her eyes away as our beach slowly transformed from virgin sand into flippered chaos. "There must be close to a thousand of the things."

I did a quick calculation in my head. "I think I read somewhere that close to a hundred eggs can be laid at one time. I guess the odds are that you're right. There were a lot of turtles that night using our island as a bloody incubator."

Conner and Pippa abandoned their post by the nest, crawling on their hands and knees, keeping pace with the baby turtles. Smiling, they inched toward the water's edge, following the haphazard trails and lurches of new life.

"This is the best day ever!" Pippa beamed, stroking the back of one tiny critter. "I want one. Please, *please* can we keep one?"

Estelle crawled like Pippa, making my heart swell as her ass swayed in her black bikini. She had no fat or womanly curves anymore, but I would've given anything to be alone, pull down her bathing suit, and take her from behind.

We'd done that a few nights ago. I'd slipped into her while she rested on her hands and knees. I'd clutched her hips and bit the back of her neck as we both turned a little savage.

I loved that her libido was the same as mine.

I loved that we liked the same thing.

I loved that she loved me.

"Can't, Pip. You know the rules. If they survive, they'll come back." Conner broke the cardinal law and plucked a baby from the sand, holding its shell so the poor thing flapped in mid-air. "Besides, they're kinda pointless. Cute, but not exactly awesome like a cat."

"Co, put that thing down." I crossed my arms. "What did we say about looking but no touching?"

He grunted. "I'm not a little kid, G. Don't talk to me like one."

"Don't care. Put him back."

Frowning, he plopped the turtle next to one of its nest mates.

Pippa pouted. "*If* they survive?" Her eyes turned worried. "What does Co mean, Stelly? They'll all make it…won't they?"

Estelle glanced at me, panic on her face.

"Don't look at me." I shrugged. "You're up."

She glowered.

I struggled to hold my chuckle. She was so damn delicious when she was mad.

"Pip, you know how the circle of life works. You know we eat fish, that we…kill…to survive. Just like we do what is necessary, some of these turtles will provide food for other wildlife." Waving at the carpet of crawling things, she added, "That's why nature has so many hatch at once. Their chances at surviving are much higher in numbers and those that don't make it…well, that wasn't their destiny."

Conner rolled his eyes. "Destiny to be dinner, you mean."

Pippa threw a handful of sand at him. "Stop it."

"All right. That's enough." Planting a kiss on Pippa's head, I said, "Let's all focus on the fact that they've just hatched, not the day of their demise, okay?"

Pippa sniffed but slowly nodded.

Conner continued to chase the babies into the sea, drawing a finishing line in the sand and cheering as each waddled over it to the gentle tide beyond.

The tension vanished, and together, we watched the miracle of life as a thousand little things trudged their way to the turquoise ocean and disappeared into its dangerous depths.

How many will survive?

How many will return to this same place and lay another generation of young?

And, if we never go home, how many times will we witness it?

Chapter Forty-Seven

···

ESTELLE

······

Blasphemy: Blasphemy is the act of insulting, showing contempt, or lack of reverence to something considered sacred or inviolable.
It's official, I'm a blasphemer.
What other word could I use for the complete switch of my emotions?
I still despaired. I still worried. I still begged for rescue.
But I also thanked. I smiled. I revelled in my new world.
Because they made it so much more real than anything before.
Taken from the notepad of E.E.

...

<u>APRIL</u>

SLEEPING WITH GALLOWAY changed my world. And not in some superficial 'he's my soul-mate' kind of way. More in a 'this man will protect me, care for me, and do everything in his power to make me happy' kind of way.

His selflessness made me do the same for him and our quality of life (despite the lack of facilities and society niceties) was the best I'd ever had.

My existence was copacetic.

Conner celebrated his fourteenth birthday, and we did our best to give him the same experience as Pippa. We lit the bonfire to signal a new year, we raided our larder for the wild mint I'd found growing last week to make a coconut milk mint dessert, and we all pulled together to laugh and joke, all while keeping the weak but constant depression at bay.

It wasn't depression that debilitated us or made us hate our life. It was depression knowing that, no matter how happy we were, Conner was at an age now where the island wouldn't be enough.

He needed friends and girls.

He needed freedom to experiment and space to get into mischief.

We could give him many things; we could teach and care, but we couldn't give him the complexities of adolescence.

Marking such occasions and sharing life events confirmed what we'd known for a while. Despite Galloway's progression with the life raft (it was half-finished and filled with potential), we were stuck here until fate decided otherwise.

Some days, it was all too much. Days when the sun irritated and the sticky salt frustrated. But luckily, those down days were soothed by happy ones, and those were what I chose to remember.

As life ticked on and Galloway and I spent more and more time in bed together, I slowly relaxed into my new world.

I allowed Galloway to learn who I was.

I no longer wanted to hide.

I told him about my family, my singing, my home.

I glossed over the tour in the USA, and only briefly mentioned the record deal because that part of my life had been so new and it was over now.

Singing and song writing were a part of me. Performing and wealth were not.

He didn't need to know about that when I had so much else to share.

In return, he told me about his dead mother, his grieving father, and the fact that his dad might not make it now he'd lost a son as well as his wife. He told me he'd studied his final months in the USA with a world-renowned architect and loved working with wood almost as much as I loved scribbling in my notebook.

My personality was no longer afraid of companionship. I was free. Which meant I no longer hid my music or songs.

I sang often.

I shared lyrics.

And the fear of getting pregnant slowly faded as my periods came irregularly, just like always. The womanly affliction didn't last for long (which I was thankful for), but at least, it showed that my body had enough nutrients to continue operating correctly and also meant, that, despite the number of times I cornered Galloway for a quickie or he dragged me from my bed in the dead of night, we were being as careful as we could.

I knew he wanted to come inside me.

I knew he struggled to pull out some nights, and when the silvery liquid jettisoned from his body to soak into the sand, he had mixed emotions.

But unless we could figure out how to make a condom, he would never come in me.

It was the price we both had to pay.

....

MAY

As weeks turned to months, we continued to adapt and evolve. Conner constantly grew as his body underwent teenage upgrades. Some nights, he was an opinionated asshole where I would happily strap his backside and turf him outside. However, others he was the sweetest kid.

He played with Pippa.

He brought me flowers.

He questioned and listened when Galloway taught him with such keen intelligence, my heart fluttered with gratitude for such a great man.

Pippa, on the other hand, stayed quiet. I couldn't compare her to the previous little girl before the crash because I didn't know her, but I *did* worry about her.

She argued or acted out very rarely. She smiled but not fully. She seemed wiser and braver than any eight-year-old was but at least, she had us. She was still young enough to only need our company and not that of punk boys or bratty girls.

Galloway continued to infiltrate my soul with how capable, strong, and incredible he was. Constantly surprising me with glimpses into his past and personality. He'd changed so much from the surly, snappy douchebag when we'd first arrived, but one thing hadn't changed.

He still refused to tell me what hung over him—what he could never run from.

It had to be something huge.

Something monstrous.

But I could never believe he was a monster.

He might've done something to justify the term…but I trusted him with my entire existence.

He wasn't a bad person.

He's not.

Some nights, I encouraged everyone to the wet sand and scratched messages for the incoming tide to steal.

Things like:

I'm grateful for fresh water and look forward to the next rain so I can have a bath. (Mine).

I'm pissed off that I can't get off this island but at the same time don't want to leave. (Conner).

I miss the turtles. I wish I could've kept one. I want a pet. Puffin and Mr. Whisker Wood aren't cutting it anymore. (Pippa).

I hope bad luck never visits us again. (Galloway).

Sharing our troubles and having them wash way helped ease our burden (I didn't know why, but it did), and I also remained faithful to documenting our life with photos and videos, becoming more selective on what to save as the memory card slowly filled up with our sandy existence.

Overall, we weren't doing too badly.

Until Galloway's fear of bad luck returning came true.

....

"Goddammit, Estelle, come back here."

Galloway's arm lassoed around my middle, pulling me back in the waves.

I giggled, pinching his forearm as it wrapped tightly around my hips. "Let me go, you sea-beast."

"Sea-beast?" His lips captured my ear, yanking me hard against his front so his erection dug into my lower back. "I'm a sea-beast now? All right, let's see what you think of said sea-beast when it wants something from you."

His hand disappeared down my back, ripping open the Velcro of his board-shorts and shoving them down his hips.

"Oh, my God. What are you doing?" I spun in his arms. The vast ocean spread behind him, the sunset losing its final vermillion glow as it extinguished on the horizon. "Stop it."

He smirked, his fingers dipping to my core and sliding my bikini bottoms to the side, exposing me in the cool tide. "I won't stop, and I would've thought it was obvious what I'm doing."

Trying to wriggle from his arms, I looked over my shoulder. "Pippa and Conner might see."

"So what?" Galloway captured my lips, swallowing my complaints as he slid one finger inside me. The coolness of ocean and probing heat of his digit unravelled me.

His tongue entered my mouth at the same leisurely pace, making me pant as my hips ignored my refusal and rocked on his hand.

His lips turned up beneath mine. "I see you've decided to stop fighting?"

I shuddered as he inserted another finger.

"You had me this morning."

"So?"

"You had me last night, too."

"I ask again...so?"

"Do you ever put that sword of yours to bed?"

He chuckled. "Sword? Oh, Stel, my sword never sleeps. In fact, it's desperate for a sheath and wants to come home to you."

His fingers slid from my body, replacing with the urgent pressure of his cock.

I arched my back, wrapping my legs around his hips. "This is so inappropriate."

Galloway licked my neck. "How? Pippa and Conner went in from their swim. They're probably having a snack and playing checkers or something. They won't be watching. Not that they can see us now the sun has set."

"They can too see us." My mouth parted as the crown of his erection slid just a little bit inside me.

My fingers dove into the long hair on his nape, twirling and tugging with demand. For all my verbal disapproval, my body submitted completely.

"Even if they can see, they'll only see us embracing in the water." He kissed me again. "We're chest deep, Stel. What goes on below the water is none of their damn business."

He thrust up, entering me in one slick slide.

"Oh..." My body folded in his embrace as my legs tightened around his hips. "God...why does that feel so good?"

"Why?" His lips circled my ear as his hands cupped my breasts, shoving aside the bikini triangles and pinching my nipples. "Because you were made for me and we fit perfectly. Nothing will ever feel as good as it does when we join."

He's right.

Not that he needed to hear it. His ego was big enough as it was.

I stayed glued to his front as he fondled me. He thrust up again, sending water rippling around us.

Sparks and fireworks detonated from where we joined, radiating down to my toes.

I shuddered. "Oh...do that again."

"Do what?" His hands left my breasts, clamping on my hips. "This?" His hips jerked, impaling me right to the base of his cock. My clit rubbed against his belly and stars twinkled behind my eyelids.

"Yes...oh, yes...*that.*"

He stood motionless; my body throbbed for more. Goosebumps rose on my arms. I didn't know if it was from having covert sex or the night breeze that always sprang up after dusk.

Either way, I wanted Galloway to warm me. I needed him.

Bowing my head, I bit his shoulder. "More."

"More?"

"More…"

He thrust but only slightly, teasing me to the point of insanity. "I think you're forgetting the magic word."

I raised my head, staring into his velvet blue eyes. Somehow, they matched the dusk-lightened sky and I swore comets glimmered in their depths. "What magic word?"

He smirked, his hips rocking in time with the sea current. "I think you know." Grabbing the back of my neck, water cascaded down his arm, flowing off his elbow. "I want you to beg."

My eyes widened as he kissed me. His teeth nipped, his tongue slinked, and any decorum I had melted from my mind.

I moaned, rocking on his body. "Please. Please give me what I need."

"Again, Estelle. Beg me." Our lips never unsealed—speaking, kissing, loving, conversing.

One arm went around me, while his other imprisoned my hip, holding me in place. With each plea, he thrust harder until ripples became splashes and we drove into each other with ferocity.

"Please…yes…oh, God. *Yes.*"

He never stopped kissing me. He knew me so well that the moment I climbed up the slippery slope of release, his pace increased in time with my panting breath.

"Yes, yes, *yes.*"

"Christ, Estelle." His nose nuzzled my wet hair. "I love you. Come for me. Please, come for me."

The friction of his lower belly on my clit and the overwhelming fullness of his cock inside ignited the dynamite in my blood.

I lost sensation of the water cradling me. I lost consciousness of who I was. All I recalled was that Galloway was inside me…just like it should always be.

I came.

And came.

And when my final crest vanished with the fallen sun, Galloway grunted and pulled out.

His forehead scrunched and his agonising groan as he came brought tears to my eyes.

He orgasmed into the salty sea, spurting milky seed far away from me, keeping his promise just like he did every night.

As we washed up and swam to shore, I smiled and laughed and gave no thought that pulling out wasn't a reliable method.

I gave no mind to the possible terror that one day soon a tenacious sperm might win the fight, regardless of our methods.

As we crawled into bed and fell asleep in each other's arms, I didn't dream of what would happen if that day ever came.

I was naïve.

I was in love.

I was *stupid*.

Our romantic swim marked the calendar as the 14th of May.

It was a day I would always remember, because, unfortunately, life wasn't done throwing us bad luck.

....

Four nights later, my tummy cramped, reminding me that my period was due and to prepare a few rags.

However, a few days later, my breasts were swollen and nipples tight and my uterus ached, granting a few spots of blood.

But no normal flow.

I stared at the clean rag that I'd shoved in my bikini bottoms and froze completely solid.

No.

No.

No.

No.

This couldn't be happening.

This can't be true.

We'd been so careful.

It's just…not possible.

It was a joke.

I smashed my eyes with my fingertips, trying to destroy every thought.

No, that wasn't possible.

It's not possible.

The concept of pregnancy was more than a silly fear. It was the scariest, terrifying, most horrifying nightmare imaginable.

And my brain couldn't cope.

So instead of thinking rationally and discussing calmly, I went into freak-out mode.

I shoved the rag back into my bikini. I yanked up my shorts. I pretended this was normal.

My body had finally used up whatever vitamins it had left and ceased to have a period. I wasn't pregnant (don't be so stupidly absurd), I was merely malnourished and island wrecked.

Yes, that was it.

I was stranded and stressed and my body had finally gone into survival mode.

I'm not pregnant.

Never.
Not at all.

....

By the end of May, I knew.

I think I'd known all along.

I just couldn't admit it.

The moment I'd agreed to a physical relationship with Galloway, I'd invited this to happen.

I'd done this.

I'd condemned myself to die.

Me.

Not him.

No one else.

Me!

Tears ran down my cheeks as I swiped at the strands of hair sticking to my sweaty forehead. The wet splash of morning sickness decorated the bush where I'd hidden to purge my breakfast.

Stupid, stupid, *stupid.*

You might not be pregnant. It might be food poisoning.

My mind ran crazy, hurling excuse after excuse for my nausea and foreign feeling body.

Despite nine months on the island, we'd only suffered tummy upsets once or twice. (I'd had a few more because of my sampling trials). But we'd all been incredibly careful about what we ate and drank, doing our best to preserve our health as much as possible.

I wanted so much to believe it was a gastric issue.

But my heart knew.

My instincts knew.

My femininity knew.

Galloway had pulled out every time, but it hadn't stopped the small amount of semen in his pre-ejaculate from somehow defeating my stupid eggs.

I was now knocked up and island bound.

All alone with no medical help or anyone to turn to.

I had to face facts.

I had to cry my tears and be strong.

I'd done this.

We'd done this.

And now, we had to live with our creation.

It was official.

I was pregnant.

....

JUNE

A few weeks passed.

And for all my bravery of telling Galloway what'd happened, I…I couldn't.

When I'd returned to camp (after throwing up again) with balled fists and fretting in my soul, I'd found Galloway carving a new spear and Conner plaiting Pippa's hair.

The scene had been the perfect family, and my eyes prickled with tears at the thought of leaving them.

Of dying in child-birth.

Of delivering a malnourished baby who wouldn't survive like these wonderful people had.

My throat closed up, and I hid my secret.

I pretended it wasn't real.

For weeks, I wore my baggy t-shirt rather than my bikini, claiming sunburn (just in case I started to show). After all, my skinny frame wouldn't be able to hide the growing bump for long.

As the days passed, I smiled and laughed and accepted Galloway between my legs all while harbouring my nasty little secret.

When we met for our midnight rendezvouses, I wanted to tell him he could come in me. That there was no point pulling out.

But I couldn't.

Every time I sucked up the courage to tell him, it trickled away at the final second.

He wasn't stupid.

He knew something was wrong with me. He watched me closely, he questioned me quietly, but he didn't push me to tell him.

I supposed he thought I'd admit it in my own time. Or who knew…perhaps, he'd already guessed?

Either way, I couldn't speak the words.

I couldn't get my mouth to form the condemning sentence…

I…am…*pregnant.*

No.

I can't.

So I remained stupid and silent.

And did something I wasn't proud of.

One night, I stalked through the plants and bushes that once upon a time, I'd avoided because of failed scratch tests or belly ache. I stood in the dark and wondered, just wondered, if I ate a few poisonous leaves…would it stop this disaster from happening?

Could I bring on a miscarriage through natural means?

Or would I kill myself before the baby had a chance to?

In a bottomless moment of weakness, I plucked a leaf from one particular bush that'd given me wicked cramping and held the foliage to my mouth.

So close.

It could all be over.

I touched my bottom lip with the bitter flavour but at the last second, threw it away.

I didn't want to die.

So why would I be so stupidly reckless when I had a chance (a very small chance) of surviving this birth? Besides, how could I possibly think of killing something created from love?

I wasn't that person. I would never be that person. Even if it meant sacrificing myself.

Striding from the forest, I never considered forcibly removing my mistake again. In fact, I made a pact to stop thinking about it so I wouldn't drive myself insane.

All month, I managed to avoid the topic, and some hours, I even forgot. That was until I brushed my breast and flinched because it was so sore. Or I touched my stomach and the strange tightness in my belly felt alien.

It seemed like only yesterday that Galloway had thrust inside me in the tide. And yet a month had passed and already nature prepared my body for its disastrous conclusion.

I only had a few months left to live. I had no illusions that I would survive such an ordeal (skinny and stranded) and deliver a healthy infant.

But my body didn't share my acid-like hopelessness. My hips gradually ached, my skin became overly sensitive, and my taste buds changed their craving.

I'd never read up on pregnancy and what to expect, and there was no way of doing it now. The only thing I could do was what I'd always done: turn to my music.

I scribbled and composed my way out of terror.

But then something even worse happened.

Worse than crashing.

Worse than becoming pregnant.

My pen ran out.

The ink ran dry.

I had no way to soothe my jagged soul and make sense of this abhorrent tribulation.

My pen was dead.

I had no more.

And that was it for my notebook.

Chapter Forty-Eight

···

GALLOWAY

······

JULY

"YOU MUST THINK I'm stupid, Stel."

She looked up from weaving yet another flax blanket (damn woman was obsessed with them) and hid behind a curtain of hair. "I don't know what you mean."

I growled beneath my breath. "Seriously, Estelle? You're honestly going to play that card with me? After the past few weeks of moping around and refusing to tell me what the hell is eating you? I'm done. I want to know. Right now."

"G...don't." Her eyes flickered to Pippa and Conner, who sat on the log tenderising the octopus I'd caught this morning. We'd learned (as we caught more) that the best way to eat the suckered creature was to smash the tentacles until they were tender; otherwise, it was just too damn chewy.

I'd promised myself I wouldn't do this.

I'd been patient.

I'd slept beside her at night. I'd tried to comfort her. I'd waited with all the bloody love I could for her to tell me.

But she never did.

And it grew harder and harder every day.

She was hurting, goddammit, and she wouldn't share the reason why.

"I'm through waiting." Throwing away the axe (where I'd been chopping excess vines from the almost-finished raft), I stood up and towered over her. "You barely look at me anymore. You don't let me touch you. You never let me watch you undress. What the *hell* is going on?"

Please, don't tell me it's over.

Don't tear out my heart and tell me you don't want me anymore.

I'd done my best to psychoanalyze if I'd done something wrong. Had I pissed her off? Did she hate sleeping me with me? Had I taken advantage of having a willing, beautiful woman share my bed?

She often joked that I was insatiable, but in return, she was too.

It wasn't just me who initiated what happened between us.

Yet I felt like the one being punished.

Running a hand through my long hair, I snapped, "Tell me. Right now. If you're through with me, just say it!"

Pippa stopped smashing the octopus, her hands falling silent as her face filled with worry. She hated when we raised our voices.

Estelle gasped. "What? How could you think that?"

"Oh, I don't know? Perhaps it's because you can't stand the sight of me anymore. You barely laugh. You're so bloody closed off I feel as if I'm living in a damn fridge around you!"

I stabbed myself in the chest. "If I'm not worth your affection anymore, Estelle, you damn well better have the balls to say it to my face so I can get on with my useless piece of a life and not constantly wonder what I did wrong."

Estelle and I didn't fight often, and if we did, it was defused as fast as it took to move whatever it was that annoyed us or obey the certain chore we'd ignored (normally me on that one), but this time, I couldn't calm down until Estelle gave me what I wanted.

An answer.

That's what I bloody want.

"Tell me. Do you hate me? Did I hurt you?" I paced, unable to stand still. "I told you I'd never hurt you, but if somehow I did, I'm so bloody sorry. But you can't keep punishing me like this. You can't shove me out of your heart just because you don't like me anymore."

I struggled for breath; the island became claustrophobic. I hadn't admitted my fears, even to myself. I'd pretended she was okay. That *we* were okay. But as days turned to weeks and she never lost the cool despair in her eyes, how could I not jump to conclusions that our relationship had run its course and she'd moved on?

Of course, she'd bloody move on.

Why wouldn't she? She was gorgeous. Smart. Pretty. Funny. Insanely talented.

Compared to me?

She was a damn goddess while I was a convicted felon who ought to have spent the rest of his life behind bars (before a bloody miracle freed him).

I'd pursued her knowing full well she was out of my league. But now, having her come to the same conclusion and cutting me off? It was more than I could goddamn stand.

Take the raft and leave.

I couldn't stay here if she didn't want me anymore.

I physically couldn't sleep beside her never being able to touch or kiss or whisper nonsensical stuff in the night.

She was mine.

She was my *home.*

And for some reason, she'd tossed me out into the scary, terrible dark with no explanation.

Estelle slowly stood up, her eyes narrowed to combat the bright sun behind me. "Can we not do this here?"

"No, we can. Right now." My nostrils flared. "Just spit it out. Go on, it's not hard. Tell me the truth."

"What truth?" Anger tinted her cheeks.

"The truth that you don't want me anymore."

She had the gall to roll her eyes. "G, you're bonkers. Why wouldn't I want you anymore? I love you."

"Funny way of bloody showing it."

"Leave her alone," Pippa said.

Conner's head wrenched up, no longer oblivious to the swirling tension cycloning around the camp. "Hey, what's going on?"

Estelle sucked in a breath, her chest rising beneath her black t-shirt.

When was the last time she wore her bikini? When was the last time she let me spoon her in bed, cup her belly, and pull her onto my cock?

Weeks, that's how long.

Too goddamn long.

"Galloway seems to think I don't love him anymore." Estelle glanced at Conner. "Can someone tell him how ludicrous that is?"

Conner scowled. "Dude, stop being a drama llama."

(I should never have told him what Estelle called me that first day).

"She's fine. Course she still loves you, man." His eyes narrowed on Estelle. Recently, his hormones had revved his testosterone to a level I didn't like. He watched my woman with a lust that shouldn't exist. I didn't want to have to kick his ass, but I would if he ever put the moves on her. She was his mother figure, not a damn wanking object.

Oh, shit.

What if Estelle shacked up with Conner? What if years passed by and Conner grew into a good-looking man and she dumped me for younger goods?

"Ah!" I clutched my head, wanting to rip into my brain and tear out such heinous thoughts.

Estelle's hands landed on my wrists, pulling my arms down. Concern and affection swam in her gaze. "G, I don't know what's brought this on, but I'm sorry if I caused it by being so quiet." Standing on her tiptoes, she kissed me.

I didn't yield.

I didn't give into the kiss.

For all I knew, it was a break-up kiss.

My back bunched and muscles quivered with the need to punch something or run.

Pippa drifted forward, standing warily a few feet away. "Please...don't fight. I love both of you. Please." Her eyes welled with tears.

Poor kid was overly sensitive to losing those she cared for.

I sighed heavily. "It's okay, Pippi. We're not fighting."

Estelle dropped her gaze, fighting the oppressive weight she'd been battling for weeks. It killed me that she didn't let me fight on her behalf. Couldn't she see I would slaughter anything that hurt her...multiple times over...and chase it into the underworld to make sure it was dead so it could never hurt her again?

My heart clambered like a rabies-infected animal. I cupped her cheek, sucking in a relieved breath as she pressed her face into my palm. "Please...Estelle, I'm begging you. Tell me what's wrong. I'm going out of my mind with worry."

A small smile lit her lips. "Well, you can stop thinking I don't love you anymore. In fact, I love you even more than I did."

I didn't know how that was possible, but I'd take it.

I'd take whatever she gave me. I'd survive on mere scraps of tenderness if that were all she could offer.

"Okay..." I brushed my thumb on her lower lip, very aware of how soft and warm her mouth was. "Tell me then...what is it?"

Her shoulders tightened, the lines that etched her forehead returned, and she couldn't keep eye contact. "It's—I mean—I've wanted to tell you...but...I can't."

Tell me what?

My heart folded to my feet. "You're...you're not sick, are

you?"

I couldn't handle the thought of her leaving me, but I would go catatonic at the thought of her dying.

She could *never* die.

I forbid it.

Dragging her to the almost-ready-to-sail raft, I grabbed her by the hips and plonked her on the wooden (hopefully floatable) platform. "We'll leave. Right now. We'll get you medicine. Whatever you need to get better."

Panic slicked my hands with sweat as I barked orders. "Conner, get rid of that octopus; we don't need it. Grab the salted fish and smoked lizard. We're leaving. Right now. Estelle needs help."

Estelle's lyrical laugh was the only thing that reached me through my stampeding frenzy. Her fingers slipped through my hair, pulling my face to hers.

Our lips connected.

Our tastes mingled.

My chaotic world found its centre once again.

Breathing against my lips, she murmured, "G…I love you. And I'm sorry for not telling you. It was wrong of me. But seeing you fear that I don't want you anymore or panic that I'm dying…I can't keep this secret." Her lips twitched into a sad smile. "Besides, it's not like I'll be able to keep it a secret much longer."

Pippa drifted closer; Puffin had magically appeared in her hands. "So…you're not sick, Stelly?"

Estelle shook her head. "No, I'm not sick, Pip." Something clouded her eyes. "However, I will need help from all of you in the coming months." She sniffed back her own fear. "I can't do this on my own."

"Do what?" I murmured. "Tell me. I'll do anything for you, Estelle. You know that."

She smiled. "I do know that. Thank you, G. Just knowing you'll be beside me is enough."

"Enough for what?"

"To face that I might not make it but I have a much better chance with my family helping me."

Might. Not. Make. It?

"What the *hell*, Estelle?"

Her index hushed my mouth, keeping me silent.

Her eyes blazed with green and brown confession. "I'm pregnant, Galloway. And I'm absolutely petrified."

....

AUGUST

I spent the following month alternating between uncontrollable rage and inconceivable despair.

Once Estelle told me, it was as if a ten-tonne weight slid off her shoulders and landed squarely onto mine.

She slept better, ate better, and she no longer hid her growing belly behind Conner's black t-shirt.

Her bikini revealed the little bump that, in ordinary circumstances would be hardly noticeable, but thanks to prominent ribs and hipbones, her belly was the only thing distended, increasing by the day.

I hated that bump.

I *detested* that bump.

But I loved it, too.

When we lay down to sleep, I traced the tightness of her skin, I massaged her lower back and made gentle love to the woman I'd given my absolute soul to.

Estelle was the reason I was still alive. And I'd condemned her to a potential death.

I hated myself.

No, I bloody *loathed* myself.

When she whispered that I could come inside her, that she was already past the need for safe sex, I lost it.

Couldn't she see this wasn't a joking matter?

I'd done this to her.

I should *never* have forced her to sleep with me.

And she wanted me to *come* inside her? The most incredible gift she could ever give me was given because I'd already taken everything.

The moment she'd said it, the mood was broken.

My erection turned flaccid with self-hatred and I left our bed to tear through the jungle to watch the sunrise on the other side of the island.

There, I went through so many emotions.

I prayed for a miscarriage before it was too late.

I bartered with God that I would never touch Estelle again if he somehow annulled the pregnancy.

I pleaded with the baby not to hurt its mother.

I threatened the little soul and cursed it to Hell if it so much as gave her bad cramp.

Amongst my loathsome terror, I also begged that he or she would be born safely.

That a part of Estelle and me would survive, blended for eternity.

I wanted our child.

I hated our child.

I wanted a baby.

I wanted to kill it.

I went through so many feelings that by the time I returned home, I was wrung out and bloody exhausted. I'd stayed away for the full day, only returning late that night when I was sure I wouldn't dissolve into a cursing tyrant or, worse, melt into ridiculous tears.

Estelle was pregnant.

With my child.

Shared genes and bodies and souls.

This should've been the happiest few months of our lives.

Not the countdown for absolute disaster.

....

SEPTEMBER

Estelle's birthday fell on the 17th of September.

That meant she'd already had one on the island, seeing as we'd crashed at the end of August. Had she remembered a year ago? Or had the crash deleted such superficial events from her short-term attention?

Either way, she tried to let it slide.

She pulled a Pippa and didn't tell anyone.

And I wouldn't have known if I hadn't commandeered her solar-charged phone and manically shot a home movie the night before.

Pippa and Conner had adorned themselves in head-dresses of ferns and palm leaves, putting on a badly acted and laughably funny theatrical performance of Fijian cannibals.

Pippa was the delicious sacrifice and Conner was the war chief seasoning his future meal.

Sprinkling sand and ash on his little sister for taste, Conner paraded around like a pompous fool, declaring how delicious his dinner would be.

Estelle and I laughed where appropriate and oohed and ahhed in suspense. Her body had already changed, rounding and filling, looking sexier every day. I hated that I found her condition beyond attractive. I cursed my cock for wanting her ten times more.

But her hormones matched mine, and the sex...goddamn, the sex reached smouldering heights.

I wanted to be careful.

She wanted me to be rough.

I wanted to take her gently.

She wanted me to take her hard.

Every time I entered her, it was like a bloody war, leading to the most intense orgasm for both of us.

And yes, I finally came inside her.

To say it didn't change my world would be an absolute understatement.

Switching my thoughts from sex to the kids acting, I swiped on the camera app only to see a blaring reminder on the screen not to forget Estelle turned twenty-seven at midnight.

I'd pretended I hadn't seen, and after everyone went to bed, I snuck out, careful not to disturb my sleeping birthday girl, and spent the entire night carving a wooden heart with the words, *'You'll always be mine,'* by moon and firelight.

It was the truth.

She would always be mine.

No matter what happened in a few months.

No matter if our baby survived or died.

Estelle would never be alone again.

Chapter Forty-Nine

. . . .

ESTELLE

. . . . . .

There comes a time when life doesn't listen to what you want.
It ploughs ahead, confident that you can't jump off the journey it's decided on.
~~I wish there was a way to change my destination.~~
Was I charging toward death?
Was I running toward motherhood?
What would happen when this was all over?
Taken from the notepad of E.E.
Final inscription.

. . .

OCTOBER

"G, I DON'T want you to do this."

"Estelle, we've been over this." Galloway refastened the vine tying his long hair back. A few months ago, we'd used the Swiss Army knife to cut all our hair. Me, Pippa, Conner, and Galloway.

The brittle, salt-tarnished lengths had been too straggly and annoying.

But it seemed the Fijian heat made everything grow faster, including our hair.

"We'll be okay, Stelly." Conner carried the crudely made oars to the sea edge. "We're just going to test it. Make sure it floats."

My heart hadn't left my throat since Galloway announced he wanted to test the life raft.

After my birthday, when he made me a delicious dinner of smoked fish, flax seeds and minted taro, and presented me with the most precious wooden heart, he'd delivered the news that if we were going to leave, we had to leave now.

I was five months pregnant.

Already, my stomach had grown and heartburn was a daily nightmare. The acid racing around my chest made me snappy, and poor Pippa was in charge of steeping concoctions, sampling the leaves we knew were edible in different preparations to see if any had antacid properties.

We had (totally by fluke) found that a small fuzzy plant helped with blood clotting and decreasing inflammation. Galloway had once again injured himself on a stupid forage into the forest with no flip-flops and stood in a patch of this furry plant while chopping down a palm tree. Instead of the wound being infected and swollen, it'd remained free of flowing blood and healed in half the time it normally would. Which was just as well because cuts on our feet lingered for months, seeing as we lived in the ocean and the salt turned the wound to sea ulcers.

We'd experimented over the course of a few months and found that boiling the leaves and using as a poultice increased its effectiveness.

We had no medicines. No antibiotics. No painkillers.

But we did have a small chance at dealing with superficial cuts without issue.

However, all of that was beside the point.

Galloway was leaving.

Leaving me and my waddling fat body to bob idiotically on the bay.

"You'll never get past the breaking waves on the reef." I hated how pessimistic I sounded, but the thought of leaving (while halfway through my pregnancy and irritable) was not on my top ten things to do.

Along with heartburn, the tiniest flutters of my evolving baby kept my thoughts turned inward. I knew I'd ignored Galloway a little the past few weeks, but that was natural…wasn't it?

My body was cooking a human.

It was only right for my mind to mature and prepare, too.

Galloway slid the bamboo raft onto the water, leaving it to float innocuously on the surface.

How many times had we swam in the tide and made love? How many times had Galloway carried my pregnant ass into the waves and washed my hair or massaged my back or kissed my lips as if I would smash into a trillion tiny pieces.

I loved him.

I love him.

He couldn't leave me.

"Please, Galloway. Don't." Tears pricked my eyes. Along with my thoughts becoming quieter and more obsessed with what happened internally, my emotions were on the knife-edge of intensity.

I bawled for no apparent reason.

I blew up over the slightest infraction.

I couldn't stand myself, let alone understand what it was like to live with a she-monster like me.

"You're only doing this because I'm annoying you and you want to run away from me." My bottom lip stuck out.

I shook my head at my dramatics, rolling my eyes at this weepy, manipulative creature I'd become, but I couldn't stop it. Whatever chemicals drenched my blood turned me from rational to insane.

Grasping his hand, I tugged him into my bulging belly. "G, I'm sorry. I won't moan anymore. I won't snap. I won't do anything to annoy you ever again. If only you'll stay. *Please*, say you'll stay."

Galloway's arms looped around me, holding me gently but firmly. The adoration in his blue, blue eyes threatened to send me into hysterics at the thought of never seeing him again.

Tears slicked down my cheeks. It probably came across as a tactic to make him stay, but I was honestly terrified of him leaving. This wasn't a trick. This was life or death for me.

"Estelle...don't." He collected my raining tears, cupping my cheeks with both hands. "I'm not going anywhere. You'll be able to see me the entire time."

I sniffed, doing my best to control my terribly tangled emotions but failing. "But...what if something happens."

"Nothing is going to happen."

"But it could."

"Yes, it could."

"Then, stay, dammit. It's not worth it."

His thumbs tightened on my cheeks. "Estelle, you're pregnant. Remember how terrified you were at the beginning?"

I tried to remember, but strangely, those past fears had been muted. I didn't know if it was baby hormones or sensibility, but I wasn't nearly as freaked out. Perhaps, it was self-preservation so I didn't go mad and try to cut myself open to avoid the horrendously painful birth.

Galloway kissed me. "Well, I'm now just as terrified. In fact, I've been terrified for months. And if I have a small chance that I can get you off this island before..." His eyes drifted to my large belly. "Well, before the baby arrives, then I'm going to do whatever I can to make that happen."

Letting me go, he strode purposely to the water.

Pippa ran to him, hugging his middle. "G, I'm with Stelly. I don't want you to go."

My heart pounded as he ducked and squeezed his island daughter.

Daughter.

Soon, he would have another son or daughter.

A fully fledged blooded and bonded fruit of his loins.

Who the hell came up with that term? Fruit of his loins.

I curled my upper lip, realising too late that my inner thoughts probably made no sense to those watching me.

Waddling to G and Pippi, I slid my arm over her shoulders from behind, tugging her close.

I needed her closeness.

Considering I'd run all my life from being touched or getting emotionally attached to others, I now craved the company.

I never wanted to be alone again.

And he's leaving me.

My tears began anew, tickling my chin as they rolled in sadness.

Galloway groaned. "Estelle, stop it. You're killing me." Grabbing my nape, he jerked me close and kissed me.

He didn't kiss me softly. He kissed me violently with tongue and taste and tantalizing torment.

Pippa squirmed in my embrace, crushed between Galloway and my belly.

We broke apart, smiling apologetically at the girl.

Galloway took the opportunity to hop onto the raft, his arms stabilising as the bamboo rolled with the current.

Conner was already on, balancing like a pirate, holding both paddles.

He passed one to Galloway. "Ready?"

With one last look at me, Galloway nodded. "Ready."

There were no spinnakers to harness the wind. No rudders to steer, no masts to steady.

Just a fateful, soon-to-be-failure.

No one listened to my protests as they pushed off from the shore and paddled away.

They crossed the bay, they approached the reef, all while standing proud on their floatable platform.

······························

NOVEMBER

We never discussed what happened that day in October.

No one said a word as Conner and Galloway swam back to shore, minus the raft and oars.

I'd been right.

The calm atoll had been a paddling haven, but when the craft reached the curling waves over the reef, it'd disintegrated beneath the smashing wet weight.

My soul hurt for Galloway's creation. My heart wept at how much energy and time he'd put into making it. I hated his crushing disappointment.

But I was glad in a way.

It wasn't that I didn't want to get off the island. It wasn't that I didn't crave medical supervision and a hospital when it came time to deliver.

But this way, the option had been stolen.

If the raft had survived and they'd broken past the reef, I would've had to make a choice.

A terribly, terribly hard choice.

Leave now…with meagre supplies and a body already stretched to its breaking point, or take my chances here and have an island birth.

As much as I feared my future, I didn't have the strength to leave the only place I knew.

I didn't have the confidence to willingly walk into the shadow of death when it was already dark enough on our piece of paradise.

Having it sink was the best thing for all of us.

Chapter Fifty

∙∙

G A L L O W A Y

∙∙∙∙∙∙

THREE YEARS BEFORE THE CRASH

"YO, MATE."

I swallowed my curse and faced the daily tormentors from E block. It wasn't an afternoon in the yard without a sore jaw or verbal abuse. "What do you want, Alf?"

Alf lumbered closer, accenting a stupid swagger that didn't hide the fact he was shorter than I was.

By three inches.

If I wanted to, I could knock the asshole out with one punch.

But I didn't.

Because the rules were you got better treatment, more choices on work, and a cleaner slate for parole if you behaved.

Alf sneered, "Come on, pussy. Today's the day." He held his fists by his face, ready for a sparring match. "You're never gonna get out anyway. Life, baby doll. Might as well have some recreational fun."

I'd schooled my face to stay ragefully cold. He wouldn't know what the words 'life in prison' did to my insides. He didn't need to know how bloody twisted I was. Part of me agreed that I'd got a fair punishment.

I'd killed a man. I deserved to never be free again.

But the other part of me hated that my victim had killed so many others and he'd never been caught. He'd had the devil on his side.

Until me, of course.

∙∙∙∙∙∙∙∙∙∙∙∙∙∙∙∙∙∙∙∙∙∙∙∙∙∙∙∙

"ESTELLE, YOU NEED to sit the hell down." I pointed at her large belly. "If you don't do as I say, I'm going to handcuff you to the bed."

Estelle whirled on me, dropping the two water bottles she'd

been carrying to give to Conner and Pippa playing in the shallows. The bottles weren't heavy, but she'd been bloody waddling all over the camp since dawn. "With what exactly? We don't have a bedhead and we don't have cuffs."

"You know what I mean."

"No, I *don't* know what you mean. How about you leave me alone?"

Whoa, what?

My heart shed its calm beat for a frenzied flurry. My voice was deceptively low. "I suggest you reassess what you just said to me."

Damn woman didn't know how to stop fussing. Her constant fretting made her tired. She shouldn't be tired. She had to be healthy and strong for the birth.

The birth.

I swallowed hard.

Every time I thought about what Estelle would face in a few short months, my temper exploded out of control. There was nothing I could do. I couldn't take her pain. I couldn't save her from agony. And I couldn't do a fucking thing if complications arose and she died.

I hated everything about this pregnancy, including the fact that Estelle seemed adamant at cutting me out of her life. "I don't appreciate being told to leave you alone when all I'm trying to do is—"

"All right, that's it! I've had enough." Her eyes narrowed, hands flew to her hips, and her face darkened beneath her honey tan. "That's all you do these days, Galloway. You follow me around muttering that I shouldn't do that and I shouldn't do this. You're constantly under my feet. At night, you want to hear insistently that I forgive you for knocking me up and that I still love you. What the hell has gotten into you? I'm not dying, for God's sake. I'm not an invalid." She poked her stomach. "You're so needy it's as if *you've* turned into the baby and I don't need this one."

I froze.

The axe in my hands, from chopping firewood, dropped into the sand.

I should leave.

I should turn around and get some air before I said something I regretted.

But the air swirled with a fight.

I didn't *want* to fight.

But this had been brewing for weeks.

We'd been off-kilter ever since the raft incident (which I still couldn't think about without cursing the wasted time) and unable to find our way back to each other.

As the pregnancy progressed, Estelle shut me out. I didn't think she did it consciously, but she'd done it nevertheless. She didn't lean on me. She didn't ask for my opinion. She shouldered more and more responsibility as if she didn't trust me to do it right.

And it made me feel like an asshole.

Because the more she didn't need me, the more and more desperate I became.

I *needed* her.

Not just sexually. But emotionally, physically, spiritually— every damn way. And it wasn't enough that she cuddled into me at night and let me do the chores she normally would.

The chasm between us confused the hell out of me.

I felt...*I feel second best.*

Somehow, the baby that I'd shackled her with (the same spawn she'd been terrified of having) had stolen the heart of my woman before it'd even been born.

"Perhaps...we should talk about this later." I gritted my teeth, doing my best to stay rational.

I bloody hated the distance between us and the fact I was the one to cause it. But I wouldn't take her bullshit quietly.

If she provoked me again...

Calm down. She's pregnant. Hormonal. Don't stress her out.

My pep talk did absolutely nothing as Estelle laughed coldly. "No. You know what? I want to talk about it *now*. You obviously have something on your mind. So spit it out, Galloway." Her chin lowered. "Unless, you're not man enough."

Okay, that's it.

Stalking toward her, I wanted to grab and shake the damn idiocy out of her. But I managed to keep my fists balled by my side. Just. "Stop it, Estelle. I don't understand why you're being such a bitch."

"What?" Her voice screeched loud enough to wrench Pippa and Conner's head up.

They paused, assessing the angry standoff between us.

I glowered down the beach. "If you two so much as move, so help me, you'll have sore asses for a week!"

Conner held up his hands in surrender. "Not looking. Not our business." Grabbing Pippa's wrist, he hauled her from the sea and walked quickly down the beach.

Smart kid.

"Don't you *dare* talk to the children like that!" Estelle pushed my chest. "Leave them alone."

Red dripped over my vision.

I'd managed years in prison avoiding the taunting for a brawl. I could do this.

She's mine. I love her. I don't want to hurt her.

"I told them to give us some space to talk. I didn't hurt them, woman."

"Could've fooled me. What did you do in your past, huh? I'm guessing it was something to do with violence. How can I trust that you won't hurt me or them?"

I. Couldn't. Breathe.

Did she *seriously* just fucking go there?

My fingers clamped over her biceps, pinching her muscles hard. "What the hell is your deal, Estelle?"

"My deal? What's your deal? You started this!"

"No, I didn't. You've been strange for weeks."

She squirmed in my hold, glaring at my fingers and her reddening skin. "Get your hands off me."

"No."

"Do as I say."

"Not until we figure out what's going wrong between us." My fingers tightened. "I feel as if I'm losing you. Is that it? You're pushing me away because you don't have the guts to tell me you don't want me anymore?"

She rolled her eyes. "Oh, my God, you're bringing that up again? How many times do I need to tell you! I love you. I want you. I'm not going to leave you!"

"Strange way of showing it, don't you think?"

"No, because you're being an arrogant ass."

"Me? You're being the stuck-up shrew."

"Don't call me that."

"Well, I can't call you what I really want to, so it will have to do."

Flyaway strands from her plait blew around her cheeks, making me want her with an intensity that only grew the bigger she ballooned with my baby.

"What? What do you want to call me?"

Don't go there, Gallo.

I hated this. We were both stressed and angry. Nothing ever came from nasty arguments. I wouldn't be cruel.

Letting her go, I put a step between us. "It doesn't matter. All that matters is us. And I'm so damn confused about where I stand." Dragging a hand through my hair, I sighed. "What is it, Stel? Why are you so angry with me?"

Something snapped in her gaze. "You want to know why I'm so angry?" She stormed toward me. "Fine, I'll tell you." Listing on her fingers, she shouted, "How about the fact that you don't let me do anything anymore. You won't let me swim. You won't let me walk. You won't let me scratch messages into the sand. And you won't let me take home movies as you say the strain of holding the phone could hurt me and I should let *you* do it." Her voice wobbled. "Dammit, Galloway, you're suffocating me and I've had enough!"

"Wow, tell me how you really feel." The sarcastic coolness I'd used to protect myself returned with a vengeance. Estelle had made me a better person and knocked down my safety crutches, but now, she was the one making me feel weak, insecure, and woefully overbearing when all I was trying to do was protect her, *care for her*, show her I loved her and hoped to bloody God that she forgave me for putting her in this awful, awful position.

"You asked!" Her cheeks blazed with fire. "Maybe you should stop being such a hypocrite and tell me what *you* really feel. Because it seems as though you have a thousand things you want to say but you're being a wimp."

A wimp?

I was a wimp?

After everything I'd done. After accepting that I'd be a cripple for the rest of my life. That I'd go to Hell for murder. That I would never have deserved Estelle if we weren't thrown together on an uninhabited island.

She called me a *wimp?*

Fine!

We were really doing this.

I wouldn't hold back for her pregnant ass' sake.

She wanted a fight?

I'll give her a fight.

Closing the distance between us, I stood to my full height, dwarfing her.

To her credit, she didn't back down, only inflated more with rage.

"You're treating me as if I don't exist, Estelle. You're making me feel like shit."

"Oh, boo hoo. You can't handle me wanting my independence."

"You call hiding your cramps and discomfort and not asking for my help independence?" I snarled. "Whatever. I call that stupidity."

"Don't call me stupid."

"Then stop *acting* stupid."

"*You* stop acting stupid."

"Christ, I can't talk to you when you're like this."

"Like what, Galloway? Like a pregnant woman? Am I not allowed to be a little strung out knowing that in a few months' time, I'm going to face the most horrendous ordeal of my life and I don't know if I'm going to survive it? Am I not allowed to feel sorry for myself when I'm tired and sore and there's so much to do just to stay alive, let alone prepare to deliver a baby I didn't want? If that's the case, then I'm *sorry* if it upsets your delicate ego, but I've got news for you. I'm so absolutely terrified that I'm not going to put on a brave face just to make *you* feel better. I'm not going to smile and kiss you when the baby is kicking my spleen like it's a damn soccer ball. And excuse me if I don't want to accept your help because it makes me want to burst into tears knowing that I can't do it myself anymore, and if I don't do it now, I might never get to do it because I could be *dead* in a few months."

Fuck.

My heart flew out of my chest and landed in the sand by her feet.

"Estelle—" Grabbing her, I wrapped my arms around her shaking form. "Don't you think I feel the exact same way—"

"Let her go, G." Conner and Pippa appeared in the treeline. They'd doubled back on us from farther down the beach.

I glowered. "Leave it alone, Conner."

"No. I was wrong when I said it's none of our business. It *is* our business. So let her go."

Estelle squirmed in my arms, forcing me to release her. I hurt so damn much that we were fighting because of the same thing.

Terror.

We loved each other, yet for weeks, we'd silently pushed each other away because of uncertainty and fear.

I felt the exact same way.

My fear killed me every hour of every single day.

I loved her, for Christ's sake. I loved her too damn much, and I couldn't survive if I lost her.

Pippa shot forward, her brother a step behind. "Stop fighting."

"We're not fighting," Estelle said, brushing aside fallen tears. "Just a minor discussion."

"Bullcrap." Conner strode to Estelle. "You're crying."

"No, I'm not. Just hormones," Estelle joked. "Honestly, we're fine."

For the first time in a while, I fully took stock of the fourteen-year-old. Coppery fuzz decorated his chin, his biceps had grown, and his voice had deepened from cute falsetto to masculine timbre.

Somehow, the kid had cracked whatever chrysalis he'd been hiding in and turned into a young man overnight.

Never taking his eyes off me, Conner hugged Estelle. Unlike when I'd embraced her, she willingly sank into his arms and kissed his cheek. "I'm okay, Co. Don't worry."

He was an inch taller than she was now and lanky muscles encapsulated her. His brown eyes filled with worry as he placed his hand on her belly. "The baby's kicking you?"

Her lips quirked. "That's what babies do. They stretch and move. It's natural."

"But does it hurt?" Pippa asked, her face full of wonder.

Estelle shook her head. "It's strange, and sometimes, I feel bruised, but it's not like an 'ouch' kind of pain."

The trio turned to face me, united once again to tell me off and cut me out.

Perhaps, it would be best if I moved to the other side of the island for the time being. Give Estelle a break from me and my emotional insecurities. She already dealt with so much of her own. It wasn't fair for her to comfort me when I hadn't been comforting her.

I stiffened as Conner pointed between Estelle and me. "Pippa and I are going to mediate. What's the problem?"

Estelle laughed softly. "That's very sweet, but seriously, it's over now." Her eyes tightened in my direction. "Isn't that right, G?"

No.

"Yes." I nodded. "Perfect."

"Whatever," Conner snapped. "We knew when our parents fought and we knew when it got so bad they wanted a divorce. It sucked. And they didn't let us help. They said we were too young to understand. But we weren't. Were we, Pip?"

Pippa dropped her gaze, scooting closer to Conner. "No, we knew. We were old enough to know why they were fighting and what it would mean for us."

Estelle sighed heavily. "Darlings, we're not getting a divorce."

"You can't get a divorce." Pippa looked solemn as if such a thing could never happen. That she wouldn't *let* it happen. But then, she shocked all of us as she added, "You have to be married to be divorced."

Married.

God, I'd give anything to marry Estelle. Even after I'd screwed up completely and made an issue out of nothing.

Estelle froze. "What did you say?"

"Married." Conner scowled. "Wait…is that what this is about? You guys were talking about getting married?"

Estelle's chest rose and fell, her black t-shirt straining against her fuller breasts. "No, that wasn't—"

"What if I wanted to marry you?" I couldn't look away from her. "What if I apologise for being an idiotic moron and get on my knee right now? Would you forgive me?"

She sucked in a breath. "What—what are you saying?"

Shakes stole my body.

Anxiety and shock and hope and disbelief.

What am I doing?

This could royally backfire.

But after finally understanding that Estelle wasn't shutting me out but merely entering self-protective mode, I couldn't have been more of an idiot. I'd picked a fight when there was nothing to fight about.

Taking her hand, I sucked a lungful of sweet island air.

And dropped to one knee.

Pippa gasped.

Conner jolted.

And Estelle moaned a little.

Staring up at her, I fell even more crazy in love with her. Her belly shadowed the sand and her skin glowed as if she'd harnessed the sun and it shone through her skin.

She was majestic.

She was terrified.

She was mine.

If she'll still have me.

"Estelle Evermore." I cleared my throat. "I'm so sorry. I'm a bastard for being so insecure and putting it on you. I shouldn't have made this about me. This was never about me. I shouldn't have sulked and worried that I'd done something wrong and smothered you with the need to keep you safe. I see now that I was suffocating you and I'm so bloody sorry.

"I'm sorry I needed more than you were able to give. I'm sorry that I haven't been there for you as I should. But if there is any way you can forgive me, you'd make me the happiest man in the world if you said yes.

"I promise to be by your side always. I'll keep you safe and cared for. I'll fight nightmares and crash land with you anytime you want as long as it means we're together.

"The reason I argued was because I feel the same way you do. I love you so damn much that the thought of you leaving me is too bloody much to bear. You own me, Estelle, and I can't get rid of the guilt. The damn guilt that *I* did this to you. That I'm the reason you're unhappy and afraid, and I'm making it worse by trying to make up for that."

I couldn't stop the verbal spewing, but Estelle squeezed my fingers. The anger in her eyes shifted to everlasting adoration and forgiveness.

My back crumpled in thankfulness.

Conner chuckled. "Way to be a pussy, man."

I threw a handful of sand at him. "Hush it."

Pippa swooned, hugging herself, her eyes bouncing between me and Estelle. "Well…say something, Stelly. Do you *want* to marry him?"

My back shot ramrod straight.

Don't say no.

Please, God, don't say no.

Estelle gave nothing away. I couldn't tell what she'd say. If it were anything like the past few months, it wouldn't be good.

However, her voice was gentle and kind, far different to the shrill yelling from before. "Say yes to what, G?"

I frowned. "What?"

"You said…in your rather large speech…'if I said yes.'" She bent forward, her plait dangling over her shoulder. "Yes to what? I need a question to give an answer."

Sunrise replaced my heart, slowly filling my body with orange and gold and happy, happy yellows.

Glancing at the kids, Conner gave me a thumbs-up, and Pippa nodded happily.

I slipped back into my world, realigned myself in Estelle's gravitational pull, and expelled every fear I'd been holding.

Estelle wouldn't die because there was no death where love was concerned.

And I loved her.

To Pluto and back.

"Estelle…would you do me the honour of becoming my wife?" I kissed her knuckles. "Will you marry me?"

She took her time.

She made me wait.

But her reply made it all worthwhile.

"Yes, Galloway. Of course, I'll marry you."

• •

"I don't know what I'm doing." Conner scowled, pulling at the neckline of the orange t-shirt we'd found in his mother's tote bag.

We'd rationed our clothing, living in one wardrobe at a time because once the cotton disintegrated, we had no way of getting more.

But tonight was a special occasion and demanded new apparel.

Pippa had chosen her frilly purple sundress and threaded yellow flowers through her hair.

I'd shrugged into my khaki trousers designated for work (but still had the shopping tags on) and topped it with a plaid shirt with the cuffs rolled up.

Estelle had struggled.

She didn't fit her shorts anymore and her belly stretched almost everything she wore. However, she'd found a few muslin scarves in Amelia's tote and somehow knotted them together into a dress-like sarong. She looked as if she'd walked from a Grecian painting with her hair coiled and decorated with hibiscus flowers.

No, she looks like a gypsy, a wanderer.

A hard to capture dream.

She'd smeared some aloe on her lips (from the small crop we'd found) and the glistening invitation against the dark honey of her skin made her eyes explode with browns and priceless greens.

I'd never craved my glasses more. I'd give anything to see her in lucent clarity.

Conner tapped my arm, dragging me from my obsession. "Dude, I can't remember my lines."

My heart stuttered as Estelle giggled. Ever since she'd appeared on the shore at dusk, I'd been besotted.

We'd all agreed that there was no reason to wait.

We wanted to get married.

Tonight was the perfect time.

The rest of the afternoon had been spent preparing, and afterward, we'd arranged to ransack our larder and have a gourmet dinner of smoked squid with some coconut milk clams.

It wasn't a flashy wedding. It wasn't a fancy feast.

But it was on our private beach with the people we loved the most.

It's perfect.

"Just say whatever you want, Conner. But at the end, make sure you ask the question I told you."

"Oh, man. That's the part I can't remember."

I snorted. "Perhaps, Pippa can help."

Pippa elbowed her brother. "Yeah, Co. I'll do it. I'll be better at it anyway."

Conner stuck out his tongue. "How do you know, smarty pants?"

"Because I could read before you could and I'm smarter. So there."

"Are not."

"Are too."

"Hey." I held up my free hand (the one not glued to my bride). "Wedding over here…can we focus?"

Estelle clutched my fingers. "Thank you, G. I feel like we didn't resolve everything this afternoon, but I'm so sorry for how I treated you, for not being more understanding of how my quietness would make you worry. I just—I needed to say I'm sorry and remind you how much I love you and how lucky I am to have you."

I didn't have a heart anymore; it'd turned into a cupid-shaped balloon and floated to the moon. "No more misunderstandings, okay?"

"Agreed."

We leaned forward at the same time, meeting for the briefest kiss.

"Hey, no kissing the bride until I say so." Conner crossed his arms. "Now, do you have the rings?"

Pippa's hand shot up, holding the knotted vines I'd done as a temporary measure. If by some miracle we got off this island, I'd buy Estelle the best ring I could afford (which admittedly wasn't much after spending most of my life in prison) and if we didn't get rescued, then I'd carve her the best jewellery I could from a coconut shell.

Pippa (bless her heart) had tried to give me her mother's ring. She'd said, between rolling tears, that her mother would want it to be worn.

My eyes had threatened to water like hers, but I'd curled her fingers around the diamond and kissed her forehead. I'd told her that the ring was hers. One day, it would be an heirloom for her daughter and it should be treasured.

"Okay, we have the rings." Conner rubbed his face. "I guess, um…the power vested in me…by um, our island and the turtles, I pronounce you man and—"

"Wait!" Pippa bounced on the spot. "You didn't ask if anyone objects."

Estelle burst out laughing.

I struggled to hold in a chuckle. "Seriously, kid, you're ruining my ego here." I slung my arm over her tiny shoulders. "Do you object to me marrying this woman and having a baby with her and giving you a little sister or brother to play with?"

A calculating gleam entered her gaze. "I don't object if it's a sister. If it's a brother, I do."

Estelle laughed harder. "Sorry to disappoint, Pippi, but I can't guarantee that and we have no way of knowing."

She pouted. "Oh. Well, in that case. No, I have no objects."

"Objections?" I squeezed her closer.

"Objections. No, I don't have any of those, either."

Conner smirked. "Honestly, and you call yourself smarter than me." He ducked as Pippa whacked him with Puffin.

We couldn't get married without the stuffed cat as our official witness.

He ducked. "Watch it!"

"Can we perhaps get back to the wedding?" I arched an eyebrow, doing my best not to laugh.

"Fine." Conner grinned. "For the record, I have no objections. However, seeing as I've had a crush on Estelle since we crashed, I'm not going to let you put a step wrong; otherwise, I'm stealing her."

My smile fell.

What?

Estelle giggled nervously. "That's nice of you to protect my honour, Conner, but I'm sure Galloway won't mess up."

Conner and I never stopped glaring.

I didn't expect it to happen, but the competition I'd feared had borderlined reality.

Conner meant what he said.

Just how deep do his feelings go for Estelle? And why didn't I pay attention?

Dropping his gaze, Conner said, "Do you take Estelle as your wife?"

It wasn't exactly the line I'd taught him to say, but it would do.

The sooner she was married to me, the sooner Conner could get over his little crush and respect that Estelle was mine forever. I pitied him that he was alone when no doubt his libido was through the roof, but I also didn't want to fight with him.

And I would if it came down to it.

Something about living on an island made animalistic tendencies rise to the surface.

"I do."

Looking at Estelle, Conner's face softened. "And do you take Galloway as your husband?"

Estelle only had eyes for me.

She gave me a heart attack and resuscitated me all at once with a single glance.

"I do."

Rubbing his nose, Conner announced, "In that case, I now pronounce you married. You may French kiss or do whatever it is that you do."

"Don't mind if I do." Grabbing Estelle by her nape, I yanked her close and kissed her.

I kissed her until my trousers were tight and lungs were empty.

I kissed her and wiped away everything that'd happened.

I kissed her with a promise that we might not have a priest or official document but this was as real to me as any ceremony.

We were married.

Until death did us part.

And even then, I'd put up a fight to keep her.

....

That night, once the kids were in bed, and we'd eaten an amazing dinner, Estelle and I headed to our bamboo sanctuary that'd become our date night and sexy time hang-out.

There, I made love to her.

I stripped her bare.

I kissed every inch.

I licked her all over.

And when I entered her, I did it as her husband.

I vowed that we were one now.

And no matter what happened, I would take care of her.

....

DECEMBER

The day of our fight and consequential marriage helped clear the air completely.

November trailed into December, and we respected each other's feelings. We were careful to be open and honest about how things were. And somehow, we became closer rather than drifted apart.

Estelle still hated when I laid down the law, ordering her not to do something. And I did my best to hide my desire to lock her in a protective bubble, settling for treating her like filigreed china instead.

She didn't like my bossiness but tolerated my demands for her to take it easy because she knew it came from a loving place. A completely infatuated place.

I forbid her from any heavy lifting.

I took over her job of collecting firewood.

I fished.

I cleaned.

I even helped her soak more flax until the softest strands were available for a baby blanket.

She barely tolerated me, but I never felt excluded if she needed some alone time. She went out of her way to make sure I felt valued and adored, and when she kissed me, she held my entire world in her palm.

We'd found balance.

We'd become a team rather than enemies.

By day, I worked on building an extension to our home, creating a lean-to that was accessible from our bedroom where the newly built crib would rest.

I just hope my skills design a better crib than a raft.

I still cringed, thinking how quickly and disastrously the bamboo platform had broken apart. Turned out, I should stick to land architecture, not boats.

By night, I massaged her back, combed her hair, and rubbed her aching feet.

I didn't let her out of my sight, and even permitted Conner and Pippa to spend the night on the other side of the island as an adventure and non-traditional sleepover, just so I could make tender love to her in front of the fire without having to traipse to our grove.

She ate what I told her to, ensuring she had her ration and most of mine to feed both mother and growing child. As she grew bigger, I grew skinnier as I refused to fish too often so I wasn't far from her.

Conner picked up a lot of my slack, taking on more duties, and restocking our pile of coconuts and water reservoirs without me asking him to.

Not once did he give me grief, and I never caught him gawking at Estelle in inappropriate ways.

Perhaps, he'd only been joking. Not that it mattered; I'd keep an eye on him just in case.

Once again, we chose not to celebrate Christmas.

The birthdays were enough to remind us of quickly passing time. However, we did plan a big meal and bonfire when the turtles returned.

We spent the night watching the massive beasts haul their bulk from the tide and repeat the same process from a year ago, laying countless eggs, doing their best for their offspring's chance, before slinking back into the sea in silence.

························

JANUARY

Pippa had another birthday.

It felt like only yesterday she'd turned eight. The little girl, resembling a washed-up princess, slowly turned into a young woman complete with long legs, beseeching eyes, and a wicked intelligence that thought outside the box and allowed us to experiment with different materials, find plants that provided pain relief for mosquito bites, and flowers that helped with swelling and sprains.

We weren't often hurt but everyday scrapes and injuries were common. She somehow morphed into the pharmacist of our island-world, constantly murmuring with Estelle about what to try next and the risks versus reward of the red and yellow flowers decorating our beach.

Our larder slowly housed a small apothecary, too. Growing with herbs and supplies as analysis turned to verification.

I had no doubt if she were back in a city with schooling and teachers, she would've been top of her class and already on her way to deciding her career.

I'd asked her a week ago what she wanted to be when she grew up.

And despite the caustic reply that she doubted we'd get off the island, she wanted to be a doctor.

She certainly had an affinity for healing and health.

Unlike the murderer I killed.

I just hoped we wouldn't need her adolescent skills when it came time for Estelle to give birth.

Chapter Fifty-One

∙∙

ESTELLE

∙∙∙∙∙∙

FEBRUARY

IT STARTED SLOW.

Painful and slow.

But with an urgency that terrified.

The skin around my distended belly rippled with pain as the contraction wrenched me from sleep.

Gasping, I jerked in Galloway's arms.

No, I'm not ready.

I'll never be ready to face this.

Another ripple tore a louder gasp from me, rousing G.

Damn, I didn't want to wake him.

He'd only fuss, and he'd hardly slept at all this past week, worrying about me, constantly looking at the calendar to pinpoint when I was due. I hated that he gave me his food, willingly hurting himself to ensure I had more than I needed. He was far too kind. Too generous. I didn't deserve it after the way I'd acted.

I twirled my flax wedding ring. Already, it was almost non-existent with wear but the weight of our marriage and bond of love seared into my flesh like a tattoo.

I adored him.

And I was so sorry this had happened when we were so unprepared.

The contraction tightened again, stealing my breath.

He roused, his eyes opened, hazy with sleep but sharp with protectiveness. "What is it?"

I shook my head, holding up my hand to signal I couldn't talk.

He shot to his knees, his eyes wild.

He acted more panicked than I did. But that was because I'd

got better at hiding my fear.

Ever since our fight, I'd been very conscious of how I came across to him. My thoughts had remained locked on my baby. He was now (as awful as it might seem) second best. I couldn't help it. It was my body making me pick the most important.

And for now, the soon-to-be-born baby was more important.

Not that I could ever tell him that because I loved him. With all my heart.

My heart had just expanded to encompass more.

The contraction faded.

I relaxed.

It could just be another false alarm.

I'd had a few of those the past week. Sometimes, it was hard to tell what was preparation and what was the rowdy baby in my belly.

I'd been afraid I wouldn't carry to full term. But by some miracle, I had. (Mainly thanks to Galloway's constant monitoring). However, I was about a week early. Was that a good thing or bad? Was the baby fully grown or not? Was it too big for my body or would I deliver without injury?

So many questions.

So many terrors.

And no one to give me answers.

I had no way to tell if it was a boy or girl, healthy or deformed. But I knew from the strength of its kick that it wanted out. It stupidly wanted to enter a world where I couldn't guarantee its safety.

"Stel...is it the baby?"

I stroked his cheek. "Don't worry about it. Just a cramp. Go back to sleep."

He sat up instead. "Let me get you some water. Do you need to use the bathroom?"

The concern and hopeful fear in his gaze undid me.

I smiled softly. "I love you, G."

His shoulders slouched. His hands came up and captured my cheeks. He kissed me long and slow, tasting and worshipping me all at once. "I love you more."

I laughed as he gathered me in his embrace. "I don't think we need to debate who loves who more."

Rearranging his grip, he hauled me to my feet. With him acting as my crutch, he guided my waddling pregnant form from our house to the smouldering fire outside.

The stars shone fiercely, determined not to give up their velvet patch as the horizon slowly brightened.

"Wait there. I'm going to get you a coconut. You need to drink and nibble on something."

I'd learned not to argue.

There was no point.

He never listened anyway.

....

The sun slowly set on the most painful day of my existence.

The false alarm hadn't been false at all and the banding agony only grew stronger and more painful as morning became afternoon and afternoon became evening.

I didn't want to eat or drink.

I couldn't move without Galloway's aid.

I was tired, cranky, and in tears fearing what would happen.

The nightmare that'd haunted me for months seemed to come true the longer I was in labour. Contraction after contraction, my body tried to deliver my child, but contraction after contraction, it failed.

My water didn't break, and slowly, my energy dwindled. I rode the pain rather than fought with it to push.

The children had spent the day by my side, alternating between bathing my sweaty body with seawater and holding fresh coconut juice to my lips. Galloway hovered like a heartsick parent, looking as if he'd happily go to war with death itself if it meant I would be safe.

The hopelessness in his gaze quadrupled my heart rate until I struggled to breathe.

And now, the moon took centre stage again, and *still,* I struggled.

How long did labour normally last for? Three hours? Three days? I didn't have much more to give if it was any longer.

Don't give up.

You can't give up.

I couldn't leave him. Leave them.

The night I'd taken Galloway as my husband was the night I'd vowed not to die in childbirth.

My place was here, by his side.

I. Will. Not. Die.

Panting through yet another contraction, I tensed until the pain subsided and collapsed into an exhausted sleep in Galloway's arms.

....

I woke to wetness and shooting sharp pain.

Galloway shifted behind me; his arms tightened around my

shoulders where he'd kept me safe, lying on his chest with my hips between his legs. The fire flickered over us, showing my swollen belly and his mangled ankle disfigured from the crash.

The pain wrapped awful pincers around me, squeezing my uterus until I screamed.

Something wanted me to push.

I needed to push.

Push.

Push.

Push!

I screamed again, giving in to the urge but coming up against more agony than I'd ever felt before.

I can't.

You have to.

I'm not ready.

You are.

I wasn't aware as Galloway moved me to stand. I didn't comprehend as I left the sandy beach and somehow ended tucked in a fetal position in his arms.

"Where—where are you taking me?" My voice was weak and wobbly. I was thirsty, so thirsty. I was hungry, so hungry.

Everything inside argued with itself. I was upside down and back to front. Too hot, too cold, tired, ready, sick, energized, dying, alive.

I don't know what to do!

Push. Push. Push.

"Your water broke in your sleep. You need to push, Estelle. And I'm going to help any way I can."

No, I don't want to. I want to believe this isn't happening.

"I want to go to sleep."

"You can't. Not until you've delivered."

"How is carrying me going to help me do that?"

He didn't reply, merely carted me down the beach and straight into the cooling sea. The hotness of my skin welcomed the salty freshness.

I sighed in relief.

Yes, that's better.

I'll just live here.

Forever.

He waded a little deeper until the water lapped his waist before reverently letting me go. The buoyancy of the water and weightlessness of no longer fighting such heaviness of my womb was sheer heaven.

The tide cradled me, swishing me back and forth as it lapped against the sand. My feet brushed the sandy bottom, but I made no effort to stand. Reclining, I tipped my head back, wallowing on the surface like a spread starfish while my belly reached for the waxy moon.

Galloway sank beside me, ducking under to slick back his long dark hair. He'd shaved with the Swiss Army knife a week ago, and his stubble matched that of a tortured alpha male with sexy, dangerous shadows.

"I don't know if it's safe being in here while giving birth." I hated to suggest we should leave after finding some comfort, but the very real fear of sharks wouldn't leave.

"I'll watch over you." He scanned the black horizon. In over a year on our island, we'd grown accustomed to seeing in the dark. Our eyesight hadn't improved (Galloway's most likely had deteriorated without his glasses) but somehow, we understood the world a little more not having electric light blinding us every time the sun set.

"Besides, we've never seen a shark in our reef before." He grinned. "You're safe."

"Just because they haven't been here before doesn't mean they won't co—" Another contraction cut me off mid-word. My teeth clacked together and my hands landed on my belly, doing my best to push internally and externally.

Heavy hands landed on mine, gently adding pressure to the struggling baby beneath my skin. I looked up, drowning in his elysian blue eyes.

I didn't speak.

He didn't speak.

But we agreed that he would help me, and together, we would survive this night.

Everything else faded as I turned inward to my task. I didn't ask where Conner and Pippa were. I didn't struggle when Galloway went behind me and supported my legs so I could squat on the sandy bottom. I didn't cry out even as my body bellowed and fought against stretching wide enough to grant life.

Time lost all meaning and I focused everything on ridding whatever alien gave me so much pain.

I wanted to sleep in peace.

"You're almost there. One more, Stel. Come on."

My head lolled on his shoulder. Air was hard to come by, and I'd never ached so much in my entire life. The stars had gone, replaced with pink-silvery light of a new sun.

His bulk warmed my back, interposed with shots of cool seawater as he breathed. His hands rested on my belly, ready to help with the final push.

I wouldn't lie and say it wasn't the most excruciating thing I'd ever endured.

I screamed so loud the sound wave skipped like a skipping stone over the glassy surface, ricocheting around our island.

That final push was hell and brimstone and the devil himself.

But the rush and relief afterward? That was the most euphoric sensation I'd ever had.

Galloway's hands left my belly, dipping between my legs to catch our child.

Raising the tiny red thing, seawater and blood cascaded from its squirming legs.

Galloway had never shared his past with me. He still refused to say what changed his heart from such a caring, wonderful man into a hardened cynic. But none of that mattered because as he held his child and patted its back to earn a squall from new lungs, a single tear rolled down his cheek.

"Oh, my God." He cupped our baby so rapturously; she was instantly promoted as priestess of his heart.

I'd done it.

I'd endured my worst fear and delivered a healthy child.

I'd given us a girl.

Chapter Fifty-Two

GALLOWAY

MARCH

THERE WAS A new dimension to our marriage.

A deeper depth.

A complicated, awe-inspiring connection.

After Estelle had given birth, I passed her our daughter and
helped her deliver the afterbirth. Once done and both mother and
child were clean, I carried the loves of my life and tied off the
umbilical cord.

Using the Swiss Army knife (sterilized in the fire), I had the
honour of separating the final link and creating a brand new tiny
human.

I did all that on instinct.

I'd never been around a newborn before.

I'd never watched what happened or what to do afterward.

But the knowledge was inside me, just like the knowledge that
I'd found my soul-mate, and together, we were invincible.

Those first few nights were hard.

I was tired.

Estelle was knackered.

Yet we had a brand new person demanding to be fed and
changed and tended to. We alternated between zombie-like
awakeness and catatonic sleeping.

Pippa and Conner were left to their own devices, and instead of
burning down the camp, they kept me and Estelle fed. They cleaned
the house, they fished, they cooked. They made me so damn proud
and grateful.

There were so many things to juggle.

The first time Estelle breast fed freaked me out until the baby settled into suckling.

The first time breakfast went through my daughter to reappear in a disgusting mess, taught us that hygiene would be paramount.

And the first time she burped and fell asleep in our arms, ensured we'd put up with anything because we were in love.

We cut up a ratty t-shirt and transformed it into a reusable diaper.

We held each other when the baby slept and sympathized when she wouldn't stop crying.

So many firsts.

So many things to learn and overcome.

By the time the first week passed, we'd recovered enough to be mildly coherent.

However, Estelle suffered a breakdown when her nipples became sore from constant feeding, and I felt utterly inadequate because I couldn't take over and prevent her pain.

All I could do was hold her, rock her, and keep our baby as clean as possible.

Our island hadn't changed.

But my God, our world had.

Late one night, lying in bed with a scarf-swaddled baby on my chest and my wife in my embrace, I murmured, "I'm so bloody proud of you, Stel."

She kissed the skin above my heart. "I couldn't have done it without you."

"Let's be honest. Yes, you could." I smiled in the dark. "But I appreciate you saying that."

She sat up on her elbows and kissed my lips. "That's a lie. I'm only alive because of your sheer stubbornness to keep me that way."

"That stubbornness is what will get us through the next few months."

She glanced at our child. "You're very adaptable, G. I look at you and think that you were born for this life. Like it wasn't an accident that you landed here."

I shrugged. "What choice did we have? It was survive or die. I chose to survive. We all did."

She ran her finger down the ridge of my nose and traced my bottom lip. "Know what else we haven't chosen?"

"No, what?"

"A name."

"Ah, yes." I chuckled. "I remember asking you about that last week and you bursting into tears saying it was too much pressure to name someone for the rest of their life."

"Yes, well." She smirked. "I might've been dealing with overtiredness at the time." Her gaze dropped as she turned shy. "I have a suggestion…if you want to hear it?"

Our daughter squirmed as I arched my neck and kissed her. "By all means, share away."

She took a deep breath. "If you hate it, we don't have to."

"You're making it sound like you want to name her something terrible."

"Well, we all have different opinions on what terrible entails."

"How about you just blurt it out, so I'm not wondering if our kid will be named Daffodil or Edwina."

She swatted me. "Those aren't terrible, terrible."

I rolled my eyes. "Come on, spit it out."

Her body tensed as she said, "Coconut."

"Coconut?"

She flopped onto her back. "Forget it, it's stupid."

Coconut.

Coco.

Sweet little Coco.

My lips twitched. "So, you prefer a fruit over a name like Hope or Faith or We'll Survive This Island No Matter What?"

She scowled. "I just told you to forget it. You're right…it's silly."

"I didn't say it was silly."

"You laughed."

"When did I laugh?" I couldn't hold back my chuckle. "Okay, now I just did, but before, I didn't."

"You smirked."

"A smirk is not a laugh."

"It's beside the point. Coconut is off the table."

"What if I don't want it off the table?"

She huffed. "What?"

"You want to name our child after something that's become intrinsic to our lives. If it hadn't have been for coconuts, we would've starved and most likely died of dehydration. They *saved* us. What better word would suit our daughter?"

"What word?"

"Salvation. Coconuts were our salvation."

"So…you *do* like it?"

"It's kind of perfect, actually."

She peeked at me beneath her lashes. "Really?"

Pushing aside the material covering the squashed face of our newborn, I grinned. "You know what? It is."

Brushing my knuckle over her warm pudgy cheek, I murmured, "Hello, Coco. Pleasure to finally make your acquaintance."

....

APRIL

I did my best for Conner's birthday—just like I'd promised.

However, the now fifteen-year-old admitted that he'd claimed Coconut as his birthday present rather than make us carve or whittle something he didn't need. He figured their names were similar enough that we'd named her after him (I let him have his illusions).

Estelle's birthday would fall again in September (I already had ideas on how to make it the best I could) and mine continued to pass in March with no fanfare because that was how I liked it.

I hated birthdays (especially knowing I was twenty-nine and the next was the big three-O). I hated being reminded of how much time I'd wasted being angry and locked up for something I would never apologise for doing but regretted with every inch of my soul. Not because he'd deserved to die but because I was better than that. I wasn't a monster like he was, but I'd become one to extract revenge.

Despite Conner's assurances that his new baby sister was enough, I made him a slingshot out of a forked twig and the elastic string that'd tied up the survival kit found in the helicopter all those months ago. For ammunition, I'd dived on the reef for broken pieces of coral.

It didn't work very well. The tension was all wrong. But we somehow made his birthday dinner of eel and taro delicious and celebrated yet another significant event on this deserted place.

That night, as dusk fell, dorsal fins appeared in our bay for the first time since we'd crashed.

Estelle froze, yelling '*shark*' as if she was still giving birth and at risk.

However, she was wrong.

They weren't sharks.

They were dolphins.

And Conner claimed their arrival as his fifteenth birthday present, too.

Our island was no longer foreign.

We'd explored every inch.

We'd navigated and adapted and excelled.

But how many more birthdays would we attend here?

How many more years would pass?

MAY

Two things happened in May that signalled just how fast Conner was growing up.

After dealing with a squirmy baby all morning, while Estelle caught up on laundry, I was free to stomp through the forest to collect firewood.

I kept my eye out for lizards and the leaves Estelle said were okay to eat, but what I stumbled across was something entirely unappetizing.

I found Conner wanking.

The horny teenager leaned against a palm tree in the centre of the island (obviously thinking he had privacy) and had his hand down his bloody shorts.

Needless to say, I hadn't stayed.

What he did with his cock was his business, not mine.

Masturbation was a common thing (especially for teenagers), but it did remind me how lacking I'd been in my fatherly duties.

When I'd finished my forage and Conner returned, much more relaxed, to the beach, I'd taken him aside and had 'the talk.' It'd been as uncomfortable for me as it had been for him. But I had to know that he knew Pippa was off-limits as well as Estelle.

The only one not off-limits (because of marriage or relation) was Coconut, and she was only a few months old. Besides, she was banned from ever having a boyfriend, so she too was off-limits.

That meant the poor kid was doomed to spend his life as a monk. However, it didn't mean he had to look like one.

Just like my hair, his had grown long enough to tie up. His copper strands had turned strawberry blond and the splattering of freckles across his nose were so dark they morphed with his tan.

He was good looking but his straggly beard was not.

We spent the afternoon in the sea as I demonstrated how to shave with the Swiss Army knife. I didn't do it often. I wasn't fussed if I had a beard or clean-shaven, and Estelle didn't seem to have a preference, either. But Conner looked so damn grateful for the lesson, I promised myself I'd continue to teach and be there for him.

After all, it was just the two of us.

Two men.

Three girls.

We had to stick together.

JUNE

I hadn't been drunk since my eighteenth birthday.

Mostly because I'd been in jail with no access to alcohol. More recently because we'd been stranded on our island.

We'd stumbled across a few papayas last month that'd been sweet and plump. The taste of sugar after so long had been goddamn delicious. We didn't get a lot of fruit on our island, probably because there weren't many birds or bats flying over depositing seeds in their droppings.

The Papaya was a luxury and I'd thought about fermenting a few to see if Estelle and I could get tipsy (if such a thing as papaya alcohol existed) but there hadn't been many and we'd eaten them all before we realised the limited numbers.

However, none of that mattered because I was inebriated.

I was drunk.

Completely.

On my daughter.

Only a few months old, she fascinated me with how quickly she grew. Her chubby arms constantly waved and fists opened and closed. She loved lying in the sand and cried if we took her from the waves before she was ready.

It seemed being born beneath the sea made her a child of the deep and she should've grown a tail rather than kicking little legs.

Her skin tanned rather than burned. The fuzzy hair on her head was as white as Estelle's. And her eyes were a mixture of vibrant blue and glowing green.

She was the prettiest thing I'd ever seen, and if Pippa wasn't carting her around being the best babysitter we could ask for, then she was in the crook of my arm babbling nonsense.

For her crazy emotions during her pregnancy, Estelle was the most relaxed mother in the world. The saying 'you need a village to raise a baby' was entirely true.

And lucky for us, we had one.

Pippa and Conner took turns playing. No one grew bored because Coco was passed around at will.

I wished I knew the developmental stages and what to expect.

When would she walk? Talk? Crawl, even.

I had no idea.

I couldn't tell if she was smart for her age or slow.

But that wouldn't have mattered anyway.

To me, she was perfect.

Just like her mother.

Chapter Fifty-Three

....

ESTELLE

......

JULY

"I WANT TO make her something. Galloway's showing us up."

I looked up from changing Coco's rag-diaper and squinted in the sun. Pippa and Conner stood in halos, dripping wet from the sea, with an armful of red and yellow flowers.

"What do you mean?" I stood up, placing Coco on my hip. She squirmed toward Pippa, who dropped her flowers and took her from me.

The two girls had become inseparable.

"I mean G's made her a crib, a damn high-chair thingy, even a driftwood horse on skates so he can drag her through the tide like a pouncy princess." Conner dragged hands through his hair, doing his best to seem frustrated but failing.

He loved G.

In fact, they'd only become closer in the past few months since Conner well and truly left boyhood for an adult.

"Well..." I spread my hands. "What are you going to do about it? Is it a competition now?"

His brown eyes lit up. "Hell yeah, it's a competition."

I laughed. "And the flowers are commiseration for the loser?"

"Nope." Stalking toward an empty piece of fuselage that we used to soak flax, wash laundry, and gather leaves, he dumped his wilting flowers and sat down. "I'm going to paint her something."

"Paint?" Curiosity exploded. "How?"

"With these." He pointed at the flowers. "I'm gonna crush them and paint her crib pretty colours. Poor baby must hate boring brown."

My heart swelled for such an amazing teenager. "You want to paint Coco a mural."

"Yep."

"And you're going to make your own paints and brushes and everything."

"Yep."

I couldn't help it. I dashed toward him and kissed his face in a flurry of affection. "I love you, Co."

He cleared his throat. "Whatever."

Fighting my smile, I left him to it.

Whatever nostalgia I'd suffered faded with every memento we made here. I no longer hankered for a tumultuous urban town. I no longer took for granted what we had.

Life had swept us away and given us so much more.

With bubbling joy and effervescent contentedness in my soul, I went for a swim with my two daughters and left my son to somehow create a masterpiece.

....

It didn't work out.

The flower petals, once crushed, turned an unhappy ochre and bruised sienna. Despite Conner trying everything to add rainwater and smear the mess into some sort of design, he didn't get the vivid colours he was hoping for.

It did make a slight difference with decorational shadows on the crib, but his disappointment broke my heart.

Galloway teased him mercilessly, but once he'd finished ribbing him, they vanished to the other side of the island for so long I began to worry.

They returned late that night with Conner proudly holding a flax woven doll complete with stringy hair. It wasn't cuddly, it wasn't exactly pretty (unless he was going for a voodoo kind of look), but it was absolutely priceless.

And when he gave it to Coco, her toothless smile was the biggest she'd ever given.

....

AUGUST

We'd found a patch of guava last week.

They were tart and juicy and far too short supply.

They'd also been the final treat we would have for a while.

Because life had been too kind to us.

Or at least, that was what faceless fate deemed.

We'd lived on our patch of dirt for two years. We'd suffered mental boredom, debilitating depression, overwhelming happiness, pregnancy, childbirth, and puberty.

Through it all, we'd kept pushing onward, determined to stay alive and not just survive.

However, instead of being rewarded for our tenacity and never-failing belief to try, to hope, to grow, we were punished far too harshly.

Whatever doesn't kill us makes us stronger.

Our daily motto was a damn mockery after what happened.

Since Coco's birth, we'd lived in suspended joy.

We swam.

We ate.

We laughed.

We daydreamed.

And every life achievement—Conner's present for Coco, Pippa's three-tiered sandcastle, and Galloway's many creations— was recorded faithfully on our video diary.

We stored memory after memory.

Hungry to remember our present while trying to forget the past.

Coconut was our future now, and she'd been born in the wilds of Fiji. We'd accepted that if we hadn't been found after two years, the chances of ever being noticed were slim.

It gave us freedom in a way to let go. To mourn finally. To grieve a life we would never see again.

Coconut excelled.

I had no idea if the pace of her development was normal, but she exploded into personality and opinions, vocal and stubborn.

At six months old, she'd already learned how to roll over and face plant in the sand. She constantly grabbed my food if I ate with her in my lap and could sit up unsupported on her little baby rug.

Her coos and babbles reached operatic levels and she held entire conversations with Pippa and Conner when they took her to the other side of the island so Galloway and I could finally have some one on one.

After so many months of healing (probably more than if I'd been in a hospital), I finally wanted sex.

To G, it'd been an eternity. I knew because he told me the first night we resumed our sexual relationship. He didn't last long and barely pleasured me with a few thrusts before pulling out and spilling on the sand.

I teased him, saying his libido didn't match his old age. That he was as potent and horny as a fifteen-year-old. But secretly, I was awed that even now, after my body had changed and silvery stretch marks decorated skinny hips and my breasts were no longer as perky, he still wanted me.

It made my world complete.

Utterly.

Totally.

Complete.

So it made the disaster that much harder to bounce back from.

We woke to smoke.

The cloying claustrophobia of burning alive.

"Get out! Everybody *run*!" Galloway was the first to spring into action. Hauling me from our bed, he stuffed Coco into my arms and shoved me from our home.

Stumbling in shock, I gasped as I turned to face our bungalow.

Fire.

The roof is on fire.

Conner appeared, dragging a panicked Pippa to join me on the sand. "What's going on?" Pippa coughed as heavy black smoke surrounded us.

I couldn't answer.

G.

Where's G?

"Galloway!"

Coco screamed as the flames turned into an inferno, licking down the walls.

Galloway appeared, salvaging supplies from the burning building. Instead of saving himself, he did his best to save our world.

My phone with all our memories soared past.

My notebooks.

Our clothes.

Stored food and painstakingly gathered supplies.

"Hold her." Squashing screaming Coco into Pippa's arms, I sprinted forward to help.

Galloway vanished inside only to re-appear with his arms full of stuff. "Estelle, get the hell away."

"No! I want to help."

The roar of the fire whipped our words, drowning us in smoke and orange light.

Throwing the items out the door, his large hands landed on my shoulders. He shoved me backward. "Stay out. I'm almost done. Take the kids to the water's edge. Just in case."

"What about you? I won't leave without you."

"Do as I damn well say, Estelle." Turning, he disappeared into the smoke-snarling abode.

"Stelly, come on!" Conner called, already carting Pippa and Coco toward the sea. The heat from the building charred the small hairs on my arms, singeing my eyebrows.

"I'm not leaving without Galloway!"

But I also couldn't go inside. Already, smoke inhalation made me cough and splutter, blinded by the vibrantly destroying flames.

Galloway threw more belongings out and vanished one last time. When he returned, he held the blankets from our beds and charged onto the beach. Throwing the blankets onto the pile he'd saved, he ordered, "Help me get this farther from the blaze."

Together, we dragged and kicked and carried our now sand-covered and mostly ruined supplies as far as we could before our lungs gave up and coughing rendered us useless.

Stumbling down the beach, we stood with the tide lapping our ankles as we watched yet another home be taken from us.

"How…how did this happen?" Tears ran down my face.

"It's windy tonight." Galloway's voice lost the silky English rasp, becoming croaky and smoke-scratched. "Some of the embers from our fire must've caught an updraft. They landed on the roof."

I pieced the rest together.

The embers landed on the flax and the reaction was instantaneous. Dried and brittle fronds—after a year of being beaten by the sun—didn't stand a chance.

Our bungalow went up in a whoosh of fiery gold, taking with it so many hours of hard work and memories.

The stars and moon wept with us as BB-FIJI burned to the ground.

As dawn approached, we didn't move.

We *couldn't* move.

We stayed vigil, covered in soot and confounded with how we would start again.

We'd been so happy.

We'd done so well.

Now…we had to start all over again.

....
SEPTEMBER

I'd like to say our deep well of eternal optimism kept us afloat. But it was hard.

Coconut became a terror as her motor skills increased, and I couldn't leave her for a moment.

Conner and Pippa took on additional chores as well as their usual hunting and gathering. Galloway layered us all with extra responsibility—turning into a task master intent on rebuilding even before the ashes were cold.

Galloway had sunk low the morning after our home turned to cinder. He'd vanished into the forest, nursing his sadness and no doubt raging at how unfair life was to those who'd already endured so much.

I worried about him (how could I not?), but I didn't chase him. I knew when someone needed their own space, just like I knew Conner and Pippa were adaptable enough to return to sleeping beneath the stars on their sandy beds and not complain.

They understood no one could've predicted or planned for this. The fire pit had been far enough away from the hut (or so we'd thought) not to be a problem. It was no one's fault. No one to blame but the sea breeze and destroying fate.

We'd sampled a better way of life.

But we'd roughed it for long enough that we were adaptable. We mourned what we'd lost, but we didn't die. We begrudged it being taken from us, but we'd survived worse.

At least this time, no one was hurt and we could start rebuilding straightaway.

Galloway's limp didn't hold him back, and he used charcoal pencils to sketch a schematic that wouldn't just give us a replacement but a small castle for our island domain.

We didn't have many assets but time was one of them.

And I had no doubt we would triumph over this new adversity.

Once Galloway had rid himself of anguish, he didn't waste a single second. He hugged his children, made love to me, and gathered his strength to start.

I did what I could.

I hauled and chopped. I obeyed and listened. Conner became Galloway's foreman and together they worked every daylight hour.

Pippa and I kept them fed and watered. In between entertaining an inquisitive baby, we plaited new roof panels and wove flooring. We gathered vines and shredded the yellow flower bark for rudimentary fixings.

Coconut was my prison guard and my first priority was being a mother. However, somehow we all pulled together and put aside our melancholy to rise from the ashes.

We would be okay.

We would have a home again.

Because we were a family.

And family worked together.

....

OCTOBER

October brought an early onslaught of the rainy season.

Our reservoirs were full to bursting and the salt grime that permanently etched our skin was washed away with fresh water bliss.

However, our new home wasn't complete, and we spent nearly a month shivering at night, soaked to the bone, while only Coco had the luxury of a hastily created lean-to covering her crib.

Our spirits were down.

We didn't speak much.

We worked from dawn to dusk, and sometimes, well past midnight.

But it was worth it.

Because slowly, ever so slowly, walls soared once again and our new home manifested from nothing.

Our depression finally took a backseat as, day-by-day, we looked forward to a new beginning.

All over again.

Chapter Fifty-Four

....

GALLOWAY

......

NOVEMBER

IT TOOK LONGER than I wanted.

It took more effort, more energy, more strife than I could afford.

But on the 24th of November, we finally moved into our new bungalow.

Not that it could be classified as a bungalow anymore.

I'd done my best.

I'd pulled on every trick I'd been taught, every architectural secret known to man.

I'd given my all for my family.

It still had flaws, but I was proud of what I'd accomplished. Proud that I'd taken the time to chip away dovetail, dowels, and finger joints so planks slotted directly into the joists instead of relying on rope and luck. I couldn't use the fancier, and frankly, better joints like mortise because of my lack of tools.

I would've willingly killed (okay, no I wouldn't because I'd never murder again) but I would've sold anything for an adequate tool-set. It would've made my life a lot easier and meant I could've got Estelle and the kids off the cold sand sooner.

But that was in the past now.

The fire.

The destruction.

All gone.

Now, we had something better.

I'd built something of stamina and stature. I'd created something that would last.

"Galloway, it's incredible. Beyond anything I could've imagined." Estelle bounced Coconut on her hip, her eyes wide with wonder as I led her through the new place.

I'd learned from my past mistakes. Instead of using the helicopter rotor blades as our main support (limited to the size and lack of numbers) I'd chosen natural resources.

If a palm tree could withstand hurricane winds and bear the weight of heavy fruits, it was good enough for me to use as our skeleton structure.

It'd taken me weeks, constantly sharpening our barely capable and blunt axe, to hack down eight palm trees. Blisters popped and re-formed on my hands and I spent many nights with Estelle as she tended to my wounds the best she could.

Getting hurt was a part of building. I was used to it. Pity she wasn't and I caused her such worry.

Conner had been a great help digging the holes required to insert our structural support. We dug and dug until I said it was enough. And once the palm trees were wrangled into position (with help from all of us), we spent the next week mixing mud and twigs with rainwater to create the best slurry I could to cement them in place.

It wasn't bombproof—it probably wasn't even typhoon proof—but it would remain standing until something worse came along to tear it from us.

Once we'd erected the main walls, the effect was a long cabin, giving plenty of space to segment into areas of use.

I didn't just want a bungalow anymore.

I didn't want a shack on the beach.

This was our home now, and our home deserved to be worthy of luxury.

It'd taken more time, but I'd created a lounge, a kitchen (or, at least, it would be if we had running water and cooking facilities), two bedrooms for Pippa and Conner on one side of the lounge and a bedroom and nursery for Estelle, Coconut, and me on the other.

I'd even made a deck at the front so we had somewhere to sit without sand creeping up our ass-cracks. But my best invention had to be the oil drum (salvaged from the storm so many months ago) that was now laboured into position with walls for privacy and a carved funnel with holes sticking from its side to act as an outdoor shower.

I'd placed the contraption at the back of the house where the run off would feed the palm trees and the drum would catch as much rainfall as possible.

We wouldn't be able to use it too often, but at least this way, we had a chance to wash off the salt-sticky ocean, even if a rainstorm wasn't convenient.

Overall, I was happy with my creation. Happy but scared that it could all disappear again.

At least, it won't go up in flames.

That'd been the first thing I'd done. I'd buried our old fire pit and relocated it farther down the beach. For extra precaution, I also erected a wall between the flames necessary for our survival and our new property.

If the wind was strong enough and luck was nasty enough, a spark could once again land on our roof.

But that was life.

It was full of risks.

We'd done everything we could to prevent it, and we couldn't worry over something we couldn't predict.

With the offcuts of timber, I'd also created stools to use around the fire so we could sit while eating rather than sprawl.

We'd left civilisation behind. Yet somehow, we'd created our version of it here.

There were no detritus of life—it was all reused.

The longing I'd had for table and chairs was gone—we had our own.

The desire to watch TV had vanished—we had stories and imagination.

And the drive to rule my own business, to give back to a world I'd failed, and prove to myself I was a better person no longer controlled me because I had a woman and children and they'd redeemed me.

I'd donated everything I was to those I loved.

I would die for them.

I would survive for them.

And nothing was better than that.

Nothing.

....

DECEMBER

The turtles came and went.

As did Christmas.

Once again, we ignored the holiday but celebrated the arrival of our flippered friends.

All of us spent the night by their shelled sides as they dug nests, laid eggs, and hauled themselves back to the ocean.

Estelle and I made love (it was almost a tradition now) in the ocean where we'd finally given into desire for the first time. We spent the night away from the kids, confident they would watch over Coco, and watched the sunrise in each other's arms.

As we strolled back along the beach to our home and resemblance of civility, we found a turtle who'd sacrificed her life for her offspring.

The leathered beast had died only a metre from the sea. She lay there pristine, so perfect and wizened, it seemed she'd only slipped into a nap.

But we knew.

Just like we knew if the kids were hurt. Or the winds had changed. Or the temperature was hotter than last month. Our perception was so much more sensitive, and we understood sleep hadn't taken her but death.

I didn't look at Estelle, but we'd been given a dilemma.

We had a turtle.

We could live because of its death.

We could eat her flesh.

Use her shell.

She would have our eternal gratitude.

I didn't know if Estelle shared my thoughts, but it didn't matter.

Because that was all they were.

Thoughts.

We wouldn't desecrate such a magnificent creature.

Wordlessly, we each grabbed a flipper and hauled her bulk into the sea. She floated serenely, slowly taken by the gentle currents.

Her body would feed sharks and fish.

She would vanish to give others another day.

But not us.

JANUARY

Pippa turned ten.

For her birthday gifts, we all contributed random things for her bedroom. Estelle made her a set of coconut vases for knickknacks and keepsakes. Conner carved a sunburst on the wall above her leaf-stuffed bed, and I wove a miniature hammock to house Puffin and Mr. Whisker Wood.

The day was good.

But the rest of the month wasn't.

Things were changing.

Things we couldn't afford to change.

We ate the best we could.

We stayed as varied as possible and constantly tried new things (sometimes to the detriment of our digestive systems), but we attempted to get as many nutrients as we could to combat the side effects of living on an island.

We'd lasted longer than I thought.

But it was inevitable.

We were all so skinny, becoming slowly malnourished.

We were all salt-covered and sun-beaten, switching from surviving to suffering.

Internally, our bodies had reached their limits.

I grew woozy if I stood too fast. I struggled to swallow.

I had vicious food cravings for things my body needed: red meat for iron, bread for carbohydrates, and sugar for glucose.

I grew tired more easily, and we'd begun to nap longer in the afternoon beneath our umbrella tree.

Even my hair felt different, less full and like straw.

Conner and Pippa continued to grow, and Coco exploded in height and energy daily. But Estelle admitted late one night that her periods had finally stopped.

That our fear of another pregnancy was over because her body no longer had the nutrition required to ovulate.

We treated it as a success.

We had sex, and I didn't pull out.

We laughed and said nature had finally given us contraception.

We ignored what it truly meant.

We loved our island and new way of life.

But it didn't love us.

It was slowly killing us.

....

<u>FEBRUARY</u>

"What's your most favourite thing in the world?" Estelle angled the phone at Conner, recording yet another home movie.

Today, she'd recorded countless memories.

Today was Coconut's first birthday.

"This little nut right here." Conner tickled Coco, who sat happily in his lap.

She didn't understand the importance of such a day or why I snuck off with her mother halfway through the festivities to make love in the same sea where she'd been delivered.

She squealed and laughed as Pippa and Conner buried her little legs in the sand and crafted her one large candle with the words

'You're our Favourite Nut' in the moulded flame.

It'd been a cute day, and we were all tired from tenderising and kebabing the octopus we'd eaten for lunch.

Estelle angled the phone in my direction. "And your favourite thing, G?"

My eyes met hers; my cock twitched. I'd had her a few hours ago, yet I could go another round. I didn't know if was the pure Fijian air or the fact she constantly teased me by wandering around half-naked in her fading bikini. Either way, she was right when she said my libido was out of control. Even with my rapidly depleting reserves.

"You, of course. You're my wife."

A year.

One full year she'd been my wife. We hadn't celebrated, but we had retied flax rings around our fingers in symbol for the ones that'd disintegrated long ago.

"And you, Pippi?" Estelle blushed, dropping her gaze from mine to focus on the lanky ten-year-old.

"Um..." Pippa tapped her bottom lip. "I think it would be our new house. I love my room."

My heart warmed.

Estelle angled the phone for a selfie, adding herself to the recording. "Well, my favourite thing is this, right here, right now. You guys and hanging out in the hot afternoon sun."

Conner groaned. "Cheesy." Grabbing Coco's hands, he rocked her on his lap as if they were rowing out to sea. "And you, little nut? What's your favourite thing?" He blew raspberries on her naked belly.

If we were ever found, the first thing we would have to do was scramble for clothes. Conner and I never wore anything other than board-shorts. Pippa and Estelle wore their bathing suits, and little Coco preferred to crawl around nude or grudgingly with a diaper.

She *hated* clothing.

Coco giggled as Conner blew another round of raspberries. "Co...co...co."

We all froze.

"Did she...did she just say her first word?" Pippa's mouth popped wide.

Estelle zoomed her phone to her daughter, waddling on her knees to get closer. "Say it again, Coco. What's your favourite thing?"

My daughter's blue-green eyes zeroed in on Conner and repeated. "Co co co co co."

"So her favourite thing is herself?" Pippa wrinkled her nose. "I thought her first word was supposed to be da-da or Pip-pa?"

Conner burst into laughter, clutching the squirmy baby and punching the air. "Wrong, suckers. *I'm* her favourite person. Didn't you hear her? She *obviously* said Co...that's me."

The ensuing war lasted all night.

And by the end of the verbal debate (Pippa couldn't tolerate that Coco had chosen Conner over her), it was undeniable.

Coco's first word was Co.

For her older brother.

Her favourite person.

Chapter Fifty-Five

······································

ESTELLE

······

MARCH

TWO MONTHS AGO, Pippa turned single digits into double and grew into a wonderful ten-year-old.

One month ago, Coco uttered her first word.

This month, we were focused on surviving the constant rain showers and thunder clouds. We spent more time indoors as fleeting morning sunshine switched to downpours in the early afternoon.

We did our best to stay occupied while cooped up inside. However, there was only so much whittling or finessing we could do before boredom became an issue.

The only one of us not struggling was Coco. Ever since she'd said her first word, she hadn't shut up. She muttered nonsense, sporadically inserting a word she heard us use.

Thank God, Galloway didn't swear as much anymore. Otherwise, we'd have a cursing infant.

One morning (when the sun seemed stronger and more likely to stick around), I got up early and attempted to have another day of fun. As the days rolled by, they morphed faster into a blur. I hated that life had accelerated way too fast.

Ever since my periods had stopped, I knew we were on borrowed time. Our bodies had used up whatever reserves we had left (making us dizzy, achy, and not able to concentrate), and unless we escaped, we couldn't live the idyllic life I'd dreamed, hidden for the rest of our days in paradise.

We had to leave.

We had to run.

And in unanimous consensus, Galloway started building another raft.

He gathered more bamboo and sat in the shade for hours plotting how best to secure it so it didn't sink like last time.

But for now, I was focused on spending the day with my family.

While they slumbered, I scooped up dry seaweed and draped it in our umbrella tree as an ugly version of tinsel and tore up pages of my notebook to fold cranes and origami love hearts for silly gifts when everyone awoke.

My songs and penned lyrics had become tools to play with rather than write in. With no pens or ink, Galloway had done his best to provide me with twigs charred in the fire to write with charcoal.

But it wasn't the same.

The loss of my writing left a piece of me hollow and smarting, but it was nothing compared to the horribleness of waking two weeks later and finding my phone wouldn't turn on.

No amount of solar power would charge it.

No tapping the battery would coax it.

We had a death on the island, and it'd taken our memories, our photos, our videos, our calendar, our very way of life with it.

The dead technology took our final piece of sufferance, pushing us one step closer to abandoning our island that seemed to have abandoned us.

We were no longer wanted here.

Once our mourning was over and every attempt at bringing the phone back to life failed, I placed the dead but so, so precious device into the carved box Galloway had made me for my last birthday.

Inside, I'd stored my expired credit cards, waterlogged passport, and the three gold and silver bracelets I'd worn on the flight.

Everything that'd seemed so important, now rotted in a box unneeded in this new existence. Gold was no longer a currency, coconuts were. A passport was no longer top possession, our Swiss Army knife was.

Funny how things we thought we couldn't live without suddenly become superficial when faced with the truth.

The truth that we entered this world with nothing and left with the exact same sum.

The only one who didn't suffer the dreaded curse of pining for their past was Coconut.

She had sand for blood and wind for breath. She could swim before she could walk (not that a few stumbles could be called walking), she craved more and more solids, and my milk was drying up, unwanted.

Unfortunately, her naps that'd allowed me time to fish or tend to our camp were few and far between as was the cooing and babbling. Her little vocabulary had transformed into a well-versed conversationalist.

Galloway had earned her second word. Da-da. And as much as I would love her to call me mummy, her girlish heart belonged entirely to G.

I adored that she'd turned from a helpless newborn into a tiny independent person, but I hated that my phone was no longer able to capture her growth and imprison her giggling chortles for me to look back on and relive happy times.

Because happy times were few and hard to come by.

Especially as lethargy and vacancy crept over us like a fog determined to smother.

We tried to fight it.

We did our best to reverse it.

But we couldn't prevent the inescapable.

Our avenue for recording was gone.

Our perseverance for living was done.

We put on a brave face, but as our bodies slowly starved and storms did their best to relocate our island to Antarctica, it became harder and harder to remain happy where everything seemed so tough.

....

APRIL

Conner shed fifteen for sixteen under a starry evening and crude jokes.

He and Galloway hung out while Pippa, Coco, and I spent the evening doing whatever we could to treat Conner like a king.

We'd all chipped in and created him a flax sleeping bag for the nights he wanted to camp away and Galloway had carved a doll with big lips and boobs, saying it was his first girlfriend.

That had earned him a punch followed by surly curses.

Two days after Conner's birthday, we lay on the sand digesting breakfast of taro and fish, and for the first time, we heard something that wasn't the wind rustling through the trees.

The loud foghorn hung heavily in the air, echoing in my ears, heralding all of us to the shore.

We stared for minutes, doing our best to squint on the horizon. If we had my phone, we could've taken a photo and zoomed in to see what lay out there (like a cheap version of binoculars).

We'd done that a few times.

Conner had repeatedly snapped images of every inch of the horizon, enlarging the photo to its maximum potential and studying for any signs of life, any other island, any hint that we weren't so alone.

Over the course of our years here, we'd seen plumes of commercial airliners, soaring thousands of feet above our head. We'd spotted a fishing trawler far, far out to sea that didn't notice our hastily burning signal fire. And imagined voices when tiredness turned our thoughts into mush.

But this…this sounded closer.

Real.

Was it a tanker? A barge? A ferry? Some sort of nautical magic that could whisk us away from here?

As the afternoon ticked on, our legs grew tired, and we sat, one by one, in the sand.

And we stared.

We stared and stared until daylight switched to moonlight and we had to admit what we'd been chanting in our heads for hours.

They're gone.
No one's there.
We're alone.

· ·

MAY

Rustling multihued feathers switched the calendar to May, donating hundreds of squawking parrots to our island.

We didn't know where they'd migrated from but we tracked the jewels creatures through the trees in awe. Pippa trailed beneath them, collecting discarded indigo and emerald feathers, while Conner climbed into the branches to see if they were tame.

We didn't look at them as food.

Merely pretty animals to enjoy.

Not that they stayed long.

As quickly as they'd arrived, they flew off.

A pandemonium of parrots in a rainbow blur.

A few days later, Pippa decided she no longer needed Puffin as a security blanket.

And Coco much preferred her flax voodoo doll, courtesy of Conner, to the tatty stuffed kitten.

I didn't know why that upset me, but it did. The faded cat was no longer wanted. No longer carted around the island by its paw.

It was discarded.

However, I gave it a forever home on our shelves in the house, sitting pride of place between the salt bowl and dried mint.

RIP, Puffin.

He'd gained new employment as our mascot.

Chapter Fifty-Six

GALLOWAY

ONE YEAR BEFORE THE CRASH

"DID YOU KNOW about this?"

I stared into the distrusting eyes of my term manager. We were all assigned a caseworker to take our grumblings and requests to the bosses.

I never summoned mine. Never had a reason to. And they'd never summoned me in return. I was a murderer serving a life sentence. There was nothing more to discuss.

Until now.

"Answer the question, Mr. Oak."

I shook my head. "No, how could I?"

"You didn't plant this evidence?"

"No."

"Yet you admitted to committing the crime?"

"Yes."

"Why would you do that?"

"Because it's the truth."

My manager closed the folder in front of him. "Well, it just so happens, the truth has been proved a lie."

My heart (that'd been dead every day since they'd imprisoned me) picked up. "What?"

"You're free to go, Mr. Oak. Time to leave."

JUNE

IT'S TIME TO leave.

We'd waited too long.

We no longer had a choice.

"I love you, Estelle." Her back bowed as I entered her.

She was hot and wet and slippery.

And always so ready for me.

No matter that it'd been a busy day of fishing and repairing the net after it snagged on coral. No matter that Coconut had been colicky and unable to rest. No matter that our happiness levels had shrivelled more and more as life got harder and harder. She never said no to me. Never made me feel like a nuisance or hindrance.

I adored her for that.

She still smiled when she looked my way. Still blew me kisses as we worked side by side. And still welcomed me to take her no matter what time of day.

I loved her.

I'd married her.

But I didn't know how much longer I could keep her.

"We'll try to leave soon," I murmured as I thrust gently into her.

Her legs spasmed around my hips, her arms slung over my shoulders. Tonight, we'd opted for quick, quiet pleasure, staying in our bark-decorated room, no energy to go to the beach or indulge in a night swim.

"Is it safe?" Estelle gasped as I withdrew and re-entered.

I didn't know how to answer her question.

So I didn't.

Plus, it wasn't exactly sexy talk, but the thought of getting off our island was paramount. It tainted everything. It was an obsession we all shared.

Everyone but Coco, of course. She didn't know any different. She ran on uncoordinated legs on the beach and swam with ungainly splashes in the ocean. Her favourite food was her namesake. Her lullaby and comfort were the island sounds.

If we left (*when* we left), she would struggle. We were the outlanders here, but if we somehow sailed back to society, she would be the interloper. A castaway baby with no birth certificate, no passport, no home.

My heart clenched thinking about stranding her there like we'd once been stranded here.

But that won't happen.

She'd have us. All of us. Conner and Pippa would live with us. Our family wouldn't change, only our current circumstances.

"Stop thinking about it, G." Estelle's fingers slipped through my hair, grounding me to her. "Only think of tonight. Of us."

My heart tightened and pleasure replaced my worry.

She was my wife.

I obeyed.

....

JULY

Time was never on our side.

It either flew too fast, hurtling us toward a desolate future. Or slowed to a maddening crawl, slowing our progress.

Despite our dedication to leaving, it took much longer than we'd hoped.

Our energy levels dwindled but the life raft slowly took shape through bleeding hands and broken blisters.

Estelle and Pippa helped.

They worked next to Conner and me as we tied and secured, tested and hoped.

I'd opted for a different design this time.

Just like I'd improved our house, so too did I tweak the original floatable (or not so floatable) platform.

This time, I'd done my best to tie the bamboo into the shape of a kayak. The hollow poles joined at an apex where we would sit and row with baby Coconut fastened securely in the middle, far away from the drowning sea.

Hopefully, the outrigger would be long enough to hold extra supplies, strong enough to carry the weight of stoppered water and blankets for shade, and fast enough to get us to a new home before we died of starvation.

However, instead of feeling proactive and upbeat, we struggled. The longer we worked on the boat, the more fear solidified. Our happiness turned heartless, demanding putrid payment for everything we'd enjoyed.

Our ill-nourished bodies had forced our hand. We had to leave if we wanted to breathe. But the thought of sailing away from the only place of value kept us restless and sleepless.

Conner, for his sixteen-year-old strength, had faded just like the rest of us. His muscles had slowly shrunk, and his ribs stood out like an unplayed harp beneath his skin.

Pippa was much the same. She hadn't hit puberty yet, and her skinny, girlish body showed no hint of womanly curves or budding breasts.

Not that our bony forms stopped us from working hard and pushing each other to the brink.

If we weren't working on the life raft, we were completing other tasks.

Estelle would cook.

Pippa would babysit.

And Conner would be up in a palm tree on look-out. We'd all become great climbers to reach the green coconuts in the fronds, and occasionally, sat in the swaying height, hoping to see rescue before we cast off and gave our lives to fate.

Our kayak was almost done.

Our time was almost up.

So why couldn't I shake the God-awful feeling that tragedy was once again coming for us?

Chapter Fifty-Seven

••

ESTELLE

••••••

AUGUST

THREE YEARS.

Three long, incredible, trying, amazing, awful, blissful, terrible years.

29th of August, the day of the crash, loomed closer.

At least, I thought it was August.

After my phone died, I had to keep a record of the days by scratching each sunset into our umbrella tree, counting the strikes, knowing in my heart we were all getting tired.

We'd survived so much: storms, fevers, stomach bugs, and a virus we'd all succumbed to, most likely transmitted by a mosquito.

Through it all, we raised a healthy baby into a toddler, a child into a young girl, and a boy into a capable sixteen-year-old.

Conner had changed from scrawny boy into gaunt young man. His copper hair was more russet gold from so much swimming and his skin would never again be snow-white but forever bronzed like an Arabian prince.

I pitied the female race who'd missed out on such a brilliant specimen and kind-hearted individual. It made me proud that Galloway and I had (in some small measure) a role in raising him.

And because of those qualities, and the fact that he was so loved by us all, it made what happened next even more tragic.

•••••••••••••••••••••••••••

SEPTEMBER

"Help! G! Stel! *Help!*"

Ice water splashed down my spine as Pippa tore into the

---

house, disrupting me in the middle of changing the tatty t-shirt that'd become Coconut's diaper. Abandoning my child, I shot upright and grabbed her quaking shoulders. "What is it? What's happened?"

Pippa could barely speak. Tears tracked down her face, horror consuming her completely. "Co. He…he…he's hurt."

Galloway charged inside, twigs and leaves sticking in his long hair, the Swiss Army knife clenched in his hand. "What? What is it?"

Taking Pippa's hand, I shoved past him. "Conner. We've got to go."

Together, we sprinted faster than we'd ever ran before to the water's edge where Conner lay in the shallows on his back. The tide licked around him, almost as if soothing whatever had hurt him. Apologetic. Sympathetic.

I *hated* the water for touching him.

I *despised* whatever had hurt him.

Slamming to his knees, Galloway scooped Conner's head into his lap, slapping his cheeks. "Conner, open your eyes, mate."

I took his left hand while Pippa took his right. We all kneeled before him as if he were the alter accepting our final prayers.

No!

This couldn't be happening.

The aura of dying wasn't real. The stench of agony wasn't true. *This isn't happening!*

Galloway tapped Co's cheeks again, rousing him. "Conner. Come on. Open your eyes."

Conner groaned; his face scrunched tight from pain. "I—can't—*breathe*."

"Co, no." Pippa sobbed. "I'll breathe for you."

"Wo—won't work, Pip…"

Terrible despair lashed her. "Come on. Don't be a jerk." Swatting at her tears, she bowed as if to give him mouth to mouth. "You're fine, you'll see."

"Pip, don't." I held her back. I couldn't fix him if she was in my line of sight. What did this? What happened?

There was no blood. No bite.

What dared hurt my son?

And that was when I saw it.

The spine, the deadly quill, the poisonous barb I'd hoped never to see again. But this time…it wasn't a minor graze on his instep but a full quiver pinpricking his heart.

A stonefish.

He'd been so careful. He fished with flip-flops. He did his best to stay where it was safe.

My hands flew up to cover my face as hiccupping horror fell from my lips.

Galloway's eyes wrenched to mine, dancing over my frozen features then to the death sentence on Conner's chest.

"Shit." He turned white. His hands fumbled on the spines of venom, ripping them from Conner's flesh as if they were grenades about to detonate.

But it was too late.

The damage had already been done.

Last time, Conner had cheated extermination. This time...necrosis had won.

This can't be real.

It can't!

My shoulders trembled as I swallowed sob after sob.

No amount of hot water and poultices would save him this time.

Galloway shifted, laying Conner's head on the wet sand and moving to his side. Weaving large hands together, he placed them over Conner's heart, ready to palpitate him back to living, ready to resuscitate and revive and reverse the horrible, horrible catastrophe.

Conner grimaced, his lips dark blue, his eyes shot red. His fingers spasmed with toxins, clawing at his throat as his body succumbed to anaphylactic shock.

He suffocated.

Right before us.

"Conner, *no!*" Pippa blew air into his mouth as Galloway started CPR.

Shock turned me into a mute statue witnessing Galloway's long hair wafting around his face with every compression, Pippa's white cheeks as she exhaled into her brother's mouth, and the warm tide never ceasing in its caresses.

A stonefish was fatal in high doses. I doubted anyone had had a larger dose.

I have to do something.

Anything.

But I knew, better than them, better than Conner, that there was nothing.

Even if we had an antidote and ambulance, there was nothing anyone could do.

The Grim Reaper had finally visited.

For three years, we'd survived together without loss. We'd

laughed, cried, kept our diet varied, and fought our illnesses with strength. We ignored every statistic saying a crash landing like ours would ensure another death before long.

This wasn't fate.

This was destiny.

It had finally found us.

To claim a life far too young.

Conner met my eyes, seawater tracking down his cheeks. "Stel—"

I captured his spasmodic fingers, bringing them to my lips. While my husband and daughter fought to keep him alive, I offered solitude and safe harbour as he slipped.

Slipped and slipped, faded and faded.

"I love you, Conner," I whispered. "So, so much."

He couldn't reply but his gaze burned brown with bravery. Reaching out, I touched Pippa's shoulder, creating a connected triangle between us. "Shush, it's okay, Pippi. I've got you."

The moment my hand landed on her skin, Pippa dissolved. Her spine rolled and tears pried from her soul. My touch blared the truth; truth she didn't want to believe.

He's leaving us.

She collapsed into gut-wrenching sobs. "No. *No!*" Her fingers looped with Conner's as she chanted over and over, "Don't go to sleep, Co. Please, *please* don't go to sleep. I can't make it without you."

My own tears made everything a water-world as I held my two children and gave into the heart-cramping, soul-tearing knowledge that we knocked on demise's door.

Galloway coughed back tears as Conner convulsed in his embrace. The teenager's heart pounded so hard, his pulse was visible in his white-shocked neck. His tan couldn't hide the spread of suffocation, turning him icicle-blue.

"It's okay, Conner," I murmured. "It's okay."

It's not okay.

Nothing about this is okay!

Pippa screamed and struggled.

But Conner couldn't comfort her.

His eyes remained locked on mine.

Brown to hazel, young to old.

This boy loved me.

I loved him.

I sobbed harder, giving him every ounce of my affection. "I love you, Conner." My back gave out as I brought his hand to my mouth and kissed him. I let gravity sway me to his venom-riddled form and I kissed his brow, his nose, his cheeks.

His eyes remained open, stealing final glimpses of this world. His skin lost life-luminosity as his mouth sucked air.

His body suffered too much poison.

His nervous system shut down.

His consciousness was the last lingering piece tethering him to pain.

I didn't want him in agony any longer.

Pulling me away, Galloway snatched me to him, hugging me, hugging Pippa as we worshipped at the feet of an angel and said farewell.

Pippa peppered kisses all over his face, murmuring promises and pacts. Galloway patted him and stroked his cheek, unable to hold back his sadness, vowing to keep his sister and me safe for him.

Conner's eyes landed on each of us as his lungs failed and his heart gave up its valiant beat.

His body thrashed.

His lips mouthed, 'I love you.'

And then…

he

was

gone.

••••••••••••••••••••••••••••••

<u>OCTOBER</u>

Conner.

I couldn't say his name without battling wet, heavy tears.

I couldn't think about him without wanting to tear apart the past and make it false, to reincarnate him from a terribly sadistic joke.

I even struggled to say my daughter's name as it reminded me too much of Conner's grin when she'd said her first word. The similarities between Conner and Coco mutilated my heart on a minutely basis.

He'd *loved* me.

And left me.

For days, I couldn't get out of bed.

No one could.

We lay frozen, neither eating nor drinking; only cracking the tomb of our sorrow to care for Coco when she squalled.

Coco.

Those two letters were forever smeared in woe.

Co.

Co.

Come back.

I'm sorry.

I couldn't understand how the quills had lodged in his chest. How had he stepped wrongly? Did he fall? Had a wave pushed him onto the reef?

Or had it just been one of those things—unforeseen, unplanned, but the tiniest mistake that cost the best of lives.

We would never know.

We'd forever wonder what stole Conner from us.

And we'd never have an enemy in which to extract vengeance.

....

The funeral was held two weeks ago, yet the pain of his loss felt only hours old.

Pippa hadn't said a word since we'd gathered on the same beach where we'd laid to rest our pilot and her parents and weighed down Conner's body for the tide to claim.

He'd looked asleep. Cold and unloved. But only asleep.

Watching the waves slowly claim him, slipping over his closed eyes and parted lips, drove me wild.

Galloway had to hold me, putting up with my fists and screams, as Conner slowly left land for sea. I craved comfort from my husband's arms but I felt undeserving. Who did Conner have to hug and kiss?

He was alone now.

That night, we didn't move from the beach. Pippa sought solitude rather than our arms, and we sat in the moonlight with silent sadness in our souls.

Once the sun rose and Conner had vanished, we added his name to the small shrine of the Evermore parents with a newly carved cross and an inscription of our everlasting love. We plucked a hundred red flowers and scattered them over the sand in his memory. And we lost each other, retreating to our private corners of grief.

The day we lost Conner was the day we lost all energy to continue.

I didn't remember much of those weeks.

I didn't remember comforting or speaking or doing more than eating when my body demanded and crying when the dysphoria grew too much to be contained.

Pippa curled in on herself, turning into an inconsolable wraith.

Galloway spent a day hunting every stonefish he could find, slaughtering them one by one. It terrified me that he would step wrong and suffer the same end as Conner.

Death didn't pay for death.

And once he'd finished, his shoulders wracked with silent sobs, crying for Conner, our future, and a past he still couldn't shake.

Even Coconut grieved.

Her questions about Conner petered out the longer we shook our heads and gave no answer to his return. Her babbling conversation turned quiet and morose as if, even at her young age, she understood that her favourite older brother was gone forever.

We'd been so brave.

We'd been so strong.

But this…this was the breaking point I feared would ruin us.

....

NOVEMBER

Grief had an awful way of lingering.

It tainted, not just our crying hearts and every thought, but I tasted it in the sky. I ate it for dinner. I slept with it at night.

After our self-inflicted solitude, we found our way back to each other.

For two months, we existed in a daze, constantly expecting Conner to charge up the beach with an arm full of freshly caught fish or proudly carry Coco to go swimming.

Pippa jumped with hope if the wind whistled in the trees, morbidly mimicking Conner's laugh.

Galloway threw everything he had into protecting Coconut. He became mistrustful of *everything,* and the light that'd shone so bright in his gaze, the same light that mirrored in mine, had been snuffed out.

For so many months, we'd beaten adversity together…now, I felt more alone than ever.

Night-time turned into nightmares. I couldn't escape them. I couldn't stop the heartache of missing him.

One star-spangled night, Galloway kissed my cheek and spooned me.

I tensed, expecting sex. Sex I wasn't emotionally ready for.

Instead, he whispered, "We loved him, Estelle. We loved him a son, friend, and brother. But we can't keep killing ourselves this way. He's gone. We're still here. We have to keep going.

"He would want us to move on. He trusts us to care for Pippa." He embraced me hard. "We owe it to him not to give up."

My tears came afresh, but this time, they weren't full of weeping acid but pure with parting.

This man wasn't my other half.

He was my heart.

And no matter what happened, that would never change.

....

Days vanished without us bothering to count them.

The rainy season pelted us, but we ignored it.

The sunshine burned us, but we paid no attention.

The constant sameness of our humid, tropical island was a mockery to our pain.

We lost sight of how to be happy, how to laugh in fear's face and survive in death's glare.

We bowed under the pressure and finally came to terms with the fact if we didn't leave, we would die.

We would die, and we wouldn't really care.

We weren't playing house on the beach.

We weren't living a fantastical dream where society couldn't touch us, everyday flu couldn't find us, and stress of work couldn't harm us.

This was real.

Conner was dead.

Dead.

We were the gateway and final destination to life and death.

We were the morgue, the supermarket, the hospital, the house, the bank, the pharmacy, the restaurant. We were *every mortal thing* and the pressure to fight had finally vanished.

....

DECEMBER

Only a few dates smudged and sullied into perspicuous recollection.

A few dates that would forever be known as life-changing.

The date Madi uploaded my song and changed my career was one.

The night we crash landed on our island was two.

The morning Coco was born was three.

The afternoon Conner died in our arms was four.

And the upcoming nightmare in our future was five.

Five dates that defined me.

Five dates that would carry such heavy, heavy weight.

Even now, three months since Conner abandoned us, we hurt just as badly.

Three months since we'd genuinely laughed and smiled.

Three months since our will to survive had dried up.

However, with death came life, and Coconut blossomed overnight. She morphed from human larvae into a chatty little girl, magically stealing our sadness and reminding us how to smile again. Her tiny cheeks and intelligent eyes acted as a balm for our smarting memories.

The tears were never far away, and Pippa was irrevocably changed. She'd become a stranger who we shared our island with. The last surviving member of her bloodline.

But life dragged us onward, patching up our wounds with hours and days, slowly healing us despite our wishes.

The turtles visited (as they did every year) but this time, no one stayed up to witness their night long laying.

We were too tired.

Too weak.

Growing weaker by the day.

One night, the urge to connect with Galloway overwhelmed me and I stole his hand to lead him to bed.

Pippa remained by the fire, staring into the flames the same way she did every night. The only time she remembered she was alive was when I put Coco in her arms. Then she would blink and converse, shedding her cape of listlessness until the squirmy toddler decided she'd had enough being the emotional medicine for a severely sad sister.

For some time, I wondered if it'd been fairer for fate to take Pippa's life instead of Conner's. She carried her family's death too hard. It might've been kinder for her to pass, to find her mother and father in the great wide ether and trade this existence for a celestial one.

But fate didn't work that way. It didn't give invitations to its upcoming events. It just orchestrated what would happen with no apology or suggestion.

We didn't speak as I pulled Galloway inside our bedroom and hurriedly undid the bows of my bikini.

Galloway's eyes burned with an intensity I'd never seen before as he shed his board-shorts and gathered me in his arms.

Our kiss was wild and furious.

Our coupling messy and violent.

And after whatever compulsion had driven us was sated, we lay in the dark and agreed.

It was time.

"We're leaving this week, Estelle. It's time to prepare the

boat."

We were saying goodbye.
Leaving Conner in paradise.
It was time to return home.

Chapter Fifty-Eight

• ..

GALLOWAY

• • • • • •

JANUARY

I'D HAD ENOUGH.

My family were dying.

Conner had already left us.

I wouldn't lose any more.

I'd never missed someone as much as I missed him.

Not even my mother or father.

Conner was more to me than a kid I shared an island with.

So much more.

And now, he'd disappeared, leaving us to deal with the wreckage.

I hated him for that.

I hated that he'd checked out and left us here.

But I hated myself, too.

While Estelle punished herself for his death, I beat myself up for ever letting Conner take so many risks.

Fishing was dangerous.

Fishing alone even more so.

What was I thinking?

Why didn't I go with him? Why didn't I take over and force the boy to stay on the shore?

I knew the answers to my questions: because Conner wouldn't have accepted my ultimatums. If he was forbidden the ocean, he would've been in trees and broken his back. If he'd been denied fishing, he would've found some other risky pastime.

It was his destiny.

Just like ours hadn't been when we'd crashed.

Pippa turned eleven but pleaded not to celebrate. She chose to spend the day cuddled in Conner's flax sleeping bag on her own.

I worried about her.

About all of us.

Grief was a constant entity poking me full of painful holes. I wanted to rope the bastardly emotion into a noose, beat it up, then hack it to pieces with our blunt axe.

I couldn't keep feeling so hopeless, so useless, so eternally sad.

So I threw myself into finding salvation for those of us left behind.

For a week, we stockpiled and prepared the kayak with food. I built a ballast on the side to keep us upright when navigating the choppy reef, stealing the design from a Balinese long boat.

Pippa helped prepare, but her heart wasn't in it. She preferred to spend her time on the beach where Conner and her parents had said farewell.

I dreaded the day when we finally disembarked.

Would she come with us or would she be unable to say goodbye? Their bodies were gone, but their souls remained on our island. And I didn't know if she'd be able to tear herself away from those she adored.

While Estelle wrapped our belongings in palm fronds and hacked down coconuts, I sailed around the atoll a few times to test how seaworthy the new vessel was. So far, the rickety, flax tied, bamboo crafted outrigger withstood enough. However, the four oars I'd made had dwindled to three.

Conner wouldn't be there to help me steer or navigate.

His loss pulverised my heart.

Our home was slowly less and less important, just a shell to abandon when we left. We were as prepared as we could be.

However, even for our forward preparation, it was water that delayed us.

January was the hottest month.

There was no respite from the humid heat.

Not one raincloud to top up our stores of drinking water.

Not one breath of wind to help guide us.

So even though everything inside said to leave, now, *this very moment*.

We couldn't.

We had to wait until we had enough to journey.

We had to wait until death visited one last time.

....

FEBRUARY

Coconut turned two.

We didn't celebrate.

Pippa had turned eleven.

She refused to celebrate.

The hot weather finally turned to showers.

We couldn't celebrate.

Because although we'd been waiting for the rain to free us, the reality had finally hit home.

We were leaving.

Forever.

However, one of us was going on a much different journey.

An unplanned journey.

A cruise up the River Styx rather than the Pacific Ocean.

Chapter Fifty-Nine

....

ESTELLE

......

As humans, we abhor death.
We're taught from birth to fear the unknown, cling to the known, and receive
our limited time on earth.
But what if that's a lie?
What if we should embrace death?
Would we be at peace knowing those that'd left us existed in another dimension?
That we weren't nothing the moment we took our final breath?
Death was my enemy.
But could it ultimately be my friend?
Taken from a carving on the umbrella tree.

...

THREE YEARS, SIX months.

Four deaths.

One birth.

Countless triumphs.

Untold failures.

Forty-two months.

One hundred and eighty-two weeks.

One thousand two hundred and seventy-six days.

And one terrified woman with the feeling of premonition on her shoulders.

Our bodies couldn't take much more but we were almost there…almost free.

However, everything changed with a splinter and a scream.

Over the years, Galloway had built many things—a firewood storage shed, rain reservoirs, and even an outhouse to keep us private when human nature called. For years, he'd hacked at branches, woven rope, and built with no complications.

So why should the morning of our departure be any different?

I couldn't explain it.

I woke with terror.

And it only grew worse as more hours passed.

Part of me believed it was because we were leaving today. We were saying goodbye and pushing off into an unknown destiny. But the other part of me believed it was for something else.

Galloway.

I'm worried about him.

I flittered around him while he tightened last-minute strappings and secured extra coconuts into the kayak. I stayed busy (like we all did) to avoid the soul-sucking memories of Conner.

Pippa helped prepare Coco, dressing her in a fresh nappy and forcing the scrambling child into an old t-shirt of hers (Pippa had outgrown most of her things), and we all stopped for lunch in the noonday heat.

Once fish and prawns had been devoured, we returned to our tasks.

Galloway headed into the trees to cut down an extra branch to use as a push-off pole and I went with him to help strip the skinny trunk of twigs and leaves.

Sweat poured down his forehead as he hacked away with our blunt axe. His hollow stomach and pronounced ribs decorated him with shadows with every swing. Finally, the chosen branch snapped, soaring to the ground.

Galloway ducked to catch it.

But yanked his hand away a millisecond later. "Crap."

"What? What happened?" A dizzy spell caught me as I shot up from my haunches.

Pressing his index to his mouth, he sucked on his injury. "I'm okay, just a splinter."

My heart rate slowed a little. He'd had countless splinters. They weren't anything to fear.

"Here, let me help." Pulling his hand from his mouth, I quickly inspected where the sliver of wood punctured his digit. A small droplet of blood welled beneath his fingernail. "It's gone into your cuticle."

Peering closer, I pressed the swollen flesh to make sure the splinter was gone. "I can't see anything. It must've just been a little prick."

"A little prick?" His lips formed a crescent smile, doing his best at joviality.

Three months was a long time after Conner's death.

Three months was no time at all.

I laughed quietly, doing my best to meet his effort. "Well, I wouldn't use the word little when calling your, eh—" My eyes went to his shorts. "I'd call my husband a very well-endowed prick."

His eyes warmed. "I'll never tire of hearing you say that."

"What, prick?"

"No." He chuckled. "Husband."

"Husband?"

"Yes, wife. Never stop calling me it."

My heart fluttered. "I won't."

Seriousness replaced fake merriment. "I mean it, Estelle. We're leaving today. Tonight who knows where we'll be. Tomorrow…we might be alive or dead."

He cupped my cheek, bringing me forward to kiss. "But no matter where we are, promise me we'll always be married."

I grasped his wrist as we kissed softly, then fiercely.

When we broke apart, I vowed, "Forever, G. You'll always be mine and I'll always be yours."

We drifted off to our remaining chores, our thoughts locked on the terrifying unknown.

....

A few hours later, when I brought Galloway some water, his forehead was burning up and a hazy film covered his eyes.

Instantly, the dizziness in my blood switched to cold-sweats. "Are you feeling okay?"

He took the bottled water, guzzling it down. "I'm fine. Stop fussing."

"I'm not fussing."

"Yes, you are. You've been buzzing around me all day. What's up, Estelle?"

He was right.

Ever since he'd hurt his finger, I'd been watching him. I couldn't stop my paranoia—not after losing Conner. If Pippa or Coco were out of my sight for too long, I choked up and dashed to find them.

Galloway was no different.

I hated that I loved them all so much but had no power to protect them.

"I'm just worried."

"Well, be worried about the journey, not me." Galloway brushed past, dumping the oars by the water's edge. "I'm fine."

He's not fine.

Something isn't fine.

But what?

"G...I—something isn't right."

He scowled. "Don't start that, Estelle. You know what today is. We're not delaying any longer."

In the past, he'd indulged my whims of instinct and listened. But today his snappy attitude stopped me from blurting my fears.

He's right.

I shouldn't make today any harder than it already was.

I smiled apologetically, clutched the empty water bottle, and forbid myself from touching his hot forehead again.

It took every reserve not to climb up his height and force him to sit so I could take care of him—to reassure myself that he was okay. Instead, I turned my back and headed toward Pippa and Coco to tick off our remaining items.

If he's still hot in an hour, I'll say something.

Only, I didn't need to.

An hour passed and he put down the axe and disappeared into the house.

Sharing a worried look with Pippa, I trailed after him.

I found him lying on our leaf-stuffed bed with his forearm over his eyes.

My heart rolled over as I fell to my knees and touched his cheek.

Hot.

So, so hot.

Bowing over him, I kissed his lips with so much fear, so much terror, I couldn't breathe. "G...what is it? Tell me. Please, God, tell me."

He groaned a little as I lay beside him, doing my best to hide my shaking. "Stop fussing, woman."

"I'm not fussing. It's gone way beyond fussing." Nuzzling his neck, I sucked in a gasp at his scolding temperature.

He's sick.

He's burning up.

He has a fever.

What do I do?

How do I fix this?

We can't leave.

God, don't leave me, G.

"Estelle, I can hear your thoughts. They're so damn loud. I'm okay...truly."

I sucked in a shaky breath.

First, Conner.

Now, him.

I couldn't handle it if he lied.

If he got sick.

If he...

died.

"What's wrong?" My voice was whisper quiet. "Tell me how to make it better."

His eyes tightened; he turned to look at me. "I just have a headache and feel a bit sick, that's all." He swallowed, his throat working hard. "It might've been the fish for lunch. Or I'm just dehydrated."

"Do you want some water?"

His lips quirked. "You're so good to me. But no, I just want to nap in the shade. I'm sure once my headache goes away, I'll be fine."

Looking through the window, I calculated our time to depart. We'd agreed on pushing off late afternoon in the hope that we'd have enough daylight to move closer to another island and it would be dark enough that we'd see flashing lights or the glow of smog from a village better than in full sunshine. Not to mention, rowing in full zenith would've been impossible.

On the other hand, setting sail just before dark might be the worst idea we'd ever had. A full night on the ocean with nothing to illuminate our path? We might row the opposite way. However, Galloway had promised he knew north from south and had a good guess which star to follow.

"Just rest, G. Get better. We can leave tomorrow. No problem."

"No, we'll leave today. I'm fine, Stel. You'll see."

The heavy depression (that never left thanks to Conner's death) wrapped a thick cloak around me.

I kissed him again, but my lips found burning skin rather than the salty coolness I knew and loved.

It took everything I had to leave him to sleep and spent the longest afternoon of my life with Pippa and Coco, whispering about the pitfalls and hopefully achievable tasks we'd set ourselves. Doing whatever I could to keep my mind from dismal thoughts.

Neither of us mentioned Galloway's sickness.

Neither of us brought up Conner.

Both were subjects far too hard to tolerate.

By the time I brought him dinner of coconut milk and squid, he was worse.

His hazy gaze had turned glassy, and he complained about the fire's brightness, even though there was no way it could affect him being so far from the house.

If he had a migraine, it was severe.

He might have swelling of the brain.

He might have a virus or meningococcal disease.

Both those I wouldn't be able to cure.

Please, let it just be overwork and tiredness.

Those I could tend to.

Those were in my realm of acceptable concerns.

Halfway through the night, when I clambered out of bed to use the washroom, I touched him again and my heart stopped.

I couldn't contemplate the worst.

I'd blindly believed (trusted) that what he'd told me was the truth. That this was a simple set-back and he would wake in full health tomorrow.

I needed him to rest.

To heal.

To get better.

To get well, dammit.

Not to get worse.

But he was worse.

So, *so* much worse.

I shook him as his eyelids fluttered.

"G, open your eyes."

He moaned, rolling onto his side. In his sleep, he'd cradled his left hand where his index finger had swollen and turned a faint shade of red.

The splinter.

Something so simple and common.

Something he'd overcome a hundred times before.

So why isn't he overcoming this one?

What's going on?

My mind went into overdrive, forcing dormant cures to rise. If his finger caused his fever, that had to be isolated.

A tourniquet.

Fumbling in the dark, I rushed to Conner's bedroom.

Tears shot to my eyes at the pristine, untouched space. No one had had the heart to remove the flax blankets or clear out the island clutter. On top of his carved belongings sat the slingshot Galloway had made him.

It tore out my heart to untie the black string from the forked weapon but I did it to save G. Clutching the fine rope, I rushed back to Galloway and slammed to my knees.

He remained fast asleep, unmoving.

I dropped the string I shook so hard, wrapping the blackness around his forearm.

How tight should I pull?

How tight could he stand it before the limb starved of blood?

Is this going to work?

Tying a hasty knot, I ran my hands up his arm, hating the tingling heat beneath my fingertips. The ever-present fear hung itself around my throat as I shook him again. I craved the beauty of electric light to douse him in brightness and confront just how sick he was.

But we didn't have that luxury; I'd even forgotten how brilliant such a device was. All I had access to was a burning fire or the silvery moon and both were outside.

We have to go.

"G, please...help me get you up."

He flinched with annoyance. "Woman, just let me rest."

"No. I need to look at you."

"You can look at me here."

"I can't see in the dark."

He groaned, clearly debating whether to yell at me or obey. Luckily, the gentleman in him was still in control and he struggled upright, letting me guide him to the fire pit.

Immediately, he slipped from standing to lying, stretching out by the comforting flames. "Just let me rest a little, okay, Stel?"

He hadn't mentioned the tourniquet. He hadn't opened his eyes fully.

His personal awareness was nil, focusing entirely on whatever he battled.

I couldn't calm my clanging heart, no matter how much I told myself not to be stupid. Not to picture the worst. Not to imagine every awful conclusion that I'd been terrified of for years.

Resting on my knees, I stroked his burning forehead, drinking my tears. "Okay, G. Rest. I'll watch over you."

And watch over him, I did.

I didn't move.

I didn't sleep.

I hardly ate or drank.

I ignored my children.

I shut out the world.

I prayed for a miracle.

For three *excruciatingly* long days.

I watched over him, just as I said I would.

I fed him.

I bathed him.
I cried for him.
I pleaded with him.
But he didn't get better.
He got worse.
And worse.
And…
worse.

....

"Stelly, you can't keep doing this. You need to rest."

I wafted Pippa away and her intolerable begging for me to eat. My stomach had stopped growling for food, my raging thirst had given up, and my heart had broken and bled out long ago.

Even Coconut couldn't reach me in my grief.

Galloway wasn't getting better.

His red finger had switched to a swollen arm. The tourniquet hadn't worked, allowing devilish scarlet tendrils to chase up his skin and paint his flesh with infection and worry. Pus seeped from his fingernail where the splinter had poisoned him and he no longer needed the fire.

He *was* the fire.

His temperature raged until he mumbled in tongues, garbled nonsense, saw hallucinations. He spoke to Conner some hours, to his mother in others. He conversed with the dead as if they were living…as if he'd already joined them.

I'd tried everything.

I'd steeped his hand in hot, hot water. I'd crushed and applied the leaves Pippa had found helped with inflammation. I mashed coconut flesh and fish into a paste and washed it down his throat with rainwater.

I did everything I could, used everything at my disposal to break his fever and bring him back to me.

But nothing worked.

Finally, on the morning of the fourth day…mere hours from when he'd hurt himself, Galloway opened his eyes and wrenched my tortured heart from my xylophone-stark ribcage.

"I'm dying, Stel."

I convulsed with the need to cry. I was *desperate* to cry. To find some avenue from the over-cooked pressure inside me.

But I couldn't.

I billowed and swelled until I was tight and achy with tears. But I couldn't let go. If I did, who would be there to catch me? Who would be there to drag Galloway back to life?

Wild, tangled hair slid over my shoulders as I shook my head. "No. No, you're not. You'll be fine." I stroked his forehead, wiped the sweat from his cheekbones, and avoided looking at his blistering red arm. "You're fine, see. You're talking. That's an improvement. You're talking to me, G. You're on the mend. See…you'll be fine. You'll be fine. I can't tell you how much you'll be fine."

Stop saying fine.

I couldn't.

"Please, G. Believe it. You'll be fine. So, *so* fine."

His smile crumpled my soul into dust. "Estelle, baby…stop."

Baby.

He'd never called me baby. Never given me a nickname other than Stel or Stelly. Now, he called me baby. Right before he decided to leave me?

He's not leaving me.

I won't let him.

Anger replaced my tears. "Don't baby me, G. You're going to get better. You hear me. You're not allowed to leave me."

Pippa appeared from the house, holding Coconut with tears streaking down their faces.

They'd heard us.

They knew yet another soul would be gone soon. And then, it would just be us.

Three females.

Alone.

All masculine energy and bravery…gone.

No!

I glowered at my adoptive daughter, wanting her gone with her pessimism and useless grief. "Go! Leave. Don't stare at him as if he's already dead!"

Pippa gasped.

For a moment, rebellion illustrated her face with war colours, but then she turned on her heel and dashed away, carrying Coconut with her.

Good.

Good riddance.

I didn't need them if they didn't believe in miracles.

Galloway will be okay.

You'll see.

Everyone will see.

He's not allowed to leave me.

The tears did flow then. Undammed and unwanted, they waterfalled down my cheeks despite my rage at them falling.

Galloway moaned, reaching for me.

I folded into him, placing my head on his chest, listening to his infected racing heart...doing its best to keep him alive just a little longer.

"Estelle, I need to tell you something. I need you to grant me absolution. Will you do that?"

I could only nod and hold him tighter, whimpering and sobbing, drenching his overheated body with my over-hot tears.

He took a while to form a sentence, to mull over the words he wanted because this was it. The final conversation we would ever have.

I knew that.

He knew that.

The damn forsaken world knew that.

Death's cold laughter existed on the breeze as my one and true love, the husband of my heart and father to my daughter, gathered his strength for salvation.

"I—I killed a man." He breathed rather than spoke; his confession barely audible. But it slithered into my chest, churning like butter, like sour milk, like fermented cream until I wanted to vomit such a sentence and pretend he was the good, hardworking man I'd given my heart to.

But I couldn't refuse him.

I couldn't ask questions or demand answers.

I could only listen and forgive so he could go to his grave one soul lighter, and hopefully, find Heaven after fearing Hell.

"I wish I could say it was an accident. I wish I could fabricate a tale of a ruined boy who made a terrible mistake. But I can't." He sucked in a rattling breath. "I can't lie to you like I lied to myself for so many years. I willingly bought an unlicensed gun. I caught the train to his house. I knocked on his door. And I hit him over and over again for what he'd done to my mother, to my father, to me. And then...once he'd paid for his crimes, I shot him."

No, no, no.

"It's okay, it's okay, it's okay."

"It's not okay. Murder is never okay. And I don't pretend to think I did the world a favour. But he was a killer, too, Stel. You have to believe me. His toll was much higher than mine. I couldn't save the patients he'd destroyed, but I could save the families left behind. He can't hurt another, and I'm willing to take that price with me."

Don't, don't, don't.

"I forgive you. I believe you've paid enough for your sins,

Galloway."

He kissed me with blazing lips. "Only you could trust me so blindly, Stel. Only you could overlook a prison sentence and corrupted past and see what's good inside me."

Please, please, please.

"You are only good, G. So, so, *so* good."

"I love you, Estelle."

"G..."

"Tell me you love me, too."

I want to.

I do.

But something prevented me.

As if those three little words would be the defibrillator to stop his heart. As if he only clung to life to hear them. Was it wrong of me to want him to remain in pain so I never had to say goodbye?

Yes, it's wrong.

Don't let him go.

You love him.

Tell him.

He deserved to hear such a thing before leaving.

I sat up.

I stared into his eyes.

I parted my lips.

And then Pippa's scream tore everything apart.

Chapter Sixty

GALLOWAY

I HURT.

There was no other way to describe it.

I was dying.

There was no point denying it.

My fingers had become terrorists, my arm a prosecuting enemy, and my body a murderer.

I'd done this to another.

Now, my body did this to me.

I'm dying.

I didn't know how I knew, but I did.

I was almost gone.

Trading blood and bone for phantom and wraith.

For days, I'd clung to strength, doing my best to fight against the ever-darkening shadow and heavy, heavy sickness. But now…now, I had nothing left, and somehow, I knew I had mere hours, maybe only minutes left.

Confessing to Estelle.

That had been my last spurt of energy.

I'd saved it.

I'd hoarded it.

Unwilling to waste my one chance at absolution.

I thought I'd be angrier. More terrified. More hurt that after so long of being unhappy, I had to leave so much sooner than I wanted.

And I *was* all of those things.

I hated leaving Estelle.

I hated letting her down.

I hated the thought of her staying on this island with no one to shoulder the burdens and hold her late at night.

There would be no voyage.

No returning to society.

Not for me, at least.

My time was up.

I hated that goodbye was such an ugly, ugly word, but I had no choice but to speak it.

Pippa's scream came again, wrenching through our sad farewell.

Estelle's leaking eyes flared with indecision, torn apart with love.

I tried to move, to seek Pippa and the reason for her anguish, but my body no longer obeyed my orders. It had a new master now. Death itself.

My racing heart (smoking with wear and tear from the infection), sprinted faster. "She's in trouble. You have to go to her."

Estelle gritted her teeth, her soul ruptured between Pippa's scream and my imminent departure.

We wouldn't be leaving together, after all.

But I would wait for her.

I would wait for eternity until I could kiss her again.

"Estelle…"

She sucked in a sob, anger mixing with her tears. "Don't make me choose, Galloway. Do. Not. Make. Me. Choose."

A seismic fissure cracked through my chest.

What an unfair situation to be in. Having to choose. Having to decide who deserved comfort when you yourself needed comfort most of all.

A heat wave resembling the surface of the sun roasted my already roasted body. "Go, baby. You have to."

Baby.

I'd never been one to use nicknames. I hated all form of generic endearment that could be transferred to another. But in this instance, it worked. Because, this time, I'd transfused the simple word with all the magic of love.

When I called her baby.

I was really telling her I loved her.

So, so much.

She was the mother of my child. The keeper of my heart and guardian of my soul, and if that didn't make her my baby, my *wife*…then I would die never knowing the meaning of what did.

Estelle threw herself onto my chest, her tears tickling my naked skin. I swore my flesh incinerated those salty droplets like a hot tin roof in a summer's rain.

"I can't. I can't leave you."

"You have to."

"No!"

I wanted so much to hug her but every inch of me screamed with pain. The most I could do was lay my hand on her head. "Baby, you must. She needs you. She has Coco. What if they're dying? Would you let them go over me?"

She stilled.

Don't answer that.

I didn't want the curse of making her verbally admit that somehow, through all my sins and failures, I'd done enough good to deserve her love over any other thing…including our own daughter.

It wasn't right.

It wasn't going to happen.

My voice tinged with anger. "Estelle, go to our children."

Her shoulders wracked with sobs.

Her hands clutched me harder.

"Go."

"No! I won't leave you."

Tangling my hands in her hair, I pulled her eyes to mine. "You don't understand." Tears filled my own gaze, wavering her beautiful face. "I'm leaving you. And you can't abandon them when I've already abandoned you."

"Don't say that! Take it back. God, please…take it back."

For a moment, I swore my heart stopped, as if testing to see how ready I was to die.

I wasn't ready.

I would *never* be ready.

But Conner would be there. We'd find each other again. I'd see my mother. And who knew…maybe even my father if he'd died of heartbreak after almost four years of me missing.

Will she die of heartbreak?

Fear electrocuted my nervous system, giving me a few more minutes. "Estelle." Her name became my rosary beads for my final prayer. "Promise me, you'll look after them. No matter what happens. Promise me, you won't give up."

Her sobs quietened as she slowly, terribly, scooped up her grief and tucked it back into her soul. "You're truly leaving me."

I wished I could say any other word than "Yes…"

I tensed against another refusal, but this time…she accepted. Curtains swished across her eyes, blocking out life-light. The steely acknowledgement and power she'd always had blanketed her sorrow and weakness.

I'd fallen in love with this woman because of her many facets and capabilities. I'd loved her every way a man could love his girl. And now, I had to commit the most cardinal sin of all...leave her behind.

Death was a divorce. The most bitter, awful divorce.

Pippa screamed again. Louder. Stronger.

And that was the end.

Estelle bent over me, her eyes locking onto mine, giving me an anchor to return to time and time again as a ghost once my immortal soul was free.

Her lips sought mine, neither moving nor kissing. Just breathing and loving and reliving everything we'd been through, every year we'd loved, every night we'd slept, every day we'd lived.

And then, she was gone.

She flew to her feet.

She vanished into the forest.

And I closed my eyes for the final time.

Chapter Sixty-One

E S T E L L E

"PIPPA!"

Don't think.

Don't think.

Don't remember.

My fists couldn't stop clenching, shaking, shuddering. My heart couldn't find its normal rhythm as I left it with Galloway as he lay dying alone on our beach.

Alone.

He's all alone.

He's left me.

The shards of my soul clinked like shattered porcelain, rattling in my hollow, hollow chest.

"Stel! *Help!*"

Pippa's voice helped me focus. I'd made a promise. Galloway had left me. But Pippa and Coconut would not.

I forbid it.

A man's baritone echoed through the trees as I charged toward my daughters.

A man?

That wasn't possible.

Unless Galloway had died and his ghost now haunted me.

Haunt me forever.

Never leave me.

If I could only have him in plasma form, I would take it. I was greedy enough to stay in love with a hallucination.

Coco's cries turned to screams as another man's voice rose.

My feet switched from running to tearing and I burst through the palms and flaxes right onto a scene I never thought would come true.

My daughters.

In the arms of two men.

Strange men.

On our island of only five.

Conner.

Galloway.

Three.

On our island of only three.

The man fighting with Pippa looked up. His startled green eyes bugged and everyone froze.

The man holding Coco mimicked our standoff, looking at his colleague, dressed in the same grey slacks and shirt with a royal blue wave on the breast pocket.

My attention to detail went into overdrive.

I noticed e..ve..ry..thing.

I observed the sweat on their temples.

I saw the crinkles around their eyes.

I counted every strand on their dirty blond heads.

I catalogued their similar jawlines and aquiline noses.

I cursed every breath they took.

Every breath Galloway would never take.

Every breath Conner would never have.

They left me.

He left me.

I'm alone.

And that was when I snapped.

These animals were hurting my children—the only people I had left in the world.

I didn't care how they came to be on our island. I didn't care if they were here to rescue us or how they'd found us.

I don't care.

I don't care.

I don't care*!*

They're dead.

All I cared about was protecting my family.

Galloway had left me.

He'd made me *choose.*

He'd given me no choice.

I wouldn't let anyone else make decisions for me.

No more.

No way.

Not with my family.

"Let. Go. Of. My. Children." I took a step forward. *"Now!"*

My grief snarled into a nasty, nasty thing, wanting to lash out and maul. I wanted blood. I wanted pain. I wanted to hurt and hurt and hurt until the hurting stopped inside. Until I could breathe without wanting to die. Until I could exist without him by my side.

The men flinched but didn't obey.

So I did the only logical thing.

I lost it.

I lost myself to tears and fears.

I charged.

I hit.

I struck.

I bit.

I screamed.

I hurt them.

I fought them.

I destroyed them for taking what was mine.

And through it all, I was no longer a wife or mother.

I was a monster.

Chapter Sixty-Two

∙∙∙

E S T E L L E

∙∙∙∙∙∙

"ONE DAY, YOU'RE going to be a big fancy singer, and I'm going to be the one scrubbing your back in an overfilled bubble bath."

I threw my sour lolly at my sister, Gail. "Wrong. You'll be scrubbing my back in a spa on some cruise sailing the Tahitian sea."

Madeline giggled. "You're both wrong. You'll be scrubbing my back as I'll be the manager of said success and skim all your royalties for my own."

I rolled my eyes at my seventeen-year-old friend.

As an only child, Madi didn't have a bestie like I did with Gail. We'd met on the first day of primary school, and I'd adopted her. Gail (who was two years older) adopted her, too.

If there was mischief to be had, we were the ones to meddle in it.

"You're all morons." I laughed. "I won't be the one singing; I'll be the one writing for others. I'm terrified of microphones and crowds...remember?"

Madi slung her arm over me, staring at our reflection as we added the finishing touches to our makeup. We were heading to a party to celebrate the end of school. She'd made me swear I would attend back in middle school, seeing as I never went to social functions.

"You and me, Stelly. We'll show 'em."

Gail joined our duo, making our matching yellow dresses a triple golden glow. "All for one and one for all. I love you crazy peeps."

...

TEARS ROLLED DOWN my cheeks, tickling my throat, wrenching me from the dream.

It'd been so long since I'd dreamt of my sister. Almost as if my mind blocked such painful memories because she'd died far too young.

So why now?

Why did death cling to me like the stench of decay?

Galloway.

The moment his name popped into my head, images of his smile, his touch, his laugh, his kiss…all spindled in my head, crushing me harder and harder into the supple mattress.

I rolled over, hugging the white pillow, sobbing my heart and soul into its starched perfection.

I didn't know how long I cried.

I didn't care how long I drowned in tears.

I would sail away on them, unmoored and unnoticed, until I met Galloway in another life.

However, I couldn't let go.

I couldn't be so selfish.

Pippa.

Coco.

They need me.

The men.

They had them. They'd hurt my babies.

Cannon firing memories shot me upright; my fists raised, searching the room for the men who'd hurt my family.

Where were they?

Where were my daughters?

Adrenaline crashed through my blood like rogue waves, searching for my victims.

But no one was there.

Was it a nightmare?

Not real?

Sniffing back tears, I blinked, expecting to see the bright glare of virginal sunshine, hear the soft *hish hish* of the tide, and fall in love with (just like I did every morning) the images of my family arguing and laughing by the cheery fire pit.

Only…

None of that existed.

Not anymore.

I was in a room.

A room!

I hadn't been in a room for three and a half years.

I was in a bed.

With sheets.

And pillows.

And creamy cotton blankets.

There was a television and curtains and wallpaper and light switches. A painting hung on the wall mocking me with delicate seahorses and anemones swaying in a non-existent current.

Instead of being relieved at finally, *finally* being found, all I focused on was *how?*

Where am I?

Who are they?

Where are Pippa and Coco?

How had this happened without my knowledge?

Throwing myself out of bed, I plucked at the white nightgown covering my salty, skinny body. My ragged bleached hair looked almost as colourless as the gown. A strange after-taste burned my tongue, and a small Band-Aid covered a puncture wound inside my elbow.

What the hell happened?

Was this heaven?

Had I died with Galloway?

My bare feet dashed across the short-pile carpet, beelining for the exit.

I passed the bathroom and slammed to a halt.

A woman stared back.

As much as the men who'd tried to hurt my family were strangers, so too was this mirrored reflection.

It took three heartbeats to recognise myself. Five more until the hurried breathing in the mirror matched mine. My eyes were wild beneath unkempt seaweed hair. My collarbones looked as if they lived within a skin layer of flying free on skeletal wings. My legs were sticks. My fullish chest was mostly flat with teardrop bumps reminding me I'd suckled Coco. I'd grown from naïve introvert to powerful mother all while combating survival.

The outlander was me.

And I'd never felt more alone.

Tears came swiftly but I didn't have time for such nonsense.

I'd cried enough.

I'd cry again later.

But for now, I had to find my daughters. I'd made a promise. Galloway had died believing I would keep that promise.

Turning away, I wrenched open the door and charged into the corridor.

Rows and rows of identical doors greeted me. Numbers labelled them from high to low, peepholes glittered in artificial light, and sideboards held seashells and sculptures of clownfish and turtles.

Where am I?

A man came around the corner in a light grey pantsuit with a tray of covered food and water.

Water.

Yes, please.

Not evergreen-tainted water from our trees or slightly earthy rainwater from our reservoirs.

Pure, pure *water.*

In a glass tinkling with ice.

Ice!

Did such a wondrous thing still exist?

"Ah, you're awake. I was just coming to get you."

My mind snapped from the water trance, and I spun around, expecting to see another person behind me.

He couldn't be speaking to me…surely? I'd never set eyes on him before, yet he spoke as if he knew me.

I turned back to face him, pointing at myself. "You're speaking to me?"

He smiled. He was older than the interloping vagabonds on my island but kindness radiated in his eyes. A stethoscope hung around his neck and his nametag gave him an address of Stefan.

"Yes, of course. You're the woman rescued from the island."

My mouth dried up.

Placing the tray on the sideboard with clownfish frolicking, he held out his hand. "Pleasure to meet you. You were awake last night, but I did wonder if you would remember. After all, such trauma can sometimes render a mind forgetful for a time."

I couldn't look away from his hand. It'd been so long since I'd touched anyone but Galloway and the children.

Conner.

His memory took me by surprise at the worst moments.

Galloway.

Both…were gone.

Tears pricked my eyes as I stared at the man's hand. Did I want to touch him? Was it safe?

But he never dropped his offering, forcing me to be brave and place my fingers into his.

The moment I touched him, splices of the past few hours attacked me.

Fainting mid-fight with the men holding my daughters.

A boat sloshing and roaring, taking me from Galloway.

Screaming as a large, looming ship accepted me into its belly.

Fainting again as I tried to fight and was held down by three men on a gurney.

Crying as needles and medicine were administered against my wishes.

And through it all, the horror of what would happen to Pippa and Coco. And how much Galloway would hate me for abandoning him so soon after he'd abandoned me.

I hadn't held a funeral.

I hadn't given him his last rites (not that I knew what that entailed).

I'd just...*gone*.

Ripping my hand from his, I swallowed. "Where are my family?"

"You mean the toddler and the girl?" He grinned. "Doing mightily well, I must say. The girl mentioned you'd been on that island for almost four years. It's remarkable that you're in the shape you are for such a length of time."

"What shape?"

"Strong and fairly healthy. Your blood-work came back with some vitamin and mineral deficiencies along with very low iron levels, but you're not dehydrated. It truly is a miracle."

"It wasn't a miracle."

He raised his eyebrow. "Oh? Were you trained survivalists before the accident?"

"No. But it wasn't a miracle. It was hard work and determination not to die."

His shoulders lowered; his face softened. "It's amazing what the threat of death can make a human achieve."

Galloway.

Waterworks tried to come again. I dug fingertips into my eyes. "Can...can you take me to them? My children?"

As long as I was with Pip and Coco, I could keep the impending agony of Galloway's death from consuming me a little longer. Long enough to figure out where we were and what this new future meant.

Stefan nodded. "Of course. That was the plan. I was going to give you lunch and then take you to them. I'm the nurse working with Doctor Finnegan." He came closer, lowering his voice. "Do you remember what the captain told you last night? Or is it a blur?"

"The captain?"

"Yes, of this vessel."

The ship.

"We're on a boat?"

"More than just a boat." His lips quirked. "You're on Pacific Pearl."

When I stared at him blankly, he laughed. "Have you heard of P&O Cruises?"

Vaguely, I remembered Madi mentioning them a few years ago as a short break leaving from Australia…to Fiji.

Oh, my God.

"You're cruising the islands?"

"Yes. We recently renovated the boat. Took eighty-four thousand man-hours in just twelve days; pretty spectacular undertaking, if I say so myself. Anyway, with the new boat, we wanted a new route. As this is the inaugural cruise since the renovation, our customers were open to trying something unusual.

"Each night, we sail to an island never visited before and check it out before letting the guests off the next day to explore."

He ran a hand through his hair. "That's how we found you. Our scouts had just traipsed through the forest to check the land for danger when they ran into…what did you call them?"

"Pippa and Coco."

I kept the fact that Coco was short for Coconut.

That was private.

"Yes. Pippa and Coco. When you came and, umm…attacked them, they radioed for back-up but then you fainted and they took the opportunity to carry you on board the adventure craft to bring you back.

"And good job, they did. You fainted because of low levels of folate, Vitamin A, electrolytes, and unhealthy levels of magnesium." His smile faltered. "You're all anaemic as well. Common indicators of overwhelming tiredness, prolonged grief, and emotional distress. Not to mention, unavailable access to food."

I didn't speak…absorbing the ramifications of such a random event. The captain had saved our lives by sheer fluke, yet he'd been only minutes too late to save the love of my life.

Tears welled again, and this time, I couldn't hold them back.

The longer I stood in society, the more manners and historical memories emerged. I remembered how to be polite even while screaming inside. I recalled decorum and how to lie to a stranger's face…all while hiding how badly I was hurting.

And I was hurting.

So, *so* much.

The introvert part of me swung into full gear, no longer comfortable or at home with people I'd woven my life with.

That was over now.

Done.

Gone.

Just like Galloway.

Just like Conner.

"I'm—I'm sorry." I wiped at my wet cheeks. "It's—it's just…"
I sucked in a heavy breath unable to tell him that along with the
three lives he'd rescued, one more was lost on the very beach
holidaymakers wanted to sunbake and drink cocktails.

Oh, no…our house.

Our things.

My memory card with countless videos and photos. My
notebooks. Galloway's carvings, Coco's doll, and Pippa's necklaces.

We'd just left them all.

I need them.

They were the only thing I had left of him. Of Connor. Of our
private world.

I never thought I'd say such heresy, but I made eye contact
with Stefan and begged, "Please…we have to go back."

His lips parted. "You do? Why? We've rescued you. No need
to worry. We'll take care of you and transport you home. Come on,
I'll take you to your daughters. I promise we brought them on
board. We didn't leave them behind. We left no one there, I
promise."

You did.

You left two souls we loved and three more we didn't know.

"You don't understand. There's someone…something that we
left behind. I can't go. Not without them."

Him.

Stefan stepped over all boundaries as he gathered me in a hug.
I remained still as stone in his embrace.

He murmured, "I think you'd better come with me."

Chapter Sixty-Three

• •

ESTELLE

• • • • • •

Enemies can become friends. Friends can become enemies.
And strangers?
They can become both at the same time.
Taken from a P&O Cruise napkin, Pacific Pearl.

• • •

"AH, HELLO AGAIN."

My spine braided into a thousand worthless knots.

Again?

I didn't know this man.

Wait…

Foggy memories swirled into clarity as the captain strode across the bridge.

Last night.

He'd come to visit me where I'd been tended and drugged. He'd said something about taking care of us. To relax. To let him fix whatever it was that needed fixing.

He couldn't fix this.

He couldn't bring back the dead.

He'd meant it to be soothing and kind.

But it'd done the opposite.

He was asking me to *trust* him. To put him in charge of my fate, turning everything I'd endured, everything I'd evolved into nothing because *he* knew better.

I was just a woman plucked from an island.

He was the hero.

I don't want a hero.

I want Galloway.

And Conner.

And Pippa and Coco and my island!

"Pleasure to see you again, Miss." The captain's black hair was peppered with grey beneath his official hat, and his trim Asian physique spoke of life upon the open seas.

His hand came out (just as Stefan's had), demanding I touch him against my wishes.

I hid my cringe, shaking quickly before tucking my hands under my arms and crossing tight. "Hello, eh…"

"John Keung."

"Hello, Captain Keung."

His button nose wrinkled. "Oh, don't worry with that. Please, call me John." His dark eyes brightened. "It's not every day we welcome a castaway on board."

What am I doing here?

I didn't have time for this. I needed my children. I needed them to keep my cresting pain at bay. I felt the tears scratching my insides, harpooning me with agonising memories.

He's dead, they screamed.

You're alone, they gloated.

I needed to hold Coco and let Pippa hold me as we both cried for the men we'd loved and lost.

I glanced at Stefan. "I thought…I thought you were taking me to see Coco and Pippa?"

He rubbed the back of his neck, disrupting his stethoscope. "I thought it was best you debriefed with the captain beforehand." Looking at John, he added, "She, umm—she can't remember much about last night. Perhaps, a re-jog of her memory is in order, sir?"

Goosebumps broke out beneath the white shift I'd been dressed in. I suddenly worried my underwear-less frame might be visible beneath.

The thought kicked my heart then ran away.

So what?

What was the point in caring?

I stood before strangers barefoot, mostly naked, and stripped of natural beauty and vitality thanks to years on a tropical island. No one cared about me. The sad little washed-up rescued girl. No one cared that I was loved and loved in return. That I was a mother. That I was a widow. That I was grieving for a son I'd lost only months before I lost my husband.

They didn't need to know.

That was my pain, and my pain was more private than my useless body.

The tears scratched harder, biting lonely teeth into my heart.

Bracing my shoulders, I said, "Thank you for what you've done for me, but I really must insist that we turn around. I need...I need to go back."

"Go back?" The captain's eyes flared. "My dear, what ever for?"

My lower lip wobbled as sobs threatened to take me. All I seemed to do now was cry. If a human body was made up of water, then I didn't have a single droplet left.

"I just do. Take me back. At once." My voice came out harder than I'd intended, using anger to patch up my terror.

Was that what G did?

The entire time he'd been gruff and argumentative; was he merely blustering with façade to hide his true fear? The fear that he'd murdered. That he'd *killed*.

He'd passed such horrendous news to me before dying. What was I supposed to do with that? Was it supposed to make me love him less? Was I supposed to hand in his crime and choose the law over my heart?

It doesn't matter now.

He's dead.

I rubbed at the bleeding hole where my heart used to be, eaten by my feral tears.

The captain followed my movement, ignoring his question for another. "Are you uncomfortable in the nightgown? I'm sorry it's slightly too big. That was all the on board gift shop had in stock."

Glancing down, I read the P&O cruise logo on the frilly collar around my décolletage (not that my boobs had cleavage after so many years).

"It's—it's fine." I swallowed against the bitterness of bereavement. "I'm grateful for what you've done."

Biting. Biting. Tearing. Tearing.

The tears grew and grew.

"I'll have a selection sent to your room. Dresses and what-not." The captain cleared his throat. "I hope you don't mind that we didn't launder your bathing suit. We decided it was probably past its use-by-date."

Yes, I do. They're memories. Not clothing.

How many times had Galloway undone those bows and made love to me?

How many times had I slipped from the black swimwear to swim beneath the moonlight bare?

I looked at the floor. "No, I don't mind."

"I'll make sure more clothes for your children are sent up, too." The captain shuffled in place. For the director and man in charge of such a vessel, he seemed nervous around me.

Was I that wild? That savage?

Apologise for hurting his men.

It took so much effort, but I said, "I—I need to thank you, Captain Keung. Thank you for finding my family. I'm sorry for hurting your crew."

"Don't worry about it. Gave them plenty to talk about." He winked. "Not every day we head to an uninhabited island and find locals."

I cracked a smile. It was what he expected. Even if it cost me everything.

Locals.

That was what we'd become.

And now, we'd been ripped from our home without a choice.

This wasn't a rescue.

It was a kidnapping.

Achy tears bruised my eyes. I struggled to hide my sob-filled sigh. "Sir...please. I'm very grateful to you. And I can't tell you what a relief it is to have medical assistance after so long. But...there's something...someone—"

I couldn't finish.

My knees gave out, and I pooled to the polished wooden floor of the bridge. The wood was so glossy it mirrored my large, aching eyes brimming with stupid, hurtful, angry, disbelieving tears.

He left me.

He left me.

I hadn't had time to grieve.

I'd had to make a choice: stay with Galloway or save our daughters. He'd made me put him second best.

And because of that, I never got to say goodbye.

"I never...I never got to say goodbye!" I couldn't look up. I couldn't make eye contact with the milling crew in the operating tower. I couldn't glance at Stefan, and I *definitely* couldn't look at the captain.

If I did, I didn't know if I'd die from the cracking, wrenching sorrow inside or kill him. I wanted to kill him for taking me from the man I loved.

I wanted to smite everyone with hurricanes and helicopter crashes for ever giving me a lover and then stealing him so swiftly.

I didn't get to say goodbye!

I wasn't over Conner's death.

And now, I had to deal with Galloway's, too.

I...I couldn't do it.

My torso fell forward, my arms wrapped around me, and my forehead bowed on the lacquered floor.

I sobbed.

I screamed.

I sounded like a typhoon.

The captain ducked to his haunches, patting my shoulder blades. It only made me worse.

A strong but kind hand pulled my chin up, forcing me to look at him. Stefan shook his head. "That's why you're so unhappy. That's why you want to go back?"

I bared my teeth, wrenching my face from his hold. "Yes! He's there. Just lying there. He's dead and I didn't bury him. The ants…God, the ants…they'll take him from me. I can't…I can't let that happen! Don't you see? He has to be with the turtles. He has to be set free. I didn't set him free!"

My garbled nonsense interspersed with ugly, ugly tears.

But I didn't care.

Just as I didn't care about my physical self, I didn't care how deranged I came across to these men. I knew what I meant. And Galloway, if his soul was chained to his dead body, he knew, too. He'd know I'd abandoned him. That I ran away without telling him I love him.

Oh, God!

My sobs became a wail.

I didn't tell him I love him!

I clutched Stefan's shirt. "Please! I have to go back. I can't do this. I have to tell him how much I loved him. How much I *do* love him. Please! You can't do this."

The captain shared a worried look. "Is she unwell, Stefan? I thought we'd explained all of this last night."

Unwillingly, I sank into Stefan's embrace, hating the way he rocked me. I didn't want his sympathy or attempts at compassion.

I want Galloway.

And unless I could have him, I didn't want anything anymore. I didn't want to live another day. I didn't want to breathe another breath without him in my world.

"We did, sir. But the trauma has hidden much of what occurred yesterday. She needs to go on medication and high-strength vitamins to boost her deficiencies. But she refused. The kids behaved, but we couldn't get her cooperation. No matter that we told her the truth. She didn't believe us then. And she doesn't believe us now."

"Believe what?" My eyes narrowed through my tears. "What don't I remember?"

"That I explained to you why you don't have to return to the island."

"Because he's dead?"

"That's what you think? Truly, think. Try to remember."

I froze. Tears turned to stalactites on my cheeks. "What—what are you saying?"

"I'm saying that you should be crying for life rather than death."

My breathing stopped for an entirely different reason. Despicable hope rose like two hundred sunrises in my ribcage. "Tell me."

Stefan let me go, handing me a wad of tissues from his pocket. "I think I'd better show you." Standing, he held out a hand to help me up.

My knees shook.

My back ached.

My eyes burned.

But I couldn't shake the thought I'd missed something. That all of this…this pain and suffering…

"Captain, we'll come back tomorrow. We can go over the bases then." Taking my elbow, Stefan guided me toward the exit.

The captain waved. "No problem. Oh, and, Miss. Please don't worry about anything. The clothing, the food, the medical attention, even your room. Everything you require is at the pleasure of P&O cruise lines." He lowered his head importantly. "Anything at all."

I should thank him.

I should show gratitude for such a gift.

But I couldn't.

Because somehow, somewhy, somewhat…my brain unlocked another memory.

Him.

He'd been here.

On this boat.

Galloway.

Chapter Sixty-Four

•••

ESTELLE

••••••

"DO YOU BELIEVE me now?"

Stefan let me go the moment we entered the tiny room with beeping noises and a single cot pushed up against the wall.

We'd descended in the lift.

We'd walked along the corridors.

We'd entered the medical wing.

And with every step, my heart slowly stole back its existence from snarling tears, welcoming hope instead.

I didn't know what I did first.

Laughed.

Cried.

Collapsed

Danced.

Perhaps, all four at once.

One moment, I stood beside Stefan in the doorway. The next, I was sprawled on his chest.

His.

The man I loved.

The man I'd left.

The man who'd died.

"Oh, my God." I kissed him. Over and over and *over.*

He didn't wake up.

Stefan came closer. He didn't tell me to climb from the cot. He didn't tell me I was crushing his patient.

He was wise.

Instead, he said, "His system is severely exhausted and the infection has stolen whatever reserves he had left. He'll wake up when he's ready. But he's alive, and we'll do everything we can to keep him that way."

He's alive.

I didn't have to choose.

Galloway was here, with me, on the ship. He hadn't gone to Conner. He hadn't visited his mother.

He was my havoc, my harmony, my only chance at hope.

I clutched him harder, kissing his warm, lifeless lips, staring into his gaunt face and sunburned nose. His long hair spread out like a crown, a mixture of browns and bronzes on white perfection.

He looked regal.

He looked dead.

But I knew better now.

I'd left behind my phone, our videos, my notebooks, and three and a half years of carvings and creation.

But I hadn't left behind my husband.

I could breathe again.

Chapter Sixty-Five

....

GALLOWAY

......

IF THIS WAS hell, then I pitied those who went to heaven.

I expected raging fires of doom and pitchforks and condemning judgements. Not the floating strange sensation of healing.

I'd said goodbye to Estelle.

I'd trusted she'd keep her promise.

I'd died the moment I lost sight of her.

Yet…noises kept interrupting my restless slumber. Pinpricks and beeping and touching, lots and lots of touching.

Fragments of dreams appeared of motorboats and rocking oceans. Which was odd as I hadn't been on a boat since my father took me fishing for my sixteenth birthday.

Slowly, I became tethered to my body, feeling more pain and more heat than before. Wasn't death the opposite? Weren't you supposed to find freedom once you made the conscious decision to…let go?

The eerie sensation of being watched and discussed came and went, along with unknown voices.

Until suddenly, there was a voice I recognised.

A woman.

My woman.

My wife.

Desperation shoved aside hot sickness; I tried to swim to her.

She was on our island, surrounded by smashing waves and snapping sharks. All I had to do was get to her and then all would be well.

I would swim the gauntlet. I would fight every shark. I would do whatever it took to keep her.

But something anchored me down.

My eyes remained shut with lead lures on my eyelashes and limbs locked in a cage.

But she understood my trial because she touched me. It wasn't a stranger or fleeting phantom.

It was *real*.

Having her touch me (when I was so sure I'd never enjoy it again), gave me peace for the first time since the splinter sentenced me to death.

I relaxed.

I stopped fighting.

My body and immunity took over, and I finally began to heal.

Chapter Sixty-Six

. . . . .

ESTELLE

. . . . . .

Who do you thank when life gives you your deepest wishes? Who do you curse when it takes away your greatest triumphs? Who do you beg when nothing you want works out? Who do you pray to when the impossible comes true?
I don't have the answer.
I doubt anyone does.
Taken from a P&O Napkin, Pacific Pearl.

. . .

THREE HUGELY IMPORTANT things happened.

One, I was united with Pippa and Coco amongst tears and wide-eyed glances at our foreign new world.

Two, we never moved apart, chaining our emotions together, staying vigil at Galloway's side.

Three, Galloway slept for two days, slowly growing healthier.

The doctors said he could wake up when he wanted. But his system was so badly depleted; it might take time for such a feat to happen. He said every energy was directed at helping the intravenous antibiotics fight septicaemia. He said G was aware and listening. That he knew I was there, touching him, talking to him, telling him secrets…singing to him.

And I believed him.

I also believed just how lucky we were to be found. How kind the crew had been to overlook my inhospitable welcome. How they'd listened to Pippa when she'd cried there was someone else to rescue as they'd bundled my unconscious form on the boat.

Two people actually.

Three.

No, four.

Pippa led the scouts to Galloway, and they'd carried his lifeless body to the adventure craft. She'd returned and scooped up the memorial shrine for her parents and Conner and stole Puffin from his shelf in our pantry.

She was the reason why Galloway was here with us. She was the reason Coco was tended to while I broke down. She was the reason my family was still together.

She'd had so much heartache that I doubted she'd laugh again. Love again. Live again. But she was young. Tragedy could never be erased, but it could be cushioned. And I would adore her as my daughter for the rest of her life.

As Galloway healed, Dr. Finnegan explained what'd happened. The tiny splinter blighted him with a bacterial condition called cellulitis. As his immune system was undernourished, the infection spread rapidly, chewing through his final reserves.

My tourniquet didn't work.

Nothing on the island would've worked.

Cellulitis was life-threatening, but in a city with penicillin, a mere annoyance. However, in the wilderness with no drugs…it was the checkered flag on the finish line.

G was moments from succumbing when the crew had placed us side by side in the rescue boat. We'd lay almost touching, bouncing over whitecaps, whizzing toward doctors.

We were tended to in the same medical room (a single ward for ship guests if they fell ill or needed emergency care). All of this, I'd known…apparently. I'd even thrown myself on Galloway's white-dead form, the moment I woke from my fainting episode.

I'd seen him.

I'd touched him.

Yet my exhausted, grief-stricken mind had forgotten him.

And now…as the monitors recorded a racing heart and the antibiotics cleared his blood, I managed a small smile as Pippa and Coco inched closer to his cot.

Last night, we'd spent it together. We'd been given separate rooms, but after so long living in house only feet away from each other, I couldn't sleep without the sounds of their breathing.

I missed Conner's breath. His vibrant energy and boundless youth.

Unfortunately, the bed we'd been given was too spongy, and after hours of restless discomfort, we'd all camped on the floor. We only took the pillows (which were the best invention ever) and snuggled close.

Coco had cried for the newness of it all.

Pippa had cried for the loss of it all.

And I'd hugged both of them. Finally strong enough to comfort them, knowing Galloway hadn't gone.

The next morning, I had my first hot shower in almost four years.

I cried.

The overwhelming sensation of flowing water, of turning on a tap and being able to drink made gratitude pour.

Unwrapping a new toothbrush and tasting minty paste for the first time in so long.

I cried.

The simple things.

Things I'd used every day without thinking were now the most incredible novelties.

Once we were clean, Pippa, Coco, and I joined the other cruise guests at the buffet. There were too many voices, too many bodies, too many of everything.

We couldn't do it after so long in solitary.

However, Stefan was our personal shadow. He instructed us to find a relaxing spot on the promenade surrounded by potted palm trees and cushioned wicker furniture while he gathered us plates groaning with waffles and maple syrup, crispy bacon, fresh mango, fluffy eggs, and the largest plate of miniature muffins I'd ever seen.

That first taste of sugar.

I cried.

My tears mingled with blueberry dough, and Pippa's moans of pleasure threaded with mine until we sounded like rabid savages.

We visited Galloway often, but he remained asleep. However, his lips twitched whenever I touched him, and his forehead smoothed when I whispered in his ear.

We were subjected to poking and prodding from the medical team. We were given tablets and vitamins and our vitals checked regularly to ensure we were improving.

For dinner, Stefan brought us cheeseburgers and French fries, roasted chicken and potatoes, braised beef and thick gravy.

For all my vegetarian ways, I sampled everything.

And I cried.

It seemed I cried and cried and cried.

I cried in happiness. In pain. In homesickness. I cried in confusion. In misery for Conner. In excitement.

So many things were changing, and we had no choice but to be swept away.

The cruise had set sail the moment we'd been found, authorities had been alerted, Morse code or telegrams (however boats transmitted messages) sent to our respective families.

The passengers had been informed of the change of schedule and given a choice to disembark at the nearest hotel in Nadi, and wait a few days for a replacement cruise, or return to Sydney with the promise of another voyage of their choosing.

To my surprise, the majority decided to return home with us. I had no idea why the captain wanted to personally escort us. He could've dumped us on a flight (gulp) or arranged other transportation.

But he wouldn't hear of it.

Our reappearance was his personal accomplishment. He'd found us and would only leave us when we were on familiar soil.

Unbeknownst to him, Galloway wasn't from Australia. Neither was Pippa. And Coco didn't have a birth certificate. We were all going to the one place I knew because I was greedy and wanted to see Madeline. I wanted to hold my friend and tell her who I'd become. *What* I'd become. And let her protect me from what would come next.

Despite my nerves dealing with so many strangers, they gravitated toward us, drawn by our celebrity status thanks to the captain announcing our unforeseen arrival. If the limited audience was this obsessed with us, what would the city be like? How hectic would our future be now we were back from the dead?

I met with the captain again and apologised profusely for my dramatics. He'd hugged me (I was hugged a lot) and said he completely understood. He pried about our tale. Asked questions. Curious as to how we'd survived.

I was reluctant to share too much. What we'd endured was ours. It wasn't a story to be told with gratuitous embellishment. It wasn't something to gloat over and determine if the re-teller could've done better.

It was our life.

And I wanted no judgement.

So instead of answering his questions, I smiled and redirected. I learned more about the P&O renovation than I ever needed. He educated me on his nautical career and showed me pictures of his two boys in Taiwan.

The photos depicted twins aged sixteen.

I'd cried.

I'd tried not to but couldn't help it.

Conner had been sixteen.

Conner had died before he could be found and now…now, we'd been taken away.

And soon…Pippa might be taken from me, too.

She was only eleven-years-old. But she acted like an adult. She knew how to fish, to cook, to build, to heal. She was more woman than any girl I'd ever met. And she was mine.

We shared the same last name through some twisty cliffhanger of fate.

But we weren't blood, no matter how much I wished it.

Our future was changing and the power I had over our destinies was no longer in effect.

I was once again just a songwriter without a pen to write.

Chapter Sixty-Seven

GALLOWAY

"I CAN'T BELIEVE it."

My father's arms (the same arms I never thought I'd feel outside prison again) wrapped tight around me.

I was free.

Free.

How?

I still didn't know.

"Did you do it?" I asked, pulling away from his embrace.

I'd been told I looked a lot like my father, but I had some of my mother, too. I'd inherited my height from him and my colouring and possibly his eyes.

Those eyes now brimmed with tears. "No. I mean...I've tried, Gal. So bloody long, I've tried. I've drawn up affidavits. I've begged for a new hearing. But nothing came of it. Not until I got the phone call."

"What phone call?"

"The one saying they'd charged the wrong killer."

"But, Dad. I'm the killer."

My father slung his arm around my shoulders, leading me from the prison gates. "We both know that, but someone...someone knew that too and decided to save you. It's a miracle, Gal. And I'm going to find the man who did this and worship him for being so damn kind."

SHE'D TOLD ME she would be there for me.

She didn't lie.

I opened my eyes, and there she was. Coco dangled asleep in her arms while my woman watched me with such concentration, I felt as if she'd yanked me from my dream with pure willpower.

Pippa stood behind her, her lips parting into a smile.

Estelle clapped a hand over her mouth as our eyes met.

Tears leaked unnoticed down her cheeks.

My emotions crested and crashed, threatening to wash me away after clinging so tightly to the rock of life.

"You're awake," she whispered. "You're finally here."

"I—" I spluttered. My dry throat was out of practice. The more I woke, the weaker I became. My scratchy throat was the least of my issues. My toes tingled and limbs ached as if I'd run for weeks with no rest.

But it didn't matter.

Estelle gave Coco to Pippa and immediately slipped into my bed. The ecstasy of her warmth as she curled into me cured me better than any sleep, swifter than any drug.

I sighed heavily as her head rested on my chest.

My left arm (the same one that'd tried to kill me) wrapped around her—needles and all.

I reached for Pippa and Coco with the other, urging them into the hug and kissing them.

Estelle's tears soaked my white hospital gown, spreading a translucent stain.

Pippa let me go, cuddling Coco. "So good to see you, G."

"You too…" I coughed. "Pippi."

Estelle shuddered, clutching me tight.

Unable to stop myself, my lips landed in her hair. I'd almost lost her. I'd said goodbye. I'd forced her to leave.

"You never said it…" I breathed, nuzzling her, loving her.

Estelle stiffened.

No reminder was needed. She knew what she'd refused me on the precipice of my death.

I understood why she did (sort of). I understood she didn't want to say farewell. Didn't want finality on something so heart destroying.

But the fact she hadn't said it broke me.

"I love you, G." Her lips found mine.

The broken parts healed.

Her lips tasted of strawberry and sugar. Her mouth moved beneath mine, chanting over and over, "I love you. I love you. I'm sorry. I love you. I love you *so* much."

"I love you, too."

We reaffirmed that we were still here. Still together. Neither of us had left. No divorce had come true. No goodbye had been uttered.

This was hello, and I wanted it to last forever.

We hugged for the longest time.

A doctor arrived but didn't interrupt. He allowed our moment before tiptoeing closer and checking my vitals.

Estelle sniffed back the dampness in her gaze, smiling with genuine ease at the doctor. Over the years, she'd told me tales of her struggle with crowds and strangers. I had no doubt being around so many would be hard. I was proud of her for being so brave.

Pippa and Coco moved out of the way as the doctor came closer. "Welcome back, Mr. Oak."

I jerked.

No one had used my last name in so long. No one but Estelle and my island family had spoken to me in almost four years.

Just staring at someone who wasn't familiar, someone I didn't know every scar, sunburn, stretch mark, or growth spurt was the strangest sensation.

"Thank you for saving…" I coughed again. "Me."

The nametag said my physician was Dr. Finnegan. His red hair gave away Irish roots even if his Australian accent didn't. "Pleasure was all mine." His eyes flickered to the machines and the drip slowly administering whatever had saved my life. "All signs are great for a full recovery. In such severe cases such as yours, I must warn you that although the infection didn't spread to your bones, it was in your blood long enough to possibly cause complications with your lymph glands and immune system as you get older. You must be careful with any future cut or graze and continue to be vigilant with insect bites and swelling. Do you understand?"

"Yes."

"The strength of the antibiotics have given your body a head start. However, you'll need to take oral medication once we dock for twenty-one days afterward. This is the higher end of the scale, but after so long with no adequate vitamins, your system is too weak to fight on its own."

Estelle said, "I'll make sure he takes every pill, Doctor. I thought I'd lost him once. I won't let him leave me a second time."

Finnegan chuckled. "Good to have you on my side, Ms. Evermore."

"Please…call me, Estelle. I told you that two days ago. You've already met my children. I want you to call them by their first names, too." Smiling, she pointed at the two girls.

I was so used to them half-naked that their matching peach sundresses were ostentatiously bright.

"This is Pippa but you can call her Pippi, and Coco is short for Coconut."

Finnegan touched his temple in greeting. "Pleasure." Bending to tickle Coco under her chin, he grinned. "So you're named after the tree that's been dubbed a miracle, huh?"

Coco giggled. "Co co co coconuts. Yummy."

Dammit, Conner.

Why did you have to die?

God, I missed that kid. He would've loved this. He would've been the centre of attention. Probably already earned a girlfriend or two.

Why was life so cruel to those most deserving?

"They are." Finnegan smiled. "They're also immensely helpful for stranded survivors such as yourselves."

Coco shook her head, rosy cheeks glowing. "No. Home."

Finnegan frowned. "What do you mean?"

For her young age of just over two, Coco had a good string of words and knowledge of questions. I doubted she could answer eloquently about her conception and birth, but I tensed. The age-old cliché that a man and woman were overcome with lust and just couldn't help themselves. That we threw caution away just to have sex and screw the consequences.

We'd tried to prevent Coco.

We'd been very aware of how dangerous such a thing could be.

But she'd come anyway.

And we loved her so damn much.

"Born." Coco tapped her chest importantly. "Home." Crystal tears glittered on her eyelashes. "Home. No like here. Swim. Turtle." Her bottom lip wobbled as she reached for Estelle. "Ma-ma, home!"

Estelle took her from Pippa, bouncing her and kissing her forehead. "It's okay, little nut. You're okay. We can swim soon. The ship has a pool. Would you like that? We can swim and I'm sure someone will have a pet turtle."

Her eyes glanced at the man lurking by the door. "Stefan, does the gift shop have stuffed turtles for sale?"

The guy shrugged. "Not sure. But I can check for you."

Estelle cringed as if she hated being an imposition. "It's— don't worry about it."

"I'll go." Pippa moved toward the man. "I know how much Puffin helped me. I forgot to bring the doll Conner made for her. She needs a friend."

Estelle melted. "Thank you, Pip."

"No problem."

She slipped out the door with the stranger. My heart went wild, hopscotching on the monitor. "Who is that? Is Pippa safe with him?"

Estelle looked at me. "His name is Stefan. And yes, I trust him."

I wasn't so sure, but Coco held her tiny arms out for me. The chance to hug my daughter overcame the fact I was hooked up like a damn robot to machinery. "Give her to me."

Estelle moved closer, carefully transferring the weight of the wriggling toddler. As she pulled away, I snagged her wrist and kissed the delicate skin. I knew she had a scar there from a scary slip with the Swiss Army knife trying to open a coconut. Just as I knew she had a scar on her knee from falling from the umbrella tree and a permanent mark on her chest from her harness when we crashed.

I knew everything there was to know about this woman.

Yet...she seemed like a stranger in her cream shirt and denim shorts. Her hair was in a ponytail and she smelled different. Not like sand and sea and sun, but more like synthetic soap and overly scented body lotion.

Possessiveness rose to claim her. To sink into the ocean and wash away the unknown; to make love in spite of death's attempt to separate us.

Finnegan cleared his throat, reminding us we had an audience. He glanced between me, my wife, and my baby. "So...you gave birth alone?"

Estelle flinched. "Yes."

"But in your check-up, there didn't seem to be any complications."

"There weren't."

"You must've been terrified."

"I was."

I jumped in. "She was amazing. So proud of her."

The doctor frowned. "So...you were married before the crash?"

None of your damn business.

Estelle dropped her eyes. "No. But we're together now."

Finnegan stroked his chin. "I must admit, that makes more sense. I couldn't understand what she meant."

"What *who* meant?" My voice was sharper than intended.

"Joanna Evermore."

Estelle turned to granite. "Who?"

Pippa's voice interrupted as she re-entered the room. "My grandmother. I told him to call her. I didn't know her number, but I remembered her name and town." She sniffed, not able to raise her gaze. "She needs to know about my...my parents...and...and..."

She couldn't hold the tears any longer. "She needs to know about…Conner."

Estelle opened her arms.

Pippa ran to her, hugging her tight.

"It's okay, Pippi. You did the right thing. Of course, she needs to know. She'll be longing to see you."

My heart hurt at the thought of Pippa being taken from us.

But that wouldn't happen, would it? We were her legal guardians. We didn't have the paperwork, but she'd been ours for almost four years.

"I returned to see if Coco wanted to come to the gift shop to pick out a toy. Not to hurt you guys." Pippa cried harder. "I miss my family. I—I couldn't keep it a secret. Not anymore. They need to know. Conner—"

My pulse quickened; I was desperate to climb out of bed and hold her.

"It's okay. I completely understand." Estelle smoothed Pippa's hair. "And that's very nice of you to take Coco. I'm sure she'd love to go."

A thin veil of normality descended as Pippa sucked up her tears. "Okay…" The thought of spending time with the toddler went beyond the nurturing tendencies of an older sister but a full-blown requirement to stop thinking about a lost brother.

How guilty were we of using Coco as a safety blanket for such heartache?

Finnegan broke the tension-filled bubble. "If you don't mind…I need to confirm something Joanna Evermore told me."

Estelle never stopped hugging Pippa, gathering Coco to join in the embrace. "All right…"

"When I told her that Pippa's aunt and uncle had been on the island and looking after her grandchild, she said Duncan never had any siblings. That he was an only child. However…I know from your medical records you listed your name as Estelle Evermore…which matches Pippa's."

The doctor looked at Galloway. "However, yours is Oak so I'm assuming, and I don't want to pry, that Estelle was married or somehow a distant relation to the Evermores before you met? Or did you perhaps change your name out of convenience?"

Pippa shot out of Estelle's arms, indignant. "She *is* my aunt. G is my uncle. I don't care what they say. They're family."

Finnegan held up his hands. "I wasn't saying otherwise, but the authorities will need to solve this."

"Solve what?" I asked.

Finnegan gave me a sad look weighted with everything we didn't understand. "When we arrive at port in a few days, you'll be interviewed by Sydney immigration. You'll be detained unless you have valid documents stating nationality and origins."

Detained?

We'd gone from imprisoned on an island to imprisoned by people?

Hell, no.

Not going to bloody happen.

"Listen, we have no documents because we crashed. We're alive because of how we pulled together not because anyone came to find us. They can take their clearance and shove it up their ass before I let them detain or separate us."

Estelle warned, "G…"

Pippa burst into tears again.

Coconut looked as if she'd join in.

Heaven had just become a nightmare.

Estelle placed her hand on mine. "It's okay. We'll work it out." She smiled bravely at Finnegan. "It will be okay…right?"

Finnegan had the grace to lie. However, his eyes couldn't stop the truth. "Yes, I'm sure it will be," said his mouth. "I'd start saying goodbye now," said his eyes.

For the first time, but definitely not the last, I wished we were back on our island.

Back home.

Where nothing and no one could touch us.

Chapter Sixty-Eight

•••

ESTELLE

••••••

TWO DAYS.

Both comprised of twenty-four hours.

Both unchanging in minutes and longevity.

Yet somehow…they blinked past.

It was always the same. If something joyous was on the horizon, days turned into years. But when something horrendous threatened, they turned into seconds.

Two days was too short.

Despite our ticking time, Galloway grew stronger.

Finnegan inspected his badly healed ankle, foot, and shin. He took X-rays and tapped his chin with deliberations.

Unfortunately, he admitted that the end product wasn't ideal.

Galloway's shin had healed from the lateral malleolus injury and his foot suffered a lis franc fracture which might cause arthritis.

His ankle however.

His ankle wasn't normal.

We already knew that.

What we didn't know was the injury was called a bimalleolar fracture. Coupled with his other injuries and the fact the ligaments and tendons had been damaged as well, meant the splint I'd done and the best care I could administer wasn't enough.

The joint had moved while healing, causing a malunion. His ankle could bear weight, but he might never be able to run or even walk without a limp. He would develop pain over time as he aged. It would be unstable and require constant awareness for the rest of his life.

Instead of being strong for G, being there while he heard the news, I broke.

I felt responsible.

I *hated* that I'd let him down.

I should've done more to fix him. I should've known how to provide better care.

However, he didn't blame me. He blamed himself. He was the one who'd coerced a pilot to fly us in uncertain weather. He was the one who'd done something karma demanded payment for.

I loved him no matter his brokenness or wholeness.

I just wished I'd been better. More able. A nurse rather than songwriter.

That night, after Finnegan delivered the news, Galloway held me close and ordered me to stop feeling guilty. I was never to think about it again.

He accepted that this was his gait now. He could run; he could walk (he might never do it gracefully or be able to dance) but he was alive and that was all that mattered.

We were given permission to move Galloway from the infirmary and into my room under the proviso he carted the antibiotic drip and fluids wherever he went.

We spent two nights curled together on the floor with Pippa and Coco beside us.

Conner's ghost never left, giving us strength to face what we must.

Galloway's system (bolstered by drugs and intravenous nutrients) excelled with healing. His natural colouring returned, his smile appeared, and every hour he felt more alive in my arms.

The medical team kept a close eye on him. And all of us underwent a dentist visit for cleaning and X-rays.

I required a few fillings as did Pippa, but overall, our teeth were in good shape thanks to our flossing and bi-daily brushing, even with old toothbrushes with no paste.

We'd done what we could to stay in physical condition.

And it'd paid of (minus the lack of weight).

On the morning we cruised into Sydney Harbour, two things conflicted me.

One, I'd waited three and a half years to return home, and it'd finally come true. I hadn't had to fly (thank God) and the cruise liner (along with its staff) had been the best integration into noisy society that we could ask for.

And two, I no longer thought of this metropolis as home. The itch to run grew stronger every wave we sailed over. Even the thought of seeing Madeline again couldn't stop my overwhelming desire to hold the captain at gunpoint and order him to return to the high seas like any good pirate.

As the loud groan of the humongous anchor splashed into the harbour and jetty mates helped tether the floating behemoth to the dock, I trembled so hard, Galloway struggled to hold me.

The captain was ever professional, donating more clothes from the gift shop (and Coco a cute stuffed turtle), accepting no charge (not that we had any money), and providing scripts of antibiotics and vitamins before granting us safe passage to land.

He also pulled us aside before we entered the gangway and stuffed a piece of paper into Galloway's hand. The random set of numbers meant nothing to me until Galloway exhaled heavily. "The coordinates?"

The captain nodded. "To return if you ever need to. Those exact coordinates will lead you back if you feel the urge."

I'd hugged him then.

I'd squeezed him so hard because he'd just given us the key to paradise.

He'd given me the power to someday collect my phone with our memories. My notebook full of scribbled songs. And the four spirits who'd died and found salvation in the salty seas and sunshine.

If our future was too hard—if our dreams turned into a disaster—we had a safe haven to run to. An island that had almost killed us. But was ours, nevertheless.

We were the last to disembark (after watching two thousand people crawl like ants) and we didn't do it alone.

Stefan and Finnegan escorted us down the gangway, handing us over to the grabby hands of the media, newsmongers, and awaiting immigration officials.

This was our new hell.

But at least, we had directions back to heaven.

One day.

Someday.

I wanted to go home.

Chapter Sixty-Nine

....

GALLOWAY

......

"CAN YOU TELL us what happened on the island?"

"Did you resort to cannibalism?"

"Where are the others who crashed with you?"

"Do you regret your decision to board that helicopter?"

"The pilot's family said you pressured him into flying when he advised it was a bad idea. Can you confirm?"

"Do you think you should be held accountable for Akin Acharya's death?"

Bloody hell, they're vultures.

Worse than vultures, rabid disgusting locusts.

"This way, please!" Someone in a navy suit flashed a clipboard above the heaving crowd of journalists.

Grabbing Estelle's waist while she cradled Coco, I pinched Pippa's elbow and manhandled, pushed, and shoved my way through the crowd.

"Tell us what happened!"

"Is it true you killed a man?"

"Why won't you confirm that you're responsible for the crash?"

By the time we made it to the glass doors of customs where seafaring passengers were processed, I was sweaty, angry, and more stressed since I was sentenced to jail for a crime I wished I hadn't commit.

My system wasn't running at top capacity and my head swam with nausea. The headaches had faded and the redness on my arm had turned to a blush rather than murder, but I still wasn't well.

We shouldn't have to put up with this crap.

We were tired.

We needed to rest.

Can't they see that?

The man who'd waved us over clanged the door, locking it the moment we were inside. Waving at Stefan and Finnegan, I was glad we'd said goodbye before this circus because our unceremonious parting was short and messy.

Instantly, we were led into a private room away from the hustle of returning holidayers, treated like suspects rather than lucky survivors.

The man's short hair gleamed like a doberman's pelt beneath the glaring electric lights; his glasses reminded me how desperate I was to replace my prescription.

My fingers itched to steal his so I might see Estelle, Coco, and Pippa in crystal clarity rather than fuzzy haze.

Motioning us to sit, the man settled at the large table and set the clipboard down in front of him.

Awkward silence fell.

Estelle soothed Coco as she squirmed in the velour chair. Poor kid wasn't used to plastics and silks and metal. She'd been raised on salt and wood, the stars were her night-lights and the waves her lullabies. This foreign, chaotic world would wreak havoc on her senses.

Hell, it wreaked havoc on mine. I'd forgotten how archaic human interaction could be. How many sensory interruptions we had to phase out in order to pay attention to what truly mattered.

I'd have to re-learn.

And fast.

"So…" I cleared my throat. "What happens next?"

The man clasped his hands. "We're just waiting on a few others, then we can begin."

A few others?

Who exactly?

An answer came ten minutes later, after a carafe of water and shortbread cookies on a three-tiered cake stand was placed before us.

A woman joined our party with an identical clipboard, taking her place at the top of the table.

A door opened and shut, reverberating in the all glass room. The *clack clack* of high heels sent chills down my back.

Pippa turned first.

Of course, it was only right.

Family was family. No matter how much time had passed.

But the way she beamed and burst into thankful tears tore out my heart and smashed it into the untouched shortbread.

"Nana!" Her chair went flying, sending Coco into a squeal of fright. Estelle turned at the same time I did, just as Pippa soared into the arms of a frail grey-haired woman with dangling pink earrings.

Her bony arms came around my child, holding her close to a scratchy woollen suit and well-worn handbag. "Pippa! Oh! I'm so glad you're okay."

I should look away as Pippa was graced with a thousand kisses, dotted haphazardly on her forehead. I should be happy that she had one surviving family member.

But I wasn't.

Because I knew the truth.

This was the last time I would be able to call her mine.

"Ah, Mrs. Evermore. Now that you've arrived, let's begin." The man motioned for her to take a seat.

However, she didn't. She remained standing with her arms around my daughter and glowered at Estelle and me. "Where is Conner?"

The interrogation had begun.

She'd not only ripped out my heart by claiming Pippa, but stomped on it, too.

When no one answered, the old woman took a couple of steps forward, dragging Pippa in her spindly embrace. "I asked...where is Conner?"

The first question...the one I'd been dreading.

Her rage increased.

Pippa cried into her nana's suit, unable to utter the words. She hadn't spoken them yet. She hadn't verbally admitted that Conner was dead. Whenever she spoke of him, she used words that were ambiguous. Deliberately ignoring the truth.

That he had gone.

That it wasn't a lie.

That he'd left her. Me. All of us.

"Answer Mrs. Evermore's question, if you would, Mr. Oak."

My attention snapped to the man running his fingers pompously on his clipboard. My instincts kicked in, sniffing for his hidden agenda. Because he had a hidden motive; I just didn't know what it was.

Estelle wiped away tears and answered for me. "He's dead, Mrs. Evermore." Her chin tilted with courage. "He died of stonefish poisoning. There was nothing we could do."

"Is that the truth?" the officer demanded.

Mrs. Evermore turned puce. "You're telling me my grandbaby is dead? My son and daughter-in-law? All dead?"

Pippa cried harder, burying her face in her nana's protection.

Come here, Pippi. I'll protect you.

Not that crone.

"What do you mean is that the truth?" Estelle balled her hands. "Of course, it's the truth. What are you implying?"

Coco sniffled and wriggled but didn't make a peep, her eyes wide with fear.

"I'm implying, Ms. Evermore, that perhaps Mr. Oak had something to do with his passing."

"What?!" I lurched to my feet. My chair screeched along the porcelain tiles.

The man and woman (who I still didn't know their names) looked worriedly at one another. "I'm just saying…with your history."

"My *history?*"

"Yes, you can't expect us not to ask that question. After all, no one was there to attest your innocence."

"My innocence?" I punched myself in the chest. My heart resembled a fire-breathing creature. "I have nothing to attest. It's the goddamn truth."

How had a homecoming become so twisted and wrong?

My head swam with weakness, my immune system draining far too fast thanks to life-sucking vampires.

Estelle stood, keeping a calming hand on Coco's head. "You're incorrect. There *were* people there to confirm his innocence. Us! I know why you're targeting Galloway and you couldn't be further from the truth. I've never seen someone so broken over another's death. He loved that boy. We *all* did. We would never hurt him. We would've died in his place if we could."

I breathed hard as Estelle held out her hand for me.

Every desire wanted to latch onto her, but I couldn't. I wouldn't use her as my safe place, not when I'd done this.

I'd caused these suspicions.

My past had superseded me.

She shouldn't have to pay for that.

Everyone stood in a rage-filled standoff until Pippa untangled herself from her grandmother and stood alone in the sea of tiles, looking younger, sadder, older than I'd ever seen. "It's the truth. Conner stood on one a couple of years ago and Stel and G saved him. They looked after us. We would never have survived without them."

She bowed her head. "My brother…he…he…" She smashed fists into her eyes, forcing herself to continue. "He loved them as much as I do. Don't spread lies when you don't know what happened."

Her grandmother gathered her in a hug, her face softening with shared grief. Her eyes met mine. "I'm sorry. To both of you."

Estelle nodded curtly. "I understand."

"I appreciate you looking after my son's children."

"I would do it again in a heartbeat." Estelle looked at Pippa. "I love her like I love my own daughter. She'll always have a place with us."

Grandmother Evermore smiled sadly. "That's very nice to hear. Likewise, my home is always open to you." Her gaze flickered to me. "Again, both of you."

Biting her lower lip, she hesitated before blurting. "Are we related, child?" Coming closer to Estelle, she added, "You have my husband's last name, yet I wasn't aware we had any relatives in Australia."

Estelle ran her fingers through Coco's blonde ringlets. "No, I don't believe so. Just one of those quirky happenstances."

Joanna Evermore closed the final distance, stopping by me. "May I?"

I froze.

May she what?

Before I could reply, her bony arms wrapped around me. "Thank you. From the bottom of my heart. My son would be proud knowing you loved his children as much as he did."

Letting me go, she gathered Estelle in the same treatment with a kiss on her cheek for good measure. "And you. I'm ever so grateful."

Estelle hugged her back when I had not. "I want you to know Duncan and Amelia were given a graceful send-off. We thought of them often, and they're free from their tragic end."

Tears welled in the old lady's overly powdered face. She would've been a handsome woman. Now, she was wrinkles and worry. "Thank you. One day, I want to hear the story of what happened. But today isn't that day."

Turning to Pippa, she opened her arms. "Today is the day I rejoice having one family member return."

Estelle sniffed as Pippa burrowed into her grandmother. "Oh, Nana, I wished you'd been there. But I have Mummy's bracelet and Daddy's watch. And their wedding rings."

Joanna met my gaze again. "You kept them?"

"For Pip and Conner." I flinched, screwing up in just a few words. Conner no longer needed such trivial things. "For you. For family."

"You *are* family, G." Pippa smiled shyly. "Always."

The rage holding up my spine siphoned away leaving me hollow and hurting. "And you, Pippi. Forever."

Pippa came to me. I dropped to one knee to embrace her completely. Her torso bent over my shoulder as we glued tight, tight, *tight* together.

Estelle came to join us.

Because we knew.

This wasn't just a normal hug.

This was goodbye.

The man in charge of this God-awful meeting cleared his throat, breaking the spell. Pippa wiped away her tears, backing into her nana.

I nodded as if it made perfect sense. We were her naturally appointed guardians, but we were also awful memories. She loved us, but whenever she looked at us, she saw Conner, our island, pain and suffering and death.

No young kid should have to see that over and over again.

I couldn't take my eyes off her but the man interrupted my sadness. "I'm sorry, I've been remiss in introducing ourselves. I'm Alexander Jones and this is Daphne Moore. We're here to make your immersion back into our great city as easy as possible."

The tone of the meeting changed.

However, instead of sitting, Estelle and I remained standing, poised as if any second Pippa and her grandmother would disappear.

Coco kept her blue-green gaze locked on us, gripping the back of her chair with tiny fingers.

Daphne asked, "Do you have your passports by any chance? That would make the process a lot faster."

My fists curled.

Seriously? They wanted to waste our time with these questions? Luckily, Estelle answered because I was about to lose it.

"No, they're back on the island. Besides, they're expired now."

"Ah, never mind." Alexander Jones looked at his clipboard. "You'll be expected to undergo a full physical, despite the captain's doctor assuring us you're all in good condition, considering the recent events."

There was no question to that nonsense.

We remained quiet.

Daphne said, "Along with the medical, you'll be expected to undergo a debrief on how you survived, what you cooked, how you sheltered, and why you chartered a helicopter in such bad weather. Search and rescue will discuss the parameters of their initial investigation when you disappeared and will have their own questions, I'm sure." She smiled thinly. "Of course, such things can wait. This is just preliminary warning of what—"

"A warning?" I tensed. "Strange choice of words, don't you think?"

Ms. Moore stiffened, glancing at her partner. "Um, well..."

"Not entirely, Mr. Oak. I'm afraid we do have a mixture of good and bad news."

Of course, they did.

It would've been too much to expect a kind welcome. Everything had to be so hard when dealing with bureaucrats and red tape.

I crossed my arms, standing over Estelle and Coconut, preparing to protect them from whatever verbal stupidity we'd be subjected to.

"One thing we need to clarify, Mr. Oak. Is..." Alex looked at his paper for the millionth time. "You're not Australian. Are you?"

I wanted to lie. To say I was Australian so I wouldn't be separated from Estelle but my accent gave me away.

My English clip that I couldn't hide.

Anyway, they already knew the truth. They had every detail they needed. I wasn't an idiot. My verdict had already been decided.

Before I had time to answer, Daphne jumped in. "Mr. Oak, you are in fact from Kent, is that correct?"

"You have our birth certificates and God knows what. Do you really need me to answer that?"

The two officers fell quiet.

These questions were a farce.

I balled my hands tighter. "Just get on with it. What's the good and bad news?"

Ignoring me, Alex asked, "And you were heading to Fiji on a work visa for three months?"

They wanted to play?

Fine.

"Yes."

"Yet you ended up overstaying by an extra three years and three months."

"I hardly call crash landing and having no way off the island a deliberate overstay."

What was with the skulduggery officials and pompous paperwork? Couldn't they empathize? Couldn't they understand what we'd been through? We didn't need this Spanish inquisition.

"That being the case, we can't permit you into Australia until necessary forms have been completed."

"What? You can't do that—" Estelle leapt in my defence. "He's mine. We're married. We have a child together." She pointed at Coco as if there was any mistaking the blended creation of her blood and mine. "See."

Alex frowned. "That does bring us to another issue. We will need to figure out what to do with the infant."

Right, that was it.

"What to *do* with her? Don't speak about her like she's an inconvenience, mate. She's my *daughter*."

Estelle placed a hand on my trembling forearm. "Its okay, G. I'm sure that's not what they meant."

"No, quite." Alex shuffled his papers. "Getting back to the point. We do require correct paperwork. Ms. Evermore is free to enter the country and as the child is clearly hers and below the age of five, she can travel under the proviso of attending the necessary meetings to arrange citizenship."

"And what about me?" I bit back my rage.

"You, sir, are a little more complicated."

"I don't see why. You say I don't have forms. Well, give me the bloody forms and I'll fill them out right here, right now."

"It doesn't work like that."

"It can work however you want it to work."

"I'm afraid that isn't the case."

Estelle clutched my hand in hers. "We're married. Doesn't that mean anything?"

"Legally?" Daphne raised her eyebrow. "You have a marriage certificate and evidence of this union?"

Estelle straightened her spine, fighting for me. For us. "For all intents and purposes. Yes. Coco is evidence of our relationship. Surely, that's enough."

"But the paperwork?"

Estelle didn't reply.

I did. "No, we don't have a damn piece of paper. But that shouldn't matter. We're not separating. End of bloody story."

The two officers stared at each other as if we were troublemakers and not long-lost prodigal returners.

Behind us, Nana Evermore couldn't stop touching Pippa. The longer Pippa stood with her grandmother, the more she lost the persona of wild urchin capable of anything and transmogrified into a scared eleven-year-old girl, bowing to her elders.

Don't be that kid, Pippi.

I knew her better than that. This was just shock.

Where was the quiet but super-intelligent young woman? Where was the witty jokester, the inquisitive sea-sprite?

I knew where…back on the island. Just like the rest of us.

Nana Evermore interrupted. "Talking of documentation. I'm assuming all ours are in order?"

Estelle's head snapped up. "What documentation?"

The immigration officers nodded. "You are correct. A temporary passport has been issued and you're free to return to America."

"What?" Estelle stumbled. *"No!"*

Coco sniffed, her face going red with ready-to-spill tears.

"You can't. I won't let you." Estelle dashed to Pippa's side. "You don't want to go back to America, Pippi. Stay with us. We're your family now. You, me, G, Coco, and Conn—" She realised her mistake too late.

Pippa's face hardened and fell all at once. "My brother is dead."

She finally said it.

I wish she hadn't said it.

"I need to be with my family."

"We are your family." Estelle grabbed her elbows, ignoring the old woman tutting under her breath. "Pip, don't do this. We'll heal together."

Wisdom far beyond her years filled her gaze. She threw her arms around Estelle. "I'll always love you, Stelly. I'll visit and call and never ever forget you. But…I want to go home."

Home.

Turned out one of us hadn't replaced that word with our island. Pippa had been the youngest to crash yet the one to hold onto the illusion of civilisation the longest. She'd been loyal while we'd traded our city lives believing our stranding was forever.

I couldn't begrudge her for that. And I couldn't let her go feeling as if she'd let us down.

Even though I suffocated inside, I went to her and wrapped her in an adoring hug.

Nana Evermore politely moved away, proving she wasn't the ogre I wanted her to be.

She was just a grandmother who believed she'd lost her entire bloodline only to find one back from the dead.

If I were in her shoes, I'd want to steal Pippa the second I could, too.

"We love you, Pippi." I spoke into her hair, smelling the Fijian breeze and coconuts of our island. "Keep your promise and stay in touch."

She nodded as I let her go. "Always, G. I'll always love you. *Always*."

I nudged her chin. "Conner and your parents would be very proud of you."

She forced a weak smile. "I hope so."

Estelle struggled to let her go, but I pulled her into my arms and held on tight. I didn't let go as Pippa gave us one final wave and took her grandmother's hand.

With a smile and promise to call when they landed, Pippa walked out of our lives for good.

It'd taken days to fall in love with her, years to get to know her, and now, we'd lost her in mere moments.

That was the worst part, but as we turned to face the officers, it turned out it wasn't the only piece of terrible news.

There was more.

"Estelle Evermore, you have free clearance to enter Sydney and will be placed in a temporary apartment until your affairs can be resonated and your death certificate revoked. Unfortunately, your home has been sold along with your belongings, but your last will and testament has been overseen by Madeleine Burrows."

Estelle jolted, latching onto new subjects. "I didn't—I didn't know I had a will. And Madi. Is she here?"

Alex shook his head. "We weren't aware to contact her. The captain of the Pacific Pearl gave no such instruction. However, your lawyer has been notified, and he advised Ms. Burrows of your safe return. I believe she will pop in to see you once you're settled."

Estelle focused on the good news while I focused on the bad. She had a home to go to, permission to take our daughter, and a friend waiting to welcome her.

Me…the jury was still deliberating.

If it were anything like the last jury I'd faced…I was in deep shit.

Every muscle locked as the man delivered my verdict. "As for you, Mr. Oak. We are aware of your ordeal, and under normal circumstances, we would offer compassionate grounds to allow entry for a time. We would overlook the fact you do not have the necessary visas and work with you to ensure future paperwork was arranged. However, you are a convicted felon. You have a criminal record.

"As per Australian law, we don't permit serious offenders into our country without a full background check and deliberation. Even then, it's never guaranteed." He peered at me over the bridge of his glasses. "*Especially* for murderers."

And just like that...I'd gone from almost dead to forbidden.

Estelle was no longer mine.

My past had finally caught up with me.

It was over.

Chapter Seventy

. . . .

ESTELLE

. . . . . .

THIS CAN'T BE happening.
I couldn't let it happen.
Galloway was mine.
I was his.
I'd delivered his daughter.
We *loved* one another.
"You can't be serious?" My voice resembled a shrill violin.
"What do you intend to do?"
The immigration officer (who'd become my nemesis) cleared
his throat. "He will be held in the detention centre for his flight
tomorrow and deported to the United Kingdom."
I couldn't stop shaking.
No, no, no...
Coco jumped off her chair, rushing on her tiny legs to grip my
thigh. "Ma-ma. Home?"
Automatically, I scooped her up, not tearing my eyes from the
asshole trying to rip apart my family.
He'd already stolen Pippa.
He wouldn't steal my husband, too. "It's okay, Coco. Don't
worry." In the same breath, I snarled, "Where he goes, I go. You
want to put him in a cage...fine. But you'll put me in there, too."
I watched my angry spectacle almost as an outsider. I saw
Galloway stiffen and his rage at my conviction. I knew he would
argue and encourage me to return home (not my home anymore)
and let him sort it out when he arrived in England.
But I wouldn't let that happen.
We'd been together every day for almost four years. I thought
I'd lost him. I'd watched him die. There was no way in *hell* I would
let them shove him on a plane and pay for a crime he'd already paid

for.

The fact I could stare at these people and stand by my husband knowing he'd killed but know nothing of the facts could be seen as blind naïvety.

But I knew Galloway.

He'd served his penance.

Even if he hadn't been in jail the past few years, his conscience and soul had paid. Time and time again.

He was purged and forgiven.

"Stel, wait." G grabbed me. "Think of Coco. They can lock me up, but I won't let them imprison my daughter." He held my cheeks with shaking hands. "Please...do it for me. We'll be together again soon."

Whatever remaining shards of my heart splintered to dust. "You don't know what you're asking me."

"Yes, yes I do." His eyes blazed with blue horror. "Do you think I want to be incarcerated again? It fucking terrifies me, but I'm willing to do what is needed to keep you safe. And if being deported is the key...then so be it."

"No, I'll fly to England with you. I revoke Australia. If they can do something this cruel, I don't want to live here anymore."

"Stel, we have to be reasonable. We don't know what will happen. I haven't been able to get hold of my father, even though the captain assured me he was alive when I gave him the details. I don't know if he's in a home or sick or where we'd end up."

Self-hatred and despicable confession trickled over his features. "I'm penniless, Estelle. I have nothing to my name. I'm broke. I won't subject you and Coco to an unknown country with no home to go to. Think of how terrified the poor kid would be. It's cold there. No beach. No sun."

He shuddered as he gathered me against him. "This is the only way. Here, she'll be confused, but at least, she'll be around things she remembers. We'll find a way back to each other, you'll see."

"You're an idiot, Galloway. Do you think she cares about the ocean when she's about to lose her father?" I punched him in the chest. "No! I won't let you do this."

The male officer came closer, hugging his clipboard as if it would save him from my furious glare. "Mr. Oak, I'm afraid the bus is here to take you to the compound. If you can say your goodbyes, I'll make sure Ms. Evermore and her child are taken to the apartment."

Galloway whirled on the man, fists clenched and murder in his gaze. A sheen of sweat hinted he didn't feel as strong as he looked. I wanted to kill everyone for stealing what progress he'd made. "Don't fucking talk to me about goodbyes. *Got it?* You'll give us the time we need. It's the least you can damn well do."

The man froze, before backing off slowly. "Fine…yes, of course."

Galloway turned, leading me away. "Get to the apartment and call my father."

"Your father?"

I remembered our conversations. Late at night, beneath the stars, still craving electric light and ice cubes, Galloway revealed a little about his family. His father who suffered viral infection after viral infection after his wife died of breast cancer because his grief stripped his immune system.

He made his father sound sickly and sad, but there was a rod of strength there, too. To remain living when your soul-mate died? I'd lived that horror for a few hours, and I'd almost broken.

I couldn't imagine enduring such hardship for the rest of my life.

"Call my old number. The captain left a message on the machine when he couldn't get through. I told my father I'd ring him when we docked. He'll be expecting a call if he got the recording."

He took a deep breath. "I haven't told you my full story, Stel, but my father will. He has everything he needs to clear my name. I don't know why it happened. I don't even really understand how. But there's a reason why I was freed after being sentenced to life. If the English courts can overthrow a conviction like that, then that same information will convince these assholes that I'm not going to murder downtown Sydney. That I had a reason. That my sentence was revoked. That my record should've been expunged. My father will help us be together."

"I—I—" The thought of talking to the man who'd raised Galloway into such an incredible person intimidated me. Who was I? I was just the woman who'd crashed with him. The woman who'd done such a bad job of setting his broken ankle he moved with a permanent limp.

I wasn't worthy.

But I'm also the woman who claimed his heart.

The woman who carried his child.

The woman who loved him more than anything else on earth.

If that didn't make me worthy…what did?

G's lips touched mine, kissing me hard. "Promise me, you'll call him."

I'd made so many promises in the past few days, I could no

longer keep track. I'd promised to leave him while he was dying. I'd promised to love him, obey him, fight for him.

I'd also cried more tears than I'd ever cried in my life, yet I still had more to shed.

"I promise, G. I'll call him. I'll get this awful mess sorted out."

His kiss turned vicious. "Thank you. Thank you for trusting me and being on my side."

"Always. I'm forever on your side."

"I love you."

"I know."

I couldn't stop my tears as Galloway kissed me one last time, kissed his daughter, hugged us tight, then disappeared with his jailers to be deported.

Chapter Seventy-One

....

GALLOWAY

......

TERROR.

That was the only word I could use to describe the feeling of walking into the holding cell. Not that it was a cell compared to the last one I'd inhabited. This was more like a basic hotel room. A proper toilet with walls (not a metal pan with no privacy), a bed with sheets (not a cot with scratchy blankets), and meals served on crockery rather than slopped into plastic moulded troughs in a buffet line.

But nothing could change the fact that for a few incredible years I'd been free.

I'd been happy.

I'd been the best man I could ever be.

And now...they'd stripped me of everything.

Stolen my wife.

Kidnapped my daughter.

Robbed me of my family.

All over again.

Chapter Seventy-Two

....

ESTELLE

......

The panic of having another control your fate. The dread of relying on strangers to fix it. The powerlessness of being alone.
That is my life.
My new life.
I want my old life.
~~*When living another day wasn't dependent on bribing and bowing.*~~
When fate was negotiable as long as we paid the right price.
Now?
I have no idea the cost of my future.
Taken from Narrabeen Apartments Notepad.

...

RING RING.

Ring *ring*.

I'd been obsessed with calling the number Daphne Moore had given me (courtesy of the information pack the captain had provided) for Galloway's father.

The entire taxi ride to my new address. The entire run from journalists as they swarmed me. Even the moment of stepping into the cramped one bedroom apartment where cool porcelain tiles decorated the walls and the kitchen bounced late afternoon sunshine with its high gloss white cabinets.

It was sterile.

Unalive.

And I hated it because Galloway wasn't there.

My prison guard left me once she was happy her task was complete. Placing the key on the kitchen bench, she murmured some nonsense apology about tearing my family apart and left.

She was wise to leave.

I'd allowed silence to be a curt form of politeness. I didn't answer her awkward attempts at small talk. I didn't glance at her when she touched Coco and made soothing sounds in the taxi.

I ignored her.

Because if I didn't.

I'd kill her.

Then Galloway wouldn't be the only convicted murderer.

My soul panged for Pippa, for my competent babysitter, while Coco screamed and cried with uncertainty over her new life.

I cooed her. I bounced her. I did everything I could to ease her tears while I yanked the phone off its cradle and dialled the number.

Everything felt too much. Too heavy. Too hard.

But I clung to the phone waiting, waiting, waiting for it to connect with my last hope.

"Hello?" a groggy voice answered.

Screw time zones. Screw sleep and rude awakenings.

I didn't bother with introductions.

I'd used up my civil refinement and had nothing left.

"Mr. Oak. Your son is being held for deportation tomorrow against his wishes. He's my husband, the father of my child, and I'm Australian, yet they won't grant him entry based on his criminal past." A hiccupped sob threatened to derail me. "Please...Galloway told me to call you. That you'd know what to do. That you had paperwork proving he wasn't what they said he was and would find a way to let him stay."

For an eternity, no reply.

Then harsh breathing as a man I'd never met teared up.

It seemed tears were in never-ending supply these days.

"Did you say you are his wife? That you have...children together? That he's *alive*."

"Yes, we crashed together. We survived and had a child. A girl. Coconut...long story. And yes. We don't have the stupid piece of paper sharing last names, but we're together. We're married. I love him with everything I have."

"My son is alive." A loud sniff. "And he has a family of his own. I don't know who you are but I adore you already."

I laughed...such an odd reaction, but somehow, calmness trickled down the line. "So, you'll help me?"

"Child...I can most definitely help you." He paused. "First, I need the email or fax number of the bastards holding my son. Second, I'll need to know everything about where you've been and how you survived. And third, I want to meet the woman who has become my daughter-in-law."

I smiled for the first time in days. "I have the business card of the men who took him. I'll recite it. But for now…my name is Estelle."

"Pleasure to meet you, Estelle."

"You too, Mr. Oak."

"No. None of that. Call me Mike." Shuffling sounded followed by a yawn. "Now…give me that bloody email address, and let's get my son out of jail. Again."

....

I'd done all I could.

I'd given cliff notes on the past three and a half years.

I'd passed on the email address required.

I hung up.

I trusted that Mike Oak would be able to spring his son out of prison for the second time and focused on soothing my neglected daughter.

Coconut took forever to settle. Even a warm bath (which was still a novelty) didn't work.

She didn't want her stuffed turtle (courtesy of P&O). She didn't want cheese (which was her favourite food ever since she'd had it four days ago). And she wanted nothing to do with the sterile, lifeless apartment currently housing us.

It was the opposite of our wild island with it sharp lines and unforgiving edges.

There was no freedom in the white, white walls.

Even I felt claustrophobic and unsettled.

Eventually, I opened the balcony door and exited the twelfth-floor dwelling two streets away from Narrabeen beach where I used to live. Late twilight and people still jogged the sandy shores reminding me this beach wasn't private. This beach didn't belong to us. From now on, we would have to share.

I sighed as if my lungs would splatter to the concrete parking lot below.

Coco toddled outside, coming to hold my leg beneath the purple polka-dotted dress the cruise line had given me.

We stood there together, listening.

Just listening.

Breathing.

Thinking.

Finding familiarity in the breeze, in the ocean, in the wideopen space of wildness.

Wave after distant wave, she calmed. Her tiny shoulders relaxed, her face lost its pinched fear, and she lay her head on my thigh, growing drowsy to the sounds of our old home.

I'd always lived near the ocean. Always connected to the watery horizon, never able to be tamed. I would never have guessed that waves would become my heartbeat, my breath, my hope.

I sighed...Pippa, Conner, Galloway...they'd all gone.

I hadn't been alone in three and a half years.

Once upon a time, I'd savoured silence. I'd hankered for peace. I'd been cruel in protecting 'me' time. Even poor Madi was held at arm's length when life became too noisy. Yet, now...I would've given anything for company. I would've swum all the way to Fiji if it meant my world returned to the simplistic heaven of before.

Before our bodies ran out of nutrition.

Before death tried to destroy us.

I wanted Conner alive.

I wanted Pippa back.

I wanted Galloway free.

So many wants....and only one would hopefully come true.

But not tonight.

Scooping up my sleep-standing daughter, I pulled the comforter off the bed, spread out two pillows, and lay on the thin carpet.

The hardness was welcome.

The pillows sensational.

We'd eaten, taken the recommended vitamins to boost our depleted systems, and, as I drifted off to sleep, I didn't notice it had been dark for hours and I hadn't once turned on a light.

I'd bathed my daughter in the dark.

I'd prepared a meal of cheese and crackers from the fully stocked kitchen by starlight.

I'd lived my life the way I had for almost four years...

In comforting moon-cast shadows.

Chapter Seventy-Three

. . . .

GALLOWAY

. . . . . .

MY INCARCERATION ENDED as fast as it'd begun.

I'd eaten the dinner provided (hotdog with relish), I'd stared blankly at the television locked to the wall (some silly rom-com), and settled unwillingly into bed (all while suffering physical cravings for Estelle).

I'd slept with her for so long that I struggled to fall asleep. The worry of how she was. The concern over Coco, the smarting agony of saying goodbye to Pippa, and the uncertainty if my dad could free me again, fermented in my chest with wicked heartburn. A headache also tormented me (a side effect of cellulitis) and my finger still felt tender.

But I shouldn't worry.

I should trust.

After all, my father wasn't the reason I'd been sprung from my previous sentence early. Even though he hadn't accepted the court's verdict and gathered testimonials from families of patients murdered by Dr. Joseph Silverstein, he'd had no power when it came to swaying cold hard evidence that I'd pulled the trigger.

However, miraculously, I hadn't been the only one plotting murder.

A few weeks earlier, another family, unbeknownst to us, had just lost their mother to a malpractice check-up. Silverstein had been the woman's physician for decades. In that time, he'd already killed twenty people (some with uncourteous service and others with full intent—prescribing deadly doses of drugs, arranging unneeded chemotherapy, wilfully killing while pretending to be a caring, worried doctor).

Only this time, when the woman went to him complaining of a

rattling chest, back pain, and trouble breathing, he sent her home with an antiseptic throat spray. He didn't listen to her lungs, take her temperature, or monitor her blood pressure. He ignored the signs of pneumonia on an eighty-four-year old woman. He denied her the most basic of treatment…the same treatment he swore to uphold with his Hippocratic Oath.

He told her to go home.

She called the next day begging for relief.

He told her to stop moaning.

She weakened.

She suffered.

A few days later, she died of complicated pneumonia with pleurisy that any other doctor would've been able to clear up (or, at least, send her to the hospital). If only he'd listened to her chest. Observed her complaints. And done what was right.

But there was nothing right about Joseph Silverstein.

He'd done the same to my mother. He'd told her time and time again to trust him. When she said she'd like a second opinion, he struck the fear of hell into her with complicated terms and jargon. He said he knew what was right for her.

All while he got off on watching her waste away.

However, that was my mother. And she was my revenge to pay.

The husband, now turned widower, was ninety-two, heartbroken, and had his own vengeance burning. After a marriage of sixty-three years, he welcomed death because without his wife…his life was over anyway.

His tale was spookily close to mine.

He bought an unmarked gun.

He boarded the train (his license had been revoked for bad eyesight), and set his electric wheelchair on fast mode as he sped to the door of the man who'd killed his wife.

Only, I got there first.

He saw me bounding from the scene with bloody knuckles and smoking illegal weapon. He watched me throw the gun into a nearby bush, not thinking clearly, and witnessed a nosy neighbour run from her home screaming for the police.

I hadn't had a silencer.

People had heard the shot.

I was seen.

The old man made a decision.

While I was chased by sirens and busy-bodies, he pressed his accelerator and wheeled himself toward the bush.

With what remaining strength he had left, he collected the weapon (still warm and laced with sulphur) and wiped away my fingerprints with his winter scarf.

What happened next was fate working once again against me.

While I was arrested and thrown, without bail, into the judicial system (breaking my father's heart all over again), the old man replaced my fingerprints with his on the murder weapon.

He ensured his wheelchair tyres were visible to the porch and tracked mud on the carpet to the body.

He returned home and packed up the gun, wrote a letter to the police claiming he'd seen me throw a few punches, then leave. That he was the one who unlawfully entered the man's home and shot him in cold blood.

He left medical records of previous instances when his wife didn't receive the best care. He contacted elderly friends who'd also lost loved ones. And finally, a pattern emerged.

He implicated himself and gave enough evidence to prove Dr. Silverstein, cold-hearted bastard and devil, was not a worthwhile citizen. He was a sociopath; a serial killer.

All of that should've saved me from going to jail.

However, the postal system lost the evidence.

Lost it.

The package stamped and marked priority was misplaced in an archaic system that charged far too much and under-delivered.

I was found guilty.

Convicted.

For life.

And that was where I stayed for five long years.

Which I accepted.

Because I'd done it.

However, one day, fate finally decided to stop playing games and the postal system found said package. It was delivered. The documents were read. The gun was investigated.

And I was freed.

Just like that.

No apology.

No compensation.

Just a stern warning that they knew that I knew that I'd done it.

That just because the man who'd sent the letter died a week after sending didn't mean they believed he'd done it. They hated that the widower's voice carried beyond the grave to redeem me.

A complete stranger saved my life.

And I had no way to repay him.

Brady C. Marlton.

My hero.

....

The cell door clanging wrenched my eyes open.

"Oak...you're free to go. We've arranged a taxi to take you to the apartment where Ms. Evermore and her child are staying."

I wanted to burst into tears.

In fact....I'd been strong for so much of my life. So angry. So full of misplaced rage. That I did cry.

I silently let go and my cheeks remained wet the entire time I signed the temporary visa permitting me to enter Australia, swallowed my gratefulness the entire taxi ride, and collapsed to my knees as I knocked on the door of apartment 12F and Estelle fell into my arms.

I'd lived three lives.

An Englishman's existence.

A felon's incarceration.

And a crash wrecked survivor's.

But none of those defined me.

Only one thing did.

This woman.

My wife.

My home.

Chapter Seventy-Four

....

ESTELLE

......

DAWN WAS WELCOMED with an orgasm rather than a yawn.

When Galloway tumbled into my arms, contrite on his knees and heavily burdened with a past he could never shake, we couldn't stop touching.

I hugged him and stroked him, and when I led him into the apartment, I kissed him.

That kiss turned into another.

And another.

And another.

The kiss turned into stripping on the kitchen counter.

The stripping turned to his lips on my sex and his tongue licking me deep.

And sunrise turned into him sliding possessively inside me, claiming me, loving me, solidifying our bond that no matter what happened, no matter who tried to break us, no matter the circumstances that tried to kill us, we were one, and together we could fight anything.

He didn't tell me how his father had cleared him.

And I didn't pry.

One day, I would.

All I knew was Mike Oak had emailed the documentation that'd given my husband his life back. Given him to me.

One day, I would demand the full story, not because I didn't believe he was a good person but because a story such as his should be told. He would forever live with what he did. He didn't take it lightly, but now, he had me and I would help him shoulder the burden of taking another's life. Even if that life was justified to be taken.

"I love you, Estelle."

I kissed his lips, arching my back and inadvertently pressing my breasts against his bare chest. We'd ended up naked on the balcony; hidden by smoky glass panels, we'd gravitated to the sound of the ocean and the comforting never-still breeze of open skies.

For so long, we'd longed for sealed doors and air-tight spaces.

But now that we had them, all I wanted was the wildness of sleeping with no windows, the freedom of rain slapping against flax, and the knowledge that everything we ever needed was within harvesting distance on our own piece of paradise.

Funny how people evolved…most of the time without their knowledge or permission.

"I understand if you want to move back to England, G," I whispered into his skin, peppering kisses among the springy hair decorating his masculine body. "Australia hasn't exactly been welcoming."

He chuckled, gathering me closer. "I don't care where we live. As long as it's together."

"We'll always be together."

"Thank God for that."

His mouth came down, and we lost each other to another sensual kiss. His cock stirred against me and the thought of making love on an open-air balcony with neighbours above who could look down at any moment barely restrained me from rolling him onto his back and straddling him.

So many times I'd done exactly that, pushing him into the surf, the tide lashing my knees as I rocked onto his body, my hands on his chest, my nails stabbing warm skin, and his eyes catching the final rays of moonshine.

We'd taken our islandic existence for granted. We hadn't seen how special it was until it was too late.

I doubted we would ever go back.

Even though I would've given anything to return.

It's funny how I've erased the hardship of the past few months.

All I could remember were the happy times.

Galloway shuffled me off him, his eyes flickering upstairs as the sounds of the sliding door opening alerted it was time to get dressed before we were arrested for public indecency. "Come on. Let's go for a shower."

I padded behind him, nude and not caring. Coco was young enough not to care about body parts, and she spent most of her young life running around naked anyway.

That will change now.

She would have to be more civilised. Go to school. Interact with others.

She was no longer completely mine.

Neither was Pippa.

So much had happened since she'd gone. I hadn't had time to reflect just how much I missed her.

Her disappearance was almost as painful as Conner's death.

How could I remain breathing after having two incredible children taken from me?

"I'm in love with indoor plumbing almost as much as I love you." Galloway winked, slipping into a joke after dealing so long with stress.

I appreciated his lightheartedness.

We needed a laugh. To remember we were still alive and deserved to seize what we had left, rather than sink sorrowfully into the past.

My heart fluttered but not because of his flirtation or the thought of getting wet in the shower but because he honestly looked happy. He looked at home with lockable doors and humming refrigerators.

Maybe I was the only one missing Fiji. Maybe I was the only one stupid enough to want something as hard as survival.

Ever since docking in Sydney, I'd wanted to ask if he'd ever contemplate returning. If there were some small chance of making it work (where we didn't die, had access to medicine and much-needed food)...would he be interested?

I wouldn't be suicidal and return to our basic home. We would need provisions, upgrades, help.

But if we had that...would he?

However, following him into the bathroom and listening to his appreciative laugh as the shower spluttered with instant hot water, I swallowed my questions.

We were rescued.

This was where we belonged.

With internet and toilets and upholstery. With phones with signals, TV with entertainment, and electricity that heated, cooled, cooked, and protected.

Not there.

We were part of society once again.

And proper city folk didn't crave untamed wilderness.

After all...we weren't savages.

Chapter Seventy-Five

· ·

GALLOWAY

· · · · · ·

KNOCK KNOCK KNOCK.

"Can you get that?" Estelle yelled from the bathroom.

We'd finished our second round of sex with her hands on the white tiled walls of the shower and me driving into her lithe body from behind, all while we drank fresh water straight from the showerhead.

It was like having a rainstorm on command, only warmer.

I loved it…but something niggled me, too.

It was wrong.

Unnatural…even though millennium of evolution said it was normal.

"Sure!" Slinging a towel around my waist, I prowled/limped to the entrance.

I couldn't see my woman, but I could hear my daughter. She squealed and the splash of her playing in the bath echoed in the bland apartment. At least, a bath didn't have stonefish or sharks or things waiting to kill her. Coco would never suffer the same awful death as Conner or be eaten by an intruder in our bay.

There were so many positives of living back in society.

So why could I only remember the bad?

The smog.

The stress.

The backstabbing and lying and nasty behaviour?

Running a hand through my damp hair, I made a note to arrange a haircut so I didn't get labelled a caveman and opened the door.

A strange woman stared back.

Her mouth fell open, her gaze dropped to my naked chest

(skinny but toned) to my low hanging towel (I couldn't get used to clothes, no matter how much I needed to wear them) then back to my eyes (that were now scanning her in the same way).

Curvy redhead with freckles (like Conner), dark green eyes, and lips painted a cherry red. "Um...did I get the wrong apartment?"

"I don't know. Who are you looking for?"

Coco suddenly spun out of the bathroom, completely starkers with bubbles sliding down her tiny body. "Catch me!"

Estelle chased after her, her purple sundress sopping wet and clinging to her underweight curves. After so long with bare essentials, she couldn't get used to underwire and underwear, either. We preferred going commando these days.

Wild feral islanders that we were.

Her eyes were alive, her face twisted into a laugh. "Come back here, you terror!"

Her smile was for me, but her gaze went to the stranger at the door.

She slammed to a stop; a hand slapped over her soaking heart. "Oh, my God."

"Oh!" The redhead drifted forward, completely ignoring me. "Stel..." Her eyes brimmed, overflowing as she reached for my wife. "Oh, my..."

"Madi!" Estelle trembled then threw her arms around the girl I'd heard so much about. "Madi...it's truly you."

Together, they slid to the floor in a pile of dresses and lip-gloss, kissing, hugging, welcoming each other back into their lives, all while Coco zipped around in butt naked glory.

Chapter Seventy-Six

••

ESTELLE

••••••

THAT VOICE.

That lilt.

Oh, my God, I've missed her.

After so long, I finally had my best friend in my arms. As we sat hugging on the tiled entryway, I expected a sarcastic quip, a punch to my arm, an insider joke. Something familiar within our dynamics of friendship.

However, she shocked me stupid when she burst into ugly sobs, burrowing her face into my neck.

Galloway froze, his delicious body shining with rogue droplets from his long hair. He cleared his throat. "I, eh… I'll leave you guys to it."

Vaguely, I was aware of him scooping up our naked daughter and disappearing into the single bedroom off the lounge, closing the door quietly behind him.

My heart went with my family, but my attention focused on crying Madeleine. "Hey, it's okay. I'm here."

"I thought—I thought you were *dead*!" Her wails tangled with my hair, knotting with every sob. "I—I—" She couldn't finish, clutching me harder. "When they called me and said you'd chartered a helicopter that crashed…I thought they had the wrong person. What were you *thinking*? Why would you do something like that! You left me!"

A smile broke my face.

A laugh followed not long after. "You mean to tell me…that after all this time claiming you don't cry at TV shows or shed a tear in books, you're crying because I've come back from the grave?"

She pulled away. Her eyes puffed red and tears glittered on her cheeks. "When you say it that way, no, I'm *not* happy you're alive."

I nodded coyly, smiling so hard my cheeks hurt. "Oh, really? So the tears…that was staged, huh?"

"I didn't miss you."

"Yeah, you did."

"Did not."

"Did too."

"It was just a publicity stunt." Her nose tipped up with airs and graces. "I know you. You'd rather go native and hide away for years rather than go on stage and sing. I'm your manager. You don't run away from your manager!"

"I can if she's a tyrant."

Her cheeks reddened. "I was *not* a tyrant."

Giggles percolated in my chest. "Do this, Estelle. Do that. We have to go shopping. We have to travel around the world together. Oh, oops, I just made you an internet star, now you must always obey me."

She swatted me, unable to hide her smile anymore. "You liked it."

"No way."

"Go on…admit it. You missed me."

"Did not."

"Did too."

"Nope."

We glared at each other, slipping straight back into awesome pointless bickering. Our fake glares switched to watery welcome and we fell back into a hug.

"God, I'm so glad you're back." She kissed my cheek. "Just next time you need your space, tell me and I'll leave. Like instantly. Not like before. I won't hound you. I promise. Just…don't try to kill yourself again, okay?"

I stroked her curly red hair. I'd always been slightly jealous of her amazing colour. Where mine had been boring blonde (not stark white from the sun), I'd felt monochromatic compared to her. Especially seeing as I favoured a wardrobe of greys and pastels, and she preferred vibrant almost garish designs.

Pulling away, I pointed at her blotchy nose. "You have snot mingling with your tears. It's kind of gross."

She pouted. "Well, you have no boobs anymore. So I think I win."

I glanced down, hastily rearranging the gaping neckline of my dress. "Just because you have double D's doesn't make you queen."

"It does." She pinched air. "Just a teeny tiny bit."

"You suck."

"No, you do."

Launching herself at me, her arms lassoed tight and her lips landed once again on my cheek. "Estelle, I'm warning you. Don't *ever* leave me again."

I laughed.

But my heart cracked.

To her, everything was perfect. I was home. I was safe. I was exactly where I'd been three and a half years ago.

But my soul was no longer here.

I'd left it in Fiji, on our beach, in our bungalow, with Conner swimming at sunset.

I didn't belong here anymore.

And I couldn't make promises I didn't know if I could keep.

Chapter Seventy-Seven

....

GALLOWAY

••••••

I WAS ALONE with two women.

Two gossiping women.

Coco didn't appreciate the loud conversation, and once Estelle and her friend had calmed down, I dressed Coco in her store bought (no longer tatty t-shirt) diaper and placed her into the nest on the floor where the comforter from the bed had turned into a hard but warm welcome.

The moment she lay down, her little eyes drooped.

I couldn't blame her.

The past few days had been immensely tiring. For everyone. I hadn't been to sleep yet (neither had Estelle from talking all night) and the antibiotics had boosted my system so fast I forgot I was knocking on death's front gate only a week ago.

I felt okay, but my energy levels were at half capacity and the temptation to nap with my daughter rather than dress in clothing (heaven forbid) and make polite conversation (kill me now) was not appealing.

But this woman was Estelle's friend. She was a part of my wife's life.

So I made the effort. I dressed. I closed the door on my sleeping infant and sat through the necessary introductions before fading into the background and indulging in watching Estelle interact with someone she loved.

It was a novelty, especially seeing her act younger than I'd seen. It was also a great way of peeking into her past and learning more about the woman I loved.

At some point, I raided the kitchen for food. The hiss of the refrigerator and blast of cold air shocked me until I remembered how modern conveniences worked.

For the first few days on the cruise ship, lights had been magical, carpet fantastical, and wallpaper so much smoother than palm tree bark on the walls. However, the oddity wore off after a while.

We'd been raised with this stuff. Almost four years away wasn't long enough to erase such imprinted memories, and I hated how easily I fell back into opening drawers for utensils and grabbing plates to eat off rather than a carved coconut bowl.

For an hour or so, Estelle and Madeline gossiped, catching up on years' worth of intrigue. They nibbled on grapes (holy hell, I'd forgotten how amazing they were) and drank coconut water from a bottle (rather than monkey up a tree and carve into a fresh one).

I sat back as a spectator, letting the wash of feminine voices crash over me as they discussed what Madi had done after Estelle's 'death.' How she'd cleaned Estelle's apartment and removed the furniture for the new owners. How she'd contacted the morgue and ran the necessary wake and send-off.

Apparently, she also took custody of a cat called Shovel Face (even though she was mildly allergic) and gave him a loving home until he passed away in his sleep a year ago.

Estelle sniffed with sadness that her pet had gone but squeezed Madi's hand in gratitude for giving him a good life.

For a while, I couldn't understand how these two women ever became such great friends. Estelle was quiet, serious, with the occasional hilarious quip that showed wit, charm, and selflessness. Madi on the other hand was loud, vivacious, and wore every emotion as if they were a decoration.

Halfway through the never-ending conversation, I investigated the fridge again and uncapped the first ice-cold beer I'd had in almost four years.

Nothing else mattered after that first sip.

I reclined in manmade comfort and drank perfect tangy beer. Which was good because Madi had a *lot* to say.

I must've dozed at some point because my eyes shot open as Estelle jolted upright, slapping a hand over her mouth. "That—that can't be right."

Madi nodded solemnly. "It is. Once your funeral was over— you would've loved the coffin I chose, by the way—the paperwork all flowed to me. You, sneaky miss, didn't tell me you'd put me as your emergency contact."

Estelle's gaze flickered to mine.

The energy around the room changed.

I pushed upright in my chair, pinching my eyes to banish sleepy cobwebs. Once again, the craving for glasses reminded me I was no longer stranded. I could go out right now and order a prescription.

But something told me I needed to hear this.

Whatever this was.

Estelle twirled her fingers. "Well, after my parents and sister died...who else did I have?"

Madi nodded sadly. "I know. And I was honoured when the lawyer called me. He said as I was the only one listed on your personal documents and the responsibility of dividing your estate fell on my shoulders. I'd already dealt with your landlord and sold off what I could of your possessions.

"You'll be pleased to know the money went to the animal shelter in Blacktown you support and I kept your jewellery." She waved her hands. "Anyway, that's off-topic. What you really need to know is the deal you signed before stupidly boarding that helicopter took control of your artistic material. They bought your previous songs off YouTube, and your written lyrics not yet recorded. They released the ones completed but sold the remaining unrecorded rights to other artists."

Estelle gasped, shaking a little. "Wow, I didn't know they could do that."

"Well, you should've read the fine print." Madi patted Estelle's knee. "Don't worry. I did, and I made sure I got everything you were owed, even if you were dead."

"But...Madi...that means..." She pressed her hand against her cheek. "Oh, wow."

"Yes, wow."

I placed my empty beer bottle on the side table, sitting forward with my hands steepled between my legs. "Anyone want to tell me what this gibberish means? Why the hell has my wife gone white?"

"Wait, *wife*?" Madi gaped.

Estelle flinched. "Oh, yeah. Um...surprise?"

"*Surprise?*" Madi's eyes narrowed. "First, I find you chose death over me. Now, I find out you got married and I wasn't your maid of honour." She clutched her heart. "You've wounded me. For life, I tell you. *Life!*"

Estelle laughed. "Yeah, yeah. Stop with the dramatics. I know I have a lot of explaining to do, but so do you. Stop teasing and repeat what you so flippantly said before." Pointing at me, she added, "Tell him so he can stop looking at me like I'm about to pass out."

"*Are* you about to pass out?" My thighs bunched, ready to launch myself from the chair. After dealing with starvation and childbirth, living with broken bones and sickness, I'd never seen her pass out.

Madi faced me, her cheeks round and rosy. "Well, Mr. 'I Still Don't Know Anything About You,' your wife is worth three million, two hundred thousand, and a few other measly dollars."

My mouth hung open. "*What?*"

Estelle shook her head. "I—I had no idea."

Madi slapped her on the arm. "Didn't I tell you you'd hit it big when I uploaded that YouTube video?"

"*What* YouTube video?" I inched further off my seat, drawn deeper into a conversation I couldn't understand.

Millions?

How?

She told me she penned songs and occasionally sang. I ran a hand through my hair. *She told me the singing tour was low key and hardly anyone went. She told me it meant nothing!*

"Estelle...goddammit, what have you been hiding from me?"

She blushed. "It's nothing."

"It's not nothing. You kept this from me." My heart literally hurt. "How could you downplay something like that? Your songs on our island. Your music. Your bloody talent. I should've known a voice like yours wouldn't go unnoticed. I should've seen past your blasé comments and dug deeper."

I stood, unable to sit still any longer. "How could you keep such a secret from me?"

Estelle never took her gaze off me as I paced. Her head tilted to one side, blaring messages only for me. "You had a secret, too, remember? And you only told me a few days ago under pain of death."

I froze. "That's different."

"No, it's not."

"How is it not? You should be proud of your accomplishments. While I should...I should—"

"What, G? You should continue to punish yourself? Find some other way to pay? You've paid enough, don't you think?"

My nostrils flared. "That's not for you to decide."

Madi stood up, waving a white pillow from the couch. "Whoa, time out you two."

Estelle and I glowered, but we stopped. The argument (wait, was it even an argument?) hovered, waiting for the smallest spark to erupt again.

Madi pulled a cell-phone from her back pocket. "Before you kill each other, let me show you."

My insides clenched to think of the sun-cracked and ancient phone we'd left behind. Pictures of us younger, fatter, and scared, slowly morphing to capable survivors. Videos of Conner. Theatrical performances of him and Pippa and newborn entries of Coco.

God, I would give anything to have that bloody thing.

I rubbed at the ache in my chest as Conner's death and Pippa's leaving weighed heavily.

Estelle laid her hand on Madi's as she swiped the phone's screen with practiced fingers. "Wait, don't show him. He doesn't need—"

I held up my hand. "Don't you *dare* say I don't need to see this, Estelle. Don't you dare."

"Don't get angry with me, Galloway." She crossed her arms. "Just because I love you doesn't mean I have to tell you everything."

"Eh, yes it does."

"No, it doesn't."

"I would agree if it'd been something stupid like you stamp collected or hoarded stuffed toys. But bloody hell, Estelle, this is major. You're worth millions. I'm worth nothing. How am I supposed to compete with that?"

The argument switched to a full fight.

"*Compete?* There is no competition, G."

"Wrong choice of words. I'm not competing with you. But how can I accept that you have so much to offer when I have nothing?"

"Really? You're truly going there? You can start by not saying you're worth nothing!" She came toward me, stabbing my chest with her finger. "And money doesn't define us, G. We were equals on that island when we had nothing. Don't take away that equality just because a bank statement has a different number of zeros."

Madi scooted between us. "Uh, I'm not entirely sure what's going on here but take this." She shoved the phone into my hand. "Watch and stop fighting."

Estelle gave her a nasty look but stepped away as I stole the phone. I cursed my shaking hand. I didn't know if I shook because I hated fighting or because I was terrified of how successful Estelle was, how capable, how wealthy when I had nothing to offer.

I was a cripple. I was a blind, penniless, cripple.

Bloody hell.

Estelle bit her bottom lip as the YouTube video loaded. "This edition isn't very good. It's not polished."

"Try saying it isn't very good to five hundred million watches, Stel." Madi smirked.

"Holy shit." My eyes dropped to the 'watched' numbers, and sure enough, 529,564,311 people had watched my woman sing with her eyes closed, blonde hair cascading over her shoulder, and the hauntiest, sexiest, most perfect melody falling from her lips, all while she played the piano.

She can play the piano?

The moment I pressed play, the outside world didn't matter.

Only Estelle.

Only her.

Goosebumps broke over my skin as the music soaked into my brain.

How could such random stringed-together sentences be so life changing? How could they make me love her any more than I already did?

She owned my heart completely.

What else could I give her but my soul?

By the time the song finished, Estelle trembled.

Why did she tremble?

From embarrassment?

From fear that I wouldn't like it?

Whatever the reason, I couldn't stand the emotional distance between us.

She needed to know how much I valued her, worshipped her.

How much I would bow to her every damn day of my life.

Handing back the cell-phone to Madi, I grabbed Estelle and hauled her into my arms. She gasped as she landed hard against my chest. "I love you." Fisting my hands in her hair, I kissed her hard, fast, and entirely inappropriately in front of an audience.

But I didn't care.

This woman was magic.

This woman was mine.

As Estelle's tongue met mine, a burst of perfume filled my nose.

Madi hovered next to us, grinning like a demented cat. "Aww, that's cute." Pecking my cheek, she kissed Estelle before giving a cheeky wave. "I'll leave you two lovebirds alone. You sound like you have a lot to discuss. Money being one of them." She cackled. "I'll be expecting a full report on the marriage and anything else you haven't told me by the time I come back tomorrow night."

Estelle smiled, her lips glistening from my kiss. "You mean, I have to tell you about our daughter, too?"

I choked. "Wow, what a way to dump it on her."

"*What* did you just say?" Madi's eyes turned to sniper scopes. "Can you repeat that, please?"

Estelle beamed. "What? You mean the bit about Galloway knocking me up and me giving birth on an island? Or the bit that we have a two-year-old daughter?"

Madi squealed in a perfect imitation of Coco. "Oh, my *God*! Where? Can I see? Where is she?"

My eyes flickered to the closed bedroom door. No doubt Coco would be awake now after that squeal-fest.

However, Estelle wriggled out of my arms and hauled her friend to the door. "Tomorrow, oh so eager aunt."

"I'm an aunt?"

"You're anything you want to be."

"You'd better be prepared for an interrogation tomorrow, Stel. You've been a seriously bad friend to leave all of this out."

"I promise to give you day by day updates."

"Starting with what the hell you were doing flying in the middle of a thunderstorm when you'd claimed you didn't want to go to Bora Bora with me?"

Estelle groaned. "Don't make me feel guiltily for wanting my own space."

"I can and I will. It's my right as your best friend who was left behind to run your dead existence."

Estelle stiffened. "You're right."

"Of course, I'm right. I'm always right." Madi paused with her hand on the doorknob. "Wait, what am I right about?"

"My dead existence. I'm officially no longer alive. All that money, the recording deal…that's in the trust with the lawyer and you're now the beneficiary. That money isn't mine."

Madi snorted. "*Pfft*, I'm only safe-keeping it for you, douche canoe. Every penny is yours. You earned it."

"No, *you* earned it," Estelle argued. "What you did for me. The apartment. The moving. Shovel Face. Madi…thank you so much."

Joking turned serious as the two women hugged.

"Don't mention it." Madi kissed her. "You'll pay me back by introducing me to my niece tomorrow."

Breaking apart, Madi opened the door. "Bye, Galloway. I expect you to actually contribute to the next conversation. It was like having a stray eavesdropping today."

I shoved my hands in my pockets. "A stray?"

"Yep. Estelle found you and brought you home. That's

normally what a stray is." Winking, she added, "Cheerio. Have fun arguing about who gets to buy the mansion."

Estelle closed the door as Madi skipped into the corridor.

She sighed under her breath. "She's never been any different. I used to grow tired watching her buzz around like a wind-up squirrel, but now, now I find it energizing."

"She's something else, I agree."

"Best intentions, though."

"Oh, I have no doubt." I lowered my jaw, watching her beneath hooded eyes. "I can't say the same for my intentions, however." The fact that our kiss had been interrupted wasn't forgotten by my lips or my semi-hard erection.

Estelle slinked over the tiles, slotting herself back into my arms. "Your intentions?"

"I don't know if I should spank you for keeping such things quiet or kiss you stupid for making our future so much easier."

Her eyes darkened at the mention of sexual punishment but guilt won. "I'm sorry, G. I'm sorry for not telling you what the tour meant."

"I'm sorry for telling you about my past and showing you the sort of man you married."

"I'm not. I'm honoured you trusted me enough."

"And do you trust me?"

"Unequivocally."

"So no more big reveals? Nothing of such epic proportions?"

She smiled. "Not that I know of."

"That's good."

"Oh?"

"I can stop being mad at you now."

"You can?"

"Yep."

"And what does that mean?"

"It means…I have another issue that needs taking care of." My body aligned with hers, pressing my hardness against her lower belly.

"Oh, yes, that's very important." Standing on her tiptoes, she kissed me. "Perhaps, I should help you with that."

"Perhaps, you should."

Our lips connected as she breathed, "Now…where were we?"

Chapter Seventy-Eight

······································...

ESTELLE

······

Money.
~~*It can't buy happiness.*~~
It can buy happiness.
But it can't buy health. It can't buy love. It can't buy a future that is priceless.
Money makes everything easier, but it can't buy dreams.
And dreams are what I want.
Taken from the New Notepad of E.E.

...

OUR LIVES CHANGED immeasurably in the next few weeks.

We underwent another medical examination to ensure the vitamins were working and our bodies were putting on necessary weight. We had a meeting with search and rescue, going over their inspection grid and discussing how far off they'd been from finding us (it wasn't that much but enough to keep us secluded). We endured more conversations with Australian immigration about our residency. Sent a massive thank you to P&O Cruises for finding us. And we visited (much to my annoyance) another dentist to ensure nothing was overlooked on the cruise.

Considering we'd been missing for three and a half years, there wasn't much wrong with us. Only a broken heart from a teenage boy's death and the empty space at night where a solemn girl used to be.

But when melancholy tried to take us over, we remembered what we *did* have.

We had each other.

We had Coco.

We were alive and found.

We were lucky.

The day after Madi visited, Galloway carted Coco and me to the closest optometrists and sat for an hour having eye exams and picking frames for a new prescription. The bounce in his step at finally getting new glasses was worth the heartache of being lost in a city we couldn't acclimatise to.

For a week, we readjusted to the busy world. We went out for dinner and gritted our teeth through loud noises, obnoxious diners, and processed food. We put up with a temperamental toddler who demanded the quietness of the beach and nightlights of the stars. And we waited (not so patiently) for Galloway's glasses to be created.

Some days, we braved the supermarket where everything we needed on the island was available within reaching distance for the exchange of money.

Money.

I had some.

I had a lot.

I'd come from an upbringing where a few thousand dollars in savings meant you were doing all right in the world. Heading to America with Madi meant I'd leapt from a few thousand to a few hundred thousand, fully believing my life was set.

But now, I had a few million.

And I couldn't comprehend what such wealth would mean.

It was all so surreal.

Coco would never go without. Galloway and I need never worry about where we could live or how we would afford it.

We were lucky.

Our hardship was over, and we'd been rewarded.

However, as each day bled into the next, I couldn't shake the feeling of depression. I was more depressed here than I'd ever been on our island (even in those terribly dark days at the end).

Here, I felt like I didn't belong.

I still cooked by moonlight, and we hadn't turned the television on once.

It was as if we'd become suspicious of such conveniences and preferred the simplified existence we'd enjoyed.

The only change we did accept was Madi.

She slotted into our lives as if she'd been there forever.

She returned the next night, and we spent the evening talking about nothing and everything. Galloway told her what we'd done to survive. I shared juicy details of our marriage. And she played with Coco as if she'd been born to be an aunt.

Most nights, she'd pop by after work to say hi and hang out.

And Galloway accepted her with charm and suavity—completely unlike how he'd accepted me. Where I'd been given the cold shoulder and blustery glances, Madi was given warmth and welcome.

Then again, according to Galloway, his frustration with me was all based on lust. Wanting me when he couldn't have me.

He didn't want Madi (thank God). But it did make me aware that for the first time, I had to compete for his affection. I wasn't the only woman anymore, and he wasn't the only man. If he popped to the store down the road for a forgotten item, I panicked wondering if he'd find another girl more attractive than I was. What if my gaunt frame and silvery stretch marks no longer held his attention?

However, he had the same fears. And we shared them one night when a nasty quip turned into a heated debate about uncertainty in our relationship.

We'd both been so stupid.

We weren't together because we'd been the only adults on our island. We were together because our souls had bonded, our hearts had glued, and our two had become one.

Afterward, things did get a little easier. Whenever Madi came around, Galloway was on his best behaviour. I guessed being on neutral territory made him behave. However, I liked to believe it was me.

I'd cured whatever festered inside him. It was still there, but he could breathe without feeling guilty. He could laugh without filling with hatred.

He'd mellowed.

But when he held Coco, he came alive.

In bed together, just before falling asleep, we often spoke of Pippa and Conner. We welcomed the memories, and when Pippa finally called us (on the cell-phone immigration had given us), we'd been quiet for hours afterward. Physically in pain with missing her.

She sounded happier. Not cured. Not content. But happier.

Being in a new place—away from us, the island, and Conner's ghost—she might have a chance at healing. I didn't know if she would be okay mentally, spiritually, but at least, physically we'd done what we could to protect her.

And I wanted her to be happy. I wanted it enough to keep our distance until she returned to us.

Night-time was the hardest.

We struggled to sleep on the soft mattress. And gave up in favour of the yoga mats we found in the apartment closet. We relocated to the lounge where Coco slept between us and the balcony doors remained open to the humid breeze and distant crashing of the ocean.

That was the only time we found peace.

True peace.

Peace that wasn't manufactured or bought.

However, we also slept in the lounge with the doors wide because Coco screamed blue murder whenever she couldn't hear the sea. If we popped into the city, she cried. If we tried to give her a treat of chocolate or candy, she cried. She truly was an earth child who found pleasure and belonging in the sand between her toes, the sun upon her face, and the simple sweetness of coconut and papaya.

"Will this get any easier?" Galloway muttered, feeding mashed-up banana to Coco.

Her tiny face scrunched up. *"No."*

"Come on. It's yummy."

"No!"

We'd tried everything, but she still wouldn't eat anything overly salty or sweet. Her palate was refined to simple, rustic food and pounded her little fists whenever we tried to introduce her to flavoured foods such as spaghetti bolognese or meat dishes.

I was a vegetarian and converted seafood lover, but Galloway was a serious meat eater. Turned out our daughter took after me in that department.

However, I still couldn't have eggplant or halloumi (not after the painful association with my family's death).

With all the loss and never-leaving grief lately, my parents and sister had been on my mind. Being back in Sydney made their demise seem so much more recent, webbing with the ache of Conner's passing and Pippa's leaving.

It's all too much.

"I think she misses Fiji," I whispered, rubbing my temples from the slight headache I'd had all day.

Coco looked squarely at me. "Fiji. Fiji. Home!"

The spoon in Galloway's hand clunked into the bowl. "I know, little nut. Fiji *was* your home. But it isn't anymore. We live here now."

Tears welled in her green-blue eyes.

I couldn't stop staring at the nutmeg brown of her tanned skin (that I doubted would ever fade), the light blonde of her ringlets, and the determined set of her pretty jaw.

She was the perfect blend of Galloway and me, holding the same cravings deep inside her.

Yes, baby girl, I would love to go home.

Galloway caught my eye.

I didn't need him to speak to understand he felt the same way.

I hadn't asked him.

I hadn't pried.

But I knew he was homesick.

Why were we here?

Why had we returned if we would trade everything for what we had before?

Before Conner died?

Before Galloway almost died?

Before your family almost perished?

So much death and yet I wanted to go back.

It didn't make sense.

We should be *happy* to be here.

Happy to be safe with medicines and doctors and people around us once again.

Tearing my gaze from his, I stood to take the dishes to the kitchen.

The moment was broken.

No mention of home was uttered.

The next day, Galloway and I spoke for the first time about where we would live. We didn't want to outstay our welcome in the apartment (thanks to the Australian government's generosity) and we needed to put down roots if we were ever going to feel comfortable here.

We discussed what he would do for work. Not because he needed to, but because he couldn't sit idle. He hadn't been able to sit idle in Fiji, and he couldn't start now.

We agreed he'd look into transferring the certificates for his architectural degree here and go into construction. However, none of that was possible until the paperwork cleared and brought us back from the dead.

My lawyer was in charge of that, including reinstating my funds and assets. I still hadn't talked to the record company, but Madi had informed me they knew I was alive and were waiting to discuss their contract terms.

So much responsibility.

So much happening at once.

I wasn't used to it. It made me want to run away and slam the door in everyone's face.

After a long day of uncertainty and endless questions, we finally got the call to pick up Galloway's prescription.

Holding Coco's hand, I waited outside the optometrist after he forbade me from entering. He returned with the box tucked in the bag along with lens cleaner and care instructions.

He wasn't wearing them.

Taking Coco's other hand, we strolled silently back to the apartment. His limp still affected his gait, but he'd become better at hiding it. A few days ago, I'd asked if we should invest in a car. I still had a valid license. It would make things easier—especially carrying groceries back to the house.

However, Galloway refused.

We weren't ready for a car.

We'd walked for the past four years. We would walk for another few more. Besides, the option of swimming all day everyday had been stolen. We weren't ready to have our feet put out of commission, too.

As we got closer to the apartment, I struggled to hold my curiosity of why he hadn't put his glasses on.

What is he waiting for?

Entering our home, he stole Coco and asked if he could put her to bed on his own.

I shrugged and left him to it, slightly miffed that he hadn't put on the glasses that he'd hankered for for so long. He'd complained so much of wanting to see his children and me in full clarity.

Now, he had the chance and didn't.

Why?

Pouring a glass of water, I padded barefoot to the balcony and stood with my eyes closed, pretending I was somewhere where walls were made of palm trees and the floor was sugar-soft sand.

Eventually, Galloway exited the bedroom where he'd put Coco down. He hadn't put her in the lounge, which meant he either wanted to talk or…

My nipples tingled at the thought of sex.

The violent hunger in my blood took me by surprise as he came up behind me and rested his chin on my shoulder. "Can you come with me, please?"

I nodded, taking his offered hand and following him to the couch.

"What were you doing? With Coco?" My voice was inquisitive as I sat down.

He smiled. "Seeing her for the first time."

"You put your glasses on?"

"I did."

"And?"

He looked at the ceiling, a glistening film over his eyes. "And she's absolutely goddamn beautiful."

My heart lurched. "She is. She's perfect."

His hand went to the cushion behind him where he'd stowed the glasses case. Taking a deep breath, he cracked it open and pulled out the sexy black frames. "Now, I need to see just how beautiful her mother is."

I couldn't breathe as he slipped the glasses on.

He kept his eyes down; adjusting to whatever prescription enabled him to see.

Then…he looked up.

His mouth fell open.

His blue irises burned.

And every molecule of love he had for me magnified.

"You're…you're—" His voice cracked.

"I'm?"

"You're so much more stunning than I ever realised." His hands shook as he traced my cheekbone with his thumb. "After so long of not seeing clearly. After so long of falling in love with a woman I knew was beautiful inside and out, now I can see her. *Truly* see her. And I can't believe how lucky I am."

I pressed my face into his palm. "Thank you. That means—"

He kissed me, slipping his fingers to my nape and pulling me close. "I can completely and honestly say that I have the most stunning wife in the world."

Our tongues joined and passion exploded.

His glasses turned askew as I clambered onto his lap—kiss kiss kissing him all over. I didn't realise how terrified I was of him seeing me. How much I relied on his hazy vision to protect that maybe, just maybe, I wouldn't be enough for him.

But now, those fears vanished.

Those fears more than vanished; they detonated in a wash of lust as I unbuttoned his denim shorts and pushed aside the bikini bottoms beneath my white skirt. (I gave up with underwear and bras).

Our lips never left each other as Galloway guided my hips up and slid himself inside me.

Our foreheads bumped as our bodies rocked and loved.

I hugged his shoulders, panting as my orgasm unravelled faster and faster.

And when he pulled back to watch me come undone, his release quaked through him so hard, so vicious, we tumbled off the couch to finish on the tiled floor.

It wasn't until we came down from our high that I noticed he'd orgasmed inside me.

We'd agreed to stop doing that until I was on contraceptive because now we were back with vitamins and rich food, my cycle would no doubt return.

However…we were no longer on our own.

If I got pregnant this time, it wasn't a matter of life or death.

A slow smile spread my lips as Galloway spread me on his chest and hugged me. "I know what I just did. And I'm not going to apologise."

I kissed his throat. "I know."

He stilled. "Do you mind?"

"About what?"

"You know what?"

"That you might knock me up again? Why would I mind?"

His reply was to squeeze me harder.

That night, after making love and dozing in each other's arms, I woke up with damp eyes and tears drying on my cheeks.

I cried for happiness found in all corners of the globe.

I cried for the loss of Fiji.

I cried for a future we hadn't decided on.

I cried for hope.

I cried for sadness.

I cried because, once again, our lives had changed forever.

Chapter Seventy-Nine

• •

GALLOWAY

• • • • • •

<u>APRIL</u>

I THOUGHT IT would be easy to slip back into society.

Easy to relax, be grateful, and embrace what we'd lost when we'd crashed.

It wasn't easy.

We'd been back five weeks.

It'd been five weeks too long.

The only unfettered joy we experienced was when my father flew over and spent a fortnight with us. He rented a short-stay apartment in the same building we'd been placed in but spent every moment in ours.

Seeing him for the first time (even though I was skinny and recovering from illness) had been the best reunion of my life.

He'd cried.

I'd done my best not to.

But feeling his arms clench around me, after I'd given up hope of seeing him alive, was the only good thing about being in Sydney.

For days, he couldn't stop staring at us, blinking with disbelief, demanding tale after tale of how we'd survived. We spoke until dawn one day, explaining the crash, my relationship with Estelle, and how free I finally felt from the guilt that'd hounded me.

Once the poignant reuniting was over, he helped us stalk the property market, searching for a new house to move into.

It was unbelievably good to see him again. But it made me sad that he was still just as lonely as he'd been when I'd disappeared. Just as heartbroken.

I caught him watching Estelle and me a few times with

reminiscent adoration in his eyes.

However, he did find solace in Estelle (they got along as if she was his daughter rather than me his son), and he adored Coconut.

His trip came and went, and it was the hardest bloody thing to say goodbye.

Seeing him put ideas into my head that had no right to be there. Ideas that manifested to obsession. That kept me up at night. That offered hope while Estelle and I struggled with Coco to re-establish ourselves back in this unwanted world.

We'd been given free rent for exactly three months. Estelle thought it was overly generous and insisted on paying for utilities. Me...I thought it wasn't enough after they'd tried to separate us.

A week ago, Estelle and I had a Skype conversation with Akin's family and we sat in respectful silence for the dead pilot. We answered their questions about his resting place, and they granted peace by assuring us they didn't hold us responsible. Akin had flown in worse weather and survived. It was just one of those things.

The newspapers continued to hound us for interviews and the paperwork required to reinstate everything was boring and frustrating. The lawyer was insistent on going through Estelle's singing assets and advised her to arrange a pre-nup.

Needless to say, she stormed out of his office.

I wouldn't care if she *did* ask me to sign a pre-nup. I had no intention of taking her money. But I also had no intention of ever letting her go, so that problem was void.

It didn't help that every day Coco was stressed. She hated concrete and metal and plastic. She hated shoes and underwear and screeched if, God forbid, we ever tried to wash her blonde ringlets with strawberry-scented shampoo.

It had to be coconut or nothing else.

She refused to swim in the apartment's tiny communal pool, and rightfully so after her skin erupted with a rash from chlorine. However, the moment we put her in the ocean (even though it was so much colder than our island), she transformed into the happiest child imaginable.

She'd build sandcastles and collect shells and roll around until she was covered in golden grains. She was at home on the beach because that was where she was born. She was birthed to the sea. She *belonged* to the sea.

How would she ever adapt to the bullying world of cities?

How would she cope with schools and being different?

Would she forever be a free spirit or would she eventually

grow up, don a suit, and become some big-wig corporate CEO?

Try as I might, I couldn't visualize my daughter in an office with a demanding laptop. I saw her as a marine biologist, hair as white as Estelle's as she tagged dolphins and tracked whales.

She was a daughter of the wild not a child of skyscrapers.

But that didn't matter because this was our home now.

....

MAY

We tried to fit in. We really did.

We went out with Madi and some of her friends.

We did our best to introduce Coco to new things, even though she wailed with frustration.

We still hadn't found a house, but strangely, we didn't care.

Coco preferred to spend every waking minute on the beach and sometimes insisted we camp out beneath the moon.

It wasn't as warm as Fiji, so we carried the blankets from our beds and slept on yoga mats on the sand. Beneath the splattering stars, listening to my daughter's relaxed sigh, I couldn't deny I was more at home here than I could ever be beneath a white ceiling and ugly chandelier.

The only thing that ruined our happiness were the dawn surfers sneering at us as if we were homeless and early beach-goers carting umbrellas and boom boxes.

It ruined the fantasy.

The fantasy that we weren't truly here but *there*.

Days passed and we did the same thing.

We explored a little more of the city.

We forced ourselves to acclimatise, to go on trains, to attend open houses even though in my heart, I knew we'd never be able to sign such a commitment.

We were lost.

Only this time, our hearts were lost not our bodies.

Despite our problems, Estelle and I grew closer.

So close in fact, I left one night while she was bathing Coco, and headed to the jewellery shop in the local mall a ten-minute walk from our block.

I withdrew some money from the account my father had reopened with the meagre funds I'd earned from working in prison.

I spent all of it.

I bought her a ring.

And I went back to the apartment and got down on one knee and proposed.

Again.

Chapter Eighty

••

ESTELLE

••••••

Being surprised doesn't mean awe or wow or even shock.
Being surprised doesn't mean you'll love it or hate it.
Being surprised means the one person you love knows you better than you know
yourself.
And that is the ultimate sign of perfection.
Taken from the New Notepad of E.E.

•••

GALLOWAY HAD SURPRISED me.

More than surprised me.

Dumbfounded me.

"I can't believe we're doing this."

"Believe it. This way…it's official. Forever." Galloway smiled, looking so handsome in a black shirt and jeans. His tan hadn't faded, ingrained into his skin after three and a half years of hot sunshine, and the black material popped with his bright blue eyes. His glasses glittered sexily and his lips curled in the perfect way, making me want to kiss him.

And kiss him and *kiss him.*

I wore a similar outfit of jeans with a black off-the-shoulder blouse. I'd fishtail-plaited my hair so it fell over my shoulder (no longer brittle from sun damage or unwashed) and secretly loved the white strands against the dark fabric.

It wasn't exactly a wedding dress…but I didn't want one. Or need one. As far as I was concerned, we were already married.

This was just a formality.

However, I adored my wedding ring.

I couldn't stop twirling it.

There was no expensive diamond, no gaudy gemstones. Just a

simple gold band with the words: *You crashed with me. I fell for you. I love you.*

It was beyond perfect and would never *ever* leave my finger.

Not even to hand it to the celebrant so she could instruct Galloway to place it on my hand with our vows.

No way. It was there to stay.

Madeleine stood behind me with Coco in her arms as Galloway turned and took my hands.

We stood in a small room resembling a beige box with an Australian flag hanging limply in the corner.

The celebrant moved to stand in front of G and me. "Are you ready?"

We nodded.

Looking at Galloway, she said, "As this is just a simple formality, I'll ask the simplest but most important of questions." She grinned. "Do you take Estelle Marie Evermore to be your lawfully wedded wife?"

Galloway licked his lower lip. "I do."

Her gaze switched to me. "And do you take Galloway Jacob Oak as your lawfully wedded husband?"

My nerves drained away. "I do."

The celebrant clapped. "In that case, I now pronounce you husband and wife. For the second time."

We kissed.

We celebrated.

We ignored the pain of missing Pippa and Conner.

They'd been there the first time we'd got married.

Now, they were gone.

We didn't have the children, but we did have that coveted piece of paper.

And the very next day, my last name changed from Evermore to Oak.

It was legal.

Chapter Eighty-One

· ·

GALLOWAY

· · · · · ·

A MONTH AFTER we got married, we still hadn't settled.

We'd done our best.

We'd given it a shot.

We'd been open-minded and appreciative and hopeful.

But now, I was over it.

I was over not being happy.

I was over being father to a cranky two-year-old who begged to return to a place that (to most people) only existed in fairy-tales.

Why should we bow to what was normal? Why should we believe that to excel in life we had to have the fanciest house, the most expensive of clothes, and the most stressful job?

Why couldn't we be honest? Why couldn't we admit that our wants and desires weren't in flashy cities and gourmet restaurants? They were in the wild open spaces of archipelagos and turtle nurseries?

That night, Estelle and I walked along the beach at sunset. Coco played behind us with her sandcastles, chatting to her stuffed turtle, and finding happiness that she couldn't find anywhere else.

The gentle swish of the tide over our toes called to me more than concrete or glass. Something intrinsic had changed forever, and I couldn't get rid of it.

I didn't *want* to get rid of it.

I glanced at Estelle, my heart quickening at how beautiful she was in her loose white dress and unbound hair. Her period had come last week, which meant she wasn't pregnant but her body was able to.

The thought both excited and terrified.

If we gave up on this life and returned to where I wanted, we couldn't have another child…unless…

The ideas that'd kept me company for months kept evolving, twisting, growing. I hadn't shared any of them with Estelle, but I couldn't hold them back any longer.

Once the paperwork was finalised and our world reinstated, Estelle stole Madi from her job as a personal assistant to a CEO and hired her to run the empire she didn't even know she had. The lawyers released control of the trust back to Estelle, but Stel made Madi joint beneficiary for her honesty and loyalty.

The record company had been in touch and requested more songs, more lyrics, more of everything. And if she wanted it, Estelle could have the career she'd always dreamed of.

And I knew she dreamed of it because I'd caught her playing the baby grand in the foyer of a hotel we'd had dinner at while she waited for me to pay.

She looked just as beautiful as she did on the YouTube video. However, something was fundamentally different. Whereas music had been her outlet and passion, now it was second place to what she truly wanted.

What I truly wanted.

What Coco truly wanted.

What we all bloody wanted.

We wanted to go back to our private paradise.

We wanted to give it all up for what we'd found there.

But we didn't have the courage to say it aloud. Didn't have the balls to admit we were willing to give up plumbing and electricity— not brave enough to say that wealth and social standing wasn't worth as much as the quality of life we'd created.

If we continued this way, we would spend the rest of our days wishing we'd been strong enough to admit what we truly needed.

I wouldn't let that happen.

I wouldn't live another day without having what I absolutely desired. I wouldn't let my daughter scream herself to sleep because she couldn't see the stars through the smog, or paddle in the temperate sea to tickle fish with her tiny fingers.

I won't do it.

Dragging Estelle to a stop, I placed both hands on her shoulders. "I have something to say. Something wild and stupid and crazy and so bloody right I can't *not* say it."

Her eyes widened; goosebumps broke out where I held her. "What is it?"

I looked back at our daughter. She raised her head, waving with a piece of driftwood rather than the bright plastic spade we'd bought her. She hated the slimy feeling of manmade toys, preferring the carved starfish I'd done last week on the balcony.

"I think we should go back."

"What do you mean? Go back?" Her eyes narrowed. "You want to be stranded again? With no help. You want to cut us off completely?"

"I said crazy. Not ludicrous."

"Then what?"

"I have an idea."

"Well, share it before I pass out from waiting."

I smirked. "The money from your singing…how willing are you to spend some of it?"

Her head tilted. "What do you mean?"

"I mean…if I asked you to trust me as your husband, would you?"

Without hesitation, she nodded. "Of course, I would."

"Okay, I have an idea."

"What?"

"Trust me?"

"You won't tell me?"

"Just trust me. Give me a few days. Then I'll tell you."

It was a lot to ask, but Estelle gave me those few days.

I made it worth her while.

....

"I'm not asking if it's the correct business decision. I'm asking if it's possible?" I clutched my cell-phone as the Fijian national on the Board of Government Assets and Sales mumbled something unintelligible.

I'd pulled every dirty trick I could to get this conversation. But it also helped that we were minor celebrities in Fiji after finally agreeing to do a small article about our life on the island.

Our glowing praise and gratefulness of such a country had gone down well with the tourism bureau and earned us a call from the Fiji president himself, expressing welcome to his great nation anytime we wanted.

Well, I wanted.

Very much.

But I didn't want a temporary vacation.

I wanted residency.

I wanted an island.

"So…is it possible?" I prompted again.

"It—it is possible. I have to ask what sort of monetary compensation it would require."

"Ask away. I'll hold."

"You want me to ask, right now?"

"Yes. This very moment."

"Uh…okay. Hold please." Annoying music filtered into my ear.

Pacing the balcony off our tiny apartment, I tapped my fingers against my thigh. Estelle had popped down to the beach with Coco to find shells for a sea-inspired chandelier.

Coco had spent the morning pouting and crying for the salty waves. She refused to play on the smooth surfaces of ceramic tile, preferring the roughness of nature and inconvenient reach of microscopic sand.

Come on. Come on.

I wanted this phone call finished before Estelle caught me.

I wanted this to be sorted before I told her.

Before I informed my family of what our future could be.

Finally, the hold music changed, followed by a short cough. "Mr. Oak?"

I slammed to a halt. "Yes."

"This is Mr. Taito from the Board of Investments for Overseas Buyers. I have to say, your request is rather unusual."

"Why? How is it unusual?"

"Well, normally a purchase inquiry is for land with more opportunity than the one you mentioned, larger, closer to other tourist islands. We are aware of your situation from the past few years and are willing to take that in to account. However, I must inform you we do not recommend—"

"That's the one I want. Deal or no deal."

"I see." A short pause followed by a gruff, "As for your other terms. Am I correct in assuming you would pay for everything you mentioned? That you would expect the Fijian government to have no involvement or investment whatsoever? You also understand that if you were successful in your request that every infrastructure would be forfeit after the deal ended?"

My heart raced.

Will they go for it?

I couldn't tell by his voice. He could be taunting me, preparing to tell me the ultimate crushing blow or he could deliver the best bloody news of my life.

"Yes, I understand. I was the one who made the clauses and conditions. I've given you the sweetest part of the deal. All I ask for is the land."

"Give me another moment, Mr. Oak."

Music replaced the conversation and I growled, resuming my pacing. A giggle sounded below as Estelle helped Coco over the wooden balustrade blocking off our apartment's car park from the road to the beach.

Come on. Hurry the hell up.

The link crackled before Mr. Taito returned. "Although your request is highly unusual, I have some good news for you, Mr. Oak."

I bit my lip as I air-punched the sky. Joy I never knew rushed through me. I'd finally grown up. Finally understood what I wanted in life, where I wanted to live, and who I wanted to share it with.

And now, I'd been given the permission to make it all come true.

Taking a deep breath, so I didn't yell with happiness down the phone, I said calmly, "That's great news. Thank you."

Mr. Taito said, "We accept your proposed terms. $250,000 US for the right to reside on the island located at the coordinates you emailed last week. The agreement will include leasehold on the land for eighty years with the option to extend if it suits both parties at that time. The contract will be drawn up and will await your signature upon your arrival into Nadi."

Mr Taito cleared his throat. "When will that be again?"

I smiled as the front door opened and Coco barrelled toward me. My little urchin. My island ragamuffin. My castaway princess.

She was going home.

We all were.

"We'll be there on Friday at eleven a.m."

Estelle raised her eyebrow as I stepped through the balcony door and scooped Coco into one arm. Her nose nuzzled my neck. "Hi, Daddy."

"Hi, Coconut."

"Pleasant flight then, Mr. Oak. Look forward to confirming and welcoming you to our country officially."

"Likewise, Mr. Taito. Thanks again."

I hung up.

Estelle dropped the plastic bag full of seashells on the table, making her way to me. "Who was that?"

My cheeks hurt from smiling. "Just a man."

"A man?"

"A man with a contract."

"A contract?"

I nodded, biting the inside of my cheek to stop from blurting. Estelle put her hands on her hips. It reminded me so much of her bossy caring attitude when we first crashed that I tripped deeper into love. "What contract?"

"A very important contract." Grabbing her, I pulled her into my other arm. Coco squirmed, laughing as I blew raspberries on her throat and kissed Estelle with wet kisses. "A contract that's possible all thanks to you."

"To me?" Her eyes widened with suspicion. "What did you do, G?"

"I spent a quarter of a million dollars."

"You what?"

"Of *your* money."

"*Our* money. I willingly gave you the right to use it as you saw fit."

"I'm so glad you trust me." I kissed her again, radiating happiness.

She squirmed in my hold. "I trust you, but I might revoke that trust if you don't start telling me what the hell is going on."

I glanced at my daughter. "Want to tell her or shall I?"

Coco's green-blue eyes popped wide as she bounced in my arms. "Tell me. Me. Secret. Me."

"Okay, I'll tell you and then you tell Mummy, got it?"

Coco nodded with utmost seriousness. "Uh-huh."

Smiling at Estelle, I whispered low in Coco's ear. "Tell her exactly what I tell you. Mummy…"

Coco paused then repeated. "Mummy…"

"You know the island where we crashed and thought we'd die?"

Coco repeated in her childish voice (minus a few stumbles and age-related discrepancies).

Once done, I whispered, "The island where we fell in love and learned what was truly important?"

That line she didn't deliver too well. But Estelle laughed and nodded anyway, my message slowly filtering into comprehension. Her mouth parted, a feral hope igniting in her gaze.

"Well…" I murmured.

"Well…" Coco mimicked.

Brushing aside her blonde curls, I whispered, "I bought it. We're going home."

Coco froze. Her eyes popped and wisdom far older than her age shone through. "Home?"

I nodded. "Home."

"Turtles and fishies and and and…"

Estelle clamped a hand over her mouth. "What—what do you

mean?"

Pinching Coco, I ordered, "You didn't tell Mummy the last part."

Coco beamed. "Island. Home. Going home. Home!"

Estelle wobbled.

I caught her.

Just like all those years she caught me and cared for me. It was my turn. Once again, she'd made it possible for us to survive. Without the money, we would be forever homesick and lost. Now…we could do whatever we wanted.

All because of her.

"Ho—how? When?" Her eyes filled with tears. "I don't understand."

"How—I called the Fijian government and explained that considering we'd lived in their country for almost four years, that technically makes us a citizen, or at least a sure bet to give a residency visa, if they felt so inclined. After all, our daughter is legally Fijian being born in their waters and all."

"And they agreed to that?"

"It's amazing what a promise of good PR will do."

Estelle blinked. "Okay, so you managed to get approval to live there…how does that give you permission to just buy an island?"

"Technically, I haven't bought it."

"Then…"

"I've rented it for the next eighty years. They'll retain ownership, but it will be in our name and no one else can touch it."

Estelle shook harder with every breath. "You—you're serious."

"I'm deadly serious."

"But what about…Madi and my singing and…Galloway, there aren't any facilities on the island. We made do but Coco needs nutrition. She needs hygiene. We all do."

The smugness inside me overflowed. "I've already thought of that."

Her lips parted. "What?"

"I'm a builder. I intend to add to our bungalow with proper structure and shelter. I'll import nails and rebar and iron for the roof. I'll install rain tanks and septic systems and vegetable crops. Anything you want, we can build, create, or grow."

"But what about life outside the island? What about family and friends? Medicine and hospitals? Schooling for Coco?"

I hugged her hard. "That's the best part. They know where we are now. They can visit; live there for all I care. And the rest, we'll have a boat. We'll have access to whatever we need."

"And Pippa?"

My soul hurt for a moment then rehealed. "She'll know where to find us. It's her island as much as it is ours. I've put their names on the contract, too."

"Theirs?"

"Her and Conner."

My heart smarted.

"You did?"

"I did."

"Can you do that? Add a deceased person to the deed?"

I frowned. "Who knows. But that's what I requested."

"Oh, my God."

"Are you happy?"

"Galloway, I'm…I'm ecstatic. I'm blown away. I can't believe this is happening." She ran a hand through her hair. "Wait, *when* is this happening?"

I smirked. "How attached are you to this place?"

"Not at all."

"How long do you need to pack up?"

"Um, is that a trick question? An hour…tops."

"In that case…"

"Tell me." She laughed, clutching my hand. "Damn, you drag it out."

"You're so impatient." I chuckled. "Three days, woman. We leave in three days."

Chapter Eighty-Two

∙∙

ESTELLE

∙∙∙∙∙∙

Home is where the heart is.
Home is where the soul is found.
Home is where the good times laugh.
Home is where the hard times heal.
Home is home and there is no place I would rather be.
Lyrics for 'Home' Taken from the New Notepad of E.E.

∙∙∙

ONCE WITHIN A song, a music lover and a broken man found the answer to life itself. They listened, they took note, and they lived happily ever after.

I looked for the messages.

I searched the face of the check-in staff as they handed us our documentation. I tensed going through airport security and flinched as I handed over my newly issued passport to board.

But nothing happened.

No strange occurrences.

No premonitions.

No warnings.

That had been before.

That had been when I was lost.

Before I knew what I needed.

I hadn't listened to the messages…but then again, maybe I had?

Either way, they led me to the most perfect future I never knew I wanted, and now, we were claiming it without hesitating or wasting a life wondering what could've been.

Coco placed her hand on the portal window of the aircraft as the final passenger boarded, the door closed, and we taxied from

Sydney airport to the runway.

My stomach tightened, unable to prevent previous memories of turbulence and terror.

This flight would not be easy for me.

But I would endure it because the destination was worth any price I had to pay.

I'd already paid.

Nothing bad would happen.

Please, don't let anything bad happen.

I wasn't beyond begging fate to be kind. And I was scared enough to barter for a safe journey.

Madi had been told in a rush of organisation that we were leaving, that she was always welcome, and the moment we'd arranged a satellite phone and internet to be installed on our island, we would stay in touch.

I would sign the offered contract. I would continue to deliver lyrics for pop stars and sing my own creations.

But I would do it from the privacy of our paradise.

She didn't know if this was a mid-life crisis or a justifiable decision. Either way, all she could do was wave us off with a fond farewell.

As the aircraft engines screamed and we launched from earth to sky, I placed my head on Galloway's shoulder and sighed.

I wasn't afraid of crashing.

I wasn't afraid of anything anymore.

This is right.

This was the only thing we could've done.

·······················

Landing in Fiji was unlike any landing I'd had before.

Unlike docking in Sydney after almost four years on a deserted island. Unlike landing on vacation full of happy possibilities and relaxation.

This landing was the landing of my heart and soul. My toes touched tarmac but my soul…it flew free, escaping into the Fijian humidity, rejoicing to finally be back where it belonged.

Galloway took my hand.

A government representative escorted us from the plane and through the terminal. Two airport services guys helped us wheel our four huge suitcases from baggage claim. This time, we'd come prepared. We had medicine, first-aid, shampoo, conditioner, toothpaste, and a year's supply of clothes.

We were really doing this.

But we would do it right without the hardship of last time.

"We have the helicopter standing by to take you, Mr. Oak."

Galloway and I slammed to a halt.

Our voices threaded as one. "No helicopters."

The guide froze. "Uh...okay."

"We'll go by sea." Galloway strode forward. "Surely, someone with a ferry can take us."

"It will be a few hours by boat."

"Don't care." Galloway scowled. "A helicopter led us to our home. I don't want another taking us to a different one."

We shared a smile as the man rushed ahead to change the plans.

Coco tugged my hand. "Want helico—copter."

I ducked to her level, brushing unruly curls from her eyes. "Believe me, Coconut, you don't."

....

The SUV stopped outside the open-air market where run-down buildings and faded shop fronts touted their wares.

We'd gone straight from the airport to the arranged meeting to sign the necessary documents for ownership. Sitting in air-conditioned luxury, we'd been officially welcomed, congratulated on our home, and transferred the funds in exchange for the deed on our island.

Our island.

We own it.

For the next eighty years, at least.

The driver turned to face us, his hand on the wheel. "How long would you like?"

Galloway opened the door, helping Coco and me out. The trailer behind us stored our many suitcases, soon to be filled with a lot more supplies.

"Give us an hour. We'll be as fast as we can."

The guide nodded as we shut the door and each took Coco's hands. We strolled down the middle aisle where sellers sat on their knees offering sugar cane and freshwater mussels.

Occasionally, Galloway would stop and buy a bag of seeds and other long life materials. We slowly gathered things we would need: a large propane bottle, a pack of lighters, matches, mosquito nets, large water containers, and items too big and heavy to bring on the plane from Sydney.

We also bought a kettle, fan, and electrical items.

Just because we'd been without for so long didn't mean I hadn't appreciated having the convenience back in our apartment.

Coco's face remained eager and inquisitive as we entered a

hardware store with bare shelves and ancient items. This wasn't a normal depot where regular supplies flew off the shelves. This was the island way of life, where old traditions still trumped new inventions and the need for bright shiny toys didn't have the same allure as the western world.

Galloway strode up the aisle, collecting a few second-hand tools and several kilos worth of nails. "You have a generator for sale?"

The local man stopped playing a pinball app on his cell-phone, a cigarette dangling from his mouth. "Generator?"

"You know…one that makes power? Preferably retrofitted with solar panels rather than diesel."

The man puffed smoke. "I think we have one."

I drifted away, taking Coco outside so her innocent lungs weren't corrupted by nicotine.

Galloway didn't take long.

He returned from the store to pass me an armful of shopping bags before disappearing back inside.

Struggling a little under the weight, he hugged an ancient dinged-up generator with a tatty cord. "This will do. At least, we can have light at night if we want it. I'm all for roughing it, but electricity now and again would be nice. Not to mention, it will make using power tools a lot more effective."

"Always so practical."

He grinned. "That's why you married me."

I leaned over and kissed him. "One of the many reasons."

....

The first glimpse of our island appeared like a mirage.

A hidden utopia belonging entirely to us.

The slap of waves on the boat's hull compounded my excitement. I would never have believed it if I'd been told I'd return of my own vocation. That I would trade everything I knew and choose a life where I'd struggled and feared but ultimately found so rewarding.

Coco untangled her fingers from mine, dashing to the side of the speedboat. High tide covered the outcropping of the reef, allowing the vessel to glide closer to the beach.

"Swim. Swim!" Coco jumped up and down, doing her best to reach the balustrade.

Galloway picked her up. "In a minute, little girl."

I moved to his side.

I shook from nerves, homecoming, and the strangest sensation of doing exactly what I was born to do.

Our island.

We'd never seen it from this perspective before.

Never knew how small it was with the ocean lapping on all sides or how picturesque it was with soaring palm trees and gleaming golden sand.

And there...tucked in the shadows of the treeline was our house.

Tears sprang to my eyes as years' worth of memories unfolded. Small layers at first, followed by sheets and sheets of laughter and tears, triumphants and trials.

We'd endured so much.

But we'd come back.

Galloway took my hand, squeezing tight, as we drifted closer.

"I can't believe we're here," G whispered. "Can't believe we're about to go home without Pippa and Conner."

The stain of sadness weaved with my giddy joy.

"I know. It doesn't seem right. But Conner's here. And Pippa will visit...eventually."

I hope.

I couldn't look away, drinking in every facet of shadows and sunshine. As pretty as the wilderness was, it wasn't practical for docking. We had no pier, no ramp or trolley to haul our multiple belongings from the boat.

But we would make do.

We had a bamboo kayak that we'd never used. A life raft to rescue us. It lay where we'd left it, half stockpiled, all alone on the virgin beach. It would finally have a use, ferrying our items to shore while Galloway guided it from the shallows.

The moment the anchor splashed, Coco squirmed. "Home!"

Galloway managed to keep hold of her as she turned ballistic. "Hey, calm down."

"Swim! Swim!"

He chuckled. "You get into the water first, Stel. I'll pass her to you."

I did as he asked, fighting happy tears as my feet kissed the water's surface then slipped beneath the warm embrace, up my calves, my kneecaps, mid-thigh. I didn't care about my shorts and t-shirt getting wet. All I noticed were the blissful welcome of my toes sinking into soft, soft sand.

This was my place.

My one true home.

Turning to grab Coco, Galloway bent over the rail and kissed me. The moment our lips touched, I wanted him desperately. I wanted to escape into our bamboo grove and rekindle our island romance. I wanted to say hello and delete the goodbyes that'd happened here.

Conner.

Pippa.

We'd called Pippa the day before we left and told her we were returning. She didn't sound surprised. If anything, she'd expected such a call.

She'd regaled her adventures of the past few weeks, her room at her grandmothers, her first day back at school. She sounded centred and calm. However, her parting words had destroyed me: *"Say hello to my brother for me."*

Coco wrapped her small arms around my neck as I plucked her from Galloway's grasp. The moment he was free, he leapt over the side and cannonballed beside me.

The spray went everywhere.

"Down. Down." Coco kicked.

The water was too deep for her to stand, but she could swim before she could walk. She was a Fijian water nymph.

Plopping her (clothing and all) into the turquoise bay, she giggled and ducked under, half-doggy paddling, half breast stroking toward the shore. Galloway suddenly scooped me into his arms. Saltwater rained from my toes.

"What are you doing?" I laughed.

"Walking you over the threshold, of course."

"That's very nice of you. However, I do believe we're past that in our marriage."

"Never past romance, Estelle."

We shared a kiss.

"Never change, G," I murmured against his lips.

"I hadn't planned on it."

"Well, perhaps…you could change one thing."

His eyebrow rose. "Oh?"

"You could grow your beard and hair again. I rather miss seeing you all wild and savage."

Ever since we'd returned to Sydney, he'd kept his hair cut to his nape and his stubble no longer than a few days' growth.

He was handsome no matter what, but there was something undeniably sexy being rugged and untamed.

"I guess that can be arranged."

I kissed his cheek. "I'm the luckiest wife alive."

"Damn right you are."

I giggled under my breath. "Has your ego inflated?"

"Not at all. Just stating facts. Because I happen to be the luckiest husband in the world."

"That's way too cheesy."

"Do you care?"

As Galloway marched toward the shore, chasing our swimming daughter, I laughed. "Not in the slightest. I love you. Cheesiness and all."

"That's the nicest thing you've ever said to me."

I pinched him. "Come on. I always say nice things."

His eyes glowed with love. "I'm gonna say nice things to you the moment we're alone."

My core clenched as the tide relinquished us to dry land.

Coco bolted up the beach, dripping wet, toward the bamboo home we'd created. Wrenching open the rickety door on hinges made of flax string, she vanished inside and came out with her carved voodoo doll from Conner. "Co's doll!"

My heart burst.

This.

This was what life was about.

Family and connection and memories.

Thank God we'd learned that lesson while we were young enough to enjoy it.

From disaster to serendipity.

Life was a journey and no one (no matter how wishful, bossy, or opinionated) could change the destination.

That was fate's job.

Our job was to stop fighting.

Because only then could we find true happiness.

....

"Wrong, suckers. I'm her favourite person. Didn't you hear her? She obviously said Co...that's me."

Tears trickled down my face as the video summoned Conner from the dead.

"He was so full of himself that night," G murmured, tucking me tighter against him as we lay in the dark. "So cocky and proud."

"He'd earned it. He was her first word."

We'd been back on our island only a few hours. We'd unloaded our cargo, said goodbye to the crew, and arranged a pick-up time in a few days to return to Nadi to buy a speedboat of our own.

As the sun set on our first day, we'd enjoyed a simple dinner of fish and coconuts, returning to our tasks as easy as if we'd been born to it. We didn't touch the canned goods or packaged produce.

We didn't drink the variety of juices or fresh water. And we didn't crank up the generator to cast away the moon-tinged darkness as it fell.

It'd taken us months to get used to modern conveniences.

And only hours to relax into primitiveness.

Coco had stitched my heart with love as she'd squeezed me so tight before bed. Her body trembled with excitement at returning where she'd been raised, back in the sea where she'd been born, back where she belonged.

Now, the island was quiet.

And Galloway and I had finally gathered the courage to open the carved wooden box and say hello to my bracelets, passport, and unfixable cell-phone. Amongst our left-behind belongings were Mr. Whisker Wood (Pippa's carved cat), and my birthday heart from Galloway.

I hated that we'd left them alone.

But now we were back, and I'd never take such things for granted again.

Together, we'd inserted the memory card with so much precious reminiscing into the new waterproof device we'd brought with us.

The first video had ruined us.

The second had decimated us.

But as we spent the night welcoming ghosts into our heart, we shed sadness in favour of thankfulness for such precious playbacks.

The day Coco said her first word.

The day Conner earned her undying affection and bragged about it for weeks. We were all so skinny and sunburned. So much wilder and on the fringe of survival than we'd thought. Yet our laughter and smiles were pure and besotted.

"I miss him." My voice fell onto our leaf-stuffed bed.

This interlude in our old home wouldn't last long. Galloway had already contracted a local building firm to camp on our island and help erect our forever house. Soon, the palm tree walls and bamboo floor would be surplus and unwanted.

But for now, I'd never felt more content.

"I don't think that will ever change, Estelle." G hugged me harder. "But at least, he knows how much he was loved. He's happy, wherever he is."

The moon crested over the horizon as hours ticked past and we watched video after video, inspected photo after photo.

And when we finally grew drowsy, my thoughts switched to the torn page of my notebook that I'd cast into the sea in a brittle plastic bottle.

Had anyone found it? Had anyone read the hardship of someone who didn't know what she'd been given?

It didn't matter anymore.

Bottle or no bottle.

Message or no message.

I'd finally listened.

I was home.

Chapter Eighty-Three

GALLOWAY

EPILOGUE
ONE & HALF YEARS LATER

"THEY'RE HERE, G."

I glanced at Estelle as she entered Coco's room.

I'd just tucked my daughter into bed, kissing her browned cheek, loving how beautiful she looked amongst driftwood furniture and her starfish-shaped bed.

She'd fallen asleep before I'd finished reading her favourite book on humpback whales.

We'd moved into our new home two months ago after a successful build with four local craftsmen. We had everything we could ever dream of and had introduced a piece of the city we'd run from. Glass and steel made up the front part of the house, soaring above the canopy, granting perfect views to the achingly beautiful vista beyond.

The abode was understated but sturdy; built on stilts if there was ever a tsunami. And at night, the glass would glow with candles, looking like a lighthouse for lost souls.

We'd even built a small turret as a look-out for incoming guests and when the sun set over the woods, it illuminated the crash site, bouncing off the broken fuselage of the doomed helicopter that'd introduced us to our chosen end.

We hadn't discarded it.

The forest was its resting spot, just like the beach was ours.

Tiptoeing to the exit, I smiled at my wife. Her stomach billowed over her bikini bottoms, a cute bump through her ebony sarong.

Four months pregnant.

However, unlike the horror of the last pregnancy, we were both calm and collected with a birthing plan in place, medical team on standby, and the fastest speedboat we could buy tethered to our newly built dock.

Her eyes glowed as I bent to kiss her.

I didn't need to ask what was here.

The turtles.

Late December had arrived, and, with perfect precision, our leathered friends had returned.

"Fancy playing nursemaid to yet another egg laying?" She smiled, looping her fingers with mine and guiding me down the open-air steps.

Our house blended modern and rustic, taking inspiration from priceless architecture that I'd studied and the natural beauty of Fiji. It could be called a tree house with its segmented zones and open-air corridors.

Shade was granted by louvers and automatic shutters, cascading away to reveal stars and galaxies at night. If it rained, we got wet dashing from the open-plan kitchen and lounge to our bedrooms.

But we didn't care.

We lived freely with no worries to ruining clothes or messing hairstyles. That triviality didn't matter.

"Want to grab a drink and make a night of it?" I asked as we traded polished floorboards for sand.

"Sure."

Coco would sleep the night away, giving us time to do whatever the hell we wanted.

I knew what I wanted.

My wife.

Together, we headed to our palm tree and bamboo house which had turned into a convenient storage for food, toys, and awesome hang out for Coco.

Soon, she'd have a brother or sister to play with.

I couldn't wait.

The large fridge where a lot of our seafood was kept fresh and locally brewed craft beers were stored ran off the solar panels I'd installed the first month we'd arrived.

Every mod-con we needed we'd implemented, plus more.

But we didn't use them often.

We'd adapted too much to let machinery rule our life now.

Gathering a basket with a few beers for me and a bottle of wine for Estelle, we made our way to the beach to watch yet another miracle of life.

Dawn broke as the turtles finished their task.

"Come swim with me." Estelle swiped sand from her legs and untied her sarong.

My mouth went dry as I gawked at her feminine form, full breasts, and belly swollen with my child.

I'd married this woman.

I would have her for the rest of my life.

Christ, I'm lucky.

Placing my empty beer bottle in the picnic basket, I stood. Snagging her wrist, I yanked her forward to kiss. "It's dawn."

"So?"

"Aren't you tired?" I placed my hand on her stomach. "Do you need to rest?"

Her eyes twinkled. "What I need is you."

I sucked in a breath as she carefully removed my glasses and tossed them onto the blanket below. Her fingers skimmed under my t-shirt, removing it in one swipe, leaving me half-naked in board-shorts.

The pinky horizon warned we didn't have long before Coco awoke and another day began.

But Estelle wanted me.

I wanted her.

I'd never say no to that.

Moving together, we waded into the tropical ocean.

As always a small pang hit me as I relived saying goodbye to Conner in this bay. His legacy meant we never (no exceptions) went swimming without water shoes. I refused to lose any more loved ones from a venomous fish we couldn't see.

Estelle moaned as she ducked under, drenching her long hair and hovering in the tide's embrace.

I copied, rinsing myself in saltwater and bobbing beside her to stare at the red and gold clouds.

The turtles had finished laying and most had returned to sea. However, a few stragglers slowly flippered past, eddying the current as their soulful black eyes judged us.

Estelle swam sedately beside a mammoth-sized turtle, hovering in pleasure as the creature slowly sank beneath the waves and disappeared.

We'd given up so much coming back here.

But we'd earned untold wealth in return.

"Come here." Looping my arm around Estelle's waist, I sluiced her into my embrace.

She giggled but accepted my kiss.

My hands roamed. Our bodies reacted. The urge to connect magnified.

But a noise appeared on the horizon, reverberating around our home.

"What on earth?" Estelle looked up, peering into the ever-lightening distance.

"It's a boat."

"I thought you'd given the builders the week off?"

"I did." I stood in the chest-deep water, holding a hand over my eyes to shield from the piercing sun. "It's not them. I don't know the motor."

"Who is it then?"

"I guess we're about to find out." Taking Estelle's hand, I guided her from the ocean and jogged dripping wet to the jetty.

We padded to the end just as the small craft pulled up and cut the engine.

My heart quit beating.

"Oh, my God—" Estelle gasped. "You came. You truly came."

"Hi, Stelly." Pippa waved shyly. "Hi, G."

Launching myself into the small boat, I grabbed her in a bear hug. "Wow, you're here." Her slight frame had filled out, skinniness replaced with budding curves, and her cheeks were no longer gaunt but rosy red with health.

She's here.

After so long.

I couldn't release her. I'd worried I'd never have the luxury of touching her again. Of calling her my own. "Why didn't you tell us you were coming?"

She hugged me back, sighing heavily. "Honestly? I didn't know if I would. It was nana's idea."

"Hello again." Joanna Evermore cleared her throat as I released Pippa.

"I—I don't know what to say." I wished I wasn't half-naked and dripping wet. The first impression wasn't the best. Did this mean Pippa would live with us again? Did she finally want to be a family?

Questions ran rampant as the skipper offloaded two small suitcases onto the dock.

I frowned. The bags were too tiny for an extended stay.

Estelle said quietly, "This isn't a home coming, is it?"

Pippa stiffened. "I'm—it's just…"

"We've come for a week." Joanna cut in. "School holidays are in effect and I asked if Pippa wanted to go somewhere. It was me who suggested coming to see you."

I wanted to hate the woman for taking away my adopted child, but I only felt grateful. "Thank you. That's very kind."

"I can't come back full time, G." Pippa glanced at the island, decorated with brand new sunshine and freedom. "But I did want to talk to my brother and do my best to get over what happened here."

Joanna moved closer to Estelle. "Her therapist said it would help."

Therapist?

The poor kid had it worse than I feared.

But she was here now.

That was step one toward recovery.

Shoving away my concerns, I transformed into honourable host. Grabbing their suitcases, I bowed. "Well, our home is your home. You're welcome anytime, you know that."

Pippa smiled, her eyes drifting to Estelle's belly. "I see you forgot to mention baby number two in your latest phone call."

Estelle held Pippa's hand as she clambered from the boat. They embraced. "We didn't know how much to share. What would hurt. What wouldn't." She kissed the girl's cheek. "But now that you're here we have so much to catch up on."

"I can see that." Pippa turned to face our house. The glass glittered with secrets and history even though it was so new.

It knew what we'd survived here. It knew how much this land meant to us.

We'd lost, we'd won; we'd scarified, and celebrated.

We would never have a second chance with Conner.

But Pippa had returned.

One day, she would be able to visit without hurting from scars that bled so freely.

One day, she would be able to say goodbye to grief.

But until that day happened, I would be there for her.

And I wouldn't waste a moment.

"Come on, Pippi." I slung my arm over her slender shoulders. "Time to go home."

....

THREE YEARS LATER

Considering we'd crashed with no expertise, no knowledge, no hope of surviving apart from sheer determination, Estelle and I hadn't done too badly.

We'd not only survived, we'd excelled.

We'd created life.

We'd lost life.

We'd learned about life.

And life had almost killed us.

But we'd won.

We'd won so triumphantly, I'd never been so happy, so settled, so sure of my place than I did right here on our beach.

Once the Fijian government agreed to lease the island, we'd officially given it a name.

Yanuyanu ni le Vitu na Vonu.

Island of Seven Turtles.

Vitu na Vonu for short.

Seven people had arrived.

One soul had been born.

One son had died.

Four people left.

And three returned.

Those first few months beneath the stars were the best nights of my life. We shed our city attire and slipped into the half-nakedness we'd embraced. We fished together. We lit a fire together (cheating with the lighter rather than damage my new glasses) and spent the days remembering the bad times, the good times, and the sad.

We were finally able to finish grieving for Conner. For Pippa. For each other. Coming to terms with what we'd embraced and lost.

As the months turned to years, I returned to the mainland often, hiring local workers to help build the infrastructure required to keep us safe and secure for the many decades to come.

Coco stopped being grouchy and cross and blossomed into a brilliant, helpful child. As her birthdays ticked four, then five, now six, she became entwined with the Fijian nationals and culture. She would never fit in with the concrete jungle of a city. And I worried about that. But at the same time…who cared?

She learned the value of hard work and the sacred connection of hunting for your own food rather than ignoring the cruelty and sacrifice of mass marketed meat.

She hung around with my construction worker's children, being ferried from island to island and attending a local kindergarten.

Soon, she would start primary school a few islands over. Estelle and I would speed over the waves every morning to deliver her and again every night to collect her. We would never own a car but what a way to commute over the aquamarine atolls of our chosen home.

We'd contemplated the idea of using the helicopter taxis that now flew regularly, but I couldn't get over the fear of what'd happened. I doubted fate would be cruel enough to crash us twice, but I wouldn't risk it.

Eventually, Coco would head away to university if she was inclined or stay here and do whatever she wanted. But that was far enough away not to be an issue.

We learned, once we'd returned, that our island was located on the boundary of the Fijian archipelago. If we'd ever had a chance to paddle on our kayak, our chances of surviving the current rushing out to sea would've been slim.

Our island was classed as dangerous, which was why it'd been uninhabited when we'd arrived. However, the journey to other islands, unseen in the distance, only took forty minutes or so by boat.

The glistening jewels of our neighbours were hidden through sea mist and heatwaves, but we'd never been as alone as we'd feared.

Money was no object (thanks to Estelle), and together, we installed rain tanks that stored years' worth of liquid; we'd planted an orchard, sugar plantation, and every edible we could grow.

We'd seeded root vegetables, leafy greens, fruits, even medicinal foliage, loving the way they grew like wildfire thanks to the heat and humidity.

The avocados and limes were yet to give fruit, but we were hopeful next year would yield a crop. However, along with the produce we introduced, we still ate island fare.

Turned out, the taro leaves that we boiled and ate in a salad (when we had nothing else) were used for that same purpose on the mainland. And the food we often ate (that we had no name for) were local delicacies such as curry leaf and bush ferns.

One thing we hadn't sampled was *nama*, also known as sea-grapes. The delicious seaweed polyps were often eaten here and an abundance grew in our reef. If only we'd known. We'd been surrounded by more food than we realised.

We asked the wives of the construction workers to come and educate us on flowers and other plant life, finally learning their true names and capabilities.

The yellow bark-stringy flowers on the beach were called *Vau* in Fijian and beach hibiscus in English. The leaves were also good for sprains and swelling, just like the plant with furry leaves we'd used, called *Botebote Koro* (goat weed).

Estelle soaked up the indigenous knowledge as if she'd turn into a natural healer. She learned that palm trees Fijian name was *Niu* and the leaves from the sparse guava plants could be pulped and used for dysentery, which was ironic because if too many of the unripe guava fruit were eaten they gave constipation.

As our house evolved with indoor plumbing, septic systems, and hot showers, we opted for the expense of installing a saline purifier and internet satellite to stay in touch with the outside world.

Our many Skype calls were to Pippa.

For so long, I'd worried about her mental health. But as the years turned her from a quiet eleven-year-old into a sensitive teenager, I knew she'd never be boisterous or carefree. She carried too much sorrow in her heart, but she had wisdom, too. Wisdom to know that life happened, and it couldn't unhappen.

She was alive. She had a life with her grandmother and friends at school. And she visited us every year and each year was easier.

Having her in our lives (even in small doses) was more than I'd hoped for.

At night, Estelle researched new skills to continue evolving our new way of life and relayed titbits of plants we didn't know, educating ourselves on our island.

It was a humbling reminder that even though we'd become so dependent on technology, we'd done okay without the World Wide Web. We'd done it together through common sense and the willingness to try.

But we were also careful.

Those ingredients meant we were able to turn plants (that at first glance didn't look edible), into a smorgasbord of eateries without an encyclopaedia or mouse click.

And thank God we had a lot of supplies, because currently, those supplies had been claimed.

Christmas, once upon a time, had been ignored.

However, since we'd been back, that had all changed.

Our finished two-story house had become more than just a home for my family but an idyllic holiday spot for our loved ones.

I was proud of that.

Proud of its unassuming position on our beach, a few metres away from our original (well, second original after the fire) home. That house was now a children's dream hang-out with hammocks and littered seashells.

Vitu na Vonu was more than just our home. This uninhabited island now housed a family. It'd evolved with us into a wonderful haven. And regularly hosted happy events within its reef-protected boundaries.

"Are you coming?" Coco popped her head around the kitchen island. Her golden ringlets were salt-crinkled and wild. "They want the lobster and told me to get you."

"Impatient, are they?"

She giggled. "Yep. Me, too. I'm hungry."

"You just had a prawn cocktail."

"Don't care. Still hungry."

I rolled my eyes. At six (almost seven), Coco had sprung into a willowy, younger version of Estelle. My wife said there were elements of me in my daughter, but all I saw was the woman who owned my heart. From the bleached blonde hair to the high cheekbones. The only thing I noticed were the eyes, which had turned more blue than green.

"Oh, and Grandpa wanted me to tell you that Finnek wants his juice."

The mention of my two-year-old son warmed my soul. The fact that my father was here to celebrate Christmas with us even more so. He'd left England a year ago, moving into a small bachelor pad I'd built on the opposite side of our island.

The side where Conner and his parents had been honoured.

My dad was still lonely for my mum, but at least, he had a family, sunshine, and a new existence to nullify the old.

"My ears are burning. Who's talking about me?"

I wiped my hands on a tea towel as my dad appeared.

In his arms sat my little boy.

The moment Finnek saw me, his chubby hands strained for me to take him. His sky-blue eyes watered with pain as his bottom lip wobbled. "Ouchie!"

I plucked him from my father's embrace. "What happened?"

"Little tyke took off too fast. Face planted in the sand and scuffed his knee. Again."

This was a weekly (if not daily) occurrence. Finnek was a walking accident. His coordination skills had a lot to be desired. While Coco took after Estelle, Finnek took after me with his lanky limbs, dark hair, and rascally smirk. We should've called him Mischief.

Luckily, his big sister never let him out of her sight.

And as Estelle had ballooned with Finnek's pregnancy, I'd never let her out of mine. We regularly went to the mainland for check-ups, and when she got too big to brave the sea, we paid the doctor to come here.

The pregnancy had no complications, and Estelle spoke about

having another birth on our island.

I'd flatly refused.

Two weeks before she was due, we travelled to Nadi and stayed in a local hotel, close to a hospital, and took it easy. We swam in chlorinated water rather than salt and ate food prepared by others.

And when she delivered, it was in a sterile room with medical professionals and every modern apparatus required if anything went wrong.

It made me feel ten times better knowing that others with expertise were helping rather than just me and a night-shrouded sea like last time.

Another benefit of spending two weeks on the mainland meant I finally took the plunge to have Lasik eye surgery to permanently remove the need for glasses.

When we'd first moved, I'd ordered ten pairs, just in case. I never wanted to go so long without seeing well again.

However, swimming crusted the lenses, sweat fogged them while I worked, and humidity wasn't kind to the hinges.

Estelle had been the one to suggest the procedure.

And I was so bloody thankful I'd listened.

"You really are a disaster, aren't you, Fin?"

"No." Finnek pouted as I put him on the kitchen counter.

Rummaging in the drawer full of creams and Band-Aids, Coco padded to the fridge and yanked on the heavy sealed door.

I glanced at her as I tended to the scrape on Finnek's knee.

I didn't say a word as she grabbed the sippy cup full of coconut water and passed it to her brother. "Here you go. This will make you feel better."

Goddammit, she knew how to overwhelm my heart with her childish kindness.

I love her.

Them.

Everyone.

My dad caught my eye.

We smiled, understanding without speaking how precious this bond between siblings would become.

Kissing my son's forehead, I passed him back to my father. "Everything going all right out there?"

Along with my dad, we'd invited the foreman who helped me build and his wife and two children. We'd also invited anyone who wanted to come from the islands closest to us, extending the hospitality to those stragglers who had no one to spend Christmas with.

It went without saying that Madeline was here. Just like every Christmas, birthday, anniversary, and any other random occasion she could find. She might as well move in with how often she visited (claiming the benefits of tax deductions to see her boss about 'work matters').

Not that I cared.

I'd grown to love the crazy woman.

Not to mention, she ran our life back in the city with military precision, keeping on top of Estelle's contracts and obligations, ferrying paperwork and interview requests from her recording company, going out of her way to ensure the symbiotic relationship flourished.

Estelle continued writing and singing and her finished recordings were sent to Madi to deliver to the music contractors or uploaded directly to iTunes for her online listeners.

Money would never be an issue for us.

Time wasn't stolen in dead-end jobs or hated commutes.

And we were able to be generous with our monetary and material wealth.

We paid for Pippa's education. Looked after her grandmother's occasional health bills, and put aside a few blue stock bonds for Coco and Finnek when they hit eighteen. Not to mention, the investment we made into the Fijian infrastructure.

We'd adopted this place just as it had adopted us.

"Yes, all enjoying the sun and beer." My dad chuckled, clasping Coco's hand to lead my children back to the beach. "We'll see you down there. Don't be too long."

"I won't. The food's almost done."

All morning, I'd slaved in the kitchen (after shooing Estelle out) to finish the Christmas seafood feast. We had so much food; I doubted we'd eat it all. But the abundance of such banquets never grew old.

Not after those first few days of starvation.

After that, everything tasted better, richer.

Finnek waved, his tears transforming to laughter as his grandfather muttered something in his ear.

"See you soon!" Coco charged outside, bolting down the ramp off the veranda to the large table where our guests waited for the main course.

Everyone but Estelle.

My lips twitched as the haunting melody of the baby grand I'd had shipped over lilted over our island.

The lobsters could wait.

My need to hold her couldn't.

Padding barefoot across the large open-plan living, my heart squeezed as my eyes fell on Estelle.

Her fingers glided over ivory and black keys, while the sounds of conversation whispered from the beach below, mingling with the clinking of cocktails, and fluttering of white gauze curtains.

Heaven.

Instead of singing a Christmas carol, Estelle sang one of her originals. One I absolutely adored and had been listened to over fifteen million times on YouTube.

I snuck up behind her and wrapped her in an embrace.

Her fingers never stopped dancing, but her head bent as she kissed my tanned forearm. "Hi."

"Hi."

"You think they're ready?"

"According to Coco, they're all dying of lobster deprivation."

"Ah, poor things. What a horrible affliction to have."

My hand drifted downward, cupping her breast.

Today, she'd dressed in a simple pink sundress but the silver bikini she wore beneath glistened like liquid mercury against her skin. "I don't know if I'll make it through the entire feast. Why did we invite so many people?"

"Because you're a sweetheart." She sucked in a breath as I pinched her nipple. "And you have no choice."

"Oh, I have a choice." I licked her earlobe. "You do, too. Fancy ignoring everyone for a few minutes?"

"Just a few minutes?" She giggled. "I think you're underestimating yourself there, G."

"When I'm inside you, I'm surprised I last more than a few seconds."

She shivered as my touch slid from her breast to capture her throat, squeezing lightly, possessively.

Her head tilted to the side, offering her mouth to take.

And I did.

We kissed slowly, sensuously, and through it all, she never stopped playing the softest lullaby.

I groaned as my shorts became far too tight for company. "Does this wanting you ever stop?"

"I hope not."

"You like having this power over me?"

"Like it? No." She smiled. "I *love* it."

"I love you."

"*I* love you."

Our lips re-joined.

"Do you think they know?" I asked, pulling away and running a hand through my hair. I'd grown it out again and the length was starting to annoy.

"About Driftwood? I guess. But only if they've been sneaky and gone where we told them not to."

My mind switched to the mongrel pup we'd rescued from the local shelter on the mainland. A scruffy cross on death row. He was currently hidden in the woods by the orchard, waiting to meet his new master and mistress.

We'd gone Christmas shopping for the children, and just like Pippa had every year the turtles came to nest, they'd begged us for a pet.

We'd finally decided to make that wish come true.

We'd also decided to make the turtle's survival that much easier for the hatchlings, and (with the Governments Conservations approval) installed a few holding tanks inlaid into the sand so the baby turtles could swim and be protected for a few days before flipper-crawling to the open sea.

"Fancy sleeping under the stars tonight, once everyone has gone?"

Estelle nodded. "I'd love that."

"Perhaps, do our Christmas wishes in the sand, like old times?"

"I'd love that, too." Her hazel eyes glowed. "You're full of great ideas today."

I smirked. "I try."

Moments like these made my life complete. However, I wasn't saying our lives were ease and glory all the time. We had rough moments (if a hurricane ripped through), we still got sick, and still argued.

But compared to what the rat race endured, we lived in utopia.

Even our children hardly moaned or complained.

Because what was there to argue about when you lived in paradise?

Nothing.

And if there ever *was* discord, our tradition of writing messages helped solve it.

If we were angry, we wrote it in the sand.

If we were sad, we wrote it so the waves could smooth it away.

It was the perfect Etch A Sketch for our problems.

"Talking of messages…" I moved back, waiting until Estelle

tapered off her music and stood. "You won't guess what I found last night when I went for a swim."

"Oh?" She came toward me, slinking her arms around my waist. "What?"

"Something you never told me about."

"Like what?"

"Like a bottle…"

"A bottle?" Her eyes narrowed. "I don't know what you—"

"A message in a bottle."

"What…" She paused then enlightenment brightened her face. "Oh, that."

"Yes, that."

She dropped her gaze. "I'm sorry. It was a low point, and I…I wasn't thinking."

"So you ripped out one of your songs and hoped someone would find us?" I cupped her cheek. "Estelle, you do know which song you tossed into the sea, right? You do know you didn't write down any details of us, the crash, anything to help them locate us if by some miracle the tide carried the bottle to help, rather than circle the atoll to wash up on the very shore you threw it from."

"I…I'm not sure. I don't remember much of that night, to be honest. I just grabbed a page, stuffed it into the plastic, screwed the cap on, and threw it." She shrugged. "I didn't mean anything by it."

"Then why were the words about us?"

Her cheek warmed beneath my palm. "What—what do you mean? They weren't about us. The lyrics were about death and darkness and pain."

"No, Stel…they weren't."

We stood silently, her eyes searching mine, trying to understand.

Dropping my touch, I pulled out the crinkled, waterlogged page from my back pocket.

When I'd found it last night, bobbing in the tide as if begging me to find it, I didn't have a clue what the contents were. For a moment, I worried some other poor schmuck was capsized and castaway, desperate for someone to rescue him.

I wasn't prepared to see Estelle's hand-writing.

Or read a song I'd never had the pleasure of seeing.

But somehow, after almost five years of bliss on an island that'd given almost four years of nightmares, it was the fautless end.

The only end.

The beginning of our new conception.

Breathing shallowly, Estelle straightened out the page and read,

"I crash landed to find him. I fell from the sky to know him. I died a mortal death to be worthy of him. I am reborn because of him.

"If rescue never comes, know I didn't need it. If help never arrives, know I didn't want it. If we die here together, be happy knowing this was our destiny.

"Don't find us. Don't mourn us. Don't weep for us. Because we were the lucky ones, the chosen ones, the only ones for each other."

Tears rained from her eyes as she looked up.

Our bodies melted together; our lips kissed softly. "I knew you loved me, Estelle. But that…knowing that even in your darkest moments, you were prepared to die beside me, that you wouldn't have left me, that you'd chosen me over life, over safety, over *everything.* You couldn't have given me a more priceless gift."

"But don't you see, I didn't give you that." Her lips curved into the sweetest, sexiest smile. "*You* did. The day you gave me Coco; the day you gave me Finnek. The day you gave me your heart, G, you made my fate shift, and all of this—our island, our home, our very existence could vanish and I would still be the happiest woman in the world because I'd have you."

I couldn't do it anymore.

The guests would have to wait.

Dinner would have to wait.

Our children would have to wait.

Taking her hand, I guided her to our bedroom and locked the door. "You have me, Estelle. You have me for as long as you want me."

Pushing the sundress straps from her shoulders, she let it pool to the floor, standing in the middle of our elegantly simple bedroom with its seashell chandelier and white bed. "Forever?"

Unbuckling my shorts, my heart switched owners, giving every remaining beat to her. "Forever.

"More than forever.

"For eternity."

ABOUT THE AUTHOR

Pepper Winters is a New York Times, Wall Street Journal, and USA Today International Bestseller. She loves romance, star-crossed lovers, and anything to do with character connection. She strives to write a story that makes the reader crave what they shouldn't, and delivers tales with complex plots and unforgettable characters.

After chasing her dreams to become a full-time writer, Pepper has earned recognition with awards for best Dark Romance, best BDSM Series, and best Hero. She's a multiple #1 iBooks bestseller, along with #1 in Erotic Romance, Romantic Suspense, Contemporary, and Erotica Thriller. She's also honoured to wear the IndieReader Badge for being a Top 10 Indie Bestseller, and recently signed a two book deal with Hachette. Represented by Trident Media, her books have garnered foreign and audio interest and are currently being translated into numerous languages. They will be in available in bookstores worldwide.

Her Dark Romance books include:
Tears of Tess (Monsters in the Dark #1)
Quintessentially Q (Monsters in the Dark #2)
Twisted Together (Monsters in the Dark #3)
Debt Inheritance (Indebted #1)
First Debt (Indebted Series #2)
Second Debt (Indebted Series #3)
Third Debt (Indebted Series #4)
Fourth Debt (Indebted Series #5)
Final Debt (Indebted Series #6)
Indebted Epilogue (Indebted Series #7)
***

Her Grey Romance books include:
Destroyed
Ruin & Rule (Pure Corruption #1)
Sin & Suffer (Pure Corruption #2)
***

Upcoming releases are:
Je Suis a Toi (Monsters in the Dark Novella)
Super Secret Series (5-6 book series)
Indebted Beginnings (Indebted Series Prequel)
***

Her Audio Books include:

Monsters in the Dark Series (releasing early 2016)
Indebted Series (releasing early 2016)
Ruin & Rule / Sin & Suffer (Out now)
Destroyed / Unseen Messages (releasing early 2016)
***

To be the first to know of upcoming releases, please join Pepper's
Newsletter (she promises never to spam or annoy you.)

Pepper's Newsletter

Or follow her on her website
Pepper Winters

You can stalk her here:

Pinterest
Facebook Pepper Winters
Twitter
Instagram
Website
Facebook Group
Goodreads

She loves mail of any kind: **pepperwinters@gmail.com**
All other titles and updates can be found on her **Goodreads Page.**

Playlist

Ain't Nobody Like You by *Felix Jaehn*
Roots by *Imagine Dragons*
Bleeding Out by *Imagine Dragons*
Book of Love by *Felix Jaehn*
Adore by *Jasmine Thompson*
Like I'm Gonna Lose You by *Mehan Trainor and John Legend*
Love Me Like You Do by *Ellie Goulding*
Starlight by *Muse*
Hearts a Mess by *Gotye*

Acknowledgements

FIRST, A MASSIVE thank you to my husband who put up with me when the issues at the airport happened (in the exact same sequence it did in this book) and just chuckled when I read into the messages warning me not to board. For not rolling his eyes too much when I stuffed my pockets with the exact same things Estelle did, and for letting me vanish for days on end into this island world where I've left a piece of myself.

This book has a lot of me in the pages. I'm an ex-flight attendant, I was lucky enough to go on a SIGNing tour not a SINGing tour in the USA, and my life changed just like Estelle's when my dreams came true with my writing. I've put my heart and soul into these pages and I hope you liked reading them as much as I enjoyed writing them.

I've taken my own life events and plaited them into this story. I borrowed my memories of enjoying a P&O Cruise around the islands with my hubby and used my mother's symptoms of cellulitis when she got sick a few months ago and ended up in hospital with such a simple but deadly infection.

I referred to experts who know the land and sea and learned so much writing this that I'd be confident I could at least feed myself for a few days if the worst ever happened.

I have to say a massive thank you to my father for his help with the helicopter crash and terminology (he's a retired Royal Air Force Pilot). A big thanks to my stepmother for her guidance in the maladies and broken bones suffered (she's a General Practitioner). And a shout out to Stone's Nursery & Fresh Island Foods in Fiji for answering my produce questions, sea life availability, and what would be edible on a remote island such as *Seven Turtles*.

A massive thanks to my beta readers: Amy, Yaya, Tamicka, Melissa, and Nikki. To Jenny for editing such a long book and to Ellen for proofreading. Thanks to Selena for running my groups so well and having my back, Glorya for her crazy support and friendship, Nina and Aussie Lisa for being rockstars, and Skye for being my bestie and reminding me how to sample foreign food.

Also thank you to Nalini Singh for her help with the Fijian translation and for becoming a friend after I've admired her work for so long.

Thank you to Inkslinger for agreeing to work with me and help run my chaotic life. Thank you to the authors I talk to daily online and all the support you've given me.

And mostly, thank you to you, the reader. If this is the first book of mine you've read, I hope you've enjoyed it. If it's a few, then I hope I'm delivering quality you enjoy. You make my dreams come true and I'm forever in your debt.

BOOK BLURBS BY PEPPER WINTERS

Complete Duology
Ruin & Rule (Pure Corruption MC #1)

"We met in a nightmare. The in-between world where time had no power over reason. We fell in love. We fell hard. But then we woke up. And it was over . . ."

Buy Now

***

Sin & Suffer (Pure Corruption MC #2)

"Some say the past is in the past. That vengeance will hurt both innocent and guilty. I never believed those lies."

Buy Now

Complete Trilogy
Tears of Tess (Monsters in the Dark #1)

"My life was complete. Happy, content, everything neat and perfect.
Then it all changed.
I was sold."

Buy Now

***

Quintessentially Q (Monsters in the Dark #2)

"All my life, I battled with the knowledge I was twisted... screwed up to want something so deliciously dark—wrong on so many levels. But then slave fifty-eight entered my world. Hissing, fighting, with a core of iron, she showed me an existence where two wrongs do make a right."

Buy Now

***

Twisted Together (Monsters in the Dark #3)

"After battling through hell, I brought my esclave back from the brink of ruin. I sacrificed everything—my heart, my mind, my very desires to bring her back to life. And for a while, I thought it broke me, that I'd never be the same. But slowly the beast is growing bolder, and it's finally time to show Tess how beautiful the dark can be."

Buy Now

Complete Series
Debt Inheritance (Indebted Series #1)

"I own you. I have the piece of paper to prove it. It's undeniable and unbreakable. You belong to me until you've paid off your debts."

Buy Now

***

First Debt (Indebted Series #2)

"You say I'll never own you. If I win—you willingly give me that right. You sign not only the debt agreement, but another—one that makes me your master until your last breath is taken. You do that, and I'll give you this."

Buy Now

***

Second Debt (Indebted #3)

"I tried to play a game. I tried to wield deceit as perfectly as the Hawks. But when I thought I was winning, I wasn't. Jethro isn't what he seems--he's the master of duplicity. However, I refuse to let him annihilate me further."

Buy Now

***

Third Debt (Indebted #4)

"She healed me. She broke me. I set her free. But we are in this together. We will end this together. The rules of this ancient game can't be broken."

Buy Now

***

Fourth Debt (Indebted #5)

"We'd won. We'd cut through the lies and treachery and promised an alliance that would free us both. But even as we won, we lost. We didn't see what was coming. We didn't know we had to plan a resurrection."

Buy Now

***

Final Debt (Indebted #6)

"I'm in love with her, but it might not be enough to stop her from becoming the latest victim of the Debt Inheritance. I know who I am now. I know what I must do. We will be together--I just hope it's on Earth rather than in heaven."

Buy Now

***

Indebted Epilogue (Indebted #7)

INDEBTED EPILOGUE is a bonus book to be read after the series.

Buy Now

Standalones
Destroyed (Grey Romance)

She has a secret.
He has a secret.
One secret destroys them.

Buy Now

References

- Stone's Nursery & Fresh Island Foods
- http://mesfiji.org/sea-turtle-nesting-season-begins
- http://www.zippla.net/they-said-coconut-oil-was-great/
- http://www.mnn.com/health/fitness-well-being/stories/7-nutrient-deficiencies-that-can-make-you-sick
- https://humblelore.wordpress.com/2013/03/18/30-uses-for-wood-ashes-you-never-thought-of/
- http://www.healthline.com/health/cellulitis
- http://orthoinfo.aaos.org/topic.cfm?topic=A00162
- http://fijimarinas.com/medicinal-plants-of-the-fijian-sea-shore/
- http://www.nhs.uk/Conditions/Malnutrition/Pages/Symptoms.aspx
- https://www.facebook.com/RealPasifik

Thank you so much for reading.